# MEET ME IN MANHATTAN

## OR ONCE UPON A TIME IN THE EAST

The Authentic Saga of Miss Etta Place,
Companion to Butch Cassidy and the Sundance Kid,
As Recalled by her Friend and Confidant
William Bartley ('Bat') Masterson

## Douglas Brode

an imprint of Sunbury Press, Inc.
Mechanicsburg, PA USA

## MILFORD HOUSE

an imprint of Sunbury Press, Inc.
Mechanicsburg, PA USA





For information about special discounts for bulk purchases, please contact Sunbury Press Orders Dept. at (855) 338-8359 or orders@sunburypress.com.

To request one of our authors for speaking engagements or book signings, please contact Sunbury Press Publicity Dept. at publicity@sunburypress.com.

FIRST MILFORD HOUSE PRESS EDITION: November 2024

Set in Adobe Garamond Pro | Interior design by Crystal Devine | Cover by Lawrence Knorr | Edited by Gabrielle Kirk.

Publisher's Cataloging-in-Publication Data
Names: Brode, Douglas, author.
Title: Meet me in Manhattan or once upon a time in the east / Douglas Brode.
Description: First trade paperback edition. | Mechanicsburg, PA : Milford House Press, 2024.
Summary: *Meet Me in Manhattan* by Douglas Brode is a retelling of the legend of Butch Cassidy, the Sundance Kid, and Miss Etta Place. The fictional story focuses on the 2½ weeks following their taking leave of Wyoming and remaining in New York City while waiting for the boat that would bring them to South America. Numerous other historic personages who were in Manhattan at that time are included to allow for an epic vision of the early 20th century.
Identifiers: ISBN : 979-8-88819-245-0 (paperback).
Subjects: FICTION / Feminist | FICTION / Romance / Historical / General | FICTION / Jewish.

Designed in the USA
0  1  1  2  3  5  8  13  21  34  55

*For the Love of Books!*

To
Shaun L. Brode

Thomas Wolfe owed his success to Maxwell Perkins
I owe mine to you

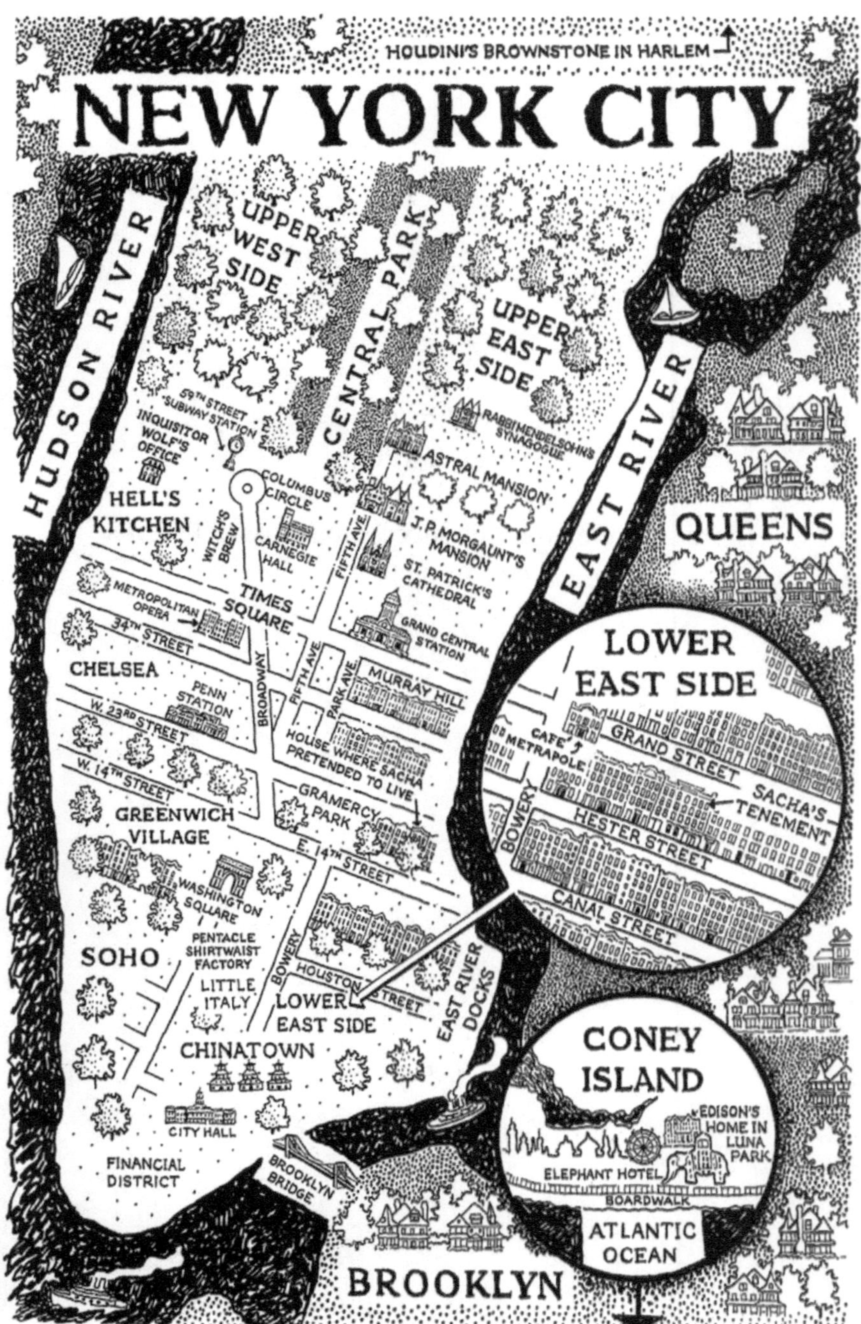


THE WAY WE WERE: New York City as it appeared in 1901 when Miss Etta Place and her outlaw lovers spent several weeks there after fleeing Wyoming.

# CONTENTS

# GLEANINGS

"You can't realize your dream unless you have
one to begin with."

—Thomas A. Edison

*

"We live as we dream: Alone. Yet while the dream
will inevitably disappear, 'the life' must
painfully continue."

—Joseph Conrad

*

"I care not what others think of what I do, but
I care very much about what I think of what
I do. For that, simply, is character."

—Theodore Roosevelt

*

"Just because you are 'a character' doesn't
mean that you have character."

—Quentin Tarantino

*

"A man's got to do what a man's got to do."

—William S. Hart

*

"When the delicate responsibilities of a goddess are
completed, the hard labor of a true woman begins."

—Colette

*

"History is but a set of lies we have decided to
agree upon."
—VOLTAIRE

*

"History interests us only in so far as it is
able to illuminate the present."
—ERNEST DIMNET

*

"Give 'history' a gentle nudge in the direction of
'myth' and it will settle down in a middleground popularly known as 'legend.'"
—NED BUNTLINE

*

"Every generation rewrites the past."
—JOHN DOS PASSOS

*

"East is east and west is west."
—RUDYARD KIPLING

*

"The West is where all Americans plan to go some day."
—ROBERT PENN WARREN

*

"The west of the old times, with its strong people,
its stern battles, and its tremendous stretches
of loneliness can never be blotted from my
mind. The second half of my life will be spent
keeping that narrative alive for generations of
Americans who never knew it firsthand."

—WILLIAM F. CODY/'BUFFALO BILL'

*

"I saw the railroad on the horizon and knew the
end was near. The wild riders and vacant
land were about to vanish. The more I
glanced around, the more a mighty doomed
pageant unfolded before my eyes. Now at
last I know it for what it was: The great
and enduring American Myth."

—Frederic Remington

*

"When I have camped in The West, the experience
caused me to want to be one with the ground,
the crystal waters, the high timber. Made
me desire to mix with the whole thing. No
longer able to separate myself from its
dark, dangerous, primal beauty."

—Owen Wister

*

"The Old West is not a place or a period in time.
Properly understood, it's a state of mind."

—Tom Mix

*

"Those who do not appreciate The West will never
comprehend the true meaning of America."

—Louis L'Amour

*

"When the history of the West is written, if it is
told truthfully, then all will know that the
Sunbonnet, not the Stetson, tamed the frontier."

—Edna Ferber

*

"Thinking back on The Great Gatsby, I have come
to realize that while set in New York, this
was really a story about 'The West.'"
—F. SCOTT FITZGERALD

*

"New York, New York, it's a wonderful town; the
Bronx is up and the Battery's down."
—BETTY COMDEN AND ADOLPH GREEN

*

"New York is the city that other cities can only
aspire to be."
—WILLA CATHER

*

"Literature without a tinge of philosophy is
worth no more than a sneeze, a cough, a
feeble joke. Genuine, worthwhile stories
are always replete with wisdom."
—MARK TWAIN

*

"Thank you for individual perception."
—MORT SAHL

# PREFACE

Though many (indeed, most) of the characters included in this book share names with historical people, this is a work of fiction. Liberties have been taken with timelines and events that occurred during the first decade of the twentieth century. Actual occurrences are here re-adjusted for the sake of narrative flow and dramatic impact. Various incidents recorded in newspapers of that era—journalism is the first draft of history, Philip Graham noted—are collapsed into a story that might best be described as "legend": partly fact, partly fiction. That has always been the case since the genre was invented by Homer and Sophocles, from Shakespeare's plays to the "history" films of John Ford. No movie about Wyatt Earp so totally rearranges and rewrites the tale of Tombstone AZ as *My Darling Clementine* (1946); then again, no film or book about that era so perfectly captures the essence of what might be referred to as "the truth."

That said, specific details presented here are essentially accurate. Life in the wide open spaces of our fast-fading Old West as well as in the then-evolving New York City lifestyle are drawn from careful research. What people wore, where they lived, what they appreciated as to entertainment, sports, and politics; and most importantly how they perceived the changing world around them. Such descriptions are intended to convey how citizens of the United States reacted to a (to borrow from Aldous Huxley) brave new world which replaced what are fondly, if inaccurately, recalled as The Good Ol' Days.

If not "reality" in a strict documentarian's definition of that term, hopefully this will present a crystallization of a remarkable juncture in time as it might appear in a midnight dream. In this context please do note that any anachronisms result from conscious decision, not accident or error.

As an old world adage has it: "The past is so difficult to comprehend that art is required to make it believable." Do not be surprised, then, to find poetic license at work here. Authors of historical (adjective) fiction (noun) have never allowed the facts to interfere with telling the truth as they see it: The only truth any of us can ever know for certain.

—Douglas Brode
November 2023

A CITY IN TRANSITION: During the first two decades of the 20th century, New York City underwent a massive changeover from horse drawn vehicles to ever more advanced automobiles . . . from the past through the present into the future.

# PROLOGUE

(BAT: OCTOBER 25, 1921)

> "Never step down a dusty street to shoot it
> out with seven men when all you're packin'
> is a single six-gun."
>
> —WILLIAM BARTLEY MASTERSON

Late that afternoon, I eased my aching bones down before a sprawling mahogany desk, planning to knock out a column for the following day's *Morning Telegraph*. As always, I enjoyed a mixture of sounds rising from the newly paved Park Row down below. The last of the timeworn horse-drawn wagons made way for a fleet of metallic automobiles just off the assembly line. I could tell one model from another by the whir of its engine. Even now, one of Walter P. Chrysler's latest 'Locomobiles' sputtered by. A glance down from my third story window revealed the car's crimson exterior, a changeover from the black Model T Ford introduced two decades earlier. That was back when I'd initially agreed to set my nickel-plated single action Colt .45 aside and take up the journalist's trade here in New York.

Echoes of the past simultaneous with sounds of the future co-mingled on this cool autumn day.

*Perhaps* that *might provide a subject for my story?*

*An aging man's views on* Modern Times *in the making.*

I might have believed, in the isolation of this spacious office, that all such activity occurred for my amusement. Here unfolded an unplanned orchestral performance rising from the street, in what had been founded as little New Amsterdam back in 1625. Gradually that quaint place receded from the public's memory, giving way to a great metropolis. Here then was the spontaneous music of a new century's heart and soul.

Heavy commerce dominated during this transitional time of day. Pale workers poured out of brick buildings to embrace the evening's myriad pleasures before retiring to the tenements; there to catch several hours sleep, only to begin all over again the next morning. People chatted about politics, the latest

A SYMPHONY OF THE CITY: By the 1920s, final holdovers from ethnic entertainments that had earlier been confined to downtown gradually worked their way up to Park Row, site of Manhattan's newspapers.

Hollywood movies, restaurants, sports, and our recent war. The sound of sleek motors merged with the snapping of whips on antique carriages dragged by sweating nags.

A lone organ grinder, positioned at the nearest cross-street with his dancing monkey, provided a reminder of those European immigrants who, during the past half-century, flowed through Ellis Island into the lower East Side. In time, the Irish, Italians, and Jews edged ever further northward. And, in so doing, altered the ethnic map of once-Anglo Manhattan.

"It ain't locked," I called out, detecting a gentle rap from the office door's far side. "Who's there?"

"Guess?" Lolly answered, casting me one of her killer smiles as this little whirlwind of perpetual motion cracked open the door and, grinning from ear to ear, peeked in.

"Ah, I know'd ya by your knock."

Her bright eyes, dark as a pair of sapphires, signaled that something special was on this young charmer's mind.

*

That had been the case when Lolly first paid me a visit two years previous. Then, a handsome comer in the sporting world name o' Jack Dempsey set out to challenge mighty Jess Willard for Heavyweight Championship of the World. That bout, which had come to be perceived as the athletic event of the year, was scheduled for July 4, 1919.

And, in all places, Toledo. The heartland! As if such a date and location might qualify boxing, however belatedly, as a legitimate sport on the order of baseball. Leastways till a short time later when the Black Socks Scandal dampened that.

For the time being, though, like everyone else, Lolly . . . Louella Parsons, then recently hired by editor Henry Lewis as our first gossip columnist for a new, jaunty breed of woman reader . . . hoped to place a bet. Figuring if anyone could advise her, it'd be the senior residing sportswriter.

*'Old Bat,' everyone called him.*

*Me!*

The dignified elderly gentleman in a derby hat, carrying a silver-tipped cane. Difficult to believe, for some, this was the same fella who nearly half a century ago shot down 21 men in ramshackle crossroad towns along the still untamed frontier.

*Yes, I finished off more than my fair share of varmints.*

*Never, though, anyone who didn't require killing.*

*

"No matter what anyone else says, *don't* bet on Dempsey," I'd told her. "Nice boy, but he don't stand a chance." As I spoke those words, I noticed Lolly's attention had divided between my prediction and an assortment of colorful adornments on the walls.

For here, displayed for all who stopped by to take a peek, I'd set in place a miniature museum dedicated to a time that had largely passed into history. Rusty spurs I'd worn on my first long drive up the Goodnight-Loving Trail. The broken pistol, in its original holster, I'd used at age 15 to shoot and kill Sergeant King after that jealous drunkard murdered our mutual lover, Molly Brennan. The badge Wyatt Earp awarded me on the day he hired an aggressive, if inexperienced, nineteen-year-old as his deputy in dusty Wichita, Kansas. A photograph of us together, two years hence, as the marshal of Dodge and sheriff of Ford county, members of the famed Peace Commission.

Back, though, to Lolly, Jack Dempsey, and my 'expert' advice? Eventually, I had to eat them words. For I'd headed out to middle America early in the summer to cover the much-heralded match. Careful to avoid everyone's eyes once I returned, particularly those of a down-hearted Lolly.

Y'see, she—like most others on the staff—had taken my lousy tip as gospel and bet accordingly. But to everyone's surprise, Dempsey won! Some fellow reporters stopped talking to me altogether. "No fool like an old fool," they whispered. To my happy surprise, Lolly proved an exception. The giddy jazz baby, always sportin' one of her short Flapper skirts, waltzed back in to see me regularly, sometimes just to chat, on other occasins for fatherly advice.

I always sensed, though, that this New Woman—as the working girls referred to themselves once they'd won the vote and could do pretty much what they pleased—took a notably keen interest in my hard-earned relics. These antiques had been hung alongside framed prints of Charlie Russell's richly detailed watercolors depicting drovers on the trail, Indians on the warpath, and the so-called cowtowns I'd helped tame.

*

About a year ago, in autumn of 1920, Lolly had arrived with the same determined look she now cast. A bright sparkle left little doubt she did so with some firm purpose in mind.

"Bat," she'd cooed seductively, those striking eyes fluttering while cat-like Lolly settled herself into a frame chair across from my desk. She moved with the assured grace of Big Town royalty, a status she'd achieved once her gossip column became a top-selling attraction. "I've just come from an editorial meeting. We're about to publish a new weekly titled *City Lights*. A departure from the usual reporting on police blotters, high finances, and sports, sports, sports."

"What else is there to report?" I lamely joked.

"This will be about *people*. 'Human interest' stories."

"Sounds like your beat, expanded into a magazine."

"Precisely! And I thought *you* might contribute."

"Articles dealing with current athletic stars?"

"Everyone who wants to learn what Bat Masterson thinks about *that* gets it three days a week in 'Timely Topics.'"

"Reckon I know what's comin'," I whispered.

"Bat, everyone in New York is still 'wild' about the Wild West. Why, the Buffalo Bill show sells out every time it's booked at Madison Square, even though Colonel Cody passed on . . . I guess it must've been three years ago."

"Four," I said, nostalgic now. "I'll never forget when . . . twenty years back . . . I walked out onstage alongside him. Once. Only once. But oh! What a night that was . . ."

"Why, you could do a nostalgic piece about Cody for the first issue, then move on to Wild Bill Hickock—"

"Draw in them thar reins, pardner," I interrupted with a chuckle, purposefully assuming a tone which Easterners associate with men from the wide open spaces. "I only met Buffalo Bill a couple o' times. Wild Bill? Never."

"No one will care. It's the *concept* that'll sell papers. Last of the old-timers telling tales about the good ol' days."

"The good days are *now*, Lolly," I replied, suddenly as serious as a hoot owl at midnight. "*That's* the truth."

"I don't understand what you mean by—"

"Sitting in my plush chair, chatting with a fine young lady like yourself? Receivin' free tickets to every sportin' event in the Big Apple. And Ziegfeld's shows, too! Dinners at Lonchamps or Luchows. Then back to my hotel suite where a soft feathered mattress and a fine, loyal wife await."

"The way you live today," she sighed, comprehending.

"*That's* what *I* call 'good.' Out west? Peel off your boots and curl up on a hard-as-rock bunk at day's end, thanking God for allowin' you to survive the past 24 hours. Dinner? Beans without beef. Worst part of all? When you had to kill a man."

"Even someone as horrid as Sergeant King?" she asked, familiar with that fabled event. An ugly incident in a low-grade Sweetwater saloon. Guns blazed on January 24, 1876, and my first shooting made its way into Texas folklore.

"When a gunfight is over, Lolly, you walk away from it. And hold your head high for the crowd to see. Then—"

"Yes, Bat?" she asked as I paused.

"You live with a memory of him in his death throes for the rest of your life. Tryin' to tell yourself it had to be, according to a set of values we believed in."

"Which was . . . ?"

"The Code of the West."

"I don't even know what that means."

"You will, if I tell you the whole tale of what we lived through in them grim territories."

"That's sure not how the stories play out in Dime Novels. Bold frontiersmen, rescuing fair damsels in distress—"

"*Curse* Ned Buntline, and a dozen other liars like him."

"Well, then!" She rolled her ravishing eyes, which I must admit were difficult to resist, even for an old fool like me. "Here's *your* opportunity to set the record straight."

"Hmmmm. When you put it that way . . ."

Now, Lolly looked absolutely inspired, her mind whirling. "This might be bigger than I realized! Once the stories are in print, we could collect them in a book. 'Bat Masterson's True Tales of the Gunfighters.' My guess? A bestseller."

"If this *were* to happen," I said after taking some time to think it through, "I'd prefer to write about those I knew personally. My mentor and best friend to this day, Wyatt Earp. Charlie Bassett, Bill Tilghman, Luke Short, 'Nervous' Neal Brown."

"Oh! How did he acquire such an odd nickname?"

"That," I insisted, not wishing to speak of such a tawdry series of events in the presence of this young lady, "is one of those things you never ever will know, not for certain. At least from my lips."

"Alright, then," she stammered, a bit taken aback. "Anyway, let's make 'em all famous!"

So, I set to work. The pieces were published during the following year. Eventually, the volume arrived in downtown stalls as well as upscale shops and sold out. That's when the bold men I'd worked with first became household names.

Or *Celebrities*, a term Lolly had recently coined.

Wyatt in particular. He sent a telegram from Los Angeles, where he and his wife Josephine resided: "Damn you, Bat! Kids show up, wanting my autograph. No privacy. Yours, W.B.E." Me? If were I to walk down Fifth Avenue, crowds rushed up.

"*More*, Bat!" people called out. "More *stories*."

*

"You must be proud that you've let the country know what you men achieved," Lolly reflected as late afternoon passed into early evening. While far below that organ grinder shut down and headed home.

"So! Tell me what bee is buzzing under your bonnet?"

"How about a sequel? Cody, Hickock, Pat Garrett—"

"I don't know," I sighed, gazing down at my desktop to a blank page I'd rolled into the typewriter.

*Maybe I was running out of things to say. Or needed to start driftin' down an entirely new trail.*

*Find a subject more important than the fight game. Maybe Marxism. And whether there might actually be another American revolution on the horizon. This one political and economic.*

"Bat? Are you quite alright?"

"No need to worry," I assured her, forcing myself to recoup from an unexpected sense of exhaustion. "Just some old wounds flarin' up again."

*Despite my words of assurance, Lolly's worried manner implied deep concern for her aging colleague.*

"Why, though, the hesitation about a second book?"

"In all truth, I may have done my friends . . . and for that matter history . . . a disservice."

"How so?"

"Well, transforming people into . . . how to put it . . . 'heroes.' In the ancient Greek sense of th term."

"What's wrong with that? America's still a relatively young country. We need our *own* heroes."

"My point is, in all truth, things weren't simple. The Good versus the Bad. Why, I personally knew desperadoes who, if events had gone differently, might now be recalled among the list of truly great men from them days."

"Wonderful! Write about 'em. What were their names?"

"LeRoy Parker and Harry Longabaugh, in particular. Back then, folks knew 'em as Butch Cassidy and the Sundance Kid."

"Think maybe I've heard of them."

"Few folks living today know that I played an important role in their lives, particularly toward the end. But all of this is . . . well . . . too personal to share."

"If you say so." Lolly looked disappointed. Then her left eyebrow arched high. "Won't you at least tell *me?*"

"I'm comfortable with that. And someday, when I'm gone—"

"*Stop* that. Why, you're in solid health for your age."

"Sixty-two! Amazed I made it this far. Anyway, when my time comes, write it. *Should* you choose to."

"I'm all ears," Lolly giggled.

"Now that I think on it, Butch and Sundance weren't what most caught my interest so much as the woman both loved."

"You've *really* got me hooked now. My favorite subject has always been remarkable females. Same with my ardent readers."

"Well, they'd sure take to the girl who rode with Butch and Sundance. Born 'Eloise,' though she hated that name."

"I don't blame her. Sounds . . . crabby."

"Changed it to 'Etta.' Miss Etta Place . . ."

A DAME TO DIE FOR: Miss Etta Place, inamorata of Butch Cassidy, the Sundance Kid, as well as virtually every man who ever gazed upon her.

# PART ONE:
# THE LAST SUNSET

"I have found myself, my work, my happiness, and
my 'way' in a life lived under the light
of Western skies."

—ZANE GREY

*Hmmmmm!*, I wondered while completing the daily chores in and around Hole in the Wall: who will I share my bed with tonight? Likely, Henry will expect me to fulfill what are referred to as "wifely duties" on his first evening back. Though ours is in truth only a common law relationship.

*Momentarily, I indulge in wishful thinking, wondering if this might be the night. And not just for lovemaking.*

*When Mr. Harry Longabaugh finally pops the big question: 'Miss Etta Place: Will you be my bride?'*

As always, his cocky grin (cliché though it may be) which in large part caused me to fall in love with the Kid at first sight, stretches from one side of that sunburnt face to the other.

Finally, the charming rogue offers me a ring.

'*Oh, yes, Sundance!*'

The ceremony completed, we two ride off into a glorious sunset. A red sky, bright with the final hints of daylight's powder blue, now laced with swirls of orange and yellow. Just as in the old fairy-tales I read to rustic scholars while still gainfully employed at my chosen profession, teaching.

*How long ago was that? Oh, I remember: five years. At times like this, feels more like fifty.*

'Woah!' a deep male voice interrupts. 'Hold on there.'

Before Sundance and I embrace and kiss, James LeRoy Parker steps between us. Broad-shouldered and the taller of the two, he extends a hand toward me, offering a lovely ring.

'*Marry* me, *Etta,*' *Butch implores.*

Silently, they wait for me to choose.

But how can I? For I love each in a special way.

*No matter. This is what I want. What every woman does, I imagine. Even more than marriage to a truly fascinating man.*

*The opportunity to choose for herself.*

* * *

"Etta?" Louise's voice beckoned from across the field. "Stop daydreamin' and get back to work!"

The stark words drew me out of my reverie. I gazed about. While rock formations surrounding our isolated retreat stretched high and mighty, no woman would mistake them for the diamond-clustered turrets on a prince's castle.

*Hole in the Wall? Aptly named, that's for certain.*

A rural slum. Eight worm-eaten cabins in a circle. A larger central log building in the middle for meetings and meals. Off toward the eastward rim, a crude barn shelters our livestock from the summer's maddening sun. Half-wild dogs run to and fro, whining or snarling for handouts. Most of the women here shout at the curs and throw rocks to shoo! them away, fearing they may carry rabies. As for me, I toss 'em table-scraps. Always had a soft-spot in my heart for animals.

The starving beasts appear ready to head back up to the hills, surrendering to what Jack London proclaimed is the call of the wild. That ancient lure of the dark forest, its treetops silver-tipped in the moonlight.

*Escape? What I on rare occasions consider doing. The curs rushing back to nature. Me? A return to town.*

That young naif accompanied here half a decade ago by two handsome gents, beckoning a bored female to follow them down the outlaw trail, does not now wear bangles and beads. Rather, outfitted in worn Levis and a rough gingham shirt. A torn kerchief holding in place the unkempt strands of my dark hair.

True also of Louise Bullock, Black Jack's latest girl. And all the other women who hooked up with the Wild Bunch.

Huh! *Mild* Bunch might be a more fitting description. They slept till noon and played horseshoes or poker all day, drinking beer from dawn to dusk. Always expecting *us* to prepare the meals and then await them in bed. Except on rare occasions when they set out for a bank job or to rob a train.

*They plan to continue doing so for as long as they can. If there's one thing they fear more than the law, it's change.*

While they're gone, we set out each morning to search this cliff-shrouded valley for rotting tree limbs to feed the fire. Later slaughtering chickens to roast, doused with home-brewed wine and fresh picked cayenne, for when the men return. *If* they return. Always have, so far.

*Which means the odds grow worse each time they ride out.*

Once back—some primitive hunger for mischief slaked—and fed, they roll us over to satisfy their other great appetite.

Louise will have Black Jack. Me? Butch or Sundance. *Always* their *choice.* Never *mine.*

* * *

"I seen a fella ride in an' hand you a letter earlier," Louise mentioned. The two of us had found a little free time to sip stale coffee before moving on to the pyramid-high pile of laundry. "Anythin' important goin' on in Nugget?"

A RURAL SLUM: Though 'Hole in the Wall' has been romanticized as the appealing hidden recluse of The Wild Bunch, the compound consisted of a series of sad cabins, randomly arrayed around a larger central building.

She referred to a small burg thirty miles to the south. Friends there would secretly travel to the Hole should news break worthy of risking a hard journey across parched badlands.

"From my friend Bowdry. You've met her?" Louise nodded. "Been working the Red Light District. Hoping to break out."

"Ain't easy, less'n a gal's got rare beauty like you."

"Thanks for the compliment. I fear it's fading fast."

"Also, book l'arnin'. That sure gives you another edge."

"Well, Bowdry's down and out. Some bum got her pregnant. A drunken doctor then botched the abortion."

"Bad, huh?"

"Seemed so, from what I read between the lines. Once the gang's back and settled in, I'll head off for a visit."

"You surely are a good friend, Etta."

"Way I figure it, a man can't be depended on when it comes to our . . . how to put it . . . *female* problems. Which, try as the boys might, they can't ever understand."

## SUNDANCE: THURSDAY; JULY 5, 1900

"Butch? You in the mood to palaver?"

"Not particularly. Been enjoyin' the peace and quiet."

"Well, that's just it. For more'n four hours, ever since you picked me up off the prairie, patched my wounds as best you could, hauled me up onto a stray horse . . ."

*Likely belonged to News Carver. Tense little fella with big sad eyes. First to get caught in the crossfire as what was supposed to be a polite train robbery turned into a bloodbath.*

"Make your point, Kid."

*As always, we'd followed the old strategy. Heaped a pile of branches and rocks on the tracks to halt the locomotive.*

"Ever since we headed back, you been whistling."

*Didn't expect anything out of the ordinary. The guards gave up their weapons. It was all supposed to be so easy!*

"And?"

*Then came the sudden sound of rapid-fire Henrys, along with the overpowering black-pepper scent of gunsmoke.*

"It ain't easy fer me to appreciate the stark beauty of this land with you blowin' yer brains out."

*I'd caught two shots in the fray. But as more bullets whizzed overhead and around, I sensed they hadn't hit me hard.*

"You know I love whistlin'."

*One shot nicked my left arm as it passed by. Another tore a hole in my leg 'bout an inch above the right boot.*

"An' *you* know I can't stand listening to it. Tell you what. How 'bout some song other than 'Oh, Susannah'?"

*Next thing I knew, my horse panicked. A second later I found myself flyin' through the air.*

"What's wrong with 'Oh, Susannah'? Why, it's the ballad our forefathers sang while crossin' this great land—"

*Then, hittin' the ground. Losing consciousness for a while as the sound of iron-shod-hooves moved ever closer.*

"Nothin.' Except after hearin' it more'n five hundred times, might you switch over to 'Down in the Valley?'"

*Figured it was all over for the Sundance Kid. Until my eyes opened and I seen Butch ride up like a phantom.*

"Sentimental hogwash."

*Then, of course, I knew things would turn out fine.*

"'Streets of Laredo,' maybe? Because, Butch . . . and I don't mean to in any way be unappreciative about you savin' my life back there . . . I may just have to *shoot* you."

*Of course, I was just blowin' off a little steam.*

"That'd sure solve the problem. Permanently!"

*In all truth, should I search my mind from here to doomsday, I can't imagine anything that might set the two of us against each other . . .*

"How 'bout 'Bury Me Not on the Lone Prairie?'"

*Why, if Butch hadn't reined in to help, it would've been back to prison again.*

"That I can perform, pard."

*As fer me? Rather be dead than behind bars!*

"Ride away, Butch. I can hear their hoofbeats closin' in."

"Forget it. We leave together or not at all."

*That's the way things were between us.*

"I understand. I'd do the same for you."

## ETTA: THURSDAY; JULY 5, 1900

"I don't mean to set you to worryin,' Louise," I said as the sultry day wore on with still no sign of the boys. "But they should've been back by now."

"That's where my mind's driftin' as well."

*I can't dwell on the possibilities. Times like this, a girl's got to think positive.*

*Or she'll lose it, like Crazy Woman Madden did. Walking off onto the prairie, talking to herself a mile a minute.*

So let me return to a happier subject . . .

*Sundance!*

Forever thinking on him, even at a time like this. More now than ever, when I can't see him. Or hold him. Recalling that even in the dark, I'd know him by his tight, hard body. How do some folks put it? Good things come in small packages.

Not that Henry's little, in truth. At 5'9", the Kid cut a fine figure. Wearing a black-leather gunfighter outfit and matching low brim hat, which I recall him sporting on that first day I ever cast eyes on Harry Longabaugh. Likewise pleasing to the eyes when decked out in fancy-tailored town clothes when we three were riding high, wide, and handsome.

*Believing our golden age would never end.*

Small? Harry? Nah! Only in comparison to LeRoy, all 6'4" inches of that muscular son of a 'B.'

*Butch!* With his angelic blue eyes and skin as soft to the touch as expensive velvet, yet with a hard as iron body. LeRoy's sweet breath smells of the dollop of honey he downs each morning. And every evening before retiring.

*For health reasons, he says. To intoxicate any woman he may encounter, I'd guess.*

On nights when my door opens and it's LeRoy standing in the light, I surrender to the devilish charm of his overgrown boy's smile and know I'm in for a night of easy loving. Not the case with Henry. Always the stain of chawin' tobacco on his teeth, overpowering me with its rawhide-like maleness.

To each his own, it says in the *Prairie Home Companion*. For Etta Place, *my* own means one or the other. Of course, respectable folk . . . *townspeople*, the sort that bore and raised me . . . disapprove.

*'Loving* two *men? Without benefit of marriage to either? Why, Eloise. That's sin without salvation.'*

*'You may be right, Mama. All the same, I have trouble understanding: How could something feels so good be* bad?*'*

*So, Henry . . . LeRoy . . . Sundance . . . Butch . . . Where the* hell *are you?*

BUTCH: THURSDAY; JULY 5, 1900

"If you like," I offered as we rode on, "we could talk."

"All finished whistlin'?"

"For the time bein.' Share what's on yer mind, Kid. Cause I can tell something's eatin' away at you."

Henry took a moment to catch his breath. If we were to palavar, now was the time. Before our throats became too dry.

"Soon we'll have to face Etta, explain what happened."

"Obviously. Your point?"

"She warned us not to try our luck again."

"What else could we do? We're flat broke."

"All the same, I'd prefer *you* break the bad news."

"Why me? She's your wife."

"*Common-law* wife.."

"Way I perceive the situation, ain't nothing separating you from the real deal but a piece of legal paper."

"Hellfire! If she and I was man and wife, I wouldn't be willin' to stand by while the two of you . . ."

"'The two of us' . . . *what?*"

"May have been me who invited Etta to ride along with us back at the start. Still, she's as much yours as mine."

"Can't argue with ya. But why should *I* be the—"

"—because I'm . . . Butch, this ain't easy to say—"

"Spit it out."

"Well, a little bit *frightened* of her."

"Truth be told?" I reckon that I blushed. "Me, too."

"How do you figure that, pard? I mean, we go and risk our lives ridin' out on jobs. But that don't phase us."

"Such dangers are part of the profession."

"Yet approachin' a teensy little gal when her eyes and shoulders are swellin' up with anger . . ."

"My guess? Most men, other than the mean-spirited sort, are pretty much the same."

"What are we good at, though, but robbin' and ranchin'?"

"I'd punch cattle again, so long as I still have Etta."

Silence prevailed for several minutes. My mind drifted back to more pleasurable times. Allowin' me to set aside the Kid's wounds and our mutual sense of failure.

"Let's face it. You and I got us somethin' none of the other boys ever did."

"One in a million."

"Yup. 'A whole lot of woman,' as the sayin' goes."

"She'd never desert us, the way Kitty Haines did Lone Star Lewis last month. Any more'n we would her."

"Why, I'd even tend to *sheep* all day, just so long as when the sun sets, things between us would continue."

"True. All that *really* matters is you, me, and Etta."

ETTA: THURSDAY; JULY 5, 1900

"Etta? Look! Here they come."

Standing a quarter mile away by the rail fence, Louise shaded her eyes with a kerchief. The near-twilight sun cast a blood-orange glaze over our recluse, momentarily allowing the hideout to appear a natural paradise. As the stifling heat of the day gave way to a cool breeze from distant purple hills, a quarter-moon then cast a vanilla sheen over our hideaway. All thoughts flew out of my head. I rushed from my cabin, joining other women in residence at trail's end.

"I got a bad feeling about this," someone mumbled.

Once I'd caught a glimpse of the mounted silhouettes, my heart set to palpitating. Butch and Sundance, heads hung low, the only ones in sight. Riding slow, as if they were in no great hurry to complete that final half mile and confront us.

"I don't see Black Jack," Louise fretted.

"Where are the others?" Kid Curry's Latina wailed.

"I don't guess they'll be comin' back this time," another woman replied, her voice full of despair.

*If this keeps up, I'll end up like her. Some day. For now, though, mine are here. That's* something!

ONE JOB TOO MANY: What would ironically come to be called "The Great Train Robbery" witnessed the end of the Wild Bunch as a pair of determined posses closed in from either side.

As LeRoy and Harry turned their sweating mounts toward the corral, several Indian lads, along with old-timers living here for wages, rushed to meet them. The makeshift group helped my boys ease themselves down, their faces despondent.

*That's when I first smelled stale blood. And knew that one or both had been wounded.*

"I told you we were pushing things," Henry all but spit at LeRoy as they plodded our way, shoulders hung low. I had a hunch his words were spoken for my benefit.

*As I've learned over five years, that's the way men are.*

SUNDANCE: THURSDAY; JULY 5, 1900

"We shoulda quit after the last haul. But, *no!* Butch says, 'let's pull off one final job and retire rich.'"

"Don't recall you arguin' with me on that point."

"Now, Deaf Charlie and Apache Dave are dead. Harry Logan, Flat Nose, and Black Jack headed off in different directions."

"Oh, then he's *not* kilt," Louise sighed.

"Kid, any time you want to ride herd over this outfit, just say the word. Till then, *I* call the shots."

As we'd agreed beforehand, I spoke my carefully prepared piece as a means of avoiding a possible argument with the ladies. For nothin' irks a man more than having to tell a woman she was right all along. And that he ought to have listened.

"What happened?" Etta asked, visibly shaken. She tried her best to make eye contact first with Butch, then me.

"I kin answer *that*," Henry stated, staring down at the bleached sand by his feet. "Joe Lefors and Charles Siringo."

*What Bat Masterson and Wyatt Earp were to Kansas back in the 1870s, these men represent in Wyoming. The territory's most feared and respected lawmen.*

Well, we'd somehow managed to escape bein' taken once more. No question, though, that in due time these Horseman of the Apocalypse would be headin' this way.

## ETTA: THURSDAY; JULY 5, 1900

Some of the other women, all hope crushed, wept for their lost loves. And for their futures, knowing this way of life had abruptly come to an end. Once a girl's fella bites the dust, she has little choice but to head for the nearest town and take up residence at a 'house.'

*A fact that separates me from the rest of them. As every gal here knows. And secretly resents.*

Yes, the brothels could prove a necessity for Etta Place down the road, as they have on occasion in my past. Yet as Louisa noted, I am unique here. Educated.

*Perhaps I will teach again. However unlikely that might seem, after such a long time riding the outlaw trail.*

Course, that's not the only thing qualified me as unique. I alone belong to two men. Once, I took pride in that. Made me feel special, like the heroine of some romantic tale. Queen Guenevere, torn between Arthur and Launcelot.

Yet the older I grew, the more I wonder if belonging to two amounts to having no man to truly call one's own. While there's still time, maybe I should decide as to which of these two overgrown children I'll spend the rest of my life with.

*But how to pick between fellows so appealing?*

## BUTCH: THURSDAY; JULY 5, 1900

"It happened this way," I began once we were inside the central building. Thick log walls, rather than the shack-like timber employed elsewhere, allowed for a sense of isolation. Etta yanked off my boots, then Henry's, seatin' both of us on a wooden bench before the fireplace. The fast crackling timber put me at ease as night set in. A prairie turns deadly cold once darkness appears.

Shaken by the news I related, desperate to do something, Louise served us whiskeys. Henry and I downed them in single gulps. Etta mosied over to the stove and prepared heaping plates of grub. Chicken 'n' biscuits, one of my favorites.

Now as always, her silence suggested an eternal sort of wisdom. For Etta, and Louise as well, understood that the one thing a man most hates to speak on is what he can't admit to himself: Utter failure as to his goals.

"We rode up, demandin' they surrender the payroll," I explained. "Fer a while, everything went well."

"Our first surprise?" Henry continued. "Fella in charge informed us that the safe now had a time lock."

"Which wouldn't open till the moment the train was set to reach its destination."

"If you'd only listened to me, Butch, why we'd have blown the damn thing open."

"Why didn't you?" Louise asked.

"An explosion might destroy the paper money inside."

"So we sat there, waitin' fer the better part of an hour," Henry confessed, his voice mournful.

"That's when two possies, twenty men apiece, maybe more, came ridin' down on us. Swift as quicksilver, and mean."

"Joe Lefors and his boys from the west," I recalled, rubbing my swollen feet, "Charlie Siringo from the east."

"*Not* demandin' a surrender. Which we would've done!"

"Why, they rode up, guns blazing, as if they'd set out to exterminate a pack of wolves."

"We! Who never killed—or even *harmed*—anyone."

"That's *terrible*," Louise exclaimed, tears flowing.

"What is this world of ours comin' to?" I asked, hoping to steer the discussion from our disaster. "Lawmen, mind you."

"My concern?" Etta sighed. "When the last century passed, all the world's 'right' and 'fair' values went with it."

"Well," I admitted in as stoic a voice as I could muster, "*I'm* surely persuaded the time has come to quit."

"As Etta here told us some time ago, Butch."

"Better late than never." I locked eyes with Etta at last. Like I used to do as a kid back in Beaver, Utah, when trying to charm my Mama out of a beatin'. "We'll begin anew."

"Good for you, Butch," said Etta. A giddy smile caused me to grasp that Etta's tone conveyed what she called *irony*.

"What about . . . *Jack*?" Louise anxiously asked as she and Etta served us a second round of dinner. "He got away?"

"Alive, last time we glimpsed him," Henry assured her.

"Will he come back?" Louise pondered, voice quivering.

"Don't count on it," Etta flatly responded when neither Sundance nor I could muster the grit to do so.

"You're right," Louise admitted.

Etta spoke, as if she'd only this moment settled on an eternal truth. "Ridin' off into the sunset with a fancy man is easy. Acceptng he's gone for good? *That's* the hard part!"

An awkward silence passed over us. I hoped that was the end of it, though Louise delivered one final stinger.

"Fer me now, Etta," she bitterly drawled. "And some day? You, too. Just wait."

"Now, don't go takin' your troubles out on *us*," I scolded Louise while rising. "No way we'd ever desert Etta."

"And that," Sundance insisted, "is the *truth*."

"Huh! Well, if you're so certain 'bout that," Louise shot back, "why haven't one of you *married* her?"

"Etta don't care 'bout things like that," the Kid replied. "Ain't that right, hon?" he asked, turnin' toward her.

I glanced over, assuming she would confirm his statement. Instead, Etta headed for the door like soaring bullet.

"What did I say?" Sundance howled. "I don't understand—"

"Men!" Louise hissed.

"Not men. *Boys!*" Etta cat-called back. With that, she left, Louise following. Though not before the latter paused to toss an epithet our way. "*Overgrown children!*"

We two sat a spell, not knowin' what to do. Or say. Like myself, I guessed, Etta suffered from stress. Alone now, we stretched our sore feet toward the fire and dozed a bit.

"Don't worry," Sundance muttered. "Things will be brighter once the sun rises."

"This time around, Kid? I have my doubts."

ETTA: WEDNESDAY; JULY 11, 1900

"We'll leave our team at the livery stable," I explained to Louise following our arrival in Nugget. We had traveled for several hours over what locals called a 'road.' In truth, the trail was a little more than a rock-strewn pathway. The two of us perched atop the wooden bench of a creaky old wagon. As our pair of mules moaned, tortured by the all but airless surroundings, we somehow made it to town. And like any good Westerners, male or female, we knew that our first responsibility was to the animals.

"You're right," Louise agreed as I pulled up before the livery stable. "No need for them poor beasts to suffer more."

I paid a silver dollar to a freckle-faced lad in a wide straw hat and dirty Levis. He promised to give the mules a thorough rub-down. As this grinning attendant did not strike me as particularly bright, I instructed him to allow our team only a small amount of water for the first hour.

"I know my job," he huffed, bringing the beasts inside.

"Well?" Louise sighed, eyes full of concern.

"Let's busy ourselves with what we come for."

We two were dressed in simple clothes of the type any pioneer woman wears to town, capped by sun-bonnets. To keep from attracting attention, we'd decided against finery or jeans as either might give us away as outlaws. For some folks—mostly town and city girls, reading Ned Buntline's outrageous accounts of romance on the range—those of our ilk might seem glamorous, daring, adventurous. A rare female who strikes out on her own, willing to die young so long as she lives wild and free. Others, as Puritanical as the mother I had known, look down their noses at so-called frontier trash.

Both views were wrong. Only those who, like Louise and I, have ridden with the west's bad boys could attest to the odd combination of highs and lows for such a female 'companion.'

WELCOME TO THE WEST: However fanciful images of a frontier town such as 'Nugget' may be in paintings and movies, a photograph more accurately captures such forlorn outposts of civilization.

"I'm nervous," Louise shuddered.

"That makes two of us."

Side by side, eyes downcast, we navigated the dirt path passing through a shabby collection of small buildings fronted by deceptively large entranceways. Dry goods stores and saloons lined each side, punctuated by an occasional barber shop, hash house, or blacksmith shop. A farm equipment emporium nestled close to a little sweets shop on one side of the street, a foul smelling bathouse on the other. Back behind us, a church, always the first building erected by folks eager to set a fine Christian standard, stood stark against a colorless sky. Its thin coat of whitewash had faded due to an unrelenting summer sun, which beat down daily on northeastern Wyoming.

"There it is," said Louise.

Directly before us awaited the brothel. This three-story building provided a bookend to the Presbyterian enclave facing it from the far side of Nugget. As some caustic observer might note, here stood the most important addition since the church. In comparison with the currently empty house of God, 'Dinty's' did not want for its own 'faithful' to arrive.

Come Sunday, the menfolk could head over to the church, silently begging the Lord to forgive their carnal sins. Some of those men had taken wives, with their families praying alongside them. Others—what we called saddle tramps—would arrive alone to likewise repent. Yet beginning early in the morning on the following Monday, one by one each would likely return here.

SUNDANCE: WEDNESDAY; JULY 11, 1900

"Howdy-do," Butch said, turning to glance my way as I stepped inside the barn. An overpowering scent of fresh hay, old leather saddles, and horse-dung nearly overcame me. None of the nine mounts stabled here whinnied as I crossed the straw-strewn floor, nor did chickens stir on their perches. Our two oversized pigs in their pokes briefly glanced in my direction, then turned away.

"Howdy, pard," I replied.

*I might've entered a morgue. That sensation wasn't about the presence of anyone. Rather, absence. Of Etta.*

Recently, Butch and I had concentrated on determining our strategy for the near future. He insisted that our necessary flight from the Hole must wait. During the following months, countless posses would be scouring the territory for the last survivors. Three riders, two men and a girl would be spotted by scouts and arrested, if not shot, on sight.

We desperately hoped the great tracker Siringo did not find his way here any time soon. If our prayers were answered, when winds covered the area with ice and snow, they'd desist. Which meant we'd remain here temporarily, then attempt to escape come spring.

"Figured you'd be stoppin' by." He cast me a feeble smile, then resumed brushing his sorrel, Apple.

"The Mexicans are cookin' up frijoles and refried beans at the big house," I mentioned. "Want to head on over?"

"Let's settle what you come here for first."

"That bein'?"

"Palaver again, while Etta's not around."

I nodded, then spoke my piece. "Here's what I think: She knows Louise was wrong in hintin' we'd someday dump her."

"Agreed."

I stepped into the adjoining stall, took up a worn brush, and set to grooming Rosebud, my palomino. Butch stepped away from his mount, pulled up a stool, and settled himself nearby.

"Tell me something, Kid. Back when we first met Etta. Did it ever occur in the wildest stretches of your imagination that some day, our feelings for her would run so deep?"

"Nah. Sixteen year old girl, standing alone on the dusty boardwalk, gazing as we rode in. Figured on a brief fling."

"Elaine, the Lily Maid of Astalot," he laughed, recalling one of the many stories Etta had shared with us. First reading out loud, she eventually guided her eager wards to do so ourselves.

"And us? A pair of Launcelots."

"Then, maybe. Less so now, I reckon. Me? Took her to be one more townie, hungry for a chance to escape the blight."

"As time goes by you acquire a sense of someone's worth."

ETTA: WEDNESDAY; JULY 11, 1900

"Bowdry's upstairs," the plump Madame—hair died orange, with large faux black eyelashes and an array of cheap jewelry crossed over her voluptuous chest—politely announced when I spoke for Louise and myself as to our reason for arriving.

*No, Madame. We are not inquiring as to employment. Not today. In the future? One never knows.*

Men of every social class came and went, wearing finery and farmer's duds, loudly bickering price with the women. And, in some cases, girls. As to the latter, their faces were as milky white as the chalk I'd employed while scribbing on a blackboard for my one-room schoolhouse filled with small scholars. In the parlor, such bargaining continued. Here, in the perfume-laced lobby, the walls were painted pink and the shabby furniture white, *de rigueur* for houses of ill-repute.

*As I well knew from sorry experience on those occasions when LeRoy, Henry, and I were dead broke between their jobs. When you come right down to it, a body's got to eat. So here's a woman's last resort, for herself and those she loves.*

"How's she doin'?" Louise asked in a hushed tone.

"Worse than I guessed," Big Sal con-fided, with sincere concern and wistful

'SOILED DOVES': In the rough and tumble West, women whose husbands had died often found themselves with no other option than working in brothels.

sadness in her eyes. "But better than I feared," she added, managing a hopeful smile.

The better part of a week had passed since Henry and LeRoy returned. I'd scrupulously cleaned, then carefully wrapped the latter's wounds, minor but potentially deadly if unattended to. Then retired to my cabin, waiting for him to join me. That hadn't happened. To my surprise, the Kid chose to bunk in his own shack that first night back. Likewise, LeRoy.

*Which provided the unexpected answer to a question I'd rolled over: Who'd come to my bower? Neither, it turned out.*

BUTCH: WEDNESDAY; JULY 11, 1900

"Kid, did you ever tell Etta that you love her?"

"Not in so many words. Figured she already knew."

"Neither did I. Funny! Had no trouble sayin' that to a dozen other women drifted in and out of my life. But as to the one I truly feel that way 'bout? It's . . . well . . . tough."

"Maybe that's the 'situation' we're facin' now. Guess a woman needs to hear that word occasionally, out loud. "

"So! Here we be."

Neither of us spoke for a while, each mullin' over the growing disconnect we felt from Etta as the days wore on. Then last night had come Etta's an-nouncement: "I wish to head into town and visit Bowdry."

*Sure. But why now? Might her motivation be less a desire to see an old friend than to get away, think things through?*

ETTA: WEDNESDAY; JULY 11, 1900

In time, a woman comes to understand menfolk if she's bound and determined to survive with them. As I'd learned, nothing makes once proud desperadoes behave more like a pair of banty roosters than a fat payroll in hand. When that's not the case, they quickly come to perceive themselves as losers, causing each of my boys to doubt his own masculinity.

Anyway, Louise and I had left them early this morning at the main table in the big house, discussing possible ideas for the future. Downing fresh coffee, hot-cakes, and fatty bacon. Their joint mood (emotionally, the two were always as one) had improved with each passing day. I gathered from snippets of their conversations that the glories of yore were done.

*Explaining why both had abandoned my bed. Each too embarrassed to try and perform with me as a true man ought to.*


SUNDANCE: WEDNESDAY; JULY 11, 1900

As to their journey from the Hole to Nugget, Butch and I agreed that any risk would be minimal. Wives and daughters of scattered ranchers traveled to town for supplies on a regular basis. Louise and Etta should go unhampered.

As to our pursuers? If they somehow located the hideout—not likely as they'd been searching for years without luck—we could spot them coming miles away. Keep 'em at bay with our Winchesters. Didn't matter how many there might be, as only a single man could approach at any time by means of the narrow passageway through high red rocks that camouflaged the Hole.

Likewise, no chance of the law starving us out. We had cattle aplenty, plenty of dried corn in storage, and a working well. When winter set in, they'd either give up and leave or freeze. Certain though to return at the first thaw. So our strategy seemed obvious: hibernate here until the early signs of spring. Then slip off before the siege resumed.


ETTA: WEDNESDAY; JULY 11, 1900

The big question now for Butch and Sundance: What to do with the rest of their lives? And, as I had become integral to their existence, mine, too. Their intentions? Noble, in an old fashioned way. Louise had been wrong. They'd surely take me with them. Yet by not including me in such decision making, I felt like a pretty piece of baggage. More cherished for its attractiveness than truly appreciated for personal value.

Once, though, the word I dreamed to hear so often during the past five years had been bandied about. *Marriage!* Though I wasn't certain whether Butch or Sundance planned to propose.

*No matter! I loved each enough to go either way. How wonderful, though, if I might make the choice!*

No doubt about it, what we three shared amounted to love. Still, a question lingered: Could even that be enough to carry us through the stormy weather on our shared horizon?

## BUTCH: WEDNESDAY; JULY 11, 1900

"Assumin' everything goes according to plan," I now said as a means of breakin' the silence, "Etta will want a fresh start wherever we wind up. A respectable life, far from here."

"No problem. Soon as she gets back, I plan on sayin' 'I love you.' Better late than never."

"Come to the same conclusion m'self."

"Did you, pard? Then think on what must come next."

"The hardest thing a man, or at least a man livin' as we do, can ever bring himself to say to a woman."

"Will you *marry* me?"

"That word could sober a fella from a ten-day drunk!"

"That bein' the case, I'll be glad to do the honors."

"Which poses a problem. Cause if marriage is in the air, finally . . . well . . . now, I want it to be *me*."

At that moment, a chill ran up my spine, even in this harsh heat. I guessed one did for Sundance as well. Time to admit the truth: Our swiftly changing attitude toward Etta could not help but create . . . well, how to put it clear and simple? A problem that must be solved. And done so in a manner that made sense for men of the West. Truly a breed apart.

## ETTA: WEDNESDAY; JULY 11, 1900

"This way." Big Sal marched upstairs as best she could in her billowing silk gown, tinted with evergreen patterns though stained from spilt coffee. On the third floor, Louise and I followed her down a hallway to the last room on the right, its slat door ajar. Sal explained that she left it partways open as Bowdry hated to feel sealed off from the world. Which, as all sensed but no one dared admit, Bowdry would soon depart.

"I knew you'd come," she exclaimed as Sal escorted us in and then excused herself. Bowdry had been here since the day of her abortion by a drunken quack as the town's 'respectable' doctor refused to operate.

*How I would like to get my hands around the doc's neck. Also, learn who had impregnated and then abandoned her!*

SUNDANCE: WEDNESDAY; JULY 11, 1900

"Tell me this," Butch said in a low voice. "If I did step aside, let you propose, then marry her . . . might we still take turns . . . well . . . *with* Etta on alternate nights?"

"Whew! Couldn't abide by that."

"Explain."

"Not easy to put in words. But . . . so long as we were wild boys of the road, she our bandit queen? That was fine. But once she and I exchange marriage vows, I can't see it."

"Which changes everything."

"Yeah."

"So, it all comes down to: How do we settle this?"

*An uneasy calm set in. For I knew what must come next.*


ETTA: WEDNESDAY; JULY 11, 1900

"Course we did, hon," said Louise, sitting herself down in a chair opposite the rickety wire-bed, piled high with musty-smelling mattresses for Bowdry's comfort. "You'd do the same if it were one of us."

I stepped to the single window, glancing down at the primitive town. People, mostly men, walked the dusty main street, off and about on their personal responsibilities, blissfully unawares of the suffering inside this tawdry room. Finally, I gathered the courage to turn and take a long, hard look at my friend. It seemed as if Bowdry had aged ten years in a few months. I tried to conceal my deep concern.

"It's wonderful to see you one last time, Etta."

Wearing a flimsy nightgown and half-covered by a sweat-stained sheet, Bowdry still wore around her wrinkled neck the symbol of that religion she'd been raised within. A Magen David, the six pointed silver star with blue embossing.

"You're lookin' pretty good," Louise lied.

"Thanks. When a woman needs to speak," Bowdry sighed, "talk her heart out, it's not a man she longs for. They come an' leave. When things go awry, only her girlfriends will do."


BUTCH: WEDNESDAY; JULY 11, 1900

"I'd like to believe we could do so over a game of cards. Winner take all, marriage-wise, nice an' friendly?"

"Can't see that happenin'," I replied.

"So?"

"Only one option left."

Neither of us could bring himself to eyeball the other. First time that ever happened in our many years together. For a spell, we remained silent. That things could come to this!

"When and where do you figure we ought to settle this?"

"Before Etta returns."

"Agreed."

"Meet me behind the corral. Shall we say . . . sunset?"

"So be it."

*We both knew Etta Place was a woman worth dying for. Or if need be, each now realized, killing to keep.*

## ETTA: WEDNESDAY; JULY 11, 1900

For three hours, Louise, Bowdry and I spoke of everything and anything. Whatever subject we happened to light on, as we women are apt to do when males are not present. At such times, females withdraw from the world that men create for us, which we are then expected to survive in. An empire defined by cold, sometimes brutal actions rather than those slow, steady conversations which we women prefered.

And so, on occasion, we must retreat to a private place of open emotions and feminine values which the opposite sex could never grasp, much less accept.

*Until, hopefully, a dreamed-of day comes when we decide it's time to take over and end their ancient codes.*

## SUNDANCE: WEDNESDAY; JULY 11, 1900

Some things can be explained; others can't. What I'm about to embark on now, to borrow one more of those bits of traditional wisdom that LeRoy and I learned from Etta, is an exercise in futility.

All the same, I felt the need to try, though likely men from the East and women from anywhere would not understand.

"That's crazy!" most people would claim. And I don't for a moment doubt they're right, at least from a certain way of seeing things. But for those who've lived their lives on the frontier, values determine one's actions. And vice-versa. What men who push westward have relied on since our first American argonauts deboarded the Mayflower and stepped down on what came to be called Plymouth Rock. They carried guns, or at least what passed for such the better part of 300 years ago.

A way of life began that day. Men carried rifles so that, as a last resort, they could get the job done, whatever task presented itself. Whether that had to do with the killing of Native people to claim the rich earth for themselves, a practice causing some of us to hang our heads in shame lately, or turning weapons on one another, as would be the case when cowboys and farmers clashed over the issue of open range.

There were those who shot first and asked questions later. They were the worst of the lot that formed the great migration. The better sort, if only by degree, hoped to find some other means to solve any unpleasant issues. More often than not, though, in the end, it all came down to the same thing: our national experience since the first European set down his cavalier's boots on virgin soil, wielding a weapon.

I don't expect a fellow who has spent his life in a solid home headed up by a fine woman, filled with rugrats scurrying in circles before the fireplace, and holding an honest job to grasp, much less accept, what would shortly come to pass here.

Likewise, women—with their more complex minds and deeper comprehension of the world we live in—would not comprehend the 'way' which a certain breed of man clung to.

ETTA: Wednesday; July 11, 1900

"When you get back on your feet again," Louise said, hoping against hope that such encouragement might lift Bowdry out of her doldrums, "you'll come out to the Hole with us."

Bowdry managed a slight smile at the thought of a longed for third act to the tragic play which constituted her life. Only once did she slip away from our talk, drifting into a troubled sleep. We two sat patiently waiting. Meanwhile, the intense mid-afternoon heat wafted in through the window. In due time she regained consciousness. Then, before we could speak again, our profound silence abruptly came to an end.

"I want the youngest, sweetest thing you have available," a self-assured male voice insisted from the hallway.

Bowdry clammed up at the shrill tone. Somehow twisting herself around on the bed, she peered through the half-open doorway. My eyes followed in that direction.

"Yes, yes," Big Sal meekly replied.

The loud man wore a beige tweed business suit, the kind a fellow could purchase only in a big city like Laramie. "I prefer a gal with blonde hair," he continued, unaware this conversation had an audience, "if there's one handy."

From my angle of vision, he appeared, as the saying goes, tall, dark, and handsome. Sporting a handlebar mustache of the type favored in those days by men of supposed distinction.

"We do have a new girl," Sal replied.

At that, Bowdry emitted a half-muffled gasp. Hearing this, the man shifted his head to observe us in the room.

"Who the hell's in there?" That's when I noticed his dark chestnut eyes. In them, I recognized what I feared most in men of a certain orientation. Outside our door stood a hard, ungiving male, possessing a heightened capacity for cruelty. We women of experience can spot them immediately. The opposite of Butch and Sundance. A virtual foil to their charming—sometimes, at least—boyishness.

## BUTCH: WEDNESDAY; JULY 11, 1900

A week ago, I risked my life to double back and save the Kid as Siringo and Lefors closed in. How did one of the old timers put it? "When you *ride* with a man, you *stick* with him." Either Henry and I escaped that valley of death or we went down fighting, as we'd always feared might someday occur.

Now? I sat in the quietude of my cabin, pistol hangin' by my side. Shortly, we'd face off and settle a situation that for us, at least, offered no other possible solution. Even though neither had ever killed a man, including our enemies.

This could not make sense to normal folks. But that term has never described our existence. As sunset colors the big sky with nature's paintbrush, we, like all true men of the frontier, will settle things in the only manner we know how.

*The Way of the Gun.*

## ETTA: WEDNESDAY; JULY 11, 1900

"You!" the man muttered, recognizing Bowdry.

"Did you think I might disappear?" she gasped.

"I surely hoped so!"

Turning sharply, he headed down the hall, Sal following. We could hear footsteps recede in the long, narrow corridor.

"That the one who got you with child?" I questioned.

"No one else but. I begged him to use *protection*, but he insisted on goin' in *raw.*"

So this strutting martinet had doomed my friend. Now, off to do the same to a younger girl. My female instinct begged me to step out into the corridor and prevent such a horrid thing from occurring. Maybe kill him with the hidden derringer Sundance had given me, always kept handy in a purse whenever I was away from the Hole.

That didn't happen. Louise, guessing what I likely was up to, sternly shook her head. I acquiesced. Make a fuss, and the law would arrive. Lest I forget, we were outlaw women.

Shivering with frustration and anger, I managed to hold myself in place. Loathing everything this self-styled 'gent' stood for: power and privilege, which we women did not share.

## SUNDANCE: WEDNESDAY; JULY 11, 1900

"Mr. Sundance? What ya readin'?"

I glanced up from where I sat in my cabin, holding a book. Ponch had cracked open the door, peerin' in with those big eyes that characterize most half-Arapho, half-Comanch kids.

"Book by America's best-sellin' writer, Ned Buntline."

"Miss Etta's teachin' me to read." Bold as brass, Ponch came closer. "May I borrow it, when you're done?"

"Actually, I've just finished."

I dropped the paperbound book on the table, rose, and sashayed over to the basin, set on a table below the clouded mirror. There I proceeded to shave and generally clean m'self.

"I can read the title," said Ponch, now holding the tattered pulp volume. "*The Last Sunset.* What's it about?"

"Happened down New Mexico way, some twenty years ago. Ever heard o' Pat Garrett and Billy Bonney?"

"*Everyone*'s heard of *them.*"

"Well, they were cowhands, workin' for John Chisum himself. Became friends, until each fell in love with the same Mexican gal. Then, everything changed. Faced off one night. Both went for their guns. History proclaims Garrett won."

"My grandfather told me. Lived in Santa Fe back then."

"Pretty much the same as what I just said?" I wiped the suds off my chin, then set to combing my hair.

"No. Grandfather . . . Old Bear . . . laughed and said it was nothin' like the way people spin the tale."

Ponch seated himself where I had been minutes before, observing my slow, precise movements as I made ready.

"Let's hear his side of it."


## ETTA: WEDNESDAY; JULY 11, 1900

"Y' know, Etta," Louise mentioned once we'd bid Bowdry goodbye, "you do have a choice as to what happens next."

"How so?"

A sudden breeze whipped dust up into our faces as we shuffled along, listless from the recent experience. As the white light of early afternoon faded, we passed by folks whose skin appeared as grey as their humble attire. People who worked hard for a living, however meager the rewards. Then ate a solid if ordinary supper, went to sleep, rose themselves up in the morning and did it all over again.

*Normal folks. Not like us.*

"Don't return to the Hole. *I'm* not."

"Figured that's why you packed a pair of bags."

"There's a stage passing through here in an hour, headin' west fer Sandy Creek. I'm takin' it."

"Anyone, or anything, waiting for you?"

"No. For me, though, the time has come."

"I admire your courage. And resolve."

"I'd love for you to travel with me. Why, we're still young enough to start over. I'm 23, though I sure look older. An' we celebrated *your* 21st birthday two months ago."

"If I *do* leave, it must be soon. But not today."

"Why so?"

"Louise, consider. If Black Jack had ridden back in with Butch and Sundance, would you be departing?"

Her eyes drifted downward. "I can't honestly say."

"You've got nothing to stay for. As for me—"

"It's always them two, ain't it?"

"If I were to leave Henry and LeRoy . . . and I doubt I *ever* will . . . I could never simply disappear."

"You'd have to tell them so, face to face?" I nodded. "The moment you tried, Etta, your will would collapse. And I must admit, they're mighty fine specimens of the male animal."

"Sure, I love them. As I know they truly do me."

"*What*, then?"

"Under those tough facades, they're like infants. I wonder sometimes if they could manage on their own."

"Maybe it's time you started thinkin' 'bout yerself!"


BUTCH: WEDNESDAY; JULY 11, 1900

"Kill one other person and you murder the world."

Etta read that to us once: Me, Sundance, and the other members of the gang. As well as those women at the Hole. Two years ago, I reckon, as we huddled by a roaring fire.

*Etta: The woman who had not only entered our lives but altered them, perhaps without us ever realizing so till now.*

Actually, I'd heard similar words years ago from my mentor in outlawry, Mike Cassidy. More on him later.

Meanwhile, as to the Wild Bunch, that had been the moment when we sensed, like eager kids listening to a fine schoolmarm, Etta had a purpose besides teaching us readin,' writin', and 'rithmetic. She shared something significant: a moral view of the world.

Not moralistic, mind you. 'Do this, and don't do that. Be good and you'll go to heaven. Bad? Hellfire awaits.' She hated that kind of talk. And the Bible thumpers who preached it.

"Harm no one," she insisted was the only law that mattered when you came right down to it.

*Otherwise? Do as you damn well please. Them that don't like it can leave you alone. As to the only universal sin? Do not take another person's life. Do so, and you are doomed.*

ETTA: WEDNESDAY; JULY 11, 1900

"My hope?" I said to Louise. "They're changing."

"Wishful thinkin', I'd bet."

"Last night, I overheard them discussing things. For the first time ever, the word 'marriage' came up."

Louise considered the implications. "Tell me this, Etta: What do you believe will happen when you return to the Hole?"

"If I guess right, they'll be waiting for me, side by side. Like gentlemen, they'll request that I choose between them."

Louise's deeply knit brow revealed her doubts. "Well, *if* this goes the way you believe, any idea who you'll pick?"

"Reckon I'll toss that about in my mind during the ride back. Likely it'll be a spur of the moment decision. Then—"

"—tomorrow'll be the first day of the rest of your life."

"That's what I dream for."

"Well, honey, I do hope it becomes a reality."

SUNDANCE: WEDNESDAY; JULY 11, 1900

Ponce related the old man's version. Garrett and the Kid had worked for Chisum, but there was nothin' to the rumor of them bein' fast friends. That was an invention of mythmakers. When Garrett left the ranch, he'd headed to Old Fort Sumner. In time, he ran for sheriff of Lincoln County. Not bein' well known, Patsy needed to establish his name. Something *big*.

Then Bonney, who had joined a rough crowd, killed a couple of men in a drunken quarrel. Garrett figured this to be his chance to make headlines in local papers. He tracked down the spot where Billy headed each night, visiting a Mexican gal. So the sheriff surrounded the adobe with a posse and waited until the Kid wandered out for some fresh air, not wearin' a gun. Pat gave the signal. The posse set to blazing away.

Garrett took all the credit. Even writin' a book chronicling the event, least-ways as he wanted others to recall it. Employin' this to rise in the local political system.

Fame and fortune. The American Dream, folks call it. Do whatever you must to reach the top of the heap. The means don't matter. It's all about reaching the heights.

"I can't imagine anything worse than a killing that's motivated by nothing but profit."

"I hear ya, Sundance. What do you think *really* happened?"

"Well, Ponch. As Butch likes to say: There's one side of the story. Then, the other. And, finally, the truth."

I assembled my most formal gunfighter outfit for the big moment only minutes away now. Black shirt, pants, boots, and hat, along with a matching leather belt and holster.

"Sundance? I like Buntline's tellin' of it."

"Makes for a better story. And that's what folks care most about. From old Adam, up to us today. Third only in importance to food and companionship, each person longs for a great tale, well told."

## ETTA: WEDNESDAY; JULY 11, 1900

As I began my reverse journey across the Badlands, a constant thumping of the wagon might have lulled me to sleep. Fearful I might fall from my seat and find myself on foot, I focused by telling myself a story. Above all others, one rated as my personal favorite. "The Wyf of Bath's Tale" from Geoffrey Chaucer's *Canterbury Tales.*

One bright morn in the days of King Arthur, when sprites and dragons still inhabited our earth, a knight rode forth from Camelot. After making a false turn, he found himself deep within a magical wood, sheltered from the sun by intertwined branches high above. Suddenly, he noticed a beautiful maiden, sitting by a turquoise pool, humming to herself.

*"You are mine, and I am yours," he said This was no coincidence. Clearly, they were destined to meet.*

Her amber eyes glanced up at the overpowering figure. Yet she feared not, sensing him to be her one true love, the swain she had moments earlier dreamed of. They sat on a hillock and drank sweet red wine from his pouch. The couple enjoyed cool breezes, engaged in small talk, and exchanged gentle kisses.

Eventually, they rose, promising to meet on the morrow. She left for her cottage while he returned to the castle.

## BUTCH: WEDNESDAY; JULY 11, 1900

Ask anyone what his or her favorite story happens to be, and that'll provide you with a key to that person's secret self. What we all want is for things to remain simple in the tales because, in the big, wide, real world everything appears confusing, however much we may hunger for black and white. Back then to New Mexico. Who was the hero or the villain; Garrett or Bonney? Depends entirely on who may relate what happened. An Australian cowboy I once met claimed we listen to the singer, not the song. Storytellers determine how we feel, what we think, and how we act as each of us attempts to live our own lives based on what we have learned along the way.

*"What do you believe to be the greatest theme of the most important stories ever written?" I once asked Etta.*

*"What it means to be human," she replied. "As the Greeks put it during their Golden Age: the end of man is to know."*

*"Know what?" I asked.*

*"The meaning of life."*

*"Which is?"*

*"Each person must discover that for himself."*

*"When he does, will The Truth save or destroy him?"*

*"Either. Neither. Both. That doesn't matter."*

*"What does?"*

*"That he unrelentingly searched for truth. His truth. For that, in the end, is what defines each of us as a person."*

## ETTA: WEDNESDAY; JULY 11, 1900

True to his word, the knight rode out again the following day, planning to beg for her hand in marriage. By noon, he had located her cottage; on its southern side, he noticed a slowly revolving water-wheel, creaking in its eternal circle. Sheep bleated their hunger to no one in particular from an adjacent corral. Hazy smoke rose from a stone chimney atop the thatched roof. The knight dismounted and gently rapped at the door.

"Yes?" an odd, unwelcoming voice called from within. The Knight stated his reason for arriving. But if he anticipated the sight of that shy maid, young Gawain encountered grave disappointment. Before him stood an old hag, her hideous eyes glaring, her crooked mouth offering a cynical smile.

"I came to visit the maid I met yesterday."

"I am she," the figure before him cackled. "Enter."

Once seated, the knight listened to her story. Some time ago, the maid had rejected a sorcerer's invitation to marry. For revenge, that evil one cast a terrible curse upon her. Half the day, for twelve hours, she could appear as her youthful self. During the other dozen, she must assume this semblance. Warts ran across her scarred forehead. Unseemly lines spiderwebbed a pock-marked face. Green, scabby lips caused Gawain to recoil.

*Might she marry the knight? Of course. The question: With the knowledge he now possessed, would he still want her?*

*Absolutely, he insisted, pledging undying love. Or, as I choose to call it, unconditional love.*

"At least there is a silver lining," she whispered. "For as my husband-to-be, you have the right to decide when I will take one form or the other. If you so choose, I will look like the beauty you met by daylight. Then, at night, become what appears before you now. Or, if you prefer, the reverse."

"But every curse can be broken," he wailed. "Tell me what must be done, and as a knight of the realm I will do it."

WHEN KNIGHTHOOD WAS IN FLOWER: Sir Gawain courts a mysterious maiden in 'The Wyf of Bath's Tale,' reputed to be Miss Etta Place's favorite story in Geoffrey Chaucer's 'Canterbury Tales.'

"Should you deliver to me the single thing in this world every woman most desires, the curse *will* be lifted."

"Name it! I will travel the wide world—"

"Ah, but there's the rub. For I cannot say. *You* must discover that elusive truth on your own."

SUNDANCE: WEDNESDAY; JULY 11, 1900

"Why'd you get all duded up?" Ponch asked.

"Seemed appropriate."

The nearer that the moment of truth between Butch and me drew, the more frequently I feared I might faint. Not owing to the possibility that I might die. That, I could handle.

*More the fear of surviving. Kill one man and . . .*

I, who had never fired a shot at a pursuing lawman. Now I prepared to do so at a man whom I considered my brother.

*Was anything . . . or anyone . . . worth that? Yes! Miss Etta Place.*

"It's sunset," Ponch observed, peering out the sun-stained window. "What's happenin' out there?"

"Mr. Butch stands at the far side of the corral."

"What's he wearin'?"

"The white suit he reserves for special events."

"He packin'?"

"The single-action Colt .44 'Mike Cassidy' presented to him as a boy. I know that fer a fact, cause Butch told me so."

"LeRoy's favorite pistol."

"You'll be usin' your Smith and Wesson, Model 3?"

"Sure know your guns, Ponch."

"Yeah! When I grow up, I want to be a gunfighter."

"The outlaw trail," I asserted, kneeling down to eyeball the child, "is fast comin' to an end."

"Oh, no. There'll *always* be banks and trains to rob."

"Won't be the same. There'll be more guards in the future, with rapid-fire rifles. Safes? Time-locked!"

"Then a new breed of bandit will come into being."

"No doubt you're right about that. A never-ending story. The details may change. The faces. But not the basics."

Sensing the time had come, I took a step toward the door. "My advice? Opt for the straight life. You may miss a lot of fun, but in the long run, it'll be for the best."

ETTA: WEDNESDAY; JULY 11, 1900

With a heavy heart, he began his quest, traveling across many lands. In the north where white-winged horses fly about in the sky like so many birds, on to an island nation in the south where cannibals lived and the sea always remains warm. Everywhere he journeyed, the knight approached the wise old ones, hoping to learn from them what he must discover. The answers were what he expected. A great fortune. A happy home. Beautiful babies. Status among other women. Power over men.

Each, he knew, was to be desired. Wisely, though, he perceived that none of these responses, so obvious, indicated the correct answer. And so a year and a day later, he returned empty-handed.

Still willing, though, to honor his commitment. When he knocked on the cottage door, the girl awaited him. Without hesitation, Gawain asked for her hand. She broke into tears, knowing this to be something more than romantic love. True love! The only meaningful form of love that existed, then or now.

BUTCH: WEDNESDAY; JULY 11, 1900

Harry Longabaugh may not have been my brother as to our flesh. Blood of my blood, that sort of thing. Still, I loved him as much as I did any of my mother's other sons. Course, I would never use that word—*love!*—whilst we were talkin', for fear I might be misunderstood. Yet here we were, a stone's throw apart, making ready to face one another. With an audience! All in the Hole had lined up on either side of our central path, ready to watch two crazy men duel to the death.

Still, long before we ever met Etta, the Kid and I vowed to never commit such a deed. We'd read our Bibles when young.

*'Thou shalt not kill.'*

*'Am I my brother's keeper?'*

The answer to the latter? Yes! As Butch proved following the worst fiasco of our careers in banditry a week ago.

"It's a man's world," someone once claimed. True or not in general, that sure was the case now.

*To anyone not born or bred in the West? What transpires next must appear utter madness. For one who walked this brutal land? The only possible solution. That may not make sense. Then again, how often does real life do so?*

ETTA: WEDNESDAY; JULY 11, 1900

"Make your choice, my husband," the girl said. "Will I be beautiful for you during the day, or the night?"

"I cannot," he sighed. "No matter how many times I think this through, I cannot choose."

"What, then?"

"It is *you* who must decide."

With that, the girl broke out in hearty laughter. "We are saved!" she exclaimed. "The curse is broken. From this day forth, I will *always* be as beautiful as you see me now."

"I don't understand," he said. "I gave you nothing."

"You have given me what every woman *most* wants: the right to choose for myself."

SUNDANCE: WEDNESDAY; JULY 11, 1900

"How do you feel at this moment?" Ponch asked.

"Bad. No matter what happens, it'll be wrong."

"You could remain inside."

"Not an option."

"Mind tellin' me why?"

"I don't have the words, Ponch. I can only put it this way: somethin' of m'self is invested in this. In time, a fella has to live up to his own idea of what a man ought to be."

"My guess? Mr. Butch is thinkin' the same thing."

Nodding in agreement, I turned the knob and opened the door. There, as expected, two lines of women and men eagerly awaited the big showdown. Willing even to risk death by a wild bullet so that, should they survive, like Ponch's grandpappy back with Garrett and Bonney, they could someday claim: *'I was there! Let* me *tell you how it* really *went down!'*

*Each, of course, with his or her own unique version of the event. As many 'truths' as there were folks assembled.*

"Good luck," Ponch said as I stepped onto the porch.

"Luck's got nothin' to do with it. Things will turn out however they're supposed to."

*Did I really believe that? Once, yes. Now? My faith in a clockwork universe is less certain. Challenged if not gone.*

I shuffled forward, down the path under a fast-fadin' sun. Butch did the same from the far end.

"Evening, Kid," he said once we were six, maybe seven feet apart, each comin' to a halt as if on cue.

"Same t' you, Butch," I replied, making certain I did not allow the pulsating anxiety inside me to show.

"Draw," he stated without emotion.

ETTA: WEDNESDAY; JULY 11, 1900

"What the hell is going on here?" I gasped.

My wagon turned the bend on the southern side of our corral, where I observed a sight so inconcievable that my mind momentarily refused to acknowledge what my eyes bore witness to.

*A dream, though I sleep not. Some nightmare that took form in my imagination. Yet did indeed play out before me.*

The women, Indians, Mexicans, and hangers-on all stood silently on either side of the trail. In-between were Butch and Sundance, right hands hanging aside holstered pistols. Apparently, neither had heard or seen me approach.

"Draw!" Butch repeated. My gaze turned to Sundance.

"I said 'draw!'" On this third time, Butch sounded fierce. Yet did I detect an undercurrent of desperation?

*They'd never argued over money or anything else. Which means this dispute must be about . . . me!*

"You first," Harry asserted, stoic as an ancient Spartan.

"Then I'll *make* you!" Butch drew his gun and fired.

"No!" I attempted to scream, but my voice would not work. Leaping down, I tripped. My scratched knees bled. No matter. All I cared about? Rising up to somehow stop the madness.


BUTCH: WEDNESDAY; JULY 11, 1900

The Kid stood, unharmed. I'd shot the hat off Harry's head. "*Now* will you draw?" I hollered.

"Sure," Sundance replied, smiling like a black cat at the stroke of midnight. Lightning fast, he did just that. A split second later, my tall white hat flew up into the air.

"Stop this!" Etta, whom I observed out of the corner of my eye, hurried close. Few among the onlookers took notice, other than a sad-faced woman who I guessed sympathized with her.

"Your turn," Sundance snapped back, as if this were some sort of wild game we played for others to relish.

*Code of the Cowboy. Way of the West. The final showdown.*

*A never-ending story for we wanderers of the wasteland. Until, at least, that day arrived when the frontier came to an end.*

"You asked for it."

I fired again. This time, Sundance winced. I could hear women swoon while children danced around ecstatically. Blood dripped from the Kid's right ear lobe. My bullet had nicked the flesh, tearing away a small piece. Harry

Longabaugh would forever wear this red badge of masculine courage. Or false pride. Depending, of course, on one's point-of-view.

ETTA: WEDNESDAY; JULY 11, 1900

"Your turn!" Sundance cackled, returning fire. A red crease appeared on Butch's flat head.

*Joking? While you're readying to kill one another?*

"No wonder the boys call you 'Kid,'" Butch snapped, bolting forward. "Won't anything make a *man* outta you?" With that, he lunged close and with his free hand whacked Sundance across the jaw, sending him flying backward.

"Stop!" I screamed to no avail. Sundance shook off the blow and rose. As LeRoy made ready to slam the Kid again, Henry dropped his gun and struck his right fist into Butch's jaw. Now it was the taller man's turn to collapse.

Sundance could have used this to his advantage but instead, he waited for Butch to regather his wits again and stand. Then, they leaped at one another like a pair of panthers. Panicked, I spotted Sundance's gun in the sand. I reached for it, raised the pistol high, and rapidly fired three times.

*Bam! Bam! Bam! That ought to catch their attention.*

SUNDANCE: WEDNESDAY; JULY 11, 1900

Butch and I paused, releasing one another, turning to see who had intervened. Each line of observers swept back, allowing room for a strong-willed, solitary woman to step forward. Me!

"Etta?" I asked sheepishly.

"Didn't think you'd be back till later," Butch added.

My guess? We must have seemed less a pair of classical warriors than circus clowns. Each trying to catch his wind while blood poured down over his lips.

"Who do you think you're fooling?" Etta shouted. "The two of you, *kill* one another? That's a laugh."

"Well," Butch wheezed, "there may be some truth to that."

"Can't you see . . . don't you realize . . . the two of you *love* one another?"

For a moment, I wondered if Butch and I might turn and face off again. For reasons I can't explain, we didn't.

"Why?" Etta shrieked. "Why do this?"

"It was all for you," I mumbled.

ETTA: WEDNESDAY; JULY 11, 1900

"See," Butch explained, "we realized that when it comes down to marriage, that ain't such a bad deal after all."

"Such a . . . bad . . . *deal?*"

"Right!" Sundance added. "But once we agreed on that—"

"*You . . . 'agreed'?*"

"We couldn't figure out which one of us ought to make a respectable woman of you."

"Which of you . . ." I stammered.

"So we decided to settle this man to man."

Tha's what I heard. What had I hoped for?

*The curse is broken. You have presented to me what every woman most wants from a man. The right to choose for myself!*

I turned and hurried to my cabin. It wasn't as if I could not speak, though in fact there seemed nothing left to say. Only that I did not wish for either to see me cry.

—INTERLUDE—

BAT: OCTOBER 25, 1921

*While explaining what occurred in the Hole, Lolly, I mentioned a writer named Ned Buntline. Re-named, I ought to say. For the man who would go by that monicker entered this world in 1821 in rural upstate New York as Edward Zane Carroll Judson. Born to a struggling lawyer who decided that his son ought to becomer a clergyman. Like so many other American free spirits, including those I'm telling you 'bout now-and I reckon myself as well—this obscure fellow considered the wide world beyond the limitations of his small hometown and abruptly decided: this may be enough for some, but I want* more.

*So, young Edward ran away from home, setting out like Huckeberry Finn to the nearest body of water. In Edward's case, that was the Atlantic Ocean. He joined the Navy under his assumed name, Buntline a reference to those ropes attached to the foot of a square navigational 'role.' At age eighteen, Ned saw action during the Second Seminole War down in Florida. He even served aboard 'Old Ironsides' herself, the U.S.S. Constitution. Whenever a violent combat concluded, Buntline would hurry below deck to write an exaggerated account of the fight, sending this off to publishers of those Almanacks that catered to the coarse tastes of our nation's least discriminating readers.*

*When Ned come home, he discovered an immense tide of devotees awaiting his next sub-literary endeavors. What to do, then, but head West, into the far lands that even then were in the process of transforming into a romantic kingdom of high adventure; at least for those stuck in factory jobs, desperate for glorious escapism to make it through the next dreary day. Arriving on the frontier, Ned headed to Dodge, following Wyatt Earp and me around in search of material for stories. Deciding to transform Wyatt into a 19th century figure of knightly stature, Ned reckoned that his own hero ought to have some special weapon akin to the long sword Excalibur. So Buntline fashioned a Colt style Army single-action pistol with an extended 12 inch barrel, named it after himself, then placed the gun in Earp's hand. Then concocted tall tales about how the bold lawman could bring down enemies from far distances thanks to the innovation.*

*Next, Ned discovered a down-and-out, whiskey sotted one- time Pony Express Rider, Indian Scout, and High Plains Hunter named Bill Cody. Inspiration struck once more: even as Ned had created his current self out of some vague idea of what the American male ought to be, he now built Cody up into*

THE LEGEND MAKER: Pop-culture charlatan/pulp fiction writer Ned Buntline poses in the garb of those Western heroes he claimed to know personally and 'imaginatively' wrote about.

*a figure of legend, Buffalo Bill. Cody's close friend, a sometimes law officer and occasional wanted man, named Hickok, soon became Wild Bill. After bringing these gents East and starring 'em in a stage show, Ned came up with an even grander concept: take the notion of P.T. Barnum's tent circuses, add to this a frontier theme, and, Voila! The Great Wild West show.*

*Cody toured the Eastern States, then England and Europe, mis-educating everyone who had not lived as an actual pioneer by providing an illusion of a swiftly-fading golden age. Those who'd spent their days toiling on farms and ranches, tending Dry Goods stores in sterile wind-whipped towns, knew better.*

*They dreamed of someday pursuing Romantic existences . . . where else? . . . in Eastern Cities.*

*I bring all this up, Lolly, not as the diversion it might seem, but for reasons that will become clear as my disjointed narrative continues. Indeed, both Ned Buntline and Buffalo Bill will become as essential to the story of Etta Place and her beloved boys . . . as I myself eventually will.*

# PART TWO: CABIN FEVER

"One morning, I fired all six shots from my revolver into the cabin wall. This was not hysteria; I did so to avoid pumping them into my pardner. Reckon that's what folks mean when they speak of 'cabin fever.'"

—Jim Bridger

BUTCH: MONDAY; OCTOBER 1, 1900

Ask any Wyomingite to relate our 'state joke' and the reply ivariably is: "In our territory, there are but two seasons. One, July and August. Rest of the year? Winter." May sound odd to hear that in the heat of a summer sun. Less so when you experience White Hell as only Wyoming knows it. A mass of ice confines a person to his cabin for what feels like an eternity. In time, a body begins to wonder if a self-inflicted bullet to the temple might be preferable to yet another day of freezing. Particularly so when you lay awake at night, shivering beneath blankets piled high, listening to the ceaseless wind. All the while, your humble refuge shakes from incessant hail that, if you listen close, seems to speak. Whispering a mean-spirited threat of encroaching death.

Perhaps the worst of it, though, is *Chinook,* an Indian term for warm winds. Westerly gale-forces that slash above, across, and around those natural towers known as The Rockies. A *Chinook* brings mighty floods powerful enough to wash away sturdy buildings. Hefty cattle that a day earlier survived an intense sleet drown in the brown muck. 'Snow eater,' the Blackfoot long ago called these sudden gusts. A girl named Wind, warm and sweet, reunites with her beloved warrior, Glaciar. *Chinook* resultin' from their explosive meeting.

*Other tribes call the woman Thunderbird or Bluejay. Always, though, the cause of this commotion is female.*

* * *

Some folks claim these disasters begin far to the west, in Hawaii. The result of the South Pacific's warmth, carried to our continent by Easterly-moving

WHITE HELL IN THE WILD WEST: Wyoming Pioneers found themselves snowbound from early November to late April, struggling to survive as blizzards wiped out ranches and, in some cases, entire towns.

winds. A powerful mass reaches our shores, then collides with peaks, melting the ice. Then a wall of water slides down their leeward sides, gaining momentum, passing through awaiting wind tunnels. These cause the Chinook to heat up again. So it is that a growing monstrosity reaches the prairie below, colliding with whatever happens to be there. You go to sleep at midnight after staring out the window at a three-foot peak of ice, only to wake next morning and observe a swiftly rising flood.

Why, even the vegetation gets confused. Buds in the ground sense this unexpected warmth, figurin' spring has arrived. Poke their hard li'l heads up through the earth, only to perish when the temperature drops again.

You know a *Chinook*, or Rain Shadow, will hit when storm clouds hover on the horizon. Only there ain't no storm. Just an unsettling calm. As a result, panic sets in.

*If you weren't already a fatalist, you become one fast. Wyoming, by its very nature, does that to a person.*

Another sign that a Chinook is near: sky appears an oily yellow in the morning, then turns gun-metal grey at noon, and finally pink as spring blossoms at evening-time. Temperatures race up and down before you can adjust to the most recent change. Inhabitants suffer headaches. Arguments break out over things that didn't seem to matter back in September. More than one man hanged come springtime for killing his partner months earlier, went to the gallows screamin': *'It warn't I. The* Chinook *done it!'*

As for me and the Kid, we avoided such confrontations. We'd been substantially sobered by Etta's reaction to our fizzled showdown. She still fixed our meals and continued our education as to the classics. But when the sun set, Etta retired to her cabin alone. And locked the door from inside.

ETTA/ELOISE: Monday; October 15, 1900

During the days following 'the incident,' which I could not wrest from my mind, I chose to remain alone as much as possible. Attempting to separate my emotions from any logical discourse. Not all that easy to do for a woman. But necessary.

So the slow process of attempting to truly understand myself demanded that I reach back to the beginning. The path that beckoned me to follow.

*No, that's not honest. The trail I blazed for myself.*

For if there is one value the frontier has taught me, and which I now believe essential to the American spirit: *always take personal responsibility for what you have become.*

* * *

"Don't be naughty," Mama pleaded once I reached the age of twelve, blossoming with the first signs of womanhood.

We lived in Hamden, Connecticut. One brisk day in early autumn, I strolled home from school in the company of a nattily attired boy who carried my books, this considered the proper way for a well-bred youth to reveal interest in a charming girl.

"I'm Gerald."

"Eloise."

"I know. I asked around."

"In all truth? So did I."

"That's funny!"

"Can I call you 'Gerry?'"

"I prefer 'Gerald.' My family is very formal."

On this dreamy golden day, the thick woods on either side of the road formed delicate tableaus of orange, yellow, and red. We halted at a point where our paths diverged. Returning my scholarly volumes, he gently placed his lips against mine.

My first kiss! I *liked* it. The experience lasted only a few seconds. Then he smiled sweetly, continuing on. Pleasantly surprised, I watched until the boy passed from sight. Turning, I found myself face to face with my mother. She towered over me, sterner even than usual, her wide walnut eyes aghast.

"Eloise, I *saw* what happened from the house."

"Oh, Momma! It felt so nice. So *good*—"

"It's sinful."

"*What?*"

"Our sect calls it 'the way of all flesh.' Surrender to a kiss, next thing you know, you're 'with child.'"

"But that's not so! For *that* to happen, I'd have to—"

"Eloise! Don't dare mouth such a—"

"I would *never* shame you and Papa."

"How easy it is for a girl to say that."

"But I *mean* it."

"Of *course* you do. Yet there will come a time when a boy tempts you to join him in the woods. Beneath a harvest moon."

"That's ridiculous," I tried to stiffle a laugh.

For some time, I had begun to doubt all my mother taught me. And our biddy teachers who insisted that nature is evil. Satan lives deep in the forest whispering for us to abandon the sanctuary of our church and join him there. Nature around, as well as inside, each. Enemy to a Puritan's soul. Resist!

*But how could a God that loves us . . . humans . . . more than any of his other creations . . . be so cruel?*

Even as such thoughts and emotions whirled within me, I felt the underside of a hard, righteous hand across my face. More from shock than pain, I broke into tears. Then shrieked in humiliation, causing my mother to swiftly step back.

## SUNDANCE: Friday; October 19, 1900

During the lazy days of August, Butch insisted that those remaining in the Hole cease their card-playing and careless jawin'. Beeves and hogs must be slaughtered, then treated with preserves before winter comes roaring along. Likwise, corn had to be harvested and stored in our weather-beaten silo. Y'see, he'd read in *The Old Farmer's Almanac* that this winter shaped up to be the worst since '82. Back then, men and beasts were all but wiped off the face of the earth hereabouts.

So, our preparations began early. Rawhide pelts were nailed to interior walls to keep the coming cold at bay. And, when the *Chinook* arrives, hold the waters out. Wood must be piled high as setting out to cut more would become impossible.

Initially, the mood followin' our showdown wasn't conducive to palaver. Butch and me weren't quite the same. We'd converse, but somehow it felt forced. I hoped that, in the dead of winter, our need to resist cabin fever would bring us together again. Not just LeRoy and myself. Etta, too.

## ELOISE: Friday; October 19, 1900

Mama appeared ready to say "I'm sorry," but sensed from my misty eyes this would only make matters worse. Next, she mustered a regretful, hopeful smile. I did not react. Then, tears forming in her eyes, she stretched out her arms. But I stood my ground, fiercely independent even then, sensing nothing would ever again be the same.

"Dinner's ready," she hastily announced. Perhaps news of a warm meal awaiting would put an end to such nonsense. As all of us do, Mama created a scenario in her mind, trusting it'd come into being if she firmly clung to her vision.

*Even as I had done this past summer, on my way home from Nugget to the Hole. Only to discover a hard truth waiting.* For the simple, if difficult, truth remains: in reality, things don't work that way. Life writes its own story.

Mama entered the house, me trudging behind. Soon we sat together in our quaint dining room. Tastefully decorated with regional paintings of whiskered governors, several framed Currier and Ives prints cut from *Harper's* magazine, and pieces of fine China, these off-white with intricate blue designs. My father, who in his simple black suit more resembled a Bible thumping preacher than the village's dairy-store owner, glumly consumed his meal of mutton and taters. Oblivious as always to the altered state of affairs.

Mama droned on. Trusting that if only she might talk long and loud enough, such banter would restore what had been our everyday lives. It didn't. That night, I slipped out a window, with a hastily assembled package of clothes, my three favorite books in a canvas bag, and a pocketful of coins.

*Never to return. Or so I believed at the time.*

## BUTCH: SUNDAY; NOVEMBER 25, 1900

"What's caught your interest, pard?" Sundance asked.

Wrapped in a bearskin coat, I had seated m'self high on a ridge, allowing for a clear view in every direction, even as snow softly fell. From here, I could spot riders from miles away. An absence of movement indicated no one rode near.

*With winter in the air, we wouldn't need to take turns on guard duty much longer. For now, better safe than sorry.*

"Been readin'," I sighed, raising high a newspaper that arrived days earlier, along with several letters addressed to assumed names, care of general delivery, Nugget. Brought here by a pal who made the ride once a week. Partly out of loyalty, if also due to a considerable payment.

"About the election?"

"That's front page news."

Sundance and I previously expressed our disappointment at not bein' able to vote in the presidential race. For McKinley, though neither of us knew much about him. His running mate? Another matter entirely. Colonel Theodore Roosevelt, during the past several years, governor of New York State. In two months, he would resign to serve in Washington, D.C. We two wanted to support our former commanding officer. Fortunately, Etta—disguised as a farmer's wife—got to cast her vote, thanks to the Wyoming Equality Act of 1869.

In this way, at least, we rough-hewn plainsmen and women were far more advanced than supposedly sophisticated folks back east, where suffrage still had not been enacted. There, men believed their trophy wives would vote as they did. On the frontier? We knew that a woman has a mind of her own.

* * *

See, back in February, 1898, we were surviving the first of our rough spells with Etta. She left Hole in the Wall at one point, headin' off to Laramie. There,

Etta landed a job as schoolteacher. That took the tar out of us. Robbing trains or banks offered no satisfaction without her. Then, we learned the U.S.S. *Maine*, an armed cruiser, had been blown up in Havana harbor. More'n three-quarters of the crew perished. They'd sailed there to protect our citizens and American financial interests once Cuba's Native people rose in full revolution against the ruling Spanish. No one was certain who torched our ship, though newspapers insisted it'd been Spain's soldiers.

*The way most folks figured: They couldn't print this if it weren't true. At the time, I believed so as well.*

"Remember the Maine!" folks shouted, figuring that this was yet another Alamo we ought to revenge. Congress put a fella name o' Leonard Wood in charge of rebuilding the army, thinned down considerably since the Civil War's end. Then, an item in the paper caught my attention. A Colonel had been assigned to recruit and train an elite division. He referred to his outfit as our military's 'special forces,' the first such since Roger's Rangers during the French and Indian War.

Loving the West and having chosen to live on a ranch, this Easterner rounded up some cowboys and Indians he had come to know. Also included were several Ivy Leagers Teddy Roosevelt met while attending Harvard. The main requirements for enrollment held that a body must be willin' to ride and shoot in the 'just' cause of liberating our nearby neighbor from them imperial Spanish.

THE HIDING PLACE: Aptly named, 'Hole in the Wall,' a snall natural tunnel allowed the Wild Bunch an all but foolproof means of disappearing into the far side of Wyoming's vast and intimidating mountains.

The Rough Riders, we were called. Funny thing (Etta might have described it as 'ironic'): once over there, we didn't do any ridin' at all. At the Battle of Las Guasima, the Kid and I (having joined under our given names) were deployed infantry style. The ship carrying our mounts hadn't arrived. When we managed to dynamite several Spanish cannon, the Colonel noted our 'above and beyond' bravery, premoting me to top sergeant, Sundance to corporal. That occured on June 24. Week and a half later, we trudged up San Juan Hill and overtook the heights. Three and a half weeks following that, we arrived home. As to Etta: impressed by our service to the country and hopin' we'd grown up, our lady-love returned.

Now? Though we felt it our patriotic duty to support Teddy, Etta insisted that showin' up in Nugget to vote would be reckless. She cited Shakespeare, "Discretion is the better part of valor." Still, we did take considerable pleasure when McK. won re-election, this time with our Teddy by his side.

## ELOISE: SUNDAY; NOVEMBER 25, 1900

Even as I became a different person that day I left home, I shed another skin when I drove into the Hole and grasped that my lovers had not grown during my attempt to introduce them to The Humanities in hopes of humanizing them. So I had set my beloved fairytales aside. Permanent-like, this time, or so I insisted to myself. Perhaps I now had to finally admit that these irresistible fools could never rise to the level of my conception for them. After watching the two face off with such ferocity, I sadly acknowledged that every one of us is a prisoner of the past. The result of our birthright, as well as all one has done and said. Also, all that's occurred, wished for, or feared. The individual self that has evolved from the seed one was at birth, plus all our worldly experiences.

How haughty I'd been at fifteen, sensing the power of my beauty, believing the universe was mine for the taking. Before the pride and poetry within every child has been beaten out by harsh reality. In time, we learn the lesson so important to the Greek heroes of their Golden Age. *Abide thee in modesty.*

*At age 21? I have no illusions left.*

## SUNDANCE: SUNDAY; NOVEMBER 25, 1900

"Something else caught your eye, Butch?" I asked, noting his interest in an item on the back page.

"Indeed. Help yerself."

Handing me the newspaper, he rambled off into the brush to relieve himself. Snug in the heavy wool coat always kept on hand for this time of year, I settled in. Didn't take me long to hone in on the story that'd left my partner feeling queasy. The piece concerned one Luke Clegg, born in 1848, Missouri. Youngest in a clan of dirt farmers from one of that state's poverty stricken counties. Same area the James and Younger boys hailed from. Violent, angry, hardened, these Southerners had joined Quantrill's guerillas during the war, continuing such bloodshed after when they weren't allowed to surrender, as those in Robert E. Lee's official army had.

*A far cry from either of us 'gentlemen bandits.'*

In 1865, the Cleggs created holy hell along the frontier. There was Amos, or Old Man Clegg, bullwhip carrying father of four outlaw sons. Three of 'em mean-spirited. That left one, a sprout: Luke. Everyone agreed he was gentle and so might have been adopted. Still, Luke tagged along after his deadly Pap.

Best of the badmen, Ned Buntline called young Luke. For more'n ten years, the Cleggs pulled off bank heists, highway robbery, railroad jobs, even a wagon train massacre. Then, they made the mistake of trying one job too many. Up in Minnesota, townsfolk sensed the threat of five unknown arrivals and reached for their rifles, firing out their windows.

In the street, holding their horses' reins, the old man died first. His boys? All wounded, though each lived to stand trial. As capital punishment did not exist in that state, the oldest were sentenced to life without parole at Yuma. Luke, 28, hadn't worn a gun. He got off easy: 25 years with the possibility of early release after twenty. Emboldened, he took up serious study behind bars. When not hammering away at some rock pile, Luke earned the equivalent of a high school diploma, then a college degree. After further study, he become a lawyer.

Paroled at age 53, Luke walked out of prison wearin' the cheap suit each ex-con receives. In the sunlight, his future appeared bright. He headed for St. Louis and set up a shingle. One prominent banker who believed in giving people a second chance at a decent life hired Luke to handle his paperwork. Well, this upstanding citizen had fathered a plain but gentle daughter, age forty-five. Luke asked if he might court her and damned if the banker didn't give his consent. The woman responded positive-like. Must have seemed, to Luke, as one of them British poets Etta loves to quote, had written: *God's in his heaven; And all's right with the world.*

Then, Luke's parole officer paid a visit. He sat Luke down to consider the fine print in an agreement that the kid had quickly signed. Had Luke waited one more year, he would've left free and clear. That was not the case. The contract included a small-print clause he, in his haste to be free, had overlooked: legally, Luke could not marry for five years after being released from prison.

"I'll wait," his prospective bride insisted, offering what Etta claims is the only love that matters, unconditional. But Luke reportedly threw back his head and laughed out loud at what he now perceived to be the utter absurdity of life. Here was the straw that broke the symbolic camel's back in the *Arabian Nights* Etta had introduced us to. Luke headed over to his rooming house and hung himself. Story on this paper's back page? Luke Clegg's obituary. Leaving me to think: *there, but for the grace of God, go I.* Or Butch.

Perhaps both. Unless we get ourselves out of this line of work once and for all. Fast, and forever.


ELOISE: SUNDAY; NOVEMBER 25, 1900

In what seems a lifetime ago now, I headed West by train. Paying for a seat whenever I could, hiding in boxcars once my money ran out. In time, I slipped down from a cattle car at a whistle stop called 'Laramie.' Not much of a town then; hard to believe in only a few years this would emerge as a major outpost of civilization. Yet here I sensed a girl with an education would have little difficulty landing a teaching job. In fact, I did. That sustained me for a while.

But the West, I soon realized, did not, as I had naively anticipated, resonate with romance. The days were long, slow, dull. Until, that is, I found my place. Or it found me, in the presence of two handsome horsemen. Slicker than molasses, they drifted by. Drawing in their reins after noticing a girl on the boardwalk, she equally fascinated by these mavericks.

'She' was *me*.

When I boldly dared ask their names, each removed his sombrero, sweeping them toward the sky in a rogueish manner, announcing themselves as Butch Cassidy and the Sundance Kid. At that moment, my old life ended, and a new world opened up. A still-innocent mind thrilled to the possibilities. I was then sixteen, arrogant enough to believe the world to be my oyster.

*Today? I only feel exhausted. Twenty-one, going on fifty.*


BUTCH: SUNDAY; NOVEMBER 25, 1900

"Well," I said, wandering back as the Kid glanced up, eyes wide with concern, "what do you make o' *that?*"

Henry didn't answer for a spell, mulling this over. Then: "There but for the grace of God go I."

"My sentiments exactly." I sat beside him, chuckling. "Maybe something like this is all we have to look forward to?"

"Now, you sound like our woman."

"*What's wrong with that?* She might say—"

"*If* she were still talkin' to us."

"My belief? This paper didn't just happen to come our way. We were *meant* to read it. And havin' done so—"

"Avoid just such a future?" He mused on that briefly.

"We'll spend the winter patchin' things up with Etta. Lettin' her know, through action and word, *she's* in charge. And if she'll allow us one last chance, we'll set aside what she calls 'masculine nonsense.' Become the fellas she needs."

"Do you think we can pull it off?"

"We have to. If we don't, it's all over."

And so we settled in for what would prove a difficult month and a half during which cabin fever took on a whole new level of misery. We tried to make things right with Etta, though she remained as emotionally distant as she was nearby in our crampled, ever more frigid hideaway.

## ELOISE: Monday; January 7, 1901

"I'll be back before dark," I told the boys, still making a point to avoid eye contact. Once more, I sat high upon our rickety wagon, the mules readied for the three-hour drive.

"God go with you, Etta," they called out simultaneously.

This time, I traveled solo. And on a considerably more disheartening mission than when Louise and I headed for town. Even as the air took on a frightful chill in recent weeks, a sense of coldness settled deep in my heart. A furtive note from Big Sal explained in fragmented English that Bowdry had passed, her burial scheduled for noon today.

So in a pre-dawn stream of moonlight, in the morning of a new day, in a new year, in a new century, once more wearing a discrete calico dress, I'd determined to attend.

## SUNDANCE: Monday; January 7, 1901

"Etta," I said after working up the courage to do so and wanting to try and set things straight before she left, "over the past month, we've feared that we are about to lose you."

"I can't say for certain what the future may bring, boys. Only that we'll talk on this once again, when I return."

"Be assured," I announced. "Come sunset, we'll be right here, waitin'. This time? No guns, no fist-fights."

"Willin' to accept *your* choice," Butch added.

"My choice as to . . . *what?*"

"Why, marriage, of course. To whomever you should pick."

"How I would have loved to hear all this the last time I rode back," Etta laughed, if without humor.

"I don't get your drift."

"That was then, Sundance. This? Now."

"It'd kill me to think I've lost your love."

"That's not what I'm saying, Henry. In all truth, I'll love you forever. You too, LeRoy. Forever and a day."

## ELOISE: MONDAY; JANUARY 7, 1901

"What, then?" he sighed, voice ripe with vulnerability.

"True love never dies. If what seemed to be true love ends, it never really was such in the first place."

"We feel the same way," Butch softly replied.

"Still, love can take different turns. Like a river, slow and steady at one point, swirling white water just around the next bend. Boys, please understand: *I'm not the person I was.*"

"We sensed that," Sundance mumbled.

"Too much has happened for me to simply go back to the way we were. Yet I'll always love you both."

"You're a very special woman."

"I appreciate that, Henry. But maybe this is the way a female . . . *any* woman . . . has to reconsider things at my age. When, no matter how much she still wants to put the decision off for another year, and then another . . . I am no longer a 'girl' but a 'woman.' I must act accordingly."

Nodding solemnly, they turned and headed back to the main lodge. After watching them enter, gait slow and shoulders hung low, I set off on the barely visible trail for Nugget, even as the first hints of daylight peeked over distant purple hills.

## BUTCH: MONDAY; JANUARY 7, 1901

"Not certain if I'm more worried about the things she said," I mumbled once we were seated at the main table, mugs filled with black coffee, "or the way in which she said 'em."

"No question we got us a 'situation' on our hands."

"Like the times themselves, things are changin'."

"Either we change with 'em, or lose her forever."

Neither of us said anything else for a spell. In time, a half-Comanch, half-Negro woman—one of the few who hadn't picked up stakes and moved on—served us tortillas and beans. Nearby, the fire sparkled and snapped, warming us a little. I reached into my pocket and pullet out an aged wallet, playing with it as a child does a toy. Where did I get this long ago?

Oh, I remember. Bat gave it to me! The worn leather reminded me of an old gambling buddy.

Wonder how William Bartley Masterson is makin' out in New York, now that he's hung up his guns and become a reporter? I ought to get a long-overdue letter off to him. While I still can, before the next blizzard hits and we're boarded up for the duration.

ELOISE: MONDAY; JANUARY 7, 1901

"Oh!" I exclaimed, as if a solution to my troubles had swooped down like a *deus-ex-machina* in some old Attican fable. Tacked up on a bulletin board located alongside Nugget's livery stable, the front page of their newspaper stated in dark block print: "McKINLEY'S INAUGURATION WILL OFFICIALIZE A SECOND TERM." While national events intrigued me, this seemed special owing to the boys' devotion to Colonel Roosevelt.

That's when I spotted a small, hand-written note that read: "TEACHER REQUIRED FOR SCHOOL RE-OPENING: Any Interested and Qualified persons, Inquire at the Town Hall."

A WOMAN'S RETREAT: Despite the crudeness of most frontier towns, tea parlors eventually appeared alongside livery stables and hardwore stories, allowing 'respectable' females an elegant getaway from the dirt and dust.

*Why, it's as if the message were set here just for me.*

Once the mules were settled, there remained an hour before Bowdry's last rites. Considering this unexpected opportunity and with a little free time, I slipped into a café that appeared cleaner than most of the others.

"Where would you like to be seated?" the hostess asked.

Several women, their middle class respectability obvious in dress and manner, sipped tea at a central table. I asked for a small booth off to the side. From bits and pieces of conversation, I learned their subjects of interest: the latest in women's fashions, recent changes in territorial politics, and a rumor that something called a Nickelodeon—some sort of picture show—might arrive in Nugget next year.

In an isolated corner of this bastion of refinement, I quietly took my noon meal. All the while pondering whether I might have happened upon a means of becoming 'respectable.'


SUNDANCE: MONDAY; JANUARY 7, 1901

"What do you figure we ought to do next?"

"Well, until Etta returns and we have that long talk she promised, maybe we'd best sit tight."

"I ain't certain. Earlier, I was reading another of those plays Etta recommended. Shakespeare's *Julius Caesar*?"

"One way of getting' your mind off our troubles."

"One line stuck with me." I opened the book and flipped to a page I had marked off by dog-earring its top.

"Men are sometimes masters of their fates."

"Tell me. What's on your mind?"

"Figurin' out a way to make everything turn out right."

"Lot harder to do than it sounds."

"I know. That's why I was hoping you might come up with something. You always been the brains of this outfit."

"Well, in all truth, an idea *has* been taking shape."

"Don't keep me in suspense, pardner!"


ELOISE: MONDAY; JANUARY 7, 1901

When Nugget's respectable ladies left the tea-house, I sat alone, other than the waitress who headed over to clean their table. All at once, as I concentrated on the boys back at the Hole and what they might be up to right now, a speech by Shakespeare passed through my mind. One from *Julius Caesar*, which I'd read many times and even taught to the more advanced schoolchildren.

*There is a tide in the affairs of men, Which taken at the flood, leads on to fortune. Omitted, all the voyage of their life is bound in shallows and in miseries.*

*On such a full sea are we now afloat. And must take the current when it serves, or lose our ventures.*

Did a teaching position offer a swift, fresh current? If *awarded the job, should I take it? Ought I to consider what's best for the boys? Or think of myself first?*

BUTCH: MONDAY; JANUARY 7, 1901

"You opened the can, Butch. Now, spill the beans!"

"We've got to leave the Hole sooner than later."

We were alone in the big room. With the exception of two hold-outs, the women had departed. Ponch and the Indian lads left to join their people for the winter. Most of the old-timers drifted off, heading south for more hospitable climes.

"You mean *before* spring breaks?"

"No. I mean *immediately*."

To pass what felt like endless hours, I had poured over everything there was to read, tearing through the Almanac several times. Which caused me to alter our plan for escape.

Sundance froze, and not from the chill. "You joshin'? We couldn't make it out of Wyoming through five feet of snow."

"Next *Chinook* ought to put an end to that. Warm up the whole territory. Temporarily at least. That's all we need."

"We'd have to move hard and fast before the next snow."

"Here's what's been botherin' me. Should Lefors and Siringo foresee our strategy, they'll move just before winter breaks. Come spring, we'll still have to shoot our way out."

"Which might put Etta directly in the line of fire."

"Right. So we must all depart here, and *pronto!*"

ELOISE: MONDAY; JANUARY 7, 1901

First came the funeral. For I would not allow some pipe dream to interfere with my reason for coming to town. As I had expected, the small, solemn event took place half a mile out of Nugget. Far north of the respectable Christian graveyard, in a half-hidden spot where all local derelicts were buried. In addition to myself, Sal, and nine girls in her employ gathered to weep over the loss of one of their own.

"Whatever happens," Big Sal whispered in my ear as four townsmen of the roughest order, eager for day labor, lowered Bowdry into the pit, "Don't let this be *your* final chapter."

"I've been thinking the same thing."

"I have great faith in you."

*Butch and Sundance? With or without them, I must crawl out from under the blanket I'd buried myself beneath.*

"So long, old friend," I whispered as Bowdry—wrapped in an oil-stained canvas sack—was lowered down to the bottom of that dark cavity. Moments later, her humble box, ungraciously covered with dirt, disappeared from sight. A self-appointed whiskey-bloated reverend arrived to read over her, as the town's most prominent man of God had refused.

"Ashes to ashes . . ."

I allowed myself to believe that Bowdry sensed my presence, she proferring a smile, a wink, and warm wishes.

". . . dust to dust."

"How can you be so certain I'll make it, Sal?"

"Because, Etta, you will refuse to fail. As always."

*That's it, isn't it? Refuse to fail and you will succeed.*

"Before you leave," Big Sal said, handing me an object covered with brown paper, "Bowdry wanted you to have this."

Confused, I unwrapped the package. Inside? Bowdry's most cherished possession. I clasped the silver chain around my neck and slipped the Star of David over my blouse.

## SUNDANCE: MONDAY; JANUARY 7, 1901

While waiting for Etta's return, we set down to do some serious reading. She had suggested that we ought to turn next to all twelve volumes of *The Winning of the West*. We did, proud that our former commander had authored this epic work. Beginning on page one, I learned that Teddy played down the landing at Plymouth Rock, as well as the Revolutionary War, in America's history. He argued that our "true origination story" began when pioneers pushed deep into the wilderness. There were peaceful encounters with Native people as well as violent ones. That was true too of the earth itself, from rich grasslands to arid desserts. Such light and dark experiences forged what in time emerged as as a common American identity.

Never had it occurred to me that 'history' might present a reader with anything but hard facts. My mind opened up to the realization that this term could include philosophical issues. For the true meaning of Roosevelt's work had less to do with what happened—when, where, and to whom—than a single overriding idea he employed to explain the past 300 years: a concept he called Americanism. T.R. perceived our basic experience as an ongoing conflict

THE ORIGINAL AMERICAN DREAMER: Daniel Boone decided that life in the Eastern territories, ever more 'civilized,' did not satisfy a deep hunger inside him, pushing West into the then unknown Kentucky territory to constantly recreate himself and begin again with a second chance of success in life.

between "savagery" and "civilization." Our true character came into being as a result of such constant give and take.

First there had been values our forefathers brought with them. If from varied lands of origin, all shared a common core of Christian belief. The woods are dark, any town brigtly lit. T.R. saw it otherwise. The West could prove beneficial for one's health, whereas smoke-filled cities smothered a man's spirit. Old Daniel Boone, whom Roosevelt cited as the first true American, lit out from a village in North Carolina to that unknown place called *Kaintuck*: the dark and bloody grounds where varied tribes came to hunt and fight.

"Elbow room," he said when asked why he had to go. Soon, other emigres from Europe followed in his path. In so doing, they re-invented themselves. And invented 'America.'

*Roosevelt viewed our ever-westward adventure as a rich panorama of a nation discovering its unique identity.*

How I wanted to discuss this with Butch. But I could sense that he now had more immediate matters on his mind. He had again returned to the much-trusted *Almanac.* "In two weeks, there will be a thaw. Expected to last three days. Then, blizzards once again. A brief window for our escape."

"If we move that fast, Etta will have no choice but to likewise leave, or spend three months here on her own."

"But will she leave with us, or on her own?"

"That, pardner, is the wild card in this fresh deck."

ELOISE: MONDAY; JANUARY 7, 1901

"Welcome back," Sundance said, the starless sky afire with incandescent hues of purple, the Hole a magical realm.

*How strange a thing is human nature! Now that I had a hope of leaving, a sudden shot of nostalgia ran through me.*

"Howdy, boys."

"What's that dangling over your blouse?" Butch asked.

"A memento from my old friend. Any objection?"

"Hell, no," Butch responded. "Jesus wore one, didn't he? Well, if it was good enough for God, it's fine with me."

*All the same, I tucked the Magen David under my blouse. For in truth I was still a Protestant, if a fallen one.*

"Will you, Etta Place, be my bride?" the Kid requested.

"Or mine," Butch asserted.

*No trace of the earlier wildness . . . the childish shows of raw masculinity . . . could be detected in their voices.*

"*Your* choice, Etta," two insisted as one.

Hating to disappoint either, I explained my newly discovered possibility. "I can't say yes; I won't say no."

"What does that even *mean?*"

"It *means*, Sundance, I'm no longer certain if I wish to marry either of you. Or, for that matter, anyone at all."

That took them back apiece. Finally, Butch replied: "As to the 'unconditional love' you spoke of?"

"My love for you is not diminished. And never will be."

"But—" Sundance stammered.

"We're not talking love now. We're talking marriage. Along with that, a whole over-ripe parcel of goods."

"What caused this turnabout?" Sundance wondered.

"Life," I responded for lack of a better answer.

BUTCH: MONDAY; JANUARY 7, 1901

A Sea Change had overtaken Miss Etta Place. If I'd been dimly aware of such during the previous months, at this point I could no longer fail to recognize her transformation. Yet I knew that whatever the future might bring, I'd try my best to adjust to whatever was in store for us.

* * *

In truth, I once experienced a life-changing moment in my past. This occurred when I reached the age of eight. We lived in Utah at the time. As a naive child, I accepted the strict morality of my Mormon upbringing. Yet we were poor—dirt poor. My only pair of jeans were worn, matted, and ripped. As I attended school each morning before heading home for chores followed by a simple meal, I came to resent the laughter hurled my way by other children. If hardly well-to-do, they were at the least neatly attired in clean outfits. For the first time, and if in the vaguest form, an idea gradually took shape in my mind: if this is the way of the world, then something's dead wrong. A body who works hard ought to at least achieve a certain level of decency if only for the honest effort.

So it was that I did something that would change my life forever. In town, at a dry-merchant's shop, brand new Levi jeans hung outside the adobe building. A price tag announced: two dollars. I didn't have two cents. But I was determined to have them pants, and more'n willing to work for them. A neighbor I knew would pay me to help out on his hog farm. So with no thoughts of taking what didn't belong to me, I yanked down the Levis and scratched on the wall: "I.O.U. Two bucks. James LeRoy Parker." According to my family's standards, If a man's word is sacred, his signature rates as holy.

Before I could finish my supper and head off to begin earning some money, there came a loud knock at the door. When Papa opened it, there stood the town deputy marshal, grim and cold. Alongside him? The merchant, eyes burning with anger. Though handcuffs were not employed, they dragged me (with my father dutifully marching along behind) to the local court. No matter how hard I tried, I couldn't convince the old judge I did not intend to steal. If that were indeed the case, why would I have been stupid enough to identify myself by name?

Mercy, or something akin to it, was the order of the day. No, I would not be confined to a cell, owing to my youth. But the incident would be recorded for future reference. And if in the following months I were to do anything wrong . . . whether by intent or accident . . . I'd be arrested once more, and treated as a two-time offender.

The jeans were returned. Papa beat me soundly. The next day I wore my torn pants and again suffered the crude humor of schoolmates, as well as a nasty round of taunts. My right fist smashed into the face of the tallest bully, at which point our teacher took me by the arm, pulled me inside, and slapped my hands with a ruler. Upon hearing of this, Papa beat me again. Bitter, I set to picking up a prized jacknife here, a bottle of pop there. Not, mind you, leavin' my identity behind. And so it was that stealing became second nature to me.

Glancing back, can I say for certain that, if figures of authority had treated me sympathetically, everything would've turned out different? Might I have settled down to a life as a farmer? I don't know. Perhaps that's one of those things in life that a body never does. Not, at least, for certain.

ELOISE: MONDAY; JANUARY 7, 1901

To relieve their confusion, I told Butch and Sundance about a meeting I'd had with the assistant town clerk. As it turned out, their former schoolmarm had up and wed, heading off to California. The town of Nugget had that very morning agreed, via a mailed contract, to hire some Missourian for the position. Next came the tricky part. This candidate could not free himself from obligations for several weeks. And, winter aside, schooling must resume. This meant a temporary person would be hired to fill in. Also, if for any reason that Missourian cancelled, as can happen, most likely the position would become permanent.

I had filed an application should they wish to interview me. When asked for an address, I replied that messages should be left at the post office, under General Delivery. If one did appear, our confederate would deliver it to the Hole.

"Where does that leave *us?*" Sundance meekly asked.

"If offered the job, likely I'll accept."

"And our *arrangements?* For the time bein', that is?"

I managed a sweet smile for the first time in recent memory rather than answer in words, allowing them to grasp that the good times, to phrase such private stuff politely, would return. And, perhaps, take on a new dimension. For my mind had lit on a notion during the trek back. Inspired by several recent French novels I'd read, penned by Colette: a daring young woman who raised eyebrows by breaking the old rules as to what was proper in print, even in bohemian Paris.

"Whether this winter will prove our final time together, or a prelude to what follows, I can't say."

"Meanin' for now everything will be back like it was?"

"Not quite. Some nights, it'll be as before. On others, I want the two of you together. What the French call a *menage*."

SUNDANCE: TUESDAY; JANUARY 8, 1901

"You awake?" I asked, once Butch began to stir. We two were in the large bed that dominated Etta's cabin. Each of us had been here before, often, though always one at a time. Last night we'd agreed to give that concept of Etta's a try.

"Never been to sleep."

When I came to consciousness, Etta had already left, off and running on her usual tasks. I clung as close to the left side of the bed as possible, my partner off on the right. A rumpled sheet in-between indicated where our lover had been.

"So . . . what do you have t' say 'bout what happened?"

"May be a long time before I can make sense of it."

"Me, I'm not certain there *is* any sense to it. I do know that the experience was . . . pleasant."

"Curious word to choose."

"You got a better one?"

"Mmmmmmmmm . . . *strange*."

"Strange in a good or bad way?"

Butch hesitated before speaking. "Good, I guess."

"You reckon what we did might rate as a sin?"

"Been rollin' that around in my mind. The Commandments clearly state that one man must not *covet* another's wife."

"So it comes down to how you interpret that word: covet."

"I always assumed it to mean the same thing as desire."

"If that's the case, then I'm guilty as charged. Likely, them words apply equally to a common-law marriage."

"That's the bottom line here. However she chooses, *if* she does pick either of us, the other will then . . ."

"Covet her. No way can *that* work out well."

"So what's to be done?"

"Good question! Sorry that I don't have a good answer."

ELOISE: TUESDAY; JANUARY 8, 1901

"I suppose it will work," I admitted after a discussion of the new strategy. "Still, I'll need to mull this over."

"We accept that," Butch replied. He rose and drifted over to the black-iron stove, heaping more grub onto his place.

*In the past, Butch would have motioned for me to serve him. Maybe, just maybe, they are indeed coming along.*

"Whatever you say, Etta," the Kid timidly ventured.

*Like Butch, I sensed Sundance chose his words carefully. But did that truly indicate the growth I hoped for, or only a temporary modification of behavior to win me over?*

"I like the sound of *that*," I admitted. "So! Got around to pickin' a place we might strike out for?"

"First, Cheyenne. Catch a train from there."

"To where?"

"East. I know how Lefors thinks. He'll assume we'll push further west, all the way to California. And pursue."

"*East*," I heard myself echo. That word held a special magic for me. A vague promise of cosmopolitan existence of the sort I'd devoured while perusing contemporary magazines.

"A new start on the Gold Coast sounds attractive to me."

"Well, Kid, as Horace Greeley put it, 'Go West, Young Man!' Problem is, that's where the law will search first."

"Besides, none of us are young anymore," I reminded him. "Those words, by the way, were first spoken by John B. Soule."

"Is there *anything* you don't know?"

"Yes! Which is why we need to talk."


SUNDANCE: TUESDAY; JANUARY 8, 1901

"We're listenin'," I apprehensively responded.

"Following our . . . how to put it . . . 'experiment' last night, I've spent the morning considering my situation. As an independent woman, and as a person."

"Does what happened change things?"

"Last night, Sundance, was about joy. Total acceptance of a natural part deep inside me that knows such experiences are not wicked as my strict parents insisted. Rather, *good*."

"You speak for me, too," Butch stumbled. "Mostly."

"Explain," Etta insisted.

"Initially, when our . . . is the proper term 'tryst'? . . . began, I been on one side of you, Sundance on the other. Each doin' his best to satisfy your . . . desires."

"Did you find that enjoyable, or not?"

"Very much so!" Butch insisted. "For once, I cared nothing 'bout my personal satisfaction. Rather, part of a team, dedicated to making sure *you* were fulfilled."

"Took the words right outa my mouth," I whispered.

"Then, without warning, we three all rolled up together. My body made contact with the Kid's, and his with mine."

"That concerned me some, too," I admitted.

Etta's eyes made clear she understood, in a way that women grasp the concerns of men but we have trouble doing with theirs. Finally, she said, "If we are to continue together, we must enter into a new phase. That will take many adjustments. Time will tell. For now, though, the more pressing business of a possible escape must be the order of the day."

"Agreed!" Butch said.

"Alright, then. California is out. Where do you suggest?"

"Chicago, maybe. Unlikely they'd look for us there. An' if so, they'd have a hard time pickin' us out in the crowd."

"As for Siringo," I recalled, "he and I played poker in El Paso once years ago. I doubt he'd even know me by sight."

"And Lefors never met us in person," Butch added.

"One problem with Stockyard City, boys. From what I hear, the area reeks of slaughterhouse blood. Scent of it carries across the city. Not certain I could handle *that*."

"Where, then?" I asked Butch.

"As far East as a body can go: New York City."

"Your thoughts on that?" I asked, turning to Etta.

"I think," she replied, eyes growing as misty as they appeared that day we first met her, "it's *wonderful!*"

ELOISE: WEDNESDAY; JANUARY 9, 1901

"In my opinion," I explained the following day, "the best place for us to head is indeed New York." I'd spent numerous hours researching this destination in magazines and books.

"Care to share your reasoning?" Butch asked.

"First, their population statistics. At current count, Chicago has nearly two million residents. Good odds for a disappearing act. But New York City's are more generous still: a whopping three and a half million folks inhabit Manhattan Isle."

"Tell me: what's your *real* motivation here?"

I laughed aloud, realizing how far LeRoy had progressed in regards to understanding me and, perhaps, women in general during the past few months. Whether Henry had advanced or not, I couldn't be certain. His naivete was essential to the man.

"I read an article in *Harper's Monthly* claiming it's a model for all cities of the future. Everything's there from restaurants and theaters to the latest styles of fashion. I mean, truly *cosmopolitan*. How I'd *love* to experience that."

"Maybe settle in permanently?"

"Perhaps. Again, no promises!"

"If we *do* try it, how are we fixed for money, Butch?"

"Figure we have a little less than two thousand. Sounds like a fortune but, believe me, it won't last long."

"We'll need twice that much."

"Well, Etta, there's our cattle. I could round up the few hangers-on here, head south as soon as the weather breaks. Sell 'em to the highest bidder, then hop a train East."

"Maybe I'll start out earlier," Sundance mused. Haven't seen my sister in ages. Love to visit her in Buffalo, New York. Then, down to the City to make arrangements for our stay."

"I have an old friend there who'll help you with that."

"For me, it all depends on that job in Nugget."

BUTCH: THURSDAY; JANUARY 10, 1901

Those final words of Etta's echoed through my mind for the rest of the day and night. I slept alone that night, Etta temporarily sufferin' from The Curse. Rising, I wandered over to the barn. There, I knew, the Kid would be waiting. Caring of his mount while expecting me to show.

Hard to explain the experience of brushing a horse to anyone who hasn't lived his (or her) life with such lofty creatures. Calm, simple, and patient, they'll remain standing for as long as it takes in a cold barn, never doubting that sooner or later, the owner will arrive and resume the ancient ritual. Then, we share a special moment. The simple act of brushing, love silently passing from person to beast. A moment in the here and now that draws a person into somethin' greater than his own self. A special feeling, physical and spiritul, that remains with you long after the act itself concludes.

"Hello," Sundance said, glancing up, smiling meekly.

I entered, slamming the thick doors against what may have been the most mournful wind I ever heard. "Howdy, Henry," I replied, eyes revealing surprise that I'd employed his given name. "Or if you prefer Harry."

"Henry will do."

*If we were to successfully escape to New York, we'd have to shed our outlaw monikers. Might as well start now.*

Kicking hunks of straw-covered dung aside, I stepped into the adjacent stall and reached for my own brush.

"Always feared someday we might lose her, LeRoy."

"Never did care for that name."

"Robert?"

"Make it James. Always wished I'd been named that."

"James it is from now on. Anyway, up until yesterday, the truth of a coming change never hit so close and hard."

"Don't jump to conclusions. All Etta indicated is that she will take the *temporary* position, if offered."

"Oh, they'll offer it. Imagine if you were on the board of directors, greetin' one candidate after another. Then, the door opens, and this rare beauty glides in—"

"Wouldn't be any further discussion."

"And why would she decline? An opportunity to leave the life that's worn her out."

"Still, recall how Etta's eyes lit up when she spoke of New York. I've seen her gazing at pictures in magazines. She fantasizes over Manhattan as if it were the Isle of Avalon."

"What are you drivin' at, LeRoy? I mean, *James*?"

"Once, long ago, we offered her romance."

"Over time, that dimmed."

"So will New York. The reality of big city life can't measure up to the paradise she's concocted in her mind."

"You'd think when one dream dies, a woman would put the whole idea out of her mind. Forever. But, no."

"For Etta, right now, the dream is The City. She's seen images of women attired in finery, livin' the lush life."

"But once she arrives . . ."

"Most of the streets in New York can't compare to that Fifth Avenue they so love to photograph. There'll be slums and such. Which will give Etta cause to reconsider."

"When she does?"

"As the old sayin' goes, 'home is where the heart is.'"

"If that's so, then when we strike out from New York to wherever we decide to head next, she'll come with us?"

"That, pardner, is my general drift."

"I can only hope you're right."

An hour later, I departed without ever getting' around to addressing the main subject I wanted to speak of: the night all three of us spent together.

Wasn't so much the strangeness of us both worshippin' her body at once. No, it was the accidental physical contact between the two of us. First time that occurred, felt like a lightning bolt tearin' through me. Then, I . . . well . . . got used to it. I'd hoped to engage my longtime saddle pal in conversation as to this.

*Yet I couldn't bring it up. I wonder why that's so?*

—INTERLUDE—

BAT: OCTOBER 25, 1921

*Before long, Lolly, I'll come into the picture. So let me intrude on this disjointed jigsaw puzzle of a tale and trace my own personal history. I ran away from my family's home in Wichita at age 15 and joined the buffalo hunters, working as a skinner for Wyatt Earp. Several years later, when Wyatt was appointed town marshal of Dodge, I served as his deputy. The good people of Ford County elected me sheriff, but after one term I moved on to sow my wild oats. Playing poker for profit and betting on, then promoting, boxing matches.*

*This is how I spent my time in Crede and other Colorado towns. Even there, though, my reputation preceeded me. Folks requested I pin on a tin star again. Occasionally I obliged 'em so long as it didn't interfere with my primary interests. Then, I recieved a telegram from an acquaintance in Dodge City. Luke Short had a problem. Though Wyatt and I seemingly had cleaned up the town, a corrupt Ring*

*we'd busted regained political power. They passed legislation redistricting the number of saloons that might open and ooperate. The laws were fabricated to force Luke, now the owner of the Long Branch, out of business.*

*Old friends are the best friends, I believe. Naturally Luke contacted me, Wyatt, 'Mysterious' Dave Mather, and other pals from the old days. We arrived, fully equipped for a showdown. When members of the Ring saw seven seasoned gunfighters, not a shot was fired. Luke could again run his saloon unfettered. We were referred to as The Dodge City Peace Commission, even posing for a group photograph, hanging on my wall today.*

*Here was a remarkable story—people standing up against the politicians—but the gutless local papers wouldn't touch it.*

PARDNERS: Bat Masterson (standing) and Wyatt Earp (seated) created the Law and Order League that tamed the Queen of the Cow Towns, Dodge City KS, in the early 1870s; their chief means of operation was strict gun control.

*Which gave me an idea! I'd long wondered if I might have what it takes to be a writer. So I started up my own little news-sheet,* Vox Populi. *My hope? Provide a paper that spoke to and for the common man. His plight, his misery, his lot in life. Aspirations and disappointments. Humanity in the raw!*

*That I'd recently taken to reading the social philosophy of Karl Marx influenced this aspiration.*

*Most folks had kind things to say, citing my personal writing style. One chap claimed I'd invented a new form of journalism, in which the author became the focus of any story. In all truth, Ben Franklin had blazed that journalistic trail a century earlier with* Poor Richard's Almanack. *But my paper folded after one glorious issue; it was too radical for local businessmen to advertise in. So, I returned to wagering on sporting events. Then, I jotted down notes while observing the slugfest between Suave Jim Corbett and The Great John L. On a whim, I headed over to Denver and persuaded the city paper's editor to publish my piece: the fight as it appeared to me, from a personal point of view. The fellow offered me a steady job on the spot, but the pay was too low.*

*More on this later. Meanwhile, let me return to the time that Etta, Sundance, and Butch left Wyoming for New York.*

THE DODGE CITY PEACE COMMISSION: IN 1881, gambler Luke Short (standing, second from left) reached out to seven magnificent gunfighters including Bat Masterson (standing, third from left) and Wyat Earp (seated, second from left) to defend the Long Branch Saloon from corrupt politicians attempting to close it down so that their own establishments would make higher profits.

# PART THREE: LEAVIN' CHEYENNE

"I believe that one carries the shadows, the dreams,
the fears of where a person has lived under one's
skin no matter how far and wide they travel."

—Maya Angelou

ELOISE: MONDAY; JANUARY 28; 1901

Despite leaving the Hole long before dawn, I nonetheless arrived late following a four-hour ride. During the night, a fierce hail had completely covered the trails. This slowed my team so much that I briefly considered turning back.

LeRoy, or as he preferred to be called James, forewarned me to expect this: the storm before the calm of the next great Chinook, already visible on our horizon. All the same I pushed on, clothes and other essentials packed high in the wagon. I refused to glance backward. How odd it felt to ride away from that familiar place without the boys bidding me goodbye. As circumstances dictated, each had lit out on his own several days earlier to handle agreed-upon requirements for escape.

Feeling dwarfed by what appeared an ever-widening white landscape, a sense of loneliness overtook me. One thought did sustain this woman who had gone by the monicker 'Etta Place' for the past five years, from now on addressing herself as Eloise Long: if things worked out and I was offered a two-week position, I'll check into the Nugget Hotel.

Never to see Hole in the Wall again, perhaps? *Likely!*

Eventually, I spotted the outskirts of the town ahead, even as oversized snowflakes commenced to falling.


HENRY/SUNDANCE: MONDAY; JANUARY 28, 1901

"Ever wonder why every last one of 'em is colored red?"

"The thought never entered my mind."

An hour earlier, even as late evening ushered in a sudden fading of the light, a crusty gentleman with a Walrus mustache and wearing a mid-priced suit seated himself across from me on a heavy barge cruising along the Erie Canal. Our destination: Buffalo. During the past five days on my zig-zag route from Cheyenne to Albany, I'd opted for one abrupt change of trains following another. Finally arriving at the state's capital, I'd shifted to this man-made waterway. A potential reunion with my sister brought me melancholy remembrances of our family from many years ago.

Then I'd head south and settle livin' arrangements for Butch—*James*—and Etta—*Eloise!*—as well as myself: *Henry!*

Fascinated by a visit to some unknown destination, I observed an occasional stark farmhouse, each surrounded by high-piled snow. Back behind every family structure, these diverse in color, invariably stood an old red barn. The Walrus-like fellow had been studying me as I gazed out the window at

'FIFTEEN MILES ON THE ERIE CANAL': Before the railroads became New York State's dominant form of transportation, visitors to Buffalo would arrive at that northwestern city by boat.

farmlands in upstate New York. The harsh night sky appeared darker than coal until passing clouds revealed a full white moon, casting an eerie glow on the fields below. The methodical beat of our ship's motor as it churned through the dark waters kept me from falling asleep.

"Well, now that I've raised the issue—"

"Custom of the country?" I replied.

"In a manner of speaking," he nodded. "Sure. But recall that every 'custom' of any 'country' began at some point."

"Surely, you're right about that."

"Are the barns all red where you hail from? Where did you tell me it was—"

"I didn't say."

"Montana? Wyoming? Your accent hints at somewhere therea-bouts." Still, I didn't offer a specific location, determined to maintain anonymity at all costs. "No matter," he coughed to cover his annoyance at my silence. "So! As to the barns—"

"All of 'em red."

"See, as a traveling salesman, I've journeyed all across as well as up and down this great land of ours . . ." The Walrus droned on.

SHUFFLE OFF TO BUFFALO: In the glory days of the Erie Canal, Buffalo served as a mighty city in northwestern New York for import and export as well as industry.

## ELOISE: MONDAY; JANUARY 28, 2001

The town hall—a massive grey-stone structure, apparently intended to signify the permance of civilization in Nugget—appeared stark as a morgue. Set high on a lonely ridge, the columned building had been all but abandoned today, owing to a predicted blizzard. As I stepped down a chilly corridor and entered the lobby, I noticed several candidates for the job. Each sat prim and proper, anticipating a turn with the all-important interviewer. None among the two women and one male made eye contact. My instinct was to turn and hurry away!

*Yet how desperately I need this position. So, despite the frigidness inside as well as out, I assumed a seat and waited.*

One by one, the others were summoned by a stiff-looking fellow with a long hollow face and scarecrow's frame to follow him down a corridor into an adjacent office. As each in time re-emerged, bundled up, then left, I attempted to read their facial expressions for some sign. None appeared uplifted.

Having been the last to arrive, I eventually sat alone. Finally, that one remaining clerk entered, directing me to follow him. We entered an undecorated room with a single frame chair, apparently a holding space for the latest applicant.

"Wait here," he flatly commanded before exiting.

BUTCH/JAMES): MONDAY; JANUARY 28, 2001

"I tell ya, Butch. I've come to the conclusion we're all of us just sittin' around, waitin' to die."

"Pretty grim outlook on life, old friend."

"Realistic, I'd say. And as to what you just called me? *Friend?* Ain't so sure it fits."

"All the same, Mike, that's how I perceive you."

"Huh! I gaze in the mirror and see a no-good scoundrel who took a wholesome Mormon boy and turned him wild."

Mike Cassidy referred to the first time we met nearly twenty years ago. I'd been fourteen, most of my hours spent working dusk to dawn on father's small, unyielding ranch near Circle-View, Utah. My folks moved us to the Seagull State from Maine when I was five, lightin' out for greener pastures only to discover yellow weeds. We owned a hundred head of non-quality cattle. They kept Paw and me busy all day, making sure every last one was well-fed and clean. Let 'em get dirty and a sudden plague may well wipe out the herd overnight.

Each evening, Mama would have a solid supper for us and the sprouts. I was firstborn, with another boy or girl arriving annually until the number reached eleven. "Go, and multiply," the good Lord told Adam and Eve as they departed paradise. My parents apparently took them words literally.

Following dinner, Paw would read aloud from the Book of Mormon for an hour or so. Loved those stories about Jesus visiting America! Then, off to sleep. Younger kids, their beds lined in parallel rows in the large room, loudly snored. My bed fit snug against a far wall. That way, if any suffered bad dreams, I'd attend to his or her innocent mind. More often than not a chorus of heavy coughing kept me awake all night. Which allowed me time to think. If there was one idea that kept passing through the mind of Robert LeRoy Parker, it was that there's got to be more to life than this.

*Out there, somewhere. Trick is how do I find it? Or do I simply wait for it to find me?*

Eventually, my Paw's strugglng enterprise failed, as most small ranches in our county already had. Draughts one year, floods the next. Couldn't compete with larger outfits able to undersell us. After Paw explained this, I saw the world from a whole new perspective. The deck is stacked against the little guy. And honesty don't necessarily pay off.

*In a perfect world, it would. Fact is, we're stuck with this real one until somebody comes up with a better version.*

ELOISE: MONDAY; JANUARY 28, 1901

As the minutes slowly ticked by, I wondered if I had been forgotten. The sound of hailstones pounding down on the roof and a swift darkening of the sky outside the window caused me concern. Then the clerk, unaware or unconcerned that I could hear, confided to his boss, "Wait'll you see *this* one!"

*Maybe I should hurry out of here fast, before—*

Before I could move, the clerk returned, now wearing a heavy over-coat. My guess? He would usher me into his boss' office, then make a hasty escape. Leaving me alone in this tomb-like building with a total stranger.

*If only Butch and Sundance were here! There I go again! Wishing for my knights to rescue me rather than save myself.*

"Mr. Ironside will see you now," the clerk announced, his tone flat and impersonal. Attempting to assure myself that any threat existed only in my mind, I resolved to convince this unknown man that I was the best qualified person.

*How does the expression go? Smart women, dumb decisions!*

As I stepped inside the office, the clerk's diminishing footsteps echoed down the corridor, offering clear proof he had scurried away. Not just from this room but the building. That's when I recognized the big man behind the imposing oak desk. And sighed deeply at the realization of precisely how vulnerable I was, at least if his memory proved sharp. Here waited none other than the tall man I observed in the hallway of Sal's house several months ago. The one, Bowdry said, who had impregnated and then abandoned her.


HENRY: MONDAY; JANUARY 28, 1901

"In Buffalo," my unrequested companion continued, "you'll also find the barns red. The question, though, remains: *why?*"

"In all honesty?" I admitted, tired of the manner in which he drew this out, "I don't care one way or the other."

I returned to my book, a Russian novel in translation that had mightily impressed Etta. I mean *Eloise*. The author, Leo Tolstoy, had (as she explained) decided that books which delight readers with love stories featuring happy endings must give way, in Modern Times, to something far more true to life. That way, readers will be made aware most illusions shatter, leaving us with a bitter aftertaste. In *Anna Karenina*, Tolstoy employed the title character to drive home his abiding point, "Romantic love will prove to be the final illusion of the Old Order." I was eager to discover how Anna's illusions about the special lifestyle a natural born beauty believes due her might eventually dim. And muse over Eloise's personal reactions.

*Damn, though, if the salesman didn't continue.*

"Once we arrive, take note of something as you wind your way through the city. Most buildings there are built of brick. Hard and solid. And, as you'll note, all . . . ?"

"Red," I sighed, guessing his drift.

"Bricks dyed red for city tenaments," The Walrus continued with a knowing wink, "and wood dyed red for country barns."

"The point you're drivin' home?"

"Simple as this: the *cheapest* dye you can purchase is red. *That's* the reason. The one and *only*."


## ELOISE: MONDAY; JANUARY 28, 1901

Recognizing him, I suppressed an urge to laugh. This is how it works in way too many far-flung outposts of what we loosely refer to as civilization. The bigger the hypocrite, the higher level to which he rises in local society. The question facing me now: would he likewise spot me as one of the two woman visiting Bowdry on that summer day?

"Haven't we met before?" Ironsides inquired. Glancing up from his paperwork, he signaled his guest—me!—to close the oak door, then seat myself across from him.

"I doubt it," I fibbed, offering an explanation that I recently arrived from Laramie, where I'd taught school. The location was true, though that was some time ago. Pushing the pile of papers aside, he eyeballed the young woman before him.

"Be that as it may," he mumbled, as if still wondering.


## JAMES: MONDAY; JANUARY 28, 1901

Once Paw sold the place for what little he could get, we packed up and, hungry for work, headed to Salt Lake City. This occurred a month following my seventeenth birthday. From then on it was day labor for Paw, me, and my two oldest brothers. Any job to pay the rent on our sad little shack. I found work at a butcher's shop. My parents nicknamed me accordingly.

One day, a big Irish fellow wearing a jaunty bowler, gun-metal blue with a bright green band, meandered into the shop. He sported a mustache so broad it stretched across his plump reddish face from ear to ear. The charmer stopped in hopes of selling cattle to my current employer. Though the small store ordinarily bought stock from a local outfit, the price Mike Cassidy offered was so low my boss found it impossible to refuse. I set at once to slaughtering the beeves out back. Before leaving, Cassidy came around, sizing me up.

"Don't figure you for a butcher, boy."

"Just doin' this until somethin' better comes along."

"Young strappin' kid like you wants to improve his lot in life, he's got to seize the reins and ride out."

"How would I even get started?"

"Well, you can lose that bloodied apron and tag along with this pilgrim. Got a spare horse and I'll be leaving this afternoon. Drive fifty head to Cheyenne. Care to ride along?"

ELOISE: MONDAY; JANUARY 28, 1901

"Well, I have gone over your references carefully," Amos Ironsides haughtily announced. "They are impressive."

"I'm glad you approve," I replied in my humblest tone of voice. If A.I. worked here in the City Hall, then likely he would not come around the schoolhouse much. "If you wish," I heard myself continue, "I could start work Monday."

Any silent prayer I'd sent up high that he might reply with a simple 'yes' or 'no' came to naught as Ironsides rose. His handsome, if hard facial features and powerful frame, clear in the light of a flickering lamp, caused me sudden concern.

"You see," he spoke following an uneasy cough, "there are *so* many candidates that I'm having difficulty deciding between them. Tell me, Eloise. What might you *specifically* offer?"

"Nothing," I hastily retorted, my tone no longer ringing with false humility. "If you think any of the other applicants might better fit your needs, I do understand. Goodbye!"

HENRY: MONDAY; JANUARY 28, 1901

I realized the salesman's presence here with me now ought to be considered a boon. For he'd shared something I truly did need to know as I set out on a whole new life.

"Are rich folk the exception? Do they choose yellow or blue so neighbors will take note of how moneyed they be?"

"You might guess so. But take it from me. The rich are stingier than the poor. Houses they build for their family may be white, blue, or yellow. But if they have a barn, it's red."

"What do they do, then, with all their money?"

"Sit around counting it. And believing that when it's their time to go, somehow they'll take it with them."

*Which caused me to wonder: if I were to someday become rich, would I become like them? Not all at once, perhaps. But over time? And without me even realizing so?*

ELOISE: MONDAY; JANUARY 28, 1901

I rose and turned to hurry out the door. Seemingly shocked by my reaction, the large man lunged in my direction, skirted around my slender body, and barred my way.

"No, No. *Please*, don't go. I only meant—"

"That it might be wise for me to profer some *incentive*?"

"Well," he muttered after clearing his throat and casting guilty eyes downward, "something like that."

Seizing my packet of references which he still clutched in his left hand, I released the contempt I held for this sort of man. "I think it best for both of us that I leave immediately."

JAMES: MONDAY; JANUARY 28, 1901

Two days after Mike Cassidy and I first met up, we rode side by side on a barely visible trail across the wide stretch of prairie. Though choking on dust raised by the dry wind, my spirits remained high. I felt free at last. Wasn't until a full week later I glanced more closely at the brands on them steers and realized they were stolen.

THE COMPLEAT COWBOY: Before heading down the outlaw trail, the youth who would become 'Butch Cassidy' embodied an easygoing lifestyle as a humble cowboy.

"Got any compunctions 'bout that, bub?"

"Don't bother me much."

"You do appear to come from solid stock."

"So? What good did it do 'em? Or me?"

"Butch, boy, we see the world the same way."

"Still, I wouldn't want to bring embarrassment on my folks. They're good people. Naive, maybe. But good."

"Then take on a new handle and follow the Outlaw Trail."

"What'll I call myself?"

"You're welcome to my name. We could pass ourselves off as father and son."

"Alright, then. From now on, I'm *Butch Cassidy.*"

"Fits ya well."

"But I do draw the line at one thing. I won't kill anyone. Not ever."

"My philosophy, precisely! Come the day of reckoning, our Good Lord may see fit to forgive a few stolen doggies. But the takin' of a life? Do so and ye be damned for eternity."

ELOISE: MONDAY; JANUARY 28, 1901

I turned, reaching for the doorknob. Abruptly, Ironsides' mighty hand grasped my wrist, holding me firmly in place.

"Release me!" I howled in my most ferocious voice.

"What's the hurry?" he replied, smirking.

"I'll have you know I am capable of defending myself."

"Are you?" he continued in a sinister tone.

"All I want is out of here!"

"But the job is yours. I only meant—"

"I wouldn't take it now if you paid me double."

That only caused him to grin more menacingly.

HENRY: MONDAY; JANUARY 28, 1901

"Now, here's why I brought this up. Figured you to be a man of the West, likely heading east for the first time."

"Speak your piece," I replied.

"No. See, if you can grasp the importance of this, rather than me telling you."

"No matter how different people may seem at first—"

"When you come right down to the basics—"

"People are the same all over."

"Anything else?"

"Oh, yes," the Walrus concluded. "Money makes the world go round."

*I'll remember that, I thought. Both those epithets. Might come in handy someday.*


ELOISE: MONDAY; JANUARY 28, 1901

"Stop!" I shouted. When he replied with a mean laugh, I spit in his face and kneed him in the groin, hard as I could.

"You *bitch*," he screamed, surprised enough by my double-barreled assault that he momentarily lost his hold on me.

"Back off," I warned, half-turning to seize the door's knob. Quickly recovering, Ironsides lunged forward. "Why, you little *snip*. How dare you speak—"

Ironsides abruptly halted, though, at the sight of a derringer which I'd yanked from my handbag with the same speed Butch or Sundance would have while drawing a larger pistol. Mine was the gun Sundance bought me as a birthday present two years ago.

*Insisting that I always keep it close. Just in case I should ever need it. Such as right now.*


JAMES: MONDAY; JANUARY 28, 1901

So my life as an outlaw began. I rode with Mike Cassidy til the day he felt too worn down to continue. That's when he bought a ranch deep in the rolling hills of Wyoming. Offered me a job as top hand, though I headed off on my own. *Now, here we stood, face to face again.* Two Cassidys. Earlier, he had paid me in greenbacks for the herd driven here from the Hole.

"Mike," I sighed, noticing a melancholy aura in his eyes. "Don't feel guilty in your old age about corruptin' me."

"But I do."

"That sure wasn't the case."

"How do you figure?" asked a shriveled incarnation of the mighty man I'd teamed up with so long ago.

"Way I see it, if you hadn't happened along when you did, someone else would have. Sooner or later. If I hadn't found 'The Life,' it would've found me."

"Well, come on in to my little study fer one last beer before you depart. We can recollect about the good old day*s.*"

"Sure. If indeed they were 'good.'"

"Well, rememberin' together, that's how they'll seem."

ELOISE: MONDAY; JANUARY 28, 1901

"Now I remember," Ironsides gasped. "Ive seen you before!" His eyes bulged. "At Sal's, visiting—"

"Dead to rights on that, mister! I watched my friend dry up and slowly die on account of you." I dared ease my way backward toward the door.

"You ornery hellcat!" he snarled. As his chest shoved up hard against the cocked derringer, my little gun went off. His brief cry of agony will forever remain locked in my memory.

*A moment later, the figure of menace lay dead at my feet. Outside, I heard the chimes sound midnight. And shuddered.*

HENRY: TUESDAY; JANUARY 29, 1901

Early the following morning, I stepped off an Erie Canal passenger boat and found myself in Buffalo. This metropolis northwest of New York City served as home to more than 325,000 citizens of all ages, second in size for the state only to The Big Apple 375 miles southeast. Once, tribes belonging to the Iroquois Confederacy hunted the bison here before those shaggy beasts were driven ever further west by encroaching white men. Then, in the mid-1700s, well-meaning, if misguided, Jesuit missionaries brought the dubious gift of Christianity and unwelcome curse of smallpox to the natives.

Thy were followed by the French, who harvested hemp and tobacco until such farmers were driven north, up to Canada, following the French and Indian Wars. Replaced by British settlers and, in time, Germans and Irish. Also, escaped slaves from the South who traveled here by way of the Underground Railroad. Always, the population became more rich and diverse. When sleek railroads drew away some of the business from raw old flatboats that transported grain and other goods along the Erie Canal, completed in 1825, Buffalo further prospered.

*Which was what I had determined to do from now on, in particular after sampling the wisdom of that unknown man.*

ELOISE: TUESDAY; JANUARY 29, 1901

I'm uncertain as to how long I stood there, frozen like an ice sculpture at some winter carnival. The gun's 'pop' had been muted by close contact with the heft of Ironsides' body. We'd been the only ones in the building and I doubted anyone in the immediate vicinity might've heard. A derringer doesn't make much noise when fired. Considering the intensity of this sudden storm, most townsfolk would be bundled in their homes, sleeping near to their raging fireplaces, thick wool mufflers wrapped around their heads. Unaware of a killing nearby.

*What to do now? That was obvious. Get away. Fast!*

Halfway out the door, I paused, then hurriedly returned. Reaching down, I removed the leather wallet from his jacket pocket. Forty-five dollars wasn't much, but would certainly add to the two hundred Butch and Sundance bequested me.

*'Maybe I'll meet you boys in Manhattan?' I'd said. How quickly things change. 'Maybe'? Now: For certain!*

JAMES: Tuesday; January 29, 1901

Sitting at the worn wooden table in the center of his humble shack, Mike asked what might be next for me. When I admitted I had no idea but that I did believe Sundance and I would meet in Manhattan, then head on to far climes outside the jurisdiction of U.S. laws, Mike excused himself for a couple of minutes, returning with a rumpled magazine.

"Received this in the mail coupla weeks ago. Some firm contactin' all the ranchers whose stock was done in by the blizzards of '82 and '84. Suggesting we relocate."

"Gonna take 'em up on it?"

"Like I told ya, Butch, I'm just bidin' my time. Lately I have trouble stumblin'. But *you*? You're still young enough to . . . well . . . re-create yourself, so to speak."

"Interesting way of putting it."

"Anyway, take that along with ya, glance it over."

Nodding, I accepted the publication. On its soft cover appeared a portrait of the lushest, most inviting stretch of greenery I'd ever observed. Appeared to me like a second Eden. Above the picture, a single word proclaimed: "ARGENTINA!"

ELOISE: Tuesday; January 29, 1901

I exited and rushed through whirling snow to the livery stable. A grey-bearded attendant eyed me with displeasure. He had hoped that his last customer would have arrived earlier, allowing him to head home. I apologized for the lateness of the hour, then snapped the reins and headed directly into a nasty gust of which blew razor sharp ice across my face.

Shortly, I was on my way toward Majestic, a larger burg twenty-two miles to the south. There, a spur to the railroad's main line had recently been completed. The following morning, I could sell the wagon and mounts for however much they might bring, then head by rail eastward to Cheyenne, on from there to New York. If I made it that far! Sleet billowed around my rig. Initially, the mules were too terrified to advance across the menacing landscape. Yet the howling tempest threatened to bury us in seconds if I allowed them to remain in place. I must get them moving.

"Haaaaa!" I screamed in the manner of bullwhackers I had observed. I whirled the rawhide whip high, bringing it down on the mules' shivering backs, though not hard enough to draw blood. Since childhood, I'd absolutely cherished animals. *More frightened of me than the storm, they pushed on.* How had Big Sal put it? I will succeed if I refuse to fail!

## HENRY: TUESDAY; JANUARY 29, 1901

"I can't believe it's really *you*, Harry," Dagmar gasped when I appeared at her door in the pre-dawn darkness, even as the children remained asleep up on the second floor. Dag used my birth name which the family had always preferred. My sister prepared an early breakfast and shortly her slender husband joined us. Ronald: a scowling fellow with thinning hair, complimented by a well-trimmed mustache and beard.

"So you're Harry? Dag's mentioned you often."

Ronald took considerable pride in explaining that that he had made a fine name for himself along the Canadian border as a dealer in dry goods. For some reason, he seemed to feel it all-fired important to convince me that he was a success.

"Sounds impressive," I responded.

From the manner in which he shook hands, graciously if hardly conveying warmth, I took him to be a stuffed shirt. We had 'em out west too. Always, though, they were townsmen, never cowboys. Soon I met Dagmar and Ronald's daughters. They were initially confused as to why this stranger stepped inside their parlor, interrupting the coming day's long list of domestic rituals.

"It's like the prodigal son in the Bible," Dagmar said, marveling, "returning after everyone had given up hope."

"Thank you for that thought," I sighed, grinning. "Though of course we're still a far piece from the old homestead."

"Be interested in hearing your story since then," Ronald said while staring at my missing ear-lobe. I sensed a threat here.

## ELOISE: TUESDAY; JANUARY 29, 1901

Ordinarily, town employees would return at dawn to the building to resume their duties. But I'd heard workers discuss shutting down their offices on account of the weather. Likely, Ironsides' body would not be discovered until Thursday, after residents managed to dig their way out of half-buried cabins.

Then, the law would relentlessly pursue me. Not, as I had previously feared, for my long-standing companionship with the boys. Suddenly that seemed a minor offense. The botched train robbery? A local, or at most territorial, crime. Unlikely Siringo and Lefors would pursue Butch and Sundance once they'd fled.

*Murder? Something else entirely. Hours ago, I was a minor figure in an unfolding play. Now? The primary villain.*

JAMES: Tuesday; January 29, 1901

Riding away from Mike Cassidy's spread, I recalled my first experiences after he and I parted trails. Not knowing what to do without my mentor, I decided to follow the pattern we'd settled on during our partnership. 'Liberating' (as Mike so enjoyed puttin' it) cattle from open range surrounding big ranches, driving them to some distant territory, selling the dumb beasts to locals known for asking no questions.

On my own, I chose horses instead of cattle, which had been the case with Mike. Always, I preferred to be around such beautiful creatures rather than sluggish, slow-moving beeves. Then, to borrow a phrase from Etta, by fate or chance, I ran into a slick fella named Matt Warren. I might've gone through life as half of a team with Matt rather than Sundance. But accident or destiny determined otherwise.

ELOISE: Tuesday; January 29, 1901

Between Nugget and Majestic, pretty much everything that could possibly go wrong did. We hadn't pushed more than a mile through the heavy downfall before I noticed a creaking from the rear end of my dilapidated vehicle. Then came a sudden thud.

"What now, God?" I wailed. There was no response.

Turning, I saw that the wagon's right side had collapsed into a snowbank. The mules, confused and frightened, halted in their tracks. Slipping down, I recognized the problem at once. The aged rear-right wheel had shattered into pieces. I could hike back to Nugget, though that might amount to signing my own death warrant. For if I aroused the populace with calls for assistance, they'd surely discover one of their prominent citizens was not at home, snoring in bed.

*No. I had to press on. But . . . how?*

HENRY: Tuesday; January 29, 1901

The Old Homestead had been in a Pennsylvania village, Mont Clare. There, Papa eked out a decent living as assistant to a blacksmith/wheelwright. Mostly, they serviced a stage company crossing the state's interlocking routes. Unlike the other five kids (I was the youngest), I essayed the four blocks that composed our corner of the world. Deciding early on *not* to find m'self a nice girl, get married, and earn a respectable living. That boy who would evolve into *me* refused to sink into such a mundane routine. Might be enough for most folks. That hardly described Harry Longabaugh.

At age fourteen, I threw in with a second-cousin and headed west with a small caravan of ten wagons. Initially, the carrot-topped captain appeared uneasy about allowin' two runaways to tag along. Understaffed, though, he agreed we could earn our keep along the trail. Grueling labor no one else wanted to perform. Shoein' horses. Gathering firewood. Doing laundry. Yet, I harbored big dreams. Soon as we arrived at their destination, I'd find a job. And, work my way up, step by step, pushing on to higher status and more money.

*Eventually I'd become a solid citizen of the frontier. Why, I might even become one of its movers and shakers.*

When Wyoming achieves statehood? Surely they'll need a governor. Only things didn't turn out as I expected 'em to. I've learned, over time, that they seldom do.

ELOISE: TUESDAY; JANUARY 29, 1901

Briefly seized by panic, I refused to surrender to the seemingly inevitable, forcing myself to assume an uneasy calm. What had great literature of the past taught me? *There is in the cosmos that which we cannot control. Also, a human ability to overcome many elements that might appear set in cement.*

Perhaps my lot was to die here, in the absolute middle of nowhere. Still, that remained to be determined. So I must take my stand and refuse to go under without a fight. Then wait to learn if victory or defeat awaits me. Might self-determination decide my future rather than destiny?

I don't know why, but at that moment I felt compelled to reach up and touch Bowdry's Star of David through my dress. At once, I felt revitalized. The wagon had been piled high with luggage containing possessions which I believed, only a day earlier, would prove essential for my future. In Cheyenne. New York. And in time, places beyond.

Suddenly, that struck me as naïve. All I require? A fresh change of clothes. The basic tools of feminine hygiene. And perhaps some make-up. *As Shakespeare put it: Vanity, thy name is woman.*

JAMES: TUESDAY; JANUARY 29, 1901

While drifting down to Telluride CO, where I planned to unload my current baggage, a sorry-looking drifter wandered into my trail camp one night, asking for a handout. After I fed him with half my evening ration of bacon and beans, he asked if he might glance over my herd of nineteen horses. Not so long as I accompanied him, I replied, with some concern. He might try and dump his worn nag and head off on one of mine. We looked 'em all over and Matt pointed out that one had the makings of a fine racehorse, if properly groomed

Hailing from Louisville, KY, he'd been a trainer on a plantation before being asked to leave over some unsavory business involving missing funds. Matt asked if we might enter into a 50-50 partnership, me owning a horse we dubbed Jupiter, he putting in the long hours necessary to turn a wild stallion with potential into a moneymaking champ. I thought *why not?*

So he accompanied me on a three day ride to the painted hills. There, we unloaded the other horses, then rented an isolated cabin. Matt soon proved the full range of his considerable talents.

ELOISE: TUESDAY; JANUARY 29, 1901

I struggled to remove the two smallest suitcases, then dragged them to where my mules stood, knee-deep in snow, braying desperately as panic and fear overtook them.

*Animals always sense death hanging in the air. When there appears no choice but to accept its descent.*

With some difficulty, I unhitched the miserable beasts from their harnesses, attached a suitcase to the back of each with canvas straps, and seized their loose reins. Employing what remained of my fast-fading strength, I forced the beasts to push forward. They initially balked, then did as commanded.

*I am unstoppable. Undefeatable.*

Were I to cease telling myself that, even for a moment, it would be all over. For me and these innocent creatures.

*However crazy it might sound to others, their well-being meant as much to me as my own.*

HENRY: TUESDAY; JANUARY 29, 1901

What little work presented itself turned out to be even more desultory than chores with the caravan: washing dishes and carting off animal dung in the town called Sundance. Sweeping bar-room floors after hours. Then scrubbing wet tobacco out of the spittoons or off the boards whenever a fellow missed. Not that I minded day labor. Only I saw no sense in it if the reward was nothin' but *more* hard work for small pay.

ONCE UPON A TIME IN SUNDANCE, WYOMING: To this day, a statue of Harry Longabaugh inhabits the jail cell that once held the young outlaw who would forever after be called 'The Sundance Kid.'

That's when the dream—my personal one like our nation's grandeur promise of eventual success through hard work—transformed into a living nightmare. Following three frustrating weeks, I said 'the hell with this,' stole a rifle, saddle, and horse, then headed off. In less than half a mile, I was surrounded by a posse. Dragged into the courtroom. Judge found the gangly youth standing there guilty on all counts and tossed me into jail for eighteen months.

As I had the distinction of being the youngest fella in stir, other inmates dubbed me The Sundance Kid.

ELOISE: TUESDAY; JANUARY 29, 1901

We traversed several miles before the next disaster occurred. A shrill whinny alerted me that one of the animals could continue no further, at least not with the suitcase. One of its scrawny legs had gone lame. The sad-eyed mule lifted up its swollen hoof as if trying to communicate his discomfort.

*I feel your pain. And adore the purity of all animals.*

My initial thought? Cut him loose and leave him here. Or end his pitiable existence with a bullet to the brain. Then, with the other mule, push on again. That's what most folks would do. And I don't blame them. Self-survival is a mighty significant motivator.

*Then again, I'm not most folks.*

JAMES: Tuesday; January 29, 1901

Wide-eyed, I watched as each day our Jupiter more fully responded to Matt's subtle moves of his talented knees, set against the horse's solid flanks. Soon Jupiter trotted and cantered at his commands, be they physical by way of Matt's stirrups against the belly of the beastor the fine art of whispering into the mount's ear. This fellow was a master.

For a while, we traveled up and down the territory, winning races more often than not. So I asked myself today: might I have become a professional at such a decent if not always reputable trade had things continued in such a manner? No question I enjoyed the rich rewards as well as Matt's company.

On days when Jupiter scored big, we had our pick of the ladies and finest food and drink. But as experience teaches, nothing lasts forever. Once Jupiter acquired a reputation, others insisted he be handicapped. So he was slowed down with weights to allow less formidable horses a chance. As this might curtail our profits, I suggested we pull a con. Accept the small sacks of bronze, then during the process of hanging them on Jupiter, replace these with identical loads of sugar.

Well, we won the race but lost anyway. While we were accepting the first-prize, Jupiter got a whiff of what was in those bags, twisted his neck around so he could land his teeth on 'em, then tore them open, sending the white crystals flying. As stunned observers rushed forward to get a look, Matt and I exchanged concerned glances, turned, and hurried to a pair of saddled-horses nearby, then rode hard and fast with the prize money as a posse formed and pursued.

*We had, in one day, transformed from horse racers to horse thieves. And there was no goin' back again.*

Somehow we eluded them and arrived at Robber's Roost, a hidden ranch in southeastern Utah that housed fugitives from the law so long as they could pay. How Matt fell out of the picture and Henry entered my life is a tale unto itself.


ELOISE: Tuesday; January 29, 1901

Instead of killing or abandoning the dumb beast, I cut the suitcase loose, allowing it to fall into a drift. Within moments, the baggage disappeared in swift-piling snow. Seizing one mule's reins in my right hand, the other's in my left, I again pushed further southward. We'd make it together or not at all. Relieved, the mule fitfully stumbled forward alongside his companion. I sensed that in their simple comprehension, they knew, even appreciated, that I had not deserted them.

When we reach Majestic, I'll sell the mules, then make my way to the railroad station. Hopefully, in time to catch the early special. And be on my way. First stop, Cheyenne. Then, with a little luck, the much fabled city-lights of New York!

*From there? The whole wide world awaited . . . if only I could make it through this one horrible night.*

## HENRY: TUESDAY; JANUARY 29, 1901

"As you can see, what people refer to as 'The Falls' is in truth an intersection of three separate waterways. There, you have the powerful Canadian Sector, merging with what for obvious reasons we call the Horseshoe Drop. Finally, the Bridal Falls, so named when the daughter of Aaron Burr, vice-president of these United States, and her fiancée chose to tie the knot here in 1801. A hundred years ago this month! Ever since, citizens of the U.S. converge at this spot to do the same. So, as many of you here today can attest to, Niagara Falls now rates as the honeymoon capital of the Americas."

HONEYMOON CAPITOL OF THE WORLD: While visiting his sister in Buffalo NY, Harry Longabaugh is believed to have taken in the remarkable sights at Niagara Falls.

"The *world*," one inebriated visitor shouted.

My sister, Dagmar, and I stood among a group of twenty visitors. Ten couples, the maximum allowed to at any one time step across a rickety suspension bridge and enjoy the most spectacular view of The Whirlpool's thick foam and swirling currents. My guess? Most of the others had married during the past few days here at the Falls. Or were newlyweds, traveling north to celebrate their recently formalized unions.

## ELOISE: Tuesday; January 29, 1901

This is it. I can go no further. As I've been trying, as have the boys, for the past month to resolve the great mystery of life—whether it's up to the self or set in place at the beginning of time—then I guess it's the latter. Because I cannot take another step.

I dropped to my knees. And set to crying as all the best laid plans of mice, men, and poor li'l ol' me . . . born Eloise Placer, self-recreated as Etta Place, lately calling myself Mrs. Henry Long . . . prepared to meet my maker in this God-forsaken spot.

*But me, being me, could think of only one thing. What will become of these poor dumb beasts once I'm gone?*

## JAMES: Tuesday; January 29, 1901

The welcome mat at Robber's Roost had the following words embroidered on its timeworn surface: "PAYING CUSTOMERS ONLY!" So Matt and I slept late, played cards, ate well, and drank our fill until the cash ran out. Then we were shown the door, invited back as soon we re-filled our coffers.

Two of the McCarty brothers, hard-case types not adverse to violence as a means to their ends—money!—rode out at the same time. Though I considered such worthless white trash contemptible, Matt and I would need companions if we were to rob the well-stocked San Miguel Valley Bank in Telluride.

"Stick 'em up!" I announced entering, while whipping out my single-action Colt. This, I pointed at the main teller, who struck me as already concerned on this bright sunny morning.

"Hey! *I* was here first!" insisted a man standing in the shadows to my right. Here stood a lean, medium-sized fella who must've arrived moments before we did with similar plans.

"No matter," I shouted back, swaying my head so as to indicate my three companions. "We got you outnumbered."

"Ain't you *man* enough to do this on your own?"

"Nobody speaks that way to Butch Cassidy."

"I just did."

"And you'd be?"

"Folks call me The Sundance Kid."

ELOISE: TUESDAY; JANUARY 29, 1901

"Missy?" a voice, resonant with a thick southern drawl, called out from somewhere in the trees. "What happened?"

Barely able to raise my head, I saw a heavyset man, covered in a woolly jacket cut from buffalo hides, moving my way on snowshoes. Numb as my body and mind were, I sensed his shock at discovering a young woman and two mules, each on the edge of collapse. Through the whirling hail between us, I somehow managed to glimpse the dark man's eyes . . .

*Masculine yet gentle, recalling those of Butch. Caring, with a reserve of strength, like Sundance.*

The precise opposite of those twin balls of arrogance and ruthlessness which had revealed Ironsides' true colors. And so I understood that salvation itself had moved in my direction.

HENRY: TUESDAY; JANUARY 29, 1901

"Harry?" Dag asked as I stumbled. "Are you alright?"

"Oh, sure. Just an old war wound, acting up."

*I couldn't admit that the pain in my right thigh resulted from a train robbery gone sour. Dag apparently remained under the impression that her brother had gone west to make his fortune in varied respectable business investments.*

Sis and me had been separated for nearly 20 years. Now, on the first day of the rest of my life? Together again. I realized how much I'd missed her natural warmth. Perhaps this brief respite with her family might set the pace for my future. Or any of an endless number of possible futures.

*What had the writer O. Henry penned in one of his stories which I'd read and, impressed, committed to memory, "The true adventurer goes forth aimless and uncalculating to meet and greet unknown fate . . ."*

ELOISE: TUESDAY; JANUARY 29, 1901

"I . . . I . . ."

"Here, little lady. Let me help ya up."

As he extended a large gloved hand, I heard the yelps of animals hurrying close. My eyes must have revealed the sudden fear that ripped through me. If I were not to die by freezing, would I instead be torn to pieces by wolves?

"No, no," he assured me. "M' *hounds*."

Instead of attacking, the pack of five Malamutes leaped high to lick my ice-covered cheeks. The warmth of their huge wet tongues relieved me.

"Where am I?" I coughed. Then, as he steadily led me and the mules forward, "And where are we going?"

"My cabin. On the northern tier of Majestic."

"That's where I was headed for," I mumbled.

"Well," he chuckled, despite the gravity of my situation, "you made it."

## JAMES: TUESDAY; JANUARY 29, 1901

"Excuse me," the teller politely asked from behind the wire-fenced window that separated him and his co-workers from those in the lounge. "But who am I supposed to turn this over to?" He indicated the canvas sack of greenbacks he'd prepared.

"Well," I said, "Just shove it through the slot and we'll figure it out." The man did as told. The Sundance Kid grabbed these goods and started for the door. "Hold on there—"

I started to follow him when an unexpected shot rang out. Turning, I grasped that an assistant teller had reached for a rifle and fired. Matt stiffened, turned my way, and managed to smile. "Well, Butch, guess this is where we part trails."

Then he fell forward, dead.

## ELOISE: TUESDAY; JANUARY 29, 1901

"How far to the train station?" I asked between frantic bouts of coughing.

"'Bout a mile."

"Oh! Please, take me there."

"You'd never make it. Nor your sorry beasts."

"But I've got to—"

"As I said, my cabin. I'm a hunter and trapper. One o' the last left in the territory. You'll be safe there."

"Thank you, mister . . ."

"Jones. Caleb Jones."

"You arrived to save me like White Knight."

"I'm hardly that," the African American man laughed.

"To me, you are." I considered what had occurred. "There must a God, after all. Or I'd be lying dead back there."

"That's sure my way of lookin' at it."

HENRY: WEDNESDAY; JANUARY 30, 1901

"Theodore Roosevelt is a devil in the flesh," Ronald Jenkins shrieked at the top of his lungs. "Should he ever become president, I'd shoot myself. Or move to Canada."

"That's pretty extreme," I responded.

"However horrid McKinley may be, Roosevelt represents everything I *most* hate about the Republican party."

This unexpected rant occurred the day after Dag and I had visited the Falls. While my sister, accompanied by her two daughters, prepared an evening meal, Ronald and I sat in their cozy parlor, legs stretched out on black-metal bars before the crackling hearth. Magnanimously, he handed me a cigar. Not top quality, but what an aspiring businessman could afford.

*How surprised he'd be to learn I'd smoked far better.*

Not wishing to seem unappreciative, I'd attempted to strike up a friendly conversation. More interested in flipping through the pages of the *Evening News,* he offered a fleeting reference to current politics. The anger in Ronald's voice caught me off-guard. Mistakenly believing he would approve of patriotism on my part, I had mentioned that I'd set my own personal business interests aside to join the Rough Riders. And, in order to avoid questioning about my missing ear lobe, lied, telling him I'd been wounded in combat with the Spanish.

"Well, he certainly impressed me as an effective military officer during our time in Cuba."

In response, Ronald howled at the very thought. "He and his 'progressives'! They'd destroy the very foundations of what our great nation stands for with their liberal ideas."

RISE OF THE ROUGH RIDER: Gov. Theodore Roosevelt left his home in New York to run with presidential candidate William McKinley on the liberal Republican ticket.

"I assume you voted for William Jennings Bryan?"

"Didn't *you*? No, don't answer that. I can't stand the thought of a Republican under my roof. And since you are Dagmar's flesh and blood, I don't want to throw you out."

## ELOISE: WEDNESDAY; JANUARY 30, 1901

"Sarry will have some hot soup for you in a moment," Caleb assured me even as my eyes opened wide. I felt myself returning to something that resembled life after hours of deep sleep. He referred to his wife, a Paiute woman whose nut-colored eyes likewise conveyed a sense of human decency.

"You're too kind!"

"Just trying my best to be a decent human being."

"You've succeeded at that. Believe me!"

A gentleman to the core, Caleb bade his wife attend to the personal chores of rubbing my body down with oils that her people of the Great Basin drew from the blood of bisons. Then, Sarry tightly wrapped me in a buffalo robe.

"My mules!" I gasped. No matter where I might travel, such beasts would always take priority over my own safety.

"In the stable. Be fit as a pair of fiddles in no time."

"Please consider them my gift to you."

"Ain't necessary. We only done what's right."

*How refreshingly old-fashioned! I can only hope that, wherever the wind blows me, there are more out there like you.*

## JAMES: WEDNESDAY; JANUARY 30, 1901

"Damn you," a McCarty shouted, firing five shots into the doomed would-be hero. Meanwhile, the head teller reached into a drawer and drew out a Smith and Wesson, shooting a round at each of the McCartys. Both fell but not before one got off a shot, bringing this bold man down. The other bank workers screamed and wept as they fearfully backed away.

"Well," Sundance asked, "what'll we do now?"

"Don't know 'bout you, Kid, but I'm getting out of here!"

He nodded. We hurried out the front door as confused and terrified citizens froze in their tracks. "For the record," I shouted as we rode off, "neither of us fired a shot."

Side by side, we made our way to Wyoming. Guess you could say that marked the end of the beginning for us as a team. Not a single day has gone by, though, when I haven't thought back to Matt, and what sort of a partnership we might have enjoyed.

*If things were different. But they never are.*

ELOISE: WEDNESDAY; JANUARY 30, 1901

While I ravenously consumed my meal, Caleb explained that in his youth, he had been one of the 'hivernants' who wintered in the Rockies between 1840 and 1860. Caleb was the first black man the Osage had ever laid eyes on. One guessed this fellow painted himself that dark shade for spiritual purposes, even attempted to rub the ebony hue away and expose his true color. When the native people realized the truth, they called Caleb 'the black white man.' From then on, many of the warriors chose to dye themselves black before entering combat with enemies.

That was during the golden age of the fur trade, when beaver and otter pelts would bring big money as trappers and their Indian wives rode down from the high country for a spring rendezvous at the bend of the Snake River. They'd be met by agents from the Rocky Mountain Fur Company who acquired skins in exchange for money or goods such as new traps and rifles, whiskey and tobacco, or truth be told the company of wanton women. The Crow were reputed to barter their wives for pile of furs. Other tribes looked down on them for such questionable behavior.

By the end of a week of wild partying, most—Caleb included—found themselves as dead broke as they had been on arrival. So off it was come fall for another season. By 1860, the Rockies were mostly trapped out. Then the hardened men and their women scattered far and wide, these two landing here.

"I'll never forget what you people have done for me," I said once the storm ceased and Caleb brought me to the rail stop in Majestic by way of their own mule-driven wagon.

"Any solid fella would've done the same."

"You and Sarry have restored my faith in men," I sighed.

"How about God?"

"I'm not yet certain. Maybe in time I'll find out."


HENRY: WEDNESDAY; JANUARY 30, 1901

"Actually," I replied to Ronald, telling the truth, "I'm not a registered member of any political party."

"Oh!" His eyes lit up for the first time since the two of us met. "Well, I'll make a Democrat out of you. Wait and see!"

"I'm aware your party opposed our involvement in Cuba's war for independence. May I inquire why?"

"As our first president stated, the United States should stand alone, avoiding 'all foreign entanglements.'"

*If I had a brain in my admittedly pretty head, I'd have learned to keep my big mouth shut long ago. But, no . . .*

"Perhaps Washington's approach was right for that moment in our history. Yet we live in notably different times. This is, after all, the Twentieth Century."

"If you refer to the modern concept of internationalism, count me out. Like Bryan, I hail from Nebraska. 'God's country' as he calls it. The heartland, full of folks who mind their own business, work hard, and earn money. McKinley and Roosevelt will open the floodgates for Chinks, Micks, Wops and Kikes to pour in."

"They're people," I heard myself respond, "just like us."

"No, no, no. We're Christians."

"So are the Irish. Or for that matter the Italians."

"Catholics," he all but spit. "*False* and, as such, *inferior* Christians. In my mind? Worse than the savages."

"You refer now to Indians?"

"I do! Roosevelt *adores* them. The blacks as well!"

"During the battle at Kettle Hill, a small detachment of Rough Riders were cut off from our main forces by enemy fire. Members of the 9th and 10th cavalry . . . Buffalo soldiers, they're called . . . volunteered to reinforce us. Without them, we wouldn't have survived. Afterwards, Colonel Roosevelt insisted that if he had his way, he'd entirely eliminate black or white companies. Have all soldiers stand side by side."

"America for Americans!" Ronald nastily snapped.

"The Indians were Americans long before we arrived."

"I find that statement offensive," he snapped back.

*I said no more. This was, after all, his home. Though it did occur to me that the sooner I left, the better!*

—INTERLUDE—

BAT: OCTOBER 25, 1921

*Lolly, before wet set Caleb aside, at least for the time being, allow me to pause and comment on the great tradition he and other people of color amassed during the settlement of the West. Firstly, he was not the only black mountain man of the 1840s. Another, named James Beckwourth, trapped in the Rockies alongside old Jim Bridger, young Kit Carson, and John Colter, the latter in his middle years then. They worked for William Asley's High Mountain Fur company originally and, in time, John Jacob Astor's more powerful American Fur.*

*Always, though, such bold men preferred to claim their own territories as independents, owing to a national tendency toward rugged individualism. The desire to strike out on one's own, employed not by some big outfit, trying to succeed as mavericks. Yet always aware they might fail, if circumstances led to that. And willing to take the risk.*

THE AFRICAN AMERICAN WESTERN HERO:
Though the character of 'Caleb' is fictitious, his personality, values, and adventures are closely modelled on those of the actual mountain man Jim Beckworth, alternately spelled 'Beckwourth.'

*Long before Beck, or 'Bloody Arm' as Crows called the man owing to his fighting skills, and Caleb, people of African descent turned the tide of our history. As early as 1778, shortly after Old Dan'l himself founded Boonesbourough and Boone's Station in raw Kentucky, it took a black man to make things work. When Boone was captured by the Shawnee, half the tribe wanted to run him through the gauntlet and bring Dan'l down with tomahawks. Chief Black Fish, on the other hand, hoped to adopt the captive as his soon. Then, an escaped slave—his name long lost—who'd married into that nation negotiated a compromise. Thanks to him, the legendary pioneer lived with the tribe until he headed back to kin. How different our nation's history might've been had it not been for that Negro's presence.*

*Following Boone, the next great explorers were Lewis and Clark, dispatched by President Jefferson to explore the newly purchased Louisiana and map it for future generations. The former's diary tells us that his slave, York, saved that white man's life three times between 1803 and 1804. Our black heroes included cowboys and lawman as well. Issom Dart and Deadwood Dick, aka Nat Love, won every rodeo competition they entered, putting their Anglo adversaries to shame. And even as Wyatt Earp and I were bringing law and order to Kansas, Bass Reeves took on the tougher chore of settling what was then known as Indian Territory, now Oklahoma.*

*Let's not forget the women! Molly Fields proved so adept with a gun that the California pioneers elected her sheriff of a mean-spirited settlement near Death Valley. Cathay Williams so wanted to do her share in what Roosevelt calls "The Winning of the West" that she passed herself off as a man and fought the Apache and Comanch as a member of the 38th U.S. Infantry.*

*Not that contributions were always of a violent nature. Born in New York as a free-woman, Elizabeth Scott Flood headed west alongside her husband after he got bit by the gold bug in the late 1840s. Though Mr. Thom died shortly thereafter from heat exhaustion, Elizabeth gathered up the nuggets and yellow dust he'd discovered, choosing not to spend the profits on herself. She used that money to build free schools for black children in those areas where the white majority refused entry to non-Anglo kids. Now, that's* my *kind of capitalism! Not raw, but with a conscience behind it.*

*Well, back to our main story. But how important it is to note the American pioneer came in all colors and included women of courage like Etta Place alongside the men.*

# PART FOUR:
# A NECESSARY JOURNEY

"The sun always shines brightest when it gazes down
on a necessary journey."

—Henry David Thoreau

ELOISE: THURSDAY; JANUARY 31, 1901

I changed trains in Denver to create a ragged rather than straight route eastward. This allowed me an hour and a half layover during which I took advantage of the surprisingly neat and clean ladies' room and then enjoyed a meal at the station's best restaurant. Lamb chops with boiled potatoes and asparagus in hollandaise sauce. What a contrast to the humble fare Sarry treated me to: a stew of whatever game and vegetables they had boiled in a bison's stomach rather than an iron kettle.

In truth, though, I'll never forget how wonderful her concoction tasted. Or how much I owed them.

While waiting, I perused the book stall and newspaper rack. The latter first, as I wanted to check if there were any mentions of the killing in Nugget. Nothing! So far, so good.

*Likely the body hadn't yet been discovered. Though when it did, all hell would surely break loose.*

JAMES: THURSDAY; JANUARY 31, 1901

"Steel and concrete!" a complete stranger confided. "The shape of things to come."

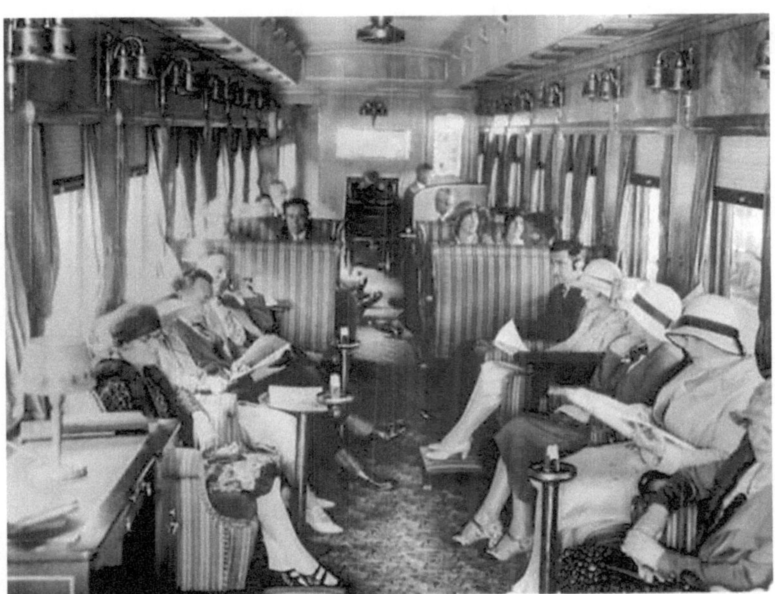

'THE TWENTIETH CENTURY LMTD.': Railroads redefined mass transportation for Modern Times, allowing travelers (at least those who could afford first class) an elegant means of crossing the country.

So said an early middle-aged man who stepped up beside me at the corner of East 4th Street and Vine, a key juncture in central Cincinatti. Earlier, I'd deboarded my train at a make-shift station. Work Zone signs announced this building was scheduled for demolition, clearing room for the more modern Union Terminal. The heavy machinery and materials for such massive construction were already in place. I felt as if I stood on an invisible bridge between the past and the future.

From the station, I'd made my way to a fine hotel just off the main business loop. If Lefors and Siringo pursued me beyond Wyoming, which I doubted, they'd search through the back alleys, where criminals hide out. Not me! Hide in plain sight, as Mike liked to say. For that's where authorities will be least likely to look for you.

With registration complete, off I'd gone to take in the surrounding city. The metal skeleton of a high-reaching building yet to be fully realized demanded my attention.

"What . . . *is* it?" I asked, caught off guard by this nattily dressed fellow's open-ness. Likely, he perceived me as a hick, arriving East of the Rockies for the first time.

"Some reporter dubbed it a 'skyscraper.' When finished, it'll reach sixteen stories high. There'll be offices for everyone from business people to doctors, lawyers—"

"Tallest I ever seen before? Four stories."

GO UP, YOUNG MEN: During the 20th Century, America would run out of 'West' to explore; The New Frontier awaited up above.

"Obviously, you hail from the west."

"That I do," I replied, reluctant to give any further details about myself. Yes, hide in plain sight. But keep your mouth shut tight!

ELOISE: THURSDAY; JANUARY 31, 1901

During the final minutes before my train was scheduled to arrive, I hoped to find some novel that might occupy my time . . . and mind . . . during the remainder of the trip.

First, I glanced over the hardcover titles . . .

*When Knighthood Was in Flower* by Charles Major caught my attention with its color-cover depicting a wrestling match between two athletes at the court of Henry VIII, ladies of the manor gazing on in fascination. Once, this would have been a natural for the romantic I had been, my mind consumed with fantasies of combat, courtship, and chivalry. Now, though, I am Eloise Long. And I know fairytles aren't for grown-ups.

Next: *David Harum: The Story of an American Life* by Edward Westcott, a retired lawyer from Syracuse in upstate New York. A jacket blurb explained that this new volume revealed underhanded tactics employed to acquire wealth by seeming men of respect who are anything but. Fascinating, to be sure. But as the premise recalled my victim, I decided against it.

*Dracula* by Bram Stoker, an Irishman who called London his home, concerned the Vampyre, a member of the Living Dead. Vlad journeys from his mountainside castle in the wilds of Eastern Europe, traveling by ship to civilied London, with plans of seducing respectable Victorian-era women residing there. To be sure intriguing, yet a bit bloodthirsty for my tastes.

Then I glanced at the paperbacks, lurid pulp fictions that appeal to the lowest level of society. Some featured crude illustrations as well as roughewn writing; these, I knew, had come to be called comic books. The cover of one caught my attention. There I was, or at least a reasonable facsimile, riding a great white stallion, grasping the reins with one hand, firing a pistol with the other. Here was the latest collection of lies by Ned Buntline, now featuring Miss Etta Place as the central character.

"All aboard!"

I'd been oblivious to the sudden arrival of my train. Impulsively, I handed the salesman a dime and took the rag with me as I hastily located my coach.

HENRY: THURSDAY; JANUARY 31, 1901

"Marta passed several years back," Dag explained when I asked about our sister. She, I, and her family sat together in the well-appointed lounge of their handsome home. "I mailed you care of general delivery in Cheyenne."

"I did receive it. And apologize for failing to reply."

"That's alright, Harry. I know *you*, even from our brief time together. Small tasks like letter-writing confounded you back then. Don't matter, now I'm sure you are alive."

*Dag almost completed her statement with the expected follow-up, 'and well.' Sensing that I suffered from severe pain, however, my sister abruptly cut herself off.*

"As to our brothers?"

"Spread across the Tri-State area, after Mom and Pop passed. Why, I've lost track of who owns our old house now."

"Just what sort of business are you involved in out west?" Ronald growled, shoving a cigar into the miniature cavern of his wide-mouth, this time without offering me one.

"Oh, a little of this, a little of that."

"Why, *that* answer ain't *no* answer at all!"

"Ronald! Harry has arrived following a long journey by train. Can't you see he's still exhausted? We'll have plenty of time to iron all such things out during the next week."

*Sorry, sis. Afraid our days together will be cut short. Your husband appears to be playing amateur detective. I'd best leave as soon as possible.*

ELOISE: Thursday; January 31, 1901

"Hello, there. Don't *you* look *nice* today!"

Fortuitously, I did appear decent, wearing a modest dress purchased in Cheyenne previous to departure. Now, here in St. Louis, an impressively attired woman boarded, marched down the aisle, glanced at this solitary female, and smiled. I guessed her age to be around eighty. 'Handsome' more accurately described her than 'beautiful.' Also: Imposing.

"Thank you!" I humbly replied, awed by her charismatic presence. "I could say the same of you."

Seating herself across from me, the lady displayed the graceful assurance of a queen assuming her rightful throne. "Ha! That's very kind, though."

"'Always be kind,'" I quoted Plato, "'since everyone you meet is likely facing a harder battle even than yourself.'"

"Schooled as to the classics? Marvelous! Though I cannot imagine what such an attractive young woman as yourself might find, as you yourself hint, so hard in life."

"Appearances can be deceiving," I sighed.

"Oh, my!" she replied, observing me with keen interest. "Tell me more!"

JAMES: THURSDAY; JANUARY 31, 1901

"This work of architectural ingenuity will be the highest west of Chicago," my current mentor, who identified himself as chief executive in charge of overseeing massive construction on this site currently covered with rubble and steel, informed me.

"Impressive!"

"In the Windy City, they've got one reaches six stories. We're mighty proud to be outdoing them."

"In New York, do they have 'em tall as this'll be?"

"Not yet. Highest I know of in mid-town Manhattan reaches ten stories, a 'twelver' rumored to be near to completion."

"I wonder why they're building 'em up now, instead of stretchin' out further on either side, as they used to."

"My guess? Proof that Turner's thesis is correct."

I must have appeared an idiot. "Never heard of him."

WHEN YOU RUN OUT OF WEST, GO *UPWARD*, YOUNG MAN!; The Ingalls Building, completed in 1903, as it appeared while under construction several years earlier.

Shaking my hand, this agreeably burly fellow identified himself as, among other things, a professor of history. A newly completed University put Cincinatti on the map as something more than just another medium-sized center of commerce along the Ohio River. Here was a city in transition! Changing so fast that most folks couldn't adjust before the latest wave gave way to the next.

*Progress, I reckon that's called.*

*A good thing, more likely than not.*

ELOISE: THURSDAY; JANUARY 31, 1901

"I've always been intrigued by what people choose to read," the matron said, peeking at my paperback. "May I ask what so rivets your attention?"

"Oh," I blushed, wishing I'd picked up anything but this. Obviously in the company of an intellectual, how much smarter I might appear holding the naturalist masterpiece *McTeague* by Frank Norris in which the previously un-challenged notion of an American Dream came under close critical scrutiny. Or *Harriet Tubman, The Moses of Her People* by Sarah H. Bradford, sharing the tale of a bold female Civil Rights activist with the wide world. For that matter even L. Frank Baum's seemingly escapist but in fact richly symbolic *The Wonderful Wizard of Oz.* Yet here I sat, holding Ned's latest pack of colorful lies. "I rarely waste time on such trash."

"Which only furthers my curiosity."

"Having heard many rumors of adventure and romance on the frontier," I said, turning the book sideways so that she could observe the title and illustration, "I wanted to learn more."

"Buntline's *Wild West Weekly*," she read aloud. "But I've been told such stories are too sordid for decent women."

"I'll never purchase another," I assured her, giggling to cover my embarrassment. "My tastes run more to women writers like that critic of the class system, George Eliot."

"A favorite of mine as well!" She further studied the words on my book's binding. "*Butch Cassidy, The Sundance Kid, and Miss Etta Place in the Golden Hills of Old Oklahoma.*"

"Fiction of the lowest order," I sniffed, tossing it down.

"But aren't those actual people?"

*Why is this woman's face vaguely familiar? I'm certain we've never met. Yet I recognize her.*

"So I've heard," I replied in a tone of disinterest.

"If I may be so bold," she continued without missing a beat while drawing out a thick pamphlet from her purse and handing it to me, "may I recommend a future reading choice?"

"*The Revolutionary.* Is this a political publication?"

"One might call it that. Philosophical, I'd say. You see . . . uh . . . oh, but I didn't catch your name?"

"That's because I didn't give it," I snapped, realizing I'd already revealed far too much.


HENRY: THURSDAY; JANUARY 31, 1901

"You ever fight Indians, Uncle Harry?" asked the eldest of the girls, nine years of age and intrigued by this visitor.

"In truth? No, Deborah. Seen plenty, though."

"Are they really 'red'?"

"More the color of copper," I answered little Sarah, younger by almost a year and a half. "Their skin's beautiful, so far as I'm concerned. Gilded by the sun, you might say."

"Are they like the cannibals in stories Mama reads us of the Seven Seas?" Debbie inquired, eyes wide now.

"Well, there are rumors as to the Kronks down Texas way. But even if that's so . . . and I ain't confirmin' it is . . . mostly, the Indians I knew were admirable people."

"You almost sound as if you prefer them to whites!"

"Well, Ronald, that isn't exactly true."

"Thank God!"

"Don't get me wrong. It isn't that I prefer Anglos."

"What, then?" he replied, exasperated.

"More that I take each individual as he, or she, comes along. And decide whether I respect that person or not."

"Where did you ever pick up such values, Harry?"

"In the place where I chose to live, Dag: The West."


ELOISE: THURSDAY; JANUARY 31, 1901

My sudden rebuke caused this uninvited companion to refrain from further conversation for a spell, allowing me opportunity to study her out of the corners of my eyes. The stately woman's wardrobe struck me as typical of well-born ladies from the civilized states a decade earlier. Then, such understated garb (now considered outdated from my readings on current fashion) suggested America's well-born educated elite.

A shirt-waist projected discretion in a wearer's personal life. The straight lines of her neat beige skirt featured a thin band of buckram at the hem, allowing for a 'finished' look. Her small, brimless felt hat served as an unofficial crown. No doubt that here sat homegrown royalty. A person who abided in humility, yet projected a deep sense of self-worth untinged by false pride. The next several hours would be spent in the company of one whose life had not in any way wound down with the unavoidable onset of age.

I noticed from a ticket the grand dame placed on the empty seat beside her that my fellow traveler would continue on to Philadelphia. My plan was to dis-board earlier, in Harrisburg where I would check into the finest hotel available.

*Hide in plain sight! Butch insists. Well, it's always worked for us in the past.*


JAMES: THURSDAY; JANUARY 31, 1901

During the past few years, my companion informed me, and with advances in construction such as the one we now gazed upon, the population here had reached 350,000. Next, the man inquired as to whether I might join the long list of residents that composed "a new Cincinatti." When I replied that my stay would be for one or two nights, he appeared disappointed.

Then, intrigued by his previous comment, I continued, "As to this 'Turner'? What is it exactly?"

The chap explained a concept that originated in academia some ten years earlier. A scholar, Frederick Jackson Turner, had delivered a speech to the American Historical Association in Chicago, in which he re-defined our United States on the cusp of the 20th century. From the day Europeans first landed on America's Eastern shores, we forged a national identity by steadily expanding *westward.* In time, that word ceased to indicate merely a direction and took on the fuller dimensions of an idea. The one that most identified Americans.

*Huh! Turner's thesis paralleled the viewpoint of Colonel Roosevelt in* The Win- ning of the West. *This fascinated me.*


ELOISE: THURSDAY; JANUARY 31, 1901

"I do apologize for being so forward," my companion said following an extended silence.

"No, no. It's only that I'm a rather private person."

"As you have every right to be! I presumed too much—"

"Let me say this," I interrupted. "I sensed that, while boarding, you singled me out from the crowd."

"True. For you struck me as a young woman of style and substance. Some-one whose conversation I might enjoy."

"That's flattering." I extended a hand. "I'm Eloise Placer Long. On my way to join my husband Henry in New York."

"Hmmmmmmm!" Her eyes tightened, the smile disappearing.

"Anything wrong?"

"Not 'wrong' so much as 'curious.'"

"Why so?"

"I notice you aren't wearing a ring."

## HENRY: THURSDAY; JANUARY 31, 1901

"You look worn, Harry. I'm worried about you!"

Dagmar sat adjacent to my bed inside the Invalides Hotel at 653 Main, Buffalo's first modern hospital complex. An hour earlier, I'd collapsed from increasing pain from an old wound. Dr. Ray Vaughn Price—most of his pink face hidden behind a goatee—employed a radical system of electrical currents to eliminate infection, a scietific advance to better our lives.

"I'll be alright, Sis."

"Guess you'll remain upstate for a spell after all."

"No, no. As I said, I've got to leave soon as possible. Places to go, people to see—"

"Same old 'Harry.' You'll never change."

"Tell me the truth, Dag. Would you *really* want me to?"

"Perhaps not," she admitted, offering a wry smile.

## ELOISE: THURSDAY; JANUARY 31, 1901

"Oh!" I felt my face turn crimson. "I lost mine. Harry plans to replace it once we're reunited in Manhattan."

"Harry? You referred to him as 'Henry' a moment ago."

"Oh, you know. John, Jack. Harry, Henry . . ."

Again, I grew anxious. For all I knew, she might be one of that new breed of female police detectives heralded in the newspapers. Or a lady reporter in search of a major scoop. So for the remainder of our journey, I purposefully gazed out the window. Long stretches of frozen forests randomly interrupted by medium-sized burgs, grey and brown with little if any colorful adornments. In time we reached the outskirts of an industrial city, where stark factories were connected by uninviting cement roads lined with grim, skeletal trees.

As the engine ground to a shakey halt, I signaled for porters. Several hurried over and seized my luggage. Casting a non-commital smile at the seated matron, I quickly exited.

That *is* that! *I won't let down my guard again.*

## JAMES: THURSDAY; JANUARY 31, 1901

In the process of searching for greener pastures, or in some cases escaping difficulties back home, a great migration characterized us a people. Go west for a fresh start. Our citizenry expecting the frontier to always be there. Problem was, having reached the Pacific Ocean as the 19th century snailed to an end, those in need of a second chance or an exciting challenge were left with nowhere left to go. Except back to where they hailed from: West to East in the 20th.

The concept struck even a fool such as me as profound. For this offered a generalized notion of the journey I had embarked on. Either east, or up. Toward the final frontier.

"So now we reach for the sky. Which is what they're doing with what will when completed be called the Ingalls building,"

"Sounds like the Tower of Babel all over again."

"Sir, I didn't catch your name."

*With a non-commital smile, I turned and walked away.*


ELOISE: THURSDAY; JANUARY 31, 1901

Discretely, I took dinner in a quiet corner of the Scranton Hotel's cafe, then returned to my room. I planned to read until I dozed off, as was my habit. Sprawled out on a luxurius bed with silken sheets and overstuffed pillows, I purused a local newspaper. As my aching bones gradually relaxed, I flipped the black-on-white pages to Section Two, where the criminal news always appeared.

*Nothing about the murder in Wyoming. Good! Or, more correctly: so far, so good.*

Now, I'll read for pleasure and edification . . .


HENRY: THURSDAY; JANUARY 31, 1901

During these past few days, Dagmar had come to view me as Etta did: her big baby boy, beloved if in need of constant care. Never though had I over the intervening years shared in my infrequent letters my true identity. I'd told Dag only what I thought she could handle. I'd wandered about, somehow never putting down roots. Now, however, Dag wanted more.

"Harry, would you please let me know what's going on?"

"Let me say this," I answered, coughing. "What you don't already know, you don't *want* to know !"

"Maybe I grasp more than you realize."

"From what I've learned, most women do."

With that remarkable sense of wisdom the female of the species apparently possesses from birth, Dag considered me closely and asked, "Why is it you never married?"

ELOISE: Thursday; January 31, 1901

A substantial piece in Section One caught my attention. Alongside lengthy details on the re-election of Presedent McKinley, a subsidiary interview introduced our former secretary of the Navy and current governor of New York, soon to be sworn in as the nation's next vice-president. In truth, I'd never paid a great deal of attention to the political scene, preferring to read fine literature and contemporary fashion in my rare moments of spare time. Yet all at once, this emergent star on the nation's horizon captured my interest.

A sickly child from a fine family, T.R. had gone west for his physical health. But what most intrigued me involved Roosevelt's declaration that the wilderness provided a potential for our return to mental, even moral, as well as bodily fortitude.

The *romance* of the West, he quipped, referred not to love stories between women and men on the frontier, in the crass Ned Buntline sense. Rather, something profound: "Though my education at Harvard may have provided an aura of what some call *sophistication* to my person, I believe that a sense of *character*, in the most essential meaning of that term, is fostered by living in the forests and on the plains. Some say that the natural people found there are savages. But I see them as pure, unaffected by the minute details of city life. The same goes for the cowboys I met and came to admire. They do not spend their time discussing the many problems that arise. Simple and straightforward, they quietly 'get the job done.' I admire that! And hope to bring such to my office."


JAMES: Thursday; January 31, 1901

"Well, Mr. Ryan! How has your stay with us been so far?"

An elegant woman, topped with radiant auburn hair rolled high like a beehive, reigned as hostess for Grande Metropole. Casually yet confidently, she hob-knobbed with its well-to-do cliente, boasting an English accent worthy of Queen Victoria. I'd noticed the lady glancing in my direction when I stopped by the lobby, pausing to observe the expansive collection of fine art. Seemingly, she sensed that I did not fit into the same mold as other guests, and so singled me out.

"Marvelous, though I would appreciate any perspective you might give me as to the rich variety."

As she explained, most of the paintings were imported from Europe. Yet recent works by rising homegrown talent were interspersed with traditional pieces to blend old and new, Europe and America, here fused within a hotel that expressed our emergent desire to dominate the world in the arts as well as industry during the exciting times ahead.

*What had a journalist written? 'The 20th Century will be the* American *century.' The Metropole certainly suggested so.*

ELOISE: FRIDAY; FEBRUARY 1, 1901

I woke early Friday morning in a state of dire physical distress. That hardly represented anything new. Ever since my first mense, the monthly curse had been preceded by malaise—miserable aches and pains—forcing me to halt all activities. However anxious to reach Manhattan, I decided to book my room for another night. I sent telegrams to the boys, care of general delivery at places on their routes, informing them.

Afterwards, I slept most of the day away, waking in mid-afternoon somewhat refreshed. Eager to resume reading the article and learn more about current issues. I treated myself to mild tea and unbuttered toast from room service and continued . . .

A story on the recently deceased Queen Victoria dominated the front page. The monarch had passed away on Jan. 22 at the age of 82. "We are not interested in the possibilities of defeat," she had announced three years after her coronation in 1838. "For the English, these do not exist."

*Such veracity, and at twenty-one: the age I'd reached. Precisely the sort of self-empowerment I must now acquire.*

Yet other aspects of her ideology left me cold. I could not accept Victoria's assessment that sexuality constituted the wicked side of human existence. As for me? How I adored our own indigenous Romantic, Walt Whitman. "I sing the body electric!" What a truly American sentiment. He had proclaimed this in 1855 while writing in the far West. Pages of his book were intended as literary equivalents to waves of grass along the great plains, each a leaf. The body and the soul are not separate sides of a person, Whitman claimed. The body *is* the soul. Our human flesh? *Divine.*

Well, that certainly did describe my state, physical or mental, after a night with the boys!

HENRY: FRIDAY; FEBRUARY 1, 1901

"Why ask *that*, of all things?" I questioned Dag.

"I saw the mournful look in your eyes when you noticed the happy couples, back at the Falls."

"*Temporarily* happy. I'd give most anything to see how they treat each other after, maybe, five years."

"It will be different. Less enthusiastic. The first thing to go, more often than not, is any sense of passion."

"Pretty much what I figured!"

"In some cases, something as good does take its place."

"That bein'?"

"The knowledge they've made a go of it. Raised a family. Shared a life together. Built something of value."

"Well, so far, that hasn't happened for me."

"No reason you can't change that, if you want to."

"That's what I been thinkin'. See, there's this girl—"


ELOISE: FRIDAY; FEBRUARY 1, 1901

As to Victoria, I admired the courage and conviction of a woman who, while little more than a child, had assumed the responsibility of running a country. Beyond that, an empire! Proving by wise decisions that a woman may well be the equal of a man, if allowed an opportunity. How surprising then to peruse Queen Victoria's final writings, re-published here. In spite of a successful 63 year reign, she confessed regret over the loss of a "normal" life. Her conclusion: "The wife owes service to her husband as the slave does to his master."

*What?!* She *wrote* that? *Despite her accomplishments.*

And: "White women should be confined to the household, remaining private, not public." For they (we?) are "not fit for labor, certainly not leadership."

*Yet hadn't her own life's journey belied such antiquated prejudices?*

"I do not consider black females or those of the lower classes to be women in the fullest . . . *white* . . . sense."

*Dismissal of other women owing to accidents of birth? My hope: Victorian values will pass along with the Queen!*


JAMES: FRIDAY; FEBRUARY 1, 1901

The stately 10-story hotel stood at the corner of Walnut Street and Sixth in the heart of a brightly lit city, attesting to the innovation of electricity. Earlier, my recent mentor had informed me that this structure was designed by architect Joseph G. Steinkamp, who opted for a self-conscious collapsing of traditional forms with the more recent Art Deco.

"Deco," the hotel's charming concierge noted, stood for "decoration." In the past, she enthusiastically explained, most big city buildings had been created with function in mind. During modern times, loveliness could exist for its own sake, allowing all living in a democracy to experience high (or, as she chose to call it, *haute*) culture. Available for those who had excelled in our capitalist system and could afford to book a room here. An elite. Not based on birth but accumulation of money. The American Dream come true, at least for a precious few. Why did my mind now drift to the majority? Those untold millions who had not succeeded in their aims, and so daily worked for humble wages?

ELOISE: FRIDAY; FEBRUARY 1, 1901

A fitful sleep helped me make it through the long day. Waking even as late-afternoon gave way to early evening, my rapt hunger for reading material had not lessened. I recalled that pamphlet offered to me aboard the train by the fascinating woman I'd briefly encountered

As if in retort to everything the late queen had claimed, contributors to this anthology railed against Victorianism. The first essay, by Voltairine de Cleyre (whom I assumed to be French), focused on the manner in which a coterie of liberal women became radicalized. The Emancipation Proclomation at last behind us, Lady De Cleyre argued in "Sex Slavery" that marriage, according to its current form (Victoria's, that is), did not significantly differ from what people from Africa had suffered in the U.S. for hundreds of years.

I thought, of course, of my relationship with the boys. How fascinating that what I so longed for a mere three months ago now struck me as highly questionable: Marriage!

HENRY: FRIDAY; FEBRUARY 1, 1901

"A woman," Dag interjected. "I guessed as much."

"Leaving Wyoming without her? That was rough."

"Will she be meeting you in New York?"

"Wish I knew. I'll be joining my business partner there. The thing of it is, he loves Etta, too."

"Etta! You pronounce her name, Harry, as if you were speaking of a goddess."

"That's how I see her. Dag, she's *so* beautiful!"

"Then let me offer some sisterly advice. A woman wants to be respected as a person as well as worshipped for her looks."

"You don't think I do? My pard, too?"

"Sounds more as if each of you obsesses on her."

"And you suggest . . . ?"

"Set 'adoring' her behind you. Learn to *truly* love her." I leaned up and kissed Dag on the cheek. "Harry. when you get to New York, and if she is there, keep in mind: You're blessed with a second chance. I guarantee: there *won't* be a third."

ELOISE: FRIDAY; FEBRUARY 1, 1901

"The New Woman," a translated section of Polish author Boleslaw Prus' novel *Emancypantki*, would be the first I'd read after boarding the train. An Asian, Meri Te Tai Mangakahia, had in 1893 penned an article "So That Women May Receive the Vote." She here declared the political process would provide the key to self-empowerment. How enlightening! Intriguing, too, that we women of the rugged west had secured this, backed by men who appreciated our full worth owing to the daily struggle to survive in a harsh environment. Compared to the 'sophisticated' East, where a gentleman's trophy wife did not have such rights. Much as in Victoria's England.

Also prioritized: Matilda Joslyn Gage's "Women, Church, State," which questioned our political and religious systems alongside conventional marriage. "Only in Conjunction with the Proletarian Woman Will Socialism Be Victorious," Clara Zetkin titled a piece challenging the late queen's insistence that Anglo women should lead lives of privilege. Also hinting that emergent feminism might be combined with the political left.

*If that were so, then I must become a progressive. As such, an ardent supporter of Teddy Roosevelt.*

*Not only in loyalty to my own rough riders. Now, as my own . . . and first . . . true political choice.*


JAMES: FRIDAY; FEBRUARY 1, 1901

The lovely lady's explanation of art continued, as she then invited me to join her for tea in The Arcadia, this hotel's quiet parlor. A charming combination of abundant plants and indoor grasses allowed guests to relax in an elegant white garden, as if outdoors. When I asked as to the unique sensibility achieved here, she took pleasure in explaining the thought-process that determined such decor.

In 1560, England's Sir Philip Sidney coined the term 'Arcadia' to define a lost Golden Age, as pastoral as Eden, which we all strive to rediscover. Once there, a jaded citizen of the city may reclaim a lost innocence and be reborn in nature. Such idealistic thinking was abandoned during the 19th century as swiftly evolving technology redefined our world. With steel and cement the essence of everyday life, Sidney's sentimentalizing of the past came to seem naïve. Replaced by a modern perception, the future is now; the future 'as' now.

Meanwhile, a philosopher named Karl Marx had formulated a 'dialectic' in which he insisted that every action must and will provide an equally powerful *reaction*. If Arcadianism had given way, and seemingly forever, to big city cosmopolitanism, then Neo-Arcadianism now emerged to counter such a modernist approach. Designers and architects set to work creating sweet, idyllic hidden places including the one we now enjoyed.

"As the Romantic poet William Wordsworth write some eighty years ago, 'One impulse from a vernal wood may teach you more of man, of moral evil and good, than all the sages can.' And so hear we sit, in Neo-Arcadia."

"Sure know your business," I said with a smile, impressed as this cultured hostess and I snacked on dainty crackers and rare cheeses imported from the far corners of the world.

ELOISE: FRIDAY; FEBRUARY 1, 1901

The final selection was by Elizabeth Cady Stanton, also the pamphlet's editor. Why, even *I'd* heard of *her*. Its title: "Solitude of Self." Beyond loyalty to the feminist Movement, which she'd been instrumental in founding, Mrs. Stanton argued that each woman must develop a strong sense of identity as an individual *person*, not limited by gender.

*Can it be coincidental that I received this anthology at this juncture? For here is the clear route for my future.*

HENRY: SATURDAY; FEBRUARY 2, 1901

I had arrived as a welcome family member, not unlike the Bible's Prodigal Son. Now, I took my leave like a thief in the night, slipping out of the house without a farewell. Not to Dag, whose existence I'd disturbed enough during my brief stay. Nor Ronald, who had eyed me closer and critically, his attitude more askance with each passing day. Or the two adorable girls. How wonderful it had been to enthrall them with tales true and tall of the west. Which, now that I'd abandoned it, came to seem a Golden Age.

As I trod the down-hill path from their house to the main drag, a suitcase in each hand and on my way into the commercial center of Buffalo where the railroad station stood, I wondered if the girls would remember me a year from now. Might both come to think of 'Uncle Harry' as a dream they'd shared once memory recreates all that happens and, as we grow older, what actually took place takes on aspects of fantasy?

With that in mind, I stopped in my tracks and turned, eager for one final glance. To my surprise, Dag stood at the largest front window, watching me go. She did not wave, nor did I. But our eyes locked in one of those precious, delicate moments when two humans communicate their love without words. In our case? Unconditional love.

ELOISE: SATURDAY; FEBRUARY 2, 1901

Once the train glided into Philadelphia, several fellow passengers disembarked. Outside, others queued up to enter the half-filled coaches for our final run into midtown Manhattan. Glancing out the window, I noticed the wide variety of attire worn by females residing in the East. This potent mix included Victoriana, simple and modest, favored by mature women; also, the free and easy Gibson Girl look. Here, old and new mixed.

Among those boarding, I spotted the older woman whom I encountered two days earlier. Her choice of garments did not fit neatly into any single category. Rather, she projected a proper but hardly prim fashion statement. Her discrete, long charcoal-grey dress, smartly embellished with a crimson scarf, visually suggested a truly independent thinker.

JAMES: SATURDAY; FEBRUARY 2, 1901

"Tell me about the Indians," my exquisite companion had inquired during one of our interludes on Friday night and Saturday morning between intense bouts of lovemaking.

"Me, being a Westerner, and all?"

"Yes! The scar that runs from the tip of your forehead all the way across to the back. Did a savage do that?"

"Hardly," I laughed, wondering if she'd believe me were I to tell the truth about that odd incident at the Hole.

"Are all of the tribes fearsome?"

"Well, Ned Buntline and Buffalo Bill Cody would sure like to convince everyone of that," I chuckled.

"But it isn't so?"

"Once, maybe. Not anymore. Indians I've met . . . mostly Arapaho, Crow, Bannock . . . strike me as havin' had their spirit broken by the way we white folks treated them."

"Now, you're sounding as 'progressive' as our upcoming vice-president," she snickered, her tone cynical.

ELOISE: SATURDAY; FEBRUARY 2, 1901

After exiting the brick station, she advanced toward my passenger car, surrounded by enthusiastic ladies of differing ages. They busily swarmed about their queen bee, as if she magically emitted signals inaudible to all but members of this Sisterhood. Each hurried as best she could to keep up with the matron's determined, if never rushed, pace. As they bid her farewell, porters hurried forward to seize her luggage. Half a dozen men in flat-brimmed straw hats darted her way. Each held a notepad in one hand, a pencil in the other. Reporters!

The woman casually waved the men away in the manner of born royalty, dismissive, though not haughty. Once outside the window, she noticed her former traveling companion peering down with keen interest and smiled. Shortly, a gesture of her white gloved hand indicated that she would like to join me. Still concerned as to my anonymity, if overwhelmed now by the flurry of excitement surrounding her, I nodded my acceptance.

HENRY: Saturday; February 2, 1901

As the train chugged along between Buffalo and New York, I had ample opportunity to consider my current position. On the one hand, we three might, when reunited, discover nothing had changed during the past week. On the other, we might find that each of us had been altered by our separate journeys.

Either way, the next two and a half weeks would prove crucial regarding our futures. Perhaps Manhattan might become our next home. Little doubt Etta would want to stay on. As for my pard and myself, chances are we'd stick, too, if she so wished. I wasn't overly concerned about Lefors and Siringo. A failed robbery attempt, no money stolen and no innocent people harmed, hardly demanded a national search.

But could Butch . . . *James!* . . . and myself ever truly be happy without ever again stretching out on the prairie, under twinkling Western stars and a ripe yellow moon?

ELOISE: Saturday; February 2, 1901

"You certainly were 'the cat's meow' back there," I said, hoping to ferret out the source of her celebrity, once this impressive peron seated herself across from me.

"A curse, not a blessing," she heartily chuckled. Just then, with a sudden surge that jostled standing passengers as well as those already seated, the locomotive pulled forward.

"May I inquire why you visited this city?"

"Well, Eloise, this past week, I traveled from Rochester to Scranton for a committee meeting. Then, off to Philadelphia, in time for yesterday's grand event. There, I delivered the keynote speech."

"Forgive my ignorance. You refer to . . .?"

"A convention of the National American Suffrage Society."

JAMES: SATURDAY; FEBRUARY 2, 1901

"Take it you didn't vote for T.R. and his running mate?"

"I'm a conservative Democratic. So, no."

"Myself? Never joined a party. But I served under the Colonel during our war in Cuba. Never known a finer man."

"Hmmmmmm. I find his approach to ethnics disturbing."

"Served alongside many Indians with the Rough Riders. Blacks, Italians, and Jews as well. In the military, a man learns fast not to judge someone by the color of his skin."

"What, then?" she asked, confused. The aura of a superior sophistication seemed ever less impressive now.

"We take the measure of a man from what he does when the chips are down. None of them fellows ever disappointed me."

"Well," she said, groping for words. "When the Wild West show reaches Cincinnati, I'll make a point to catch it."

"If you're lookin' for spectacle, Cody won't disappoint."

"You mentioned that you were heading on to Manhattan?" I nodded 'yes.' She added, "Maybe you'll catch it there?"

"Not likely. After living in the reality of the frontier, I don't care to see a fantasy version."


ELOISE: SATURDAY; FEBRUARY 2, 1901

"I read about that organization in the pamphlet you so generously provided. And was suitably impressed."

"We are a group of varied people. Mostly female, plus several enlightened men.

"Oh," I gasped. "I just realized where I've seen your face before. In national magazines!"

Here was the person so many men as well as those women who steadfastly supported traditional causes proclaimed an enemy of marriage and morality, Victorian style.

"I'm Susan B. Anthony," she sweetly said.


HENRY: SATURDAY; FEBRUARY 2, 1901

"Next stop, Grand Central Sta—*ah*—tion!"

The conductor barked out our destination in a raspy voice known as the New York accent, halfway between a high wolf whistle and a low cough. Not everyone in the city, I would soon learn, spoke so. Those of the upper-classes

A SPOKESPERSON FOR WOMEN'S SUFFRAGE: Susan B. Anthony
led the march for women's rights to vote at the turn of the century,
sensing (and assuring) that a new America was about to emerge.

avoided common speech. Like Boston's bluebloods, citizens who lived on Fourth Avenue and shopped on Fifth were trained from childhood to speak in the manner of a reigning elite.

No, this was the voice of the people. Those who, like the mighty industrial machines ever more present in any metropolis, performed the grunt work that kept an enormous system running, hopefully like clock-work. Those grey men in blue overhauls handled dreary labor in the city streets and forlorn factories which even thick iron and cold steel couldn't accomplish without the presence of muscular arms.

Just such a person was our train's engineer, up front in the locomotive, was invisible to us in the coach, but our very lives depended on him. Here, on this randomly populated vehicle, the speech of everyday folk included our conductor marching up the aisle punchin' tickets. And though I hailed from the west, I felt a certain kinship.

ELOISE: SATURDAY; FEBRUARY 2, 1901

"I've never before been face to face with a celebrity."

"That, and a nickel, will purchase you a five cent cup of coffee in any diner all across this great land of ours."

"No, really! I . . . I . . ."

"Relax, Eloise. I'm a *person*. No more, no less."

"You don't take yourself seriously, then?"

"Heavens, no. I despise those who achieve some level of fame and are overly impressed with themselves."

"What *do* you take seriously, then?"

"My mission! To do whatever I can to make our country, and the world, a better place in the coming century."

## JAMES: SATURDAY; FEBRUARY 2, 1901

I dozed off for a spell. When I awoke, she was gone. The only trace that a lovely woman had shared my bed during a long night's journey into day: with her lipstick, she had scrawled on the bathroom window, "Ships that pass in the night!"

I lay in bed for more than an hour, which is not my way. Sundance? Or, as I should say now, Henry Long! Give him an excuse to keep from rising for another minute and he'd embrace it. Me? Ordinarily up with the first crack of dawn.

Today was different. This marked the second day of the second month of the second year in a new century, the start of an era which promised growth, change, enlightenment. If the recent past had witnessed a gradual demise of the way things were, the future ought best be viewed with cautious hope. As for me? I couldn't wait to get going on whatever trail awaited me next.

## ELOISE: SATURDAY; FEBRUARY 2, 1901

"Should I assume you were thinking of your husband?"

"Oh! I was distracted there for a moment. Excuse me."

We spoke of her illustrious career. And several ideas I'd absorbed from her essay, which offered me a glimpse into an alternative world. We ordered raspberry ice water and vegetarian sandwiches. I finished mine more swiftly perhaps than I ought to have in the presence of a cultivated personage. Eventually, I'd found myself listlessly gazing at passing scenery as farmlands gave way to drab suburbs.

"Nothing to be 'excused' for. Only, the curious look on your face as you peered out struck me as . . . well, wistful."

"In fact, yes. The thought of Henry and myself reuniting after a week apart does weigh on my mind."

"And of course replacing your missing wedding ring." She nodded at the appropriate finger and that object's absence.

"As to *that* . . . may I be entirely truthful?"

HENRY: SATURDAY; FEBRUARY 2, 1901

As for me, sitting on the half-filled coach and about to arrive at my destination? Merely one more face in the crowd that would shortly pour into the already busy streets and avenues that criss-cross the much fabled Isle of Manhattan. The time had come to visit The Big Apple and witness what all the hooplah was about. Here awaited an island where, some 400 years ago, a bunco artist—the first, if hardly last, to arrive on these shores—purchased fertile land from local natives for a small box of colored beads. And set into place the future history of a country that, however difficult this might be to admit, had prospered owing to such exploitation.

"Can't wait to get a look at the station's insides," I said with a smile as the conductor stepped close.

"You will not be disappointed," he responded with a wink.

ELOISE: SATURDAY; FEBRUARY 2, 1901

"If there's one attribute I appreciate, it's honesty."

"Henry and I aren't *married*. Not officially."

"I see." She sounded neither surprised nor judgmental.

"You grasped that yesterday, didn't you?"

"In all truth? *Yes*."

"Yet you said nothing."

"I didn't consider it my business to do so. Once in Manhattan, will you and 'Harry,' or 'Henry,' or whatever you call him, resume a 'common-law-marriage'?"

"Funny you should ask. He's actually requested we now make it legal. With a ceremony and ring. The whole package."

"If I may be so bold as to ask: will you accept?"

"It's . . . well . . . *tricky*."

"I'm all ears. And we still have some time left."

JAMES: SATURDAY; FEBRUARY 2, 1901

Without Etta's influence, I mused as my train continued to roar eastward, I'd be one more member of the vast crowd. For as I came to realize, relaxing between the mussed sheets at my hotel, that Etta . . . *Eloise!* . . . was with me even now. This was particularly apparent, if in an odd sort of way, after sharing a bed with another woman, who briefly impressed me with her seeming worldliness. But that lady's outlook on life struck me as simplistic.

*Suddenly, the truth dawned on me. Ever since that day when Sundance and I met Miss Etta Place five years ago? She did not so much join us as she* recreated *us. For the better!*

## ELOISE: SATURDAY; FEBRUARY 2, 1901

Without revealing the identity of either man, I explained my difficult situation in detail. There was Harry, or Henry. The dark, suave Westerner, who once swept a naïve girl up and away in his firm arms. And LeRoy, now 'James,' like an older brother, friendly and warm if on occasion my lover as well.

Now, both hoped for marriage after five years of such an unconventional—some might say immoral—relationship.

"Many women would envy you."

"Well, these truly are *remarkable* fellows."

"They certainly *sound* special! Not that I would expect anything less, in light of your own catalogue of qualities."

## HENRY: SATURDAY; FEBRUARY 2, 1901

I'd already heard of the station's recently redesigned interior, modelled on a Vienna palace. Paintings, statues, a man-made waterfall, as well as cut glass chandeliers. "Rumor has it no station in America is located in a larger building."

"*Three* buildings," the conductor corrected me. Observing my wide-eyed fascination, he shared some big city knowledge. "A trio of railroad depots, linked together fifty years ago, when that master of industry Andrew Carnegie bought out the previous owners and added inter-connecting corridors."

"Can't wait!" I exclaimed.

"You're going to have to," he kidded, "at least for a minute or so longer." I took that to be a New York sense of humor. Clearly, I had a great deal of adjusting to do.

'NEXT STOP, GRAND CENTRAL STATION': Arrivals to Manhattan, trains and entered New York City through a modern Xanadu intended to reflect the glories of the coming century.

ELOISE: SATURDAY; FEBRUARY 2, 1901

"That's quite a compliment from a person of your renown."

"How marvelous that you chose the term 'person,' not 'woman.' I dislike gender-specific categorization."

"My, but you are 'to the point.'"

"Most Suffragists are. It's characteristic of how we see life and our situation in the world."

"Please explain."

"Devoid of sentiment and romanticization."

"That's exactly what *I* suffer from! I've lived in a dream world where white knights ride to the rescue."

"Likely, as much a glorious creation as those stories Mr. Buntline invents about the West. In that book featuring Butch Cassidy, the Sundance Kid, and Miss Etta Place—"

"Oh," I interjected, purposefully cutting her off. "But I would *love* to learn more about the Movement,"

"Once in New York, I'd be delighted to teach you."

JAMES: SATURDAY; FEBRUARY 2, 1901

Something about a long, leisurely train ride causes a body to set any recent troubles aside, as well as worries regarding what may lie ahead. Be it the smooth movement—so different from that of a stagecoach, bouncing up and down with every turn on the trail—or perhaps the sound of the mighty engine, roaring ahead with industrial assurance. You come to feel momentarily released from time and space.

Half-asleep, I overheard small-talk between husbands and wives, mainly concerning family matters. Nearby, well-groomed ladies traveling together discussed current trends in fashion. Businessmen, secluded in tight cliques, analyzed the state of the economy, specifically any impact the incoming McKinley/Roosevelt administration might have on the stock market.

All the while, I took in the thick, rich scent of quality cigars enjoyed by fellows in tall Lincoln-esque hats. Such types tended to sit alone, quietly reading newspapers while maintaining a discrete distance from the general riff-raff.

*They were mighty capitalists. Men defined by money.*

*That's the way it's always been. Then again, as we enter a new era of human interaction, might it be time for a change?*

ELOISE: SATURDAY; FEBRUARY 2, 1901

"That would be wonderful! I'm so confused."

"Share, dear."

"Well, I know that the late Queen Victoria would condemn me for living with Henry, without benefit of wedlock."

"As to common law marriage, our great inspiration, Mary Wolstonecraft, lived in such an arrangement for years."

"Oh, didn't she write *Frankenstein?* I adored that novel."

"You refer to her daughter, Mary Wolstonecraft Shelley. 'The Modern Prometheus' does include arguments first articulated by the mother. Among them, 'state-sanctioned marriage as a legalized form of imprisonment for women.'"

"*Whew*! Perhaps the Queen read each of Mary's work and felt a need to rail against them."

"Why, you're sounding like a Suffragist already!"


HENRY: SATURDAY; FEBRUARY 2, 1901

While others rose from their seats to retrieve luggage from over-head racks, I remained still as the conductor spoke on. Soon, he enthusiastically told me, I would be treated to the greatest example of what educated folk referred to as Neo-Renaissance architecture in the U.S.A. An earlier station, which for more than half a century serviced those heading into or away from New York, had degenerated with time and misuse. A successful capitalist, Andrew Carnegie, responded by financing the most costly construction project in the city's history. All shops, restaurants, waiting rooms and 'indoor out-houses' were gutted. A relic of the 19th century gave way to a harbinger of the 20th.

As the country had been generous to him, Mr. Carnegie announced the time had come to return some of that largesse. 'Enlightened capitalism,' he called such a system. Yet, notably, his name was prominently displayed everywhere.

*Social responsibility combined with a self-conscious legacy. Struck me as right and proper for the U.S.A.*


ELOISE: SATURDAY; FEBRUARY 2, 1901

"But there's more! Mary resented that 'should a woman be born beautiful, so much the better for her. At least, for the first twenty or so years.'"

"I recently turned twenty-one," I sighed, realizing that our conversation was relevant to this time in my life.

"How much easier to live in the lap of luxury. Though everything becomes difficult . . . near impossible, at times . . . when a woman dares say, 'I will not depend on protection by the man in my life . . . *if* I choose to have one . . . rather, I must learn instead to always protect myself."

"It's as if you've read my very mind!"

"That, or aided you in solidifying your thoughts."

"Oh," I exclaimed, completely forgetting for the moment my precarious position. "I think I'm going to *love* the East."


JAMES: Saturday; February 2, 1901

Off on their own, a large clan of country folk, in casual work clothes, huddled close. The elderly patriarch delivered a rundown on prices for corn, tomatoes, and other vegetables to his demure wife. Their seven children appeared interested only in fried chicken and apple fritters, packed away in a wicker basket. The mother dutifully served these foodstuffs to her brood. Practical people did not waste funds on train fare.

*As such, recalling my own onetime family. Now, shadow figures in vague, fading memories. Part fact, part fiction.*

Then there were the porters, all black. Attending to the whims and wishes of white people, me included. Though I knew this to be the way things work, I couldn't help but find such a system . . . well . . . *wrong.*

Gradually, a notion come to me that here, in this coach, existed America itself, relentlessly pushing ahead even as our locomotive did. A diverse nation, come together as one. The United States in miniature, as T.R. might put it.

Halfway between my own past and future, I'd have several weeks in Manhattan to try and figure out where I stood with our woman, the Kid, and most significantly, the world. And, perhaps most important of all, my own self.


ELOISE: Saturday; February 2, 1901

"Here's my address," my mentor said while drawing a business card from her purse, "and the hotel's phone number."

"This is where I'll be staying," I responded, scratching our already-set boarding house's address on a slip of paper.

"One way or the other, we'll be in touch shortly."

Moments earlier, we'd deboarded the train, awaiting the porters with Susan's luggage. I carried only a loose sack of clothing strapped over my right shoulder.

"This is . . . well . . . beyond my wildest dreams!"

"I look so forward to introducing you to a special sector of Manhattan. Where remarkable people are building a future in which enlightenment will spread as it has not since Emmanuel Kant's philosophy changed the world a hundred years ago."

"Oh, yes! I've studied his work. A new reliance on Reason, yet balanced by an acceptance of one's senses. That's the sort of world I wish to inhabit.

"Perhaps, Eloise, you'll play a part in helping to shape it."

## HENRY: SATURDAY; FEBRUARY 2, 1901

Shortly, I stepped into the main lobby. Gas lamps on display here during the previous decade were gone, replaced by electric lights everywhere. Their white-hot radiance poured down from elegant arrangements on high-reaching walls, bannisters, and the ceiling itself. Such vivid details allowed this immense cavity the appearance of an ongoing winter carnival.

*Suggesting to oncoming visitors like myself that Manhattan offers a holiday each and every day.*

That's when I noticed my old gambling partner, settled into a second life as a respected journalist. Leaning on his famous silver-tipped cane, a brown derby set jauntily atop his head. Awaiting my arrival, as he had assured me he would.

"Howdy," I said with a smile, all the many years since we last met blowing away like fading leaves in an Autumn wind.

"Hello Kid," Bat Masterson replied, eyes twinkling.


## ELOISE: SATURDAY; FEBRUARY 2, 1901

"Oh! But I may only be here for several weeks."

"Owing to Henry?"

"In part, I guess. Though I have determined to choose my own path from this point on."

"Well, that gives me some time to try and persuade you to remain here, with or without him. Or should I say *them*?"

No doubt the boys would, at this point in our long and complex relationship, do precisely as I requested. If I were to stay here and agree to resume our earlier sharing of one another, they'd agree. Or if I informed them I wanted to marry one or the other, they'd somehow deal with that.

Now, though, a wild card had entered my life. I was a wanted criminal. The wise thing to do was to depart as soon as possible for foreign shores, as Butch had suggested.


## JAMES: SATURDAY; FEBRUARY 2, 1901

Now pushing fifty, Bat appeared considerably older than that. My first impression? He'd left any trace of youth behind once he abandoned the west. As to that cane? The living legend born William Bartley Masterson up in Queebec back in 1853 had required such a third leg ever since taking a bullet in his right thigh during his first gunfight.

OLD SOLDIERS NEVER DIE; THEY JUST FADE AWAY . . . : Friends and
family of Bat Masterson noted that the once robust man had aged swiftly
after moving to Manhattan; Bat provided the inspiration for 'Sky Masterson'
in Damon Runyon's "Guys and Dolls" stories.

"The ravages of civilization," he sighed, seeing right through an ineffectual
attempt to conceal my reaction to his appearance as I approached him and
Henry, standing together, jawing.

"If you say so, Bat. For the moment, I feel entirely re-invigorated by the
present grandeur. Eloise 'll love it!"

"Miss Etta Place?" Bat mused. "She'll sure be a sight for these sore eyes!
Arriving today as well, you said . . ."

Smoke and steam billowed from mighty engines just beyond the thick glass
doors, drifting in every time they opened wide for yet another pageant of incoming and outgoing passengers. I marveled at the variety of humanity. Rich,
poor, middle-class—dudes in business suits, farmers in overalls—united for one
brief, if notable, moment in Grand Central Station. All likely unconscious of
the meaning I read into the situation.

"Speakin' of her," Henry mentioned, "she was wondering if maybe we
ought to settle down here permanently."

"Might fit her. Being educated and all, You and Henry? Can't see it. You
two would be like coyotes, caged in a zoo."

*That wasn't what I wanted to hear. Perhaps because I knew it to be the truth.*

ELOISE: SATURDAY; FEBRUARY 2, 1901

"And so we're together again," I called out, immediately spotting both of
my boys along side Mr. Masterson, whom I did not initially recognize. I'd only

met him twice, when he had returned to the frontier following adventures else-where. He appeared to have aged considerably during those two years. "Thank you so for all you have done for us!" I said, referring to the preparations he'd made for us once Butch contacted him.

With a smile, I rose on my toes to kiss his rough cheek. Next, I embraced Henry, then James, my lips meeting each of theirs. A part of me wished to tell one, then the other, how much I'd missed him. At the same time, though, I wanted to explain that things were different now.

HENRY: SATURDAY; FEBRUARY 2, 1901

"Wouldn't have believed it if I hadn't seen it with my own eyes," James announced at the majesty surrounding us as he, Bat, Etta, and I left the row of raw steel platforms and entered the main lobby. Here existed a city within a city.

"I seen it and *still* only half believe it," Bat replied.

For here we were, standing near to an ivory statue of a stark naked woman, perched on a half-shell in the middle of an resplendent marble fountain. Sur-rounding this object of high art, plush seats were scattered, occupied by ladies and gents with newspapers in one hand, a beverage in the other. All the while, an eleven-piece symphonic orchestra performed. Many passersby, heading to or from the platforms and overwhelmed by gusts of steam heat, momentarily halted to marvel at the rare splendor. Others stopped to sit a spell at tables covered with white linen clothes, each featuring a vase of long stem roses. Finely attired waiters hurried from a grand mahogany bar to their customers, deliver-ing exotic drinks and crab cocktails.

*Why, a man could get used to such finery. Even a wild fella like myself. That is, the self I once was.*

—INTERLUDE—

BAT: OCTOBER 25, 1921

*As my role in this tale is about to become considerably larger, let me bring you up to date. Talk about the luck of the Irish! Soon, I received a telegram from a mil-lionaire in New York City. Over the years, George Gould Mullins had made more than his share of enemies. Word had it a hired killer had been contracted to blow the rich man's brains out. Mullins needed a bodyguard. After reading several of Ned Buntline's novels, he came to the conclusion there was but one man for the job: me. I telegrammed back, requesting an unsightly sum.*

*To my amazement, Mullins agreed. Next day, I set out for New York by train. First class! That was in 1895. Serving as Mullins' guardian angel with my cane in place of a sword. We became fast friends. He was a great fan of the West and relished my admittedly long-winded tales of the old days.*

*All true, Lolly. Give or take a fib or two.*

*To eliminate the threat of assassination, Mullins and I worked closely with the new Police Commissioner, Theodore Roosevelt. We three became inseparable. Once Teddy and I rounded up the conspirators threatening our mutual acquaintance, we spent many a summer day fishing, conversing, and imbibing bourbon and branch on my boss' yacht.*

*One afternoon, Mullins asked T.R. if he had further political ambitions. Hell's bells!, he exclaimed. Why, I'm heading for the White House in due time. His own pappy had told him as a child, "Son, it doesn't matter what you do in life. What counts is that you're the best at it. Which means you must reach the top of the heap."*

AN AMERICAN HERCULES IN HIS PRIME: Bat Masterson, the man who became a legend in his own time; a jack of many trades (lawman, frontier scout, boxing promoter, journalist, etc.) and master of each.

HOW THE WEST WAS (ALMOST) LOST: Buffalo hunters headquartered in Dodge City in 1876 reaped huge profits from the skins they collected, but their actions threatened to annihilate the American bison and the indigenous people who relied on them for food and shelter in the form of teepees.

*So T.R. turned and asked what I'd prefer to do with the remainder of my life, now that buffalo hunting and the like were a part of my past imperfect. I shared a secret dream I held as a result of my brief experiment in Colorado to write about athletic events for a newspaper, if they paid enough.*

*Raised eyebrows revealed this gave Mullins an idea. "Well," he said, "the editor of the* Morning Telegraph *is a good friend. Want me to speak on your behalf?"*

*The following morning, I was in that fellow's office at the paper's Park Row building. He asked to see my portfolio. I handed him copies of the single issue newspaper from Dodge and the boxing story out of Denver. He read 'em over and chuckled.*

*"Why, I learned more about* you *from these reports than I did anything you were supposed to be covering."*

*"If I'm wasting your time, Mr. Lewis, I'll leave."*

*"No, no. I loved it! You're hired. We'll have you write a column that includes sports and other topics as well. I like the idea of stories about the modern metropolis as told by a man of the Old West. You start tomorrow."*

# PART FIVE:
# FIRST BITES OF THE BIG APPLE

"New York City, seen for the first time, reveals to an arriving visitor the wild promise of all the mystery and beauty in the world."

—F. Scott Fitzgerald

ELOISE: Saturday; February 2, 1901

A transom brought us to a quiet, out of the way, neat, if nondescript, boarding house at 124 West Twelfth Street in lower Manhattan. This located us at the northern tip of what locals called The Village, once reputed, I knew, for a grand style of living during the dimly recalled gilded age of the 1870s. More recently renowned for its art colonies and bohemian inhabitants.

*How enthusiastic I was to visit every nook and cranny.*

Bat and the boys were eager to spend a night on the town. Though invited to join them, I did not feel up to it. My bones still ached; hot flashes plagued me below the waist-line. So like a pair of overgrown boys—the quality I often criticized them for but also cherished—they danced off into the fading light to enjoy those unique experiences that men so cherish.

Not, though, before we briefly set into motion what would become an ongoing discussion as to the future.

WHERE THEY STAYED: Butch, Sundance, and Etta resided at this boarding-house, located at 124 West Twelfth Street; though the name of the actual proprieter is known today, the character of 'Kathryn Trumbell' is entirely fictitious.

JAMES: Saturday; February 2, 1901

We'd been met at the front desk by Mrs. Trumbell, a tall redhead whom I guessed to be forty-ish. Also, a giant of a youth, identified as her nineteen-year-old son, Samson.

"Welcome," the owner said with a sly smile.

I wondered if perhaps the lady of the house bought our story. That is, Eloise supposedly traveling with her husband, Henry Long, and her brother, James. All friends of the renown Bat Masterson, the three of us visiting the city for several weeks on "business." More likely than not, she considered it a stretch for such folks to board here rather than at one of the lavish mid-town hotels.

"Our pleasure," I replied, noting that this Mrs. Trumbell eyed me up and down. Likewise, I couldn't help but notice her lush figure. Or enjoy her notably feminine movements when she fulfilled my request to lock an envelope, in which I'd placed most of our funds, in the lobby's steel safe.

As to our arrangements, I would stay in a single room on the third floor, directly across the hall from the supposed married couple, occupying a larger suite. Once settled, While Bat waited in the lobby, we broke a clammy silence as Eloise insisted on addressing the elephant in the room: life beyond our temporary stay here. Already, I'd suggested in telegrams that Mike Cassidy had offered what might be the perfect solution: South America. Would Eloise agree?

"I will remain with you til the boat leaves for Bolivia, or whatever destination you may have in mind."

"First stop: Argentina!" I announced. "There, a whole new world will open up for us. We can begin again fresh!"

"Will you accompany us?" Henry anxiously asked.

"That, I'm not certain."


ELOISE: Saturday; February 2, 1901

"What's to decide? We three—"

"Hear me out, James! As you know, things change."

"Sounds as if your trip has been life-altering."

"True, Henry. And certain events which occurred before my leave-taking must be discussed."

"We're here for ya, whatever you decide."

"I knew that even before you said so, James. And do appreciate such loyalty."

"We'll take what happens step by step," Henry added.

"Meanwhile, all three of us made it here. That's the most important thing. We'll have time enough to talk soon."

"Well," James said. "I guess we ought to join Bat for whatever he has planned."

"Boys' night out? Well, have yourselves a good time."

## HENRY: SATURDAY; FEBRUARY 2, 1901

I felt comfortable leaving Eloise alone, as Trumbell's Boarding House was clearly located in a safe area. The Village, at first glance, struck me as looking less like a part of this mighty city than a tree-lined (Mulberry, to be specific) hide-away, resembling a middle-American town in, perhaps, Ohio.

We three traveled by trolley to a borough Bat identified as Brooklyn, housing what Bat claimed to be the best open-air boxing venue in New York. Constructed as part of an elaborate amusement pier previously known as SeaSide Park, the area had recently been rechristened Coney Island. We arrived even as the first hint of stars appeared in a darkening heaven highlighted by strands of pink, not unlike the cotton-candy on sale here.

"There's a lot more at stake," Bat whispered to James and me as we sat ourselves in the bleachers as the bell rang and Round One commenced, "than which fella wins this fight."

I hoped to hear more, but silence descended on the crowd. The two boxers left their respective corners and met in the center of the ring, fists raised.

## ELOISE: SATURDAY; FEBRUARY 2, 1901

For a while, I drifted off to sleep. Then, the cramps returned, more intense than before. Awake if uneasy, I lay still in the bed, praying for this to pass. When it did not, I pulled myself together, rose, and sat before the single table in what would be James' single room, mine for this one night when privacy mattered. I turned to the final essay, penned by editor Elizabeth Cady Stanton. She had chosen as her subject a gathering of like-minded women and men, 307 in number, held more than half a century ago in upstate New York at a village named Seneca Falls. Among the attendees: Frederick Douglass, the one-time escaped slave who rose to prominence as an abolitionist leader in Massachusetts before the great war.

As Stanton's carefully chosen quotes from that great man revealed, he, too, perceived ownership of people and the current state of matrimony as parallel variations on a false arrangement.

*In more recent years, though, and at long last talk of enlightenment filled the air. How I would love to be a part of this oncoming revolution, headquarted in the very city that I had just now entered!*

JAMES: SATURDAY; FEBRUARY 2, 1901

Waltzing forward with the grace of a dancer, "Dandy Jim" Buckley lived up to his nickname. At a height I guessed to be 5'6", weighing maybe 150 well-proportioned pounds, the youth kept his head raised high. Jim's baby-brown eyes scrutinized his opponent's frame as Jim tried to anticipate what the big fella might opt for next. Then, the youth moved in fast as a bullet for a strategic punch. As to "Brawlin' Jack" Darby, here stood an impressive mass of bone, flesh, and muscle. At least a foot (maybe more) taller than his fiery opponent, with ten more years of living under his belt, this fighting machine likely weighed in at 225 pounds. Enormous fists were covered with ribbons of leather and tightly wrapped cloth, as were his opponent's, these safety measures now a legal requirement.

Darby swung wildly as Dandy Jim pranced about. All in the arena sensed that even a single well-connected blow from Darby might send Buckley down and out for the count. You might've heard the proverbial pin drop as the gathered sports fans waited to see what might occur next.


ELOISE: SATURDAY; FEBRUARY 2, 1901

With slavery officially outlawed in the U.S., the time was right for liberal voices to decry marriage. If not the institution per se, as with slavery, then at least in its current form. Human bondage for an entire gender.

Now to be rethought. Appropriately, as I recalled my own once all-encompassing desire to wed. Had that indeed been the case only a few months ago? Difficult to believe! A desperate desire to officialize a union with one or the other of my boys and a hunger to make the choice had given way to a pressing need to decide whether marriage remained a desirable option.

"The history of mankind is a history of repeated injuries and usurpation on the part of man toward woman, having in direct object the establishment of absolute tyranny over her."

*How Elizabeth Cady Stanton's words resonated with me! The 'new' Etta, or Eloise, or whatever I called myself.*


HENRY: SATURDAY; FEBRUARY 2, 1901

"Kill 'em, Brawler," a drunken lout with a hoarse Bowery Boy accent shouted from the back row. The cheap seats! Bat had arranged for us to sit five rows back from the ring, square in the middle: the best possible spot for observing a match.

What surprised me? A number of handsomely attired middle-class men, some accompanied by respectable women, were among the 200 or so in attendance. On the frontier? Gladiatorial matches consisted of back-alley confrontations, performed for the roughewn pleasure of crude men. Yet here in New York, boxing apparently snailed its way toward legitimacy. My guess? Bat Masterson played a key role in this.

"You can take him, Buckley," a refined-looking gent in a pin-striped suit stated in a considerably more couth tone.

Three-minute rounds were interrupted by sixty second breaks. No limit had been imposed as to the number of such carefully spaced confrontations. A match continued until one or the other could lunge forward no more, demonstrated by his fallng down, barely alive. If indeed he did remain so.

## ELOISE: SATURDAY; FEBRUARY 2, 1901

First and foremost, the Victorian rule that insisted on obedience of wife to husband must be cast aside in favor of equality. Well, women on the frontier had demonstrated their worth on farms, ranches, and other endeavors day after forlorn day. On the prairie, a woman constantly proved her true value. As to big cities? Upscale wives were pampered while their poorer urban counterparts had little time to consider voting rights. No wonder the right to vote had first been won in the west.

Stanton insisted a modern woman, however respectable her status, must be free to find employment should she so choose. How I appreciated that neither Henry nor James objected to my possible return to teaching. Primitive as either might be, they were Westerners who perceived a wife as a partner, not some status symbol to be enshrined in a virtual castle. If men still dominated women, my boys were at least the best of the lot.

## JAMES: SATURDAY; FEBRUARY 2, 1901

For the first half-hour, The Brute seemed destined for an easy win. Stalking his opponent like a monster from mythology closing in on a menaced hero, Darby's relentless punches sent the shorter contender staggering backward again and again. But by the sixth round Darby, now winded, slowed down. At last, Jim Buckley came into his own, moving ever faster. To the crowd's amazement, Jim's feet tripped the light fantastic. Sudden, swift blows to Jack's face and sharp jabs to his vulnerable stomach impacted on the weakened tub of guts. This strategy by Buckley caused Darby to sweat buckets, backing off toward the ropes.

"Like David versus Goliath," Bat happily noted.

A PUGILIST'S DREAM COME TRUE: Coney Island's sports venue allowed boxing, previously reserved for street thugs, to reach the vast American public.

## ELOISE: SATURDAY; FEBRUARY 2, 1901

I could no longer believe that my meeting with Susan B. Anthony qualified as random. As when I was young, I felt that destiny specifically chose me for an important mission. Had I discovered it during my flight to Manhattan?

*Susan B. Anthony might be a person to some, a source of inspiration to others. To me, she signified my fate.*

Susan struck me as a woman . . . person . . . who might well be president. A female in that role is a dream that could, should, *must* be realized. I understood, as Cady Stanton did, that for the moment it would remain necessary to support such progressive men as McKinley. And, in the near future, Teddy Roosevelt.

## HENRY: SATURDAY; FEBRUARY 2, 1901

During the eleventh round, the tide turned again. Darby grasped that he must move quickly if he were to survive, much less win. At this point, he set to slugging away swifter than any of us might have guessed the big fella remained capable of. Though Dandy Jim crouched low, slipping in close for a swing, one of the Brawler's mighty paws landed on the smaller man's forehead. The crowd gasped in unison.

'Never say die!' must have been Jim's credo. Somehow the comer lasted another four rounds, looking more like a worn-out punching bag with each passing moment. The end became clear to all present when Jack's right ham-fist connected with Jim's face, never again to be described as 'handsome.'

"Damn!" Bat all but spit. "That sets the fight game back at least ten years."

ELOISE: SATURDAY; FEBRUARY 2, 1901

"We are such stuff as dreams are made on," Shakespeare claimed in *The Tempest*, "our little life rounded by dreams." Never in the life of Etta Place, aka Eloise Placer, aka Mrs. Henry Long, did that quotation ring so true as when I fell into an uneasy sleep. My mind experienced a full tsunami of conflicting ideas and emotions. Swiftly, I lost all sense of consciousness, settling deep into the clean sheets.

How I wanted to disappear into the worlds within worlds that apparently existed in this magical city. How I needed to escape as swiftly as possible before the law closed in. Could I resolve the delight I experienced when reunited with my boys with a conflicting desire to have Susan mentor me on the ways of women who set old fashioned relationships aside?

No way could I even imagine what might occur next. Yet I would face the future, if with trepidation. tempered by my natural courage. My mantra—I refuse to fail!—had seen me through the worst blizzard in Wyoming's history. Now, that must be the case with the winter weather, figurative and literal, here in Manhattan.

JAMES: SATURDAY; FEBRUARY 2, 1901

"Please explain what you said back at ring?" I asked Bat once we were seated in a snug seaside shack. Along with large pitchers of beer, the place served something unique to this pier, nicknamed by locals as a "Conie": grilled frankfurters, buried beneath crumbled cheese, fresh-chopped onion, and a sharp tongue-burning mustard imported from Bavaria.

"Remind me," Bat mumbled as we considered the selection of available brews on the crude hand-written menu. Instead of a traditional cloth, our table was covered with brown butcher-board paper, easily disposable after any party left. This venue represented a casual retreat for male visitors.

A crimson sky, observed through a panoramic horizontal window, provided the fitting backdrop for our view. Giddy folks of all ages promenaded along the rough slat boardwalk or mingled on an adjacent beach, despite the chill. Not far to the northeast stood Stauch's Baths, infamous for catering to men who enjoyed close proximity with other men.

*Which caused me to remember that Butch and I would share a bunk tonight. Without Etta 'Eloise' in-between. Something that in all our years together we'd never once done.*

Didn't particularly want to think on it until the time came. Other than the recent fight, my mind concerned itself with our woman. Soon as she's up to it,

'I LOVE THE NIGHT LIFE!': A predecessor to Disneyland and other upcoming theme parks during the day, 'Luna Park' offered endless attractions for adults once the sun set

we must bring her to this marvelous enclave. Bat assured me that when we all arrived together, his wife Emma included, our little company would partake of the more upscale offerings at Coney's top spots. These of course appealing to women as well as men.

ELOISE: SATURDAY; FEBRUARY 2, 1901

Slipping into an ever deeper, darker sleep, I envisioned myself on a raft at sea, high blue-green waves capped by salty white tips swirling about as the relentless current drew me toward a rock-strewn shore. Reaching the beach, I crawled up onto barren land. An undertow threatened to drag me back into the roaring sea but I would not succumb.

"Etta!" James's voice called from somewhere distant.

"Eloise!" Henry loudly screamed. "This way."

Unable to keep my eyes open owing to the punishing salt spray, I managed to rise up and force myself to step in the direction from which their voices beckoned. As I approached a hill, at last I managed to raise my eyelids slightly. And, thanks to a stroke of lightning, make out the two high on a rise.

*They sat together, arm-in-arm. Stark naked. Each a prime example of American manhood. Seemingly so happy together.*

HENRY: Saturday; February 2, 1901

"As to the fight's importance," I reminded Bat.

"Ah!" he explained. "I was hoping against hope Buckley would win. Either of you gents care to guess why?"

"You bet a big wad on him," Butch ventured.

"Good guess," Bat replied with a laugh. "But, no."

"We're all ears," I responded.

"My plan is to take boxing out of the back alleys and move it first to Coney Island, then on to Madison Square Garden." Bat referred to midtown's recently completed mecca for sports and spectacles. Even now, Buffalo Bill's Wild West performed there to crowds drawn from every social class.

With rare breaks to consume the hearty Coney and drain his mug, Bat rambled on. Around us, on the rustic wood walls, hung framed photographs of muscular boxers, each assuming a studied pose to reveal the classical lines of his physique.

Bat explained that he now involved himself with everything from publicizing events to serving as referee. What most disturbed him? Mindless brutality, a hangover from the past. This had resulted in several cities, eager to achieve full respectability, going so far as to outlaw boxing. Few people believed The Fights might ever emerge as a national pastime such as baseball. Nonetheless, Bat dedicated himself to making that seemingly impossible dream come true.


ELOISE: Saturday; February 2, 1901

The words I'd hurled at them months earlier came back to haunt me now, "Can't you two see that you *love* one another?"

"Join us," Butch and Sundance simultaneously called out.

"I want to," I heard myself answer, "but I can't."

"Why?" the boys, speaking as one, demanded.

"I must make my own way now."

"We are here for you, now and always," Henry insisted.

"I know," I wept, loving them, yet longing for freedom.

"Let us help you through this cruel night," James added.

"I don't know what I ought to do," I howled in confusion.


JAMES: Saturday; February 2, 1901

In 1890s New York, Bat explained over the roar of a now unruly crowd, pugilism had been the sport of choice for the lower classes. A typical bare-knuckles encounter between moustachioed Bill 'The Butcher' Poole and his rival Johnny

'Old Smoke' Morrissey, whose long yellow and orange head of unkempt hair recalled Viking raiders from ancient legends, would last all day and into the night. The unrestricted violence continued until one or the other was knocked flat. There were few rules, the match 'called' only in case of a police raid. But too many members of the force were open to bribery for that to prove likely.

"But some twenty years ago, an Englishman known as the Marquesse of Queensbury civilized the fight game, at least in Britain. Combatants there were required to wear padded gloves, thicker with each passing year. A fight can be shut down by The Ref without a knockout if he deems this necessary to avoid damage."

"That sure's not what we witnessed tonight."

"Right you are, Henry. My aim? Bring 'the Queensbury Code' to our country. We Americans are still more attune to violence, owin' to our four-hundred-some-odd years of taming the frontier. But we're coming along. As you saw, decent working-folk attended, as well the usual street toughs."

"Even some finely dressed females!" I piped in.

"You *would* notice *that*," Henry sighed. "So what happened here this evening constitutes a setback to your plans?"

"The gentleman went down; The Brute won. In my column, I will phrase what occurred so as to hint that there will be another day, another fight. And, in time, things *will* change."

"Sounds to me like you're not so much *reporting* the news as you are *making* it."

"I'll tell you boys a little secret," Bat whispered. "Public may not realize this but that's the way things work. Sports, politics, theater? We Gentlemen of the Press are not witnesses to history so much as its primary avatars."


ELOISE: SUNDAY; FEBRUARY 3, 1901

Initially, I wasn't certain whether or not I'd feel well enough to join the boys for breakfast. The extreme chills and aches were gone, though my stomach remained queasy. So when they left the suite and stepped across the hall to check in on me, I sent them on ahead. This allowed me time to perform my toilet and dress. Eventually, I made my way down the hardwood spiral staircase, a holdover from a previous period of brief-lived prosperity before bank-runs ended the gilded age. Then, fine mansions fell into the hands of the middleclass as a once wealthy citizenry sold off their fabled haunts.

As I reached the ground floor, certain now that I would indeed be able to go out and about today, Mrs. Trumbell met me. The attractive, if no longer young, redhead eyed me with curiosity. In truth, everything about Mrs. Trumbell's projected attitude of lighthearted accommodation struck me as feigned. My guess: she mistrusted us, particularly me.

"Your *husband* and *brother* await you by the window," she greeted me with a broad sweep of her right arm, as well as a hint—purposeful, it seemed to me—of disbelief in her tone.

This further increased my fear that she suspected I was someone other than whom I claimed to be. I must keep in mind that sooner or later, the eastern papers would carry the story of a man found murdered in Wyoming. The key suspect: a woman.

*And while there was no known photograph on record that might be published, likely the fugitive was Etta Place.*

After accompanying me to the boys' table, our hostess moved on to other guests. At this moment, I made a decision not to share (yet) the horrific fact that altered everything: I killed a man. Instead, I gave way to a compulsion to savor life while it remains possible. I will enjoy this day!

## HENRY: SUNDAY; FEBRUARY 3, 1901

James had risen early, as he often did during the decade of our partnership. He'd said nothing as he went about his morning ritual, washing and shaving at the cracked marble sink. My best friend could never be described as a morning person. Try to wrangle James into a friendly conversation before he'd downed three cups of black coffee, you'd be met with a barrage of profanities. Loud, lame, angry insults. In time, he'd mutter some half audible responses to whatever you brought up. Minute by minute, the inexplicable anger resided and he once again became good ol' Butch, grinning from ear to ear.

But it wasn't a lack of small talk that concerned me. Rather the absolute silence. Not a whistle much less a word. When James stepped away from the toilet to dress and I took his place before the mirror, that emptiness continued.

In time we headed down the stairs, side by side, only this time not discussing whatever came to mind. Mrs. Trumbell sat us down for breakfast, inquiring as to where our "lady friend" might be. Neither managed anything more than a mumble in response. Finally, Eloise appeared. And, as if on cue, each of us sensed the need to put on an elaborate show, pretending that not a thing might be different from the day before.

Only, I guessed that deep down James sensed, even as I did, that our lives would never again be quite the same following the previous night's experience.

ELOISE: SUNDAY; FEBRUARY 3, 1901

"Well, *Eloise?*" James asked once I sat down.

He referred to the serious subject I had broached but not fully revealed.. While gathering my wits, I toyed with a soggy waffle drenched in maple syrup on the fine China plate Mrs. Trumbell had set before me. Momentarly, I felt faint owing to the sickly sweet smell. The boys, sensing my anxiety, paused politely as to both their breakfasts and any further questioning, waiting for me to recover.

"Whenever you're ready," Henry whispered.

"Alright, then. Here goes—"

We all fell silent when Mrs. Trumbell approached like a sudden gust of wind, flashing a broad if (to my perception) theatrical smile. She drifted to our corner nook, a fresh pot of tea in one hand, coffee in the other. The magnetic hostess, adorned in a garish silk outfit which she likely believed made her appear classy, paused to glance at my handsome boys.

"There's more where that came from," she gaily said, indicating their plates. "Let me know if you'd like another helping of anything. We love to eat well around here!"

Either blithely unawares that we were on the verge of entering into an intense discussion, or sensing this but unconcerned as to our personal situation, she stood in place.

"Thank you," Henry replied. "We're fine."

"Everything is first rate," James assured her, hinting that Mrs. Trumbell was free to move on to other guests.

"I have one demand," I said once she took her leave, "which must be met if I am to remain under this roof."

"Well," Henry said. "We're all ears."

"Though we will spend time together, I must also be free to explore the city on my own."

"You've always had your independence."

"Now, James, I'll require it more than ever."


JAMES: SUNDAY; FEBRUARY 3, 1901

Shortly Bat arrived, delighted at the unseasonably warm weather and eager to guide us on a grand tour of The Big Town. First, he ushered us onto a horse-drawn Omnibus. Eager to share his love for what had recently come to be called The Big Apple, Bat explained that in time New York City would entirely transition to mechanical modes of public transportation. Cars were mass-produced on an assembly line in a nearby borough, Queens. Taxi cabs and buses would be up and running by early summer.

*Too bad, I thought, that we must leave without witnessing such marvels. Manhattan sure does get under one's skin.*

We four seated ourselves high atop in the open air section during our thirty street trek northward. From here, we could best view the skyline—charming old buildings in the classic style juxtaposed with higher, leaner ones representing the modern approach to architecture—while riding toward what our host informed us would be the heart and soul of an emergent Manhattan: Midtown.

"Now, it's time for some fun!" he announced as we all disboarded at what I took to be a major traffic stop, numerous omnibuses converging at a busy corner.

ELOISE: SUNDAY; FEBRUARY 3, 1901

The intersection of Broadway, 42nd Street, and Seventh Avenue was, as Bat explained, where the vast middle-class converged on Sundays. No rich folks here and no sad poverty-stricken types. Hard working people regularly employed at every business, trade, and industry imagineable. Sunday represented the longed-for holiday when even six-day-a-weekers enjoyed time off for enjoyment, once they'd visited the church of their choice.

We picked our way through narrow streets, bustling with folks sporting their Sunday best—in some cases gaudy and garish, in others low-key and pleasingly understated. Some paused to pick up overpriced items from food carts. The scent of slow roasting meats—grilled chicken, bacon, and brisket; beef frankfurters, pork rinds—blended with diverse others ranging from freshly popped corn to cherry-flavored soda.

Many of these people-in-motion were like us headed for the fabled Longacre Square. This marked a notable halfway point between Lower Manhattan's rough areas, in particular on the East and West Sides, and the high-society residencies arraigned in townhouses commencing at 59th Street. I'd encountered the term 'Melting Pot' in my readings, yet how fascinating to see the concept in action: gentlemen in hand-tailored business suits passed by blue-collar fellows in jeans, though on such a day they wore only their cleanest and best-pressed. The women displayed everything from fine lace to simple cotton dresses as they paused to purchase caramel apples and frozen bananas. Emergent America in embryo, I reflected on the rich tableau before me.

Enjoying the varied sights—fat men in clown costumes, beckoning families to enter a brightly lit menagerie; young girls in scandalously short skirts, winking

ALL ROADS LEAD TO MID-TOWN MANHATTAN: Between 1900 and 1901, Little Old New York completed its transformation into The Big Apple, with 'The Great White Way' at the epicenter of diverse entertainment and excitement.

at single fellas while arranged along the bottom of steps that led to adults only pleasures—we turned a corner and found ourselves at the intersection of Union Square and Broadway. Here, clip-joints offered souvenirs including cheap models of the Miss Liberty statue. One makeshift storefront featured a guaudy sign, "The DeFLY Portrait Studios." Though my companions took no notice, I experienced a sudden desire to have our pictures taken. To share with our children, should we have some in the future. And, if not, to immortalize the final days when we three were, like Alexandre Dumas' musketeers, all for one, and one for all.

## HENRY: Sunday; February 3, 1901

"Now, *there's* a face worth immortalizing," the proprietor announced, eagerly waving to Eloise. She giggled outright at his outrageous costume: a pink straw hat, vanilla jacket with multi-hued stripes, and pantaloons the color of lemonade.

"I'm not certain that'd be wise," James whispered.

"As for me, pard, I wish we hadn't allowed ourselves to be photographed with three other of the boys." I referred to an 1899 image taken in Texas that did not include Eloise.

"We'll keep 'em carefully locked away in our rooms," she suggested. "I do so want to have a remembrance of our time in New York."

"NOW, SMILE FOR THE CAMERA . . . " Sundance and Etta pose together; at least twelve photographs were taken featuring them and Butch in various combinations and also singly; though the photo-shoot did take place, the character 'DeFly' is fictional.

First, Bat whittled the price down to less than half of what Mr. De Fly initially indicated. We chose a package with portraits of each of us singly as well various combinations. At Bat's suggestion, we did not pay until the process of developing reached completion, which stretched on for two hours. Meanwhile we feasted on Shepheard's Pie at Gallagher's, a nearby Irish pub. while washing our meal down with green beer. Eloise enjoyed the simple fare, her appetite returned.

A thought crossed my mind, "I *love* New York!"

## ELOISE: SUNDAY; FEBRUARY 3, 1901

With the finished photographs (marvelous, in a rich sepia tone) in hand, we drifted wherever our collective whims drew us. Eventually, Bat took his leave. His wife Emma, whom I looked forward to meeting, would be preparing dinner. A dutiful husband, he didn't wish to arrive home late. How fascinating that the onetime prince of pistoleros had settled down to a normal life. Perhaps that remained a possibility for my boys as well.

At this point, our party of three leisurely headed back downtown. We stopped in our tracks, though, when we reached 23rd Street. A considerable crowd had amassed in front of one of the larger newspaper offices along Park Row, where Bat had his office. As curious (some might say nosey) as any others we joined a growing throng on the sidewalk.

"This better be good," James muttered, tired from the day's activities, growing grouchier by the minute.

"If it weren't," I smirked, "there wouldn't be so many people about, would there?"

JAMES: SUNDAY; FEBRUARY 3, 1901

"Both of you stop arguing," Henry insisted. "Come on!"

With me leading, we squirmed our way to the front of the crowd. Standing near to the street, a rich assortment of gents and several women accompanying them had assembled. This tight company appeared determined to complete some sort of project. Individuals wore everything from an overcoat in a Scotch plaid pattern for one jaunty fellow to a gypsy-like arrangement of mismatched silks on a dark complexioned woman. Likely, these were some of the non-conformists known to gather in parts of New York. Notably, the fascinating characters surrounded a large box-like contraption, covered with a thick black cloth, set shoulder-high on a tripod. No question this was a camera, if far more intricate than the one we had posed for earlier.

"Let's try it again," a medium-sized fellow instructed his team. His lower face featured an untrimmed mustache, each end jauntily turned upward in the Italian manner which Eloise explained had recently become fashionable. Also, he wore a beret of the type favored by Basque immigrants. So New York offered a melting pot of fashion as well as people.

Several feet away, a neatly-dressed couple stood chatting on the sidewalk. The man wore a tweed sack-coat with matching brown sweater vest. His trousers featured a recent innovation, turned-up cuffs. She embodied the Gibson Girl look, projecting an illusion of casual glamour. A low neckline revealed lovely breasts to the extent that decency allowed. Her tight skirt displayed an hour-glass figure. Shiny red patent leather shoes enclosed the woman's petite feet. She smoked a cigarette, this daring for any female to do in public. They gazed across the street, keenly obsrving the mustachioed man in charge. At the sound of their leader's officious voice, they stepped forward.

ELOISE: SUNDAY; FEBRUARY 3, 1901

Daring to approach the group's ostensible leader, I mustered all my charm and asked what was happening here.

"Listen, lady, we're busy trying to make a movie," he snapped, turning abruptly to dismiss one more nosey intruder. Only to find himself face to face with my misty eyes, perfectly chiseled cheekbones, and a killer smile I'd appropriated from the stage-star Sarah Bernhardt, whose image I had admired in magazines. All these appealing elements collapsed into the persona I offered the world.

*And, in particular, the world of men.*

"Oh, I'm sorry," I cooed, feigning a retreat into the anonymity of the crowd. "I shouldn't have interrupted."

"Hold on a minute," the man gasped, signaling with a nod for me to step closer. "You oughta be in pictures!"

"If that's a compliment," I responded, "thank you!"

"Make no mistake about it, sure is . . . uh . . ."

"Eloise Long." I gestured for the boys to join me. "This is my husband, Henry, and my older brother, James."

"Oh," the man said, failing to hide his disappointment. "Hello," he added, extending his right hand for a shake. "I'm Grover J. Lakeland of the Black Maria Moving Picture company."

"As to your suggestion? I already *am!*"

I fumbled through the large manilla envelope containing our dozen images, selecting one of me posed alone.


HENRY: SUNDAY; FEBRUARY 3, 1901

Caught up in the excitement of the moment, Eloise boldly handed the image to Lakeland. This perpetually anxious man, whom I guessed to be thirty-ish, accepted the photograph, studied it closely, then glanced at our woman.

"The camera loves you," he announced.

"Why wouldn't it?" James asked. "My sister's gorgeous."

"Indeed, sir. But natural beauty doesn't always come across when filmed. In Eloise's case? Yes!"

"Boss?" a crew member called out from where he stood behind the camera. "It's that time!"

"May I hang onto this?" Lakeland asked rhetorically, shoving the picture into his jacket pocket. I moved to stop him but he had already stepped away, intent only on his work.

"I'm not keen on that," James said, but Eloise only brushed off his concern. "A.C.? Florence? Start forward . . . *now!*"

Lakeland waved his arms wildly, recalling the conductor of a symphony I once attended with Etta. The couple did precisely as told, avoiding eye contact with Lakeland, the camera, and the surrounding crowd

## ELOISE: SUNDAY; FEBRUARY 3, 1901

A diagonal movement brought the pair ever closer to what I hadn't noticed until now: a large metal grate in the 23rd Street sidewalk, halfway between the lavishly designed Academy Museum of Modern Art and the dull box-like Lichenstein Store. The latter conveyed function and economy; the former reeked of style. The oddness of their juxtaposition, the ornate beside the practical, seemed to me representative of the city itself.

"What *is* that thing?" I asked, indicating the grate.

"They call it a 'hot-air shaft,'" James explained. "I seen one once in San Francisco—"

"Saw!"

"—*saw* one," he continued with

"ANYTHING GOES!" The increasing desire for sexual freedom of 'New Women' was introduced to the public at large in the short film "What Happened on 23rd Street."

an obvious hint of pride in his knowledgeability as to modern marvels. In the midst of all this intrigue, he'd temporarily forgotten my insistence on maintaining proper grammar at all times for anonymity's sake. "When the newspapers' printing presses inside the building create too much heat for safety's sake, pipes carry the excess energy out under the floors, then release it up into the air. Watch!"

## JAMES: SUNDAY; FEBRUARY 3, 1901

At that moment, A.C. and Florence stepped onto the grate. The two, now putting on an elaborate show suggesting a married couple out for a stroll, feigned a sudden argument.

"You're angry, A.C.!" Grover Lakeland called out. A.C. struggled more intensely to project such a heightened emotion.

"What's my motivation?" A.C. asked under his breath.

"How about this? You don't get a paycheck come Friday if I'm not happy with the results."

"Got ya, boss!" the performer meekly replied.

"How'm I doin'?" Florence asked, disguising her question as conversation with A.C. to keep the illusion alive.

"Good! But he's hurt your feelings. *Terribly.* Think on that and it'll show on your face. You gettin' this, E.S?"

"You bet!" a team member replied. He had slipped his head under the cloth to gaze directly through the camera lens. A colleague gripped the odd contraption with both hands, holding it steady. Meanwhile, a third man cranked a handle on the machine's right side. Mutely, his lips counted the seconds to coordinate the steady speed of his hand motion.

ELOISE: SUNDAY; FEBRUARY 3, 1901

"Here we go!" Lakeland shouted as a sudden burst of steam rose high from deep within the grate. A.C. feigned shock while Florence melodramatically gasped as her dress flew upward, revealing attractive legs and a shocking stretch of thigh. Observing, male members of the crowd called out happy or angry epithets, delighted or offended by this modern display of sensuality. Several women covered their eyes in horror, though I noticed a few peeking through the spaces between their fingers.

"Scandalous," a mortified female voice insisted.

"Never seen nothin' like it," a tolerant young man said.

"Movie people!" spat a nearby man wearing old-fashioned black garb worthy of a New England Puritan minister, my own father included. "Just you wait. You'll all burn in hell!"

"So what are you watching for?" I called back over my shoulder. James, Henry, and several others gents laughed. The self-righteous man cringed at my taunt yet did not leave.

"Cut!" Lakeland shouted. "A.C., Florence? Places!" He turned to consider the crew. "Get ready for the next take."

JAMES: SUNDAY; FEBRUARY 3, 1901

"They're making a 'flicker,'" Henry whispered in my ear, all and any concern about our previous night together gone, at least for the present moment. "A batch of pics taken one after the other. When developed and shown in rapid succession, they'll convey a sense of movement to an observer."

Lakeland disengaged and stepped close. Smiling at Henry, he said, "Never heard the process more charmingly related. Have you three ever watched a movie?"

"Nope. But friends who'd been East told me about 'em."

"Oh! You're a Westerner, then?"

"My husband, brother, and I travel extensively," Eloise interrupted, clearly fearful Henry might reveal too much.

"Interesting!"

He chose to say no more, at least for the moment. For the next hour the team repeated the motions over and over. Grover Lakeland informed us between these 'takes' that they recorded multiple verions of the same simple action, in case varying sunlight caused one to appear less vibrant than required. Or if, during the developing process, a 'take' was destroyed.

ELOISE: Sunday; February 3, 1901

As time went by, the business of making a movie—so exciting, at least initially, to the spectators—gradually lost its lustre. One by one, they grew bored and drifted away, heading home or on to other distractions. Some spoke excitedly about this rare occasion while others complained about the amorality that movies might encourage. Eventually, we three were the only remaining observers. Lakeland declared that the light had waned, precluding more takes. He dismissed the team, instructing them to return to Orange, across the river.

"If you folka aren't doing anything, maybe I could take you to a Nickelodeon, so you can observe some of my work?"

"Actually, we do have plans," James fibbed.

"We'll cancel them," I stated in a voice that left no room for argument. "This intrigues me!"

HENRY: Sunday; February 3, 1901

When we reached the corner of Broadway and 31st, I experienced my first peek at a Nickelodeon. The large building that contained several dozen such medium-high devices stood midway between a garish honky tonk saloon on one side and several carry-out restaurants featuring international foods—curries from India, rice dishes from China, fish 'n' chips from England—on the other. In the vicinity, open-air shops offered inexpensive items ranging from mass-produced clothing to French (or so they claimed) perfumes. Also, Persian-style cigarettes with multi-colored paper wrappings and thin gold bands on which a smoker's lips would be placed, suggesting worldliness.

"Even in San Francisco's Chinatown," I commented to Eloise, "I never saw nothin' quite like *this*."

"*Anything* quite like this," she corrected me.

A handful of men dressed in white uniforms and matching caps passed out handbills detailing the goods or services awaiting at various businesses. "Ignore 'em and follow me," Lakeland insisted, weaving in and out of the throng.

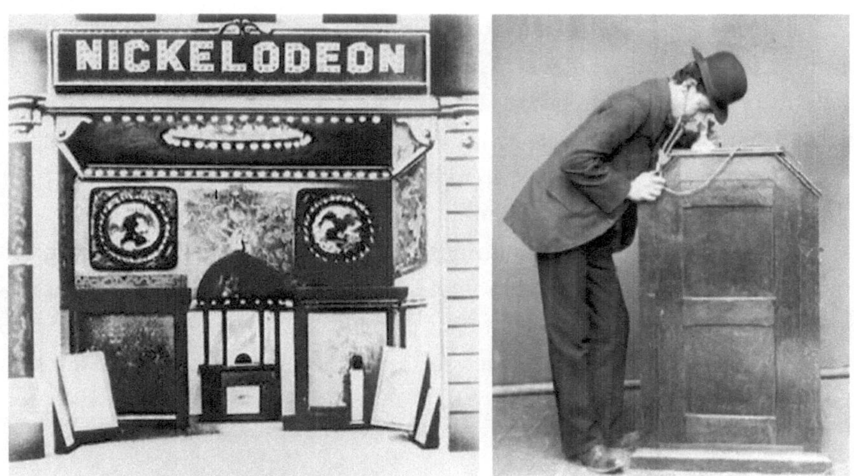


"PEEK-A-BOO, I SEE YOU!" Visitors to the Nickelodeon would stand before a box-like contraption and gaze in at flickering single still images that suggested continuous movement; in some cases, sound was also featured.

"We know enough to do so," I called to him through the flotsam and jetsome of humanity. Made me uncomfortable when such a city slicker assumed us to be green.

ELOISE: SUNDAY; FEBRUARY 3, 1901

Lakeland led us along a twisting path through the mobs of people. Along the way, several tawdry women standing in front of swinging doors reminded me of hardbitten soiled doves on the country's far side. An overpowering smell of cheap beer and the vulgar shouts of drunks likewise identified a lower-class milieu.

"So not all of New York is 'sophisticated.'" I quipped, my dream of Manhattan as a contemporary Camelot challenged.

"People are people," Henry sighed. "Don't matter where they live. Styles in wardrobe may change. And the backdrops. But human nature, as I have learned, remains the same."

"You are something of a philosopher," Lakeland noted.

"Not everyone from the west is ignorant," I informed him, just in case that 'aside' had been intended in a sarcastic manner. The look in this man's eyes revealed a belated sense of understanding that he'd best watch his tongue around me.

At last, we reached a more stately building, whitewashed with dark evergreen trim. A high, wide sign above its entrance read: The Edison Emporium. Here, a host in a tuxedo greeted potential customers, croaking, "Movies!"

"Allow me a moment," Lakeland whispered once we stepped in by way of a chrome and glass revolving door. He left us by a popcorn vendor. Overwhemed by the scent of this steaming-hot salt-laced treat, Henry purchased a bag which we three shared. Lakeland, meanwhile, headed over to a central desk. Behind it stood an officious looking fellow in a cotton visor.

"Hello, Mr. Lakeland," he humbly said.

"Howdy," Lakeland magnanimously replied. After he leaned down and spoke softly to the cashier, the employee nodded, then pushed forward a high pile of nickels. Lakeland signaled for us to join him. When we did, he distributed the five cent coins, pointing at a row of high-perched wooden boxes, these arranged side by side along the far wall.

### JAMES: SUNDAY; FEBRUARY 3, 1901

"I read about these contraptations in *Harper's*," Eloise noted. "We're in for something special, boys."

"Slip a nickel in the slot, then peer in and prepare for a journey to exciting worlds far from where we currently stand."

At the level of an average adult's chin, each machine featured a viewing device that resembled a set of binoculars. Leaning down, I dropped a nickel in; a single photograph appeared. In it, a mustacheod young man and a long-haired lady gazed deeply into each other's eyes. A split second later, this picture flipped downwards, replaced by another in which the two appeared closer together. As this process continued, and the speed by which one image replaced another increased, man and woman shifted closer ro one another and kissed. Not . a quick

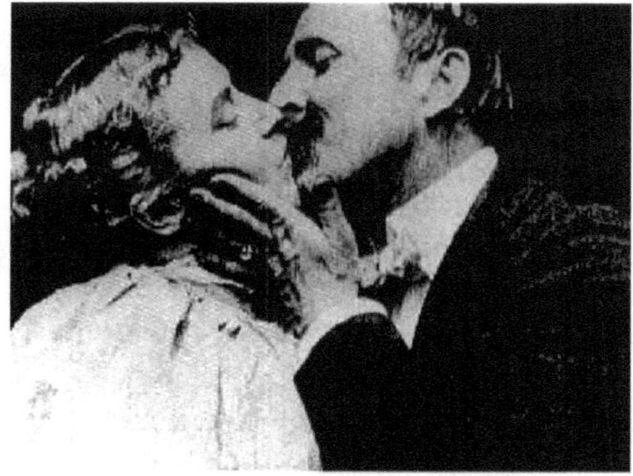

'A KISS IS STILL A KISS': The John Rice/May Irwin kiss, lasting between ten to twelve seconds at Nickelodeons, created a controversy; damned by social conservatives as potentially destructive to late-Victorian morality.

peck, rather a meeting of the lips that ran on longer then I would've guessed might be socially acceptable. They continued to nuzzle until the transition between successive pictures ceased. The experience lasted about twelve seconds.

"What do you think, James?" Lakeland asked, all at once standing beside me as I stepped back, blinking rapidly.

"Kind of shocking, don't you think?"

"This may have been hot stuff a year ago. Now? Mild. That's why we must push the envelope ever further with the sort of daring movie we shot earlier today."

ELOISE: SUNDAY; FEBRUARY 3, 1901

"How quickly folks adjust to a new era," I noted.

"That's true of progressives. The conservative element would like to shut The Flickers down and run us out of town."

"New York isn't all that different from the rest of the country, then?" James mused.

"I said it before and I'll say it again," Henry insisted, "People are the same all over."

"Yes," I agreed. "Half of the population embraces change while the others live in fear of anything new."

"Do you own the studio that makes these 'movies'?"

"Heavens, no. Mr. Edison does. Thomas A."

"His name, I *do* know," James said. "But I'm intrigued, what was the reaction when 'The Kiss' made its premiere?"

"Newspapers ran editorials claiming that the barbarians had seized control of our culture. 'Lascivious' and 'utterly 'degenerate,'' the *Times* railed. 'Christian Civilization is doomed,' a scandal sheet announced. Ministers warned their flocks to avoid Edison's peep shows as they would the plague. The Klan threatened to protest when we shot our next film."

"The result?"

"Ha! The louder such bastions of morality screamed, the larger our crowds. Cause there's nothin' people want to taste more than the latest example of 'forbidden fruit.'"

HENRY: SUNDAY; FEBRUARY 3, 1901

On then to my choice. *The Execution of Mary, Queen of Scots,* a recreation of that historic moment when the great lady's head was severed from her body, shocked me with its graphic realism. *It's only a movie,* I told myself.

Still, I was entirely convinced. After all, as folks say, *Seeing is believing.* Now, apparently, more'n ever!

Henry had taken in a flicker in which President William McKinley delivered a speech. "Only pictures, of course. No words," he commented, slightly disappointed.

"We're working on that," the filmmaker confided. "At our Jersey studio, technicians are creating a system that'll allow us to coordinate Edison's phonograph recordings with movies on celluloid strips created up in Rochester by George Eastman."

"Sight and sound," Eloise marveled, clearly impressed. "What will you fellas think of next?"

"We're also developing a color film stock. Meanwhile, we make do by assigning artists to tint each individual image."

"How many shots would that entail?" I wondered out loud.

"We've settled on twenty-four frames per second as the best possible means to realistically suggest movement."

ELOISE: SUNDAY; FEBRUARY 3, 1901

"How do you guess folks will react after seeing what you shot today?" I asked. "I mean, a woman exposing her legs!"

"Think back to the Holy Joes we encountered out west," James cut in. "They'll want to see it for themselves first, then howl to their followings to stay away."

"In truth?" Lakeland chuckled. "There's no such thing as 'bad' publicity. That's the first rule of show business."

"How cynical," I sighed. "But I guess if all you want is to make a lot of money—"

"I'll tell you this," he cut in, looking me up and down in a manner that made me feel vaguely uncomfortable. "We'd make plenty more on the next if *you*'d played Florence's part."

"No, no, no. I've seen many an actress on the stage, so I'm aware how skilled one must be to perform convincingly."

"In all truth? No Broadway actress will have anything to do with movies. They consider our work to be 'junk' fit only for the moron masses. So we hire anyone who's willing to step in front of a camera. But only if they have what I call 'it.'"

"What's . . . '*it*'?" I ventured.

"A charisma audiences sense right off. In a man, we look for what my boss James White calls 'a quiet confidence born from assurance of his masculinity.' A girl? She must be—"

JAMES: SUNDAY; FEBRUARY 3, 1901

"Stunning!" Henry blurted out.

"Well, sure. But what we want is . . . let's see, now . . . to quote Mr. Edison, 'a supreme aura about her.'"

"Self-confidence?" Eloise asked.

"More like 'self-*possession*.' Both men and women adore her, but she appears utterly self-consumed."

"That's true of Eloise," I said without thinking first. She cast me a look that could've drawn blood. No question it had been a mistake to say this in front of a stranger. Not, mind you, that my statement was in any way incorrect.

ELOISE: SUNDAY; FEBRUARY 3, 1901

"Anyway! I brought you here to witness what we've achieved so far. What you see on display: a weight-lifter, showing off his muscles? Terrific, two years ago. That was then. This, now. Already, folks want more."

"And you're the man who'll deliver the goods?"

"You said it, Eloise. Ever greater sensation means—"

"Ever more profits," I finished for him. "What's next?"

"What we shot today will be our final 'little flicker.' Now, I'm set to direct *story* pictures. Ten minutes long. Maybe twelve. We'll shoot the exteriors on celluloid film across the river in Jersey's open stretches, employing the new Kodak camera. The interiors, meaning scenes set inside a room, we'll complete in our studio, The Black Maria."

"*That* sounds menacing," I shuddered.

"Nah, just a big barn covered with tarpaper, and a roof that can be opened, allowing sunlight to pour in for filming. Mr. Edison, got the idea from a gifted Frenchie named Georges Melies. Only our boss brought the concept to a new plane."

"What a truly remarkable man this Mr. Edison must be."

"Indeed, Henry." Lakeland again turned to me. "Now, I can't make any promises. But I want to share your picture with Edison. If you were to stop by for a visit, you might even meet the Genius of Menlo Park!"

"May I assume that James and Henry are also welcome?" I asked, wary after my horrific encounter with Ironsides.

"Sure," Lakeland said, sounding disappointed.

HENRY: SUNDAY; FEBRUARY 3, 1901

"Why such special treatment for *us*?" I asked.

"Because, Henry, I'd like to give Eloise a screen test. We'd photograph you, like in DeFly's studio. Only *moving!*"

"And if I pass this . . . 'test'?"

"We were going to use Florence for the female lead on our next project. I got a hunch you'd come across stronger."

James and I exchanged concerned glances, worried about our anonymity. Lakeland noticed this and said, "Maybe we could employ you two as bit players." He drew a business card from an inside pocket and handed it to me. "Well, lady and gents?"

"Guess it'll be okay, if *we're* there," James mumbled, a hint of uncertainty in his voice.

"Oh, my God!" Eloise guffawed, rare for a woman known to be subtle and self-contained. "I'm going to be . . . if not an 'actress' . . . what term do you 'movie people' prefer?"

"We're going to make you a *Star.*"

—INTERLUDE—

BAT: October 25, 1921

*"Vivid flashes of lightning dazzled my eyes, illuminating the lake, making it appear like a vast sheet of fire," a 16-year old girl named Mary Wolstonecraft Shelley wrote in 1816. She put these words into the mouth of the anti-hero of her gothic romance; he called Victor Frankenstein, based in part on her husband, the poet Percy Byshe Shelley, an amateur scientist experimenting with the powers of electricity to revolutionize the world. Attempting to create a superman, Victor only manages to make a monster. Yet there is a tragic sense of nobility to Frankenstein's failed effort. Which explains why the young lady subtitled her book "The Modern Prometheus." Here is a rebel who robs a power from God himself and delivers this source of glory or destruction into the hands of men.*

*Such experiments can be traced back at least to our own Benjamin Franklin. For in 1752—sixty-four years before that revolutionary novel would be written on the shores of Lake Geneva in Switzerland—the good doctor tied a key to a kite to learn whether a remarkable force in the skies might be harnessed for mankind's betterment. Only in our century, though, has a true genius emerged to bring that life-altering idea to fruition at the inception of Modernism. He is, of course, the mental giant, Thomas Alva Edison, aka the Genius of Menlo Park.*

*Today, his innovations—the light bulb, phonograph, long-range communications—are about to be joined by actualization of what humankind has been playing with since early examples of homosapiens painted images of eight-legged wild game on cave walls, depicting the men pursuing such beasts with four legs. The illusion of movement; a believable if impossible sensation that a single picture can move, today attained by running numerous images across an electric light source that projects them, one by one, onto a screen.*

*To again quote Mary Shelley, "Nothing is so painful to the human mind as a great and sudden change." Yet if Edison's presentation of 'cinema'—from the Greek word for movement—appeared to suddenly spring into being in 1901, that was not the case. For centuries, experiments were enacted in England, France, and, in time, our own country. But it is Edison with his total harnessing of electricity for functional or artistic endeavors who made the modern motion picture theater possible. First he had his crew shoot a 'movie' about firemen rescuing a woman and child from a burning building. The heroes were all real, captured on the fly as they roared down a street. The victim was played by a performer positioned on a Black Maria set holding a rag doll. The scenes were intertwined in the editing room and proved convincing to the public. Next up? A more ambitious attempt to tell a story. Edison and his colleagues decided on a costume piece based on a widely publicized event that caught the public's interest. Based on a true tale that had occurred earlier that year in the wilds of our last frontier, Wyoming. Involving several notorious outlaws and the bold lawmen who put an end to their transgressions . . .*

THE MAN WHO INVENTED TOMORROW: Motion pictures and recorded music were among the array of contributions overseen by Thomas Alva Edison.

# PART SIX:
# WELCOME TO
# WASHINGTON SQUARE

ELOISE: Monday; February 4, 1901

I didn't sleep much during what seemed like the longest night of my life. So many things vied for my attention: what to do about the boys, together or singularly; the law now pursuing me, which I would eventually need to inform Henry and James of; and most of all Susan, with her generous offer . . .

As if I needed anything more on top of that? Sunday's invitation to stop by the Black Maria for a screen test.

If not the fairytale I had once, in my girlish naivete, hoped to transform my life into, then the unfolding events struck me as an American equivalent of one of those remarkable tales of Wessex shires penned by my most beloved male writer, England's Thomas Hardy; that rare male author who could create flesh and blood women, rather than the usual misconceptions. Tess of the d'Urbervilles in the novel that bore her name. Eustacia Vye in *Return of the Native*, and Bathsheba Everdeen in *Far From the Madding Crowd*. Each a raven-haired beauty like . . . well . . . *me*. How deeply I'd associated with each while reading.

Born if not into poverty, then on the outside peering in at her local aristocracy. *So* hungry to be a part of that life, which appeared off limits. Until, at least, a series of unlikely incidents suddenly opened up that world to her. Only though if she employed her brain, as well as her beauty, to navigate the myriad dangers she must survive on her upcoming life's journey. Even as I must do now.

JAMES: Monday; February 4, 1901

"You definitely have changed," Henry sighed as he shaved before the suite's mirror, contemplating our companion called 'Eloise,' now very different from 'Etta,' and not only in name.

Earlier, I'd completed my morning constitutional, as city folk refer to preparing for the upcoming day, in my room. Then I crossed the hall to learn if my companions were ready for our next sojourn. I sat puffing a Havana cigar while waiting.

"You think so?" Eloise replied. She ran a brush through her sleek hair for the hundredth time, momentarily pausing to peer out the window and observe what shaped up to be yet another bright, sunny morning. Unseasonably mild for February.

"I agree," I chimed in.

"Boys," she said, laying her tool down, Eloise's demeanor now serious. "Understand: I've undergone a Sea Change. And I'm not just referring to our move to a big city. It's . . . oh, how to put it? *Internal.* My eyes and mind have been opened wide to a whole range of possibilites."

"All I know is that the woman we reunited with at Grand Central was not the one we parted from back at the Hole."

Eloise held up a a book. This was, she explained, a gift from Susan B. Anthony, her unexpected, if welcome, traveling companion for several days. A volume that addressed the concept of female independence.

"Well, we're all for *that*," Henry responded.

"Sure!" I added. "We don't want to fence you in."


ELOISE: MONDAY; FEBRUARY 4, 1901

"Listen to these words by a philosopher, J.S. Mill: 'the legal subordination of one sex to the other is fundamentally wrong in and of itself. In our time, it must be perceived as one of the chief hindrances to human improvement.'"

"Wow!" Henry declared. "Sure does have a way with words."

"You speak them, Eloise, as if you wrote them yourself."

"That's only the beginning, James. 'The old order must, if we are to move forward, be replaced by a principle of absolute equality, admitting no power or privilege.'"

"You memorized that?" Henry exclaimed once Etta quoted the piece without glancing down. She replied with a wink.

"Etta . . . *Eloise!* . . . is sure the equal of any man," James observed. "And don't we know it!"

"Yes. But, now . . . ?" Henry hesitantly asked.

"I've got to go out and change the world so that every man comes to see things the way you two do!"

"Sounds fine," James said. "Except—"

"—where does that leave us?" Henry finished for him, my once bold caballeros of yore now reminding more of Lewis Carroll's comedic Tweedle-dee and Tweedle-dum. Me? Alice, soaring upward in size after biting into a magic cookie.


HENRY: MONDAY; FEBRUARY 4, 1901

Eloise's eyes were filled with passion of the sort I had not noticed there since the day we'd first encountered her. A gut sensation told me this did not bode well for our future.

Of course James and I must tell her about what had occurred. Our lives together were always based on full disclosure. But how might we approach Eloise on a subject neither of us had been able to broach with the other? Yet the presence of the absence of such conversation weighed heavily on me. Last night, I had feigned deep sleep to avoid entering into her arms.

"Let's talk further over lunch," James ventured. "So whereabouts would you like to visit today?"

"Actually, I'll be leaving you momentarily." Eloise then raised in the air a page of handsome personal stationary. "I found this slipped under the door when I awoke at dawn."

"What is it?" I asked.

"An invitation to join my new friend for lunch at her hotel. Just imagine! Susan B. Anthony conversing with *me*."

"Alright," James mumbled. "But keep in mind: Beneath the invented character 'Eloise Long,' 'Etta Place' exists."

"Don't *you* forget that before I invented, then became 'Etta Place,' I was born and raised as Eloise Placer."

Her voice sounded curt. Yet with a sweet smile she kissed each of us, then exited. Soon James headed downstairs for beakfast. For once, I wasn't hungry. Then the severe pains I'd experienced in Buffalo suddenly returned. I carefully navigated my way to the bed and sat down.

ELOISE: MONDAY; FEBRUARY 4, 1901

"It's magnificent," I gushed to Susan B. Anthony. We chatted together on a flower-laden, tree-lined promenade in front of a stately four-story hotel. Devoid of the ostentation that adorned grander sites I'd observed, this building recalled a wistful style of architecture much admired in Vienna a century ago, familiar to me from intense studies.

"We who call it home think so," she responded, smiling. "A close friend awaits us in the dining room."

"Marvelous," I responded, enamored with the charms of the establishment and its quaint surroundings. "I'm starving!"

What had originally been three row-houses between 32-36 Streets were now inter-connected via a series of fashionable corridors. An even larger extension was now under construction at a nearby juncture known as University Place.

"Let me mention at once," I said as we made ready to step inside the quaint hotel, "this is on *me*."

"No, no. After all, it was *I* who requested *your* company."

JAMES: MONDAY; FEBRUARY 4, 1901

"Well, pard, let's get movin'," I said, after chowing down on ham and eggs while reading the morning newspaper. To my surprise Henry lay on his back. "Good Lord, Henry. What—?"

"I imagine this is how Doc Holliday felt before the consumption took him. Though I don't think I've got T.B."

"*What*, then?" I wondered, seating myself in a plush chair.

"That's what I have to find out. Goin' to see a doctor."

"How'd you locate—"

"While you were eating, Mrs. Trumbell stopped by. On learning I was sick, she sent Samson to make an appointment."

Henry tried to rise but couldn't. "Don't worry. I'll get you there, one way or the other," I assured him.


ELOISE: MONDAY; FEBRUARY 4, 1901

A loud noise distracted us. I turned to observe a nearby work crew, half a block down the street. Laborers in worn overalls climbed a ladder to remove the hotel's old sign. 'The St. Stephen' marquee would give way to 'The New Albert.'

"Is the change to honor Queen Victoria's widower?"

Susan shook her head. "I can understand why you might assume so. Actually, this property is now owned by Albert S. Rosenbaum. Considering his religion, Albert felt it appropriate to play down the hotel's former Catholic ties."

"Oh! The rumor is true, then," I blithely asserted as a well-appointed doorman waved us into the lobby. "The Jews really do own everything of value in New York City?"

A faint gasp on my companion's part revealed that I'd made a gaffe. "Eloise," Susan explained, "that's the sort of prejudicial thinking our organization hopes to eliminate."

"I'm *so* sorry!" I responded, breaking into tears. "Do understand, please! I've spent the past five years ... nearly six, now ... in the west. I've lived in Texas and Wyoming, where people considered me more educated than most. I Even taught school, on occasion. But I *do* realize everything exists in contrast. Here, I must seem the lowliest rube."

Susan drew a white linen handkerchief from her handbag, gently drying my eyes. "We are what we are, Eloise, until we decide to *do* something about it."

"As for Jews, I've only met one. My dear friend Bowdry, now deceased." I considered revealing the Magen David I wore beneath my dress but decided that might be a tad too melodramatic. "So if I'm prejudiced as to Jews, it's in favor of them!"


HENRY: MONDAY; FEBRUARY 4, 1901

As Bat had explained on our way home from Coney and the Fights, James, Eloise, and I were staying in one of New York's varied unique areas. For here in Greenwich, people perceived themselves as apart from the great metropolis.

Located on the Lower West Side, this district offered an oblong series of blocks bounded by 14th St. to the north, Broadway on the East, Houston to the South, and the Hudson River off to the west.

During the 1890s, stately houses near Washington Square were owned by rich descendants of early British and Dutch gentry. A subdued existence dominated during what folks still recall as the Gilded Age. Then, most such American aristocrats lost their money in a string of sudden stock market crashes. Reluctantly, the old-timers sold off grand buildings they once assumed would remain part of established family dynasties for generations to come. Members of this fast-fading elite drifted off to rebuild their lives. Many stalwarts settled in on the northern shore of adjacent Long Island. Meanwhile, The Village was overtaken by artists, poets, dancers, intellectuals, and the like. If less classy in appearance than during that now legendary era of largesse, tradition, and status, its current environs did strike me as colorful, exciting, and innovative.

ELOISE: MONDAY; FEBRUARY 4, 1901

"Now, let me introduce *my* mentor," Susan said as our host seated us at a circular table, across from a far older woman than herself. "Eloise, meet my friend, Elizabeth Cady Stanton."

My right hand quivered. The lady, whom I estimated to be in her early nineties though vibrant and alert, half-rose to shake, then settled back down into an elegant chair. A matching oak table had been delicately set with a white tablecloth and brightly polished fine-dining utensils. The tall headwaiter approached, asking whether we cared to peruse the wine list.

Remaining silent, for fear of making a further fool of myself, I allowed these esteemed ladies to pick.

"I think you'll enjoy *this*," Susan winked..

"If you chose it," I tactfully replied, "I *know* I will."

Shortly, we were sipping an exquisite Chardonnay. The dry refreshment offered an elevated version of what passed for white wine back on the frontier. In Denver and San Francisco, I'd tasted claret, though nothing close to this in quality.

THE MENTOR'S MENTOR: Elizabeth Cady Stanton initiated many aspects of the Suffragist agenda that Susan B. Anthony would thereafter bring to fruition.

"Susan mentioned you've read one of our anthologies? Do share your thoughts."

JAMES: MONDAY; FEBRUARY 4, 1901

As Henry and I strolled along well-attended boulevards to the scribbled address, we witnessed a gypsy-like existence of Bohemians in colorful outfits mingling with professorial types in smart Scotch plaid jackets. Small buildings housed fortune tellers, tattoo artists, book-stalls, and many massage parlors.

"I for one could stay here for the rest of my days, at least if I still have some left."

"We'll let the doctor determine *that*, pard."

It seemed now, despite our altered names, that we were Butch and Sundance once again, as if Saturday night had never happened. But in the back of my mind, a little voice insisted, yes, it did.

And, someday soon, you two must face up to that fact. And talk things through.

ELOISE: MONDAY; FEBRUARY 4, 1901

"Where to begin . . . ?"

Bound and determined not to commit another faux pas, I concentrated on choosing my words carefully, phrasing each statement in hopes of meeting their high expectations.

"Your choice, dear," Elizabeth softly encouraged.

"I am so committed to the women's suffrage movement as described in several of the essays that you shared with me."

Gazing into each woman's eyes in rapid succession, I felt a sense of relief; clearly, I was off to a good start.

HENRY: MONDAY; FEBRUARY 4, 1901

Taking our sweet time in the surprisingly mild weather, James and I made our way to 174 Second Avenue. The doctor's office, we learned, was located on the ground floor of a stately two-story brownstone. Worn by the passage of years, the building struck me as gloriously shabby, pretty much summing up my vision of The Village. As it turned out, the Doc, 'I. Washington,' held office hours three days a week.

I shared with James what Mrs. Trumbell had earlier told me. I.W. spent most of his time working as a consultant at various city hospitals specializing in eye and ear conditions, likewise attending The Village's colorful locals rather than pursuing a lucrative practice by tending to the wealthy. Sounded like a straight-shooter, as we referred to such dedicated types out west. I looked forward to meeting him.

ELOISE: MONDAY; FEBRUARY 4, 1901

"Eloise, when we met for a second time, I'd just left a national convention of the Women's Movement. We Easterners finally resolved our differences with the ladies of the south, who likewise demand the vote for themselves but remained wary of becoming involved in racially-oriented politics."

"Fortunately," Elizabeth added, "we are entirely united now as to the movement's central goal: women must be treated as 'equals' under the law with men."

"As our Constitution clearly states," I dared add.

"Thus," Susan concluded, "to deny a woman the right to vote is anti-American."

I sensed they believed me to be a Western woman of good standing. How might they react if they were to learn I'd ridden with outlaws, worked as whore, and shot a man dead?

JAMES: MONDAY; FEBRUARY 4, 1901

"Please take a seat," the nurse, a young woman of color, said. With a bright smile, she directed us to a small, if well-attired, lounge. Various magazines were spread out on a rectangular glass table for patients to enjoy while waiting. "Dr. Weinstein will see you momentarily."

MANHATTAN'S BOHEMIA: As the gilded age came to an end, 'gypsies, tramps and thieves' as well as avant garde artists and self-styled philosophers made their home in Greenwich Village, filled (like Paris' Left Bank) with books stalls.

"James," Henry whispered as we hunkered down, other folks seated nearby. "I thought his name was *Washington*."

"So?"

"Weinstein! Doesn't that mean he's a . . . Jew?"

"Well? Anything wrong with that?"

"Course not. You know that warn't my drift."

"Here in New York, Henry, you're going to come into contact with people from everywhere. Get used to it."

"Apparently! Why, to tell the truth, I didn't even know that a Negress *could* become a nurse."

"Live and learn, pard. Welcome to a whole new world!"


ELOISE: MONDAY; FEBRUARY 4, 1901

"We ask for justice, we ask for equality. We ask that the civil and political rights which already belong to white male citizens of the United States be granted, and *guaranteed*, to women and our daughters. Forever!"

"Elizabeth is a considerably gentler soul than I. My choice of term would not be 'ask' but 'demand.' For when all women join together, we will emerge as a mighty force to reckon with. Then, our voices *will* be heard!"

"Indeed. There shall never again be another season of silence until women have the same rights as men."

"I wholeheartedly agree with absolutely everything you say," I announced, fascinated by their ideas as well as the precision with which such intellectuals expressed themselves.

*Now I knew what I most want! To join them in this cause.*


HENRY: MONDAY; FEBRUARY 4, 1901

"You're suffering from 'Caarh,'" Dr. Irving Weinstein, a medium-sized man wearing thick glasses, informed me. "An inflammation of the mucous membrane that causes excess phlegm to rise and collect in the cavity of your throat."

"Can you cure it, Doc?"

"Unfortunately, no. The condition is permanent."

"Oh, Lord!"

"Hold on. Here's the good news. I can prescribe drugs to relieve the congestion."

"Any side effects?" James ventured.

"They'll make your friend a little drowsy. He'll have to expect from now on that suddenly, without warning, he may need to find a place where he can sit down and recover."

ELOISE: MONDAY; FEBRUARY 4, 1901

"What an honor this is! But let me ask: why *me?*"

With a laugh, Susan explained, "Boarding the train, I noticed you were dressed differently than the other women. They wore frilly blouses and elaborately tailored skirts."

"I did feel a bit out of place."

"Nonsense! For then, there was *you*. The rustic shirt and basic skirt announced: I am not old-fashioned nor am I a 'new woman.' I am *me*: take me as I am or leave me be."

"I'm afraid you over-estimate my consciousness of such things. In all truth, I didn't pick my wardrobe as a fashion statement. Only what seemed most comfortable for travel."

"Better still!" Elizabeth replied. "Practicality, not ostentation, is the way we Suffragists prefer to dress."

JAMES: MONDAY; FEBRUARY 4, 1901

"Will this disease eventually kill me, Doc?" Henry asked.

"Not likely. Yet there are precautions you may take to lower the risk. You speak with a Western accent. I'd suggest a return to the wide-open spaces where the air is cleaner."

"Don't reckon that's an option."

"Hey, Doc," I piped in. "Would South America do?"

"Now that you mention it, that might prove perfect."

"Thanks for everything," Henry said, rising to leave, pausing to shake the man's hand. "Doc, may I ask a question?"

"Speak your piece."

"Why did you change your name?"

"That occurred far from Manhattan," the Doc chuckled. "While practicing medicine in the Deep South, I discovered that attempting to 'pass' as best I could would lessen the resistance many people hold toward my religion and race."

"You mean being a Jew is considered *both?*"

"Yes Mr. Long. According to our self-perception."

"Fascinating," I noted as we two exited. "I'd sure love to learn more about you people while we're in town."

"I want to learn about *everything* New York has to offer," Henry added, clearly relieved that he hadn't received a death sentence, restored now to high spirits.

ELOISE: MONDAY; FEBRUARY 4, 1901

"Up until today," Bat announced in a strident tone, "I believed we had a 'situation.' Now? More a 'catastrophe.'"

"Apologies for not mentioning this earlier . . ."

When in the mid-afternoon I'd returned from lunch, I learned at the front desk from Samson that the boys had left. The towering youth informed me that Mr. Masterson had arrived and awaited me in the lounge. At once, I guessed what this must be about: word had reached him at the newspaper about a killing out in Wyoming, credited to Miss Etta Place.

Indeed, Bat sat still as a corpse in a quiet corner, scowling with concern. Seating myself across from him in the otherwise deserted room, we spoke in whispers.

"Must've had your reasons for remaining mum on this."

"Indeed. So! When will be the story be printed here?"

"Tomorrow's early edition."

"I'd best inform the boys tonight."

"No, hold off. No need to send them into panic yet. I need to mull this over, figure out what to do next. They each need a good night's sleep. Morning will be soon enough."

"Whatever you say."

Suddenly I felt faint, owing to too much wine at lunch and the now prominent reality of my sad situation.

"Come on," Bat said. "Let's get out of here. We'll find someplace more private to talk."


HENRY: MONDAY; FEBRUARY 4, 1901

On our way home, we stopped by a pharmacy to fill my prescription, paused to sip cold beer at one of the numerous outdoor venues, then visited one of the Village's bookstores. There, James purchased a recent arrival bound with a red ribbon. This, he mentioned, would provide me with something to engage my mind while bedridden, which the Doc assured me shouldn't be for more than a day or two. A back cover blurb explained that Owen Wister's story was set in 1880s Wyoming.

"Seemed an appropriate choice," James chuckled.

"Just so long as it's not one more load of buffalo chips on the order of Ned Buntline's tall tales."

I did have high hopes for this volume, though. For one of the most admired of all Western painters, Fredric Remington, had provided an illustration for its cover. Like the author, and for that matter Teddy Roosevelt, Remington was a born Easterner who had traveled west and fallen under its spell.

## ELOISE: MONDAY; FEBRUARY 4, 1901

"I have to fight the sense of utter hopelessness that now circles me." I admitted once Bat and I were again seated. Now, we occupied a shadowy corner of the British style tea-house, quiet and elegant, located a block west of Washington Square.

"As a professional gambler, I know it's more important to play a bad hand well than a good one poorly."

"The obvious solution would be for all three of us to remain in the suite as much as possible."

"I'm not so sure. Other guests might notice and wonder why you keep so isolated. Likely set them to gossiping."

"Well, I did have an invitation to visit Mr. Edison's studio in Jersey, perhaps appear in one of his flickers." I explained to Bat about the meeting with Mr. Lakeland.

"That could just work! If you spend most of your time over in Orange, there's less likelihood people will take to whispering Just be certain to keep those photos from DeFly's locked up tight."

"Oh, Bat! I didn't think to mention . . ." Summing up my courage, I mentioned that I'd given one to Lakeland.

"Can things get any worse?" he groaned.

## JAMES: MONDAY; FEBRUARY 4, 1901

I tucked Henry in bed at three o'clock, the way Eloise would've done were she here. Course, that made me think once more on our personal if still private entanglement. Part of me longed to sit nearby and talk it out. But Henry appeared so worn I decided against that, at least for the time being.

"Can I bring you up a plate of food?"

"Thanks, but no. My appetite ain't restored yet."

"*Isn't*," I reminded him with a wink.

Leaving Henry alone, I headed downstairs to discover that the noon meal had concluded. So, I took off to find a nearby place. The choices were plentiful: Greek, Middle Eastern, Mediterranean among them; the former prominent, with Little Italy but a stone's throw away. A hearty bowl of pasta in a rich Bolognese sauce, accompanied by an imported Sicilian beer, filled the empty space inside me. Then an espresso satisfied my appetite and set me to considering how nice it would be to settle here.

Afterward, when I returned, Samson still stood at the front desk. Eloise had not yet returned. Once upstairs, I entered the suite, asking, "You any better?"

"Considerably," Henry said, sitting up in bed with the book held tightly, as if it were a talisman.

ELOISE: MONDAY; FEBRUARY 4, 1901

"Once, Eloise, while scouting for Custer and The Seventh Cavalry up in Montana, I found myself face to face with a half dozen or so Lakota warriors on horseback, forming a virtual wall. Before I could turn my pony and retreat, I heard more riding up from behind. So I whipped out my Navy Colt, cocked it quickly, and told myself, 'Bat, m'boy, you got a *choice* to make here. You can do the dumb thing and try to outfight them; or the smart one: point that pistol toward your head and blow your brains out, for that would be better than Sioux torture.'"

"And the point of this nostalgic fable is . . . ?"

"I'm still standing, so you can surmise I kilt 'em all. Point is: if I were carrying a piece now, I'd likely use it on myself."

"This shouldn't be that big a problem, Bat. When I ferry over to Jersey for my screen test, I'll ask for the picture back."

"Maybe I'll calm down once you have it in hand."

Bat reached into his inner-jacket pocket, pulling out a thin box of Gay Boy cigars. These were his favorites; the tobacco company had approached Bat for permission to feature a portrait of him in derby hat and a dandy's outfit, carrying his infamous cane and smoking one as their logo.

"Know what Mark Twain said about cee-gahs?" I asked.

"Got me there, girl, though do I love his books."

*"If a good smoke isn't allowed in heaven, I have no intention of lettin' God to talk me into goin' there."*

"Hah! Wouldn't be surprised if, in time, the so-called New Women of the 20th Century abandoned cigarettes for 'em."

"That gives me an idea. Do you have another, for me?"


HENRY: MONDAY; FEBRUARY 4, 1901

"Good yarn?"

"Pardner, here's the truth as we knew it, in plain and simple words. Long days of hard work and rare nights of glee."

James pulled up a chair and listened intently while I retold, in my own words, the saga's opening chapters. "These aren't the good men or bad of Dime Novels. Every fella is—well—a mixture of the two. Revealed in shades o' grey,"

"Precisely how I recall things."

"I know. Seems such a long time ago, already."

"Time's a funny thing, Kid. Supposed to be flat as the numbers on a watch and steady as the hands that move from one digit to the next. That's just not so. Minutes and hours and then days, months, and years all get mixed up in one's mind."

"For me, making love with Etta . . . Eloise . . . causes hours to whisk by as if they were mere seconds."

I laughed out loud. Then the mention of the kind of action that takes place in a bedroom caused me to go silent. For now, everything had altered in that department.


ELOISE: MONDAY; FEBRUARY 4, 1901

"Alright, girl. Let's talk about the ramifications of my paper and others across the country printing news of . . ."

Bat did not appear comfortable with saying 'the murder.' Or expressing his understanding that U.S. Marshals would be tracking and pursuing me, even here. I breathed in deeply before broaching yet another issue.

"That may be, but there's yet *another* 'complication.'"

"Oooooh! Can't *wait* to hear *this*!"

"I've come to believe New York City is where I belong. I want to make my home here, with or without my boys."

"That," he marveled, following a pregnant pause, "won't be easy for a murderess on the run."

"Believe it or not, I shot that man in self-defense."

"Guessed so, even before you told me. I know you to be a woman of fine character."

"I so appreciate that! But may I ask a favor?"

"Shoot," he said with a touch of irony.

"Next time you say something so nice, could you please refer to me as a 'person' rather than a 'woman'?"

"Ah! So our Etta . . . Eloise . . . is a Suffragist?"


JAMES: MONDAY; FEBRUARY 4, 1901

"Does this fella, 'The Virginian,' hone to the straight and narrow? Or, like us, ride the outlaw trail?"

"The former. But his pardner, Steve, rustles cattle."

"From the look in your eyes, I'd bet this 'Steve' was the character you associate with."

"Got me there. Anyway, The Virginian catches Steve, lets him go, but as top hand demands that Steve never steal again. Particularly from their own employer's ranch."

"Figure I know what's coming."

"When he catches Steve a second time, there's no mercy."

I'd heard the phrase, "East is east, and west is west," before. Now, though, it took on a whole new meaning. People may, as Henry insisted lately, be the same all over. Still, there's no denying that where you are at any time has sway over how you think and act. The West insisted on its own unique way for better or worse. Code of the Cowboy.

THE GREAT AMERICAN NOVEL: In his turn of the century tome, Owen Wister broke with the sentimentality of Ned Buntline's dime novels to offer the unvarnished truth as to what 'The Cowboy Way' had been all about.

ELOISE: MONDAY; FEBRUARY 4, 1901

"Setting this city's allure aside, the longer you remain in Manhattan, the worse the odds are of you gettin' caught."

"My head tells me you are right. Yet from the day I was a little girl, I've always followed my heart."

"Keep in mind: you aren't a little girl anymore."

I managed a smile at Bat's blunt honesty. "True. Yet in the past two days, I've fallen in love not only with this city, but the exciting century that's coming into being."

"I say, better alive in some place far away than winding up in jail. Or even executed."

Before I could muster a response, I spotted a lone woman observing us from the partially open front door. I hadn't noticed her presence before, as she'd been shrouded by the entranceway's thick drapes. Now, though, no question that it was Mrs. Trumbell. I guessed she'd heard everything.

HENRY: MONDAY; FEBRUARY 4, 1901

"Way I look at it now," James mused, "the west isn't only a place. During our years in Wyoming and elsewhere, it somehow got inside us. And wherever we go, it'll be there always."

"For better or worse."

"Which of the two do you believe it to be?"

"Not sure. Eloise knows, at least for her. My guess? She believes that the longer we three remain in New York, those 'bad boys' we used to be will mellow."

"Allowing us to become the men she want us to be."

"Question is, are those the men *we* wish to become?"

"Comes down to a choice, really, between changing and getting to keep her, or clinging to the past and losing her."

At that moment, the door opened, and Eloise stood there. She could tell by the looks on our faces, as well as the few words she had overheard, that the time had come to talk.

## ELOISE: MONDAY; FEBRUARY 4, 1901

Bat left me at the boarding house's front door and headed back to work. I attempted to enter as discretely as possible, avoiding the eyes of other boarders: two women who took no note of me and a gent who smiled broadly. But only, I assured myself, owing to my natural charms. Mrs. Trumbell stood behind the desk. Though I guessed that she might confront me here and now, it was not the case.

"Welcome back, Mrs. Long," she surreptitiously said.

Without a further word, I hurried up the stairs and into the suite, learning all about Henry's physical condition. No matter how much it disturbed me to know of his suffering, I was relieved to hear this was not life threatening.

"Please tell us, Eloise. Where do we stand with you?"

"You refer now to the issue of marriage, Henry?"

"Far as I'm concerned," James responded, "the three of us *are* married. In the most meaningful sense."

"A slip of notarized paper means nothing to me," Henry agreed. "We love you. And know you love us."

"Boys, things are extremely complex at this juncture."

"With *you*, things always are."

"Have been, from day one," James added.

Previously, James had requested Mrs. Trumbell's son bring our dinners upstairs. As I tipped the hulking youth, he stared at our little party as if we were sideshow freaks. This caused me to wonder if he (after speaking with his mother) grasped who we were. No way of telling, at least not yet. We silently ate, then set the dishes outside the door to the suite.

I took Bat's advice and put off mentioning the story that would appear in tomorrow morning's paper. As he had said, they'd be better able to deal with that after a full night's sleep. Yet I shared with them what I had told Bat.

JAMES: MONDAY; FEBRUARY 4, 1901

"Alright, fellas," Eloise began. "Let's get to it."

Then, like a sudden tornado sweeping over a flat, stark prairie, she let loose with a tirade: head versus heart. The relief of escape as compared to the desire to remain here. She then unloaded her concerns and questions about not only the immediate future but so much else that mattered. Did she wish for the sweet life, all the things that money can buy? Or would she rather be a serious person, living in simplicity, dedicating herself to a greater cause?

Is it even possible to cling to the glorious sensation of loving two men or has the time come to choose between them? Then again, might it be time to strike out on her own? If we were all to stay, would she want to continue living with us, or find a room of her own and see us only on occasion?

*When might she choose? Likely, what with Etta being Etta, I knew she wouldn't decide until the last possible moment.*

ELOISE: MONDAY; FEBRUARY 4, 1901

"Well, boys, there you have it. Your turn."

"If the future remains to be seen," James responded, "I want to make your stay here as happy as possible."

"My view as well!" Henry added.

"So tell us what you most want to do."

"First, I'd like to own a piece of Sterling Silver from the city's finest jewelers: Tiffany's."

"May I ask," James inquired, "why a woman who's no longer certain she wants to marry would covet such a token?"

"Recall that I did not say *a ring*."

"Duly noted."

HENRY: MONDAY; FEBRUARY 4, 1901

"The following weeks will determine if this sojourn will serve as the beginning of an uncertain future together or the grand finale for what once was. That's why posing for photos at DeFly's was so important to me."

"That was a mistake."

"Yes, Henry. A whim, which I am subject to."

"Anything else besides Tiffany's?" I cautiously asked.

"While here, I wish to dine at Delmonico's. I read that it's the finest restaurant in the city. Maybe the world."

"All of us out in the open? That could be *suicide*."

"'Hide in plain sight,' you used to claim. Let's do so. If we arrive wearing the spiffiest duds that Manhattan has to offer, no reason anyone might take a second look at us. Rather they'll assume we're high-class tourists."

## ELOISE: MONDAY; FEBRUARY 4, 1901

"Anything else?" James asked.

"When I deboarded the train, I noticed colorful posters plastered on the station's walls, announcing that Italian opera star Enrico Caruso has arrived to perform at the Met."

"That's been the big buzz here at the boardinghouse," Henry said, "along with Buffalo Bill's Wild West."

"I want to ride to the opera house in a fine carriage and experience for myself the greatest voice since Jenny Lind."

Each shrugged. "If you're willing to jump off a cliff to enjoy a grand time," James said, "we'll leap with you."

At that moment, I heard someone's footsteps from outside the door. "Who's there?" I asked.

"Me," Samson drawled. "Came by to collect the dishes."

*Maybe that was the case. We couldn't know for certain. Perhaps, though, he'd been listening all along.*

## JAMES: MONDAY; FEBRUARY 4, 1901

What had Samuel Clements written in one of those books Etta encouraged us to read? Oh, sure: The more I learn of human nature, the more I appreciate my dog. Well, I haven't had the pleasure of petting one in a long time. Sure do agree about humans, though!

The midnight hour was closing in as I left my companions and headed across the hall alone. How wonderful the warmth of a female body would feel beside me. But Eloise was with Henry and likely would remain so for the duration of our stay.

*If that were the case, at least the Kid and I would not have to deal with the situation that arose Saturday night.*

"Don't turn on that lamp," a female voice whispered from the dark interior. Gently closing the door behind me, I could make out the shape of Mrs. Trumbell, naked betwixt the sheets, in a brief flash of light from the hall outside.

"What are you doing here?" I gasped.

"Three guesses," she laughed. "First two don't count."

ELOISE: Tuesday; February 5, 1901

"Hey, handsome," I whispered in my lover's left ear, nuzzling the prickly skin along his neck. "Wake up."

Henry stirred, straining to open his eyes. A wide yawn caused his face to momentarily contort. As a result, my own fine Adonis resembled an ancient-world Minotaur, at least for several seconds. Coming to full consciousness, he blinked before focusing on me, seated on the bed beside him.

Briefly, Henry smiled. Then an anxiousness appeared in those beautiful eyes. "Sorry 'bout last night."

"Don't be silly! Could happen to anyone."

"Not to me," he shivered. "Never has before."

"Stop!" I took his head in my hands and drew it toward my breast, kissing him again, this time square on his forehead. "You were in pain! That explains everything."

"Maybe," he shrugged. "Eloise, until I'm recovered, maybe me and James ought to switch rooms. He wouldn't let you down."

"Nonsense! But speaking of your pard? Last night, at one point, while asleep, you called out: 'Butch?'"

*Immediately, I knew I'd said the wrong thing. Henry looked . . . well . . .* threatened.

"Maybe y' heard me wrong," he mumbled.

"Maybe," I lied.

An idea passed through my mind like a tumbleweed whirling across a barren stretch of desert. Those words I had called out upon discovering the boys facing off on the last sunset at the hole: *Can't the two of you see that you love one another?*


HENRY: Tuesday; February 5, 1901

"As to James," I mentioned, eager to break the stoney silence that had settled in, "he up yet?"

"I stopped by his door and heard not a stir from inside."

Always, Eloise appeared lovely. Now, though, I realized that in a fine silk dress, she surpassed all expectations.

"You're lookin' particularly glamorous today."

"It's for my screen test! Earlier this morning, a note arrived from Lakeland stating that someone from the company would await me at the Jersey ferry station and provide my transportation to their base in Orange. Earlier, while you were still asleep, I headed out and purchased this."

"Okay." Straining to pull myself together, I attempted to rise, but the pains I suffered yesterday returned.

"You're to stay in bed! Doc's orders, remember."

"Guess it's alright, so long as James escorts you."

"Actually, there's been a change of plans."

Though Eloise's voice remained measured, something in her manner suggested concern as to my possible reaction.

"I don't understand."

"Well, considering your health issues, I contacted those new friends I told you about."

"Uh-huh."

"Anyway, they agreed to accompany me to the river by way of a tram, then across on the ferry."

"I see."

"Oh, Henry, isn't this remarkable?"

Forcing a smile, I nodded in agreement.

## ELOISE: TUESDAY; FEBRUARY 5, 1901

I managed to keep tears from fallng down my cheeks by biting my tongue. For if I were to let loose and bawl as my emotions encouraged me to do, no doubt Henry would respond in kind. The melancholy in his eyes could not be ignored

If there's one thing I've learned during my years on the outlaw trail, it's this: *a man will do anything to keep himself from crying. Especially in front of a woman.*

Makes him feel less a man. Particularly one who has spent time in the West. Though I'd like to believe that, during the months since their planned shootout, I'd begun to draw each away from that sort of attitude.

So I maintained my pose of self-control, turned back, and kissed him again as if all were right. He and James must come to accept that now, instead of doing most everything important with them, I'd be spending ever more time in the company of women. Something I very much looked forward to.

## JAMES: TUESDAY; FEBRUARY 5, 1901

"Stop that whistling, Butch Cassidy. It's annoying."

"Sorry," I replied, a moment later realizing precisely how Mrs. Trumbell had addressed me. "What'd you just say?"

"You heard me, lover."

"Now, wait a damn minute!" I stepped away from the narrow mirror where I'd been shaving. The lush, mature woman remained sprawled across the bed amid twisted sheets, looking a little worse for wear following our long night together.

"No, *you* wait," she insisted, any false sense of humility that previously served her purpose gone. Here was a person who felt powerful, revelling in it. "The jig is up, desperado!"

Part of me wanted to deny her accusation. Yet the sheer impossibility of that caused me to surrender. "How long have you known?" I asked, sitting up.

"From the beginning, I guessed something was awry when Bat Masterson showed up here, of all places, to reserve rooms for visitors. So I perused the news-papers from the last six months. Read about the demise of the Wild Bunch. Then I picked up one of Buntline's books about the friendship between Bat and Butch. Wasn't difficult to put two and two together."

"So! Where does that leave us?"

"That's a considerable stash of money that's locked away in my safe. If, when you three are ready to leave and want to retrieve the money, you might leave say half of it with me. That'd prevent my visiting the police."

—INTERLUDE—

BAT: OCTOBER 25, 1921

*First thing in the morning, I kissed my wife (still half asleep) on her cheek, made ready to face the day, and rode an omnibus to a confluence of the Bowery, East Broadway, and St. James Place; also Oliver, Mott, and Worth. Here, all roads converged at a centerpoint called Chatham Square, northernmost tip of Park Row. Twelve years ago, many of the city's rapidly-sprouting rogue newspapers set up shop at this crossroads.*

*Varying competitors printed everything from respectable editorials to gutter-level Yellow Journalism. As to my employer, the* Morning Telegraph *offered a mid-ground of reportage, somewhere between those extremes. We may not have been as progressive as The New York* Times, *which heralded the positive contributions to business and culture of recently arriving immigrants. Nor though did we stoop as low as William Randolph Hearst's* The American-Journal, *inciting irreponsible outrage over such newcomers, accusing all of criminality.*

Our editor, William E. Lewis, believed (as did his two brothers, co-owners of the operation) in a balanced view. I whole-heartedly agreed.

*"Mr. Masterson?" an aloof secretary, who lorded it over her wide metal desk at the reporters' entrance, called out as I stepped inside. "Mr. Lewis wants to see you at once!"*

*Her words stopped me in my tracks. Little doubt as to what might be so important, the very thing that haunted me all through the night. Just this morning our paper, along with every other, had carried the story of Etta, referred to as a Wyoming's Bandit Queen.*

Why, she might be hiding in a shadowy corner of our own metropolis, the article implied. Citizens, lock your doors! Better safe than sorry.

*In lieu of a photograph, the newspapers printed fanciful sketches depicting the femme fatale astride a mighty roan. Etta! Whom as I recalled had mostly cooked and cleaned for her irresponsible fellas. Point is, alarmed visitors from every borough of New York now flooded into our offices. Half the population claimed to have spotted her. And wanted the reward money, a thousand dollars, if they helped locate Etta.*

Hearst's rag had gone so far as to run a headline: Etta—Mania! Likely, Lewis had somehow discovered that in the old days I'd befriended Butch and Sundance. He might even have an inkling that, were they currently in town, I'd be the very person they would have contacted.

With considerable trepidation, I headed upstairs to his office, expecting the worst.

THE SCRIBES OF PARK ROW: Unlike those rare 'star reporters' such as Bat Masterson, who had an office all to himself, most reporters worked in crowded quarters in an immense and often stuffy room.

# PART SEVEN: BEAUTY IS A WITCH

"Beautiful women believe they, and they alone, are allowed to write their own rules. More often than not, the world of men proves them correct."

—Thomas Lanier 'Tennessee' Williams

ELOISE: Tuesday; February 5, 1901

"I can't believe it," I marveled with an enthusiasm that caught my companions, Susan and Elizabeth, off-guard.

"Believe *what*, Eloise?"

"Susan, I'm going to be in The *Movies*!"

"Let's not jump the gun," Elizabeth cautioned me. "Keep in mind! You've been promised a screen test. Nothing more."

"Oh, but it *will* happen. It must! I just *know* it."

"We both of us hope you are not let down."

*Why the sudden lack of support? I'd assumed these ladies would be happy for me.*

At ten o'clock, we three had crossed the murky Hudson on one of several ferries heading to Hoboken and back. There awaited our transportation, arranged by the Edison Studio. Not the expected horse-drawn carriage but an open air motor-car, fresh off the Kidder company's assembly-line in New Haven. A few miles from where I spent my childhood.

*Might mother be there still? If she even remains alive.*


HENRY: Tuesday; February 5, 1901

"What do *you* look so exasperated about?" I asked as James rushed into the suite, eyes wide with excitement.

"Look and see!"

He drew a large envelope from his inside jacket pocket. "Spent mid-morning over at the docks. Booked our reservations on a tramp freighter to Buenos Aires. We'll be leaving early on the 20th, boarding the night before."

"What?"

"On arrival, we'll search through Argentina for our private paradise. If that don't work out? Next stop, Bolivia."

"Hold on," I coughed, managing to rise despite the obvious pain. "Isn't that a bit premature?"

"Hmmm?"

"I was under the impression, and I believe Eloise is as well, that we're still in the process of deciding what happens next." With difficulty and much coughing, I began to dress.

"At this point," James exclaimed, "Eloise's independence has become irrelevant." He tossed a copy of the morning paper on the bed where I sat, slipping into my socks. "Lefors and Siringo will likely arrive in a day or two."

"I'm still not convinced," I responded before checking out the story, "they consider us important enough to pursue."

Struggling to step into my trousers, I glanced down at the banner. A front-page story announced that Miss Etta Place of Wyoming had murdered a leading citizen in a small frontier town, then disappeared. A national search had been initiated with a $1,000 reward posted. As deputy U.S. Marshals, with authority far beyond Wyoming as to capital crimes, Lefors and Siringo would be on their way, if not already in New York.

## ELOISE: TUESDAY; FEBRUARY 5, 1901

Our driver informed us that this shiny vehicle had been purchased the previous week by Mr. Edison himself. The fellow (whom I recognized as a member of the film crew on Sunday) took considerable pleasure in pointing out notable buildings we passed along the way: a modern canning company, a spacious park where working families could picnic come Sunday, a four-story department store of the type springing up in the East.

"In ten years," he announced, "most of the trees and brush you now see will be gone. Jersey will be industrial."

The youth introduced himself by his nickname, *E.S.* He had been hired by Mr. Lakeland as a jack of all trades, with no previous experience as to filmmaking.

"Sounds like The Movies are none too particular as to who they hire," Susan commented in a surprisingly snooty tone.

"Oh, not to worry! You see, Mr. Edison is about to change all that with his next film. So I'll have a hand in creating something that will astound the world."

"If you say so," Elizabeth coldly responded.

## JAMES: TUESDAY; FEBRUARY 5, 1901

"I don't get it," Henry coughed, once he was able to speak again. "Why didn't she tell us?"

"From what I've gathered of Etta, or Eloise, or whatever we chooe to call her, my assumption would be that she wanted the three of us to enjoy a carefree time in Manhattan for as long as it might possibly last."

"But of course that comes to an end with this."

"The marshals have no authority outside the U.S. No matter what Eloise said, once she sees this story, I have a feeling reality will hit her, hard and fast."

"Now I wish we were leaving sooner."

AMERICA'S ORIGINAL MOVIE STUDIO: Edwin S. Porter and other pioneers of the industry shot all 'interior' sequences for their early films inside this roughewn building, later editing these with on-location shots.

"My thought precisely. But all vessels departing before the 20th were booked solid."

"Which means—"

"Fifteen days to go. And the clock is ticking away."

ELOISE: TUESDAY; FEBRUARY 5, 1901

On we went, then, the four of us, bouncing along the rough, pebble-strewn excuse for a road. Little more than a glorified trail of the sort my boys and I once traversed. E.S. assured us that such paths would be paved with cement surfaces during the following year. Less than twenty minutes later, we arrived at Edison's complex, a series of disorganized shacks, mostly indistinguishable in appearance, arranged in an uneven circle. These were surrounded by hemlock trees, which provided the tannic acid that, over the past decade, allowed shoe and boot factories to put Jersey on the country's economic map.

"This is it," E.S. announced, slowing down the car.

Admittedly, I half-expected some sort of magical kingdom, brightly lit up with dazzling electricity. Perhaps not all my heady illusions were abandoned during that difficult cross-country journey. I momentarily experienced a sudden sense of disappointment.

*Will I ever divest myself of such impossible dreams? Or are they essential to my most basic self?*

HENRY: TUESDAY; FEBRUARY 5, 1901

We agreed to further discuss the matter of the killing over dinner with Eloise. In the meantime, we spoke of the future should we three make it out of Manhattan together.

"Once we arrive in South America," I said, more or less thinking out loud, "we'll be able to scout around and find some obscure territory where no one's ever even heard of 'Butch Cassidy and the Sundance Kid.'"

"Reckon we could earn an honest living," James replied.

"About time! Meanwhile, we do have our grubstake. More'n two thousand dollars. My guess is that down in Bolivia, or wherever we end up, that oughta buy us a cattle ranch."

A dark look crossed my pardner's face, as if I brought up a subject he didn't yet wish to address. Momentarily, I considered trying to draw whatever difficulty he might be dealing with out of him. But, no. James would tell me what had happened when ready to. Clearly, though, this had to do with our grubstake, which I knew to be safe for the time being. Downstairs, in Mrs. Trumbell's safe.

ELOISE: TUESDAY; FEBRUARY 5, 1901

We learned from E.S. that the majority of these simple constructions were scientific labs. The sole stand-out turned out to be a large, oddly shaped barn-like building. Covered from top to bottom with tar-paper, The Black Maria featured a roof that could be raised high by pulleys or, if so required, rotated sideways. This, E.S. explained, allowed sunlight to pour in for shooting daytime sequences. As to a scene set at night, the crew only had to lower the top a bit, creating a darkened image on the film stock, this referred to as Day for Night.

"But why would you give the place such a horrific name?"

Smiling, E.S. informed us that the crew came up with that on the first day of its employment. Workers were reminded of what it felt like inside a police paddy-wagon should they be arrested while inebriated. Such small prisons on wheels were referred to as Black Marias throughout the Tri-State Area.

"It's seven years old now," E.S. continued, helping each of us in turn to step down. "After this film, we'll replace it with our new Manhattan studio. High up on a skyscraper's roof, featuring an innovative glass dome that will allow us greater control over the lighting. Inside the New York venue, which is now under construction, technical advances will add diversity to photographic effects. Light and shadow will be effectively manipulated for greater artistry."

"'Art' strikes me as a highly elevated term for such a primitive entertainment form," Elizabeth noted.

"Just wait, Ma'am. We're the pioneers of a new form."

JAMES: TUESDAY; FEBRUARY 5, 1901

"So it all comes down to—"

"Eloise Placer Long," Henry sighed.

"Soon as she returns from Jersey, we'll show her the newspaper, though Eloise will likely spot it before then."

"Maybe she already has."

"Either way, that ought to knock any crazy notions of staying here in New York out of her head."

"If it were any other woman we were talking about, I'd agree. But . . . follow my drift?"

"Course I do.."

"The good news is that we got us a one of a kind lady. The bad? We got us a one of a kind lady."

ELOISE: TUESDAY; FEBRUARY 5, 1901

"I'm ecstatic!" I told Mr. Lakeland as he exited The Black Maria, joining us. "When do we begin?"

The sense of confidence he had exuded several days earlier while shooting on the streets was gone. Crew members who followed him out mumbled about problems they'd encountered during the morning hours. Clearly, things had not gone well.

"The process is moving slower than anticipated."

"Sorry to hear that."

"It's typical. When making movies, the first rule you learn is: anything that can go wrong will."

"I'll remember that, if we do work together."

"Also, time is money. This'll set Mr. Edison back a bit. In the end, though, I'm sure we'll show a decent profit."

"Well," Susan sanctimoniously announced, "it's no great achievement to make money, if that's all you want in life."

"Nothing against making money," E.S. drawled, "but I'm convinced we're about to create something important."

"No reason for you three ladies to sit here while we prepare. E.S.? Give our guests the 'royal tour.'"

HENRY: TUESDAY; FEBRUARY 5, 1901

"You don't sound any better," James noted as, without any warning, I took to coughing and hacking. The thick phlegm had risen in my throat. I forced it back down, if with difficulty. While I did, my partner whistled away, as was his wont.

"Hand me a glass of water, will you?" I asked, once I'd regained my voice. "Along with two of 'em?" I pointed toward the indigo bottle of pills on our bureau.

"Other than that croak," he asked, bringing my medicine and the liquid over, then seating himself, "how you feelin'?"

"Moderate. I'll be up and about tomorrow."

"A note from Bat arrived. He hopes to spend Wednesday with the three of us."

"I'll be back on my feet by then."

"Meanwhile, did you get any further in that novel?"

"Yeah! A pretty lady from the East name of Molly Brennan steps down from the train to work as the new schoolmarm. All local menfolk crowd close, our hero included."

"Sounds vaguely familiar." A hint of irony underlined James' voice, as our own woman from the East came to mind.

"Let me share with you what transpired."


ELOISE: TUESDAY; FEBRUARY 5, 1901

We enjoyed an early afternoon promenade starting at the red brick home of Mr. Edison, a remarried widower with three children. The stately house, isolated within beech, elm, and black spruce trees, had not been visible when we first drove up to the compound. E.S. informed us that The Genius of Menlo Park had overseen its location so that he would be near to all the experimental stations, yet allowing his family some privacy, provided by this natural camouflage. Even in winter, shorn of their leaves by the temperature and winds, this thick range of woodlands served to set Edison's home off from his complex.

"Mr. Edison shares the handsome residence with his second wife," E.S. informed us. "Daughter of a Midwest industrialist. That gentleman markets our concepts to the public as commercial products."

"How fascinating," Susan quipped with a touch of cynicism.

"A marriage of convenience," Elizabeth added.

*So it is true: money does make the world go around. Not, apparently, that Susan or Elizabeth approve.*


JAMES: TUESDAY; FEBRUARY 5, 1901

As Henry read, I found myself fully absorbed in the tale. Specifically, easygoing Steve's corruption by cattle rustler Trampas. In time, Steve joins the villain but is caught and tried by onetime saddle pals. And, in the morning, hung. As for the cowboys, they'll likely never speak of that incident again. Not

DEMOCRATIC CAPITALISM, AMERICAN STYLE: Buildings of various sizes and shapes could be found throughout Menlo Park; Thomas Edison's stately home, situated relatively nearby, served as a virtual castle from which he could observe (and on occasion mingle with) his 'serfs' at work.

that they'd forget Steve, or remain silent about him. Around a campfire some mellow evening, one of the boys would bring up the fun they'd all had together.

'Steve sure was a good ol' boy,' someone would laugh. The others might join in, spinning more tales, each to became a bit more outrageous every time the fable would be repeated.

*Women harp on the rough spots when they converse. But not men. Especially Western men. Cause that's not our way.*

ELOISE: TUESDAY; FEBRUARY 5, 1901

We continued clockwise along a circle of considerably less impressive buildings. Inside each, 'team members' (as Mr. Edison referred to his workers) were even now creating the essentials for America's future. Inventing those items that the human race had somehow survived without up until today. Yet which, once on the market, people couldn't live without.

"Might we step inside, for a closer look?"

Though E.S. did not think it proper to interrupt, even briefly (so mission-like was their dedication), our guide encouraged us to peek in several windows. In one shack, a three-man team attempted to perfect the alkaline storage battery that would provide a power source for non-gasoline cars and revolutionary communication devices still in the planning stages. In the shop next door, gifted craftsmen put finishing touches on a vastly improved incandescent lamp.

'TEAM MEMBERS AT WORK': Various employees of Thomas Alva Edison set about perfecting diverse inventions, most based on harnessed electricity.

"And to think that I bear witness to this," I marveled. "The creation of the future, even as it occurs."

## HENRY: TUESDAY; FEBRUARY 5, 1901

Seems to me most fellows choose to avoid the dark news out there, while women insist on hearing and discussing every troubling detail. A female can't know, to paraphrase one of the old-time Greeks whom Eloise introduced us to, if the truth will save or destroy her. Still, she'll search for it until everything's out in the open. For that's their way.

As basic to the female mind as the opposite is for the manner in which a gent's head works. Something in our make-up insists that we avoid the inevitable for as long as possible.

Naturally, rumor as to what the Virginian oversaw spread through the valley. "Did *he* do it?" Molly, dumbfounded, asked a Western woman whom she had come to depend on for advice.

"Somebody had to," her companion replied. "The Virginian was in charge of the posse that caught Steve. Think of it as a difficult chore that naturally fell to him."

## ELOISE: TUESDAY; FEBRUARY 5, 1901

At the following stop, E.S. mentioned that those inside were close friends and, as such, wouldn't object to a brief visit. We entered an oblong recording studio where, to my amazement, the sound of Enrico Caruso—The Great Tenor, as opera critics hailed him—rang out loud, strong, and clear.

"Figaro! Figaro! Figaro!"

The star, whom I hoped to see perform in *Rigoletto*, stood before a microphone, recording an aria for Mr. Edison's phonographic machine. In awe, Susan, Elizabeth, and I exchanged thrilled glances, aware we bore witness to a momentuous occasion. This innovation would allow people everwhere to purchase recordings and listen whenever they chose in the privacy of their homes.

*Culture available to the masses at a reasonable price. Democracy combined with capitalism. Leading to a much altered life in the 20th Century. Hopefully, a better one for all.*

"No, no," Caruso assured us, his florid Italian and broken English augmented by E.S.'s translation. "you are not interrupting. We were about to take a break. Wino? Birro?"


JAMES: TUESDAY; FEBRUARY 5, 1901

"Oh, no!" Molly gasped, horrified that the rumor had turned out to be true. She reached for the pioneer woman's hand to steady herself, experiencing the vein or iron pounding hard beneath that strong female's wrinkled flesh.

"Molly, try to understand. If we don't put the fear of God into these lawbreakers, you couldn't teach school. Why, you couldn't even ride a mile in safety from your own cabin."

"Oh, but he was only a poor, silly youth."

"You have no cause to feel sorry for Steve. Feel sorry for *him*. A man that did his duty, no matter how distasteful."

"*Duty?* To *lynch* a man?"

"Look around! Out here, we have no police, no courts, no jails. No *law*. So we have to make our *own* law."

"Well, I suppose if you live out here long enough, a person becomes callused and hard."

"That's not true. Can't I make you see? What went down was law and order, frontier style. The only law we got. Molly, we're building a *country* here. More'n just that. A *nation*."


ELOISE: TUESDAY; FEBRUARY 5, 1901

The imposing (more broad and wide than tall) figure whom I took to be in his late-20s collaborated with Edison's crew to immortalize The Voice for the emergent Victor company. "Multi Bellisimo," Caruso sighed, gazing up and down my torso much as a common workman on the street might do.

*Rich or poor, handsome or plain, smart or stupid, genius or ordinary. All men have at least one thing in common. They fall to pieces at the sight of a beautiful woman.*

Not that we beautiful women—no false modesty on my part, now or ever—are immune to the appeal of men. Only it isn't obvious physical attractiveness that matters most to us

*Always, I have been drawn to men with something special. A unique quality, be it a legendary outlaw or a great artist. A man considered to be remarkable in whatever his field may be.*

HENRY: Tuesday; February 5, 1901

"Y'see, James, before that, Molly planned to leave for the East. But after listening to such a seasoned female who has survived the prairie's bleakness, she decides to stay."

"Molly's adjusting to the frontier."

"And its Values. Not just for men. Applies to *everyone*."

"You got me on the edge of my seat, Kid. Whoops! Ain't supposed to call you that. *Or* use the word 'ain't.'"

"Well, The Virginian asks for her hand in marriage, even vowin' to abandon his search to locate and kill the no-account Trampas. Man and wife will find themselves a quiet refuge deep in the purple hills. Build a farm, raise a family."

"And so they lived 'happily ever after?' Hogwash no better than the sentimental stuff Ned Buntline turns out."

ELOISE: Tuesday; February 5, 1901

In truth, looks don't matter all that much to a woman, though surely James and Henry must be described as handsome. Yet that wasn't what drew me to them or why I stayed with the boys even when things were at their worst. The opposite of men, we females fall in love with the essence of a man.

As to Caruso, his forehead might be considered a bit too broad; his nose, notably prominent; the mouth wide, marked by thick lips. Indeed, that collection of features might cause an objective onlooker to find him unattractive. But my reaction, like that of every female, must be described as subjective.

Like 'Butch' and 'Sundance,' Enrico Caruso struck me as magnetic. There existed inside him a greatness. A talent. A gift from God or Nature or whatever you choose to call what's out there. In his case, that voice; the art that flowed out of him and mesmerized the masses, myself included. So, in a manner of speaking, I experienced love at first sight for Enrico Caruso.

HENRY: TUESDAY: FEBRUARY 5, 1901

"That's where you're wrong. See, it don't stop there. For while he and Molly are in town making preparations, Trampas shows up. Drunk and ornery, the saddle bum taunts that if The Virginian fails to meet him for a shoot-out at high noon, he's a coward. Hearing this, our hero heads back to his room and buckles on a gunbelt, setting his Colt .45 into the holster."

"How does this impact on his woman?"

I continued reading.

"Let's get away, Molly begged. There's still time."

"I *can't.*"

"But, *why?*"

"I don't know. Can't explain it logically. All I know is, I feel I've got to stay."

ELOISE: TUESDAY; FEBRUARY 5, 1901

"Grazie," I responded, employing one of the few Italian words I knew. "My friends and I are thrilled to meet you in person." I said this in hopes of calling to his attention the dignified if aged matrons.

"The Great Tenor has eyes only for you," Susan whispered.

"You have indeed made a conquest, Eloise," Elizabeth purred. "Though I'd guess he's not the first."

"You can add me to the list," E.S. sheepishly admitted, casting his shy hazel eyes downward. At that moment, Caruso whispered in Italian to E.S., who grasped the opera star's meaning and nodded. "Mr. Caruso requests that you join him Saturday evening. Attend the grand premiere, then spend the remainder of the evening in his company."

"Tell him, yes!" I unhesitatingly responded in the excitement of the moment, "I'd consider that an honor."

*Oh! But I've already asked the boys to escort me. I wonder: will they be appreciative at not having to go, or jealous that I choose to do so with Caruso himself?*

JAMES: TUESDAY; FEBRUARY 5, 1901

"That's just your *pride,*" Henry continued reading. "Your foolish, narrow-minded *male* sense of honor."

"Yes, Molly. Only I ain't so sure it's foolish."

"Come away with me. Do this *one* thing? For my sake?"

"Anything *but* that. See, I haven't a choice."

"This story certainly does hit home," I cut in.

"Yeah! Molly insists this is too much to ask and swears she won't wait. He departs, faces off with Trampas. When that skunk shoots first from hiding, The

Virginian fulfills his mission and plugs Trampas, then wanders back to the hotel. Molly's there. She'll stand by her man, now and forever."

"She becomes a Western woman. As our Eloise did!"

"The question for us: has bein' in the East for even this brief time changed *our* girl back to what she once was?"

## ELOISE: Tuesday; February 5, 1901

"Mr. Caruso further requests your company for the remainder of his stay in Manhattan," E.S. translated.

"That," I flatly stated, aware Susan and Elizabeth were listening in and closely observing me, "will not be possible."

E.S. appeared stunned, Caruso also taken aback by my rejection. The Opera

THE GREAT CARUSO: Italy's most beloved opera star traveled to America bringing European culture to the masses, also recording his voice for posterity.

Star well knew his status as the current toast of the town. Why, most any woman in this city would be overwhelmed, including many married ladies.

*I too was impressed. If not surprised. I'd heard such offers before, and often. A part of me wished to say yes.*

All the same, I did not want to completely sever ties with Henry or James, they still an important aspect of my life. Likewise, I felt the two ladies scrutinizing me, eager to learn whether under a cloak of womanhood I were merely one more giddy girl, dazzled by male charm and celebrity.

## HENRY: Tuesday; February 5, 1901

All at once, the strength that had returned to my system while reading evaporated. My body felt weak; my mind lost its sense of sharpness; the phlegm suddenly rose in my throat and I was overtaken by a coughing fit.

"Easy, pard," James said, his voice forceful yet gentle. He rose from his seat and came closer, setting the palm of his right hand on my forehead to determine if a fever were present. The sensation calmed me, as if Eloise had done so.

"Let me help you slip under the covers," James whispered as his strong hands guided me into a horizontal position.

"I think it's best if you go." For now the memory of what had occurred Saturday—which I'd only recently succeeded in forcing out of mind—returned.

"No. As Mike Cassidy said, 'When you ride with a man—'"

"—you stick with him," I managed to reply.


ELOISE: TUESDAY; FEBRUARY 6, 1901

"I'm so terribly sorry," Mr. Lakeland explained when we returned to The Black Maria, "but the camera is not working."

"Stuff happens," I shrugged, coining a phrase I'd often employed out West, though back then I didn't stay 'stuff.'

"Would you be willing to return tomorrow?"

"If that's what's required of me, yes. I want to see the process of a screen test through and learn the results."

"I for one believe it'll be a success," E.S. ventured.

"There'll be a working camera when you return," Lakeland assured me.

"I can ferry over to Manhattan," E.S. volunteered, "and pick another machine up at our warehouse there."

"It's decided, then. Tomorrow, as early as possible."


JAMES: TUESDAY; FEBRUARY 5, 1901

We remained curled in each other's arms throughout the afternoon. Outside the suite's window, daylight burned bright, then faded. The first hints of an oncoming evening became visible when the soft blue sky slowly turned grey.

Gradually, Henry began to stir. Impulsively, I reached out and once more placed a palm on his forehead. The heat I'd detected there hours earlier had faded, his fever broken. I noticed the sweat on his chest evaporating as I slipped out of bed and dressed. All the while, Henry coughed loudly as he regained consciousness. Anxious now, I did what I always do when stressed; I whistled.

"Not 'Oh, Susannah' again," Henry kidded.

"Always been my favorite."

"I remember."

"You ready to talk about this?"

"Guess we have to, now that it's happened again."

"Yeah. I so wanted to believe that Saturday night was some kind of crazy accident. A one-time thing."

"Now we know that's not true."

"You . . . embarassed?"

Henry shook his head. "Relieved, actually."

"We'll speak more on this as time goes by."

"And share . . . whatever you call it . . . with Eloise."

## ELOISE: TUESDAY; FEBRUARY 5, 1901

"You don't seem particularly pleased," I said to Susan and Elizabeth as we crossed back to Manhattan, a red-orange nightscape providing a rich background to the Big Apple's ragged skyline. At evening time, the city—dappled with silver thanks to electric lighting—struck me as a far horizon with all but endless possibilities for entertainment and enlightenment, old-fashioned buildings juxtaposed with new needles pointing upward.

*But that's the old Etta, a hopeless romantic. Somehow, Eloise must move beyond such girlish thoughts.*

There are more poor people in Manhattan than there are of the sort that I've come in contact with. That's the reality. The poor. The criminal. The disenchanted. Lost and lonely. A thick crowd of strangers, passing one another without making eye-contact. Living inside their skins, hiding away from one another in the small rooms of overcrowded tenements. That's the greater reality I must seek out in New York. And I will!

"We're concerned, Eloise," Susan admitted.

"This may be a glamorous new sort of industry. Still, it strikes us as a bit . . . *well!* . . . superficial."

"If you do win the role, won't you have to spend most of your remaining days in East Orange?"

"Well? Yes, I imagine so."

"We had plans to introduce you to our friends. In time, you'd become a member of an elite society."

"That won't be possible if you choose to become a . . what did they call it? . . . 'movie star.'"

"Surely the money will be plentiful, and the status exciting. But wouldn't the process of making movies divert you from the truly significant issues facing us?"

"If you feel that way, why did you agree to accompany me?"

"Women supporting other women," Susan insisted.

"Yes! That's what the Movement is all about."

*Elizabeth's motherly tone caused me to think of my own Mama for the second time. I found myself seized with a desire to see her again.*

## HENRY: TUESDAY; FEBRUARY 5, 1901

"Anything bothering you boys?"

"No!" James and I lied simultaneously.

"Sure look like you're each mulling something over."

"Speaking of that," I hurriedly said, wishing to change the subject, "you look distraught."

"What I didn't need now was another 'choice' to make."

"Share," James encouraged her. Eloise explained the latest problem to arise: should she embrace life's serious side or go for the gold? Once we'd discussed this, I asked:

"Eloise, why didn't you tell us about the killing?"

"I can't answer that."

"Why not?"

"Because I'm not certain myself."

"My call? An arrest warrant for murder leaves you with no other options than to make a hasty escape."

At that point, James rose and excused himself, claiming we'd continue this another day. Once he entered the hallway, I sensed that he had not closed our door tightly. I struggled to rise, cross the room, then lock it.

"Don't bother," Eloise offered. "I'll take care of that!"

As Eloise reached the door, we each heard a female voice call out from James' room, "Welcome back, lover."


ELOISE: WEDNESDAY; FEBRUARY 6, 1901

"Show more emotion!" Lakeland called through his megaphone as I rushed onto the stage. I'd been instructed to feign shock at the sight of an unconscious railroad man, face down on the floor, hands tied behind his back. The painted backdrop had been designed to suggest the inside of a whistle-stop station, with crudely sketched wooden planks. All the same, I tried my best to make the character seem believable.

"I was worried about overdoing it."

"Bigger is better," insisted my director. "Without sound, you must express every emotion through your face and body."

"More like a mime artist than a stage actress?"

"Hadn't thought of that. Now that you mention it? Yes!"

For my screen test, I'd been cast as a simple girl who carries a pail of lunch to her father, the station master. On arrival, she realizes that a crime has occurred. Panicking, she (*I*) prays that her Pap may be yet alive. Her tiny fingers struggle to untie the rope that binds him.

"Next *take*," Mr. Lakeland called out.

This time, to please him, I also tore at my hair.

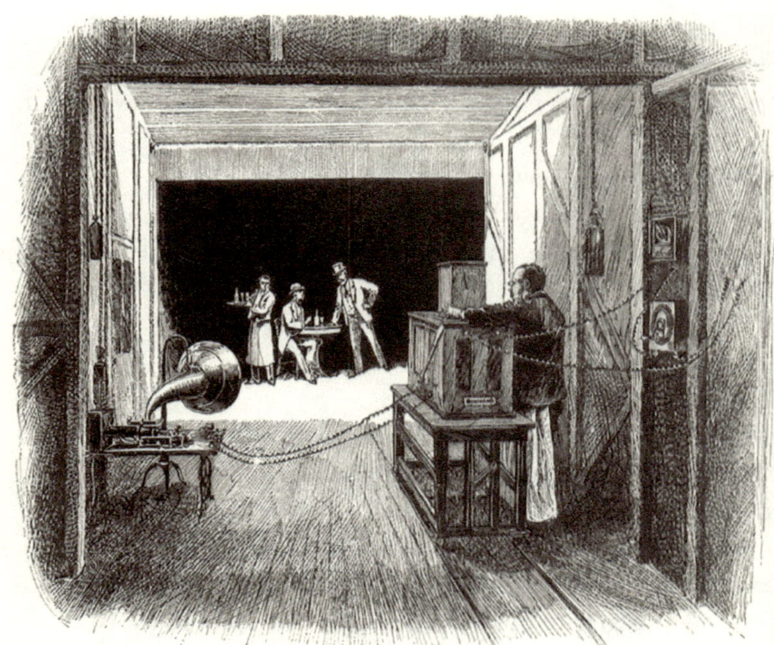

MAKING MOVIES: The Black Maria featured a raisable roof to control the amount of light filtering inside and suggest morning, noon, and evening shots.

"Eloise certainly is coming across effectively," I heard Elizabeth confide to Susan, both seated at the studio's rear.

We ran through the scene several times. E.S. dutifully recorded each rendering until Lakeland rose and announced they had enough. During the next 48 hours, Eastman's celluloid film stock would be processed. Then the executive producer, James White, would view the footage and decide whether or not I came across effectively in the role.

*Should I win the part? The American Success Dream all long for but few achieve. Yet the decision to be made by men.*

The project (as I'd learned moments before the screen test commenced) would be a Western. Titled *The Great Train Robbery,* it would chronicle that day when the Wild Bunch met its end. I had to hold myself tight to keep from laughing out loud. After all, could anything be more fitting than that?

'Fitting' or, as my sense of the absurd dictated, ironic.


JAMES: WEDNESDAY; FEBRUARY 6, 1901

"It's an attractive entrance," I observed as we stepped through a high-reaching revolving glass and steel doorway.

"Wait until we're inside," Bat chuckled.

Moments earlier, Bat, Henry, and I deboarded a transom at the corner of Broadway and 13th. Earlier still, our host had stopped by the boarding house, eager to whisk us off. Grasping Henry's sickly condition, Bat suggested that only he and I ought to head out. Insisting he was well on the way to recovery and didn't wish to miss a thing, Henry swiftly rose and joined us as we cautiously exited.

"I have a feeling you got something important on your mind," I mentioned. Bat led us through the establishment, the air hazy owing to thick cigarette smoke. We settled down at one of the few open tables, which he explained he'd reserved in advance.

"That's the understatement of the year!"

ELOISE: WEDNESDAY; FEBRUARY 6, 1901

Over the mild objections of Susan and Elizabeth, I requested that E.S. take us back to the recording studio so that the Saturday date with Enrico could be confirmed. He appeared delighted, insisting that while he wished to become familiar with me as a person before our date, he could not join me for supper this evening owing to a full dress rehearsal. But The Met would be in the hands of those in charge of settings, props, and the like on Thursday. This left him free and Caruso would be honored to escort me to Delmonico's, the city's finest restaurant.

"When you join Mr. Caruso for the evening," E.S. said, "these gentleman must accompany you."

I now realized that a pair of tall, silent, mustachioed men stood all but invisible in the shadows at the room's far side, monitoring everything that transpired. Sporting long black overcoats and high top hats, they resembled a team of stark morticians. Never before had I seen such stern eyes.

"They're Mr. Caruso's bodyguards," E.S. noted. "The Met hired them to insure his safety at all costs."

"Smart move," said Susan. "One fanatic is all it takes to ruin absolutely everything for everyone."

"Indeed," Elizabeth complied. "Why, even the two of us have received death threats and considered hiring protection."

"Actually," E.S. sighed, "it's worse than that. The Black Hand has already extorted Mr. Caruso out of 15,000 dollars."

"That's terrible! But what's the Black Hand?"

HENRY: WEDNESDAY; FEBRUARY 6, 1901

Earlier, while James had been shaving, I rolled over in my mind whether or not I ought to tell him Eloise had, the previous night, noticed that Mrs. Trumbell awaited him. As his pardner, I felt it my duty to share this, so when Eloise decided the time was right to confront him about this . . . she, after all, slept with no man other than us, singly or together . . . he'd have had time to prepare.

But I chose not to. For months now, Eloise had lectured us on the need for total equality between women and men. And that only if she were convinced we had at last attained such a relationship would Eloise even consider remaining with us.

*Well, Eloise was my 'pardner' as well. As such, I owed loyalty to her as much as I did to James.*

If, when she did tear into him about Mrs. Trumbell, it became clear I'd spilled the beans, that might turn her against me. I didn't want that to happen.


ELOISE: WEDNESDAY; FEBRUARY 6, 1901

"The Black Hand is a syndicate of Sicilian gangsters, headquartered in Little Italy," the taller bodyguards said.

"A force of evil," his partner added.

I listened with interest as those around me revealed the extent of organized crime on the East Coast. And realized that the current common knowledge among old-time Anglo New Yorkers—which held all immigrants responsible for the recent surge in violence—was wrong-headed. The majority, honest folk, were financially preyed upon by La Cosa Nostra. 'Pay or die!'

"Not that organized Crime is nothing new here," Elizabeth explained. "Back when the English first re-named this city New York, there existed such a violent element."

"Even previous to the British invasion of 1664," said the slightly shorter bodyguard, "Don't think for a moment Little Old New Amsterdam was the postcard paradise we recall today."

"People choose to forget dark elements from the past," E.S. sighed, "so they can envision 'the old days' as a Golden Age."

"Like Camelot in England," I mused. "We picture a grand castle with high towers, banners waving from turrets. When in truth there were nothing but mud huts."

"Only when the cold facts slip from memory do we grow nostalgic for the past and turn it into legend," Susan said.

JAMES: WEDNESDAY; FEBRUARY 6, 1901

I marveled at sparkling chrome everywhere. Why, the very walls mutely announced here awaited a state-of-the-art eatery. Everything I'd learned about Modernism appeared present.

"Welcome, Gentlemen," Bat said, "to Horn & Hardart's."

A sweet young hostess seated us in shiny new chairs that recalled the sleek exterior. Yet we were arranged before a simple wood table, covered with a home-spun red and white linen cloth of the type I associate with heartland eateries.

"Here's the latest innovation in contemporary dining," Bat added, "but with a touch of the past as well."

"Proof of the puddin' comes with the tastin," Henry noted with a broad grin, obviously eager for a late lunch. He had hardly consumed anything during the past day and a half.

"I don't think you'll be disappointed," Bat assured us with a twinkle in his eye that suggested something special was about to occur.


ELOISE: WEDNESDAY; FEBRUARY 6, 1901

The bodyguards explained to me why their presence was necessary, considering a particularly ugly development that had arisen. "As to Mr. Caruso," the taller one said, "the criminals plan to kidnap him during a downtown event on Friday evening. Their consigliere, known as Lupo the Wolf, is a mad dog killer, capable of anything."

"When did you learn this?" I gasped.

"Caruso and those in charge of the Met were threatened more than a week ago," the other bodyguard explained. "The managers naively paid the full amount asked for to the Mob."

"But that didn't end the threat?"

"First thing you need to know about organized crime," the shorter body-guard said, "is that their greed knows no bounds."

"Despite an old cliché, there is no honor among thieves. Though of course an innocent young thing like you would not know anything about the criminal class."

"Of course not," I said, biting my tongue.


HENRY: WEDNESDAY; FEBRUARY 6, 1901

Inside the restaurant, I observed varied city folk busily consuming their meals. Most such customers sat alone. This suggested to me a characteristic of life in New York: an omnipresent aura of isolation among multitudes crowded into the twelve-mile-long, two-and-a-half mile wide isle known as Manhattan. It made sense, once I turned the situation over in my mind, that life in these parts would be the opposite of how things work back in Wyoming. There, owing to the sparsity of people, a handful of locals rushed to join one another at meal time, as hungry for human company as they were for grub. Here, those who stepped inside seem relieved to vacate the busy and Oh! So noisy streets. As if seeking a temporary oasis.

A society of strangers, as I perceived them. On Sunday, I'd witnessed the bright side of big city life. Here was the down side of modern city dwelling: The Lonely Crowd.

ELOISE: WEDNESDAY; FEBRUARY 6, 1901

"Lupo's minions," the taller guard noted, "threaten not only to kidnap Mr. Caruso so that he cannot play the Met. If another $25,000 is not turned over they'll slice his throat."

"You mean, kill him?"

"No, missy. In a way though, worse. They'll allow him to live but he'll never be able to perform again."

"Why doesn't he simply skip Friday's appearance ?" Elizabeth asked, Susan nodding in agreement.

A MODERNIST APPROACH TO LUNCH: The Automatic brought technology into the eating habits of Manhattanites.

"We begged him to. But The Great Tenor is a man of honor. He gave his word that he would sing to the working class folk who can't afford tickets to the Met."

"I wish he'd change his mind. Yet I admire him for that."

"I don't think you ought to visit Delmonico's with him," Susan warned. "The gangsters might make an attempt there."

"The mobsters couldn't know of that date as we've just now arranged it," Caruso said, his English notably improved over the past day.

"Call me headstrong, ladies, if you wish. But I wouldn't miss dinner at Delmonico's with Enrico Caruso for the world!"

"Besides, we'll be there," the taller bodyguard added.

"Believe me, we're more than able to counter any threat."

JAMES: WEDNESDAY; FEBRUARY 6, 1901

"Let's order," Henry suggested. I glanced around the establishment, sensing that something seemed 'off.'

"What're you looking for?" Bat asked, his tone mercurial.

"To tell the truth, *waiters*."

"There are none," he guffawed. "That's why I brought you here. Take a look at New York's first fully-automated eatery."

Moments later, we approached the western wall, featuring row after row of rectangular-shaped metallic compartments, each shielded by a glass door. Peering inside, I spotted a chicken pot pie contained in one venue, meat loaf with mash potatoes behind another small pane of glass, and a pork chop with creamed corn nearby.

"I don't get it."

"Watch! And witness the miracle of modern technology."

Bat reached into his pocket, pulled out a nickel, and inserted it into a slot. The glass window opened on its own, thanks to an attached spring-like device.

"Like the Nickelodeon," Henry marveled, "only dispensing food rather than entertainment."

"Impressive," I admitted. "But I must say . . . I miss having some pretty girl with a broad smile stoppin' by to take my order."

An invisible cloud descended on Bat, resulting in a rare instance of concern. "To tell the truth? So do I!"

"*Progress*," I sighed, "for better or worse."

ELOISE: WEDNESDAY; FEBRUARY 6, 1901

Suddenly, it occurred to me: I had not requested the portrait of myself that Lakeland borrowed, despite Bat's insistence that I must do so. I'd sworn to myself this would be a priority of the first order when (if) I returned. Yet on my original visit I'd been overwhelmed with everything from my meeting with Caruso to the disappointment of our cancelled filming; and, on the second (earlier today), the screen test left me exhausted. Then came the frightful disclosure of the Mafia's plot, as well as the unexpected dinner invitation. So I had allowed this important detail to become lost on two occasions.

"This afternoon," Susan said on the ferry. "Elizabeth and I will be joining several friends to plan an upcoming meeting of our society. Would you care to join us?"

"For the latter? Oh, yes!"

"But not today?" Elizabeth asked.

"Today, I'm going to spend the afternoon shopping for a glorious outfit to wear at Delmonico's. Have you been there?"

"No," Susan replied in a less than happy voice. "Their policy is that women not accompanied by men aren't welcome."

"Oh!" I responded with sincere concern.

HENRY: WEDNESDAY; FEBRUARY 6, 1901

I'd chosen the turkey croquettes, a favorite from back when I was a kid. My pard ordered an immense bowl of split pea soup with ham. Bat picked spaghetti and meatballs, which he explained had become a favorite with New Yorkers following the arrival of Italian immgrants during the past twenty years.

"You said we needed to talk," James reminded Bat.

With that, our mentor reached into his inner jacket pocket and drew out a rectangular leather wallet. This, he tossed down on the table. The two connected halves stretched wide-open, revealing a silver shield badge inside. "Never thought this would happen, but I'm back to my old trade. Secretly this time around. Lawman, all the same."

"Should I assume you're here to arrest us?" I croaked.

"Ain't gonna happen."

"Don't tell me you want us to turn Etta over?"

"She, happily, is *not* an issue, at least not for me."

"What, then, in the name of God, is going on here?"

—INTERLUDE—

BAT: OCTOBER 25, 1921

*Several hours earlier, Lolly, and following a hard bare-knuckled knock, Lewis opened his office door and waved me in. Framed testimonials to the paper were mounted on all four walls. Happily, I detected no trace on the man's time-worn face to indicate that my worst fears were true and the jig, at least concerning my outlaw friends, was up.*

*In fact, Lewis appeared relieved to see me. "Bat," he drawled, "say 'hello' to an old friend."*

*With that, Lewis gestured toward a medium-sized, heavy-set man sporting a thick moustache, seated nearby.*

*"Governor Roosevelt?" I extended my hand for shaking. "Or, should I say, Mr. Vice-President? Good to see you again."*

*"At this moment, Bat, lost in some odd, irritating place between the two. However! Yes, it's me."*

*I was aware that the eminent politician, quickly rising from statewide to national prominence, had recently assigned Lewis to edit his speeches for an upcoming volume. This then provided an official excuse for T.R.'s presence here today.*

*The motivation for summoning me as well remained unclear for the moment.*

LAW AND ORDER: During his final days as Governor of New York, vice-president-elect Theodore Roosevelt enlisted journalist Bat Masterson to serve as a secret agent against organized crime.

"Bat," Lewis explained, "Teddy—you and I can refer to him so when the three of us are alone—is here on a most pressing issue that jeopardizes law and order in our city."

"I'm all ears."

"We are on the verge of rioting in the streets. Before traveling to Washington, I hope to do whatever may be necessary to end this imminent threat."

"When I became aware of this, Bat, I thought of you. May I assume you anticipate what T.R. refers to?"

"Of course, Mr. Lewis," I answered, relieved that this meeting had nothing to do with Etta. "The Immigrant Dilemna."

Each of us knew that these admired companions rejected the vicious prejudices against diverse people—Jews, the Irish, Chinese, Italians, and African-Americans from the Deep South—now pouring into New York. As the number of ethnic arrivals quadrupled, the established Anglo population—mostly Dutch, German, and English—came to feel threatened.

A boiling point had been reached when prominent members of the Old Order employed their influence to manipulate the uneducated masses, in some cases leading to street violence. As a result, legislation to restrict further immigration was now a serious subject of discussion in Congress, despite the fact that we were indeed a nation of immigrants. Why, even the Indians had crossed over from Europe on a now-gone landbridge.

"What we must immediately set about doing," the vice-president elect spoke in a majestic tone of voice that assured me T.R. would, in due time, win the nation's top spot, "is to convince the citizenry that the so-called Immigrant 'Problem' is a myth. The majority of recent arrivals enrich us."

"Which means," Lewis added, "we must crack down on the small number who do indeed threaten our way."

"I assume you're referring to La Cosa Nostra?"

"You assume correctly, Bat."

With that, Roosevelt handed me a silver badge along with official documents, signed and sealed. "I'm appointing you as federal marshal for the Fourth District of New York."

"Just like old times," I sighed.

# PART EIGHT:
# EAST SIDE, WEST SIDE . . .

"When I'm in New York, I just want to walk down the streets and feel this remarkable sensation that the city generates . . . it's like, I'm in a *movie*!"

—RYAN ADAMS

ELOISE: Wednesday; February 6, 1901

First, I paused at a newspaper and magazine shop, pouring over advertisements of varied local shops specializing in women's wear of the highest order. The outfit I chose must be ultra-contemporary, *tres chic* in a modern way.

One establishment all but leapt up off the page. This shop, the first of its kind in New York, had opened during the past year in anticipation of Victoria's demise. As a new century dawned, America was ready to cease imitating the conservative English and emulate that liberal nation across the channel. Naughty France, where the mantra has long been: *Viva la difference!*

In the final decades of the nineteenth century, a belief in freedom extended from that country's radical politics into the daily lives of ordinary people. Middle-class citizens now aspired to pleasures previously reserved for the elite. This movement, journalists heralded as *Tout-Paris*: Unbounded joy, free love (including the carnal variety), available for all.

*A magical aura that had appeared in the last years of the 19th century. A decade of liberty for all. And perhaps even for Americans, beginning in Manhattan.*


JAMES: Wednesday; February 6, 1901

"You're telling us this *why*?"

"Because Henry, I want you both to become my deputies."

"That's . . . *nuts*."

"So nuts, James, it might actually work. Out west, the army claimed, 'It takes an Apache to track an Apache.' Well, I figure former outlaws like yourselves would be the best assistants to help round up those I'm assigned to arrest."

"Well," I chuckled, "it'd certainly give us something to occupy the time we have left here."

"Also, you will be paid."

"Sounds good to me," Henry shrugged. "Tell us more."

"An honest Italian cop in Little Italy, name of Joseph Petrosino, will be collaborating with us. So I'd mostly need you at nights, leaving you free to be with Eloise by day."

"What's our first assignment?" I asked.


ELOISE: Wednesday; February 6, 1901

*La Belle Epoque* referenced the nickname of a fabulous era. While burrowed in at the Hole, I obsessed over the scandalous novels by a daring new Parisian author, Colette. Responding to the bleak Victorianism across the channel, she encouraged women to enjoy, rather than repress, their rich sensuality.

Experience sex not only to bear children and satisfy their lords and masters, but also for self-fulfillment.

Colette favored a primal neo-Paganism. She called for readers to embrace "the exotic" from ancient times. Such mind-and-body experiments drawn from the Far East had recently been introduced to Europe by Sir Richard Burton. His translation of India's *Kama Sutra* offered an alternative to the West's notion that spirituality and sex ought to be considered oppositional. Thereafter, post-impressionist painters celebrated the female form on canvas, even as Colette had in words.

Might *La Belle Epoque* cease to be merely the name of a shop but, as in France, emerge as a way of life here in the U.S. too?

HENRY: WEDNESDAY; FEBRUARY 6, 1901

"Well, Enrico Caruso, the Italian tenor, arrived a week ago to perform at the Metropolitan Opera House."

"That much, we know," James nodded. "Eloise is determined to catch the gala on Saturday evening."

"You two aren't planning to attend, I hope."

"She requested we hire a carriage and ride there in fine style," I explained. "You don't approve?"

"Henry, The *Morning Telegraph* has already acquired that photograph of the two of you with the gang. Arrived too late for tomorrow's First Edition, so they're holding it until Friday. Once it's published, people might recognize you."

"And grasp that the woman currently traveling with us must be Etta," James deduced.

"Heard through the grapevine that Lefors and Siringo are in town looking for her. They have no notion of what she looks like. But you two, with a beauty, would be a dead giveway."

"Huh," I sighed. "Let me consider that."

"As always, I'll do the 'thinking' for the both of us. Say, Bat, if Eloise goes alone, shouldn't she be safe?"

"She'd appear to be one more elegant Manhattanite."

"That's the solution, then. We have to convince Eloise that, no matter what we promised, we can't accompany her."

ELOISE: WEDNESDAY; FEBRUARY 6, 1901

Crinolines, *Polonairres*, bustles, and *dolmans* of every imagineable size and shade! Displayed on mannequins or draped from hangers along the lilac colored walls of this cramped little shop. How the incongruous array of fashion dazzled a first time visitor. In this case, *me*, the small-town girl from rural New England who had transformed into an outlaw, now hoping to ease into high society circles of modern Manhattan.

"I'm here. I'm actually here!" I crowed. Other female customers peered at me from behind their Oriental fans as if I were a cross between a silly child and an escaped lunatic.

While at the Hole, I'd labored as a scullery maid, short-order cook, and horse-doctor, if never in fact a true outlaw. Often, I'd wondered why other women, none more beautiful than myself, were able to pick and choose among such exceptionally feminine choices for morning, day, and evening wear.

*Why not Etta Place? I asked myself. Well, now . . . why not? The moment is ripe.*

JAMES: WEDNESDAY; FEBRUARY 6, 1901

"My guess? Eloise is independent enough now that she won't mind so long as she gets to see the show."

"Likely James is right about that. Which would free us up for the service you request. Bat, you mentioned Caruso?"

"Roosevelt hoped Enrico's performance might demonstrate to long-time New Yorkers that Italians offer great culture."

"You expecting problems?" I asked.

Bat explained the difficult situation. Lupo the Wolf planned to kidnap Caruso at an upcoming street festival set for Friday in Little Italy. Our job was to make certain that crime did not occur.

"If the Mafia were to succeed, Hearst's tabloids and others like it would have a field day, stirring up moderate Anglos. If they were to join with the cult of anti-Italian extremists, violent confrontations might rock the city."

"Well," I said, "maybe we can help prevent that!"

"Just think on it," Henry added. "Butch Cassidy and the Sundance Kid, only this time on the side of law and order!"

ELOISE: WEDNESDAY; FEBRUARY 6, 1901

"I literally want to knock a man's socks off."

"You've certainly come to the right place."

Mademoiselle Mimi, owner of *La Belle Epoque*, had greeted me at the door. And, with an aura of supreme confidence, bade me follow her deep into the rich collection. Gowns and dresses on display were augmented with frills and furbelows with the potential to transform a girl into a goddess. Here were those elegant fashions I'd observed, in my frontier haunt, portrayed in the pages of

VIVA LA DIFFERENCE!: A new freedom for women, first expressed in the novels of Paris' Colette, led to more eroticized fashions during la belle epoque (1880-1915) and soon appeared in Manhattan as well.

*Les Modes*, France's premiere magazine for bold females not only in that country but the world over. Around me hung daring ensembles which, but a year or two earlier, were available only in those boutiques which lined such Paris boulevards as rue Halevy, Avenue Auber, and Place Vendome.

"I'm *amazed!*"

As for American females, our pioneer heritage of freedom allowed us to step away from traditional attitudes and enjoy ourselves in a way our English sisters were hesitant to do. I might not be the first to push into this glorious frontier of fashion. Yet I planned to be one of the original *avant garde* pioneers.

HENRY: WEDNESDAY; FEBRUARY 6, 1901

"But, Bat, doesn't Caruso already have bodyguards?"

"Yes, Henry. I've learned that the Met hired several. But our presence can only increase his degree of safety."

"Alright, then. We'll make our excuses to Eloise as to Saturday's big premiere. As well as Friday."

"I'll need you Thursday night as well. We must make a preliminary study of Little Italy."

"That's a bit more difficult," James mused. "Eloise asked if we'd bring her to Delmonico's. It will be our last chance to step out in public before our picture goes to press."

"Well, you'll have to disappoint her."


ELOISE: WEDNESDAY; FEBRUARY 6, 1901

Evening gowns fashioned by such designers as Jeanne Paquin and Madeleine Cheruit encouraged 20th century women to embrace their inner femaleness. Mademoiselle Mimi explained that such a wardrobe offered not only an attractive appearance for an evening but a costume, as if the wearer were a performer.

Who (or what) do I wish to be tonight? A celebrated aristocrat from Vienna? A mysterious seductress out of Transylvania? An exotic geisha newly arrived from the Far East? Why, I might become anything, if for a single night. Then, cast that role aside to assume a different persona on the morrow. No matter how hard I try, there will always be an element of Etta Place which, deep down, desires to have her everyday life transform into a romantic fantasy.

*Is this true only of me? Or might it also be essential to the female of our species? In our very nature, ever since Eve.*


JAMES: WEDNESDAY; FEBRUARY 6, 1901

"We have to talk," I said as soon as Eloise joined us in the suite, carrying a large package. Henry and I hurried to the door and help her carry it in.

"I know!" she said, ecstatic. Once more, we would take our dinners here to avvoid contact with other boarders. "So much has happened today that I don't know where to begin."

"Let's start with this," Henry said, pulling out a chair for Eloise. I poured her a cup of coffee. "We won't be able to take you to Delmonico's tomorrow night after all."

"You boys are off the hook for that one." She then rambled on about having met the great Caruso in person.

"Oh," Henry gasped. I felt relieved there would be no angry words, yet exasperated to think our Eloise would be stepping out on the town with such a notable companion.

"As for Saturday, Bat told us that a picture of the Wild Bunch will shortly be published in the paper."

"If you were seen arriving at the Met in our company, people would assume you are indeed the accused murderess."

"Not a problem. You see, Enrico—"

"You're on a first-name basis already?"

"Yes, James. Got a problem with that?"

"You, seeing him Thursday *and* Saturday? Yeah, I do."

"That so?" In a second, Eloise transformed from a happy young woman to a harridan. "How about you and Mrs. Trumbell?"

"Huh?" I responded, taken off guard.

"Eloise heard that lady's voice the other night, James."

"Well?" Eloise relentlessly continued. "Isn't what's good for the gander also appropriate for the goose?"

"I been meaning to tell you," I stumbled.

ELOISE: THURSDAY; FEBRUARY 7, 1901

I arose to discover yet another envelope had been slipped under the door of our suite. This one was from Caruso, with details as to when he would arrive for our evening on the town. However much a feminist I considered myself and aware Susan and Elizabeth might turn up their noses at such superficiality, I burst into tears of joy. As Henry uneasily slept, I dressed and descended. In the lobby, I penned an acceptance and paid Samson to hand-deliver it to Fifth Avenue and Central Park.

In fact, the Plaza—still under construction with less than a quarter of the work completed—was not officially scheduled to open for another five years. America's own great palace would emerge as witnesses passed by every day, eager to keep track of the progress. Meanwhile, the owners learned of Enrico's arrival and invited him to stay, as their guest, in a completed section. With the understanding that, before they officially opened, he would provide a glowing advance review.

*Who first said that the business of America is business?*

I'd say nothing more about James' all-too-true betrayal; a 'betrayal' more owing to the secretive manner in which he entered into a tryst with another woman than the act itself. Still, his decision to bed down with her changed everything. Whether I would consummate my relationship with Carosuo, I had not yet decided.

Most likely, if James hadn't done so first, I would think of my upcoming dates as nothing more than harmless flirtation. Now? One more choice to consider. For this afternoon, I'd put such thoughts aside for another day on the town.

HENRY: THURSDAY; FEBRUARY 7, 1901

Late Thursday morning, we entered into yet another demimonde within the sprawling metropolis of New York: Tiffany's at 15 Union Square. What Bat refers to as the *hoi polloi*—ordinary folks, welcome enough over at Coney Island—drifted on by. Several paused to gaze in the window but none had the courage to enter. For here stood a highly guarded bastion, exclusive to the money-based aristocracy. Armed guards were stationed on either side of the entrance to 'discourage' browsers.

"Why the long look, Bat?" Eloise asked as we, apparently passing the test of a guard's scrutiny, were ushered inside. "After all, this is democracy, American style, in action. You work your way to the top, and you're welcome anwhere."

"Power and prestige," I added, "derived not from a birthright as in Europe but a person's accomplishments."

"It's like this. Some say that because the rich get ice in the summer, even as the poor do in winter, it all evens out. Me? I just can't see it that way."

"Why, Bat Masterson. You almost sound like a Marxist!"

"Make no mistake about it, Eloise. I'm a card-carrying member of the American communist party."


ELOISE: THURSDAY; FEBRUARY 7, 1901

"Bat, are you kidding?"

"No. Decadence, which some consider divine? To me, such stuff distorts all serious values."

His solemn words failed to diminish my unbridled joy. Meanwhile, a tall, gaunt man in an expensive tuxedo greeted us with a facade of superiority. He did not deign to look any of us squarely in the eyes, far too aloof for that.

"This is your moment," James whispered, coming alongside.

"Oh, but you two will shortly know how I feel now. Next, you'll purchase some proper duds at Brooks Brothers."

"What's *that*?" Henry asked with a hint of concern.

"The finest clothiers in New York City, *that's* what!"


JAMES: THURSDAY; FEBRUARY 7, 1901

Henry and I wandered around Tiffany's like a pair of bulls in the proverbial china shop. Our eyes drifted over the seemingly endless array of diamond rings, earrings, and other spectacular (and spectacularly expensive) items displayed on dark velvet, sparkling like stars in a midnight-black sky.

"Keep in mind," Bat said in a stern, if sympathetic, voice, "two house-rules are strictly in effect here." He sounded like an old mother hen, worrying over a brood of chicks. "First, cash only. Second? Note that every object has a small card, attached to it by a string, listing the price."

"Same as everywhere," I replied.

"Here, though, there's no haggling. We're not in Santa Fe, debating the cost of a pony with some wily horse-trader."

"How sophisticated!" Eloise marveled. I could tell from Bat's slumped shoulders that he did not appreciate her term of choice. The grand scale of city life at its loftiest levels did also bother me a bit. Perhaps without realizing it until this moment, I'd come to share Bat's values.

"You don't approve?" Eloise asked.

"Style without substance never impressed me much."

As for Henry, he said nothing. But the manner in which his eyes lit up suggested he saw things much as Eloise did.


ELOISE: Thursda;, February 7, 1901

We spent the better part of an hour examining the items on display, always with male clerks hovering close to make certain these clients of somewhat questionable appearance did not attempt to steal anything. Henry laughed that off while James cast his killer-stare at each critical observer. Bat, meanwhile, remained at a safe distance, monitering the human encounters unfolding before his wise eyes with the scrutiny of a philosopher. This allowed me a more definite sense of what I did desire: an object to transcend superficial beauty with a practical function.

"Perhaps the young lady would find *this* to her liking?" one supercilious employee suggested, indicating a .23 Carat diamond ring as if only a jejune hick would argue.

"I think not," I replied, more supercilious than he.

Eventually, I settled on a silver-lined lapel watch I could display on a dress in a broach-like stickpin manner. Form and function together. Why, even *Bat* could not object.


HENRY: Thursday; February 7, 1901

Next, we were on to Brooks' at the intersection of Catherine and Cherry streets. Here was the institution, Bat explained, where Ready Made Suits had been invented half a century ago for an ever more casual citizenry. The 'sack-suit' offered a single size to function for gents of differing physiques. More recently still, imported Madras from India increased the global appeal of men's attire. Yet classicism had not entirely been abandoned.

Brooks earned its reputation as the most revered men's clothing store in New York since its founding in 1818 by the family patriarch, Henry. Today, his sons carried on the grand tradition. An icon from this shop's earliest days had been mounted above the door. The Golden Fleece, a sheep suspended on a ribbon, signified the high quality of wool sold here.

"Shortly, they'll move to the corner of 44th and Madison."

"Is there *any* institution in New York that's *not* changing its location to midtown, Bat?"

"St. Patrick's Cathedral, Henry. But as it's already in midtown at 5th and 51st, it doesn't need to."

"Any advice before we start selecting?" I asked.

"Only one restriction here. As Abraham Lincoln wore a black suit from Brooks on the night of his assassination, they'll never be sold here again out."

"Never say never!" I responded, drawing on memories from our notably different existence on the plains, when in a fit of competitive anger James and I faced off with six-guns.

ELOISE: THURSDAY; FEBRUARY 7, 1901

James settled on a three-piece maroon suit with the 'tailored formal look.' This offered a striking compromise between the current cosmopolitan flair and more roguish Beau Brummel trend which dominated during the previous

CLOTHES MAKE THE MAN: Any fellow could project the aura of a born-to-the-manor gentleman if he could afford to purchase his outfits at Brooks Brothers

century. When Henry couldn't make up his mind, I selected for him a coffee-and-cream colored jacket with the popular four-button look, also a natty vest to be worn above the high-waisted, slightly baggy trousers, thus providing a smart contrast. These choices, the attentive, if vaguely remote, salesman insisted, were all the rage now in Paris, London, and Berlin.

"Dapper!" I observed.

From this point on, my boys would appear to be upscale Manhattanites, diminishing the possibility of recognition.


HENRY: Thursday; February 7, 1901

"Well, Henry," Butch commented, "I'm sure *feelin'* good, seeing myself in such a suave outfit. But I can't forget what Masterson said. 'There is style and substance.' Gazing at my new look implies the former."

"Still, this is the United States. Where even the poorest cowpoke can, with brains and persistence, rise from obscurity to importance. Perhaps even us!"

"From vulgarity to elegance," Eloise added, "achieving this by pulling one-self up by one's own boot-straps."

"But what about those born without the natural gifts? Who will never know success! Don't they count?" Bat asked.

"My point precisely," James said. "In due time, Bat, be sure to explain how this Marxism will relieve poverty."


ELOISE: Thursday; February 7, 1901

After returning to the boarding house, James and Henry changed their clothing, saying they required less notable outfits for a low-key night out with Bat. As day passed and evening approached, they took their leave. I bade them goodbye for several hours and stood before the mirror, slowly slipping into my ensemble. Beneath the elegant gown, my body transformed step by step into the semblance of a goddess. A tightly bound cotton corset forces a woman's natural form into an hourglass shape, resulting in a faux image of perfection. Over this, a silk chemise adds a sense of luxuriousness. As do stockings, also of silk, enhancing already shapely legs.

Devices of precious whalebone and manufactured steel, hidden in the corset's construction, furthered the sense of impossible glamour. Beige stitching of the most subtle and intricate design camouflaged these, implying that the ideal appearance could be actualized. Yet I doubted that, once I'd arrived at Delmonico's, I'd be able to consume their legendary cuisine. The intense tightness of my costume likely will make it difficult to part my lips and breath, much less eat.

My low slung bustline would be exaggerated in size by padding and wire supports. Mademoiselle and her attentive team had encouraged me to pick a vanilla gown which, augmented with a mahagony sash, would draw eyes to my waist. Why, I thought, I appear to be a walking work of art.

## JAMES: THURSDAY; FEBRUARY 7, 1901

"Well, boys," Bat exclaimed, his tone even more sardonic than usual, "earlier we saw the heights of modern Manhattan. If that struck you as heaven on earth, here is hell itself."

Minutes earlier, Henry and I had followed Bat back to Park Row, from there continuing southward. How amazing that a solid, respectable area as the one we left could exist little more than a stone's throw from the worst sort of poverty. For soon we found ourselves in a nasty rat-infested area known as The Five Points. Rotting breweries left over from the early 19th century, when lofty businesses clustered around the once clean waters of now stagnant Collect Pond, had been converted into ramshackle tenements for the poorest of the poor.

Sad souls gathered along Park and Center Streets to the north, framed on either side by Bowery and Canal. Many of the faces we witnessed—the rare children as well as plentiful adults—displyed ashen or yellow and green faces, the latter signs of jaundice. Most wore dirty rags.

"If Fifth Avenue struck me as a dream come true," I said, "this is worse than any nightmare I've ever experienced."

## ELOISE: THURSDAY; FEBRUARY 7, 1901

Throughout my elaborate makeover, a sense of guilt seeped into my mind. I recalled a discussion with Susan concerning my wardrobe when we first met on the train:

*"The simple blouse and basic skirt announced: 'I am not old-fashioned nor a new woman. I am* me; *Take me as I am or leave me be,'"* she had later reflected on my appearance.

Was I a traitor to the cause that enthralled me? Or is it possible to embrace the best of both worlds? And have it all?

## HENRY: THURSDAY; FEBRUARY 7, 1901

A hundred years ago, Bat explained, tanneries, factories, and slaughterhouses generated prosperity for German residents. In time, industrial waste seeped into the nearby body of water and turned its natural liquid into a poisonus trough, large black flies whirling about during the day. I could momentarily close my

WELCOME T|O THE FIVE POINTS: If the sewer rats don't get you, observers claimed, the Dead Rabbit gang members will!

eyes to avoid the horrific sight; I could not hold my breath long enough to avoid the putrid smell.

"Even as the middle-class Germans scurried to leave, recently freed African Americans from the South settled here, as this and Harlem to the north were the only areas where Anglos had no interest in living. They arrived penniless and could not find the means to rise above that station. Then the Potato Famine of the mid-19th century sent refugees from the Emerald Isle in search of a new and, as they naively believed, impressive beginning. When they poured through Ellis Island, immigrants were greeted by signs proclaiming 'NO IRISH NEED APPLY!' displayed in windows. As always, those people who had arrived earlier were resistant to change.

"Go back where you came from!" they shouted. Only at the lowest of the low neighborhoods, Five Points, did newcomers find flophouses willing to accept them. For here, in-place residents did not harbor the prejudice or pride which allows any strata of people to feel superior to another. All were the lowest of the low. The suffering masses in all their angst."

"Yes!" James muttered, his disgust at the thought that human beings could be forced into such a horrible level of daily existence, "I must learn more about Marxism. And do so soon!"

ELOISE: THURSDAY; FEBRUARY 7, 1901

"Where are your bodyguards?" I asked Enrico as a driver in full tuxedo drew the carriage, pulled by four white steeds, to a halt before the boarding house. Wearing a tuxedo so elegant that it put the fine duds my boys had purchased at Brooks to shame, The Great Tenor sat in stately perfection in the velvet-lined back seat. I'd waited patiently by the sidewalk, under a street lamp, my silver lapel-watch reflecting its light.

"They are close but invisible," Caruso answered as his driver dismounted to courteously lift me up and into the cab. "The greatest protectors are never seen until needed. Until then? They see all, hear all, and say nothing."

Now, I felt safe. Nothing could diminish this night of a female's most wonderful fantasy come true.

HENRY: THURSDAY; FEBRUARY 7, 1901

"If the rats don't kill you, the Dead Rabbits will."

"Can't imagine what *they* might be."

"Deadliest gang around. Fifty years ago, they fought a turf war with encroaching members of the Bowery Boys. Look down and you'll find blood stains on the cobbled streets, *if* you scratch away dung deposited there by feral cats."

"Is *this* where we are headed?" I sighed. "Because I don't think I can handle—"

"Merely passing through. We'll swerve over to Mulberry, where the Italians call home. There, too, you'll encounter rough areas on Elizabeth and Spring, but nothing so . . . well . . . morbidly depressing as here."

"Once we arrive?" inquired James.

"I'll introduce you to a policeman dedicated to bringing law and order to the southern-most sector. Joseph Petrosino is Teddy Roosevelt's great hope for salvaging Little Italy."

ELOISE: THURSDAY; FEBRUARY 7, 1901

Originally founded in 1827 as a humble, well-regarded pastry shop at 23 William Street, the then-penniless Delmonico brothers, Giovanni and Pietro, offered quality products at fair prices. Hard work paid off over the following years. In time, their cousin Lorenzo expanded the enterprise into an elegant restaurant. Here then was *their* American Dream. Their deepest hope transformed into reality by sweat, blood, and tears, knowing the odds were against them. More entrepreneurs go belly-up than reach the heights. There are no guarantees in life, particularly when capitalism intersects with democracy. The Delmonicos refused to fail and succeeded.

Not long ago, the Queen and her consort Albert visited here during their American tour, afterwards announcing that Delmonico's ranked with the finest establishments in Europe.

*Did they proclaim this after paying for a fine meal? Or as Enrico Caruso would do for the Plaza, make such a lofty statement in return for a free ride?*

*As the saying goes: The rich get richer . . .*

JAMES: Thursday; February 7, 1901

As we stepped into Little Italy, a downtown area north of Canal, citizens joyfully strung bright electric lights on store-fronts similar to those which dominated their home city of Naples. Situated along Mulberry, Broome, and Houston, grocery stores offered imported oils, cheeses, and salamis from the Old Country. Also, tailor shops, fruit emporiums, barbers, wine merchants, shoemakers, and sellers of handsomely crafted boots. Here were the haunts of working people which made up the majority of 10,000 residents who, over the past two decades, had crowded into tenements best described as basic, yet in no way downtrodden as in nearby Five Points.

There were offices for professionals as well: doctors, dentists, lawyers, apothecaries, music teachers. All educated in Italy, briging their fine-honed skills with

STREET FESTIVALS: Residents of Little Italy would set all hard work aside to enjoy several days of dancing in the streets, wining and dining along the avenues, also paying homage to one of their beloved saints.

them across the turbulent ocean. Such varied places of business—high, low, middle-class—recalled the Old World in daylight hours, illuminated by night in modern 20th century grandeur. Most notable of all were banks on every streetcorner. Locals, Bat explained, were reluctant to trust their hard-earned funds to the Germans and English who preceded their own people into lower Manhattan.

In stark comparison to the Five Points, here lived ambitious immigrants, desirious of being accepted in the U.S. if without abandoning traditional elements they held dear. A happy compromise. Which, as Eloise noted on several occasions, is the key to success in life.

## ELOISE: THURSDAY; FEBRUARY 7, 1901

The fabled restaurant I would soon experience firsthand stood on the corner of 2 South William, in close proximity to New York's bastion of economic power: The famed Financial District. As I glanced at the sign announcing an adjoining street, 'Beaver,' I wondered why such a rural term had been chosen for this prestigious location. Then, I recalled that our country's climb to enormous wealth began when William Henry Ashley and his Rocky Mountain Fur Company bartered for pelts with Native People during the 1820s. Metal tools, tobacco, and (if illegal) guns and powder in exchange for valuable furs. But as this was big business, any sense of mutual cooperation soon ended. In the mid-1840s, entrepreneur John Jacob Astor ceased such trade, instead dispatching a small army of mountain men, like my benefactor Caleb, up into the Grand Tetons to trap for beaver, mink, and other varmints.

Numerous fortunes were made, until the fashion-trend for men's beaver hats and women's fur-lined outfits declined in favor of silk attire from the Far East. Always, as I have leared, the times change. At which point any business, no matter how solid for a period of time, fades into oblivion. If one element does remain constant, though, it's that money makes the world go-around, no matter how swiftly the desired products alter.

## HENRY: THURSDAY; FEBRUARY 7, 1901

Momentarily, the Napoletanos set aside life's daily routines out of mind. The people were ecstatic now for a celebration. As Bat explained, back in September, the residents had held their first religious feast in honor of San Gennaro, also known as 'Januarius.' For three days, music resonated on carefully cleaned streets. In late evening, people danced in the moonlight. Vendors sold regional favorites: sausages on sticks; bisque tortoni, an ice-cream favorite; and pasta augmented by eggs and bacon. Pantomimists and jugglers vied for attention. Wine and beer were passed around. Yet those in attendance had quieted when a holy procession, led by the area's most respected priests, passed along the Shrine Cathedral of Anthony of Padua at 154 Sullivan, a popular gathering place.

The event had been so well-received that the citizenry chose not to wait a full year for the next such celebration. So the community leaders proclaimed early February as the season to commemorate 'Blaise,' patron saint of wild animals. According to legend, 300 years after the death of Christ, Blaise inhabited a lonely cave, where he persuaded a jackal to lay down in peace beside a pig.

Residents now preparing for tomorrow's festivities struck me as deeply moved by the profound implications of that saint's anniversary as they were eager to enjoy the earthly pleasures of food and drink. If only the mild weather held!

ELOISE: THURSDAY; FEBRUARY 7, 1901

As we approached, I noted stately marble columns, rumored to have been transported here from the ruins of Pompeii. And felt a tinge of disappointment when Caruso informed me that even now, the current owners were in the process of shutting down this iconic site so as to re-locate at Fifth and 44th, in midtown, the city's new heart. What a thrill though to realize I'd be among the final guests to dine and drink in the original building.

"Look!" someone on the street shouted. Apparently, word had spread that the great Caruso, scheduled to appear during Little Italy's feast tomorrow, had reserved a table to dine here tonight in the company of a mysterious beauty.

"It's him!" people roared. "It's him! It's *him*!"

"How they love you!" I gushed to my companion.

In truth, I basked in the Great Tenor's glory. After all, I was his woman of choice. Thanks to beauty. Shallow, superficial, transitory, yet all-powerful female beauty.

"I come from the common folk. They know that. And do love that one of their own could reach such heights of success."

*But what of the multitudes who don't possess some great talent? And will never know the bounties we enjoy tonight?*

*What rewards could they possibly look forward to?*

JAMES: THURSDAY; FEBRUARY 7, 1901

"It seems almost Edenic," Henry marveled.

"True," Bat sighed. "But every garden has its serpent."

"You're talking, now, about The Black Hand?"

"Right, James. There aren't that many Mafiosos, at least not yet. But such 'mustachios' run things here."

"Decent people labor in obscurity," Henry added, "while criminals prey on those who produce things of value."

"That's why we're here."

With that, Bat led us down a stairway into the recesses of an unmarked building. In the cellar, candles protruding from holes atop old jars offered flickering light within the darkness. Blinking, I found myself in a private wine bar known by locals as Giovanni's. The silver-haired owner, his robust old wife, and the small handful of Neopolitans who frequented this recluse were, as Bat had explained, insistent on challenging La Cosa Nostra.

*Always, the forces of good require a strong leader. I was about to meet him: Joseph Petrosino.*


ELOISE: THURSDAY; FEBRUARY 7, 1901

All at once, the crowd surged toward our carriage. If for a brief moment I had felt thrilled by such fan worship, seconds later their Tidal Wave push against our vehicle caused me to fear such adoration might threaten our lives. The horses began to shiver and whinny with sudden fear.

*I feel as threatened now as when I'd became lost in that blizzard back in Wyoming. Apparently, every 'world' contains its dangers.*

"Back off there," the driver screamed, seizing his long, thin whip, snapping it at the mob. His strategy worked. Men and women made way as we proceeded to the stately entrance.

*But was this what I wanted? To be a contemporary version of Marie Antoinette, a pampered princess and lovely adornment to some prominent man?*

Once more, I felt my mind and spirit challenged. Who am I? And what sort of woman—person!—do I wish to become?


HENRY: THURSDAY; FEBRUARY 7, 1901

In the bleakest corner of this dim hideaway, a brooding man sat alone in an isolated booth. Precariously, owing to his lofty reputation, we joined this revered law officer known as 'The Dago.' Such a nickname, if spoken by hostile Anglos, would constitute an insult. But the title had been coined in irony, expressing adoration from those living in this district. A champion, in the grandest sense. A common man who achieves heroic status by daring to challenge an abiding evil.

HAUTE CUISINE COMES TO MANHATTAN : The elegance of Delmonico's interior, as well as the superb quality of their offerings, brought a new level of sophistication to dining in New York City.

Doing so not for personal gain, but in humility. The community threatened, an individual must rise to the occasion.

*A chill passed over me as I approached. For the first time in my life, I felt unworthy to meet another person.*

ELOISE: THURSDAY; FEBRUARY 7, 1901

"I've pre-ordered a series of 'small plates,'" Enrico confided as a distinguished host seated us in the most formal dining room I'd ever entered. We would enjoy the specialities of the house, invented here: a Wedge Salad with sliced bacon, Lobster Newberg, Chicken a la King. The near-raw Delmonico steak with the house's acclaimed pan-fried potatoes. And Eggs Benedict, all presented in miniature servings.

"Tapas style," my date confided. "Developed in Spain, specifically Barcelona, for truly sophisticated diners."

As a grand finale, Enrico explained, there would be Baked Alaska, the glorious creation of head chef Charles Ranhofer back in 1867. A dessert considered worthy of royalty.

*Which is precisely what I felt like. Though not without qualms about achieving such status.*

JAMES: Thursday; February 7, 1901

Joseph Petrosino, at forty-one years of age, bulky as a bulldog though a mere 5'3" in stature, possessed steely grey eyes that conveyed his religious-like conviction to not only halt the Mob but gain full respect for his people in America.

"Though my given name is Giussepe, refer to me always as Joseph. Born in Sicily, I identify as a ciizen of the United States. Since my grandfather and I made the crossing, I claim loyalty to no other nation. This does not imply that I forsake my Italian heritage. So, I am 'Italian-American.'"

"Do understand," I said. "While in the West, my partner and and I were . . . well . . . *outlaws*."

"Bat Masterson and Theodore Roosevelt explained this. But I know that neither of you have ever taken a life."

"Our view? Kill one person and you murder the world."

"Also, you never stole from the common people."

"Only banks and railroads," I assured him. "Capitalists."

"I was hoping that in aiding you," Henry nervously said, "we might make up for some of our past indiscretions."

"And," Petrosino added, "in so doing, redeem yourselves."


ELOISE: Thursday; February 7, 1901

"You are the most beautiful woman present."

"Thank you, Enrico. For there is much competition."

In fact, every woman in Delmonico's rated as a great beauty, adorned in sublime fashions that indicate a trophy wife or date. In some cases, perhaps, mistress. Power and money on the part of a female's companion earned her the right to enter, each a prize to some financially successful male. As Susan and Elizabeth mentioned, had they arrived together, even such distinguished ladies would be turned away.

No matter how passionately I wanted to enjoy this evening, I found myself overcome with guilt. I considered myself a traitor to the grand cause. And to my own sex.


HENRY: Thursday; February 7, 1901

As we learned, this native of Compania was but a child when his grandfather, who brought the youth to America, died after a fast-moving street-car on Grand Street ran that man down. Joe might have become one more boy of the back alleys, depending on thievery and violence to survive, had not an honest

Irish judge proclaimed the drunken driver, a distant relative of himself, guilty of manslaughter.

Deeply moved by the orphan's plight, the Judge invited Giussepe into his home as an adopted family member. This led to a quality education for the maturing youth. As a result, Joe came to believe in and accept our country's most essential paradigm. Success could be achieved by means of dutiful study and hard work, a value system that extended to the most humble immigrant, specifically, himself. As he had proven.

The Irish Judge had convinced Joe that there were indeed people in the world who would always do the right thing. As an adult, Petrosino chose to live by such values.

ELOISE: THURSDAY; FEBRUARY 7, 1901

"Should you change your mind, Eloise, my invitation remains open."

Enrico Caruso all but purred as we finally completed the remarkable dinner. In truth, I'd managed to enjoy small tastes of the treats in spite of my restrictive costume.

"You refer to . . . ?" I replied, caught offguard in part as a result of the bountiful champagne, particularly the extra dry brut which served as our aperitif.

"How I would love to have you join me at the Plaza—"

"Oh! *That* . . . I almost forgot."

"Might you reconsider your decision?"

"In all truth? Yes."

Caruso appeared shocked, having been silenced only the other day by the absoluteness of my decision. Of coure, I could answer in no other way then, what with Elizabeth and Susan present. When alone with Enrico? Again, things change.

"I'm delighted," he exclaimed, ecstatic now.

"Calm down, Enrico," I said with a smile. Despite my own status as a fugitive from the law, and his as an international celebrity, all power was mine now. "Do not mistake me. I said 'yes' to whether I *might* be willing to 'reconsider.'"

"Even that small compensation offers me hope!"

"Don't think I'll return with you tonight. That's not in the cards, as a gambler might put it."

No question that becoming the lover of such a great man appealed to my female pride. Still, I would have answered 'no' had not James betrayed me. If he could claim such freedom, then so might I. The only question: Would I choose to?

"By the way, Enrico whispered, "look closely at the entrance and you'll see one of my bodyguards standing in the shadows to insure safety. The other? Quietly seated at a single table, watching over us from another perspective."

"They are remarkably effective," I admitted.

"Best in the business. In town, as deputy marshals on a federal issue, though also Pinkerton men, so the Met was able to engage these professionals to also protect me."

"Who are these men?" I asked, suddenly fearing the worst.

"Charlie Siringo and Joe Lefors. Ever hear of them?"

JAMES: THURSDAY: FEBRUARY 7, 1901

"Here's the plan," Bat explained. "Caruso will arrive at the feast at six to accept a special award. We know, thanks to informants, that several of Lupo's *soldati* will then attempt to kidnap him. Incredibly, the courageous artist volunteered to arrive anyway. The four of us, as well as Joseph's Italian Squad of 'untouchable,' cops who cannot be bought, will be scattered about. We know what The Wolf and his Soldati look like. When any of them makes a move, we'll pounce."

"But what if something goes wrong and they do kidnap Mr. Caruso?" Henry asked.

"That will not happen. See, I have a back-up plan, one so secretive I cannot share it even with you. This will protect Caruso even if things do go awry. Trust me."

## —INTERLUDE—

BAT: OCTOBER 25, 1921

*Lolly, if I've given you the false impression that deep prejudice from established Americans toward newcomers began during* fin-de-siecle, *as a direct reaction to incoming people from Italy, let me correct that. A few years previous to the vast tide of Mediterraneans, a blight wiped out crops of potatoes on the Emerald Isle, climing more than a million lives in 1847 alone. By 1852, two million people had deserted the Auld Sod to avoid starvation*

*"Coming to America," they hopefully shouted from railings of lumbering vessels that had carried them across.*

*"Irish Prohibited!" read signs in broken windows of the decrepit East Side tenement buildings where the near-penniless desperately hoped to find refuge. These areas had been settled by the English, and their long-term hatred for and prejudice against Gaelic people had migrated with them to New Amsterdam, which they conquered and recreated as New York.*

*"Go back where you came from!" shouted many English Protestants at incoming Irish Catholics. Let's not forget, though, that similar slogans had been hurled at the Brits by the original German settlers, even as the Dutch had scorned them; earlier, the Indians resenting 'Amsterdamers.' Whoever showed up along this chain were despised by those who settled before and eventually proved hostile to the next wave.*

*In time, Lolly, a local, then regional, and inevitably national political party formed. Proud of their prejudices, they referred to themselves as "Know Nothings," purposefully oblivious to the cultural riches brought to these shores by diverse foreigners. Conversely, those in power in New York during the middle of the past century, a corrupt organization known as Tammany Hall, set out to woo the recently arrived Irish, increasing their influence by sheer numbers. If hostilities resulting from this initially had been verbal, shortly the growing hatred led to street violence. A Protestant, Bill "The Butcher" Poole, challenged Catholic leader Patrick McLaughlin to a duel during the 1854 Mayoral Election. The shoot-out that claimed Poole's life spilled over to generalized chaos on Canal Street.*

*Such violence carried over even to Poole's funeral, when Protestant members of the Bowery Boys fought with the Catholic Short Tail Gang during The Butcher's burial. In time, the Tweed Ring, which had been siphoning ten percent of all money spent by the government on public necessities, fell out of favor, the worst offenders jailed. Recall, though, an old saying, "The more things change, the more they stay the same."*

*Swiftly, a new 'ring' assumed control of Manhattan's politics, even more corrupt than their predecessors. Today, they are in league with William Randolph Hearst, who employs his influential newspapers to turn both English and Irish city dwellers against the Italians. Base appeals to the ignorant masses is the most effective means of maintaining power by corrupt forces hungering for total control.*

*For those currently in power understand that the easiest way to rouse the rabble in support of themselves is by manipulating the current public's fears of an Incoming Other. Whoever 'The Other' may be at any one point in time.*

'WHY DON'T YOU GO BACK WHERE YOU CAME FROM?': In turn, Irish, Italian and Jewish immigrants, expecting to be welcomed as they arrived at Ellis Island, were ridiculed and marginalized by earlier (Anglo) New Yorkers.

# PART NINE:

# ...ALL AROUND THE TOWN

"London is self-satisfied, Paris cynically resigned.
But New York is forever *hopeful*; always, it believes
that something good is about to show up."

—DOROTHY PARKER

"There it is, kiddies," Bat bitterly announced. "For all to see." He had arrived at Mrs. Trumbell's boarding house shortly after four a.m., delivering to us the *Morning Telegraph*, featuring a photo of five suited outlaws.

"That's sure us on the right and left, seated," Henry said, glancing down at the image of a well-attired quintet.

No one else was up and about yet. Not even ever dutiful Samson, who set the home fires burning each morning. Still, Bat took no chances. Rather than approach the front door, kept locked for another hour, he had wisely headed around back and climbed up a metal ladder. Traversing the shaky frame roof, Bat entered through a window adjacent to the bed where we slept. No sooner had Henry and I hurriedly dressed than 'the Kid' rushed across the hall to wake James.

"I've never seen you this upset before."

"Well, you can thank your pompous lover-boys for that!"

"They should never have had that picture taken."

"How about you? Have you retrieved that DeFly shot yet?" I lowered my eyes and shook my head. "Well, that's just dandy. Why'd you pose for it in the first place?"

"Vanity," I admitted.

A PICTURE IS WORTH A THOUSAND WORDS: Five of the gang members duded up and posed for this picture while in Texas; that's intense Harry Longabaugh seated on the far left, garrulous LeRoy Parker on the right.

HENRY: FRIDAY; FEBRUARY 8, 1901

"Don't answer it," I could hear Mrs. Trumbell whisper at the sound of my knocking.

"Got to," James insisted, sensing something important was at hand. "Be there shortly, Henry." I could hear footsteps as he retreated to the suite.

"If Lefors and Siringo happen to be in town," I coughed once James had joined us, "this will refresh their memory."

"Oh, they're here. No doubt about that!" Eloise then told us of her meeting with Caruso's intimidating bodyguards at the Edison Studio, and her date's casual admission of their true identity last night.

"From the frying pan into the fire!" Bat marveled at the absurdity of our situation. And, perhaps, life itself.


ELOISE: FRIDAY; FEBRUARY 8, 1901

"So what happened when you came face to face with your pursuers?" Bat asked, once he'd adjusted to the new reality.

"Nothing. Without ever having seen a picture of Etta Place, they had no notion whatsoever."

"I'm trying to take all of this in," James said. "As Deputy Marshals, Lefors and Siringo are in New York for the sole purpose of arresting 'Etta'. As Pinkerton men, they've been hired to protect 'Eloise' with their very lives."

"One more example of what I call irony," I laughed.

"The situation now is," Bat stated, "with the image of your boys circulating, if all three of you are seen in public together there'll be no question as to her identity. We must do something about your living arrangements."

"I might as well remain here," James said. That caused me to angrily eyeball him, then glance away.

"That should suit your purposes," I sniffed.

"I don't mean it the way you think I do."

"Have to go some to convince me of *that*."

"Then let me try."

At last James revealed the latest fly in the buttermilk that could sour everything we worked so hard for. First, Mrs. Trumbell had figured out our identity early on. Then, on the first night she and James had spent together, our landlady demanded half of our funds to guarantee she would not reveal us to the authorities and claim the reward.

"Is there *anything* in this 'foolproof' plan that hasn't gone wrong?" Bat scowled, drifting around the suite in circles.

"No," James said. "It's what sailors refer to as 'a perfect storm.' Absolutely everything has turned against us. Chances of our survival are, essentially, nill."

JAMES: FRIDAY; FEBRUARY 8, 1901

"I bet she'll betray us at the last moment."

"She can't, Eloise. Were Mrs. Trumbell to reveal our identities to the police after we pay her off, I'd tell them of her blackmail scheme and they'd seize all that money."

"Maybe arrest her as well," Bat contemplated.

"So she *can* be trusted, if not for the right reasons."

*I did withhold from them another reason for my confidence in Mrs. Trumbell. The degree to which, after the latest bout of lovemaking, her eyes suggested an emergent vulnerability.*

"If I were to to remain here alone for the duration of our stay," I said, avoiding Eloise's angry eyes, "I can shave my mustache, dye my hair, keep my hat pulled down low over my forehead, and come and go by the fire escape. With Eloise and Henry located elsewhere, we may just have a chance."

ELOISE: FRIDAY; FEBRUARY 8, 1901

"Well, fellas, one solution does come to mind."

"We're all ears," an exasperated Bat said.

"Here it is, then. I've been invited to stay with Enrico Caruso at the Plaza until he sails home."

"That, I'm not comfortable with," Butch grumbled.

"If there's one person here who has no right to say anything about it," I hissed, "it's *you*."

"Say, what's this all about?" Bat questioned.

All eyes turned to James, who hung his head and admitted that he'd become 'involved' with Mrs. Trumbell.

"Alright, alright," Bat intervened. "My best guess? As Caruso's booked into the royal suite, there will be an extra bedroom. With an inner lock on the door to insure a guest's privacy. Would you be comfortable with that, Eloise?"

"Those are the only terms under which I'd join him. If I should decide to unlock the door, it must be *my* decision."

"You're the one who gets to make *all* the choices now."

"Wasn't *me* who suggested that you bed down with—"

"The main issue here," Bat interrupted, "Eloise, would you be comfortable taking Caruso up on his offer?"

"Yes," I replied, surprising them and myself as well.

## HENRY: FRIDAY; FEBRUARY 8, 1901

"It's Dag!" the voice on the phone whimpered.

"Oh!" I exclaimed in surprise. "Hi, Sis."

A moment after Eloise made her decision, Samson rapped at the door, stating that someone had called long distance for me. And that if I were to come downstairs I could take it in his mother's office, currently unoccupied. I hurried down.

"So!" Dag said. "Shall I call you 'Sundance'?"

"I assume the Buffalo newsapaper reprinted the picture?"

"All dressed up as if on the way to your own funeral."

"Don't laugh. That may yet be the case."

"Believe me, Harry. I don't find this funny."

"Dag, how were you able to locate me?"

"You left some papers in your room when you hurried off. One included the address of where you'd be staying."

"Better destroy that before your husband—"

"That's why I called. It was Ronald who first found it."

"Did he alert the police?"

"No. Ronald left by train several minutes ago. It's scheduled to reach New York in six hours. He intends to locate you, follow you to her, then claim the reward money."

"It's okay. I'll change my location right away."

"As for Ronald? Do what you must. Though try not—"

"I've never killed anyone. And I don't plan to start with family, even if it's strictly by marriage."

"Thank you for that. One more thing? *Marry* that girl!"

## ELOISE: FRIDAY; FEBRUARY 8, 1901

Bat offered to accompany me to the Plaza for my lunch date with Enrico. However appreciative, I had embarked on a journey toward self-sufficiency. Before noon, I left all three in the suite, discussing their secretive plans for this evening. Shortly, a Hansom cab carried me up Fifth Avenue to 59th. There, I deboarded, discovering myself in a remarkable example of architectural splendor. If only partly constructed, I sensed that this hotel would upstage all others in New York with its grand conception and mid-town location.

Jauntily, I ascended the steps, covered with a delicate coating of snowflakes from an early morning flurry. A tall doorman, wearing a forest-green suitcoat

THE CROWN GLORY AT CENTRAL PARK:  The Plaza, seen here at its completion in 1905, was still under construction though accepting rare elite borders at the time of Miss Etta's visit; middle class New Yorkers skating in Central Park could only imagine the garden of delights to be found inside.

with beige trim and black silk top hat, smiled. He beckoned me forward, nodding with understanding that I was among the precious few invited to enter the Plaza at this early stage. For Bat had called Caruso in advance to inform him of my upcoming arrival.

Glancing around, I observed passersby slowing their pace to glimpse America's royal palace in embryo. Charming too was the existence of Central Park across the street; a lush garden similar to those in Europe, there designed exclusively for the pleasure of the upper-classes. By establishing such a glorious recluse within our modern metropolis, liberals like Roosevelt made it possible for ordinary city people to enjoy a taste of The Great Outdoors. Here I witnessed evidence that 'democracy' was not merely a political ideology but an everyday reality. At least when in the hands of the enlightened wealthy like Teddy.

Once inside, I hesitated in the main corridor. Workers prepared boutiques for customers yet to come. Everything from top-of-the-line jewelery and the latest in women's fashions to international gourmet foods. How large a fortune, I wondered, had already been invested in this 250 foot high, 400 foot long, 20 story symbol of New York as the world's key destination? The city of cities! What Rome had been during its golden age, all roads . . . symbolic as well as physical . . . would lead here Yet I felt a pang of sorrow for the masses that would never enter the Plaza. Or Tiffany's and Delmonico's. Was democratic capitalism the best possible political system? I wonder!

JAMES: FRIDAY; FEBRUARY 8, 1901

"That cuts it," I shouted once Henry told Bat and myself the news of our latest threat, his soon to arrive brother-in-law. "We were never meant to get out of this alive."

"Calm down," Bat commanded, "and let me think on it."

Shortly after noon, we strolled over to the intersection of Eighth Avenue and Hudson, wearing overcoats with large collars yanked high, hats pulled down almost to our eyes. Bat suggested we chow down at McFlannery's, an Irish pub at the corner of Bleeker and Sullivan. Once inside, we knocked down Guinness Stouts at the bar, then found a shadowy corner table.

"Fellas here are so busy talking sports, politics, and women I don't guess they'll even glance our way," Bat said. Just in case, though, I kept my hat angled low and collar up.

ELOISE: FRIDAY; FEBRUARY 8, 1901

"I'm here to meet Mr. Caruso for lunch," I announced to the female concierge. Her eyes revealed what I took to be a hint of jealousy. Likely miffed that she, certainly attractive, was not the one chosen to dine with the world's greatest tenor.

"Come," she said with an aura of indifferent politeness.

From the reception area, I followed her into an even more splendid inner-lobby. Cut-glass chandeliers and intricate gold ornamentation were situated alongside portraits of well-known Manhattanites. Everything sparkled and shimmered with 'class.'

"Beauty is a witch," Caruso said, rising to greet me.

"Ah! You know the Bard as well as Verdi."

"Yes. Likewise, I discover you are well-read as well as lovely. So we are both pleasantly surprised."

HENRY: FRIDAY; FEBRUARY 8, 1901

"Emma and I reside in The Delivan, Henry, near midtown. The only other residents are the owners, an elderly couple. As I recall, they haven't opened a newspaper in maybe five years. And there is a spare room in our suite."

"What about you, James?"

"I'll remain in my room and inform Mrs. Trumbell that she can rent the suite out to others. Since we've already paid for the entire stay, she'll doubtless take delight in doubling her money."

"That's not all she'll delight in," Bat smirked.

"Let's not get into that now."

I smiled in agreement and downed another beer. All at once James' eyes turned melancholy. "I wonder if our girl will ever return after sampling the high life with Caruso."

"At this point," I responded, "my guess is that she'd prefer we refer to her as a 'woman' instead of a 'girl.'"

ELOISE: FRIDAY; FEBRUARY 8, 1901

"I must say, Enrico, your command of the English language has improved by leaps and bounds."

"E.S. is a marvelous instructor. Enough, though, on that. I want to learn more about *you*."

"There isn't much to tell," I lied.

"I doubt that."

"Some day, when we know each other better, perhaps I'll share with you the strange story of my life."

"I wouldn't be shocked to learn that the entirety of it is signified by your choice of a single piece of jewelery."

He referred to the silver-lined lapel watch pinned to my outfit. "There's a long story behind this."

"One of many 'long stories' I wish to hear. If at your pleasure, of course."

"Congratulations! You just said the right thing."

JAMES: FRIDAY; FEBRUARY 8, 1901

Back in my room, I felt lonely, as if a grey cloud rolled in and perched directly above my head. I knew in a few hours I'd meet Bat, Henry, and Officer Petrosino to perform our duty. Yet I slipped into a deep depression. For absolutely nothing seemed certain anymore.

*What if Eloise could not forgive me? If she and Henry leave together, is this how I'll feel all of the time?*

For five years, I'd counted on spending most days with one or the other of those people I—well, maybe it's time for me to admit it to myself outright—loved. Days! And, in truth, nights as well. I'd come to depend on it. But, now . . . ?

ELOISE: FRIDAY; FEBRUARY 8, 1901

So! I sat across from a splendidly attired Enrico in the Palm Court. Though most tables remained vacant, each had been covered with a fine white cloth.

A lavish vase of hand-picked flowers brought rich color to ours, setting the standard for a future of elegant early afternoon *liaisons* for the wealthy.

"Pleased?" Enrico asked.

"Delighted," I responded.

As they previously had at Delmonico's, Lefors and Siringo stood guard, partially concealed by rich velvet drapes. Ready to die protecting Enrico Caruso and his intended paramour. And, once this task had been accomplished, move on to their original reason for journeying here: Arrest Miss Etta Place.

As Lewis Carroll wrote in *Alice*: Curioser and curioser.


HENRY: Friday; February 8, 1901

"Welcome to our humble home," Emma Masterson whispered as Bat ushered me in. They inhabited a suite of rooms in a quaint low-key building adjacent to yet apart from ever-buzzing Times Square. The adored reporter could, following a day's outing, retreat to an unostentatious neighborhood lined with tall maples, his loving wife awaiting him.

"How kind of you to receive me here!"

Outside, the quiet street had been empty when Bat and I deboarded a Transom. A refined older gentleman answered the door, apparently accepting me as what Bat suggested earlier . . . a visiting cousin from Canada. And how pleased I was to learn a rear entrance would allow me to slip in and out unnoticed.

"Oh, Emma's a little mother always," Bat chuckled while opening the door to the side room where I would stay. "She'd be lost without some forlorn critter to look after."

Two dogs and three cats roamed about as if they owned the place, eyeing this intruder with interest. Emma, I learned, had rescued them from the street. "I can't pass by one of these abandoned creatures without stopping to pick it up." My mind turned to Etta, identical in her caring for animals. "Luckily, Bat doesn't mind."

"Listen to Emma. *Mind?* Hardly! The great generosity of her *spirit* is what most made me want to marry this woman."

*Marriage! Something I hadn't thought about for a while. Now that the subject had been raised, I considered his words and knew at once he was right.*

*And worried about my relationship with the girl . . . woman . . . I loved.*


ELOISE: Friday; February 8, 1901

"Speak your piece, Eloise."

"You received Bat's message. Are you . . . *comfortable* . . . having me occupy a bedroom of my own?"

"Absolutely! And have no fear! Should you choose to share my bed at any point, this will indeed be *your* choice."

"Again, that's precisely what I hoped to hear."

We began our afternoon meal with cold crab and lobster cocktails, accompanied by raw fresh-shucked oysters. However much I had admired the less elaborate hotel where Susan and Elizabeth resided, I could not deny being overwhelmed by the luxury surrounding me.

## JAMES: Friday; February 8, 1901

I fell into an uneasy sleep, which made matters worse. I don't know how long I'd been drifting in slumberland when I woke to the sound of people across the hall. Pulling myself together, I staggered to the door and opened it part-way.

"Hello, Mr. Ryan," said Samson. He stood at the entrance to the suite with a small suitcase in each hand, an unpleasant looking stranger beside him. As Samson unlocked the door and carried the man's luggage inside, the intruder turned to face me.

"Mr. 'Ryan,' my ass. I know who you are, Butch Cassidy."

So here was the despicable Ronald whom Henry had warned us of. Dag's husband appeared as I'd imagined. A social climber who still owned the first dollar he ever earned, anxious to collect a quick bundle by tracking down and turning in the love of my life by bird-dogging me or Henry to her.

Love of my life? *Maybe now I should say one of them. Hard as it was to admit, that's also how I felt about the Kid.*

## ELOISE: Friday; February 8, 1901

"Does everything meet your expectations?"

"That, Mr. Caruso, is the understatement of the year!"

Enrico escorted me to the guest room. Lefors and Siringo had accompanied us up the stairwell; now, they discretely remained in the hall, allowing us to converse privately. My host stood outside the room's open door as I placed my few belongings in a closet. Shortly, we sat in a cozy corner.

"I've downed cheap white wine with Mandarin food in San Francisco's Chinatown and sipped rare vintages with parsley-seasoned rack of lamb on Nob Hill. But never, and nowhere, have I tasted anything to compare with this."

"Etna Blanco, from Sicily. Bottled in 1882."

"The scent reminds me of peaches, apricots, and jasmine, all delicately mixed together."

"How perceptive! Its unique taste results from a balance between Catarratto and Carricante grapes, which achieve their special smokey quality from local volcanic soil."

"There is so much you could teach me!"

"And, I'm sure, you 'me' as well. What you said only a moment ago hints at a woman who has led an adventurous life."

"In a manner of speaking, perhaps."

How disappointed you would be to hear the truth. Might your illusions be shattered if I were to tell you about my strict, hardworking, untalkative father? Or my dominating Puritanical mother, so often on my mind of late? Or my time in the west, spent scrubbing the floors, washing my men's clothes, preparing their food, and gathering firewood?

## HENRY: Friday; February 8, 1901

In truth, Emma Masterson was not a gorgeous woman on the order of Eloise. One might even refer to Emma as plain. Her presence with us now caused me to vividly recall some of the seductive women Bat romanced in the past: dance hall hostesses, female gamblers, cowgirls, wives of wealthy businessmen . . .

As much a 'bad boy' with the opposite sex as he'd been a good man when it came to enforcing law and order, I'd have wagered that in time Bat would settle down with some lady who, like ours, qualified as a perfect beauty.

Then again, the lovely inamorata of James and myself must also be acknowledged as a person of character. Eloise is that rare woman who offers the best of both.

So, I thought, another player has entered into our ensemble as we perform scenes without benefit of script in this ongong pageant. Would it end in comedy or tragedy?

Time would tell!

## ELOISE: Friday; February 8, 1901

"I've been up and I've been down," I sighed, revealing more than I should. "Believe me, up is better!"

"I must say I find you fascinating."

*This is moving too fast! I've said too much, too soon. As I did with Susan on the train.*

"Enrico, would you mind terribly if I were to excuse myself and take a nap? This has been an exhausting day."

"Not at all. Though I may be gone when you awake, off to a rehearsal. Order anything you wish from room service."

He leaned forward, kissing me gently on the cheek. My guess is that next time around he'd go for my lips. In all truth, I wouldn't mind that. And wondered how I might respond.

JAMES: FRIDAY; FEBRUARY 8, 1901

"No, no," Mrs. Trumbell quickly responded, appearing now at the top of the stairs. "This gentleman is James Ryan."

"Or so he says," Ronald sardonically replied.

"See for yourself. Check the sign-in log at the desk."

"Don't care what name he gave. I saw the picture in this morning's paper. And here he stands, now, before me."

Uncertain how to counter this, Mrs. Trumbell turned to me, eyes frantic, while Samson shivered with concern.

"They say everyone has a double somewhere in the world."

"Nice try, Cassidy. But it won't hold water."

"Whoah! I'll have no conflict between my boarders. Come on, Samson. We have work to attend to downstairs."


ELOISE: FRIDAY; FEBRUARY 8, 1901

A rapping at the suite's main entrance drew me from my late-afternoon nap. Enrico and I had consumed a full bottle of wine; the after-effect left tipsy.

"Yes?" I hesitantly responded, for the unexpected visitor might be friend or foe. I rose from fresh sheets and lilac-scented pillows, staggering to my room's door.

"Miss Placer?" Lefors inquired. But with Enrico gone, shouldn't both bodyguards be standing on either side of him, wherever he might be? "You have a visitor."

Unlocking, then opening the door, I was surprised to see Samson standing awkwardly between Lefors and Siringo. For a moment, dumbfounded by his presence, I could not form words.

"This young man has requested to speak with you," Lefors continued. "Do you know him?"

"Yes!"

"Would you like me to accompany him inside," Siringo politely asked, "or do you prefer to be alone?"

I considered the possibilities as swiftly as my shakey mind would allow. "I'll meet with him in private."


HENRY: FRIDAY; FEBRUARY 8, 1901

With evening's descent, Bat and I left the Delivan and proceeded on our way downtown. All around us, stark white flakes set against the natural black curtain of night offered a silent warning that the weather had turned colder. By the time we reached Mulberry, the flurry had increased in intensity, making it all but impossible to see more than a few feet ahead. I wondered if this would hamper our secret operation. Clearly, though, residents of Little Italy had no intent of allowing such a distraction to interfere with their feast. Celebrant people roamed the street, appearing as ghosts through the freezing sleet that now swirled around us.

"Welcome," Petrosino flatly said, nodding at us in amusement. We resembled an array of nearby snowmen built by children. As Bat and I shook snow off our overcoats, James emerged from out of the unexpected blizzard.

"Mr. Caruso," Bat questioned, eyeballing the celebrity, "are you *certain that* you want to go through with this?"

"I will—*must!*—take the risk."

"Perhaps this night we'll bring down the Mob," I said, a moment later seized by a coughing fit.

"Only a beginning," Bat corrected me.

"The good fight must start somewhere," Petrosino added.

At that point, I noticed James warily glancing back over his right shoulder, and asked, "What's wrong?"

He explained the situation with Ronald. "I used the rear exit, but thought I spotted someone trailing me."

"Maybe you lost him in the storm," I said.

"Let's hope," Bat replied.


ELOISE: FRIDAY; FEBRUARY 8, 1901

"There was a confrontation in the boarding house an hour ago between Mr. James and a new arrival named Ronald."

"Thank you for sharing that, Samson."

"I know who you are, Mrs. Long. That is, Miss Placer. I mean, *really* are. And I want you to know I mean you no harm."

"But your mother—"

"She doesn't know I'm here."

I could do as most women would in such circumstances and pretend to be unaware of his feelings. But that's not my way. Samson's adoring eyes revealed his fascination with me.

"Relate to me what transpired between them."

Samson told me of Ronald's intention to claim the reward. Things had just gone from bad to worse.

"Whatever happens, Ma'am, I will protect you."

*Another admirer. Well, I can use all the help I can get.*

JAMES: FRIDAY; FEBRUARY 8, 1901

Shortly, we arrived at Spring Street. Across the way stood a high elevated podium, half-buried by the fast-fallng snow. Here, in front of a majestic church towering above the city within a city, Caruso was scheduled to address the crowd. Assuring his countrymen that such hard-working folk would in time be accepted into America's radical paradigm for living. The grand welcome he'd receive, not only in Little Italy but on the following evening uptown at the Met, would pave the way for a brighter future as to ethnic minorities.

At this moment I felt like the protagonist in an epic novel. If I should die this night, I would expire as a hero rather than a wanted man. That would provide a fine legacy.

ELOISE: FRIDAY; FEBRUARY 8, 1901

"What the hell is going on here?" I demanded of Lefors and Siringo, whom I bade enter the suite once Samson left.

"Not sure what you mean, Ma'am," Siringo replied.

"You know *exactly* what I mean. Enrico planned to attend a rehearsal. Why are you two here?"

Siringo gave Lefors a look I knew all too well, for such an exchange had occurred more than once between Butch and the Kid over the years. *There's no use putting off the inevitable. Time to state the truth as plainly as possible.*

"Mr. Caruso did *not* go to the Met while you slept," Joe admitted. "When he departed, he headed downtown."

"Without his bodyguards? Why?"

"Be assured, Mr. Caruso has a police guard. He insisted we remain here to insure your safety. He's in Little Italy."

HENRY: FRIDAY; FEBRUARY 8, 1901

Along our way, Henry and I paused to purchase deep fried *zeppoles*, the scent of such sugar-coated donuts impossible to resist. A block and a half further on, we washed these down a with glasses of *Pietramerana*, an inexpensive Tuscan wine.

"Well," Petrosino said as we reached the church where a delighted throng awaited Caruso, "the ball is rolling."

"It's *showtime!*" Enrico announced, summing up his courage and pushing forward. Joe accompanied the tenor as he shuffled through the flurry. As if in a dream, perceived through a glass darkly, the two swiftly became indistinguishable in the whirling downfall.

ELOISE: FRIDAY; FEBRUARY 8, 1901

Lefors and Siringo took turns, filling me in on details that apparently everybody had been aware of except me. Caruso had grown concerned that Soldati, likely spying on him, were aware I had moved into his suite at the Plaza. He could not, Enrico had confided to the body-guards, take any chance of harm coming to me. Knowing he'd be surrounded by the Italian Squad, the Tenor decided his own bodyguards must remain here.

"Oh, but that's so risky!"

"Bat Masterson will also be there, with several special agents he recruited for this operation."

At that instant, the full scope of this assignment became crystal clear. Why, Bat's 'special agents' could only be Butch Cassidy and the Sundance Kid! That's why they were secretive!

HENRY: FRIDAY; FEBRUARY 8, 1901

Beneath high-strung lights, where then-recently washed laundry had been set to dry in the sunlight early that very morning, the people sang out in joyous anticipation. Might I ever become such an easy to please citizen? Or Butch? Also, the woman we adore; now drawn to the bright lights of show business, the serious-minded social order of Suffragists, and an offer to be the pampered paramour of a famous celebrity? At this moment, it seemed hopeless to go on believing Eloise would choose to remain with us here or sneak away in twelve days to sail for unknown climes. But enough of this!

*I must put all such notions out of mind. There is a job to be done that takes precedence. And* total *concentration.*

ELOISE: FRIDAY; FEBRUARY 8, 1901

Once again, my bodyguards stood outside the suite. Yet as soon as the door closed behind them, I hurried to the closet and searched through Enrico's clothes hanging there. A casual man's suit, though way too large for me, seemed the best option. I slipped into it, pausing only to grab the purse containing my small pistol.

No way would I allow things to proceed without me! The days when Etta Place, or Eloise Placer, might be willing to remain at some safe spot were long gone. Why, before this night is over and done, I may even become a living embodiment of the adventures depicted on the cover of Ned's pulp fictions. In reality, live up to that invented image. I could picture the title page, *Bandit Queen of the Old West's New Exploits in the contemporary East.*

JAMES: FRIDAY; FEBRUARY 8, 1901

"You look deeply concerned," Henry confided as we watched a snow-covered man step up onto the platform, heartily greeted by members of Little Italy's elite: religious leaders, revered statesmen, wealthy bankers, artists, and scholars.

"I'm alright. Hoping this goes according to plan."

All around us, temporary booths offered various walkaway foods for sale to a horde of celebrants. Hero sandwiches, meatballs on sticks. Sweet *Crostata* on one corner, freshly shucked clams at the next. Attempting to remain anonymous with collars raised high, we watched as all five members of the Italian Squad strategically positioned themselves nearby. If the law and order officers weren't able to halt the expected kidnapping, our assigned role was to rush in and do the job. I could only hope—and pray!—we were up to the task.

ELOISE: FRIDAY; FEBRUARY 8, 1901

After wrapping myself in an overcoat, a back exit allowed me to leave unnoticed. Following an alternative corridor to the one guarded by Lefors and Siringo, I reached the stairs and descended. Next, I rushed through the lobby filled with women and men conversing there about the sudden and unexpected snowstorm.

Then on to Fifth Avenue. From there I headed southward, even as a gust of wind slashed sleet across my face with the force of a Bowie knife. Still, I pushed on, passing several people as bundled up as myself. Why, this is as horrific as that night when I made my way from Nugget to Majestic. Still, I continued ahead then; I will again now.

HENRY: FRIDAY; FEBRUARY 8, 1901

"James," I said, trying to contain a cough, "I've known you long enough to tell when my pard is in a bad way."

"Maybe I'm just scared! I mean, this is a lot more risky than any stunt we ever pulled."

All around us, carnival games of chance appealed to adults. A small carousel, a scaled down ferris wheel, and a miniature wooden roller-coaster provided mild thrills for ecstatic children, unphased by the ever more intense downfall. Over on Prince Street, the procession of religious pilgrims added a solemn note to the proceedings.

"Never knew you to be frightened of anything."

"Alright, then. I'm supposed to observe the crowd for possible suspects but I can't stop thinking of our woman sharing a suite . . . maybe a bed . . . with another man."

"Join the club."

"To be completely honest? Lately, it's been difficult to stomach the thought of her with *you* every night."

"I wouldn't let *that* bother you," I coughed, thick mucuous returning. "This isn't easy to admit, but I haven't been able to . . . well . . . *perform*."

"You? That's hard to believe. For how long?"

"Ever since that first night you and me bunked together."

## ELOISE: FRIDAY; FEBRUARY 8, 1901

I switched over to Third Avenue and slowly progressed several blocks southward. That's when a terrifying sensation overcame me. *I was not alone!* Someone trailed behind, closing in quickly. Which sent me into a sudden panic. Overcoming that fear, I reached into my purse and gripped the small gun. I'd used it before. If necessary, I will again now.

"Stop!" I commanded while turning to face my stalker, "or I'll shoot." I pointed the pistol at a burly male figure emerging from the whirling snow.

"Mrs. Long, it's only me."

"Samson?"

"Yes, Ma'am."

MANHATTAN'S WORST WINTER EVER: The blizzard described in this novel actually occurred in 1888, (re)placed in 1901 as a self-conscious anachronism.

Calming, I returned the gun to my purse. After a brief pause, Samson took several hesitant steps forward.

"What are *you* doing here?"

"Promised to protect you. Waited outside the hotel to see if you might venture out. When you did, I followed."

## JAMES: FRIDAY; FEBRUARY 8, 1901

"Something's wrong," I said, pointing to the elevated platform. I made out a pair of swiftly moving figures, cloaked by the white blanket of snow. They scurried up the ladders on either side, closing in on the speaker like wolves in the night. Shocked, Henry and I froze in place. Meanwhile, Bat pushed forward in that direction, heavy precipitation hindering him.

"Come on," Henry urged me, attempting to follow. But a moment later a seizure overtook him. Gasping for breath, Henry lost control and fell backward, landing hard on the concrete.

"Henry! Come on. you can make it."

I tried my best to help him up, but Henry did not rise or even respond to my plea. Might our noble endeavor fail owing to something as seemingly inconsequential as post-nasal drip?

## ELOISE: FRIDAY; FEBRUARY 8, 1901

"Thank you for such loyalty, Samson. Now, regarding the bodyguards you met outside my suite. Any sign of 'em?"

"Not that I noticed."

"Good! Hopefully they think I'm still inside, sleeping."

"Where you headed?"

"Little Italy. It's too complicated to explain."

"Wherever you go, I'll follow."

"Understand, then. This may be dangerous."

Samson shrugged, in no way deterred. With that, I nodded for my latest conquest to join me and set out once more.

## HENRY: FRIDAY; FEBRUARY 8, 1901

For an indeterminate time I lay still, attempting to grasp whether any bones, particularly my spine, had been shattered. That would have brought a swift end to the Sundance saga! At the least, I felt gratitude to whatever it is that makes this world go around that I suffered no severe pain. Momentarily, I ought to recover and rejoin the good fight.

"Come on," James pleaded as hailstones bounced off me. "I need you now, Kid, more than ever."

Blinking, I managed to stand. James took hold of my hands and helped me regain a steady-footing.

"Caruso's gone!" shouted someone in the crowd. We turned toward the platform. The heavyset guest of honor no longer stood among the others. People scattered, likely believing Enrico had vanished into thin air, so effectively had the Mafia performed their strategy.

"Damn it!" James cursed.

ELOISE: FRIDAY; FEBRUARY 8, 1901

"Look!"

As Samson and I hurried down Third Avenue toward its juncture with East 17th, I abruptly halted. A trio made its way through the sleet, no one else near. Clearly, two men were forcing the other against his will. The third struggled to pull free, but those who held him pushed their victim onward.

"What's happening?"

"Mafiosos, Samson. My guess? They've abducted Caruso."

"What should we do?"

"Follow them. Let's try and keep out of sight."

Samson nodded and trudged along beside me. The three men, barely visible now, pushed northwesterly on 13th Street to Bryant Park. We followed, even as my face iced over. At last, they swerved, then proceeded onto Charles, halting in front of a formidable grey-stone building. The presence of an immense blue Star of David, similar to if considerably larger than the one I secretly wore, identified this as a Synagogue.

JAMES: FRIDAY; FEBRUARY 8, 1901

"Let's circulate," said Bat as Henry recovered.

With that, the three of us split up, each heading in a different direction. Meanwhile, the celebratory mood, so generalized mere minutes ago, abruptly gave way to horror. Soldati were known to randomly set off bombs in a crowd, making it impossible for law officers to function.

"This is bad," I repeated over and over.

After wandering about without achieving a thing, my instincts led me back toward the platform where I'd last seen Petrosino. As a professional policeman, he'd likely know what to do next. Yet every time I attempted to push forward, a wave of panic-stricken people drew me further back.

"You don't understand," I shouted, "I've *got* to get through. Got to!"

ELOISE: FRIDAY; FEBRUARY 8, 1901

Each Soldati drew a pistol and aimed it at the abductee's head, forcing their captive up cement steps and past the hard-wood doors. Their consigliere, Lupo the Wolf, had likely worked all of this out in advance, he aware that those of the Hebraic faith believed a Temple's entrance must never be locked. For such a place represented Israel itself, their homeland, to its congregation.

I had learned enough about Judaism from my late friend Bowdry to understand that according to their faith, the next day begins as darkness sets in. Now, Friday transitioned to Saturday; *Shabbat*, the Sabbath.

"Clever of the mobsters," I noted, "to choose this place. The one location the police would never think to look."

"What do we do now?"

"Find Bat and the boys and lead them back here."

HENRY: FRIDAY; FEBRUARY 8, 1901

Turbulence filled as well as surrounded me. The extreme temperatures caused another rush of phlegm. I wheezed, I hacked; I tried to spit but the phlegm had hardened in place. Amid the frightened masses, several people revealed the milk of human kindness by pausing to catch hold of my body as I fell. I nodded sincere appreciation but signaled for them to hurry on. No innocent bystander must be harmed tonight.

Perhaps I have, as Eloise encouraged me to, changed. A man now, not 'the Kid.' With a sense of social responsibility.

How I wanted to impress her by doing the right thing.

ELOISE: FRIDAY; FEBRUARY 8, 1901

"Was that the church of the Jews?" Samson asked as he struggled to keep up with my hurried pace.

"Yes. They call it a Synogogue. Or Temple."

"I do know that they are terrible people."

"What?" I gasped, stunned.

"They killed our Lord!"

"Oh, for Christ's sake," I howled, immediately laughing at the odd appropriateness of my words. "Who told you that?"

"My mother."

"Do you believe everything she says?"

"Of course."

"Why?"

"'Cause she's my mother."

Momentarily, I wanted to strangle him for expressing such a second-hand prejudice. Then, it occurred to me that I had made just such a stupid remark in front of Elizabeth and Susan. So I was hardly in a guiltless position to cast the proverbial first stone.

In fact, is anyone? My forementioned mentors, perhaps. I couldn't imagine that either suffered from the same limiting attitudes that we less enlightened people . . . Samson, his mother, and for that matter me . . . needed to discard before the human condition could progress to a higher state.

If indeed doing so were anything more than a pipe dream.


JAMES: FRIDAY; FEBRUARY 8, 1901

With difficulty, I forced my way past the obstacles, human and natural, and approached the wooden construction. As I did, the five untouchables surrounding their leader suddenly scattered. Each rushed down some nearby street. A singular figure remained in place. Little Italy's hero!

"Tell me what to do, Joe," I called out, hoping to be heard amidst the ever more tempestuous wind.

"You don't understand," the man replied.

That's when I grasped the truth. Bat had withheld one key piece of information even from Henry and myself. For wearing Petrosino's uniform stood . . . Enrico Caruso! The two had switched overcoats while tightly enclosed by the Italian Squad. No doubt they planned this switch ahead of time. Caruso was, thankfully, safe after all.

But what would happen to downtown's most lauded cop after the Soldati arrived at their secret destination, only to learn they'd abducted the wrong man? I shivered at the thought.


ELOISE: FRIDAY; FEBRUARY 8, 1901

I spoke over my shoulder to Samson, continuing forward in hopes of reaching the central city. "Perhaps in the time I have left in New York, I'll be able to offer you a history lesson," I called back over my shoulder.

"You mean it ain't true?"

"Samson, how did Jesus die?"

"Nailed to a cross."

"Right. And Jews never executed people by Crucifixion. Their condemned were stoned to death."

"Then who—"

"The pagan Romans. They crucified any Jew considered a threat to their imperial rule over Israel."

"You're saying," he stammered, "that Jesus was a Jew?"

"Your mother never told you that?"

"No."

Apparently, Mrs. Trumbell chose to keep her innocent Samson closeted from the complex reality of the world. As my own mother had, so long ago now, attempted with me.

*Mama? Do you yet inhabit this world?*


HENRY: FRIDAY; FEBRUARY 8, 1901

"I don't get it," I gasped at the sight of Enrico beside Bat and James as I returned to Little Italy's dominant square.

"Here's what you and I weren't told," James said, swiftly explaining the previously secretive element.

"The Untouchables are trying to locate them," said Bat.

"Never send a man to do a woman's job!"

We turned to see, of all people, Eloise emerge from the crowd, Samson doggedly following behind.

"What in the name of God are *you* doing here?"

"Same thing as you. Protect Caruso. Hello, Enrico."

"Belissima! You cared enough to hurry here despite the risk? I'm more impressed than ever." Caruso lurched forward, took Eloise in his arms and hugged, then kissed her. She responded in kind, more emphatically than I'd expected. James and I, deeply concerned now, exchanged furtive glances.


ELOISE: FRIDAY; FEBRUARY 8, 1901

"Samson and I were fortunate enough to happen upon two Soldati and a man we mistook for Enrico. We can take you to the Synagogue on Charles Street where they are hiding him."

"Well, Eloise," Bat smiled, "you *are* becoming the true hero of this odd adventure."

One by one, each squad-member drifted back, expressing regret for not being able to locate their leader. When Bat informed them of my discovery, they expressed deep gratitude.

"You are a woman of courage," stated one.

I basked in their appreciation. No longer did I feel like a lovely manqué, fit only to be observed and desired. I ranked as an equal among them. That's the sort of admiration I now crave.

"Fellas," Bat assured them, "we'll turn this setback to our advantage. I want you to spread out again, inform all the locals about what's happened. Convince them that this is their chance to strike a mighty blow against La Cosa Nostra."

JAMES: FRIDAY; FEBRUARY 8, 1901

With Bat, Henry, Enrico, Samson and myself following, Eloise hastily returned to the Charles Street Temple. Arriving at the steps, Bat proceeded up to the doors. Employing the legendary silver-tipped cane, T.R.'s secret agent rapped hard enough to make his presence known to all inside.

"This is Bat Masterson, Lupo. You're trapped."

"We've got Petrosino," a snarling voice answered. "Try anything and we'll shoot him down like a dog."

"Do that and we'll take no prisoners. I'm not bluffing."

The doors flew open. There, in Caruso's dark overcoat, stood Joe Petrosino. On either side, unsavory characters glared down, each Mafioso holding a gun to Joseph's head.

ELOISE: FRIDAY; FEBRUARY 8, 1901

"The taller one on the left," Enrico whispered, "is Antonio Misiano, The Enforcer. On the right, the stout fellow? Salvadore Cincotta. He functions as The Brain."

"How could you possibly know that?"

"They accompanied Lupo to the Kensington, where I first lodged. After their threat and a hefty payoff by the Met, we decided it would be wise for me to change hotels. The Plaza proved perfect as it is not yet officially operating."

At this point, the man I assumed to be Lupo the Wolf emerged. A cleft chin, bulbuous nose and deeply furrowed forehead defined the face of this menacing *cappo*. Though of medium-build, Lupo exuded a sense of abject evil that sent a chill through my system. The worst badmen I'd encountered on the frontier seemed rank amateurs compared to this crimelord.

"You and your men back off, Masterson. Do so and we'll release Caruso. If not, his blood is on *your* hands."

HENRY: FRIDAY; FEBRUARY 8, 1901

I froze, and not only due to the weather, as a wall of silence briefly separated us from our antagonists. Then from behind came the sound of people hurrying up the streets and avenues. Turning, I could distinguish five groups. Each had, as its clear leader, a member of the Italian Squad. A vast sector of the community, women and men furious at the intended threat to a hero, followed every policeman.

"There you are, Lupo. The *people*! Try and lick *that*."

A harried looking man whom I took to be around fifty, wearing a yarmulke and *tallis* that identified him as a Jew, broke through the mob. "I am Rabbi Cohen," he said. "Who is doing this sacrilege to our Temple?"

"An enemy not only of your faith," Eloise responded, "but we Christians as well."

Even such a ferocious figure as the Wolf, his yellow eyes burning, cowered at the crowd's magnitude. The citizenry would not be coerced into silence on this memorable night.

"To think you had the key role in creating this wonderful moment," Enrico admiringly confided to Eloise. She glanced at him adoringly. Even as, a long time ago, she had at me.


ELOISE: FRIDAY; FEBRUARY 8, 1901

"Drop your guns," Bat commanded. Lupo realized he had no choice but to obey. The Wolf signaled Misiano and Cincotto to follow suit as he released his pistol. Once they had, the Italian Squad rushed forward, handcuffing each.

"You win this round, Masterson," Lupo hissed.

"I had no doubt we'd lock you up someday."

"Hah! My lawyers will have me out by morning."

"Then I'll just have to arrest you again."

"Listen to Lupo, now," he shouted, less to Bat Masterson than James, Henry, and myself, "I'll be avenged on you yet!"

The Five Untouchables marched the scowling Mafiosos away as Petrosino turned to address the crowd. Caruso mounted the steps and stood beside the cop. The people's cheers inspired me to a new, wondrous sense of self-respect.

*Yes, I am beautiful. But I am* more *than that tonight!*


JAMES: FRIDAY; FEBRUARY 8, 1901

"I know most of you can't afford to attend my concert at the Met tomorrow," Caruso added. "So, to express my graditude for your courage and support, I will now—despite the snow—perform great arias for *you*, my people. My *countrymen*."

"'La donna e mobile' from *Rigoletto*," a woman requested.

"Won't we freeze to death out here?" Petrosino asked, as always concerned for the safety of his neighbors.

"Please," Rabbi Cohen asserted. "Step inside our Temple so these devotees can enjoy your voice in a warm place."

"That's most generous," Caruso responded.

"Perhaps tonight commences not only your own revolt against the Mob but also a fresh start between our peoples."

"Wouldn't *that* be wonderful," Eloise sighed.

ELOISE: FRIDAY; FEBRUARY 8, 1901

"Rabbi, may I speak with you for a moment?"

"Of course, young lady."

"First, I wanted to express my own appreciation for such a generous offer. But tell me, how did you decide so quickly?"

"Let me relate a little story," the egregious man said, his human warmth clear to me from a generous smile. "Ten years ago, in the Old Country, I served as Rabbi for a small congregation in the Pale of Western Russia. A fenced-in area where we Jews were permitted to establish residency."

"Oh! As for the rest of the country?"

"A few, our most highly educated men, could remain in cities beyond the Pale for extended periods of time. Those not so fortunate were only allowed to enter a town if our business proposals convinced those White Russians in charge such an exchange would serve their own best interests."

"That's *horrible!*"

"Thank you for such a sympathetic reaction."

"Makes me think back to the Wandering Jew in the Bible's 'Book of Esther.'"

"Oh! You know something of our heritage, then?"

Despite the extreme cold, I hastily unbuttoned my coat and seized my own Magen David, bringing it forth. "A close friend of mine, of your faith, gifted me this upon her untimely death. I never remove it."

"I am indeed touched to learn this."

"Please, though, continue with your story."

"Russia had entered into a terrible economic depression. Advisors to Czar Nicholas II knew that the starving people were on the verge of rebellion. Bolsheviks—those who had read the work of Karl Marx—persuaded the masses to march and then riot in the streets, many crazed with hunger."

"I know of this Marx and intend to learn more."

"In addition to ordering the massacre of protestors, the czar's advisors devised a ruthless strategy. Administers spread false rumors that our country's many problems stemmed from the Jews, who secretly controlled the wealth, though most members of my nation lived in poverty. Peoples of immense Russia were largely uneducated and easily manipulated to turn their wrath away from the government, instead rallying against us."

"Your people served as the scapegoat."

"A group of angry peasants stormed our little town and burned the Synagogue to the ground. I did not know where we might conduct our rituals. Then, a rare, sympathetic Christian leader—most such religious men hated us—knocked on my door. He explained that as his people prayed on Sunday, we were welcome to use the church for services on our Sabbat."

"Even in a world gone mad, there remain good people." I thought of Caleb, and how he and his wife restored my faith in humankind. The rabbi's experience paralleled my own.

"I wept. And took him up on his offer."

"So tonight's invitation to these Catholics provided payback for that good deed?"

"'What goes around comes around.'"

"Rabbi, I'll only be in New York for another week. But if I am able to make time, may I visit you and learn more?"

"As our people believe, 'My house is your house.' And to us, a house only has meaning if it is also a home."

A home! Wouldn't that be comforting! Such a feeling I had not experienced since the day on which my mother slapped me! Some scribe once insisted you can't go home again. I wonder!

—INTERLUDE—

BAT: OCTOBER 25, 1921

*The great lawmen of the West—Wyatt Earp, Bill Hickok, Charlie Bassett, Bill Tilghman, Luke Short, and without false modesty myself—have become a part of American folklore. And, Lolly, thanks to your insistence, I had a hand in creating their legends. The time has come now to do the same for those 20th Century figures who did their best to clean up Eastern cities. Most notably, Joseph Petrosino.*

*Indeed, if I live long enough I'll write a series of stories about his anti-crime crusade. And I don't use that final word lightly. Joe pursued the Mafia, particularly Lupo the Wolf, with a fervor that in my mind can only be described as religious. He dedicated himself to bringing down La Cosa Nostra. And if, in the end, he failed to achieve that, then his attempt to transform such an idealistic dream into reality must be recognized for what it was: a quixotic mission that when told and re-told will inspire future generations.*

*Joe was the first Italian to be accepted into the New York Police Force at a time when most cops were either recent Irish immigrants or long-time Anglo residents. His road was not an easy one; many on the Force ridiculed him as a 'Greaser.' Rather than turn bitter, as a lesser man might, he took it upon himself to end such prejudices among those who wore blue. Volunteering for dangerous assignments, Joe earned promotion to full sergeant by the then-commissioner, Theodore Roosevelt. As a progressive, T.R. insisted the contributions of ethnic Americans be acknowledged by such advancement. In time, Joe worked his way up through the ranks to lieutenant.*

*The incident involving Enrico Caruso raised Joe's already lofty reputation to a whole new level. But by far his noblest mission, self-imposed at that, was yet to come. In 1903, Joe set his sights on Vito Cascio Ferro, a low-level Soldati primed to take over the rackets, particularly the lucrative gambling and brothel franchises managed by Lupo until his demise. After a long and perilous pursuit, Joe arrested Ferro for murder. But the system, being what it is, included people in power who were anything but 'untouchable.' Ferro's high-priced lawyers got him acquitted. Joe became so despondent that his squad members worried their leader might hand in his badge. They didn't know Petrosino as well as they thought.*

*Discovering that Ferro had returned to his Native Sicily, Joe became convinced that La Cosa Nostra in downtown Manhattan was not an independent mob but an extension of what Sicilian locals long referred to as* Paliemmu. *If this was the case, the organization not only included distinctive families but evolved into an international synicate. Each localized gang connected with each of the others as a massive confederacy that, from wherever one might be located, looked to Old World families for leadership.*

*Enough on Joe, at least for the moment. But so that we don't veer away from Butch, Sundance, and Miss Etta Place for too long, let me return now to them . . .*

THE ORIGINAL 'UNTOUCHABLES': Joseph Petrosino (far left) and his Italian squad took on The Black Hand during the early years of the 20th century.

# PART TEN:
# SWEET LAND OF LIBERTY

"This nation will remain the land of the free only so long as it is the home of the brave."

—Elmer Davis

HENRY: Saturday; February 9, 1901

"So that's her," I sighed, standing a few feet from the water's edge, James and Eloise on either side as we observed the Statue of Liberty. The previous night's freeze had abated. With the rising of the sun, the snow melted, flooding many sidewalks. As Caruso would be in rehearsal throughout the day, Eloise joined us to visit this symbol, created by an artist in our fellow democracy across the sea. Signifying America as the beacon of hope for the world's downtrodden, Lady Liberty stood tall and proud in the harbor adjacent to Ellis Island. There a recently arrived ship now dispatched a new wave of immigrants.

"Sure takes one's breath away," James mused.

"Especially when you consider that, for such an icon, he chose a female."

"I suspect you're quoting your friend Susan B. Anthony."

"No, Henry. I am able to form my own ideas."

"You read up on the Statue, Eloise? Please share."


ELOISE: Saturday; February 9, 1901

"Well, the French hoped to solidify our bond as the two lands of freedom. So they built a smaller version to remain there and sent this larger one here."

"How high does she reach?" James wondered.

"Nearly 350 feet. When folks erected her five years ago, the statue had a natural copper color. The splotches are due to a gradual oxidization. In a few years, she'll be sea-green from top to bottom."

"Tell us more!" Henry sounded appealingly boyish again.

"Well, note that her right leg extends forward. She doesn't appear to be standing still while raising the torch, rather pushing ahead. Freedom for all in the future. Women as well as men. People of color treated the same as whites . . ."


JAMES: Saturday; February 9, 1901

We eased our way through the small group of visitors, two dozen women and men at most, to a series of food stalls. These entrepreneurs had set up makeshift shops nearly a quarter of a mile back from the water, under a high protective stretch of elms. Though the branches hung naked now I imagined how lovely this park would appear come spring, when greenery blossomed. And, the following Autumn, richly colorful. No question that New York is a magnet which draws me close.

Next we learned about what locals referred to as 'fast food.' One booth run by an Italian family sold pasta with tomato sauce in paper cups; meatballs cost extra. Nearby stood a tall Mandarin, offering free egg rolls as an enticement to purchase meals from his stall. 'Knishes' were available at a stand run by an elderly Jewish couple, boxty and bacon at the Irish wagon across the way. A black man from Louisiana peddled dirty rice mixed with red beans and Cajun sausage. A Native from the Pawtucket people on Cape Code roasted multi-colored ears of Indian corn over a blazing fire, serving them swathed in butter. Then we sat on a bench, sampling the unique cuisines. "Perhaps such fabulous treats will in time provide the means for Americans to accept one another."

"That's a lovely sentiment, if extremely naïve."

"Oh? Would you care to explain further, James?"

HENRY: SATURDAY; FEBRUARY 9, 1901

"How long do you think folks as different as these will remain side by side without hostilities?"

"Why not *always*?" I asked hopefully.

As if in response to my innocent question, a tightly knit group of more than fifty people, mostly men in white suits but women in colorless garb as well, came marching along the wet sidewalk. With angry eyes, they observed ferryboats arriving. Aboard stood the latest wave of Italians. The mob raised clenched fists, not only at these newcomers but also at the towering statue. Some sang hymns in unison. Others carried signs, "Great Whore of the Harbor!" I was stunned to realize the work of art which so inspired me to view our future positively caused others to express their fury at oncoming change.

"Curse the false Christians," an older man shouted as immigrants stepped ashore. Having passed through the admission process, they were terrified by the unexpected hostility.

"What's *this* all about?" James asked a nearby fellow whom we guessed to be Italian owing to his Old World *cioppa*—an overcoat colored bright blue with a crimson lining.

"Bible thumpin' Protestants," the fellow muttered under his breath. "They *despise* Lady Liberty even as they do us."

"Why?" Eloise asked, aghast that anyone might find fault with what she had described as an example of neo-classic art. The purest values of the ancients rethought for the present.

"Bartholdi, the sculptor, was Catholic. They perceive the Lady as a threat to their basic principles."

"That is . . . *crazy*," James reacted in shock.

ELOISE: SATURDAY; FEBRUARY 9, 1901

"But they are all Christians," Henry said, confused.

"Protestants claim we Catholics place too much emphasis on the Virgin Mother, which they perceive as a return to the pagan practice of goddess worship. Protestants revere only the male sky god and His son. So they despise the female statue."

"Women are worshipped or condemned in this 'bold' new 20th Century, as we have always been," I realized.

"Apparently, these old-time Anglos forget that America was discovered by Columbus, an Italian sailing for Spain. And I read somewhere that Columbus may have been a Jew. Many nations arrived before the Dutch, Germans, and English ever ventured onto these shores."

*My insistence on educating the boys paid off. The former Sundance Kid now expresses himself like a true scholar.*

JAMES: SATURDAY; FEBRUARY 9, 1901

"Earlier still," Eloise added, "Norsemen loyal to Freya, pagan goddess of fertility, arrived here in long ships."

"In truth," I said, "everybody comes here from some place else. Even the Indians! We're a nation of immigrants."

Just then, another and larger group hurried near. Women dressed in black carried signs, "Equal rights!"; "Universal Suffrage." Many wore small buttons. As they passed us on their way toward the protesters, I noticed stark white letters embossed on each little metal circle, "N.W.S.S."

"Catholics?" Henry asked, more baffled than before.

"Not necessarily," said the vendor. "These are members of the National Women's Suffrage Society. They are determined to remove the old stigma of women as evil corrupters of men. As a result, they protest those Protestants protesting Catholics, even though the members are themselves mostly Protestants."

ELOISE: SATURDAY; FEBRUARY 9, 1901

"Well," I announced with a sigh as both groups eventually left and any potential for violence dissipated, "here is where we part company again, for a while."

"When will we see you next?" asked Henry, concerned.

"Not certain. This evening, I'll ride to the Met in a carriage, then sit in a box along the mezzanine. After the opera has concluded, Enrico and I will return to the Plaza."

"Anything scheduled for *after* that?"

"No, James," I answered, ignoring his embittered tone.

"Bat mentioned visiting Coney Island tomorrow."

"Wouldn't that be terribly risky, Henry?"

"He's come to agree with me on the notion of 'hide in plain sight.' Says that if we're all together, men and women, his wife Emma too, and we keep to ourseveles, others will be so busy with their picnics that they won't even look our way."

"And if they do, Bat believes their reaction would be, 'Looks like them but couldn't be.' Besides, we'll dye our hair, shave our mustaches, and wear thick iron-rimmed glasses. Then find a secluded spot far from the crowds."

"Alright, then. If you're willng to risk it, so am I."

## HENRY: Saturday; February 9, 1901

"James, Henry . . . Butch, Sundance . . . meet the future vice-president of these United States." So said Bat Masterson.

After departing from Lady Liberty, we two headed uptown to Bat's hotel, opting for back streets. I kept a watchful eye out for Dag's husband but did not spot him. Now, we were ensconced in Bat's parlor, where Emma served tea. With us sat yet another man whom T.R. introduced as James E. Wilkie, the Secret Service agent assigned to insure Teddy's safety.

"Howdy, Colonel!" we each responded in delight mixed with concern. What could possibly be the reason why our onetime commander requested that Bat bring us together again?

## ELOISE: Saturday; February 9, 1901

"The meeting will now come to order," Susan announced, tapping an oaken gavel after assuming a seat alongside Elizabeth in front of the assembled group. Some fifty other women, fashionably dressed in an understated manner, enjoyed wine and light fare accompanied by smart conversation in the New Albert hotel's handsome, if low-key, private salon.

"Indeed," Elizabeth added as all present quieted down and took their places. Seated at the far left side of the room, I breathed in deeply, honored to be included, yet once more fearful that in such company I'd likely appear a rube.

Earlier, I'd been introduced to a wide assortment of females with careers in academia and the arts. One elderly woman from Russia, an expert on classical literature, taught a series of courses at varied Manhattan universities. Likewise, a young artist from Spain expounded on an innovative movement called Cubism, offering to mentor me were I to remain here.

"How I would *love* that!" I gushed. Then sadly added, "Likely, though, I'll be leaving New York eleven days hence."

JAMES: SATURDAY; FEBRUARY 9, 1901

"Boys, good to see you again. From what Mr. Masterson has told me, you performed commendably last night."

"We did our best under the circumstances," said Henry.

"Your lady friend as well from what I understand."

*This silenced us. Had Bat disclosed that Miss Etta Place remained in our company?*

"Well—"

"Relax, Henry. Let T.R. do the talking."

ELOISE: SATURDAY; FEBRUARY 9, 1901

I must note, six men were in attendance, each dressed in the shabbily genteel wardrobe associated with underpaid, if highly-praised, professors: woolen jackets with an Old Irish air worn above contemporary gabardine slacks. These were augmented by ties featuring Scotch plaids and Indonesian Batik. Before the meeting commenced, I'd buzzed about like a bee rushing from one sun-drenched flower to the next. Anxious, as ever, to listen in on *everything*. Momentarily, I felt 'at home.'

HENRY: SATURDAY; FEBRUARY 9, 1901

"I tried my best to keep Eloise's name out of it, fellas. But considering the impressive role she played in apprehending Lupo, the Colonel deduced that Etta must be included."

"So!" I wondered. "Where does that leave us now?"

"Well," T.R. admitted, "this is becoming complex. And since I'm scheduled to begin work in D.C. sometime next week, that doesn't leave much time to deal with our *situation*."

"Hopefully, we three will be on a boat by then."

"So our noted journalist here has informed me. James, as outgoing governor of the state, I do have some power to help keep Etta undercover until your departure. My way of saying 'thanks' for such above-and-beyond duty. Yet as incoming second-in-charge of the country, I must not do anything that might taint the fine reputation of my running mate."

"A double-bind indeed," I nodded. "We're sure sorry to put you in such a difficult spot, Colonel."

"Been in worse, including the Cuban affair. I haven't forgotten how the two of you rallied our troops!"

"Just doing our job," James asserted.

"Let's take a little hike over to Madison Square Garden," said T.R., smiling as he rose, all of us dutifully following.


ELOISE: SATURDAY; FEBRUARY 9, 1901

There had been one minor disappointment. The first hour would be given over to business matters. So mundane issues of red and black finance consumed a considerable amount of time. This might have been a convention of stock-holders for a vast corporation. Still, I bade my time, waiting for social issues to emerge as the key topic of conversation.

"Should we raise the annual cost of membership?" Susan asked the attentive members.

"Or gather additional funds by printing and selling more copies of *The Women's Bible*?" Elizabeth suggested.

Before long, I grew bored with such cold figures. The Movement's impact on today's popular politics had been what I longed to hear more about.


JAMES: SATURDAY; FEBRUARY 9, 1901

We five swiftly marched in tandem from the Delivan to Madison Square, an immense complex now ten years old. The 'Garden' stretched from 31st to 33rd Streets between Seventh and Eighth Avenues. Along the way, T.R. and Bat took turns filling Henry and myself in on the landmark's history. This 'Second Garden' replaced an earlier venue erected in the mid-1870s by P.T. Barnum. People had arrived to catch circus freaks and Europe's high-wire artists; wild animals and clowns. In time, that gathering place proved dangerously ill-equipped.

Though the legendary showman claimed all was well with his created 'world,' serious-minded progressives willing to spend funds for the general good insisted that the leaky, decrepit building be razed. So a decade ago, in its place arose this masterwork, designed by architect Stanford White. His genius for creating art which also served a practical function had not been restrained by financial concerns. J.P. Morgan, Andrew Carnegie, and the Astor family organized a coterie of enlightened millionaires. These were capitalists with a conscience, believing in both beauty and safety as a means of uplifting the common folk.

Back at the Hole, Etta had insisted that James and I read a three-hundred-and-fifty-year-old tome by Sir Thomas More, revered British statesman and, in time, saint. This seer coined the term 'Utopia' to define a possible future city in which the citizenry, from leaders to day-workers, engaged on a quest to achieve an ever-elusive perfect state. Perhaps that long ago dream would at last reach fruition here in Manhattan, during our own unfolding century. 'Hope springs eternal!'

ELOISE: SATURDAY; FEBRUARY 9, 1901

As they droned on, my mind wandered back to Liberty Island and the nasty confrontation. In comparison to the exquisite surroundings and exclusive group of people here, the incident struck me as more representative of our everyday world and its problems. That vast plain of survival on which The Great American Unwashed survive, a potential for violence always bubbling just beneath the calm surface of normal life.

Now, I eagerly awaited the detailed recounting of dollars and cents, incoming bills and outgoing funds, to conclude. How enthusiastic I was to learn more about the meat and potatoes of Suffrage and my opportunity to be a part of it.

Yet as I observed the meticulously dressed ladies around me, one concern arose. There were no women of color present. Perhaps that's nothing but a coincidence; still, this struck me as . . . well . . . curious, considering what Susan and Elizabeth had earlier told me about the necessity of all women coming together as a force for society's improvement.

HENRY: SATURDAY; FEBRUARY 9, 1901

In the Garden's most exclusive rooftop club, we sipped imported coffee, laced with cognac. Capped by a high tower, this friendly fortress was designed in the popular Beaux-Arts manner. T.R. explained, "A Parisian Ecole—*school*—developed this approach during the mid-to-late 1800s. They employ basic concepts from classic styles re-imagined with iron and glass."

"I'm coming to understand the modern sensibility," said James. "The best of the old rethought in the present for our enlightenment."

"Didn't know you to be so articulate," Bat marveled.

"Everything that's best in me, or my pardner, comes by way of our woman," I admitted.

"To be entirely honest," Butch chimed in, "a gorgeous lady further schooled me during a Midwest stop-over."

"Therein lies a tale, I'm sure," T.R. laughed.

ELOISE: SATURDAY; FEBRUARY 9, 1901

Next, my mind drifted back to the Edison Studio. The 'shoot' (as assistant director E.S. had informed me) would commence early next week. If I were to receive confirmation that I'd won a role (James would deliver this message to me once it arrived at the boarding house) I would accept. In part as a means of slipping out of sight from busy Manhattan. Also my growing fascination regarding this emergent industry.

Once more, as so often occurred in my life, I was likely to come face to face with a demanding—life altering!—choice.

That at least struck me as preferable to allowing others, mostly men, to make choices for me.


JAMES: SATURDAY; FEBRUARY 9, 1901

After passing uniformed guards, we entered the Garden proper. Inside, Bat pointed out specific areas, including an elaborate theater where as many as 1,200 tuxedo-and-gown types could attend a full-scale Shakespearean production, replete with the elegance and grandeur once confined to performances in London. Next, I marveled at an indoor baseball field, where teams could play rain or shine. Nearby, an arena allowed 8,000 folk to watch a Barnum and Bailey circus in all its vulgar glory. Or the current attraction, Buffalo Bill's Wild West.

I remembered my lover of one night telling me how she planned to see that spectacle when it arrived in Cincinnati, largely as a result of having bedded down with an authentic cowboy. Then I chuckled. For she had asked if I might catch the show while in Manhattan. I'd guffawed at that.

What had I told my lover then? "That'll be the day!"


ELOISE: SATURDAY; FEBRUARY 9, 1901

"Now, we will open the meeting for discussion."

"I, for one, wish to hear from a fresh voice," suggested Elizabeth. "Would our invited guest care to begin?"

Breathing in deeply, I rose, determined not to embarrass myself. Yet eager to address an issue ripe in my mind.

"This morning, I witnessed an ugly confrontation. A group of old-timeers protested against Lady Liberty as a symbol of democracy and the incoming immigrants."

"Yes, indeed," a lady announced. "I was there."

"Wonderful! To welcome in the newcomers?"

"Not so much that," the lady responded. "Rather to defend the idea of a woman as the icon of American values."

That took me aback. "Considering the Protestant-Catholic conflict I witnessed, let me ask, what is your organization's position on Religion?"

HENRY: SATURDAY; FEBRUARY 9, 1901

"Head 'em up," a mounted vaquero instructed drovers as they herded cattle over a dirt-covered floor. "Move 'em out."

For a moment, I might have believed I was magically transported back to Wyoming. Cowboys, Indians, and their horses roamed the area. Even a herd of buffalo, all brought East for the delight of those excited to witness first-hand the Seventh Cavalry ride to the rescue of an Overland Stage, pursued by Native people. Bugles loudly blared, accompanied by war-whoops.

However gifted Buntline may have been at spellbinding his readers, when it comes right down to it: *Seeing is believing.*

Such thoughts passed through my mind as an older man approached. His high-reaching ten gallon hat, long silver laced hair, elegantly drooping mustache, and neatly-trimmed beard left no doubt as to this person's identity.

"Boys," T.R. said, "meet Colonel William F. Cody."


ELOISE: SATURDAY; FEBRUARY 9, 1901

Much buzzing among members consumed more than a minute before Susan spoke. "We welcome all Christian women of our social class to join with us in our movement for suffrage."

"Though I, for one, do insist that Catholic women of Latin origins must be perceived as 'inferior Christians,'" an elegantly attired matron insisted, rising. Numerous others in attendance nodded in agreement. "The same with Negresses."

I couldn't believe what I was hearing. Prejudicial remarks here, at what I understood to be a bastion of enlightenment?

"Susan? Elizabeth?" I stammered. "You could not agree with such a statement, as I'm aware of your movement's early support for abolition of slavery. And your joint commitment to freeing people of ethnicity from bondage."

"Me, too!" the matron fervently insisted.

"So I assume that in 1870 you argued in favor of the Fifteenth Amendment amendment, assuring the right of black men to vote?"

"If you check the record," Elizabeth corrected me, "we all of us opposed it. And decried its passage."

"What? I . . . can't comprehend—"

"The Fifteenth Amendment did not so much as mention our gender's right to vote. At the time, when asked to argue in favor of passage, I announced, 'I will cut off this right arm of mine before I work for or demand the ballot for the Negro male, though not we women as well.'"

"But wouldn't black men, having been so long suppressed, join the movement for women's suffrage?"

"That is the precise opposite of what I believed would occur," Elizabeth explained, her voice now fierce. "I ask now as I did then, 'What will our daughters suffer if these long degraded black men are allowed to win suffrage, then prove themselves even worse than our Anglo-Saxon fathers when it comes to granting women the right to vote?'"

"Elizabeth! Whose rights are you willing to put down in the process of defending those of all women?"

"Not *all* women," the matron insisted. "At least, not yet. Perhaps when the Negro has been educated to our level—"

"What do you mean by 'our'?"

"We are speaking," Susan softly but firmly replied, "of white women. And only those white women who have achieved at least middle-class status."

"All Mediterraneans are Catholic," yet another voice rang out, "therefore inferior to we who are truly 'white.'"

"Women like those gathered here today," Elizabeth continued, "who have become as educated as possible in a male dominated society."

"Perhaps in time," the matron assured me, "when black women and men have further evolved thanks to guidance by righteous white women . . . and by that I mean Protestant women . . . then we might reconsider—"

*'Evolved'? I have never encountered a more 'evolved' person than Caleb, a man who achieved wisdom as to the world without ever attending one of those colleges.*

REVIVING/RE-INVENTING HISTORY: William Frederic Cody leads his performers in a run-through of the Wild West show that captured the hearts of Americans and, in time, the world as well.

"At this moment in time," Elizabeth concluded, "educated, virtuous, white women are more worthy of the vote."

"But what if the Negro people, women and men, don't wish to be transformed into white people other than the color of their skin? Shouldn't they be free not only from slavery but to form their own identity, and a distinct culture, within the context of America, even as you have?"

I was met with a stoney silence and askance glares. Clearly, this Movement represented something entirely other than the what I had assumed. I suddenly felt dizzy.


JAMES: SATURDAY; FEBRUARY 9, 1901

Bedecked in fringed buckskins, with a glorious red, white and blue kerchief loosely arrayed around his worn neck, as well as a pair of silver Colts dangling in holsters from a black leather belt, here was the living legend himself. The flesh-and-blood fellow matched descriptions from paperbacks I'd read. Not that Cody needed Ned Buntline or anyone else to sing his song. He'd been a scout, adventurer, lawman, hunter and so much more . . . Still, I would've guessed he might be a bit taller.


ELOISE: SATURDAY; FEBRUARY 9, 1901

"Again, and please forgive my ignorance! But I am curious, what is the group's position on Jesus Christ?"

"Do we perceive him as God's only son? Not necessarily."

Susan then went on to explain, "However, we agree with everything Jesus proposed. His 'way' is *our* way. Which is why we identify as Unitarians."

"Jesus instructed his followers," Elizabeth continued, "the proper way to love God is by loving one another."

"We call this secular humanism. Respect every person as an individual and you follow the right path," Susan concluded.

*How fully I agree with that! But how totally I disagree with their belief in the inferiority of ethnic people.*

*An hour ago, I entered this meeting with certainty that I'd found my 'place' at long last. Now, I'm more confused than ever.*


HENRY: SATURDAY; FEBRUARY 9, 1901

As we all sat talking together, the absence of Ronald for the past day and a half weighed heavily on my mind. Like James, I'd expected to at some point spot him dogging us.

"First and foremost," Bat announced, "we must find a safe place for Eloise once Enrico boards the ship to Italy."

"That's where I come in," Cody explained. "When that date arrives, we'll secretly move Eloise from the Plaza to Madison Square. Annie Oakley's under stress and requires a rest. She could shift to the Plaza while Eloise occupies Annie's room."

Next, Cody mentioned Frank Butler, the reigning marksman in Bill's show until Little Miss Sureshot arrived. Annie soon emerged as America's most beloved female star. The two married and, as popular figures, were considered fair game by Yellow Journalists who in print figuratively urinated on celebrites to sell papers. The worst of the bunch was William Randolph Hearst, who published 'rumors' (manufactured by his cynical reporters) that Frank had grown jealous of Annie's notoriety.

True or not, the public believes what it reads, much to the chagrin of the loving couple. The problem for Cody was dealing with disappointed fans when Annie felt the need to retreat and spend a few days on her own. Well, if Eloise were staying in Annie's room, might she be willing to portray Little Miss Sure Shot in the show?

ELOISE: SATURDAY; FEBRUARY 9, 1901

"What is the organization's first order of activism?"

"Suffrage, of course," someone in the crowd called out, "and, following that, higher education."

"That," I responded, "is something I *completely* agree with. I want to learn about *everything!*"

"Your ambition is as appreciated as it is charming," Susan said in what I took to be a superior tone of voice..

"What do you consider the other most pressing issues?"

"Alcohol must be prohibited in these United States," insisted one middle-aged, conservatively dressed matron.

"What?" I asked, confused. For during my marvelous lunch with Susan and Elizabeth, we sipped a superb white wine. Also, fine wine had been served here today, mere minutes ago.

"The mistreatment of women and *children* by men addicted to hard liquor is widespread," a younger female insisted. "Once armed with the vote, we can pass a Constitutional Amendment and close down the saloons and manufacturers."

"Don't you agree?" the matron asked in a less than pleasant tone, her eyes critically observing me now.

"I . . . why . . . *no!*" I stumblingly replied.

JAMES: Saturday; February 9, 1901

"Eloise can ride with the best of them," said Henry, "but she could never hit flying targets by rifle like Annie."

"Frank Butler will take care of that," Cody explained. "He'll hide in the shadows and fire real bullets while Eloise shoots blanks. The audience will never know the difference."

"That's not very fair to ticket buyers," I noted.

"No," Cody responded. "But it *is* 'Show Business'!"

"Well, we appreciate all you are doing for our woman."

"Our pleasure," said Bat. "Her courageous action on the night we arrested Lupo—"

"Speaking of that," Henry asked, "is he behind bars?"

"Wish that were the case," T.R. frowned. "Attorneys already have him out on bail. But he will indeed go to trial."


ELOISE: Saturday; February 9, 1901

"If we women must relinquish the luxury of a glass of wine with dinner," Susan said, "that is a small price to pay for elimination of widespread pain suffered by our gender."

"But we all enjoyed such drink only a moment ago!"

"Why not?" the matron stated. "It's not illegal. Yet!"

"And when prohibition occurs," Elizabeth joined in, "the violence toward women and children will end."

"I'm not certain that's the case."

"How could it *not* be?" a woman shouted from the back.

"Well, let me paraphrase an old Danish saying, 'When wine is legally banned, men will sin the more in secret.'"

"You have no problem," Elizabeth asked, voice critical, "with a man 's freedom to walk into a bar and consume liquor, then return home intoxicated and potentially dangerous?"

"What most bothers *me*," I admitted, "Is that such places are restricted. In my mind, we ought to fight for the right to drink alongside the men. Isn't that true 'equality'?"

"Tell me," a male attendee inquired, "would you *really* want to enter a saloon and knock down raw rotgut?"

"Not necessarily! But the other night, I dined at the legendary Delmonico's as the guest of a respected gentleman. Had I shown up on my own, or with some female friend, I would have been denied entrance. Now, *that* does offend me!"

HENRY: SATURDAY; FEBRUARY 9, 1901

"So tonight's the big night," James sighed. After he and I parted company with the others, we proceeded side by side in the direction of Mrs. Trumbell's. He whistling, me coughing.

"For Eloise, you mean?"

"Yeah. From the Plaza to the Met and back again."

"So what will the future bring?"

"Guess we'll have to wait and learn."

"Hopefully, Eloise will show at Coney tomorrow."

"Oh, she'll be there. No doubt 'bout that."

"Yep. *Always* true to her word."

"That'll never change. But whether we'll learn that she's still ours, or instead heading off to Italy with Caruso . . ."


ELOISE: SATURDAY; FEBRUARY 9, 1901

"What's your point, dear?" my self-appointed adversary replied. The matron pronouced that final word with calculated disdain.

"Only that *total equality* is what I believe women ought to crusade for. The right to vote or merely enjoy a snort."

"Do you have any idea how many women are abused by alcoholic husbands each and every day?"

"I'm sure. But there are also situations in which women who drink violently assault their men."

"Name even *one* such case," a disgruntled man called out.

"'Calamity' Jane Canary and James Butler Hickock of the Dakota territories. Likely you've heard of them? Well, whenever Martha Jane reached for a bottle, he'd show up the next day bruised. Never once the other way around."

*Oh, God! Have I've given my Western identity away? Why can't I ever learn to keep my big mouth shut!*


JAMES: SATURDAY; FEBRUARY 9, 1901

"Hey," a New Yorker in a subdued orange felt derby hat, a loosely fitted three piece charcoal grey suit, and patent leather shoes addressed us as Henry and I passed under the Washington Square Arch. "Did anyone ever tell you that you fellas look just like Butch Cassidy and the Sundance Kid?"

"Since that picture of them was published in the paper," I replied, "we've been hearin' that constantly."

"The resemblance in amazing," he marveled.

"Maybe we just might be them," Henry suggested.

"Oh, sure. Almost!"

"Well, why not?"

"If they are actually are in New York, they'll be hidden away deep in a cellar someplace."

"Course you must be right about that."

"Well, gentlemen, have a good day." Smiling, the spiffy Manhattanite wandered off to his own personal adventures. And we proceeded to our own.

ELOISE: SATURDAY; FEBRUARY 9, 1901

"That's merely an exception which proves the rule," a woman on the meeting room's far side insisted.

Susan assumed a defensive tone. "For expediency's sake, we *have* forged an alignment with the Prohibition forces. If we assist Carrie Nation, she and her anti-alcohol activists will join our cause to win the vote. There is strength in numbers!"

"But most men, even the best, enjoy a drink now and then. Won't this stance turn the most liberal-minded fellows against Suffrage if they know it will lead to Prohibition?"

"That's a risk we must take for now," Susan pronounced.

"It all sounds so *political.*"

"Precisely, Eloise," answered Elizabeth. "*Everything* in life, as you will learn, is political."

"And, as Charles Warner put it," Susan hastily finished, "'politics makes for strange bedfellows.'"

I sensed a hesitancy about aligning with the Suffragists, owing to their elitist attitude as women of privilege and now this as well. I would walk out of this meeting, which I had so eagerly anticipated, as emotionally downtrodden as I had been thrilled upon arrival. Could I accept their position on this issue, which I disagreed with entirely, for the sake of the vote? I wasn't certain. This, I'd have to think about, long and hard.

But not until tomorrow! Tonight will be a fairytale come true as a lifelong dream of glorious romance transforms into reality, at least for several wonderful hours.

—INTERLUDE—

BAT: OCTOBER 25, 1921

*Regarding Joe Petrosino, the man and his significance, I've explained how he eventually grasped the Mafia's wave of influence was not local, regional, state-wide, or even an infection on our own national turf. In fact, La Cosa Nostra had emerged*

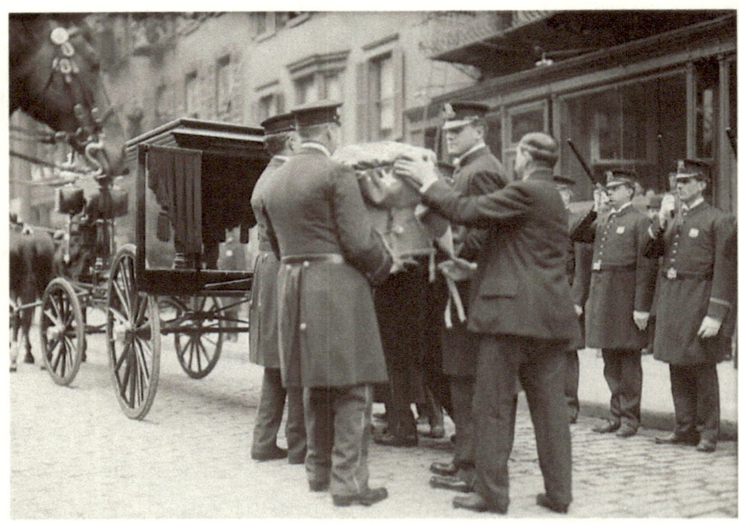

FUNERAL FOR A HERO: When Joseph Petrosino was murdered in Sicily while attempting to prove that the Mafia had transformed from a local gang into an international crime organization, his body was sent back to New York for a burial worthy of a great man.

*as a global network. One which, if left to its own devices, might in due time control the world. Yet when Joe encouraged Manhatten's newspaper editors to print an expose, they refused on the grounds of insufficient evidence.*

*So Joe set to acquiring documentation on Ferro and others whose journeys back and forth across the ocean would prove his theory. With such proof in hand, he could force the media to belatedly alert the world as to the full extent of "organized crime." That's when Petrosino received orders (some say from Roosevelt himself) regarding a secret mission. Joe traveled to Palermo to amass the ultimate proof that this yet-invisible threat did exist.*

*A note from some anonymous informer promised the very information Joe sought if this American detective would arrive alone at Sicily's isolated Piazza Marina for a midnight appointment. Smelling a rat but unable to resist the lure, Joe agreed only to find his arch enemy patiently waiting. Petrosino did not 'go out' without a fight, getting off a single shot before bullets sent him rolling down the steps.*

*Yet the assassination that ended the career of this dedicated hero did not have its intended effect. Immediately, several inspired reporters printed articles claiming that Petrosino's murder had been ordered by members of the Morello and Terranova families; their agents resided not only in Palermo but also New York and other American cities. As a result, papers across America decided to likewise publish the story. In death, Joe achieved the victory that had eluded him in life.*

*Not only was The Mafia international, the world now knew. More threatening still, local crime lords remained in contact with, and owed loyalty to, a yet unknown boss of bosses in The Old Country.*

*As a result, the very nature of crime-busting altered. America's own Federal Bureau of Investigation soon challenged the Mafia. Why, even those who'd fought J.P. admitted begrudging admiration for him. On his death-bed several years later, Ferro confessed to killing one whom he respected as "a most gallant man." Theodore Roosevelt provided an appropriate epitaph, "Here was a great and good man. I knew him for years, and he did not know the name of fear." In my own column, I noted, "Because of his work, nearly a hundred gangsters from Little Italy have been deported. Because of his crusade, he had become a marked man. Yet the public uproar against La Cosa Nostra and demands for a police unit willing to fight them here, there, and everywhere proved that Joe did not die in vain."*

*What I have told you tonight, Lolly, is the true story of how Joe's pledge to bring down the Black Hand began. As well as the prominent role a woman of integrity played in it. A woman whom to this day, in abject irony, is along with Belle Starr and Pearl Hart known far and wide as a notorious Bandit Queen.*

# PART ELEVEN:
# SATURDAY NIGHT AND SUNDAY MORNING

HENRY: SATURDAY; JANUARY 9, 1901

"Look," I said as I followed James into the lobby. At the check-in desk, a sealed envelope awaited on the counter, with "ELOISE LONG: CONFIDENTIAL" embossed across its center. In smaller print, a return address had been scribbled on the top left-hand side: "G.L. Lakeland; c/o The Edison Studio."

"Likely, an invitation for Eloise to report for work."

"Don't know that for certain. Could be a rejection."

"Hah! Ain't likely."

"Not considering how he eyed our woman last Sunday."

"Anyway, now we have competition from the serious-minded Suffragists, the glamour of moving pictures, and the seductive lure of a world-famous lothario."

"Let's hang in there and hope for the best." I picked up the letter. "Meanwhile, what to do with *this*?"


ELOISE: SATURDAY; FEBRUARY 9, 1901

Cinderella in her coach, with the pistoleros, Lefors and Siringo, rather than mice transformed into drivers. So I thought to myself as an elaborate Hansom swept me through a delicate snowfall. Off not to Prince Charming's castle (in a manner of speaking, I'd just now departed such a palace, the Plaza), but the Metropolitan Opera at 39th and Broadway.

Here would begin every smalltown girl's (and, more likely than not, many grown women as well) most fantastical dream of a wondrous, even perfect, evening.

First, as Caruso's guest of honor while the world-class tenor performs the villainous 'Duke,' a heartless seducer of women, in *Rigoletto*. A sordid spectacle of forbidden love and anguished lust adapted to opera seventy years ago by Giussepe Verdi and a gifted librettist, Francesa Maria Piavi. Derived from a tragic tale by France's literary giant, Victor Hugo, whose *Les Miserables* had enlightened me as to the extent many people suffer under the world's money-based system.

*Rigoletto*, I knew to be a story that examines the give-and-take between a cosmic fatalism and an individual's free will. These the opposing concepts I've struggled with my entire life, and which have reached a point of no return ever since my arrival in New York.


JAMES: SATURDAY; FEBRUARY 9, 1901

"I'd imagine that, like me, you'd love to tear it open and know for certain," said Henry.

"Yeah. But to do that would be to betray a trust."

"And, likely, we'd lose her forever."

So James slipped the missive, still tightly sealed, into his inner-jacket pocket. Tomorrow, he'd hand it to Eloise at our Coney Island reunion.

*Then we'd discuss the implications for our mutual future. If there would indeed be one following her sojourn tonight.*


ELOISE: SATURDAY; FEBRUARY 9, 1901

Elegant women and men halted in their promenade toward the great magnet of The Met to turn and gaze at the dazzling beauty rumored to be Caruso's inamorata. Prestigious members of families of industry, politics, and democratic capitalism—the Morgans, Vanderbilts, and the Roosevelts among them—were all momentarily spellbound by *me*. Each man wishing he could share my company tonight. Every woman dreaming of a ride in Caruso's spectacular carriage . . . of being *me!*

All these nouveaux elites here, together, on what would be recalled as the moment when Manhattan earned its reputation as the heart of world culture. How I adored it!

*Once upon a time in Manhattan!*

A mere frontier community several centuries ago, when buffalo still roamed and Native Longhouses were plentiful along tranquil lakeshores. The land later owned by wealthy Dutch, German, and English farmers. Then, industry appeared. The machine age began. Technology. Modern Times. *New York, New York*: And me at the center of everyone's attention at this prime moment in the city's history.

*Every dog has its day, as the saying goes. Unless, as Bat once quipped, there are more dogs than there are days.*


HENRY: SATURDAY; FEBRUARY 9, 1901

"Come on upstairs for a drink," James suggested. "I don't cotton to the thought of being alone right now."

"Ah, maybe I should head back to Bat's place."

"What for?"

"Safety's sake. Don't know who might be spying on us."

*That's what I said. The real reason, tempting to me yet also terrifying, I still could not express in words.*

"Is that what you really want to do, pard?"

"No," I admitted, following him up the staircase. "I'm not in the mood to be alone, either."

*Once more, our openly admitted devotion of Miss Etta was augumented by what we still found impossible to articulate.*

ELOISE: SATURDAY; FEBRUARY 9, 1901

Tonight, attendees would sit in three tiers of velvet-lined boxes, they constituting the new order of things in an emergent Manhattan. More than two decades ago, these recently wealthy families—having proceeded from rags to riches through such 'vulgar' endeavors as management of railroads—were denied the honor of purchasing seats at the Academy of Music opera-house, located on the northwest corner of East 14th Street and Irving Place. In that uninspired structure, built in the 1850's, only the Old Guard—Anglos, Nords, and pure Teutons, able to trace their bloodlines back to founders of New Amsterdam—were permitted to enter, 4000 at a time.

Meeting one night at Delmonico's, the new giants of industry collectively created an alternative paradigm City in which money, hard-earned as well as inherited, would be equally respected. How uniquely *American* that would be! They were proven correct. In an incredible irony, The old Academy's status diminished. Once revered families looked on helplessly as their fortunes were lost in a series of stock market losses and bank failures. As a result, ticket sales dropped.

Make way for the future; The Met supplanted its predessor as the Big Apple's foremost hub of European-style culture, fittingly adjusted for 20th Century patrons. As for the Academy, that once renown earlier venue fell into ruin. Reduced to a home for Vaudeville and then, on a lower level still, Burlesque.

ART COMES TO MANHATTAN: Opera in N.Y.C. was at last salvaged from the old elite and offered to the nouveau riche as the balance of power shifted from 'birthright' to 'success,' American Dream' fashion.

*Proof that what goes around* does *come around. Also, that absolutely nothing lasts forever.*

JAMES: SATURDAY; FEBRUARY 9, 1901

"What . . . in the name of God . . . has happened here?"

As Henry and I ascended the stairwell to the second floor, we chanced to meet Mrs. Trumbell. She stood stock-still by the suite's half open door, weeping. Our landlady glanced over at us and, with a weary sweep of her hand, pointed inside.

"Look!" she commanded.

We stepped closer and turned in unision to do so. There, bawling like his mother, stood Samson. As Henry and I entered, we grasped the cause of such consternation. On the hardwood floor lay Ronald's lifeless body, face down, his throat sliced. Blood trickled onto an Oriental rug.

If nothing else, I now understood why Ronald had not been following me around the city.

ELOISE: SATURDAY; FEBRUARY 9, 1901

How fitting that as Enrico stepped onstage, this modern celebrity and 'serious' artist mirrored those who had arrived to hear him. Born a peasant and self-trained, not a graduate from some esteemed musical academy. Now adorned in an elegant silken costume, he let loose with a shattering baritone.

*In America, and the brave new world even now emerging, a man's origins mean nothing. Worldly accomplishments? Everything!*

And, as I basked in the proceedings that would inevitably follow this performance, shortly to become my bedmate.

There existed the public persona of Enrico which anyone who could afford a ticket might experience. Also, a secret side of this man-of-the-moment that would belong exclusively to *me*. Why? No other reason than that I was born beautiful.

*How superficial are the ways of the world. Yet, I must add, how fortunate— blessed even—am I to possess this quality!*

HENRY: SATURDAY; FEBRUARY 9, 1901

"But who—?" I asked, shaken.

"Isn't it obvious?" James replied. "Recall what Lupo the Wolf vowed when Petrosino arrested him."

"I'll be avenged on the lot of you!"

"Somehow, his minions must've learned we reside here."

"So the Soldati showed up, assumed the man they happened upon to be either you or me, mistakenly murdering Ronald."

"With the other scheduled as their next victim."

"That, or . . . *Eloise*."

*My partner and I shuddered at the thought that any harm might come to her. Particularly if our decision to work as deputies led to such an atrocity. That'd make us complicit.*


ELOISE: SATURDAY; FEBRUARY 9, 1901

"My Night with Enrico Caruso!" What a headline that might make for Bat's column, if I dared risk exposure. Would I truly belong to The Great Tenor tonight? Body and soul . . .

If that were so, though, why did I pin on the watch my boys had gifted me, keeping them near in spirit?

Then, out of nowhere a wild thought occurred:

*What would your mother say if she could see you now? Would she be amazed, horrified, or perhaps a bit of both?*


JAMES: SATURDAY; FEBRUARY 9, 1901

"What am I to do?" Mrs. Trumbell gasped. "Should word of this get out, no decent people will ever board here again."

"Calm down," I commanded, as always assuming the role of leader. "Has anyone else seen the body?" The desparate woman shook her head 'no.' "Maybe we can keep this quiet."

"But how—"

"First things first. Let's clean up the evidence."

"Wouldn't it be wiser to contact Bat? Or Petrosino?"

"Do so, Henry, and we'll completely expose ourselves. We might even be blamed for what happened."

"Which wouldn't bode well for Eloise."

"Oh, God! Oh, God! Oh, God!"

"Easy, Samson," Henry sighed. "We'll get through this."

"We're agreed, then," I asserted, closing and locking the door. I slipped off my jacket, drew several towels from a nearby rack, and knelt to begin the gruesome task of removing all trace of the crime.


ELOISE: SATURDAY; FEBRUARY 9, 1901

How frustrated, I knew, Enrico has been. So near and yet so far from his heart's desire. Though perhaps 'heart' is not the most appropriate organ I should reference.

I'm sorry, dream lover. *But, can you understand?*

How horrible it would have been to surrender too soon. Allow you to you think of me as another easy conquest. As we ride back to the Plaza in our Hansom, those twinkling stars in the midnight-blue sky illuminate our storybook moment. Proving dreams can come true. If only, though, on rare occasion.


HENRY: SATURDAY; FEBRUARY 9, 1901

"I want to call Dag, let her know what happened—"

"Hold off, pard, at least for now. Go wet more towels."

"What about the body?" asked Mrs. Trumbell.

"Don't worry, mother," Samson insisted. "I'll wrap him in a rug, carry the corpse to the river, and dump it there."

"Oh, that my boy should have to perform such a task."

"Do you think that'd be for the best, Mr. Long?"

Following a moment of silence, I nodded yes.


ELOISE: SATURDAY; FEBRUARY 9, 1901

I will not let my mind stray to those issues that caused me such consternation earlier today.

I will block from my memory those downtown streets where members of the Mafia flexed their muscles.

I will not consider the boys, or my love for each.

I will not think on the bigots who protested the arrival of immigrants in the shadow of Lady Liberty.

I will not harp on the possibility of instantaneous celebrity should I win a role in Edison's movie.

*I will embrace the moment. And seize the day. Or, more correctly, the night.*

*I will not worry about the Movement's stance on alcohol. Or the base prejudices that infect even such an elite crowd.*

As the Persian poet Omar Khayyam described an evening such as this, I will surrender to the realm of the senses.

*'A glass of wine, a crust of bread, and thou,' Enrico. Not in some wilderness but at the as yet unfinished Plaza. A 20th Century Xanadu that, when completed, will overlook the isle of Manhattan. And silently suggest to all who witness its magnitude: work hard. Refuse to fail. And perhaps, if luck is with you, you will someday achieve the status to step inside.*


JAMES: SATURDAY; FEBRUARY 9, 1901

"Try your best to avoid anyone outside," I cautioned Samson, still shaken. "Most particularly law officers."

"I know all the back alleys between here and the Bowery."

With that, Samson crawled through the rear window, the tightly wrapped corpse draped over his left shoulder. Cautiously, he made his way down the rickety fire escape. I watched until Samson disapeared from sight, then turned to face the others.

"Tell me what to do, pard," whispered Henry.

"In a few minutes, take the same route as Samson. Then make your way to Bat's." Shortly, Henry, too, was gone.

"I can't handle being alone now," Mrs. Trumbell sobbed.

"You won't be. I'll remain here until your son returns."

"And afterward?"

"I'll head across the hall and try to get some sleep."

"In the meantime, please . . . *hold* me."

I did as requested. She whimpered but did not cry again. Then, to my surprise, Mrs. Trumbell said, "If only we could be here like this . . . *forever!*"

"You mean, you, me, and all the money in your safe?"

"I'd settle for you alone."

For the first time, I sensed a glint of humanity in her. As well as a possible solution to one of our problems.

ELOISE: Sunday; February 10, 1901

*My dear Eloise . . . if that is indeed your name?*

*What a divine pleasure to meet such a remarkable woman! Whoever you are, by the time you wake and read this, I will be gone. To spend the remainder of my time in New York at the Kensington, where I was scheduled to reside until Roosevelt explained an attempt to kidnap me there would be likely.*

*Last night was a dream come true . . . for you, I hope and trust, as well as for me . . . and, as such, a once-in-a-lifetime experience. For to try and repeat the bliss we knew must fail. Such a special union can only occur once.*

*In fact, Eloise, I do share my life with a woman, and have done so for the past three years. Her maiden name, Ada Giachetti, she like me is a native of Naples. A person of my own heritage and nationality. Moreover, we have a two-year-old son whom I worship more than life itself.*

*Now that the planned abduction has been thwarted, I'll no longer require bodyguards. Mr. Lefors and Mr. Siringo are free to return to the mission that brought them to New York—their pursuit of the outlaw woman, Etta Place.*

Etta . . . Eloise?

*Might the similarity of these names be coincidence? Or are you indeed the heroine of Mr. Buntline's lurid books?*

*I do not know. Nor do I wish to. I so love a mystery!*
*Despise me for this, if you will. Or if you must.*
*Or love me, if you choose to, as I do you.*
*Cherish our time together. And, as the poet Wordsworth put it, draw strength from what remains behind.*
*Yours eternally, Enrico.*
*P.S. I hope you will not be annoyed that I have taken a single object to remind me of you.*

How horrified I was to discover my silver-lined lapel watch missing. Adding, as the saying goes, insult to injury.

HENRY: SUNDAY; FEBRUARY 10, 1901

When Bat first brought James and myself to Coney Island, I made a mental note. We must return to this Pleasure Trove with Eloise. Now, thanks to an untimely thaw and the unique quietude of an early Sunday morn, we decided to take the risk.

For once, Bat's wife accompanied us. Emma proved to be in considerably higher spirits than our own inamorata, Eloise, who appeared moody and distracted. Lost in thought, less upset or angry than aloof. Unable to enjoy the gaiety around us as ordinary folks, arriving from church services, gathered here to pursue an aspect of life ever more accessible to the vast working classes: *fun.*

Of a simple and relatively inexpensive sort. Yet 'fun' all the same. A weekly holiday for the masses.

"Etta?" I cautiously asked. "Are you alright?"

"I'm fine," she curtly responded. Obviously, that was not the case.

"She'll tell us in her own good time," whispered James.

ELOISE: SUNDAY; FEBRUARY 10, 1901

The five of us had met at ten o'clock near a towering ferris wheel. An eighth of a mile away, The Switchback Railway—a reconfiguration of one of those compact trains in use over at Pennsylvania's coal-mining fields—whipped visitors in wide circles on America's first thrill ride. The weather did not prove pleasant enough to swim, though enough sunlight passed through grey clouds to make for an agreeable sojourn.

"So wonderful to finally meet you in person," said Emma.

"My sentiments exactly."

How surprised I'd been to discover that Mrs. Masterson was not the sort of glamorous woman I'd expected. Her ovular face appeared heavily made up, as if to cover old scars.

"I understand you're staying at the Plaza!"

"I was," I managed to answer. "Not now."

"Oh!" Sensing this was a subject I wished to avoid, Emma asked no more questions, to my great relief.

## JAMES: SUNDAY; FEBRUARY 10, 1901

At noon, we unpacked Emma's picnic basket, enjoying cold chicken, garden salad, Boston-style beans, and crisp home-baked bicuits. We sat in a circle on beach towels. In time, Henry and I played with a large inflated ball, such items available for rent at numerous concession stands. Eloise and Emma exchanged small talk. Bat sat apart, watching over the situation as an unofficial sentry. We had chosen an area far from most visitors who crowded together along the sandy beach, observing the tide as it methodically swept in and out.

Nearby children sipped root beers or stuffed Nathan's hot dogs into their faces. Those whose parents could afford the 15 cent expense were treated to pony rides or a turn on the new tilt-a-wheel. Cheerfully, my partner and I tossed the medicine ball back and forth until we grew bored. At that point we slipped off our shirts, engaging in mock fisticuffs.

"They truly were *made* for each other, don't you think?" I heard Eloise confide to Emma. Something in the manner in which she spoke filled me with dread, though I wasn't certain why.

"BY THE SEA, BY THE SEA . . .": Even during the winter months, Manhattanites would head for Coney Island's shoreline, taking advantage of occasional mild weather to enjoy a day at the beach.

ELOISE: SUNDAY; FEBRUARY 10, 1901

"As the saying goes," Emma noted, "boys will be boys."

"But don't at least a few of them transition to manhood?"

"Sometimes, when Bat and I are alone, I think that may be possible. Shortly, though, he's up and off to the gym to watch fighters spar. Or heading out to
round-up more bad-guys."

"Yet still we go on hoping."

Soon, James and Henry tired of their mock boxing match and seated themselves on either side of Bat. They conversed about pugilism, amateur as well as
professional. Meanwhile, I attempted to come to grips with a new dimension to
their long relationship: a heightened physicality I'd become ever more aware of.
One more issue for me to process on this difficult 'morning after,' so to speak.
My long-dreamed of fantasy now suddenly concluded; stark reality once again
setting in.


HENRY: SUNDAY; FEBRUARY 10, 1901

"Watching you two dance on the shore gave me an idea," Bat said, eyes
twinkling with inspiration.

"Share," I replied.

"As you well know, I've been trying to discover some way by which I can
raise the respectability of my favorite sport."

"And our clowning around set you to considering that?"

"Necessity is the mother of invention, Henry."

"Where are you goin' with this?"

"Well, James, as I see it, the best way to accomplish my goal would be to
stage a big match in Madison Square Garden."

"But how could you make something like that happen?"

"Keep in mind, Henry. Buffalo Bill loves to introduce famous frontiersman
into his mix. Bill Hickok and Texas Jack Oluhandru, among 'em. Even the late,
great Sitting Bull."

"Rumor is that he'll soon add blacks," I said, "to give the public a true sense
of the west's full spectrum."

"I surely hope so! Well, boys! What if as a special treat Cody were to host
Butch Cassidy and the Sundance Kid as guest stars?"

"What might we be expected to do? Shoot it out?"

"James and I know from experience that won't work."

"Nothing so deadly. How about a boxing match?"

ELOISE: SUNDAY; FEBRUARY 10, 1901

"Hah! The tried and true face-off, if this time without guns." I responded as Emma and I moved our towels closer.

"What's wrong with that?" asked Henry.

"The very thing I've been trying to draw you away from."

"Well," Emma noted, "at least no one ends up dead."

"You're forgetting that Siringo and Lefors are in town."

"They stopped by my office to say 'hello.' Now that their duties as Caruso's bodyguards are finished, James, their only interest is in arresting Etta for murder."

"My guess?" Henry said. "Once they learn of the bout you propose, they'll attend, hoping to locate her there."

"So what?" I interrupted, growing intrigued by the idea. "I'm set to play Annie Oakley that night. They'll think I'm her. 'Etta' will be 'gone,' for all purposes."

"When would you schedule this for?"

"The evening before you sail. Soon as Eloise is done with her exhibit, we'll spirit her out the back way, then down to the docks. After the match, you and Butch will join her."

"In my opinion," Emma laughed, "such a ruse is just crazy enough that it might actually work."


JAMES: SUNDAY; FEBRUARY 10, 1901

We relaxed in relative tranquility for the remainder of the day, each privately considering this odd yet appealing strategy. As evening descended, one by one the multitude of visitors packed up their beach umbrellas and picnic baskets, heading home or moving on to the many diversions offered by Coney at night. The park brightened with low gaslights, a holdover from *its quaint past* as well as recently installed lines of bright electric lights. Past and future overlapping.

Now, everything from ballroom dancing and elaborate stage shows to games of chance and wax museums lined the boardwalk. These attractions, also 'The Fights,' presented the masses with a variety of possibilities until the midnight hour.

We passed by such distractions, intent on choosing a restaurant from the dozen or so available. Bat suggested a popular favorite, Rudi Hollerbauch's Old World Emporium, which he described as a lavish and well-regarded biergarten. Bat explained that visitors could enjoy a broad perspective on the passersbys through its oversized windows.

ELOISE: SUNDAY; FEBRUARY 10, 1901

Diners displayed fashions from native lands: Caribbean hues of turquoise, yellow, and pink; Mediterranean shades of orange, brown, and beige. Also present were a few Asians, Native Americans, and Africans. Most, though, were of the white working class, drawn from the city and new suburbs, stretching ever further eastward across Long Island. I noticed that each group kept to their own, forming tight little cliques, ignoring if tolerant of the others. America in miniature.

*Wouldn't it be better still if they mixed and matched? Then, we might* truly *become the world's melting pot.*

HENRY: SUNDAY; FEBRUARY 10, 1901

Pretty young blondes in Bavarian costumes darted about, jotting down orders, shortly returning to deliver meals to eager customers. Old World folk songs were performed by a seven piece band; the musicians, positioned on an

INTERNATIONAL CUISINE: A wide variety of ethnic possibilities, ranging in price from cheap to expensive, were crowned by the grand German-Austrian 'palace.'

elevated stage, were dressed as Alpine mountaineers. I recognized one piece, "Schwesterien," I'd heard played at a tavern down in Gruene, Texas.

"I have something to deliver," James whispered to Eloise while the rest of us glanced over an elaborate menu. Rudi's offered pitchers of an imported German brew, Zwickl Festbock, from a 400-year-old world brewery, as well as authentic middle-European fare. Heaping platters of sauerbraten in gingersnap gravy, hot and cold potato salad; Schnitzel with spaeztel.

As a hearty eater, I couldn't wait to get started. James, however, showed no interest in the meal. Eloise's eyes lit up with anticipation as he drew the letter from his inner-jacket pocket. She accepted the missive, hesitating, eyes shut tight for a long time before daring to open the envelope.

"So?" James asked following a lengthy silence.

"I've got the job," she sighed with an odd combination of relief and anxiousness. "*If* I choose to take it."


ELOISE: MONDAY; FEBRUARY 11, 1901

Early on Monday, I arrived at The Edison Studios where E.S. again escorted me to the Black Maria. Once inside, he led me to Mr. Lakeland's office, then exited. Waved in by the executive, I found myself inside a stale, cold circular room.

"Good morning, Etta."

"Same to you, Mr. Lake—"

"Anything wrong?" he asked as I took a seat across from a desk cluttered with scripts, rolls of film, and props for the upcoming project, including several Colt .44 pistols.

"Only that my name is 'Eloise.'"

"Oh, that!" He laughed; I sensed a hint of cynicism. "See, in this industry, the moment a person is cast, the director ceases to address that actor by his or her given name. Rather, the 'role.' See, that's who you'll be playing."


HENRY: MONDAY; FEBRUARY 11, 1901

"I didn't expect to see you again, Henry," the tough cop said as we sat together in a dim Little Italy eatery.

"Nor I you, Joseph. But I must ask a favor."

"You were essential in capturing Lupo and his thugs, as well as rescuing me. There is nothing I can deny you."

Over cool beers and plates heaped high with Genoa Salami, black olives, and red onions, along with garlic bread fresh from the oven, I related what we discovered at the boarding house. A man had been murdered in cold blood. He was family, that foremost in my mind. Second? He died in my stead.

"There, Joseph, but for the grace of God go I."

"You can't be certain that the Mafia killed him."

"Recall the Wolf's threat. Now, I must respond in kind."

ELOISE: MONDAY; FEBRUARY 11, 1901

"Still, why did you choose *that* name in particular?"

"Since the day we shot your screen-test, a great deal has transpired. You are aware, I assume, that the newspapers have printed a photograph of Wyoming's legendary Wild Bunch?"

"I did see that, yes."

"Now, as I've already told you, the film we are about to shoot . . . no pun intended! . . . was inspired by that gang's disastrous final robbery."

"But I auditioned for the role of a girl who discovers her telegraph-operator father tied up by outlaws."

"Well, we've reconceived the project, as well as your part, owing to this unexpected free publicity."

"I'm all ears," I said, trying my best to conceal a shudder of fear.

JAMES/BUTCH: MONDAY; FEBRUARY 11, 1901

"Mr. Cassidy! May I have a moment of your time?"

At noon, I'd exited the boarding house and headed toward Park Row to speak with Bat. As I passed under the Washington Square Arch, a figure bolted forward from the thick shrubbery. His sudden appearance shocked me, though not nearly so much as that he'd addressed me by my outlaw monicker. "You must be mistaken, sir. I'm James—"

"You're Butch Cassidy of the Wild Bunch and you know it. More significantly, so do I."

"If you're referring to the picture in the newspapers the other day, believe me; you aren't the first person to stop me on the street owing to the resemblance. So if you'll excuse—" I attempted to navigate around him but the incorrigible fellow countered my movement. We stood face to face. "I *know* you!"

"My name's DeFly. Does that ring a bell?"

I struggled to recall where I'd heard that. Then it came to me. "You're the photographer who took those portraits a week ago."

ELOISE/ETTA: MONDAY; FEBRUARY 11, 1901

"Originally, we intended to make a five to ten minute feature. Now, we're hoping for twelve minutes running time, presented in what will be Manhattan's first movie theater."

"Oh! You won't be sending it around to Nickelodeons?"

"That era has peaked. In France, a pair of brothers named Lumiere developed a machine that allows films to be projected onto a screen by way of a directed light-source."

"My, my. What *will* they think of *next?*"

"Sound. But back to the present. Initially that girl who freed her father was the only female in the script. Our expanded version will include Etta Place, lover of Butch Cassidy and the Sundance Kid."

"Etta Place," I stammered, biting my tongue. So if I continued with the project, I would be playing . . . me*!*

HENRY/SUNDANCE: MONDAY; FEBRUARY 11, 1901

"When they realize they've murdered the wrong man, Joseph, they'll come back for me."

"I could round up all three and hold them for a limited time while their lawyers petition for release. Bat mentioned you'll be sailing shortly. You'd be long gone before—"

"That's not what I want."

"What, then?"

"I'm going to kill each before I leave."

"Please, my friend," Joe gasped. "Do not speak so—"

"This is *personal.*"

"Henry! Now you sound like one of the Mafiosos. Such vengeance, La Cosa Nostra refers to as *Vendetta.*"

"Where I hail from, we call it the Code of the West."

ETTA: MONDAY; FEBRUARY 11, 1901

"The Maverick Queen. A beautiful female desperado. That will add a whole new dimension to our film."

"And to your box-office profits."

"Hey! You *are* catching on to contemporary Show Biz."

"But if your focus is on the robbery, how can she—"

"E.S. and I have, in our recent pictures, been toying with a new concept we call 'the cross-cut.' We'll shoot the robbery first, then another sequence in which the paramour will be at Hole in the Wall, dreaming of her lovers."

"And intercut them later, in the editing room?"

"You *do* understand the process! Well, we're all agreed. You're perfect for that role."

BUTCH: MONDAY; FEBRUARY 11, 1901

"How'd you track me down?"

"No need to go into it now. The point is, here I am."

"Do your damndest, but be aware. The authorities in New York have no reason to arrest me or my partner."

"You're forgetting something."

From beneath his overcoat, DeFly whipped out a copy of one of the photographs. There, clear as the light of early morn, were we three: me, Sundance, and Etta, all smiling.

"Oh, no."

"Pinkerton agents Joe Lefors and Charles Siringo are in Manhattan searching for her even as we speak. The only problem for the lawmen is that nobody can identify the 'lady' by sight. But they will should this image fall into their hands."

ETTA: MONDAY; FEBRUARY 11, 1901

"I came here today to accept the role that I auditioned for. But, now? Perhaps I ought to withdraw."

"Why? You have all the necessary qualities: Beauty, a keen formidability, piercing dark eyes, a pleasing shape—"

"But for a lady like myself to incarnate a *criminal*?"

"We want you and no one else for the part."

"Sorry, but, no. I'm leaving."

"Nobody's stopping you."

"First, though, I'd like my picture back."

"I'm not sure where it is. And I do not have time now to embark on a search. Be here next Tuesday morning. That's when we begin our shoot, with or without you."

"You'll return it then? Whether I play the role or not?"

"That's what I said. You'll head back to Manhattan, now?"

"Actually. I'm decided to travel to Connecticut today."

"On business?"

"More on the order of a sentimental journey."

SUNDANCE: MONDAY; FEBRUARY 11, 1901

"I want to know more about the three men who kidnapped you. Let's begin with one of them."

"Which—?"

"Doesn't matter. It's like choosing which rat I'm going to shoot first at the city dump."

"But this goes against the grain of everything I believe in. Law and order. Due process. A fair trial."

"We tried that Friday night. A lawyer sprung them."

"They will have their day in court. I promise you—"

"Not if I get to them first. Give me something, Joe. The smallest detail. Something for me to go on."

"I can't," he all but wept.

"You can. You must! Remember what you said only minutes ago? You owe me your life. Alright, then. Honor that debt."

—INTERLUDE—

BAT: OCTOBER 25, 1921

*No one is ever born with a name like 'Lupo the Wolf'; a man must earn such a title. Which is precisely what Ignazio Saietto did following his birth in Palermo on March 21, 1877. Most Sicilian-born members of The Black Hand carved out niches for themselves in New York, Chicago, and other cities with a speciality: loansharking, bank and armored car robberies, various forms of thievery ranging from street crime to break-ins, murder for hire, prostitution, gambling, and shake-downs, to name a few. Lupo, though, proved himself a true exception from the moment he stepped off an overcrowded boat and set foot in lower Manhattan. Others already established in Little Italy—most notably Giusepe "Old Clutch Hand" Morello*

*with his vast crime family—were rendered obsolete by Saietto's all-encompassing ambitions and the wily strategies he developed to corner the market on every racket.*

*For those original Mustachios in their sharp white suits and multi-colored ties, as well as members of the other developing Five Families, Lupo presented a far more dangerous threat than the police. Once having risen to the very top of the criminal heap, he stretched La Cosa Nostra's influence from their downtown haunts all the way to Harlem, above 110th St. There, the neighborhood's black residents, with their unique*

THE FIRST 'GODFATHER': Lupo 'the Wolf' lorded it over Little Italy until the U.S. government shipped the Mafioso back to Sicily, circa 1902.

*jazz clubs, were forced to operate under the greasy thumb of what had come to be called The Mob.*

*Other crime bosses hired thugs to carry out their dirty work. Unlike them, Ignazio enjoyed performing executions (often preceded by torture) personally, with more than 60 credited to him. Salvatore Maranzano, a much-feared Don, first used The Wolf monicker for Lupo when that older, flamboyantly dressed musketeer of the downtown streets realized his traditional approach of grandeur to the citizenry could not compete with Lupo's rapacious, capricious, pugnacious style.*

*It's doubtful any of the former bosses, including those I've mentioned, would have attempted to kidnap a beloved figure like Caruso. For to do so spit in the face of the Italian people. That explains why during the foiled abduction the working class rose up in anger. Such immigrants respected their homeland and its favorite sons. There were, after all, limits to what one could accept, even from The Mafia. You see, Lolly, previous to Lupo, members of the criminal world had referred to themselves as Men of Respect. No such term could describe the Wolf. It mattered not to him that Enrico reigned as Italy's bright light in the cultural scene; the Tenor was perceived as prey. Nothing more, nothing less.*

*Even today, he exists beyond the reach of the law. And continues to spread his activities beyond Manhattan. Informers report that he currently runs a sophisticated counterfeit ring up in the Catskills. Lupo spent bundles of cash in isolated villages to buy the silence of Protestant Bible thumpers residing there. Power walks; money talks.*

*For that is the true goal of the Mafia today—to not only dominate crime in big city America but rural enclaves as well. At which point the Mob becomes synonymous with Big Business.*

*Lolly, I share this so you can fully comprehend what sort of a man . . . if that term applies . . . Lupo was twenty years ago. Then, a young turk who scoffed at attempts by T.R., Petrosino, and myself to curb him. Even as an easygoing cowboy nicknamed Sundance dared take on the Black Hand's leader. Harry Longabaugh's temper stretched to the point that he would willingly embark on a mission to do something he never had before—coldly take the life of another person.*

# PART TWELVE: STRANGE HOMECOMING

"Which among us is not forever a stranger and alone
after leaving the place where we were born?"

—Thomas Wolf

"Next stop, New Haven," the conductor announced.

Minutes later, I stepped down onto the northern shore of Long Island Sound. During my girlhood, my parents seldom left the Village of Hamden, several miles away. There, we lived in one of many little stone houses built by Eli Witney to insure that his factory workers enjoyed a decent and clean if simple home. "Spreading the wealth around a bit," as that giant of industry phrased it. A capitalist with a conscience, welcoming profits, yet eager to 'give back.'

But as to *my* family. In those days, several times a year Papa would hitch up the mule to our buggy, then off we'd trot to spend a day in what, to me, seemed a true and vital center of civilization. Boasting 35,000 residents, New Haven ranked as one of the more cosmopolitan small cities on the East Coast. Now, the population had in the five years since I last visited The Green—our local nickname for a 'common block' which served as the area's business hub—grown by leaps and bounds.

So I delayed my intended journey northward for an hour. This allowed me to take in 'Lighthouse,' an intimidating off-white tower with a strangely shaped black top. Also Yale's oldest campus housing quarters, where the current students hurried from classes to parties as their predecessors had on opening day in 1701. East Rock Park invited tourists to observe a stark reminder of our prehistoric past, oblong natural formations still standing in what once had been the domain of the Quinnipiac. Those native people fished in the harbor and grew maize as the mainstays of their existence.

Recent constructions included red brick factories, where cotton gins were mass produced. Throughout the city, elm trees stood tall. These were not indigenous but had been planted by local officials to create a comfortable environment with plentiful shade. Long before New York's liberals determined to transform their metropolis into a Utopia via urban planning, New Haven's founding fathers eyed their own prospects in much the same manner: a better future for all thanks to constant economic growth.

How fascinating to contemplate that I was not the only link between Connecticut and Wyoming. For here, Samuel Colt manufactored the deadly pistols which those on the frontier daily put into action. Apparently, as to East and West, one could not exist without the other.

I chuckled at the thought that I, once a willing fugitive from this peaceful enclave, had become famous—in all truth, *infamous*—on the nation's far side, yet now returned to try and recapture something I'd lost along the way.

## BUTCH: MONDAY; FEBRUARY 11, 1901

"Sit down," I commanded Sundance.

"Uh, oh," he snickered, as if to cover any concern. Moments earlier, Henry had arrived at the boarding house, clearly wishing to discuss some important subject. But on sensing the deadly seriousness of my manner, he stepped in and took a chair, awaiting whatever revelation I'd deliver.

"Fire away, pard. At this point, I can't imagine—"

So I told him of my earlier confrontation with DeFly. Me, Etta, and the Kid, together in a single photo. End of the line for our woman should DeFly contact the police, unless we prevented such a thing from happening.

## ETTA: MONDAY; FEBRUARY 11, 1901

I hired a horse and carriage, then set off on the old road leading to Hamden. Still a rural pathway, I guessed that in another five years this would be covered over with cement. And where wild grass grows and tall trees reach skyward stores and businesses would in their place appear; homes, schools, churches; nature shorn away in the name of progress.

On the way, I passed Westhille, the city's Jewish suburb. Close to but notably apart from the area's Protestant-based population, the latter descended from Pilgrims who arrived here in 1637. In time, Jews had arrived from Europe, initially a small trickle, though more plentiful by *fin-de-siècle*.

"Why do the men wear those odd little black caps?" I'd asked Mama when the three of us passed through the pleasant ghetto ten years ago during a quiet Sunday ride.

"Modesty to God," she answered, her tone most respectful. "The Jews are deeply religious."

As far back as then, I'd been curious to know more about these people.

## SUNDANCE: MONDAY; FEBRUARY 11, 1901

"Why doesn't he contact the authorities and collect the reward at once?"

"Greed. Figures to blackmail us for even more money."

"Thought your lover already had a claim on our stake?"

"You thought right."

"So . . . what do we do now?"

"That's what you and I must discuss."

"You start the ball to rolling, pard. I'm *lost!*"

## ELOISE: MONDAY; FEBRUARY 11, 1901

"They're called yarmulkas, Eloise. They represent the Jews' daily sense of humility to their Lord."

"Is *their* Lord the same as *ours*?"

"Yes and no. It's complicated."

"Explain, Mama!"

"Some day. When you're old enough to understand."

"But I want to know *now!*"

"That's my daughter," Papa chuckled.

So Mama related as best she could the key differences between the Old Testament's Yahweh, whom we Christians shared with the Jews, and Jesus the Son, a concept widely rejected by Hebrews nearly 2,000 years ago, creating the great schism.

*When I return to New York, I must look up Rabbi Cohen and learn more about these fascinating people.*


BUTCH: MONDAY; FEBRUARY 11, 1901

"Well," I said, concerning Mrs. Trumbell, "the lady in question' plans to pay me a visit tomorrow night."

"Well, then. Considering your masculine persuasiveness, any possibility you can talk her out of the blackmail plan?"

"In truth, Mrs. Trumbell has suggested she wouldn't be averse to me remaining here with her."

"Those blue eyes of yours do work wonders!"

"So maybe I'll take her up on the offer, though only if she agrees that she and I will keep my share of the stake and no more."

A long silence. Then, "Meaning Etta—let's return to that name, too—and I would leave without you?"

"As they say, 'All good things must come to an end.'"

"That'd be tough on her."

"Maybe. Though she's discovering her own path."

"Even if that's true? It'd be tough on *me.*"

"Me, too," I softly replied, averting his eyes.


ETTA: MONDAY; FEBRUARY 11, 1901

Little appeared changed in the village, other than the addition of several more factories, such places of industry side by side along with dignified buildings dating back to Colonial times. I turned down a narrow dirt path, precisely as I recalled it, leading over a rise toward an isolated house.

Pulling up in front, I hauled in on the reins at the sight of a woman I knew to be forty years of age. I did not immediately recognize her, my mind insisting this must be an elderly person who resembled someone who had exerted much

OUR TOWN, U.S.A.: Even after the turn of the century, some small towns such as Hamden CT. managed to retain their sense of a simple village, apparently all but unawares of the changes taking place nearby.

influence over me. As she tended to a flower bed, yanking weeds, I noticed movements of her spindly legs and long arms—those minute gestures we are often unaware of but identify a person to the onlooker—as my mother.

She rose from this earnest task, unaware of the visitor quietly observing her. Clearly tired, she approached the door, sweeping pebbles off the mat with a broom so old I could believe it to be the one she used long ago. Considering her practicality, that might well be the case.

"Hello, Mama," I announced myself, the prodigal daughter returning at last.

## SUNDANCE: Monday; February 11, 1901

"Now, it's your turn," said Butch.

"Not sure what you—"

"Stop meandering and share what's torturing you!"

"Butch, I've decided to kill Lupo the Wolf and his companions. Even as 'The Virginian' did Trampas."

"That was a novel, Kid. This is life. Real life. And believe me when I say they're entirely different things."

"Perhaps. But I came to ask for your help."

"My help in . . . ?"

"Wiping such scum off the face of the earth."

ETTA: MONDAY; FEBRUARY 11, 1901

"Well, a body's got to eat. So sit yourself down at the table. You recall where it's at, don't you?"

That was Mama's less-than-warm welcome to the daughter she hadn't seen in six years. Why, though, expect anything else?

"Yes, Mama. As you'll recall, I possess a keen memory."

Mama! Always rigidly moral; ever certain she was right about everything; frantic when anyone dared note this might not be the case.

Mama: Traditional in values, resentful of those who went his (or in my case her) own way. Never mean-spirited, doing what she did out of love. A hard, cold kind of love. Yet love all the same.

BUTCH: MONDAY; FEBRUARY 11, 1901

I considered Sundance long and hard, wondering if perhaps my best friend had gone stark raving mad. Then I rose, staring down toward the floor so as to avoid eye contact. All the same, I could feel his eyes on me. Sundance coughed; I anxiously whistled.

"Any song but *that*, Butch."

"Ooops! Forgot how you hate 'Oh, Susannah.' Explain how you arrived at this, Henry."

"Let's begin with The Bible."

"I'm listening."

"Which states, 'An eye for an eye, a tooth for a tooth.'"

"You forgettin' another line from the same book? 'I am the Lord, thy God; Vengeance is *mine*.'"

ETTA: MONDAY; FEBRUARY 11, 1901

As I assumed a seat at the table—the same spot I occupied when this quiet refuge had been my 'place,' no pun intended—Mama brought me a bowl of beef stew from the worn stove.

"Tastes good."

"Never concerned myself much about that. Meals are only a necessary requirement to fill the empty space inside."

"Well, that's yet another difference between us. I see food as . . . hmmmm . . . an art form, at its most refined."

"God almighty. Where did you pick up such notions?"

Always sure her vision of the world is the only fit 'way' anybody ought to live by! My Mama. Blood of my blood.

SUNDANCE: MONDAY; FEBRUARY 11, 1901

"Keep in mind," said Butch, like the teacher of a one-room schoolhouse lecturing an erstwhile student, "Wister's novel takes place in the nineteenth century. We're pushing into the 20th—"

"Stop speaking as if I were a child. I know that."

"—which will have a system of life, and accompanying values, all its own."

"Maybe this will be my way of wrapping up the past."

"Figurin' you'll then be free of it?"

"Maybe. Your take on it?"

"You'll be right back where you were at the Hole. Having achieved none of what Etta refers to as 'growth.'"

"There's what you think, pard, and what I think. And somewhere in-between the two, there's the truth."

"Right! The trick is recognizing the latter when you face it."

"Do so, and you've achieved wisdom."

ETTA: MONDAY; FEBRUARY 11, 1901

"You're lookin' healthy, at least."

"So are you, Mama."

"Don't lie. Less of me here with each passing day."

Had I expected to rediscover Mama as I perceived her while a child, larger than life to a little girl? Or had the years shrunken her? I couldn't tell. Maybe that's always the case when you try to go home again. The past is another country. Even if the place hasn't changed, you have.

"If you prefer, Mama, I can turn around, leave, and exit your life. This time, forever."

"I'm not going to beg you to stay. Nor will I order you out should you choose to remain."

She wants a reunion—a reckoning, perhaps—as much as I do, but can't bring herself to say so. I must accept her as she is or depart, my motive for coming here left unfulfilled.

"I'll take that as the nearest to an invite as you are capable of extending."

BUTCH: MONDAY; FEBRUARY 11, 1901

"Bat Masterson and Joe Petrosino will take care of The Wolf and his cohorts in their own way, in their own time."

"That's like saying The Virginian didn't need to kill Trampas. Sooner or later, some lawman would."

"More or less."

"You're missing the point. He *had* to do it."

"Mind tellin' me why?"

"Well, a man's gotta do what a man's gotta do."

"Come on, Kid! Don't fall back on that time-worn cliche."

"Ronald was my brother-in-law. He may have been a skunk. Now, that don't matter."

"What does?"

"He was Dag's husband. I feel responsible."

"Family," I muttered under my breath.

## ETTA: MONDAY; FEBRUARY 11, 1901

"For how long do you care to stay?"

"Three days, counting what's left of this afternoon. At noon on the 13th, I must return to New York."

"Is that where you've been living all this time?"

"No. Only for the past week and a half."

"Didn't think so."

"Why is that?"

"Eloise Placer was bound and determined to achieve fame and fortune in her lifetime. Had you been in Manhattan, no doubt you'd be a flashy showgirl in a variety theater, a rich man's pampered wife, or president of an important company. One way or another, I'd have heard."

The stew consumed, Mama rose and headed back to the oven. Soon, she returned with a steaming-hot apple pie.

"Where's Papa?" I asked all of a sudden.

"Buried in the old cemetery beyond the village square."

"Oh! I didn't—"

"'Know?' Not surprised. Doubtless, you must've had plenty of distractions to keep your mind and body occupied."

"That's true."

"Men, I'd imagine," she said contemptuously.

## SUNDANCE: MONDAY; FEBRUARY 11, 1901

"Have you stopped to think how Etta will react?"

"'Course I have. Even worse than when she arrived as you and I were about to shoot it out back at the Hole."

"Should you succeed—and there's a great likelihood one of them will bring you down—if she gets wind of this, my guess is our woman will have nothing more to do with you."

"A calculated risk I'll have to take."
"Not if you abandon this crazy plan."
"If I go through with it, would you tell her?"
"Henry! How can you even ask that?"
"Sorry. But I must know. Would you?"

ETTA: Monday; February 11, 1901
"You're correct about the men, at least in part."
"Even as a child, you flirted with local boys."
"As I recall it, they approached me."
"People see things the way they choose to."
"That holds true for you as well, Mama."
"Enough! You were speaking of your experiences."
"Would you believe I once taught school?"
Mama silently considered this. In time, she stepped to the window, peering
out as the late-afternoon sky dissolved from a pale shade of blue into the pastel
rainbow of colors that marks the onset of evening-time.
"I'm impressed," she said, if without enthusiasm. "So! That all of it?"
I hesitated before honestly replying, "Hardly."

BUTCH: Monday; February 11, 1901
"How can you even ask me such a question?"
"That's not the point."
"What is?"
"I need to hear it from you. Whether you'd tell—"
"I'd die first. But Etta's got a knack of sensing things."
"I hear ya."
"Enough of this nonsense, then?"
"Think of it this way, Butch. If Etta were ever to find out, that would likely
make her all yours. Right?"
"I don't want to get her that way. She must choose."

ETTA: Monday; February 11, 1901
"Didn't expect so," Mama all but cackled. "Can't imagine you being satis-
fied with the prim and proper life for long."
"As judgmental as ever?"
"I am what I am, Eloise. Take me or leave me."
"Once, you'll recall, I did the latter."

"Still, you came back."

"Felt I had to."

"Why? Guilty conscience?"

How difficult to answer, "Yes. At least, in part."

SUNDANCE: MONDAY; FEBRUARY 11, 1901

"Fair enough. But as for you not accompanying me? What happened to, 'When you *ride* with a man—'"

"In my mind, that was the second most significant of the values we lived by."

"Top of the list?"

"Kill one man, you murder the entire world." That took me back a bit. "If you were walkin' into a showdown in which enemies—wouldn't matter how many of 'em there were—waited in ambush, I'd be there by your side."

"In such circumstances, you'd shoot to kill?"

"Without hesitation. But this is another thing entirely."

ETTA: MONDAY; FEBRUARY 11, 1901

"Don't go expectin' me to say 'I'm sorry' for slapping you that day I caught you with your lips up against a boy's."

"Never did I believe you would apologize to anyone for anything."

"*Never* apologize," Mama announced with a sense of pride that struck me as misguided. "It's a sign of weakness."

"To me? Of *strength*."

"How do you figure?"

"The human element. None of us are perfect. Anyone can err in judgment."

"Like you did? Leaving without so much as a 'goodbye'?"

"You know as well as I do, Mama, that if I'd said that, you'd have tied me up to hold me here."

"Would've been the best thing in the world for you."

"In all truth?" I laughed. "I sometimes think so myself."

BUTCH: MONDAY; FEBRUARY 11, 1901

"We still have nine days until the ship sails," Sundance said, rising to leave. "Who knows what'll happen between now and then?"

"Not so sure I'll be takin' that trip after all."

"Why? As you said, likely Etta won't want me after I eliminate the Wolf."

"Kid, I'm ever less certain she'll show up at the docks next Tuesday night, no matter what we do."

"As you so often say, we'll have to wait and find out." Without a backward glance, he started for the door.

"Don't go," I heard myself say.

"Huh?"

"I don't want to be alone."

A shudder passed over his form. "What if—"

"Whatever happens, happens. Stay! Please?"


ETTA: MONDAY; FEBRUARY 11, 1901

"Mama, as this may be the last time we'll ever meet, at least in this world—"

"I'm planning to stick around for a while."

"—we might come to some sort of an understanding."

"Mend the fences, as farm-folk put it?"

"Something like that."

"Well, they say 'good fences make for good neighbors.' If you'd like to bunk in your old room, we'll be 'neighbors' in a manner of speaking for two nights and three days."

Without warning, I broke into tears. For an extended moment, I couldn't catch my breath, much less speak. My eyes closed tight; I thought I might faint. Until I felt a pair of withered arms embrace me. And realized Mama had stepped around the table, now holding me close. Like she did when, as a child, I grew fearful during the midnight hour of goblins, ghosts, and things that go bump in the night.

"Oh, Mama!" I managed to gasp between sobs.

"It's alright, Eloise," Mama said, her voice softer than before. "Welcome home."


SUNDANCE: TUESDAY; FEBRUARY 12, 1901

"Three," Butch said, waking.

"Huh?"

"Last night makes three. Three times we—"

"Didn't know you were keepin' count."

"Weren't you?"

"I guess so."

"Want to talk about it?"

"Not certain I'm able to yet." I avoided eye contact.

"I know what you mean. Let me ask, then. This in any way alter your feelings toward Etta?"

"Not at all."

"I was referring to *physical* feelings."

"I understand. No."

"Me, neither."

"Don't seem possible it wouldn't."

"Yet it don't."


ELOISE: TUESDAY; FEBRUARY 12, 1901

"Please tell me, however difficult this may be. Did Papa die quietly in his sleep, or was the end painful?"

"It's difficult to say. You see, Eloise, your father took his own life."

"Oh, no!"

"I wouldn't have told you if you hadn't asked. But since you did, I have no intention of lying."

At mid-morning, we two stood in the small cemetery just beyond the Village Square, where buildings ranging from the timeworn livery stable, an original saloon, and a historic hotel stood alongside contemporary factories and stores.

"I asked. Tell me, though . . . *why?*"

"That's difficult to answer."

"I'm a big girl now. I can take it."

"In all truth, I'm not certain."

"Did he experience a business setback?"

"Nothing like that."

"A serious illness?" Mama shook her head 'no,' then took my right hand in hers to my great surprise and greater relief.

"*What*, then?"


BUTCH: TUESDAY; FEBRUARY 12, 1901

"Alright, Kid. Let's try to hash this out."

"You first."

"This change things between *us?*"

"That's what I was wonderin'."

"Up until today, whenever this occurred, we ignored it."

"All the same, I think Etta may have caught on."

"Now that she's left Caruso's, she'll be around us again. If she hasn't already, sooner or later, she'll—"

"Don't forget, Etta will bunk over at the Garden."

"Likely, I'll be stopping by to see her."

"Not me. I couldn't face her just yet."

ETTA: TUESDAY; FEBRUARY 12, 1901

"Your father always seemed settled, content, and free of any concerns."

"He was a man of few words; that much is true."

"Never once can I recall him worrying about problems that arose daily. Finances, local politics, and such."

"He appeared happy, as if in a world of his own."

"Appearances can be deceptive, Eloise."

"Tell me about it! If there's one thing I've learned from life, it's that few people are in truth what they seem."

"That well describes your father."

"Mama! What are you driving at?"

SUNDANCE: TUESDAY; FEBRUARY 12, 1901

"So you're actually going through with your plan?" Butch asked as I made ready to leave.

"Don't see any alternative."

"Let me try again to reason with you."

"Nothing you can say or do—"

"Pig-headed, as ever."

"Likely. But I can't help bein' me anymore than you can help bein' you."

"Got me there."

"Or Etta, Etta."

"And that, as one of her favorite poets put it, is the way of the world. Congreve, I think."

"Whoever the author is, sure holds true."

"That's always the way with great poetry, I reckon."

ELOISE: TUESDAY; FEBRUARY 12, 1901

The day had turned unseasonably warm, one more of those sudden jerks in temperature that characterized this odd winter in the East. Unconsciously, I reached up and undid several of the tight buttons on my modest dress. In the process, my hand brushed against my Magen David, causing it to slip out.

"Oh!" Mama gasped.

"Don't trouble yourself about that," I laughed. "It's a keepsake from a dear friend, long gone if never forgotten."

"The Star of David," she muttered.

"If you're concerned I may have married a Jewish man, Mama, that isn't the case."

"That's not what I was thinking."

"What, then?"

"Eloise, I can't!"

"Mama? You *must*."


BUTCH: TUESDAY; FEBRUARY 12, 1901

"Hang on, Kid," I said as Sundance neared the door. When he turned back, I'd already slipped into my pants and was in the process of reaching into the closet for a clean shirt.

"What's this about?"

"Changed my mind. I'm going with you after all."

"No."

"What?"

"I said, 'no.' Don't want you tagging along after all."

"Ah, stop it, Sundance. We been facing things together for more years than I can count. If you're so doggone set on—"

"No," he asserted, more adament even than before.

"Explain yourself, then."


ETTA: TUESDAY; FEBRUARY 12, 1901

"When you were little, Eloise, we would sometimes speak about the concept of fate."

"That's perhaps my greatest legacy from our time spent together. My mind has often pondered the idea of destiny."

"Be more specific, please."

"Whether such a force exists, or if life is nothing but a succession of random occurences."

"At this precise moment, Eloise, I finally know for certain. Everything that happens does so for a reason."

"Mama, I have no idea what—"

"The Magen David. It's a *sign*, Eloise!"


BUTCH: TUESDAY; FEBRUARY 12, 1901

"We've come to a parting in the trail," Henry announced. "I've made up my mind as to which way I'm headin'."

"So? I'll follow that path as well—"

"It's not the right one. Leastways, not for you."

"I think I know my own mind."

"This time, it's me who does. Everything you said last night? That's what you believe. Now you're surrendering to blind loyalty when you must be true to your own self."

"My choice to make."

"No, pard. Mine! I won't allow you to walk down a road to hell, as you believe the outcome of this will be. Sorry, but this is for me to do. Right or wrong. Alone."

ETTA: TUESDAY; FEBRUARY 12, 1901

"Here it is. Eloise, I'm Jewish, as was your father."

I can't imagine how long I stood stock-still, trying to understand. I found myself overwhelmed; not in either a good way or bad. Rather, so amazed that I could not react.

Yet one idea did gradually take form in my mind; *on some level, I sensed this all along.* Not that I was Jewish. That'd never occurred to me, even if it helps explain my fascination with that faith. Rather, that I was *different*, somehow.

Not in an obvious way. As a schoolgirl, I sat in the middle of our humble classroom, anonymous. But as our current teacher droned on about readin', writin', and 'rithmetic, a notion emerged, despite my show of conformity. I am with you here and now. But not of you. I must find my own way in the world. And develop values that are essential to *me* even if incomprehensible to others.

SUNDANCE: TUESDAY; FEBRUARY 12, 1901

"Well, Henry . . . Harry . . . whatever name you go by; You made it."

"I don't get your drift."

"Should you go back to calling yourself 'Sundance,' you'll need to drop 'the Kid.'"

"Mind explaining?"

"You've grown up. What I see standing here is not, as Eloise claimed both of us to be, an overgrown boy but a *man*."

"Tell me, Butch Cassidy, in your infinite worldly wisdom, what's the difference between the two?"

"A man . . . a *true* man . . . cares more about what's best for someone he loves than for his own well-being."

"Reckon that's what Eloise means by unconditional love."

"Right. And in refusing my aid, you've proven that you are now capable of precisely that."

## ETTA: TUESDAY; FEBRUARY 12, 1901

"Tell me more, Mama. Please?" Neither of us had been able to converse at the graveyard but now that we were back home, perhaps that would be possible.

"We were happy, for a long time, in Westhille."

"Never knew you lived there."

"You were an infant. Hamden came later."

"Why leave?"

"The Klan. Spreading their doctrine of hate from saloons to churches, school-houses, political rallies. Anywhere people may congregate and listen to those who would gain power by turning simple if frustrated folk into an angry mob. All they need is a scapegoat. More often than not, it'll be the Jews."

I thought back to everything I'd learned in New York since that incident at Lady Liberty's harbor. And came to fully understand the most terrible truth of all. The faces may change; those who are the victims of hatred in any one decade may become the oppressors during the next. Always, though, there must be a target for the mob's anger.

"In New York twenty-five years ago? It was the Irish. Today? Italians."

"Sit back and wait. In time, it'll be *us* again. Just a matter of time before someone gains power by convincing those who can't think for themselves that we're the cause of all the world's woes."

## BUTCH: TUESDAY; FEBRUARY 12, 1901

Then, he was gone. Leaving me alone. Not that being by oneself is always a bad thing. I can recall nights on the prairie when, employing my saddle as a hard pillow and with a single Navajo blanket spread over me, I enjoyed the solitude. A cow-pony, legs gently shackled with suede bindings grazing in the moonlight, my only company.

*Alone, yes. But not lonely.* The two aren't necessarily one and the same.

Now? It's as if terrified cattle were rushing toward me in a stampede, after a crack of lightning set them off and running. I imagine Sundance and Etta felt the same way.

To fill time, space, and an oppresive silence, I began whistling. Not "Oh, Susannah!" which I'd performed so many times that Sundance once jokingly threatened to shoot me.

Now, my mind drifted to a ballad expressing not the glory of heading west but the fear of oncoming death. That and many other aspects of a cowboy's life, "Streets of Laredo."

"Once, in the saddle, I used to ride daily.

Once, in the saddle, I used to ride 'gay.'"

ETTA: TUESDAY; FEBRUARY 12, 1901

"All of what you've just shared with me. Was any of this connected to Papa's suicide?"

Mama nodded, then related the whole story. "Some, like us, fled Westhille. Others chose to remain, whatever horrors rained down on them, from barn burnings to harassment of the rabbi. They took a firm stand; this is our village, our little world inside the greater world of America. Your father felt the same, yet he believed our safety mattered most."

"Explaining why," I whispered, "we hid in plain sight."

"We survived by moving and pretending to be Protestants. Prospered, even. Yet every day, I could tell by the melancholy look in his eyes, and a slump in Papa's shoulders, that he felt . . . how to put it—"

"Guilty."

"Yes. For in denying his . . . well, *roots* . . . he lost his *identity*."

"Did he speak to you of this?"

"Never. Your papa was not a talkative man. But we had a way of communicating without words. So, when one day he seemingly out of the blue—"

"No more, Mama. Please. That's all I can handle."

"How will you deal with this going forward?"

"By telling myself that, when I depart in the morning, tomorrow will be the first day of the rest of my life."

SUNDANCE: TUESDAY; FEBRUARY 12, 1901

"Mr. Long, may I please have a minute of your time?"

I'd exited the boarding house and was on my way back to the Mastersons' hotel to smoke, down a drink, and think things through. A voice from behind caused me to slow down.

"Samson? That you?"

"Sir, we need to talk."

"I can't imagine what about. Your Mama—"

"This has nothing to do with her."

"Alright, then. I'm listenin'."

"First, let me apologize. When you and Mr. James were speaking upstairs, I stood in the hallway, listening."

"So now you know everything. Might as well address me as Sundance from here on. Any cover I had is completely blown."

"This has to do with your plan to kill them Mafiosos."

"Now, hold your horses, boy. Less you know about that, the better. You don't want to mix with La Cosa Nostra."

"But that's just it. I *do!*"


ETTA: TUESDAY; FEBRUARY 12, 1901

Sunday morn, standing before Lady Liberty, I'd perceived myself as a sympathetic observer of what humankind's darkest nature can do to others. Now? I identified with the victims.

"Your Papa and I decided you must not grow up living in fear. So we recreated ourselves here, from assumed names to to our supposed religion. And hid away in this obscure corner of the world."

"For better or worse."

"For the better, certainly, at the beginning."

"Then, in the long run, the worse."

"Papa eventually doubted his choice. And could not continue on knowing that for our sakes he betrayed the most fundamental truth about himself."

"Unconditional love for us drove him to loathe himself."

I must take the first step in handling this revelation. No longer wear my Star beneath any day's outfit. Rather in plain view, for all to see, annoucing who I am. Now that I finally know, for certain.


BUTCH: TUESDAY: FEBRUARY 12, 1901

"Mr. Cassidy, may we resume our conversation?"

"Sorry, I'm busy," I said to DeFly as once more he approached me. I'd headed north from the Village to visit Bat; see if I could persuade him to go to extreme lengths, if necessary, to keep Sundance from fulfilling his mission. Lock Henry up, maybe, for the next five days. Until the time to depart at last arrived.

"Time's a-wasting. Pay, or—"

"Die?" I interrupted. "You with the Mafia now?"

"No, no, no. I want only money, not blood."

"I'll get it somehow. Just give me time—"

"That's the one thing you don't have. I'm aware of your plans to sail away—"

"How could *you* know of *that?*"

"I have my ways. Do you want the police to see this?"

Smirking, he again waved the photograph in my face. Proof positive that the woman claiming to be 'Eloise Placer Long' was indeed Miss Etta Place. Wanted for murder.

ETTA: TUESDAY; FEBRUARY 12, 1901

"Tell me, Mama," I said over coffee. "Backtrack, now, if you will. While in the ghetto, how did the bad times begin?"

"At first, there were rare incidents most of us wrote off as nothing more than nasty mischief. The windows in Jewish-owned shops were smashed during the night. Bullies stopped our menfolk on the street and picked fights."

"And you accepted that?"

"We were naïve. Thought if we ignored these conflicts, in time they'd lose interest and leave us alone."

"Things don't work that way."

"Tragically, you are correct. The longer we overlooked such offenses, the more their hostility increased. We were among those who left."

"Explaining the combination of strict Puritan values and unbending Victorian ideals I was subjected to."

"We thought it for the best. Believe that, Eloise."

FORCE OF EVIL: Though the terror tactics of the Ku Klux Klan are often associated with the Deep South, white supremacists also threatened blacks, Jews, Italians, Irish, and Asians in the northeast.

"Mama, ever heard this old adage? 'The road to hell is paved with good intentions.'"

HENRY: TUESDAY; FEBRUARY 12, 1901
"Mind tellin' me why you're so eager to take part in something that might get you killed, Samson?"

"Miss Eloise. Can't stand the thought of anything bad happenin' to her."

"She does a pretty good job of lookin' out for herself."

"Maybe. Maybe not. I ain't sure that she could've made it through all that went down the other night in Little Italy if I hadn't followed along to protect her."

"There may be some truth in that."

"If you go after them, and fail because you have no back-up, they'll come after her next. You don't know Little Italy as I do, Mr. Long! Every nook and cranny."

"You make a good point," I said, wavering.

ETTA: TUESDAY; FEBRUARY 12, 1901
I took a long nap in my room, but found no peace there. Dreams haunted me, some recalling the events of the past year from nearly freezing to death in Wyoming to dining with the Great Caruso in Delmonico's. Then there were premonitions of what might occur should I journey to South America. I pictured myself as a pagan goddess in a primitive land. Or as an impoverished woman on the run, bounding over snakes, gators, and warthogs as I desperately attempted to flee.

"Are you alright, Eloise?" Mama asked. She had heard me groaning as I rolled between the fresh sheets.

"Only a nightmare. Thanks for checking, though."

"I used to do so when you were a child. Remember?"

"Course I do. Only then I feared ghosts and monsters."

"If you like, I'll stay here all through the night. You can tell me the story of your life since that day . . ."

"It's a long tale," I warned her. "And complicated."

"They always make for the best stories, don't they?"

BUTCH: TUESDAY; FEBRUARY 12, 1901
"So I can count on your help? When he returns to the Delivan, you'll him into custody for vagrancy or—"

"No, Butch," Bat interrupted. "I can't."

"What?"

"Legally? Sure. But it's not my 'way.'"

"I don't get you."

"Butch, you've told me that what Miss Etta wants most of all is to make her own choices."

"Yeah. So?"

"Think of Sundance, then. If I were to do what you ask, I'd be taking that away from him. Now, if you'd like me to discuss this with him—"

"Further talk will not change his mind."

"Like Etta, he must choose the path for his own future."

"Hate to admit it, but I guess you're right about that."

ETTA: WEDNESDAY; FEBRUARY 13, 1901

Mama listened while I rambled on, all night long. Through the window I watched the sun rise as I concluded my saga. Then Mama kissed me on the forehead before heading to her room for some belated sleep. Momentarily, I lost consciousness. In due time, the grandfather's clock below sounded the noon hour.

"Eloise? Breakfast is ready."

"Be right there, Mama."

We ate in silence. Then I returned to my room, packed what clothes I'd brought with me, and with a small piece of luggage in either hand, stepped back down the stairs, through the main room to the porch. Mama had hooked up my carriage to the horses, the rig awaiting me out front.

So I faced Mama for what I knew would be our final meeting. And noticed that she now wore a Star of David around her neck. Notably tarnished, she must have kept it hidden away all this time. Not anymore. Mine likewise now dangled in plain sight.

"Maybe my coming here has had a positive effect on you?"

"Two days ago, I claimed I'd never apologize for what I did long ago. I've changed my mind. I am sorry for that slap."

"Me, too. For leaving without a word. No doubt I would have left sooner or later, me being the free spirit that for better or worse I am. But I apologize for running away."

We embraced. After that, I hoisted myself up and rode off. Not allowing myself to cry until I'd turned the bend.

## —INTERLUDE—

BAT: OCTOBER 25, 1921

*On at least two occasions now, Lolly, I've mentioned the name of William Randolph Hearst, and not in a positive way. Today, he's achieved his goal of building the country's most influential newspaper chain, which may impress many but not me. Happily, I—and you—are employed by a daily that for more than two decades has expressed progressive values regarding those people pouring in through Ellis Island. As you know, Hearst's rags do the opposite.*

*Following his first experiments with the San Francisco Examiner, the equivalent of a toy handed to a spoiled boy by his wealthy dad, Hearst settled down in New York. There, his paper succeeded financially by providing the prototype of Yellow journalism: selling papers with no concern for moral consciousness. Hearst printed exposes of celebrities in which sensationalism took precedence over viable facts. Ugly rumors sold papers. For him, it was as simple as that.*

*Shortly before the beginning of my tale, Hearst called a meeting of his top editors to choose a popular figure as their next victum. 'Annie Oakley!' all agreed.*

THE GREAT MORALIST: William Randolph Hearst preached old-fashioned morality in his newspapers but kept film actress Marion Davies nearby as his secret mistress.

*This Ohio-born dirt poor kid, blessed with an uncanny knack for shooting, had become a symbol of old-fashioned proprietry for middle-Americans in search of a female hero from the fading frontier, though in truth Annie had never been near the wild west.*

*As a result of Bill's show and Ned's Dime Novels, people looked to her as an icon of unapproachable integrity. If the Hearst chain could bring her down, that would prove they possessed the power to annihilate anyone. This would serve as a warning to politicians in each political party. Pay proper homage to Hearst or expect to be ruined. And for many years to come, elected officials did precisely that.*

*So a story appeared, claiming that America's Sweetheart was a fraud. Purportedly, Annie had been selling her 'favorite rifle' to gun collectors for large sums, passing off one after another worthless piece as a valuable treasure. According to Hearst, in a manner that implied rather than stated offensive behavior so as to avoid law suits, Annie necessarily went this route to pay Frank's (supposed) gambling debts and rumored (but never verified) drinking and sexual peccadilloes.*

*While Frank shrugged off such lurid attacks, Annie was unable to. If even one person believed this trash, she'd be crushed. And wanted to disappear until the scandal blew over.*

*How could she ride into the ring for another performance fearing there were those in the bleachers who doubted her? This brief interlude, Lolly, is necessary that you understand Annie's desperation at the moment in time our tale took place.*

*Also, in hopes that wherever your own career leads you, you'll never ever write for William Randolph Hearst!*

# PART THIRTEEN: THE WAY OF THE WORLD

"To refuse the sweets of life because they soon must leave us is as preposterous as to wish we had been born old, because one day we must become that."

—William Congreve

HENRY: Wednesday; February 13, 1901

That day of our first discussion concerning the Mafiosos I'd asked Samson to think his offer through carefully. Now, I found the youth waiting on the boarding house's rickety steps. "Let me be your guide," he begged.

"I'd be too worried about you, Samson. More likely than not, I'd get myself killed worrying about you."

"I can provide another pair of eyes, sir. Make certain no one gets you from behind."

"If I do agree to take you along—remember, I said if—promise you'll back off when—"

"Yes!"

"I, and I alone, will do the shooting."

"You're the boss. *But*—"

"Uh-oh!"

"Hear me out? If anything should go wrong . . . if some how, some way, one of the three gets you before you can do him in . . . is it alright if I finish the job?"

"To insure Miss Etta will not be threatened?"

"Right."

"Under those circumstances, yeah."

"Thanks, Mr. Sundance. I won't disappoint you."


ETTA: Wednesday; February 13, 1901

"Rabbi, do you remember me?" I asked once an assistant had accompanied me to the Temple's executive office. Smiling, grey-haired Rabbi Cohen bade me enter with a friendly wave.

"Of course I do. And I did guess you would return."

"The last time you saw me," I said, taking a seat across from him, "I believed I was a Christian. Now, I know myself to be a Jew. And want to learn more."

"I see you have already acquired a Magen David."

"Oh, I've had that for some time. Legacy of a deceased friend, which I previously wore beneath my clothing. Now, I know myself to be a member of your nation."

"Well, where to start?" He turned in his seat to point at a delicate box mounted on the back wall. "This is called the *hakodesh*, essential to our places of worship. Simply put, a reconstruction of the Ark of the Covenant, which encloses the scrolls we refer to as our Torah."

"Share with me, please, the basics of our faith."

"Nothing is more holy than the Ten Commandments. Beyond any obvious restrictions . . . 'Though shalt not!,' that sort of thing . . . they require each of us to accept a One-ness with our all-encompassing God Yahweh. Deep respect for fellow humans as well as every living thing in the world He created. Most significantly, an adoration of the family."

"Defining the experience I have recently undergone."

"Then your arriving here now is what we call לְרוּג," Rabbi Cohen spoke the word in Hebrew and knew from my reaction that I did not comprehend. "What Christians call 'fate'; ancient Mediterraneans 'destiny.' Those of the East, 'Kismet.'"

"The names may vary. Not the idea behind them."

"That's because it is universal to humanity. Every race perceives it in their own unique way."

BUTCH: WEDNESDAY; FEBRUARY 13, 1901

"So now there's *two* people trying to blackmail us," I told Cody after relating my recent meetings with DeFly.

"Stay calm," the old-timer insisted. "If I'm right about the upcoming match between you and Sundance, there'll be a huge turn-out. First, that picture in the papers created a buzz. And beginning today, advertisements will be posted all across Manhatten isle."

"So it's set for six days from now?"

"Yes! Following our big event, we'll sneak you off to the docks, with Etta already aboard."

"*If* she chooses to sail," I mumbled.

"Butch, tell me! What's eating away at you?"

"Ah, Henry's got some crazy notion in his head."

"Care to share?"

"Maybe. Not just yet."

"When and if you're ready. Butch, this *will* work out."

"I can only hope you are right about that."

"Hope," he agreed, "and pray!"

ETTA: WEDNESDAY; FEBRUARY 13, 1901

"Additionally, we study the Kabbalah. An ancient text that helps a Jew complete his life's journey with dignity and righteousness. Containing the *sefirot*, which offers wisdom that connects each of us to the essence of Yahweh."

"Sounds similar to what Christians call a 'soul.'"

"Fair comparison. Significantly, though, this must be appreciated in relationship to *Keter*, or the Divine Will of God."

"This, a person's acceptance of what we cannot ourselves control, and must
accept as 'given.' Tell me more!"

"*Chesed*: the ability to adore all in God's kingdom."

"How wonderful."

"*Tiferet*, a sense of harmony that includes humility as to one's own self with
gratitude to God for what a person has received, freeing us from covetousness
as to others."

"I look forward to furthering my education."

"And in time assume your role as a Hebrew woman?"

"Well, that too, of course. But you see, I'm a former school-teacher. At
some point I would want to become a rabbi."

With that seemingly innocuous statement, the eager smile disappeared
from Rabbi Cohen's face.


HENRY: WEDNESDAY; FEBRUARY 13, 1901

"It's me, Sis," I whispered into the lobby phone once the operator connected me with Dag's home-receiver up in Buffalo.

"Oh, Harry," she stammered. No doubt Dag had learned of Ronald's death.
Perhaps his body had been discovered and identified by policemen, who contacted the next of kin.

"Try and stay calm," I begged.

"I'm alright. What happened?"

"Murder most foul. I don't want to go into the details."

"All I ask? Word of honor that *you* did not kill him."

"I can swear *that* on my eternal soul. This I promise you, Dag. Ronald's
death *will* be avenged."


ETTA: WEDNESDAY; FEBRUARY 13, 1901

"I'm afraid that wouldn't be possible," the rabbi said.

"Why not?" I asked.

"Because we believe a woman's place is in the home."

"Then you perceive women as inferior to men?"

"Not at all! We *revere* women. As the home is more sacred than a place of
business, a wife and mother's duties are far more exalted than a man's dealings
in the financial world."

"Oh."

"You sound disappointed. Are you one of the feminists who believe women should abandon such a traditional calling?"

"I agree with some of what they say. Not all."

"Explain, please."

"I believe each woman, like every man, must come to terms with herself as an *individual*. If she truly believes her place is at home, good for her. The workplace? That's fine, too. But I don't think any group—women or men; religious, racial, or social movement—should dictate to any person what's acceptable."

## BUTCH: WEDNESDAY; FEBRUARY 13, 1901

A hard, swift rap at the door announced someone wanted to join us. A moment later, a short squat man bolted in. He wore buckskin trousers, a multi-colored serape, and a high-reaching black satin top-hat with a red-and-blue feather dangling from its brim. No real Westerner would dress in such a flamboyant manner. Which left little doubt who this must be.

"Hello! Take it you're Butch Cassidy." He hurried over and extended a meaty hand for shaking. "I'm Ned Buntline. Bill hired me to create the greatest promotional campaign ever. We're going to re-invent show biz—"

"Stop! What Sundance and I agreed to was a boxing match."

"Oh, that too," he continued jovially. "Entertainment, sports. All part of the wide new world of public spectacle."

"Why not throw politics in as well?"

"That, too! Why, when T.R. eventually runs for president I'll sell him as America's Cowboy Politician!"

Sensing friction, Cody stepped between us. "Let's focus on what needs to be done in less than a week."

"I agree, Bill. Now, Butch! if you'll accompany me, I'll take you to wardrobe where they'll design your costume."

## ETTA: WEDNESDAY; FEBRUARY 13, 1901

"Eloise, a lost section of text from Genesis claimed that the first female was not Eve but Lilith."

"I'm aware of that name, though I've never come across her full story."

"That's because you read Christianized versions, edited to accompany the New Testament."

"As to the original?"

"Grasping that Adam felt lonely, Yahweh created a companion. Adam's opposite if equal. As with the first man, God scooped up a helping of raw earth and molded Lilith. She revealed herself as cruel and wilfull. A cannibal who gobbled down their babies. She was banished to the dark woods where she howled at the moon alongside wolves."

"I can guess where this is going."

"Again, though, Adam grew lonely. This time around, God, learning from his previous mistake, removed one of Adam's ribs. From this, he fashioned a second wife. Eve: an extension of man. Not evil, like Lilith. Flighty. Illogical. Well-intentioned if often misguided. Yet she was content to cook, clean, and bear children—"

"Please excuse me," I mumbled while rising and heading for the door. "I'm afraid I'm going to be ill."

SUNDANCE: WEDNESDAY; FEBRUARY 13, 1901

"Harry! What are you planning?"

"To punish the men responsible for Ronald's death."

"Do you mean," Dag hopefully asked, "round them up and turn 'em over to the authorities?"

"I can't take the chance they might be set free on bail. Ronald was done in by men . . . very *bad* men . . . who were planning to murder me. In truth, I remain vulnerable. As do my best friend and the woman I spoke so admiringly of."

"How does that legitimize you doing the same to them?"

"I'm personally responsible to insure justice is done."

"Harry, listen to me! Ronald should never have traveled there. If my husband had stayed at home, he'd still be alive."

"Maybe that's how an Easterner sees it. Not me."

"How any *civilized* person would."

"Sis, I didn't leave the West behind when I came here. Something of it remains inside me. And likely always will."

ETTA: WEDNESDAY; FEBRUARY 13, 1901

Lost in conflicting emotions and thoughts, I desperately needed to speak with another woman. Less certain than I had once been that Susan or Elizabeth would be the best choices, I'd taken it upon myself to pay Emma a surprise visit. She welcomed me with hot tea and fancy biscuits. As well as talk, talk, and more talk.

Precisely what I hungered for.

"You can't imagine how much this means to me," I said. We sat in her small, pleasant lounge.

"Like you, I'm aware of the limitations involved in sharing one's feelings with a man. *Any* man!"

"Huh! Even with one as exceptional as Bat?"

"He certainly is that. And yet . . ."

## BUTCH: WEDNESDAY; FEBRUARY 13, 1901

After Buntline's wardrobe crew finished bedecking me, I stood before a set of mirrors to get a look at myself in the costume I was supposed to exhibit while stepping onstage. Stretching high upon my head sat a ten gallon hat of the type no cowboy would wear, other than the Drugstore variety; all sizzle, no steak. Hanging from either side were faux horsehair strings, more decorative than functional.

"Well," Ned enthusiastically asked, "what do you think?"

For a shirt, they'd bundled me up in a bib-style item, the fabric a purple chambray with oversize buttons. Richly colored designs were arranged across the upper chest. Over my shoulders, a soft suede jacket had been neatly set, long strips of fringe hanging from either arm.

"Butch? *Say* something!"

Instead of rough boots, I wore Seven League style shiny black ones that made me look like a phony swashbuckler in some backwater performance of *The Pirates of Penzance*. As if this weren't enough, golden spurs—twice the size any drover would wear—jingle-jangled whenever I moved.

"Thanks, but no thanks," I replied. "I agreed to a boxing match. But—"

"Butch, you have to understand. This is *entertainment*."

"Maybe. But I'm not about to spit on my whole life."

## ETTA: WEDNESDAY; FEBRUARY 13, 1901

I rattled on about all that weighed heavily on me. With great good patience, Emma listened to every word. "When I spoke of the Movement, Emma, you reacted. May I ask why?"

"To be honest, I have mixed emotions."

"Surely, you can't object to a crusade for the vote?"

"Of course not. Any fair-minded person, men as well as women, would rally around such principles."

"Is it their alignment with the Prohibition cause?"

"To a degree. More significant, though, is their firm opposition to a woman's right to legal abortion."

"What?" I gasped, taken entirely off-guard.

For a brief moment, I found myself transported back to that lonely graveyard outside a weatherbeaten Wyoming town. Watching as the remains of Bowdry, denied a clean and simple operation, were lowered into unhallowed ground.

## SUNDANCE: WEDNESDAY; FEBRUARY 13, 1901

"I need information on the mobsters, Joe!"

"Alright, then! I'll tell you this much about Antonio Misiano. 'The Enforcer' has a sweet tooth."

"More," I begged.

"Please, Henry. No!"

"You owe me, Joe. You said so yourself. And Eloise! Could you live with yourself if anything—"

"Why not keep her hidden until you three depart?"

"That's all up in the air now."

"This is so difficult—"

"I know you are an ethical man. But measure a remarkable woman's worth against a piece of street scum—"

"Okay! One more detail. Wherever The Enforcer conducts his business—Lafayette Street in the West, Bowery on the East, Kenmore to the North, or Worth in the South—he always stops for a treat."

"Be more specific."

"Misiano invariably heads to Mulberry Bend Park, where the finest cannoli in all of Little Italy can be found."

"The best place for such a dessert?"

"Battaglia's. There! I will say no more. For if I do, my own soul will be as doomed as yours, if it isn't already."

## ETTA: WEDNESDAY; FEBRUARY 13, 1901

"Oh! I assumed you knew. Susan B. Anthony and Elizabeth Cady Stanton are firmly opposed to legalization of abortion."

"I . . . was unaware of that," I stammered, even more let down in my heroes than earlier.

"It's the most significant reason why me, and other like-minded women who also support universal suffrage, have not and cannot join their cause."

For a long moment, I sat stock still. "Do you happen to know, Emma, why they've taken such an extreme stand?"

"Wouldn't be fair for me to speak for them. Bat mentioned you've become friends with the leaders. Go to them. *Ask.*"

"I will. And now believe that perhaps a sea journey to a whole new world isn't such a bad idea after all."

BUTCH: WEDNESDAY; FEBRUARY 13, 1901

Chinatown, as Emma explained, emerged during the mid-1880s. Those Asians who naively journeyed to America in hopes of prospering during the gold rush of fifty years earlier found themselves in virtual slavery. Many labored at laying track for railroads. The Iron Horse reduced once proud citizens of China to the lowest level of America's poverty-stricken working classes. Profits for fat cats at the top were enormous; yet those at the bottom could barely afford food and shelter. To escape their daily hell, hoardes of Chinese migrated to New York.

Like other minorities, they collected in the lower East Side. Here, Asians survived with their culture intact while honing to a basic American precept, the abiding dream that defines us; work hard, wait patiently. And trust that, even when all hope for success appears lost, in due time such true earnestness will result in financial triumph.

ETTA: WEDNESDAY; FEBRUARY 13, 1901

Emma and I had met up with Bat and the boys in front of the newspaper building. Then we all drifted into Chinatown. Two square miles of crowded tenement houses on major avenues and slimmer cross-streets aligned with threatening alleys no sane person would dare enter. Contrarily, shops resided on brightly-lit avenues where visitors could purchase small trinkets, as well as stores for residents to buy food and clothing imported from their homeland. And eateries where all—locals and tourists alike—were welcome.

Kenmore and Delancey streets to the north, Worth to the South, Allen further eastward, and Broadway on the West Side bordered this gaudy district. Delicate rice-paper lanterns hung from facades, punctuating the darkness with seductively bright shades of yellow and red. On every set of steps leading up to a mysterious loft or down some dark cellar stood statues of fierce dragons. Our destination: a lavish restaurant known as Chinese Palace, located at the center of Pell, a diagonal street stretching from Mott down to Bowery.

"I find it exotic!" Sundance proclaimed, gazing at icons of black and crimson ogres on the building's exterior. A scent of opium defined the vast interior as we were escorted in by a silent hostess, she lovely in an understated floral Cheongsam Quipao wardrobe, to a secluded corner booth Bat had requested.

"Don't say that in front of the servers," Emma cautioned. "You may mean it as a compliment, but these people wish to be accepted as Asian-Americans. *Not* marginalized in any way."

A WORLD WITHIN A WORLD WITHIN . . . : Chinatown existed as one of numerous ethnic neighborhoods in downtown New York.

## SUNDANCE: WEDNESDAY; FEBRUARY 13, 1901

"How did your sentimental journey go?" Bat asked Etta.

"Would you prefer the short or long version?"

"How about a medium-sized rendering?" Butch suggested.

"First, I discovered that I am, in fact, Jewish."

A sudden silence fell over our small circle of friends as each attempted to absorb this information. Now, though, we understood why Etta wore the Magen David in plain view.

## ETTA: WEDNESDAY; FEBRUARY 13, 1901

Though my announcement had been met by a brief period of quietude, it struck me as non-judgmental. Just as I'd expected from trusted friends like these. I felt at peace with them.

"Well," Sundance half-kiddingly offered, "so was Jesus."

At that, all chuckled good-naturedly. I understood Butch and Sundance well enough to know they'd remain open and accepting. And, even if I had doubts about certain Hebraic traditions, I was blood of Israel's blood, this my birthright. I must accept that fact even while forging my own unique and original identity as a person.

BUTCH: WEDNESDAY; FEBRUARY 13, 1901

Fascinated, we listened to Emma's short history of the area. Similar to nearby Little Italy, where *Soldati* for Don Ferranzaro had engaged with those representing Don Masseria, those men first cousins, for total supremacy. Here too, competing crime families demanded protection money from simple, hard-working residents. On occasion, street soldiers representing the On Leong and Hip Sing Tongs battled to determine which would reign supreme.

In-between such turf wars, these gangs earned their protection money by insuring Chinatown's streets were safe, as with La Cosa Nostra. And no place was safer, ironically, than a neighborhood dominated by some Mob. One thing the Mafia, the Tongs, the Under Shtik in the Jewish community or The Westies among the Irish, would not tolerate? Disorganized crime. Such lowlives feared the gangsters more than they did the police.

ETTA: WEDNESDAY; FEBRUARY 13, 1901

"May I order for all?" Emma eagerly asked.

"You're the gourmet in this crowd," Bat responded. Emma suggested four massive entrees, accompanied with bowls of hot rice and piles of imported oranges. We would share this feast while sitting cross-legged on a plush car-pet around a low table. The boys and I had sampled Chinese food at humble eateries out west, but nothing comparable to this. The Cantonese speciality called Dim Sum, with its rich dumplings, varities of seafood, and small cakes nearly caused me to swoon on its arrival. Hot Pot from the Chongqing Province featured meats and vegetables in a mild broth steamed slowly for the subtlest flavor. An entire duck had been smothered in sweet sauce. A platter of Sichuan Kung Pao Chicken arrived with dried chili.

"Enjoy, enjoy, enjoy," Sundance announced in an unusual tone. I wondered if he had been up to more this afternoon than he admitted. "For tomorrow we may die." 'Sardonic' struck me as the term to describe his mood, uncharacter-istic of him.

SUNDANCE: WEDNESDAY; FEBRUARY 13, 1901

The meal was accompanied by an assortment of teas. Each, an elderly man in a silver outfit with a blood red Phoenix embossed on the chest area explained, was shipped from a unique territory in their homeland: Dragoon Oolong, Black Zheng, Plum Flower, Eight Treasures, West Lake Green Tang.

"Good food without fine drink is like a day without sun-shine," he insisted. Bat read from the list of choices, Green Ginger, Asian Summer, Singapore Sling among them. We became so entranced with his elaborate descriptions that I remained only vaguely aware that numerous women, outfitted in conservative black clothing, had collected at the entrance, their eyes blazing with anger.

ETTA: WEDNESDAY; FEBRUARY 13, 1901

"We'll begin with beers. Let's order Tsingtao, a rich and hearty speciality; Lao Li, emboldened with sorghum—"

"Bat," Emma whispered, her voice quivering, "I—"

"Then we'll move on to wines. My favorite is from the Han Province, a variation on yellow-rice—"

"Uh-oh!" Emma's concern caused me to gaze about the cavernous room as panic gripped Asians and Anglos alike.

"Finally, we'll sample the hard stuff," Bat continued, still unawares. "Baijiu, invented by Yi Di, the great lady of the First Dynasty—"

Suddenly, a virtual army of mainly middle-aged women spread out through the building's interior. Next, they rushed through the cavernous room, darting from table to table, knocking beverages to the floor.

"Ah, no!" Bat shouted. "It's the Prohibitionists."

BUTCH: WEDNESDAY; FEBRUARY 13, 1901

Diners leaped up from their places and rushed toward the exits. An older female, the only invader wearing a sky-high hat, stood back and observed as her minions wreaked havoc on the premises. She resembled a stark-eyed eagle seated atop a saguaro cacticus out west. I recognized her at once from photographs in newspapers. This was Carrie Nation, scourge of all men and *women* who believe that alcohol is not in and of itself evil.

"Spare not one bottle of the devil's brew," she howled. Carrie Nation wore Pince-Nez glasses set tight across the bridge of her nose and wielded a large axe.

As Carrie Nation's companions drew small hatchets from purses to smash the lavish adornments, their leader raised her own larger axe high. Edging forward, she brought it down on a table covered with the house's specialties. Her blow smashed the furniture, sending food and drink flying. Now, people screamed loudly. One lady fainted, swiftly carried out by her frantic male escort.

ETTA: WEDNESDAY; FEBRUARY 13, 1901

"We will end this era of free-flowing alcohol even if we have to do so place by place," Carrie Nation insisted. The waiters, initially frozen in shock, now darted about, attempting to apprehend the intruders. But Carrie Nation moved at an unexpected speed for a person of her age and heft, rending the sleek rosewood bar into scrap-wood. Then, as if out of the very air, two dozen men in luminous black silk robes swarmed into the building. Some waved swords high. Others aimed 'dogs' (rifles) and 'pups' (pistols) at the Prohibitionists.

These Tong warriors, Emma explained after it was all over, were highbinders, so-called as each man's hair had been tightly knit atop his head to avoid any interference with their swift movements. Whirling like dervishes, they appeared strangely graceful, all but defying gravity. At once, most of the temperance women rushed for the exits.

"They are Boo How Doy," Emma continued as we limped away, "street soldiers representing the Hip Song Tong." I gazed back and observed the restaurant as it burned to the ground, a result of rice-paper lanterns falling from their hangers amid the chaos and then exploding. "When a threat appears, so too do these enforcers."

SUNDANCE: WEDNESDAY; FEBRUARY 13, 1901

The entire action consumed several minutes, though during the scuffle it seemed an eternity. To my amazement, no one on either side died. Yet more than an eatery was lost here. The right of people to determine how they choose to live their lives had been challenged by a minority that steadfastly believe *their* 'way' is the *only* way.

## —INTERLUDE—

BAT: OCTOBER 25, 1901

*Depending on one's point-of-view, Carrie Nation was the finest or worst woman of her time. No question she must be ranked among the most important. At the cusp of a new century, old-fashioned values were challenged by emergent identities for females. Members of he Prohibition Movement wanted all temptations removed for both genders while The 'New Women' demanded total freedom of choice. The Suffragists found themselves caught in the middle. Meanwhile, this ultra-conservative influencer swung her huge axe. The clout was felt everywhere in America*

*On the positive side, she might be thought of as an early crusader for women's best interests. Carrie insisted corsets, worn to trim their figures for the delight of men, did harm to the wearer's internal organs. Mrs. Nation opposed long-standing organizations derived from Christian theology (which she herself devoutly adhered to) should they, like the Freemasonry tradition, exclude females. She also created a shelter for battered women and their hapless children.*

*Then again, and for me this is unsettling, Mrs. Nation claimed to be inspired by Jesus; her 'mission' religious as well as social. See, Lolly, I've never appreciated Bible Thumpers. I hold to the concept that we ought to do good for our fellows because it's clearly the right thing, without bringing the Lord—if He (or She) exists—in on the deal.*

*A native of rural Kentucky, later raised in the backwoods of Belton, Missouri, C.N. hailed from a family of supposedly solid farm folk. In truth, though, on her mother's side, a strain of delusional behavior led to that woman's eventual institutionalization. She'd come to believe herself to be Queen Victoria and took on aristocratic airs, parading while wearing a makeshift crown in public. Carrie's own seemingly admirable dedication must be contrasted with the possibility that she was, like her Mom, flat-out crazy.*

*Carrie Nation's first marriage to Dr. Charles Gloyd collapsed due to his chronic alcoholism. For this had led to his utter failure as a father to their daughter, Charlien. The divorce caused Carrie to identify drink as the primary enemy of all civilization, particularly the conventional family unit. A devout minister named David Nation proved a more appropriate choice. First in Texas, then Kansas, they crusaded for Prohibition. As this could only occur if women won the vote, Carrie's Nation aligned itself with the feminists. Here existed a world-class irony, considering*

THE LOST CRUSADE: Considered a hero by some, a villain by many, Carrie Nation led the movement to ban alcohol in the U.S.

*that Movement's left-wing leanings and de-emphasis on the traditional man/woman relationship.*

*Yes, Prohibition did pass a year and a half ago. But as a frequenter of underground clubs like yourself knows, drinking did not decline. Honest producers of wine, beer, and liquor were driven out of business. The Mob filled the gap, increasing in power by providing ordinary people with what they want, legal or not. That's when Lupo "The Wolf," previously a nasty street thug, transformed into Little Italy's reigning Caesar. As mentioned before in this rambling narrative, the road to hell is lined with good intentions. Remember that, Lolly, long after this night is over, even after I've gone to that big ranch-house in the sky.*

# PART FOURTEEN: BRIGHT LIGHTS, BIG CITY

"Sleepy Hollow is quaint, charming, and idyllic; yet nothing in New York State can compare to the thrice-renowned and delectable city I choose to call 'Gotham.'"

—Washington Irving

ETTA: Thursday; February 14, 1901

"You're . . . Annie Oakley!"

"And you must be Etta Place."

"I feel as if I'm standing in front of a mirror."

"We do look alike. *Amazingly* so."

I'd arrived at Madison Square Garden to make the final arrangements for my stay, also to plan for the evening of February 19th, me scheduled to perform as Annie, before my boys engaged in their boxing match.

"Perhaps I'm your doppelgänger."

"I have no idea what that even means."

"It's Germanic. Refers to a good person's evil twin."

"Well, Etta," Annie laughed, thrusting her right hand forward for a shake, "I think you may be confusing my . . . what to call it . . . 'popular image' with my real self."

"Who *are* you, then?"

"One more woman, trying to survive in a man's world."

"*That*, I can relate to!"

"Likewise, I'd guess you aren't the bloodthirsty bandit portrayed in Dime Novels."

"Spent more time cleaning and cooking than outlawing."

"As for me? Right now, I'm trying to distance myself from the smear campaign Hearst's newspapers are running."

"Why not fight back?"

"I've tried, believe me. A lawsuit went nowhere owing to his influence and power. Right now, all I want to do is get away."


BUTCH: Thursday; February 14, 1901

"Happy Valentine's Day, lover," Mrs. Trumbell whispered, waking me from a deep sleep. I sat up in bed and rubbed my eyes, attempting to determine whether or not the madness of the previous evening had only been a bad dream.

"Mmmmm . . ."

"Take your time, big fella."

We can build skyscrapers that touch the heavens, adorn them with electric lights, drive automobiles down newly-paved streets. And, if we so choose, call this progress. Yet that is but an illusion. For the dark side of human nature will never be entirely eliminated. A hairy ape remains inside each of us. Explaining the monster that did indeed exert its power last night. The obvious proof is that we remained prisoners of the past. Violence the tool of the intolerant, ten thousand years ago or today.

ELOISE: THURSDAY; FEBRUARY 14, 1901

"So, Etta. You're the lover of two outlaws?" At that, I nodded. "Married to either?"

"No. Not, though, that I haven't been asked!"

"No need to explain."

"But I do note a hint of disapproval in your tone."

"In truth, I did not let Frank so much as kiss me until we were engaged."

"Oh, my!"

"Nor anything more than that before our marriage."

"You really are a 'good girl,' then?"

"Reckon it's the way I was raised."

"That's how I started out as well. Though life led me down a different trail."

"How odd, then, that you'll soon impersonate me."

"Life is filled with ironies. Bill Cody tells me you're willing to show up earlier that morning at the Black Maria and pretend to be me."

"I'm not certain why I revel in that," she giggled in a coquettish manner, "but I do."

LITTLE MISS SURESHOT: Annie Oakley achieved celebrity status as the virtual embodiment of Western women; ironically, she had never ventured onto the frontier before becoming a 'show-woman' in Cody's Wild West.

"Maybe inside every good girl there's a naughty one just itchin' to slip out, if only for a day."

## SUNDANCE: THURSDAY; FEBRUARY 14, 1901

"It isn't too late for you to go home, Samson," I said. Moments earlier, we'd positioned ourselves in an alley across the street from Battaglia's pastry shop.

"No, Mr. Long. I have my reasons for being here."

"A crush on Miss Etta?"

"That's part of it," Samson replied, embarrassed.

"If anything goes wrong, don't say I didn't warn you."

"I'm a big boy, now. I'll take my chances."

"That doesn't merely make you 'a big boy.'"

"What, then?"

"You're putting your life on the line for what you believe. No matter how young, as of today you're a *man*."

## ETTA: THURSDAY; FEBRUARY 14, 1901

Had things gone differently, and I'd been discovered by Cody, Miss Oakley alone on a bleached boardwalk in a dreary frontier town that day when Butch and Sundance moseyed in, I might be a national treasure; she a fugitive.

Maybe each of us walking this earth resembles an empty vessel at birth, waiting to be filled by experience in the world. And whoever a person becomes is determined by those events encountered on one's singular journey. The greatest of all adventures turns out to be self-realization. As the ancient Greeks, in their infinite wisdom, insisted: The end of man is to *know*.

*And, I believe, that's even more apt for women.*

*Also, there's nothing more significant to 'know' than one's own self.*

## BUTCH: THURSDAY; FEBRUARY 14, 1901

"Did you buy me flowers?" Mrs. Trumbell joked.

"Wasn't what I delivered for the past ten hours enough?" As she nuzzled close, I waxed serious. "We need to talk."

"Uh-oh!"

"Don't worry. It's all for the best."

Sensing my intensity, she raised her head and took on a different tone. "I'm listening, James."

"Why not call me Butch?"

"I prefer James."

"That'll do for the time being."

"So? I'm waiting . . ."

ETTA: THURSDAY; FEBRUARY 14, 1901

"Huh! Know somethin', Etta? I think if we had met years ago, we might've been best friends."

"Got a feeling that before long we'll be separated by forces beyond our ability to control."

"Well, then, let's make the most of the time we have."

"My sentiments exactly."

SUNDANCE: THURSDAY; FEBRUARY 14, 1901

Cautiously, I stepped into the rectangular shaped venue. A small entrance-way on the street opened into a tunnel-like interior that stretched to the far back wall and rear door. A withered lady in black dress and shawl, with a silver cross dangling around her neck, stood behind the long bar. Displayed across its wooden surface were desserts the shop had become renown for: torta della non-na, the "grandmother's cake" with six layers of pie and berries, its top brushed with Masapore Cream; from Tuscany, pumpkin-gingersnap Tiarmisu, an el-egant pastry enriched by pie nuts, powdered vanilla, and lemon zest. Honey and Hazelnuts topped a cone of glistening white custard.

And, of course, more variations of Cannoli than a visitor could compre-hend on an initial visit. Tube-shaped shells of fried pastry stuffed with Ricotta, or cream, or a luscious mixture of the two. Cannoli embedded with chocolate chips, snow-like sugar, and chopped pistachios. Cannoli! The one weakness of the Mob's primary Enforcer. A brute with no idea that on this particular day, such indulgence would mark the final chapter not only of a deep obsession with sweets but his reptilian existence.

ETTA: THURSDAY; FEBRUARY 14, 1901

"Life sure takes strange turns, don't it? Tell you a secret, if you promise to keep it to yourself."

"Of course, Annie."

"Part of me wouldn't mind continuing our switch. Sometimes, I fantasize about sailing off to a whole new world for a fresh start."

"But other than this unwarranted attack by Hearst, you have . . . well . . . a perfect life."

"Do I?"

"A beloved celebrity, generously paid to perform what you most enjoy, happily married to a tall, dark, and handsome man."

"Nothing's ever what it seems on the surface, Etta."

"I should have learned that by now! Maybe that's what sustains us. Hoping the ideal is out there and achievable."

"Frank's uncomfortable that I overshadow him as a Wild West star. And it's possible those rumors of his affairs aren't entirely false."

"But you appear so perfect together."

"We put on a most convincing show."

"Hah! Welcome to the club."


BUTCH: THURSDAY; FEBRUARY 14, 1901

"Alright, then. Mrs. Trumbell. We'll—"

"My first name's Kathryn."

"That being the case, maybe you might want to address me by my actual first name."

"Isn't it 'James'?"

"LeRoy."

"A cowboy named 'LeRoy'? You've got to be kidding."

"Nope."

"Why don't you use it?"

"When I was young, people laughed."

"Even as I just did."

"I'll deal with it."

"Alright, then. From now on, it's LeRoy and Kathryn. Got a nice ring to it, don't you think?"


ETTA: THURSDAY; FEBRUARY 14, 1901

"E.S.! What are you so happy about today?"

Once again, Lakeland's young assistant drove me from the ferry station to Menlo Park. We were alone this time as I had no longer felt the need to ask Susan and Elizabeth to accompany me. At last, I was truly coming into my own, without need of chaperones, male or female.

"I'm sorry! Is my whistling annoying you?"

"Not at all. I have a dear friend who loves to blow his brains out. What intrigues me is your exuberance."

"Oh, but you must understand. We are on the threshold of an exciting future for motion pictures."

"Really? Well, I'm all ears!"

SUNDANCE: THURSDAY; FEBRUARY 14, 1901

"Don't move," I commanded, drawing my gun while entering the shadowy establishment. The hulking, dark-suited Mafioso froze in place across the bar from the old woman. His ruddy, pock-marked face provided a contrast with her beige skin; her cheeks spiderwebbed with lines that revealed a hard if honest life. His own covered with scars from a history of street combat.

"Please leave," Samson instructed the frightened lady. She appeared confused as to what was happening. A robbery? But that was impossible. Hadn't she paid her protection money, and on time? Then, her strained eyes drifted over to me, holding a large revolver, unlike anything previously seen south of Broome Street.

A Colt .45; 1888 'Peacemaker' model. Yes! That was the gun's distaff nickname. No, this was not a robbery.

ETTA: THURSDAY; FEBRUARY 14, 1901

"Mr. Lakeland mentioned that *The Great Train Robbery* will be projected on a screen before a full audience."

"True! But there's more to it than that."

"Are you referring to color and sound?"

"Even now, technicians are attempting to realize these possibilities. In time they will enhance filmmaking."

"But you're thinking of something else?"

"Within a year or two, we will produce movies that run twenty minutes or more. With longer stories and complex characters, as well as communicating ideas."

"As is the case with plays. And novels."

"Each a legitimate art form. As movies soon will be!"

BUTCH: THURSDAY; FEBRUARY 14, 1901

"You suggested the other day, Kathryn, that you might reconsider the stakes if I were to remain here?"

Her eyes expressed surprise of a most pleasant order. "You'd actually consider that?"

"Things have changed a great deal since last we spoke."

"Clearly!"

"So it's something we can talk about."

"I don't want your pity."

"That's not the emotion I'm experiencing. Or offering."

"Like I said," all lightness suddenly gone from her husky voice, "I'm listening."

Again, I revised my conception of Kathryn Trumbell. Not a simple chess piece on the board-game of life, blocking our route of escape. Like Etta, a woman. Moreover, a person.

## ETTA: THURSDAY; FEBRUARY 14, 1901

"E.S! Are you suggesting movies might transcend mere entertainment and someday equal literature and theater?"

"Yes! Film as an *original* art form, grand as the novel or play. Yet unique in its manner of storytelling."

"What will qualify movies as that," I wondered, "rather than a modern extension of the legitimate stage or books?"

"Editing!" he joyously explained. "Mr. Lakeland will shoot the robbery sequence outdoors in Orange. Meanwhile, I'll film your scenes inside the Black Maria. Once the rolls are developed, we will intercut them."

"That much, I already grasp."

"In the movie, we'll sweep the viewer from one place to another in a fraction of a second, then back again."

"Nothing quite like that exists in the arts, does it?"

"That's what I mean by an 'original' art form. Unique, if worthy of equal consideration with all the pre-existing ones."

"E.S., how long have you been mulling this over?"

"Since the day I saw my first flicker and fell in love with movies. Not only watching or helping to make them. The very *idea* of movies."

"Pictures that move," I muttered.

"More accurately, still pictures that *appear* to move."

## SUNDANCE: THURSDAY; FEBRUARY 14, 1901

The Mafioso's black-as-olive eyes registered that, on a primitive level, he sensed his oncoming demise. I'd caught him in a rare moment of vulnerability when the smell of fresh-from-the-oven sweets caused Misiano to forget everything else.

"Ooooooh!" the woman gasped. Moving faster than I would have believed possible, she whirled down the narrow hall and out the back way. Samson returned to the front and locked the door, yanking down a black shade over the window.

"Go ahead," I hissed, indicating the treats. "Take one."

"What?"

"You heard me," I insisted.

ETTA: THURSDAY; FEBRUARY 14, 1901

"What a wonderful way to phrase it," I sighed. "Have you experimented with the concept yet?"

"We did so last month with *Life of an American Fireman*. First, we shot footage of real heroes at work saving lives. Then, inside the Black Maria we filmed an actress screaming, clutching a rag doll. Next, we spliced the two strips of developed film with one another. The illusion 'worked' for our test audience. They 'believed' what they saw."

"E.S., I have no doubt you'll emerge as one of the great pioneers of this new art form."

"I can only hope I'll live up to *that*."

"Should it come to be, might I know your full name?"

"Porter," he responded. "Edwin S. Porter."

BUTCH: THURSDAY; FEBRUARY 14, 1901

"Our grub-stake in your safe amounts to a little more'n $2,000. The plan, at least until recently, was to invest it all in a cattle ranch after we reach South America."

"Any specific destination?"

"Well, Patagonia sounds like a strong possibility."

"All three of you, as in the past?"

"That was the notion. But we respect each other as . . . how to put it . . . *individuals*, as Etta likes to say."

"Which means . . . ?"

"Any one of us has the right to pull out, take our third of the money, then do as he or she chooses."

"And you suggest 'now' might be the time for a split?"

"Like we say out west, every trail has an end."

ETTA: THURSDAY; FEBRUARY 14, 1901

"Have you decided?" Lakeland asked, ushering me into his office, indicating for his distraught visitor to take a seat.

"Yes," I replied, nodding. "I will take on the role, with one stipulation. The shoot, must conclude by next Tuesday."

"Sounds do-able. But why are you suddenly so specific?"

"It's a long story."

"Share with me an abridged version."

"Alright. I'll likely be leaving New York by boat early on the 20th. I must board the previous night."

"May I ask how and why you reached this decision?"

"That's my business."

"I don't agree. And I'm not at all comfortable with your playing 'Miss Etta Place,' then disappearing from sight."

"Now, Mr. Lakeland, it's *your* turn to explain."


SUNDANCE: Thursday; February 14, 1901

"Do as you're told."

For a moment, Misiano froze in place. When I pointed my pistol toward his face the hapless man randomly seized a large cannoli from the rich assortment.

"Now, *eat!*"

Following an awkward pause, Misiano obeyed my command. He chewed the cannoli before swallowing, then instinctively licked powdered sugar off his fingertips.

"Help yourself to another."

"What—"

"Do it."

"*Why* . . . ?"


ETTA: Thursday; February 14, 1901

"Have you forgotten my plan to make you a star? What a waste it would be to feature you in this film, the public at large falling in love with you. And wanting more."

"You don't know that. Not for certain."

"I have no doubts. After all, we're investing a great deal of *money* here. What a waste if we couldn't capitalize on further projects with our newly created 'star.'"

"Apparently, I didn't think it through."

"And now that you have?"

"Money makes the world go around!" I bitterly chuckled.

"That's the way it's supposed to be."

"I'm not so sure. No question it's the way things *are.*"


BUTCH: Thursday; February 14, 1901

"We're Etta's best friends. As well as each other's."

"Almost sounds like you three are 'family.'"

"In every respect but blood."

"How I admire that. And envy you."

"You've never felt that way in a relationship?"

"LeRoy," Katheryn responded, her voice breaking in much the same manner that Etta's did when on rare occasion that equally strong woman would without warning begin to cry, "This is turning into something more than I initially expected."

"Life's funny that way."

"For you, too?" she inquired, her brown eyes hinting at a vulnerability I was only now becoming aware of.

"Yes. And, *yes*, I do honestly mean that."

"Why, this changes *everything*."


ETTA: THURSDAY; FEBRUARY 14, 1901

"So, you can appreciate our dilemma?"

"Indeed! In that case, I'll bow out and leave now."

"Nobody's holding you here."

"If you'll simply return my picture, I'll—"

"Are you referring to this?" Lakeland reached into the desktop drawer, removing the photograph in question.

"Well, there isn't any other. So—"

"That's not exactly true," a voice spoke from behind me.

I shifted in my seat to view DeFly, smirking while proferring several of the other portraits he'd taken during our first day out and about in New York. Me and Butch, me and Sundance, and me with both of the boys. Proof positive of my identity. As such, all it would take to hang me if I didn't do precisely what these wolf-like characters demanded.


SUNDANCE: THURSDAY; FEBRUARY 14, 1901

Perhaps at this moment of truth, the gangster's mind returned to his childhood. Long before he found La Casa Nostra, or it found him. Is it possible that, had this shivering excuse for a man turned left rather than right on a Palermo street some forty years ago—entered a church rather than wandering into a Mafia safe-house—he would not have become what now stood before me?

*That's one of those things in life you never will know. Not for certain.*

"Why?" he asked again in abject terror, as to my firm insistence that he down one sweet after another.

"Because I want you to experience your own private heaven before I send you to hell for eternity."

ETTA: THURSDAY; FEBRUARY 14, 1901

"Oh, my God!" I gasped. "How did you—"

"Wasn't all that difficult to put two and two together," DeFly flatly stated. "Or to connect with Lakeland."

"What do you want?" I heard myself asking. "If it's money, you'll be disappointed at how little I—"

"We're interested in the profits we can make after we've built you into the world's first great film star."

"Also," DeFly added with a leer, "You have more to offer a man than money, if you catch my drift."

BUTCH: THURSDAY; FEBRUARY 14, 1901

Kathryn Trumbell lay beside me thinking. I could tell that by watching her eyes: intense and turned deeply inward. Every time this woman had previously gone silent, she'd been scheming. How to retain as much of our cash as possible? Now her mind apparently drifted to other concerns than her own well-being or that of her beloved son. No doubt these still mattered. For the first time I did as well.

"I'm impressed," she firmly stated. "Understand, LeRoy, up to this moment I thought of you three as a pair of flighty outlaws and the loose woman they'd hooked up with."

"Scratch any surface, you'll find something deeper beneath."

"So you're seriously suggesting you might remain here?"

"'Suggesting.' That's the right term. Nothing's set."

ETTA: THURSDAY; FEBRUARY 14, 1901)

"You're a very handsome woman, Etta . . . Eloise . . . whatever name you go by," DeFly observed.

"Have no fear that we'll surrender you to the police," Lakeland added, "just so long as you do as told."

"Of course not. That wouldn't serve your purposes."

"Which you now perceive as . . . ?"

"To use me sexually whenever you choose, when you aren't exploiting my appeal as a source for profits."

"Remove any notions of leaving New York from your mind," DeFly threatened. "You'll continue on here—"

"This is blackmail—"

"True," Lakeland laughed. "Still, a minor crime, compared to the murder rap you face should you refuse our offer."

SUNDANCE: THURSDAY; FEBRUARY 14, 1901

"Go home. Wash yourself, from the top of your head to your toes. Then burn the towels and your clothes."

"Yes, sir."

"But don't . . . and I mean this, Samson! . . . do *not* tell your mother what went down here today!"

We were in an alleyway off Mulberry, hurrying there after I fired the fatal shot. I'd had no idea the bullet that sunk into The Enforcer's face would cause the skull to explode like an over-ripe melon. Pastries elegantly arranged along the bar, the white walls, glass windows—indeed, most everything present—transformed from its natural color to bright crimson.

Blood splattered on my face though incredibly my suit remained unstained. Owing to the angle at which the shot had penetrated Misiano, pieces of pink cartilidge had reached Samson. The boy had yelped like a surprised puppy, then staggered out onto the street, me following close behind. I'd seized Samson by the jacket collar and guided him away from the gruesome scene. Once we relocated in this hiding place, I drew a handkerchief and attempted to wipe his face clean.

"That was terrible," he wept.

"I warned you," I replied.


ETTA: THURSDAY; FEBRUARY 14, 1901

"Be here next Tuesday morning, bright and early."

"And should I choose not to?"

"You can run but you can't hide," DeFly replied.

"Either way, I lose."

"That's one way of looking at it," Lakeland laughed. "But are we, and the fame and fortune that will come your way, really that awful?"

I'd rather hang, I decided, than share myself with either of you. But I did not, for safety's sake, say so. Instead, I falsely nodded in acquiescence.


BUTCH: THURSDAY; FEBRUARY 14, 1901

"You realize this is the first time we've been together outside of the Boarding House, Kathryn Trumbell?"

"Yes. Refreshing, don't you think?"

She and I were seated in The Ashkenkazi Bagel Nook, a Jewish luncheonette on the corner of Delancey and Orchid. Hebrews settled in this area beginning in 1881, following the assassination of Russia's czar, Alexander II, by violent

THE LOWER EAST SIDE: Jewish immigrants achieved a delicate balance between Old World traditions and a desire to succeed within The American Dream of upward mobility through financial success achieved by hard work

Marxists hoping to incite a revolution. As had happened before, if never so blatantly, the country's Jews—most of whom were attempting to balance their identity as a people with a necessary adjustment to Russian conventions—were falsely blamed, then targeted as victims in the form of horrific *pogroms*. Persecution became so intense that many of Russia's Jews hastily migrated, many choosing The New World.

And so we found ourselves here, today. In yet another little world within the great patchwork quilt of cultures, ethnicities, and religions that constituted Manhattan.

ETTA: THURSDAY; FEBRUARY 14, 1901

"So you have me right where you want me."

"Ah! At last, you grasp the situation."

"Alright, then. I'll be here Tuesday morning."

"Just what we expected you to decide."

*Well, we'll have to wait and see about that! For I still have some games left to play. As you will shortly learn.*

SUNDANCE: THURSDAY; FEBRUARY 14, 1901

"Now, do as I say. Get back to your mother's house." Samson nodded. "And don't come near me again. Not ever."

"I can't promise that," he mumbled.

"Why?"

"I committed myself to this. And I'm not quitting."

"Listen, you fool," I began. Then I stopped short. For I recalled a saying Butch later shared with me that Mike Cassidy told him back when they first hooked up:.

*When you ride with a man, you* stick *with him. Way out west and, apparently, here in the East, too.*

"Alright, Samson," I softly replied. "We'll see."

Once he'd hurried off, I realized that however correct my advice may have been, I couldn't take it myself. Words were necessary to put my first-ever killing into some sort of a perspective. Ordinarily, I would have rushed to find Butch. But following our previous conversation, I ruled that out. What I needed was someone older, more versed in the ways of the world. So instead, I headed toward Park Row. Likely Bat would be in his office. I needed his wisdom now more than ever.

ETTA: THURSDAY; FEBRUARY 14, 1901

"You were so happy this morning," E.S. noted as he drove me back to the ferry, "yet so profoundly sad now."

I pretended to sneeze into a handkerchief while wiping away tears. "It's nothing for you to be concerned about."

"I don't agree," he responded in a tone fraught with emotion. "I overheard everything they said."

"Oh, E.S.!"

"I won't let them get away with this."

"But how could they be thwarted? With that photograph—"

"I'll swipe it from the office between now and your departure. Then return it to you." Immediately, I made eye contact. In response, the genial fellow added, "No strings attached!"

"But if you're caught, that might end your career."

"I won't be."

I didn't mention the other pictures DeFly had in his mid-Manhattan studio. For I was fearful E.S. might try to break in and steal them as well, only to wind up dead. Perhaps, though, Butch and Sundance might pull off such a risky scheme.

After all, they were a pair of professional thieves.

BUTCH: THURSDAY; FEBRUARY 14, 1901

As Kathryn and I discussed our options for the future, we snacked on coffee cake, potato pancakes ('latkas') with sour cream, smoked herring ('kippers'), and 'blintzes,' a rolled pancake filled with sweet, tangy cheese.

"There is so much to sample here in New York, LeRoy, that I would love to share with you." Her eyes appeared hopeful.

"It's an appealing possibility," I admitted.

"Understand, I'm at a vulnerable point in my life. You are sincere as to all you've said?"

"Indeed. But don't forget—"

"We're still in 'the talking stage.'"

"Which will continue for the next several days."

"When do you believe a decision may be reached?"

"Knowing me and my longtime companions," I chuckled, "not until the last minute."

ETTA: THURSDAY; FEBRUARY 14, 1901

"Mr. Lakeland will personally direct the train robbery sequence. He's learned that the Pinkerton detectives, Lefors and Siringo, are here in New York. And convinced them to to play themselves."

"Can this get any crazier?"

"Not likely."

"What next? Butch and Sundance cast as the outlaws?"

"Not a bad idea, come to think of it."

"You know, E.S., I've often thought of my life as a novel. With me, of course, as the central character."

"Everyone's guilty of doing that."

"My point is, if any novel or film ever became as contrived as my actual life has, no one would believe it."

SUNDANCE: THURSDAY; FEBRUARY 14, 1901

"I've . . . done something . . . bad."

"How bad?"

"*Bad* bad. I need to talk."

"Catholics say that confession is good for the soul."

"Likely they're right. If such a thing even exists."

"Don't you believe in God anymore, Henry?" asked Bat.

"No idea now what to believe or not believe in."

"Most folks feel that way these days."

"Bat, you think maybe confession will work for those of us who aren't members of that denomination?"

"Well, there's a Jewish doctor in Austria who believes that in our time, a patient can talk to *him* instead of a priest. Confession, with God removed from the equation."

"What does he call this?"

"Psycho-analysis."

"Maybe that's the way it has to be today. In what Etta insists is an 'ever more secular society.'"

"For those of us whose faith has been shaken? Yeah! Sigmund Freud's transformation of the spiritual into the scientific. Same old method with a contemporary title."

"So it's true, then."

"What?"

"The more things change, the more they stay the same."


ETTA: THURSDAY; FEBRUARY 14, 1901

"Oh, how I loathe Lakeland and DeFly."

"Bitterness doesn't agree with you, Miss Etta."

"'Bitter' is what I do not want to become. Though life's unexpected twists and turns are moving me in that direction."

"Try not to let that happen." E.S.'s eyes welled up with tears. "I'd so hate to see a woman as lovely as yourself surrender to the *darkness*."

"I'll try, E.S.," I assured him. "Let's wait and see what comes next. After all, time hasn't run out."

"True. But it sure is closing in fast."


BUTCH: THURSDAY; FEBRUARY 14, 1901

"Three names," Kathryn mused.

"Huh?"

"You're the only man I've ever met with three different names: Butch, James, LeRoy."

"Maybe I'm three men, all inhabitin' one body."

"Oh, my. You've just revealed something personal."

"Now, if only I can figure which is the real me—"

Kathryn leaned across the circular table and gazed deep into my eyes. "If you do choose to stay, LeRoy, perhaps I might help you determine that."

"I like, admire, and respect you, Kathryn Trumbell."

"But don't 'love' me, as you do Etta Place?"

"Keep in mind, she and I, along with Henry . . . Harry . . . Sundance . . . have more'n six years of history."

"Huh! He has three names as well."

"Never thought about it that way. But, yeah."

ETTA: THURSDAY; FEBRUARY 14, 1901

"Well, there's one thing Lakeland and DeFly won't be counting on, E.S. I hadn't planned to tell you this—"

"I'm listening."

"It won't be me who arrives on Tuesday morning. Annie Oakley will assume my place, costumed as 'Etta.'"

"Where will you be?"

"At Madison Square Garden, making ready to perform as Little Miss Sureshot later that evening."

"And when the show ends?"

"Off and running, though God alone knows where to."

"Glad to hear you still believe in the Lord."

"That was merely a figure of speech."

"Maybe. Then again, maybe not."

"With you around, perhaps I may yet regain my faith."

SUNDANCE: THURSDAY; FEBRUARY 14, 1901

"First, did you take pleasure in killing Misiano?"

"None whatsoever."

"Good. For if you had, you'd be lost to us forever."

"Yet I feel no shame, Bat."

"Tell me, how do you perceive the moment, in retrospect?"

"A hard job that had to be done."

"This, I understand. Back in 1877, when I was sheriff of Ford County, Kansas, my brother, Ed, served for a spell as Dodge City's chief constable. While attempting to disarm several drunk cowboys, one of the rowdies fired a pistol and claimed Ed's life. When I learned what happened, I hunted the man down and shot him."

"Everyone knows that story. Made you famous."

"That's one way of lookin' at it."

"There's another?"

"Confirmed that I had the killer instinct. Anyway, what you said—'I took no pleasure yet I felt no shame'?—same with me, way back then. That's somethin' in our favor."

"Yet I feel such *guilt*."

"At least, though, you've learned your lesson?"

"What d'you mean by that?"

"You won't pursue the other two?"

"Wish I could say that's so. But I vowed to complete this before leaving. And I aim to."

ETTA: Thursday; February 14, 1901

"I'll be glad to play my part in your ruse and help you anyway I can. By the way, guess who's assigned to film the boxing match later at Madison Square Garden? Me!"

"That's wonderful." As with Samson days earlier at the Plaza, I impulsively leaned over and kissed E.S.'s cheek.

"I'll accept *that* as full payment," he blushed.

I've done it again! Relying not on my brain to extract myself from a difficult situation but a superficial blessing. My good looks, once again. How did Western writer Bret Harte put it?

*Oh, I remember, 'There is no gift that requires as little exertion to work its wonders as a woman's beauty.'*

BUTCH: Thursday; February 14, 1901

"Don't overrate me, Kathryn," I said, gazing into her now mellow eyes, appreciating the sincere affection found there.

"LeRoy, you're the perfect man for me."

"I'm anything but perfect, as Etta could tell you."

"You didn't listen closely enough to what I said."

"Not sure what you mean."

"I've learned that nothing, and no one, is ever perfect."

"So—"

"—I said 'perfect for *me*.' All my life, I hoped to find such a fellow. Always disappointed and moving on—"

"Then . . . ?"

"You came along."

ETTA: Thursday; February 14, 1901

"We've each of us had a rough day," Bat announced. "Let's head out and try to enjoy ourselves. Any objections?"

There were none, of course. As we rode in a carriage to a northern sector, Bat waxed rhapsodic on our destination. The area called Harlem had been constructed at the previous century's mid-point when investors predicted an upscale enclave reaching three square miles northward across 110 St. would prove irresistible to incoming Midwestern families. Well-to-do folks arriving from heartland locations like St. Louis hoped to take part in the big business conducted in Manhattan. But when a national recession and bank failures halted that migration, handsome buildings were left to rot.

Meanwhile, an unforseen population shift occurred. Many African Americans in the deep south, no longer willing to tolerate their status as third (at best) class citizens, headed for northern climes in search of work: Chicago, Newark, Detroit, and of course The Big Apple. Buildings in the now all but abandoned Harlem district (its name derived from a Dutch settlement that flourished there some 250 years earlier) could be purchased at bargain-basement prices. Over the following quarter-century, properties that included Morningside Park—bounded by Central Park North to the south, the Hudson River to the West, 155th Street at the Harlem River further north still, and Fifth Avenue on the East Side—transformed into an ethnic neighborhood akin to those we'd already explored downtown.

"What the locals refer to as a Renaissance has taken place here," Bat continued. He explained that, finally freed from the shackles in the South—once physical, now invisible, yet still in place—African Americans at last achieved a modicum of liberation in the North. In this self-contained community a concept called The New Negro emerged. Paintings by Aaron Douglas, poetry by Langston Hughes, and music by Joseph Lamb led to an evolving identity based on total freedom of expression. Cast away the old rules of what can or can't be accomplished; do what comes naturally in art as well in life.

An innovative musical form had developed, drawn from southern minstrel shows and cakewalk performances, remixed for the new century; unrestricted as to syncopation thanks to jazzy experiments and ragged rhythms. The genre's fitting title: Ragtime. A smooth piano base for such sounds (church gospel styles, as secularized in road houses and juke-joints) had been augmented by brass and woodwinds.

"If in the past," Bat concluded, "American music offered nothing more than inferior imitations of formal compositions from Europe, here you discover in embryo the true soul of our nation: gettin' down-and-dirty-and-true-to-life with a wild beat. A fitting soundtrack to accompany modern city life."

## SUNDANCE: THURSDAY; FEBRUARY 14, 1901

To claim that African Americans lining the streets of Harlem were flamboyantly dressed would be an understatement. The women—mostly tall girls though a few were pleasingly plump—wore crop-waisted dresses I'd read about but not yet seen. These, I realized, were not merely casual outfits but fashion statements. A means by which a female could convey her personal philosophy on life. "It's a brand new century in a city of the future: *Anything Goes!*"

Raspberry-hued berets (of the type Etta informed me had been popularized by French women a decade earlier) topped the heads of many strolling by. Feather boas added a giddy flair. Zoot Suits for men consisted of high-waisted, wide-legged pants, and long overcoats draped over a fellow's shoulders, this an influence borrowed from Latinos on the West Coast. Vanilla-colored Panama hats with wide yellow bands added to the sense of a style derived from far-flung sources, including a sultry Caribbean influence.

"Who's that center-stage?" I asked Bat. The dazzling finger-movements of an ensemble's pianist performed magical music' unlike anything I'd ever heard.

"That's Scott Joplin, from Arkansas. Two years ago, his composition 'The Maple Leaf Rag' became the first example of this type of music to be recorded."

"What's he doing in Manhattan?" I wondered.

"Scott's visiting New York, playing a gig while deciding if he ought to move here permanently."

"He'll sure find a welcome-mat awaiting."

"'Maple Leaf' became a cross-over hit," Emma added. "The disc sold well not only to members of the black community but whites, too. At least, liberal-thinking folks."

"I'm loving it," I laughed, forgetting all my woes in the whirlwind of rapidly changing sights and celebratory sounds.

ETTA: THURSDAY; FEBRUARY 14, 1901

"That's Jack Johnson," noted Bat, pointing to a tall, handsome fellow sipping champagne with friends at a nearby table. "Great boxer, celebrating a recent victory."

"Bat predicts that in time he'll break the color barrier and bec ome the first black heavyweight world-champion."

That's when it struck me. Other than Johnson, every man and woman enjoying food and beverage along with the heady music and uninhibited chorus line of lithe and lovely dancers was as white as us. "I don't get it. Where are the locals?"

As it turned out, Club DeLuxe had been 'discovered' by wealthy midtown Anglos. They flocked to Harlem after hours to take in what had become 'all the rage': Rag, both the music and the lifestyle surrounding this innovative sound. As a result, though, locals could no longer attend most clubs owing to strict outdated city regulations banning any mixing of the races. African Americans

ACROSS 110th STREET: The fictional 'Club DeLuxe' in this narrative is closely modelled on the actual Cotton Club, where African American performers dazzled Anglo audiences that flocked to Harlem to enjoy the sights and sounds of Ragtime; in fact, the 'real deal' could be experienced on the streets and in underground ethnic enclaves.

instead settled for cellar clubs, 'The Underground.' What we experienced, I realized, was not 'the real deal' but a facsimile created for well-to-do visitors. A tourist trap, simply put.

"Why does Jack Johnson rate as an exception?"

"The fight game made him wealthy. Simple as that."

Money does indeed make the world go around! And, if I should agree to sail for South America, things will be no different. People *are* the same everywhere.

*Apparently, I have indeed learned something about the way of the world over the past several weeks.*


BUTCH: FRIDAY; FEBRUARY 15, 1901

Kathryn and I slipped back into bed. I realized after a brief spell of trying to make love with this lush and eager woman that I would not be able to perform.

"It's not you," I sighed. "It's me."

"Should I assume you're missing Etta?"

"That's not it."

"You're certainly thinking of someone other than me."

"True," I admitted.

"Alright, cowboy. Tell me what's bothering you."

I could not yet speak of the secret Henry and I shared. If we hadn't been able to raise the subject with Etta, how could I do so with a virtual stranger? Likewise, there existed another issue; whether or not I ought to join my pardner on the vengeance trail. So I poured out my heart to Kathryn about the latter problem in lieu of love-making. As I did, the look in the woman's eyes revealed her to be a sympathetic listener.

"On the one hand, there's my loyalty to Henry. And the sense that I ought to stand by him, right or wrong."

"As compared to your loyalty to your own self. You can be true to values basic to your existence—"

"Or?"

"Honor your commitment to the most important person in your life. Or, at least, one of two."

"There you have it. Damned if I do; damned if I don't."


—INTERLUDE—

BAT: OCTOBER 25, 1921

*Once, a reporter from a competing paper asked my wife, Emma, for an interview, focusing on what it was like to be the bride of a celebrity. "If anyone expects a typical Westerner," the fellow wrote of her, "he will be much mistaken. Of medium*

*height, Mrs. Masterson is a woman of retiring disposition. A lady from Philadelphia whose great loves in life—other than her husband—are housekeeping and reading."
Well, that might have been true of the Emma he met. But behind that demure façade existed a true female trailblazer.*

*Her father, John Walter, established himself as a successful teamster in Pennsylvania before losing his life as a yankee soldier in 1863. Six years old at the time, Emma quietly lived with her mother until meeting a professional foot-racer from Minnesota named Ed Moulton, "The Gopher Boy." Their chance encounter led to a hasty marriage in 1873. While touring the country, Emma raced against Ed in sprints, wearing wildly colorful costumes to attract large crowds.*

*Daringly for that time, Emma decked herself out in revealing tights, so men and boys bought tickets even if they had no interest in racing as a sport. Fans then paid hard cash to be photographed beside the charismatic woman. One local journalist described her as "the equal to any man" on the field, and "notably unashamed of her body despite lingering Victorian values surrounding her." When Emma competed with her husband, more often than not she proved victorious. Strong women hanker for equally strong men so eventually she dumped the loser and moved on. In time, to me.*

*Emma's career was cut short when she began to suffer from asthma as well as a previously undiagnosed case of epilepsy. These took a terrible toll on her appearance, but that sort of attraction . . . which had initially drawn me to her . . . no longer*

TWO OF A KIND: Emma Masterson, wife of Bat, joined him for a life of adventure during their youth, then shared his twilight years as the two became celebrity Manhattanites in the early 20th Century.

*seemed important. Emma had guts; when I backed young Bob Fitzsimmons in a middleweight title fight in New Orleans, 1891, Emma refused to accept the rules of a 'male only' audience, dressing in one of my suits to observe the match.*

*Though she got herself arrested for that little stunt and spent a night in jail, I proposed while she was still in stir and married Emma the day of her release. Didn't matter to me whether or not Emma was legally divorced from Ed. That's when she, her looks further faded but a strong sense of self glowing more radiantly than ever, decided to become the sort of cultivated lady she'd long admired from afar. Scoffing at playing bridge with other females, Emma read the classics and discovered her until then dormant propensity for intellectuality.*

*Once we moved to New York, she hosted gourmet dinners for such guests as the Roosevelts. Her looks were diminished once more when, suffering a fit as she stood near the stove, a pot of boiling water poured over her. Briefly, she worried that I might be uncomfortable with her current appearance. In fact, this situation only made me more aware of how devoted I was to Emma, the remarkable person, as well as Emma, the once lovely woman.*

*Someday, Lolly, I hope you will find a man worthy of sharing your life. Be sure that his love for your inner beauty exceeds that for your good looks!*

# PART FIFTEEN: LONGTIME COMPANIONS

"The love that dare not speak its name."
—Lord Alfred Douglas

ETTA: Friday; February 15, 1901

"Well, if anyone can pass herself off as Little Miss Sureshot, it's certainly you," Frank Butler told me when we were introduced by Cody and Buntline Friday morn. I had risen early, completed my morning constitutional, and taken a quick breakfast of hard cooked eggs and milk so as to be right on time for our rehearsal, which would last till noon. When I appeared before the trio in the Garden's grand arena, I wore the gaudy cowgirl costume Annie appeared in each evening: soft buckskin vest and dress, embroidered with rhinestones. Hardly what I had worn as a true Western woman but perfectly attune to what an audience of Easterners expected.

"If I could pass myself off as her for you, then I reckon I can make it work with anyone."

How easy it was to grasp why women of all ages in the towns and cities which Bill's Wild West passed through developed huge crushes on Butler, much to the consternation of his devoted wife. For Frank was cut from the same metal as other men of the far plains whom I had known. Taller and rougher around the edges than my Butch and Sundance; more on the order of Lefors and Siringo, the shootist boasted one of those long drooping moustaches that represented for people with little if any knowledge of the way things really were a fantasy on the fading frontier. Men dreamed of being him; women swooned while observing him from rickety seats, convinced he personified a last example of 'real men' from our romantic past.


SUNDANCE: Friday; February 15, 1901

"Stop talking like a nineteenth century gunslinger, Kid," Bat growled when I joined him at his office early in the morn to talk again. "We're in New York City and this is the 20th."

"A man can't stop being what he is."

"No? Look at me. Haven't I changed?"

"Less that, I'd guess, than adapted."

"Alright, then. If I did, so can you. And Butch."

"He more likely than me."

"You're selling yourself short."

"I have a solid sense of my strengths and weaknesses. The world is passing me by."

"If you believe that's the case, then it's true."

"Don't go all philosophic on me, Bat."

"More a case of common sense. I'm beginning to believe the reason you're heading down this vengeance trail has less to do with family than something deep inside *you*."

"Care to elaborate?"

"I think you want to go down fighting in a high noon shoot-out to avoid what's coming in four days."

"That hurts."

"It's not the Mafiosos you want to kill, Henry. Far as I'm concerned, it's something deep within yourself."


ETTA: FRIDAY; FEBRUARY 15, 1901

"Here's how we'll do it," Cody explained. "First, you and Frank will ride a pair of high-stepping steeds, waving to the crowd. The Rough Riders of the World will follow, each holding his reins with one hand while wildly firing a six-shooter, filled with blanks, above his head. Following ecstatic applause, you'll dismount beside Bat and myself."

"After which I'll perform an exhibit?"

"I'll toss glass decanters up into the air," Cody continued, "slowly at first, one by one . . . then, ever faster . . . while you plug away with your Winchester .73. shooting blanks."

"Got ya."

"While I fire real bullets from a carefully arranged spot off in the shadows," Frank concluded.

"Let's hope it works. Then what?"

"Once finished, step back as our grunts remove all Western paraphernalia from the center and set up a ring. As the crowd shifts attention to that, and we introduce the infamous pugilists, you'll slip back through the curtain and out of the building, where a carriage will be waiting."

"I see a flaw in the plan."

"Tell us," Frank asked with concern.

"Me, making it from the arena to the cab. But if Lefors and Siringo get wind of the switch, won't they hurry here and nab me before I can get away?"

"You're right," Cody admitted. "That, we must work on."


BUTCH: FRIDAY; FEBRUARY 15, 1901

During the early morning hours, we had met again in Mrs. Trumbell's private parlor. Owing to the developing feelings between us, I felt comfortable asking Kathryn to reveal more about herself. Her true identity, compared to the carefully created portrait which she offered to the world. And hid behind. As in fact do all of us, each in one's own unique manner.

"I'm a single, and in all ways singular, woman, battered about by life. I may not be as young or pretty as Etta—"

"You look mighty fine for a woman of . . ."

"Forty-two."

"You could easily pass for forty-one."

She responded with a combination of cynical humor and mild resentment. "Thanks, I guess. But make no mistake about it. If things don't work out well for your companion, in twenty years Etta will be like me: mere flotsam and jetsom bouncing about in a hard, cold world of men. Most uninterested in any woman once her sweet bird of youth has passed."

"Perhaps you're right."

"At twenty-one, a female may be confused and ready to make choices. Two decades later, she's desperate. Two spouses ago, the future did seem as bright, rich, and open to me as it does for Etta at this moment. Now . . ."

ETTA: FRIDAY; FEBRUARY 15, 1901

"Forgive me for asking you to use your mind," Owen Wister had written in his preface to *The Virginian*. "It is a thing which no novelist should expect of his readers."

Following several hours of rehearsal in the arena with Cody and Frank, I'd retired to Annie's room. There, as I had noticed earlier, sat a copy of the very book my boys were buzzing about, likely left there for me by one or the other of them. Anxious to discover what had so caught their interest, I breezed through the text.

As I read on, the opening words took on a deeper meaning. I sensed that, beyond the narrative, here I encountered not merely one more romantic adventure on the West but a true novel of ideas. The author employed his wide-ranging (no pun intended) ensemble to illustrate a rough-hewn yet strict code by which people once defined themselves via the display of quiet grace under extreme pressure. Leaving each reader to decide whether or not that 'way' necessarily came to an end with what Frederick Jackson Turner labelled the closing of the frontier, or if such values might continue into the 20th. That is, if they were principles that belonged not only to an already bygone time and place, but America itself.

SUNDANCE: FRIDAY; FEBRUARY 15, 1901

"Go away!"

"I can't, Joseph."

"I've told you too much already. And because I did, a man is dead. Shot down like a dog—"

"One less bum to dirty Little Italy's streets."

"That's not for us to decide."

"You lock 'em up daily. And some are executed."

"Following trial by a judge and jury."

"Joseph, please! *Help*. I'm in too far to quit."

"The Wolf knows what's happened. Word on the street has it that Lupo dispatched Cincotta to execute you."

"That solves my problem. I'll allow that mobster to trail me until I catch him."

"The person you will 'catch' is yourself, Henry. The true victim of this vendetta will be The Sundance Kid."


ETTA: FRIDAY; FEBRUARY 15, 1901

Like Molly Wood, a recent arrival from Vermont, I felt a certain horror (despite my own years on the frontier) in grasping that the man to whom she has become attracted will, when push comes to shove, hang his best friend. Initially, the Virginian's quietude struck Molly as aloof. And as such offensive. Then she (and I) realized this was not the case.

The hero, a man of few words, had been driven by what he considered an unavoidable responsibility. His duty to giddy, lovable Steve had reached its conclusion when The Virginian caught the boy stealing cattle from the Judge's ranch a second time. One discretion could be discounted owing to Steve's immaturity. Now, Steve rated as an outlaw, in need of elimination every bit as much as Trampas, the boy's corrupter.

*A true hero walks his own lonely path. And does what he, after careful consideration, believes to be correct. No matter whether others agree. For he must live with himself afterwards. That is the true measure of a man.*


BUTCH: FRIDAY; FEBRUARY 15, 1901

"First husband? A sad, pathetic loser who squandered his money and most of mine with business schemes gone wrong and late-night gambling fiascos in smoke-filled rooms."

"I assume things didn't improve once you left him?"

"Hardly! Second a slick fella who promised me everything, then run off without a trace."

"You comfortable sharing the specifics?"

"The bastard took one look at our son and realized Samson was not quite right as to mind or body. Next thing I knew Ernest was gone."

"I've encountered such men in my own time."

"With him out of the picture, I could either roll over and die or stand tall and fight, tooth and nail, to survive. My main priority was Samson, he more important to me than my own life."

"As Etta would put it, you refused to fail."

"Whatever I did . . . and some of it was pretty sordid, before I saved enough to purchase this place . . . I did for my boy. Any hope for personal happiness long since forgotten."

"Ain't necessarily so."

"If you choose to stay, LeRoy, maybe in time you'll convince me of that."

## ETTA: FRIDAY; FEBRUARY 15, 1901

Eventually, Molly managed to accept the hanging. But when her man set aside their wedding date to enter into a duel with his enemy, Trampas, she momentarily believed this final machismo indulgence could not be tolerated. The Virginian must choose between a violent deed in the world of men or the softness and tranquility Molly offered. Yet he did not buckle. True to his code, there was no decision to make. For a cowboy, it all comes down to one single value: a man's gotta do what a man's gotta do. And The Virginian knew full well what that meant.

On the streets of Medicine Bow, The Virginian shot down Trampas in a fair fight. And to her own surprise, rather than flee, Molly awaited his return. The task at hand completed, he laid down his gun, as she requested. Together, they traveled to her home town in New England, he now willing to transform from hero to Everyman for the remainder of his life. As Wister noted in closing, "Bennington probably was disappointed." The citizenry lined up to witness a legend step down from the train, only to be surprised that her companion was not the wild-eyed broncho-buster they anticipated from her letters, "merely a tall man with a usual straw hat. This was dull."

*Does a man of the West cease to be such should he move East? If Butch and Sundance were to remain here, would they shortly grow dull as well? And, if so, how might I react?*

## SUNDANCE: FRIDAY; FEBRUARY 15, 1901

"I've got a queasy feeling about this," I said as Samson and I checked out one Little Italy street after another. Mid-day approached; most men remained in their places of business, awaiting the lunch hour. Women, having completed their grocery shopping, returned to cramped apartments, there to to slave over the laundry before preparing an evening meal. Kids were still in school try-ing to concentrate, wishing they were outside, running wild. Momentarily, the neighborhood existed in eerie silence. That infamous calm which preceded an inevitable storm.

"I don't like it either. Want me to scout ahead?"

"Too risky, Samson. Stay here. But keep your eyes open so the Mafioso can't close in from behind."

"I checked. Nobody back there."

"That means he's up ahead somewhere."

With that, Samson rushed ahead before I could stop him. Moments later, he disappeared down a side street. I admired his courage. And envied his youth. Suddenly, I felt very old. And dog tired.


ETTA: FRIDAY; FEBRUARY 15, 1901

The 'unknowable' Virginian; now a humble guy named Jeff. Those mas-culine values he once embodied—the very aspects of Butch and Sundance's behavior that so often offended my female sensibilities—were nowhere to be seen. Jeff now ready to integrate himself into ordinary life.

*Will the East civilize such a man, in the best sense of that term, or only tame him, in the worst?*

If we were to leave America and sail off, might we three be born again in Bolivia, or wherever we find ourselves? Then live out one of the oldest of human fantasies . . . a second chance at life. That abiding dream, of course, represented the heart and soul of America, a nation founded by people who weren't happy with their lives and insisted on trying again. In the previous century, everything seemed so simple: 'GO WEST, YOUNG MAN.' And woman! Now, we've run out of wide open spaces. As a result, everything strikes us as more complex. Where should we go now?

Why, for all I know, maybe it's to the moon! Americans will always hunger to find and travel to the next frontier. Why? Because it's in our nature.


BUTCH: FRIDAY; FEBRUARY 15, 1901

"Do you know where he is now?" I asked Bat. A growing concern for Sun-dance caused me to seek out our mentor in the small coffee shop on Park Row where I knew he often took his noon meals. We huddled together in the recesses of this crowded diner, filled with cigar-smoke and the loud chatter of men in temporary isolation from the outside world. Which also meant from women. Momentarily happy in their man cave.

"Not certain. Sundance stopped by the office earlier."

"Admitting that he was the one who killed Misiano?"

"I knew that, Butch. Without a byline, I wrote the final draft of the story. I did keep his name out of print."

"Thank Heaven for that."

"Set such high-falutin' matters aside. In the here and now, we got us a 'situation' that's about to explode."


ETTA: FRIDAY; FEBRUARY 15, 1901

It occurred to me now that Molly did not capitulate, which would have disappointed me in the character who had come to life as if she were a flesh and blood woman. No; not any more than myself should I depart with either or both of my men. With difficulty, Wister's romantic couple had arrived at a compromise, necessary if they were to step into the future with 'the desired other,' as Wister put it. A sense of equality evened things out.

At the conclusion of any great novel, a reader closes the volume in the regretful manner of bidding farewell to a dear friend. And which, like such a beloved companion, may be renewed at some time in the future merely by bringing the volume down from its safe place on a shelf. So I set the book down with a greater appreciation of the two cavaliers who had shared so much of my life. Owen Wister had provided what, despite my years in their company, did not naturally reveal itself: a delineation of the manner in which an elite breed of men men remain true to one's essential conception of self.

Even as I, to fully grow from girl to woman, must do now.


SUNDANCE: FRIDAY; FEBRUARY 15, 1901

"Prepare to die, killer of my companion."

I turned and spotted Salvadore Cincotta stepping out from an alley on Mott Street. His gun pointed toward my head from little more than six feet away. My weapon felt like a useless weight in my right hand. Should I try to raise the pistol, Cincotta would immediately fire.

"Before you pull the trigger, know this; I harbor no regrets for eliminating such filth from the world."

"So I face a man of conviction and courage. Know then that I admire who and what you are even as I take your life."

"You gonna talk, talk. You gonna shoot, shoot."

As I stood in place, wondering if I would hear the blast before I died or if my life would be snuffed out before that sound bore into my consciousness, two things occurred to me. First, Samson would by now be somewhere up ahead and likely escape the coming violence. Second, Etta and Butch were free to become a conventional couple. As Bat once put it, 'Everyone dies. Some of us get to choose the time and place.' Well, if this is *it*, at least I'd do so with a smile on my face. I'd gone as far as possible in reaching the goal that I'd set for myself.

ELOISE: FRIDAY; FEBRUARY 15, 1901

"When you ride with a man, you *stick* with him."

"I don't understand," Susan replied. She, Elizabeth, and I sat together in their hotel suite, sipping tea and chatting. I had chosen to wear my Magen David openly during my latest visit. The two had eyed it curiously upon my arrival, though never chose to make a comment. Still, each woman's pair of eyes revealed what I had learned at the Suffragist meeting. Though both stood against stereotypical thinking and broad prejudices against the Jews or any other ethnic group, these feminist leaders perceived themselves as part of a privileged class; eager to help all ethnics rise up in the world, though not necessarily inclined to include any of us in their small, tight circle of friends.

As to Susan's reaction to my sudden statement, I replied, "The men in my life said that often. It has something to do with each fellow's sense of what it means to be a man."

"In the machismo sense?" Elizabeth asked, deep concern in her voice and manner. "How I abhor such thinking."

"As do I! But, *no*. Something far more meaningful."

"Are you having second thoughts about the Movement?"

"I'm having second thoughts, Susan, about *everything*."

"We thought you'd made such progress," Elizabeth sighed.

"Was it in truth 'progress' or merely 'change'?"

"That depends on one's point-of-view."

"I'm still developing my own."

"As a woman?"

"Of course. But also as a person."

"Explain, please?"

"As an individual. Yes, as a woman, for that's an essential part of me. Also, a Jew. If not necessarily referring to religion, then bloodlines, as I've only recently learned. Next, I must decide as to my own approach to politics. I am who I am."

"We respect that," Elizabeth duly noted.

"Considering what you said about people of other ethnicities and diverse religions, would you still even want to continue mentoring me?"

BUTCH: Friday; February 15, 1901

"Fire," I shouted while turning a corner and arriving on the scene, the dismal situation clear even as I raised my gun, "and I'll do the same."

As Sundance glanced diagonially to grasp who had spoken, his eyes met mine. He, Cincotta, and myself formed the three points of an invisible triangle; what in the old days along the southern border we referred to as a Mexican standoff. Like Henry, the Mafioso had been surprised by my intrusion. This allowed my partner enough time to swerve and draw his pistol.

"Thanks, Butch."

"You'd have done the same for me."

We three stood stock still. Likely, Cincotta's mind worked at this moment as did my own, and Sundance's as well. Do I dare shoot first? Or ought I wait for someone else to initiate the coming bloodshed?

ETTA: Friday; February 15, 1901

"It's only a matter of time til we expand our horizons," Elizabeth responded. "We could begin doing so with you."

"It would help if you'd consider converting, of course, to Unitarianism, which most of us now follow," Susan added.

"I'm uncomfortable with that suggestion. At this point in my life, I want to be accepted without restrictions."

"Etta, everything you say sounds so personal."

"I'm aware of that, Susan. Once, I believed in objective reality. That we each of us perceives the world in much the same manner as everyone else."

"Now?" Elizabeth queried.

"If there is indeed such a thing as objective reality, I no longer believe that any person, limited as to perception, can ever know it. So I've developed a theory of my own. *Subjectivism*: an acceptance that each of us lives in a world of our own making, which exists only in that specific individual's mind."

"The last time we spoke, you were so adamant about your dedication to the basic values you learned as a child."

"That was then. This, now. Things change."

"You aren't comfortable with the Protestant vision of life in which you were raised?"

"No. Nor, as I've learned, with every aspect of Judaism."

"What then?" Elizabeth queried, confused.

"I'll take what strikes me as 'right' from each faith as I find my own way in the world. I guess it comes down to this: I don't wish to become a member of any one group, be it based on gender, religious, social, cultural, political, or what have you. I am determined to live my life as a unique person on all levels."

SUNDANCE: FRIDAY; FEBRUARY 15, 1901

"We can all walk away from this," Butch insisted, at last breaking the overpowering silence. "No one need die today."

"You are wrong about that," Cincotta replied. "He killed one of my own. Our sense of honor demands retribution."

"Back off, Butch. Now, he and I are evenly matched."

"I have no intention of letting you kill him in cold blood, any more than I do of allowing him to murder you."

"That does not matter," a fourth voice called out.

"What . . . ?" I gasped.

I'd been so intensely focused on the stand-off that I'd missed the approach of yet another player in this mad game. For now, a pair of figures hurried down Hester. Lupo the Wolf held a pistol to Samson's forehead. The youth, aware these were likely his last minutes of life, openly wept.

"Welcome, my consigliere!" Cincotta announced.

"If either of you moves," Lupo said, "I blow this boy's brains out."

Suddenly, everything appeared altered. For an innocent life was at stake. If necessary, we both of us must sacrifice ourselves to save Samson. If we'd learned anything from life, it was this . . . when push comes to shove, a person must do the right thing. Or, at least, what strikes him as 'right.'


ETTA: FRIDAY: FEBRUARY 15, 1901

"Let's have this out once and for all," Elizabeth stated. "What's on your mind right now?" Her tone implied that the time had come for them to grasp where I stood on major issues, and vice-versa.

"Well, as to that fundamental belief my boys espouse, I've been wondering of late if such values also apply to women."

"Surely, that's been the case with Susan and myself. We've stuck together through thick and thin."

"And how I admire you for it! As to the men you meet, though, and who enter into your lives? What of them?"

"I never felt comfortable around members of the other gender," Susan explained. "Marriage did not interest me."

"My husband was a wonderful man. What primarily attracted me to him was his abolitionist stance. After the war he joined me on the Suffragist crusade. We happily shared our lives."

"Following his passing?"

"I met Susan."

"Ever since, we have fulfilled one another's needs."

With that, they proudly gripped one another's hands. And at last I understood the breadth and depth of their coupling.


BUTCH: FRIDAY; FEBRUARY 15, 1901

"Set that boy loose and you can shoot me down," Sundance responded, raising both hands high, still grasping his gun in the right. I prepared to drop my pistol if our adversaries allowed us hope that Samson might survive.

"He's seen too much to live," the Wolf insisted.

"If that's the case," I interjected, "so have *they*."

Warily, the Mafiosos glanced from side to side. Residents of the neighborhood—men, women, children—appeared on the street. Other Neopolitans observed with fear and fascination from behind corners of buildings or through shop windows. For here was history in the making.


ETTA: FRIDAY; FEBRUARY 15, 1901

"Let me ask, Elizabeth: Was Mr. Stanton a teetotaler?"

"He enjoyed a drink now and then."

"But not to the point of becoming abusive?"

"Never!"

"How, then, can you favor Prohibition? When your own marriage proves not all men who drink are dangerous."

"I'll repeat what I said at the meeting. The most important issue is the vote. We can't win without Carrie Nation's support."

"Tell me! The men in your own life were never abusive?"

"I'd have left either or both had that been the case, Elizabeth! More likely, shoot them dead."

"Do you now refer to 'Eloise Long' or 'Etta Place'?"

"How long have you known?" I gasped.

"I guessed that very first day on the train."


SUNDANCE: FRIDAY; FEBRUARY 15, 1901

"Don't listen to 'em," screamed Samson. With a deft movement, he swirled and kicked Lupo in the crotch, then tore loose, frantically dashing toward me.

"Drop down!" I shouted. "You're blocking my shot."

"Mr. Longabaugh!" The boy shouted just before the bullets began to fly. "Help—"

Cincotta aimed at the kid but before that Mafioso could get off a shot, Butch fired. His bullet ripped through Cincotta's right arm, scoring this horrific afternoon's first blood. The soldati tossed his pistol into the air and, as it fell back down, seized the piece with his left hand. Simultaneously, The Wolf took aim at Butch, this action distracting me from the boy's plight. I fired fast and nicked Lupo on the left leg, causing his own shot to go wild.

Next, Cincotta let loose at Butch, the two rounds barely missing my pardner's head. As the Mafioso's legs crumbled beneath his bulky frame, Cincotta emitted a shriek of pain, squatted low, and somehow managed to fire at Samson.

ETTA: FRIDAY; FEBRUARY 15, 1901

"On some level," I admitted to Susan, "I guess I've known all along that you'd seen through my masquerade."

"Break with your outlaws, once and for all," Elizabeth implored. "Remain here with us. We'll steer The Movement toward a greater emphasis on inclusion."

"We are aware of the reward for the capture of Etta Place. And we will dedicate ourselves to creating an entirely other personage, allowing that unfortunate fugitive to disappear."

"Maybe that would be possible if it weren't for your stand on abortion. I cannot grasp how any woman can define herself as a feminist, yet fail to support a woman's right to choice."

"The intensity of your voice suggests that once again you speak from experience," Susan observed.

"Indeed!" I said, my mind focusing on Bowdry. "The friend who gave me this Magen David died from a botched illegal abortion. She was one of those downtrodden lower-class women you have at least up until now considered unworthy of joining your elite organization. As well as a Jew, even as I now know myself to be."

"As you will recall from our first lunch together," Susan insisted, "I despise all prejudices toward those of your nation."

BUTCH: FRIDAY; FEBRUARY 15, 1901

As Samson dropped, I turned sideways and got off a round at Cincotta's head. Onlookers screamed in panic, some turning to run away, as it exploded into tiny shards that flew in every direction. Meanwhile, I shifted positions to center myself and bring down Lupo only to realize he was gone from the scene; headed off down one of the myriad alleys that line Mott and Hester. Sundance and I rushed toward the fallen Samson, my pard reaching him first. The youth whispered a few words before he passed. Sundance wept.

"You done your best to save him. That's all any one can ask from a man."

"If it weren't for my vendetta, that boy would be alive."

"That's true."

"How am I supposed to live with that?"

"Even I can't help you there, Sundance. But in declaring so, you've taken responsibility for your actions."

"What if it ain't enough?"

"You'll have to find some other reason to go on living."

ETTA: FRIDAY; FEBRUARY 15, 1901

"Alright. How then, Eloise . . . *Etta* . . . could we as devout Christians accept the purposeful ending of a life?"

"You are who you are. I accept that. Understand, please, that I am who I am. You have your truth; I, mine."

"We do respect that."

"You'll be leaving in several days, then?" Susan asked.

"At this point, I don't foresee any other options."

"If that's the case," Elizabeth softly responded, "may I invite you to spend this single night with us?"

Momentarily, her question—invitation, in truth—left me speechless. I surprised myself by responding, "I'd like that!"

SUNDANCE: FRIDAY; FEBRUARY 15, 1901

"I'm doomed," I repeated as Butch and I sat alongside the East River. Finally, I removed my hands from my eyes and gazed at the wide city-scape, focusing my attention on the Brooklyn Bridge. A cable model, its structure had been enhanced with suspension elements. This massive modern innovation connected The Bowery, where we had fled, to King's County, directly across river, providing easy access from one borough to another since its inauguration some twenty years ago. Now, we crouched in its long curving shadow, attempting to put the brutal incident into perspective as evening's first pastel colorings appeared above the high and wide skyline.

"If that's the case, so am I."

"No, no, no. You do not need to suffer from any guilt."

"You shot one yesterday; me, today. It evens out."

"*You* did so in a fair fight. I executed a man as he pleaded for his life. It's different. And poor Samson—"

A BRIDGE TO THE FUTURE: By connecting Manhattan Isle to Brooklyn, this technological innovation not only provided easy access between New York buroughs but altered people's lifestyles by re-inventing the concept of 'time' necessary for everyday economic transportation.

"You didn't recruit him. The boy volunteered. He knew the chances he was taking. And you avenged a family member."

"But I didn't! That's the whole point, Butch."

"You lost me there, Henry."

"The Mafiosos *didn't* kill Ronald."

"Who did, then?"

"Samson! He whispered that to me before he died."


ETTA: SATURDAY; FEBRUARY 16, 1901

As I woke in the middle of the night, with each woman on either side, we three nestled close and warm under the crisp sheets, I attempted to make sense of my sudden decision. And ponder what I ought to do next with my life, now that my range of experience had been broadened beyond anything I expected even a day earlier. Might I accept, as these ladies had, that a satisfying existence could be had without the presence of men? Or did I still want Butch, Sundance, and at times both with me even as Susan and Elizabeth did as to one another?

As time passed, I became ever more conscious of the totality of the commitment between these two people whom I so admired despite our severe differences in opinion. And, as morning approached, my thoughts extended to Butch and Sundance as well. Part of me, I must admit, had initially been threatened by the full extent of their relationship, I now fully aware of the depth of their commitment. A love as deep and sincere as each felt for me, or me for either of them. Further complicating matters as I must shortly decide whether I remain here or leave with those boys who had, perhaps, finally matured into men.

*I must accept, even adapt to, their Code. Even as they ought to embrace my most basic values.*

*Submission out of the question. Compromise the key.*

BUTCH: SATURDAY; FEBRUARY 16, 1901
"What?"

"*Samson* killed Ronald!"

"In a misguided effort to protect Etta," I gathered.

"I murdered a man for violating my family but did so to avenge a crime he did not commit. I'm doomed!"

"If only Bat were here. He might offer some words of wisdom. As for me, I'm . . . *lost.*"

"Not as lost as me."

"Let me help you up," I said for want of anything else.

"Maybe Bat will still be awake when I get to the Delivan," Sundance said, rising. "I need his advice."

"You're not going there."

"What?"

"I'm bringing you back to the boarding house." Arm-in-arm, we stepped away from the sordid neighborhood where rats and thugs wandered, searching for easy prey.

ETTA: SATURDAY; FEBRUARY 16, 1901
The Bible tells us that humans, like the animals on their way to Noah's Ark, should walk two by two. If I ever believed that, I now know that three by three may offer more possibilities for self-realization and long-time satisfaction. Three women; a woman and two men. .

To liberate myself, entirely, how necessary it was to join with Susan and Elizabeth if only for a single night. All and any differences aside, I had come to love them. What happened between us had been not only pleasurable but fulfilling for me.

*Yet I did not want to eliminate men from my life. Onward, then, with the process of forging my unique identity.*

SUNDANCE: SATURDAY; FEBRUARY 16, 1901

"Guess it's time that we spoke of this to Etta," I said to Butch the following morning, after leaving his side and shaving before the mirror. He meanwhile slipped out of bed and lowered his face over a bowl of water, Butch's favorite means of waking himself up quickly.

"She knows, Sundance."

"You tell her?" I asked, turning to face him.

"Course not. Etta senses things. Recall what she said back at the Hole, that day we were waving pistols in each other's faces?"

"Can't the two of you see you love one another?"

"Still, I reckon we ought to set her down—"

"—and talk about this openly? Yes."

"Do you figure she'll think less of us as men?"

"*More*, I believe. Discovering something about ourselves she's intuited for some time."


ETTA: SATURDAY; FEBRUARY 16, 1901

"You could go on playing Annie forever," Frank commented following another intense morning of rehearsal.

"Knowing how truly appealing she is," I replied, "I'll accept that as a compliment."

We sat together at lunch alongside the cowboys, Indians, and various laborers who attended to changes of scenery in this vast showplace. Nightly in this huge oval were performed diverse acts that included the Overland Stage pursued by bandits and a lavish recreation of Custer's Last Stand. Only here, Cody rode to the rescue at the last possible moment in a fanciful finale.

*Which explains why people prefer entertainment over reality. In life, most everything that can go wrong does. But with a show, folks anticipate . . . and more often than not get . . . a happy ending.*

Our reward for all the hard work? Seared beef ribs, piles of roasted corn, apples and pears grilled on iron skillets, and huge bowls of yellow rice with hot Spanish seasonings as well as chopped peppers and onions . . .

"My guess? Annie envies you, heading off to new and unknown climes."

"Did she say that outright?" How close Frank Butler's words came to what Annie had privately confided.

"Not in so many words. But I can read her moods."

"Same with me and my fellas."

"Would you ever consider switching places?" he abruptly asked. "Wouldn't have to be permanent. Once this commotion blows over, you could then travel to South America while Annie returns here. What matters most now is a successful getaway."

"Are you figuring that while Annie is out of the country, I'd be your bedmate?"

"Well, I sure *could* imagine something of the sort."

"I can tell you this. If I were to stay, anything that occurs between us will be my call to make."

"I sensed that before you put it I words, Etta."


BUTCH: SATURDAY; FEBRUARY 16, 1901

"I missed you last night," Kathryn sighed as I stepped into her parlor, a small recluse decorated with old Currier and Ives prints and blue tinged fine china.

"Same here," I mumbled.

"I saw Sundance enter with you, and guessed there were matters that had to be addressed. So, I did not intrude."

"That was a part of it." I took a seat as Kathryn indicated for me to do while she poured us cups of coffee.

"Something wrong, LeRoy? You look . . . shattered."

"You picked the right word. Kathryn, have you seen the morning paper yet?"

"No. I haven't had an opportunity to—"

"Thought not. I'm glad I reached you first."

"What," she inadvertently laughed, "is so all-fire . . ." At that moment, her eyes flashed with trepidation. "Samson?"

"Yes," I whispered, glancing down.


ETTA: SATURDAY; FEBRUARY 16, 1901

"Is Bat here?" I asked as Emma answered the door, hoping against hope he was not so we might once more converse alone.

"He was called over to Little Italy. Several men were killed on Mott Street yesterday. He's assigned to cover it."

"Oh, how awful," I responded.

"Afterwards, Bat's scheduled to meet Butch and Sundance at the Church Street Gym to coach them for Tuesday's bout."

"Well, care to listen to my latest round of problems?"

"I'll fix some tea."

As Emma set about that task, I nestled into the couch's plump cushions and blurted out one trauma after another. I still loved the boys but had discovered I could respond to women. I longed to support The Movement but couldn't commit owing to their stand on a woman's right to control her own body. Fame and fortune in The Movies drew me toward the limelight yet I abhorred the domination by men I'd doubtless experience there. The possibility of switching places with Annie had been broached but this too involved yet another male's expectations. Specifically, her husband Frank.

"All that to deal with and you're still standing?"

"Hang on! I have not yet begun to whine."

Aware now of my Jewish bloodline, I adored the grand heritage but nonetheless rejected the religon's limitations as to women. I loved The Sweet Life offered to me, yet my heart went out to the great masses who had so little.

"I have to warn you. Women who can't be satisfied with what's possible in the real world often end up lost, alone, and with nothing."

"That would be the ultimate irony, wouldn't it? Yet—"

"No need to tell me. I know what you're thinking."

"Do you, then?"

"Yes. 'I want it *all*.'"

For some reason I began to laugh, if without any good humor. Fearing I might at any moment surrender to madness.


SUNDANCE: SATURDAY; FEBRUARY 16, 1901

"I've come to a decision," I informed Bat. He and I stood together on Mott Street now, watching Joe Petrosino and his Italian Squad comb the surrounding avenues for evidence.

"Alright, then. Share."

"When Butch and Etta set sail, I'll remain here."

"Whew! How'd you arrive at *that*?"

"My greatest wish right now is to see the two of them happy, cause I know I never will be."


—INTERLUDE—

BAT: OCTOBER 25, 1921

*During the past century, small circuses wound their way around the country, stopping in each little burg, offering a show to folks starved for entertainment. In one of those towns, a successful businessman stepped out of his three-story-high emporium*

THE WAGONS ROLL AT NIGHT: By horse-drawn carts, later trains and eventually trucks, owners of small circuses brought their sometimes seedy if always appreciated entertainments to the nation's small towns

*to watch the free parade. Smoking a cigar more expensive than most other locals could afford and dressed in a snazzy suit, he took in the clowns, acrobats, and best of all the long line of animals from around the world.*

*When the procession finally concluded, most townspeople ran along after the performers, eager to purchase tickets to the evening's show. But this canny businessman lingered on the boardwalk just outside his store, eyes drawn to a thin fellow wearing the grey overhauls of a janitor. He tailed that parade with an enormous broom in one hand and a big bucket in the other. Unbeknownst to most of those present, he quietly went about his unsavory task: cleaning up all the dung that zebras, giraffes, elephants, tigers, and other creatures had deposited on the old cobblestone road through town; pushing the droppings into piles, then depositing such refuse into his container. Always moving forward, repeating this process at regular intervals. Doing so with an unrelenting pace and determined look in his eyes, gathering up every bit so the village's main drag would be as clean as before his company of players arrived.*

*Mightily impressed by the integrity of this worker and his commitment to not only completing his chore but coming as close to perfection as possible, the businessman now approached the stranger. "I've just lost my manager," he told the young man, "and I would like to hire you for the job. For I greatly admire as serious a worker as yourself."*

*Humbly, the worker thanked the businessman for his kind offer but declined, stating outright that he knew absolutely nothing about running such an establishment. "Doesn't matter," the businessmn said. "what impresses me is your commitment. In no time, I could teach you the tricks of my trade."*

*"Thank you sincerely, sir. But . . . no."*

*"Why, just think! A week from now you'd be wearing a fine suit, making ten times as much money, and addressed as 'sir' by a dozen employees."*

*Again, the putrid fella firmly shook his head 'no.'*

*"Do you understand the opportunity you're turning down?" the businessman asked, more perplexed than ever.*

*"I do."*

*"Then why not accept my offer?"*

*"What?" the worker replied. "And give up* show business?"

# PART SIXTEEN: NO BUSINESS LIKE SHOW BUSINESS

"It's a man's world and show business is a man's meal, with women generously sprinkled through it like overqualified spice."

—CARRIE FISHER

"If we can't take your mind off all those problems *here*," Emma insisted, "I know where we just might." Unable to come up with helpful advice, she'd insisted we go out on the town.

So we arrived at the Manhattan Theater, 102 West 33rd St., directly across from Greeley Square at Sixth Avenue. Finally, I had an opportunity to visit the burgeoning district where people headed for escape from their problems, big or small. Vaudeville had won respectability as family entertainment, in comparison to seedy, disrespectable burlesque. Not that Vaudeville was devoid of sensuous females on parade. Here, though, blonde, brunette, and red-headed long-stemmed American beauty roses strolled across the lavish stage not in trashy outfits but glamorous costumes. The lovely young women sported contemporary felt hats adorned with multi-colored feathers, showing off their stuff before more than a thousand ticket-buyers at any one time.

"If you do remain in New York, perhaps you could win a job as a showgirl," Emma commented as we slipped into rich velvet seats the color of creamed coffee, set off against dark hardwood frames. I noticed an extremely well-dressed man, seated two rows behind us. The gentleman's eyes focused on me. A glimpse

GIVE MY REGARDS TO BROADWAY: In addition to revolutionizing entertainment for the masses, Vaudeville significantly altered social and cultural sensibilities with its presentation of ethnic performers to the mass audience.

of his face—chalky, as if he spent far too much time indoors, with ears slightly bigger than his head could comfortably handle—made clear Emma's words had registered.

"With your looks, you'd have no trouble getting hired," he (though a total stranger) dared note.

SUNDANCE: THURSDAY; FEBRUARY 14, 1901

"When I allow myself to think selfishly, I imagine what it would be like if Etta and I were to head off on our own."

"And when you're better-self speaks?" asked Bat.

"Allow Butch and Etta to leave together."

"That all of it?"

"No. Perhaps it'd be best for Butch and myself to make the journey alone."

"Pardners forever?"

"That," I responded, turning away, "and more."

"Oh," Bat sighed, comprehending the full extent of our current situation at last.

ETTA: SATURDAY; FEBRUARY 16, 1901

There were no scheduled times for the seemingly endless line-up that constituted Vaudeville. Opening at ten in the morning and closing at midnight, every such house featured continuous spectacle, drawn from whichever acts were currently in town. Customers arrived and left according to personal whim or other obligations. I watched as a quintet of acrobats from India tossed one another high in the air. Emma had been correct; their skills allowed me to momentarily forget my issues.

Entertainment is a drug. One that most everyone can afford and which leaves no obvious after-effects. We indulge in such distractions not because we choose to but because we must. Escapism is not merely a desire but a necessity when the world threatens to close in too tightly. Following such a giddy interval, a person regains the necessary momentum to push forward again once outside the theatre. Alternative choices—actual drugs including opium—dim the senses momentarily but do inconceivable damage.

Not so with a stage show. Or a movie. Each provides an appealing interlude between stark encounters with bleak reality.

BUTCH: SATURDAY; FEBRUARY 16, 1901

Kathryn sat still for several minutes, as if acceptance of this sudden, unexpected finality was impossible. Then she rose without warning and shuffled around the room.

"I loved him so, LeRoy."

"I know that."

"—and now he's gone."

"I hope you won't find what I'm about to say offensive. Rather, try to draw strength from this. Now, you have *me*."

Kathryn's eyes reacted as if a bolt of lightning shocked her back to reality. Confused, she responded, "But you're scheduled to depart—"

"No. I'm not going. And that's final."


ETTA: SATURDAY; FEBRUARY 16, 1901

As if the succession of brief acts weren't enough, there was the theater itself, truly an Xanadu come to life. A vast spiral staircase, incandescent lighting, wrought-iron details, stained glass windows, low hanging gargoyles worthy of Paris' Notre Dame, and immense murals displaying mythological sirens in the act of luring sailors to their doom. Elegantly attired musicians occupied the pit; red-velvet curtains were held in place by rich gold braid.

Emma and I watched and listened as singers and dancers, displays of pantomime, Shakespearean monologues, adorable child performers, and pie-in-the-face comics held theater-goers spellbound. Then the mood changed drastically as a short, handsome, dark-haired fellow stepped center-stage. And took my breath away. *Magnetic* best described him. The house fell silent as this charismatic presence instantly won everybody in attendance over with an irresistible smile and subtle hint of danger.


SUNDANCE: SATURDAY; FEBRUARY 16, 1901

"Well, there's Joe. You could turn yourself over to him."

"Not yet. Plenty of people are depending on me. Cody's got a lot of money invested in the upcoming bout. And you're counting on this to uplift pugilism. I'll play my role. Once the fight's over, I'll give myself up."

"Man plans; destiny determines."

"I believe life is a series of random circumstances."

"Well, if you're wrong about that, fate may yet make make mincemeat of your proposed scenario."


ETTA: SATURDAY; FEBRUARY 16, 1901

"Hello," the young man announced. "I am Harry Houdini"—at this point, many guests broke into spontaneous applause—"here to dazzle your eyes and mind as never before."

"He's the current darling of the Vaudeville circuit," Emma explained, realizing I had no notion as to the fellow's identity.

"But first, allow me to introduce you to a new form of popular entertainment that is about to take the world by storm. I assume you have visited Nickelodeons and individually gazed through their lenses to watch a flicker? Now observe the latest advance in moving pictures . . . films projected on a screen for viewers to enjoy together as an audience. Watching movies as a communal experience will be the wave of the future."

BUTCH: SATURDAY; FEBRUARY 16, 1901
"What . . . ?" Kathryn gasped.
"I'm not going."
"LeRoy, you planned this upcoming journey so carefully."
"You need me more than Etta does."
"That's beside the point."
"No. It *is* the point."
"You're mistaking pity for love. And I'll have none of that. I won't accept charity from anyone."
"Pity isn't a bad word. It implies the ability to *feel*."
"Well, there's more than one kind of feeling. Love's yet another."
"Maybe they're two sides of the same coin?"
"No. Always, I'd be wondering if you had stayed out of a sense of responsibility. What I want—*demand!*—is love from any man who enters my life."

ETTA: SATURDAY; FEBRUARY 16, 1901
"Here is a film imported from Paris, where a fellow magician turned moviemaker named George Melies has recorded for posterity the greatest of all 'tricks.'"
With that, Houdini stepped to his left even as the curtains parted to reveal an immense white screen. The houselights dimmed; at the auditorium's rear, a projector hummed and clicked while directing a beam of light through a strip of sequential images, rapidly replacing one another. Still pictures whirring by so fast that a viewer actually believed he or she was witnessing motion and action.
The onscreen setting: an elegant flower garden with a vast painted mural of columned Grecian buildings provided the backdrop. Then, within the movie frame, a smiling middle-aged man, accompanied by a lovely lady in an evening gown, stepped up onto a stage.
"Here is the filmmaker, accompanying Jehnne d'Alcy as a feast for the eyes, though enjoy her while you can. For now you will be treated to a spellbinding marvel developed some years ago by Robert-Houdin. Enjoy *The Lady Vanishes*."

FROM STAGE TO SCREEN: George Melies filmed his Parisian stage act (his wife played the title character) so that the illusion might be seen worldwide.

## SUNDANCE: SATURDAY; FEBRUARY 16, 1901

"Hello, Harry."

I returned to the boarding house and discovered my sister patiently waiting out front. Dressed in the customary black associated with mourning, Dag explained that she had traveled here by train to make arrangements for the transportation of Ronald's corpse back to Buffalo. Dag appeared more shaken than saddened. Understandably! For I had not sensed any great love on her part for her husband.

Now, that was over. Suddenly, arbitrarily over. How she might organize the remainder of her life remained to be seen. Clearly, though, Dag appeared anxious to talk, so I escorted her to a teahouse two blocks west of Washington Square. Though I wished to offer my support, Sis—as always more concerned for others, particularly family, than herself—broke the ice.

"Tell me more about you and that young woman."

## ETTA: SATURDAY; FEBRUARY 16, 1901

This movie appeared within the framework of the current stage show, as such representing an illusion contained by a vaster, more inclusive theatrical experience, a film within a play. In the flicker, Melies spread a newspaper on the floor, then placed a chair atop the strewn pages. He coaxed the apparently anxious Jehanne to seat herself, then drew out a foreboding cape from hiding.

Next, he covered her form completely with that free-flowing garment. Finally, Melies waved a wand over the draped woman, then swiftly whipped the cape away, revealing a white skeleton where the petite d'Alcy sat a moment earlier. We in the theater's audience gasped as a collective. And, as the projector ceased its incessant whir while the house lights rose, applauded this remarkable trick.

BUTCH: SATURDAY; FEBRUARY 16, 1901

"Hello," the tall, clean-shaven, neatly attired young man said in an appealing Pennsyltucky accent. He approached me in the boarding house's corridor, his angular face alabaster, dotted with several iodine colored freckles which caused him to appear childlike. "I'm E.S. Porter. Is Miss Etta here?"

She had indeed mentioned a brilliant fellow who would serve as second unit director when filming commenced on *The Great Train Robbery* over in Jersey, then head to New York to later that evening capture Cody's show, including our boxing match, for posterity.

"Last I knew she was at Madison Square Garden." Locking eyes with E.S., I at once sensed that he could be trusted.

"I'd head uptown but I've got to get back in the Black Maria. Would you make certain that she gets this?"

ETTA: SATURDAY; FEBRUARY 16, 1901

"Now, it's my great pleasure to repeat this feat for you, on our own stage. *Live!*" Houdini stepped backward as a focused light revealed what none of us had yet noted: A chair, all but identical to the one in the movie, with a similar shawl on its seat. From behind an adjacent curtain, a young woman stepped forth to join the magician.

"Oh, my," I gasped, realizing her identity.

"Our special guest: Little Miss Sureshot, Annie Oakley. Don't forget; Miss Oakley currently stars in Colonel Cody's Wild West at the Garden. That pageant will conclude its run Tuesday evening with the much anticipated boxing match between Butch Cassidy and the Sundance Kid."

Moments later, she and Houdini repeated the routine before our very eyes. In a flash, Annie Oakley disappeared.

SUNDANCE: SATURDAY; FEBRUARY 16, 1901

"Tell me, does Etta know what has occurred?"

"I couldn't work up the courage to tell her, Dag."

"Well, do so. As soon as possible. Let her decide whether or not that finally cuts it for you two."

"Do you really believe Etta might still choose me once she's aware of what a terrible thing I've done, taking a person's life for a crime he did not commit?"

"I have no idea. But I can tell you this. If she loves you—truly, dearly, fully—she'll find a way to."

"Unconditionally," I muttered under my breath.


ETTA: SATURDAY; FEBRUARY 16, 1901

"Excuse me, young lady. But may I have a moment?"

After Emma and I took in several more acts, she left for the Delivan. I watched her exit the brightly-lit lobby, then headed for the stairwell, hoping to make my way backstage and speak with Annie. Before I could, the gentleman who sat behind us approached, likely hoping to pick up a seeming 'modern girl.'

"Sorry, but I'm in a hurry—"

"No doubt you take me for a musketeer of the streets. In truth, I'm a far more serious admirer than that."

Such a unique looking man! His jet black hair, which I guessed to be dyed, had been trimmed and shaped into a high pompadour of the dated Beau Brummell style. He struck me as someone of importance, self-confident, even a bit arrogant.

"You have five minutes. Make it good."

"That's all I'll need," he brightly responded. "Please accompany me to a coffee shop just around the corner."

"In truth, I prefer tea."

"Then that's what you'll have. And before you finish a single cup, you'll understand—"

"Can you be a bit more precise as to—?"

"Certainly!" He handed me a business card identifying him as Florence Ziegfeld, talent agent and theatrical manager. "This is your lucky day! You've just been 'discovered.'"


BUTCH: SATURDAY; FEBRUARY 16, 1901

E.S. handed me an 8 X 12 inch manilla envelope. "What's inside?" I asked with some trepidation.

"Look and see," he answered with a genial smile.

A moment later, I held that photographic image which Etta had, well-meaning if unwisely, handed to Lakeland last Sunday.

"How did you manage to—"

"That's not important. It's no longer a danger."

"Yeah, but other prints and all the negatives are still over at DeFly's Studio. As long as they exist—"

"Perhaps I ought to break in and steal 'em. Maybe—"

"No, no, no. I wouldn't want *you* to take that risk. This calls for a . . . well . . . professional, so to speak."


ETTA: Saturday; February 16, 1901

"I've seen your name in the papers," I told Ziegfeld once we were seated opposite one another in a nearby cafe. "You're the fellow who's building a new entertainment center?"

"Yes! Where Sixth meets Broadway. A soon-to-be-actualized landmark on the Great White Way."

"You'll go up against all the established venues?"

"Actually, I'm going to blow them out of the water. My plan is to create a majestic palace to showcase acts so remarkable that other theaters won't be able to compete."

"That's certainly *ambitious*!"

"Only the finest stars will be invited to perform. I visited that theater today to observe Harry Houdini."

"I found him magnificent!"

"As did I. As soon as The Ziegfeld is up and running, he will work for me. As will all the giants of Vaudeville."

"How will you win them away?"

"Money!" he said. "I'll pay three, four times the amount they're currently earning. Five if necessary."

"I feel naïve for having asked."


SUNDANCE: Saturday; February 16, 1901

"We have to talk," Butch said once I'd rejoined him. We were scheduled to arrive at the gym in less than an hour. First he shared the photograph, allowing me a sense of relief.

"But there are others," I reminded him. "At DeFly's—"

"That's where *we* come in."

Butch explained the basics of his developing plan. Late tonight or into the early morning hours, he and I would slip inside that building, search until we found any prints and the negatives, then destroy them. At which point all hard-evidence would be eliminated, freeing Etta to decide what she wished to do next.

"Now, Butch, let me talk. This is serious."

"Yet another road-block?"

"The opposite. I've thought this over carefully. When you and Etta leave Tuesday morning, I plan to stay here."

ETTA: SATURDAY; FEBRUARY 16, 1901

"The main attraction will be a glorification of the American girl. Tall, lovely young women, their natural beauty enhanced by dazzling costumes. Scads of diamonds . . . the real deal, mind you . . . draped across expensive gowns, richly colored feathers enhancing the image."

"Wasn't that what I witnessed earlier?"

"I'll take the concept to an infinitely higher level. The most gorgeous females in America, parading under spotlights with colored filters highlighting each living-dream on parade."

"Certainly sounds spectacular."

"A Ziegfeld Girl will embody our nation's updated equivalent of Aphrodite. A flesh-and-blood Venus on the half-shell, so to speak. That gives me an idea! Perhaps I'll have my team create faux shells for the girls to emerge from. Wouldn't *that* be something?"

"You certainly are a visionary, Mr. Ziegfeld."

"I'll offer an illusion of the perfection every American male hopes to achieve though cannot in our everyday world."

"Then, he heads home to his wife. Perceiving her as a sorry disappointment in contrast. Inspired by fantasy only to then be frustrated by reality."

BUTCH: SATURDAY; FEBRUARY 16, 1901

"I've been thinking that it ought to be the other way around," I interrupted. "Me who stays."

"Damn! Here we go again."

"I thought you'd be pleased."

I explained my recent discussion with Kathryn. And that if I remained, everything ought to fall into place. For us and Etta and Henry. Happy endings all around.

"I don't know," Sundance sighed.

"*What* don't you know?"

"Anything! I've never felt so confused in my life."

"Well, we agree on one thing. We must get our mitts on DeFly's photographs. Because they threaten everything."

"No argument there. Say! What we'll do tonight will be just like the good old days."


ETTA: SATURDAY; FEBRUARY 16, 1901

"Let me explain how you will fit into my plans."

"Mr. Ziegfeld—"

"Call me 'Ziggy.' Everyone does."

"Alright, then . . . *Ziggy* . . . you see me as a prime candiate for one of your 'Ziegfeld Girls.'"

"That's the understatement of the year. Why, I had a difficult time concentrating on Houdini's act with you seated in front of me."

"I'll take that as a compliment."

"You'll be the centerpiece. Why, we'll bring the gaudy sophistication of a Parisian show to Little Old New York."

"Would I be required to act, or sing—"

"There will be others, picked owing to their talent, for that. Eddie Cantor to sing, Fanny Brice performing comedy—"

"What would *I* be expected to do?"

"Slowly cross the stage with a combination of a casual stroll and an aloof strut, appear in elaborate make-up to project a combination of the 'Girl Next Door' and an international woman of mystery. Smile and pout. Simply: be beautiful."

"That's what I thought."

"What do you say?"

"I say: *No*"


BUTCH: SATURDAY; FEBRUARY 16, 1901

"Think back to the Hole, Henry. That day when we almost shot it out as to who would marry Etta."

"Back when marriage still seemed possible."

"If there's one thing we learned from the incident, it's that each of us would die rather than kill the other."

"Agreed."

"Well, we can solve this without anyone dying."

"I'm listenin'."

"Whoever wins the boxing match gets to go with Etta."

"I don't think she'd accept that. Last thing Etta wants is to be a trophy. She must choose."

"Yes, but we don't have to tell her."

"Whoever loses the match will then announce he'll remain behind? While she leaves with the victor, if indeed that's what she wants?"

"That's the plan."

"Sounds fool-proof."

"I know. That's what worries me."

"Cause always, as they say down Texas-way, there'll appear a fly in the buttermilk."


ETTA: SATURDAY; FEBRUARY 16, 1901

*"But, why?"?"*

"Ziggy, I'm aware of my physical appeal. And I'm not one of those hypocrital women who take delight in pretending to be unaware of their impact on men."

"Women, too. Curiously, I've noted that females in the audience are as fascinated by glamour girls as are the men."

"I realize both genders are in awe of elegance."

"You speak in such a worldly manner!"

"Please understand. What you offer me is a career—"

"With handsome payment!"

"—based entirely on one quality: my looks."

"What could be more important than that?"

"Intelligence. Commitment to a great cause—"

"That's not what the Ziegfeld Theater will be selling."

"Precisely. And while I don't mind being appreciated for my beauty, I refuse to be reduced to a mere object."


SUNDANCE: SATURDAY; FEBRUARY 16, 1901

"Straight right," Bat called out as I danced about in a pugilist's square located in the Church Street Gym on Park Place, five doors down from the *Morning Telegraph* building.

"Got ya." I swung and almost connected though Butch slid aside too quickly for me to land.

"Butch?" Jack Johnson shouted. "You will be the Wild Bull. A 'Swarmer.' Move aggressively, always within close quarters. Go for his gut, then follow up with a circular swing to the jaw."

We'd arrived together at two p.m., our coaches awaiting. Each mentor appeared enthusiastic about the big match.

"Think back to Coney," Bat coached me. "You'll be the 'out boxer.' A general of the ring, in full command. Move Quickly, take up your best possible position, and then, jab, jab, jab! He's the wild bull. You're the matador."

ETTA: SATURDAY; FEBRUARY 16, 1901

"Annie?" I whispered, after bidding Ziggy farewell. And, in spite of what I'd just asserted, self-consciously employed my feminine charms to convince a theater guard to allow a notably attractive visitor to slip backstage by spellbinding him with my eyes and manner.

"Etta?" She hurried down a shadowy corridor on the third floor and embraced me. "What are you doing here?"

"I might well ask you the same question."

She explained that her appearance had been arranged by Buntline, always eager to further publicize Bill's show.

"Annie, may I ask one more favor?" She nodded assuringly. "Will you introduce me to Houdini?"

"Well, he's a notably private person," Annie explained. "But I will make the request."

BUTCH: SATURDAY; FEBRUARY 16, 1901

"Don't punch," Bat insisted. "*Slug!*"

That is, be a brutal Hun who wastes his opponent with relentless ham-fisted swings, delivered in rapid succession.

"How's this?" I asked, increasing my energy level.

"Employ relentless 'power shots,' as opposed to the swift combinations Henry relies on." Surely, such polar approaches would bring a crowd to its feet.

"Jab now!" Johnson instructed Sundance.

"Cross," Bat shouted, leaping to his feet and waving.

"Counter, Kid. Counter!"

"You two are swinging so hard," Bat observed, "that I could almost believe you're becoming *serious* about who wins."

"As well as who loses," I muttered under my breath.

ETTA: SATURDAY; FEBRUARY 16, 1901

I followed Annie until we reached a door with the words "HARRY HOUDINI: DO NOT DISTURB!" emboldened in large block print. Rolling her eyes, Annie gently rapped.

"Who the hell is it?" a less-than-friendly voice roared from inside. But when Annie identified herself, the man opened the door, respectfully greeting America's most adored celebrity.

"Harry, a young lady would like to meet you in person."

"Oh, no," he howled. "Not another autograph seeker!" But when Houdini turned to consider me, everything changed. "Do come in," he said, stepping aside as Annie left the two of us alone.

Here we go again, I thought. Female beauty could conquer the world! Quickly, though, I realized my assumption might have been wrong. For Houdini hadn't been magnitized by my face, rather my Magen David. And, I noticed at once, he wore a similar one.

SUNDANCE: SATURDAY; FEBRUARY 16, 1901

"So that's the current plan," said Butch after summing up our decision regarding Etta and the match. At four, Bat had insisted on a ten-minute break for fear one of us might drop dead in the ring.

"Huh!" He sat a long time in silence, mulling this over.

"Well?"

"On the one hand, it's the most awesomely idiotic idea you've come up with yet. Which is going some!"

"On the other?"

"For the life of me, I can't think of anything better."

ETTA: SATURDAY; FEBRUARY 16, 1901

"You want me to make you disappear Tuesday at the Wild West show? I love it! Let's discuss the details . . ."

Seated in Houdini's small dressing room. I shared my difficult situation and the one flaw in our otherwise cracker-jack plan: a proper means of my vanishing. I held nothing back, for the sincerity with which Harry Houdini expressed his loyalty to one who shared his ethnic origins left no doubt I could trust him. For I was a Jew in terms of bloodlines, same as this celebrity. We are a people, a nation. And so, as I was swiftly learning, we help one another when a need arises.

BUTCH: SATURDAY; FEBRUARY 16, 1901

"*My* guess," Bat mused, "is that at the last moment, Etta will decide to remain here. New York's her home now."

"If so, maybe Sundance and I will head off together."

"From what I've observed recently," he responded, refusing to allow his eyes to meet mine, "that might be for the best."

MAGIC MAN: Harry Houdini hoped that his tricks and illusions would not only entertain the masses but also convince Anglo audiences that a Jewish performer might become one middle-America's popular 'celebrities.'

ETTA: SATURDAY; FEBRUARY 16, 1901

*What is a Jew?* Shakespeare's Shylock asked. Now, I found myself pondering the same question. Bloodlines or beliefs? Both? The traditions that reach back more than five thousand years? Some other element I have yet to discover?

And so my journey continues. Two journeys, in fact. My inner search for self and the need to discover a destination where I may spend the remainder of my life.

Meanwhile, Houdini shared with me the secret to the trick that allowed a woman to disappear instantaneously in front of a large crowd. Or, at least, appear to. The magician's sudden entrance into my life at this precise moment seemed serendipitous.

Could it merely be coincidence? Hard to believe when I pause to consider the remarkable train of events of the past two weeks. Perhaps this is my fate, revealed to my following what I took to be a simple excursion for some entertainment.

If so, what next?

SUNDANCE: Saturday; February 16, 1901

"I've come to beg your forgiveness," I said flat out to Joseph Petrosino in the underground bar where we'd first met. Following a day consumed with sparring, my mind drifted to the decent fellow who had gone against the grain of his conscience to aid me. Doing so, according to his values, at the risk of losing his soul. I'd arrived here to face him, man to man. And apologize.

"Not necessary."

"To me, Joe, it is. I wrangled information out of you despite your resistance. Leading to three deaths."

"As a Catholic, I believe no one is innocent. We are all sinners. Even of our most revered brethren. That's why our priests confess to other priests."

"Confession! Bat claims whatever one's faith, if any at all, it's good for the soul."

"You're sounding as if you do believe in a higher power."

"Well, as yet another wise man put it, there's no teacher like experience. And I've had a bellyful of that recently."


ETTA: Saturday; February 16, 1901

"You're saying Harry Houdini will be with you, Cody, and Masterson?" chuckled Ned.

"That's the latest development."

"This is too good to be true! Why, even *I* wouldn't have thought to add *him* to the mix."

"Here's a complete plan of what Houdini will require." I handed Ned the drawings and instructions, encouraging him to swiftly pass them to the Garden's construction crew. "This requires a trap-door be built in the main platform for an illusion originally designed in Paris by Buatier de Kolta."

"Even *I've* heard of *him*."

"This will allow me to slip down under, crawl out back through a tunnel, then disappear from the building."

"From there, off to the ship, then Bolivia."

"*If* I do so decide."

"Still uncertain?"

"Me? *Ever* uncertain!'


BUTCH: Saturday; February 16, 1901

"Everything is set," I told Kathryn once we were alone. "Today, I convinced Sundance we'd engage in a true bout once in the ring. Whoever wins sails off with Etta."

"Maybe *she* should have the final say say as to that!"

"I'm all in favor of a woman determining her own future. So she will then get to choose: leave with whoever wins, or head off on her own. Or, if she prefers, remain here."

"There's something you haven't told me yet."

"I'm going to throw the fight, Kathryn. As the rounds go by, I'll appear to tire. Then, for a finale, I'll open up to let one of Harry's jabs hit me hard. And take the fall."

"Instead of a sporting event, folks 'll witness a show. So everyone lives happily ever after?"

"I've done everything possible to make that happen. For them, as well as you and I. So let's hope so."

"And maybe pray?"

"Can't hurt," I responded.


ETTA: Saturday; February 16, 1901

"Annie, remember when you shared your fantasy of slipping off somewhere to begin your life over again?"

"How could I forget? We all of us have our illusions."

We sat alone in the dressing room. I could not forget what Frank had told me and hoped to learn if Annie might consider such a move.

"Did you really mean that?"

"But as to me accompanying your boys? Etta! I'm a wife with extremely traditional values."

"I understand."

"And I'm not entirely comfortable with you and Frank becoming a 'team,' if you follow my drift."

"Course I do."

"Let me think this over, Etta. Carefully!"

"Please do."


SUNDANCE: Saturday; February 16, 1901

"Henry," explained Joe, "each of us suffers from a universal human stain which can be traced back to Adam. That doesn't mean everyone will eventually burn in hell."

"I was raised a Christian but I know little of your denomination. How, according to Catholicism, to avoid that?"

"By what we call Redemption. First, confess your sins, with honest regret."

"Though you aren't a priest, I already have. To you."

"Next, go out in the world and do something that's good and selflesse."

"I can do better than that. I'll abandon my dreams to insure the happiness of Butch and Etta."

"But how to manage that?"

"Come Tuesday night, I'll purposefully throw the fight."

ETTA: SATURDAY; FEBRUARY 16, 1901

"Who's there?" I called out. Annie had left for the Plaza. Cody and his cohorts fed the animals, then drifted off to their rooms. The vast silence was broken only by the braying of beasts in their stalls and corrals. Suddenly, I sensed a presence in the room. Something, or someone, moving about in the darkness.

"Your death-knell, little lady, come to meet you."

I shuddered with recognition as this intruder lit a match, illuminating his face. As if Satan himself had materialized, there stood Lupo only a few feet away.

"I wouldn't be too sure of that!"

Without hesitation, I reached for my purse, visible on a nearby table during those fleeting seconds before his match's glimmer could expire. From it, I drew my pistol and pointed it at the menacing figure. Lupo's eyes revealed shock. Likely, he'd expected me to fall into the traditional role of a woman who could not protect herself with no male nearby.

"Aaaaaah!" he yelped in surprise a split second after I fired. In the darkness, the intruder made his way to the exit and retreated from my little sanctuary, slamming the door behind him.

—INTERLUDE—

BAT: OCTOBER 25, 1921

*Now that Etta is making ready to appear in the Wild West, let me note there existed William Frederick Cody of Le Claire Iowa, born of a woman, long before 'Buffalo Bill' emerged as a platonic creation from the mind of Ned Buntline. The former incarnation—by 1901 aged, alcoholic, and in constant need of doctors to relieve the pain of old war wounds—had little in common with the latter until he adorned himself in an extravagant buckskin outfit. For the show must go on. Then, what was left of the man born in 1846, Bill stumbled out of his dressing room, mounted (with help from assistants) his lean roan, and rode out into the latest venue, transformed from an ill old man into heroic myth by the magic of limelight.*

*The failing example of flesh and blood instantaneously revitalized into a figure of national stature.. For Cody had replaced both Boone and Crockett as the dominant symbol of a country forged by its experience with the frontier. The Wilderness. The West, always one step beyond where any American currently stood.*

*Elements of The Cody Legend could be traced back to his personal history. As a boy, Bill rode with the short-lived Pony Express in those days leading up to the War Between the States. Later, he served in varied occupations including hunter of bison for the railroad workers and scout to Custer and Crook during the Lakota Wars of the mid-1870s. Like his father Isaac, Canadian born as was I, Bill had a good heart, opposing slavery and in favor of the rights of Native People. Always though a storm cloud circled the bright blue sky against which our key narrative had been set. Even the Congressional Medal of Honor bestowed on Bill for killing Cheyenne*

THE IDEAL AMERICAN MALE INCARNATED: Though William F. Cody had served as a pony express rider, frontier scouter, and Congressional Medal of Honor winning soldier, he became 'a legend in his own time' only as entrepreneur Ned Buntline transformed a half-fogotten historical hero into national symbol of masculinity, U.S.A. style

*Chief Yellow Hand during the Battle of War Bonnet Creek would be tarnished when doubts as to Cody's bravery were raised. Congress demanded he return the award. Which he, believing his reputation to be ruined, did. That honor would in time be returned, a legacy restored.*

*Where then, Lolly, is the truth, so essential to a reporter like yourself? To answer, let me again temporarily abandon our primary tale and offer a seemingly unrelated anecdote. On the Nebraska frontier, a lawyer rose to the highest levels of prominence as a senator, based solely on his supposed killing of a notorious outlaw: 'Liberty' Valance, had long menaced a sad little settlement known as Shinbone. Decades later, when a reporter finally sat the then-elderly politician down for an interview, the "great man" at last admitted the truth. In fact, a companion had shot Liberty down, doing so from an alley. Now, Senator Ransom Stoddard apparently hoped to earn belated redemption after a lifetime of personally profiting on a grand misperception.*

*My point? The reporter tore up his notes and threw them away. America remained a young country still, in need of creating its own heroes. Like Greece and its hero Heracles, England's Arthur, France's cult of Charlemagne, or Spain's worship of El Cid. The United States required our own such stories if we were to survive as a nation. For that is impossible without role models to inspire the multitude.*

*"This, sir, is the West," the reporter assured the feeble old timer. "When the legend becomes a fact, print the legend!"*

*Whether that decision was noble or naïve, courageous or cowardly, or for that matter right or wrong, it served its purpose. And though you yourself live in the East, Lolly, I ask you to keep that in mind when someday long after I'm gone you must decide whether to retell Etta's story, or not.*

# PART SEVENTEEN:
# THE GETTING OF WISDOM

"We don't receive wisdom; we must discover it for
ourselves after a journey through time and
space which no one can take for us."

—MARCEL PROUST

BUTCH: Sunday; February 17, 1901

"Run this by me again," I said to Etta as she, Henry, and I gathered together in the boarding house. This occurred early Sunday morning. Shortly, me and my pard must return to the gymnasium for another day of sparring. Etta would head to the Garden for a grueling afternoon of rehearsals. Following that, we three were scheduled to meet Bat and Emma in the East Village. Bat assured me, when I made my request, that Kathryn was welcome as well.

"When I prepared for bed, Lupo the Wolf appeared in my room. I have no idea how he slipped in, but there he was."

"I'd imagine a La Cosa Nostra consigliere would be experienced at breaking and entering," Henry quipped.

"I heard him scream out in pain. Then frantic scurrying in the darkness."

"The problem is," I noted, "he escaped."

"Well, there was blood aplenty on the floor."

"I myself put a bullet in Lupo yesterday, so that's two wounds," I added. "That ought to at least slow him down some."

"If he's dead we'll read about it in the papers," Henry said. "If not, he's out there, somewhere. And a threat."

"When I told Cody, he assigned a bodyguard to remain with me during the next couple of days. One of the new hires, just arrived from the West. He'll be arriving here soon to accompany me back to the Garden."

"Any assistance will be greatly appreciated."


ETTA: Sunday; February 17, 1901

"Etta," Sundance said, no longer able to meet my eyes with his own, "I've been meaning to share something with you."

"Not certain this is the right time or place!"

"Quiet, Butch. I want to hear what Henry has to say." And so he informed me of the details which had been withheld from me till now regarding his Vendetta, then awaited my response. "In truth, I've been considering the Cowboy Code as of late. Maybe this'll surprise you, but I've found elements in what you profess that deeply touch me."

"May I ask what, in particular?" Butch wanted to know.

"The fierce loyalty to a 'pardner.' Also, an admirable determination to stay true to one's deepest sense of self."

"Even as we've learned to appreciate your values," said Henry.

"I'm wondering if your 'Way' defines America at its best. Anyway, I will somehow deal with this."

SUNDANCE: SUNDAY; FEBRUARY 17, 1901

I could sense Butch shivering in trepidation as I told Etta what had become of Samson. Was forgiveness even possible?

"Allow me a moment to digest this." Her eyes revealed great concern. The silence threatened to crush us all.

"Etta's got to know the whole of it, Henry. See, it was Samson, misguided fool that he was, who murdered Ronald. As for the second Mafioso, *I* shot him down."

Etta mulled that over for a while before speaking. "We're all killers. I took down a man back in Wyoming, and may have done the same to the Wolf. How hypocritical it would be for me to judge you. The way I see things now? Every person walking this earth is Cain, at least by implication."

ETTA: SUNDAY; FEBRUARY 17, 1901

"Wow!" Butch whistled. "That is profound."

"When I was little, my parents taught me that life is simple. There's right and there's wrong. Do the one and you are heaven-bound. Surrender to the dark side and hell awaits."

"That's pretty much what I learned," said Sundance.

"Only it's not like that."

"It ought to be." Sundance lamented.

"Yes, Henry. But it's not."

"Welcome to the real world," Butch humorlessly laughed.

"Your vision of life is mighty dark," said Henry.

"Like you, I'm searching for the meaning of life."

"My greatest fear?" Sundance sighed. "There is no meaning."

"Welcome to Modern Times," Butch responded.

"Maybe not," I concluded. "Maybe we're all of us searching a bit too hard. Perhaps 'the meaning of life' is, simply, life itself."

BUTCH: SUNDAY; FEBRUARY 17, 1901

"There are still the images at DeFly's Studio to deal with," Etta next reminded us.

"Let Butch and me handle that," said Sundance.

"Lefors and Siringo are closing in," Butch added.

"Everyone at the Wild West is doing their utmost to provide a means of escape for me should they arrive on Tuesday evening."

"We'll survive this," Henry insisted.

"Whether two days from now we remain together or go our separate ways, boys, we'll each possess the shared memory of our years in the West. We were a force of nature."

"When I was a kid, my most Puritanical teacher insisted, 'Nature is what we were put on this earth to rise above.'"

"Yet another tired sentiment, Henry. Dostoevsky penned, 'Drive nature out of the door and it will fly right back in again through the window.'"

ETTA: Sunday; February 17, 1901

"You!" I gasped while stepping out the front door of the boarding house having allowed the boys to exit first.

"You?" The man, clearly my bodyguard, declared.

"I never thought to see you again," I said, not certain whether I might laugh or weep with joy.

"Same here!" Caleb responded. For this was the former High Rockies mountain man who had rescued me from a blizzard! Circling back into my life when I most needed him.

"What are *you* doing here?" I inquired.

Caleb explained the situation. Several weeks after my departure, he received a letter from Nate Salisbury, business manager of Buffalo Bill's Wild West, requesting that Caleb travel to New York and join the company. Some time ago, Ned Buntline had told Salisbury about a hivernant who long ago partnered with Hugh Glass and Jim Bridger during the height of the fur trade. A search for his identity revealed that Caleb and his woman, Sari, lived in obscurity somewhere in Wyoming. As the husband and wife always wanted to see the world, they agreed. So here he stood.

A wonderful coincidence? Or, might I hope and believe, something more significant? And, if so, proof perhaps that there may indeed be 'meaning' to life after all? How had Alexander Pope put it? "Hope springs eternal in the human breast." True. Without that, we couldn't push on.

SUNDANCE: Sunday; February 17, 1901

"Peak-a-boo," Bat insisted. "Raise your hands up to your face like a baby playing a game. Move your head from side to side to throw your opponent off-kilter, then take a sudden jab at his nose.."

I nodded in affirmation dancing about before Butch. Out of the corner of my eye, I noticed that many hangers-on here at the gym had gathered nearby, intrigued by the match.

"Counter that with a brutal offense," Jack Johnson told Butch once we'd each pulled back to our respective corners at the sound of the bell. "Slip inside and wear him down. You holding up okay, Sundance?"

"Yeah. Thanks for asking, Butch."

Following a quick break to catch our breaths, we resumed sparring. Butch came forward throwing punches. I back-peddled, shifting from side to side. Then moving in hard and fast, grasping what pain this inflicted on my pard. Hating myself for hurting him. For even at such a moment of masculine conflict, I loved this man.

ETTA: Sunday; February 17, 1901

"Hello," Enrico Caruso sheepishly said as, in response to a sudden knock, I opened the door to my dressing room.

"Oh!" I gasped, stunned to realize that people from out of the past would continue to haunt me in the present.

"Yes, it's me. May I enter?"

I found myself nodding yes, then stepped back to make way. With a nod, I signaled to Caleb, standing guard outside, that this visitor meant me no harm. The Tenor entered and, as I closed the door, his expression conveyed vulnerability.

"I figured you'd be halfway back to Italy by now."

"I was unable to leave. Though I boarded the liner with my family, I grasped the truth. And returned to the dock."

"What precisely are you driving at?"

"Forgive me! And allow me back into your life."

BUTCH: Sunday; February 17, 1901

"This might just be the fight of the century," I heard Bat tell Johnson. "These guys are really *good*."

"They're naturals. If we could persuade 'em to stay in New York, we could turn 'em into professionals."

That statement remained with me throughout the day as we continued sparring. I wondered, might this be another option?

Up until now, I believed that throwing the fight would be in everyone's best interest. But during the rest of our practice bout, I felt some of that machismo which earlier had motivated all my efforts once again rise to the surface.

What would happen if we matched off at Madison Square and I were to forget all my planning, hungry only to win?

A SPORTING FELLA'S RETREAT: As boxing became ever more acceptable to the mainstream, gymnasiums dedicated to the sport sprung up in New York and other major cities.

## ETTA: SUNDAY; FEBRUARY 17, 1901

"So you think you can re-enter my life, just like that?"

"It took courage on my part to even try."

"I ought to slap your face."

"Do so, if you wish."

So I hit him full-force, if with an open hand. And, a moment later, found myself crumbling into his arms. Crying and laughing simultaneously as the irresistible Enrico held me close once more.

"This is the last thing I need right now."

"I'll leave if you want me to."

"Make a move toward that door and I'll kill you."


## SUNDANCE: SUNDAY; FEBRUARY 17, 1901

"Let's talk a while, Henry," said the lady of the house.

Following an exhausting day of practice, I'd returned to the Mastersons' apartment to clean up and prepare for an evening in the Village with the others, as proposed by Bat. To my surprise, Emma awaited me, indicating for her guest to sit.

"I'm listening," I responded, a bit intimidated.

"There are forty-eight hours left. Decision making can't be put off much longer."

"I'm the wrong person to tell that to. It's all up to Etta."

"That sounds fine, in the abstract. But Etta's a person of emotions as well as ideas."

"You describe her perfectly."

"My concern is that she'll continue to roll this over in her heart and mind until the last possible moment."

"More'n likely."

"But not necessarily the best way to handle the situation. No matter how much you respect her rights."

"You suggesting that the three of us talk it through? Get every last detail out and in the open?"

"Exactly. Bat's made arrangements for this evening—"

"Our final day . . . and night . . . in New York."

"Promise me you'll both speak freely with her? Share your precise thoughts, not what you believe to be best for her?"

"I guess, in the end, that's the way it'll have to be."


ETTA: SUNDAY; FEBRUARY 17, 1901

We kissed. Angrily, at first. Then, tenderly. Then with the passion we'd known on that glorious night spent together. Purposefully, I bit his lip. Caruso yelped; I took perverse pleasure in his pain, and licked away a drop of blood before he recovered and drew back.

"That hurt?"

"Yes!"

"Good! It was meant to."

If only he hadn't kissed me on my forehead, gently but firmly, I might have regained my sense of self. Instead, I once more embraced him.

"Can you ever forgive me?"

"Yes. No. I don't know."

"What *do* you know?"

"At this moment? Absolutely *nothing*."


BUTCH: SUNDAY; FEBRUARY 17, 1901

Bat Masterson had, weeks earlier, been scheduled to speak on the subject of Marxism. Now we were set to join him at a small, underground meetingplace in the East Village. The issue of communism had been raised often during the past two weeks. I remained largely ignorant as to its precepts other than that a redistribution of wealth so as to eliminate the concept of poverty would elevate the working-class to a higher level of existence. The exceptional person would thereafter take a backseat; the common man reconceived as the true hero.

"Are you certain I'll be welcome?" Kathryn asked once I'd returned to the boarding house.

"Yes. It's time Etta came to know you as I do."

"And what, pray tell, is that?"

"Something other than a fearsome menace."

"You're still in love with her. I can hear it in your voice, feel it in your arms even as you hold me tight."

"I'm firmly committed to remaining here with you."

"I must be certain the man in my bed is not there just to be an old-fashioned gentleman."

"I'm telling you this *will* be as you wish."

But how will Kathryn react when I inform her I've committed to spend Monday night with my known lover Etta and longtime companion Sundance? Will she accept this, or perceive it as an act of betrayal?

ETTA: SUNDAY; FEBRUARY 17, 1901

"So what are we going to do now?" I asked of Enrico once our furtive lovemaking had concluded.

"Come away with me."

"Your family. Did they de-board as well?"

Firmly, he shook his head. "I sent them home without me." Enrico explained that he'd told his wife a lie. Legal issues had arisen involving the Met that would keep him in America for at least another week.

"What do you propose?"

"I will provide for you for the rest of your life. A villa will be at your disposal. Your years will be filled with luxury and security."

"Am I supposed to take your word for this?"

"Have no fear. I will put what I offer in writing before we set sail to dismiss any doubt."

"And I'll spend the rest of my life as a whore."

"That's such an ugly term."

"What do you prefer?"

"*Courtesan.* In my homeland, this is a position of lofty status."

"But never as your wife."

"I am Catholic. Divorce is not possible."

"Well, Enrico, far as I'm concerned, a courtesan is merely a whore with a fancy title and a higher price tag."

SUNDANCE: SUNDAY; FEBRUARY 17, 1901

"God is dead," I mumbled once Bat arrived, joining Emma and myself in their lounge.

"You been studying Nietzsche, Henry?"

"Not yet. But Etta's read articles in magazines and shared that theory with us. He's next on my to-read list."

"Alright. Tell me, what do you make of that statement? Taken completely out of context and only for the time being."

"I don't know what to think anymore. About anything."

"Do you believe this modern philosopher meant that one day Yahweh, a transluscent old man with a long white beard and remarkable powers, seated on a high cloud, would suffer a heart attack?"

"No," I responded, laughing at the thought.

"What, then?"

"More like . . . the whole 'concept of God, as it's been around for thousands of years now, no longer 'works.'"

"Why might that be?"

"As we move further into the 20th century, new developments in science and technology make it ever more difficult to perceive the world as people once did."

"Remove the Grand Illusion," said Emma, speaking for both she and her husband, "and civilization crumbles."

"Didn't John of Old insist 'the truth will set us free?'"

"Yes, Henry," Bat concluded. "The difficulty comes in determining where freedom leaves off and chaos begins."


ETTA: SUNDAY; FEBRUARY 17, 1901

"Hello, Rabbi."

I stood at the door to his office, peering in. Rabbi Cohen sat at his desk, the Synagogue deserted.

"Hello!" he said, dancing eyes revealing delight that I'd returned. "Didn't expect to see you again."

"Likely, I'll be leaving New York soon. I wanted to stop by and apologize for rushing out the other day."

"Don't be silly," he exclaimed, shifting in his chair. "In fact, this is most serendipitous."

"Oh?"

"I've been thinking about you since that day. You see—"

BUTCH: SUNDAY; FEBRUARY 17, 1901

"You look stunning," I said to Kathryn as she descended the staircase. "And your choice of color is perfect." She wore a dazzling red dress, most appropriate for the event.

"I shouldn't be going out at all. With Samson not yet buried, I ought to stay here, in black for mourning."

"Samson would want you to seize the day, so to speak."

"That's what I've been telling myself. And it's not some sort of shallow entertainment we'll be attending."

We strolled together, on yet another unseasonly pleasant evening, downtown to the address Bat had given me. "How much do you know about 'communism'?" I inquired.

"Enough to be aware it threatens a great many of our fellow citizens. Everyone's supposed to share everything?"

"That's simplifying it, but . . . yes. An attempt to make people equal in a way democracy has failed to do."

"But in the U.S., doesn't our Constitution ensure equality?"

"This goes further. Marx claims that for a state to function, each person must perform his own labor, with each and every job perceived as equal in value. When this is the case, a society runs like clockwork."

"Sounds reasonable."

"Well, if that's the case, ought not each of us be paid the same, no matter what type of work we do?"

"A doctor who studied for nine years, paid the same as a janitor on his first day?"

"That's the theory."

"In a perfect world, perhaps. We live in the real one."

"You don't believe this could ever work?"

"Uh-uh. See, you'd have too many janitors and precious few doctors."


ETTA: SUNDAY; FEBRUARY 17, 1901

Moving slowly, as if the rabbi were older than the fifty or so years I had estimated upon our first meeting, he made his way to a corner table. There, a faded photograph had been placed, encased within a silver frame. Affectionatly, he carried it over to where I sat so that I could fully appreciate the portrait of a proud and happy family. Within the grouping, likely from some twenty years earlier, the Rabbi—clearly young at the time—wore a suit and stood beside a comely woman holding a baby. The child, less than a year old, offered a faint smile.

"Your family?"

"Yes. My wife Miriam, and our daughter Rachel. Taken shortly after we arrived at Ellis Island to begin what was supposed to be our great American adventure."

"Supposed to . . . ?"

"On board the ship, in steerage, little Rachel was exposed to sickly people and unhealthy conditions. Within two weeks of this portrait's sitting, our little one . . . left us."

"Oh! Rabbi, I'm so sorry."

"Rachel would have been just about your age now had she survived. The first time we met, I was struck with the thought that were Rachel still with us, she might well resemble you."

"I'm flattered to hear you say so."

"Then you came back and told me of your great discovery regarding your heritage. That night, I shared with my wife the news. A wonderful Jewish girl, attempting to find herself in a turbulent world, had come to me for advice."

"Your concern deeply touches me."

"My wife and I would like to invite you to join the Jewish community that we oversee. Re-invent yourself here in lower Manhattan, embrace your Hebraic identity. We know of many eligible young men eager to meet a nice young woman such as yourself. Miriam and I would mentor you as we would our own daughter if, by God's will, Rachel were returned to us."

Momentarily, I could not find words, so overwhelmed by the sincerity of his generosity. However . . .

"But your insistence that there can be no female rabbis—"

"I spoke without considering carefully enough. Things do change; the world alters around us. Everything might be different in the future. And, believing in destiny as I do, perhaps you have arrived for the purpose of initiating such overdue reform? And might emerge as New York's first female rabbi?"

## SUNDANCE: Sunday; February 17, 1901

"First and foremost, you must understand that the economic structure determines *everything* in our social discourse. This idea forms the basis of Marxism."

Bat had met us at the door and guided our party into a retreat located a dozen blocks northeast of Delancey between Tompkins Square and the East River. In a dimly lit cellar deep beneath a crumbling old building, we listened intently as he addressed nearly twenty attendees. Several wore suits; most appeared to have drifted here from the Bowery.

"Most essential to this paradigm is the common worker, yet that person exists at the bottom of the fiscal barrel. This has been accepted for millennia but is now challenged."

We sat around a wooden table, brown bean jars with candles atop substituting for lamps. In addition to our landlady, another newcomer had joined us— the rabbi we'd met in Little Italy at the feast. Etta had spoken with him earlier in the day and invited him to come along as her guest and learn something of current politics emerging not very far from his own people's neighborhood.

"Your mentor certainly is a convincing speaker," Kathryn whispered to Butch. The manner in which they glanced at one another left no doubt that a true intimacy had developed.

"I've suggested to Bat that he go into politics," Emma mentioned. "But he insists he can have more fun as a sports reporter and secret agent for the police."

"This is far too abstract for me," I confided to Etta. "I can't follow anything Bat's saying."


ETTA: SUNDAY; FEBRUARY 17, 1901

"The first precept," Bat continued, "is that human beings are animals. An advanced species, to be sure. But animals all the same."

"This is connected to Darwinism," Emma whispered to our table, "and the theory that we are an evolved variation on the apes."

"As such, desperate to survive both as single beings and a race, we must fulfill basic needs essential to the individual but also to the community at large."

"Help me out here, Bat," said Sundance. The hollow looking women and men, devouring a humble meal while nodding in agreement to all Bat said, now considered Henry. "Won't you put that in terms a cowboy like me can understand?"

"Like the lower animals," Bat responded, "food, drink, and shelter from nature are primal needs. Also, though, and a step above the other beasts, clothing, and housing. And, reaching further still, intellectual activity and artistic satisfaction."


BUTCH: SUNDAY; FEBRUARY 17, 1901

"What we choose to call 'the history of civilization' was born from our necessity to produce the means by which such requirements can best be met."

"How would you define the process?" I asked.

"*Labor* is the preferred term. Human existence, when properly understood, involves the struggle between people and nature to furnish products essential for society to continue."

"Some animals do that," Etta chimed in. "Ants, bees. Have since creation."

"Humans alone are *conscious* of their labor; *why* we do what we do to survive. Which implies that we created civilization to simultaneously satisfy both its animal *and* uniquely human needs."

"So," the rabbi reacted. "Now, he challenges the Creation story Jews and Christians alike believe?"

"My guess?" Etta responded. "In the Modern Sensibility, that's considered a dated fairytale."

"That's it for me!" the rabbi shouted while rising.

"Within a Capitalist system, human consciousness raises the question: Why do the majority engage in hard labour while receiving but a minimal amount of the produced goods?"

"Even as a small elite," I heard myself say, "reaps the rewards while performing the least amount of work."

"And with the ever wider circulation of books that spread ideas," Etta deduced, "adding to a heightened awareness of the common man's plight, a worker's revolution is inevitable."

"Precisely," Bat nodded. "One that would truly render all men equal by eliminating the current class system."

"Isn't that what we've achieved in America?" asked Henry.

"No. We've challenged the old *caste* system. The American Dream insists that people *can* transform from rags to riches. The class system remains."

"But Marx notes that few do," said Etta. "The rest go without riches, many living in poverty."

ETTA: SUNDAY; FEBRUARY 17, 1901

"So why don't the Russians embrace democracy," Kathryn questioned, as yet unable to grasp the concept that now made sense to me, "even as the French did following our own revolution?"

"Because democracy invariably entails capitalism. The Russian intellectuals looked to our nation and realized that our system fails to fill every empty belly."

"So they turn to Marx's writings from 1850 and decided to give communism a try," Emma deduced. "For if no one gets rich, then no one goes without."

SUNDANCE: SUNDAY; FEBRUARY 17, 1901

"Gotta admit," Butch drawled as he, Mrs. Trumbell, and I left together, "Bat makes a damn convincing argument."

"How can you say that? Why, outlaws like we used to be are Robin Hoods. We stole from the rich and gave to the poor. How could we have done so if there weren't any rich people?"

"First off, I don't recall us sharing much with anyone."

"We paid the folks who worked at Hole well."

"But that's the very point Bat was making. Then, *we* were the capitalists, dolling out only what we deemed proper."

"Well, I been rich and I been poor. Rich is better."

"I take it you aren't inclined toward this Marxism."

"Nope! You?"

"Just think on it! We might eliminate poverty forever."

"If I believed that were possible, pard, I'd be all for it. Were all folks as fine as my Sis Dag, this just might work. But for every one like her, there's another on the order of my 'dear' deceased brother in law. And you can't deny that's so."

ETTA: SUNDAY; FEBRUARY 17, 1901

"Well?" Emma asked as we strolled through the mild night with Bat between us. "Share your impressions."

"Mixed emotions!" I said. "On the one hand, I agree that poverty ought to be eliminated. That, and hunger."

"That's what Marxism is all about."

THE SHAMEFUL SIDE OF THE CAPITALIST SYSTEM The moneyed elite as well as middle/working-class population largely remained oblivious to the poverty that haunted Manhattan's slum neighborhoods

"Yes, Emma. But I find it . . . naïve. Would geniuses like Thomas Edison endeavor to improve life were it not for that rich carrot hanging just beyond the proverbial mule's reach, enticing him to pursue the dream?"

"They should!" Bat insisted.

"There's what people 'should' do and what they 'would' do. My guess? No reward; no work."

"I just realized," Emma said. "You're against idealism."

"True. On the other hand, I believe the world around us can be improved. Yes, I'm a realist. But also an optimist."

BUTCH: MONDAY; FEBRUARY 18, 1901

"Be careful not to touch anything," I said, though we each wore thin cotton gloves. "Can't leave even a trace of fingerprints or anything else that might identify us."

We had, in the wee small hours of the morning, jimmied open the back entrance of DeFly's studio and slipped inside.

"I can't make out much, with only the light of the moon seeping in through one window."

"When we find the room where he keeps the negatives and duplicate prints, I'll light a match so we can see better."

Silent as a pair of foxes hunting for prey we continued on. The cabinets were marked with dates so it didn't take long to locate the one from that Sunday. With infinite care to avoid making noise, we opened the drawer and searched.

"They're not here. What could have happened to 'em?"

"Pard? Look there!"

On the floor, tight against the far wall, lay DeFly's body. His throat sliced; blood drained everywhere. A pair of wide if dull eyes stared into nothingness.

"Someone got here before us," I whispered.

"Yeah. But who?"

—INTERLUDE—

BAT: OCTOBER 25, 1921

*I've been trying to figure an appropriate time, Lolly, to fill you in on the Pinkerton men who had traveled east in pursuit of Etta. Charles Siringo and Joe Lefors always truck me as equal in grit, smarts, and that calculated determination it takes to track down the cleverest among the west's outlaws.*

*So let me tell you first about a personal meeting with Siringo shortly before I left the frontier. Late one night, I sat across from the 6'6" Charlie in an Ellsworth KS*

THE PROFESSIONALS: Less known than Bat Masterson and Wyatt Earp in large part because they were never romanticized in print by Ned Buntline, Charles Siringo and Joe Lefors were among the most respected lawmen in the West.

*saloon playing poker. Doc Holliday dealt when not coughing into a handkerchief, owing to consumption. In consideration of that grim dentist's reputation with a gun, nobody dared complain.*

*Well, when men gather around a poker table for hours, they talk between hands. Charlie, drinking more than he ought to, suddenly waxed sentimental. Shared that his old man had been an Italian immigrant. Charlie's Mama? From the greenest place on earth, Ireland. So the big fella turns out to have been part and parcel of the great American melting pot.*

*Siringo spent fifteen inconsequential years as a ranch hand in his hometown of Matagorda, Texas. Dull days and slow hours were broken only by annual long-drives up to Kansas. In time, though, Siringo would pin on a badge. He helped Pat Garrett capture William Henry Antrill, alias 'The Kid,' in Lincoln County, New Mexico, circa 1881. Thereafter, Garrett wrote a letter of recommendation to Alan Pinkerton, manager of a Chicago detective agency. That ever-scowling fella came to be known as The Private Eye, owing to an oversized image of an ocular membrane central in his advertising logo.*

*As for Joe, he's best known for capturing a cold-blooded killer named Tom Horn. That gun-for-hire had murdered a simple farmer, fourteen-year-old Willie Nickell, during the range war in Johnson County. Attempting to preserve open range, wealthy cattleman persecuted incoming squatters mounting barb wire fence to protect their crops from wandering beeves. Just how Lefors obtained a confession from Horn, no one can say. Likely, Joe beat it out of the so-called 'regulator.' Horn was hanged.*

*That was good enough for Pinkerton, who hired the Texan born in 1840 and teamed him with Siringo. So they came at The Wild Bunch from two sides during the Wilcox Train Robbery, shooting down Kid Curry and most of the other boys. That left Butch Cassidy and the Sundance Kid as the gang's last survivors. Siringo and Lefors announced they wouldn't relent until they had those two behind bars. So it was that all four ended up in Little Old New York even as the city transformed into The Big Apple.*

*And, along with Miss Etta Place, became involved in the making of an early Western movie,* The Great Train Robbery.

# PART EIGHTEEN: AS TIME GOES BY

$$\infty$$

"In one way, at least, Time is like a River: You cannot
touch the same water twice, because the flow that
has passed will never again return."

—Marcus Aurelius

ETTA: Monday; February 18, 1901

"Miss Etta? You alright in there?"

I woke, in Annie's room at Madison Square Garden, to the sound of Caleb's voice. Nightmares of the Wolf returning to my personal retreat had woken me more than once during this long, lonely night. Such dreams worsened as I suffered from headaches and a nasty pain down below, as if it were time for my monthly, though that seemed unlikely.

"I'm . . . Okay, I guess. Come in, Caleb."

He cautiously opened the door. "What's the matter?"

"Nothing. Everything. I—" At that moment, I did what no woman ever wants to do in front of a man, vomiting all over myself and the bed. The rancid scent proved overpowering.

"We'll get you cleaned up good," Caleb assured me as Sari joined him and the two set about caring for me as well as cleaning up the mess. "Then I'll ask Colonel Cody where to find a doctor."

"No need for that, Caleb. I know of one Sundance visited down in the Village. He's the doc I wish to see."


SUNDANCE: Monday; February 18, 1901

"May I ask what's got you so intrigued?"

I spoke to Emma as I joined her at the breakfast nook in their suite. Mrs. Bat Masterson sipped coffee while reading a book called *A New Type of Vision* by Bishop George Berkeley, a writer I hadn't heard of.

"A remarkable tome," she remarked, reaching for the coffee pot in the center of the table and pouring me a cup.

"By yet another contemporary author altering the way we perceive the world?"

"In fact, a predecessor by more than 250 years. The first philosopher to consider the then-emergent science called physics and form an original perspective on what's actually 'out there,' compared to what we believe."

"I'm all ears."

"Alright, then. And since you phrase your request in that manner, let's start with the idea of 'sound.' Berkeley wrote, 'If a tree should fall in the forest, and no one is around to hear, is there a sound?' Share your reaction, Henry."

"Of course there is. Sound's . . . *sound*."

"Not according to Berkeley."

ETTA: MONDAY; FEBRUARY 18, 1901

Caleb and I rode in a transom headed downtown to the office of the doctor Henry had spoken so highly of. That he was a Jew added to my interest. Might I learn something further as to our moveable nation, as well as what ailed me now?

"Well, our rubes have nearly completed the additions your magician friend required. When the moment of your 'vanishing' arrives, I'll be waiting outside for you."

"May I ask, Caleb, why are you so good to me?"

"It's in my nature, I reckon, to treat people kindly."

"With no thought of a reward?"

"None at all. And I add, 'Amen!' to that."

"As to that, let me ask, Do *you* believe in God?"

"Never crossed m' mind not to."

"Caleb, are you aware that many citizens of the world now doubt whether or not a supreme being even exists?"

"Sure. Got nothin' to do with me. I walk my own pathway."

"I envy your confidence."

"You can regain yours, Miss Etta. Force the doubts out of your mind. Focus on what's good in the world, not the bad."


BUTCH: MONDAY; FEBRUARY 18, 1901

Gradually, I regained consciousness and focused on Kathryn Trumbell, beside me in bed. "That was . . . well . . . wonderful!" she sighed, glowing with satisfaction.

Doubtless, a nearly infinite number of women had said that to a nearly infinite number of men on a nearly infinite number of mornings similar to this. Sometimes, common-place expressions prove to be the truest.

"For me, too." Likewise, I responded without originality. "So! Are you convinced now?"

"Let me say," Kathryn answered with a coy flirtatiousness that included raising of an eyebrow and rolling her eyes, "you're a lot closer than two days ago."

"How can I make you 100 percent certain?" I asked.

"I'm sure you'll achieve that tonight, LeRoy!"

"Kathryn," I mumbled, grasping the trap I'd just set for myself, then blindly stumbled into, "We have to talk!"

ETTA: MONDAY; FEBRUARY 18, 1901

"Dr. Washington, I presume?" I asked. In the waiting room I'd introduced myself to the nurse.' She accompanied me down a hallway to the main office while Caleb stood guard outside.

"I'd prefer you call me Weinstein," he said, taking note of my Magen David.

"You don't choose to wear one, doctor?"

He spoke as if we were family; all our people brothers and sisters, ever on the lookout for fellow Jews who enter their lives and require mentoring. So the doctor informed me of the prejudice he'd ecountered over the years.

"Why fight battles when you can avoid them?" he concluded.

"That's one way of looking at it."

"You don't agree?"

"Still making up my mind on that one! For now, I'm willing to take the risk. As to the future? I'm not yet certain."

"Should we ever chance to meet again, tell me how that works for you. It's a mean world out there."

"I've experienced that. Yet on rare occasion, I've met people who restored my faith in humanity, if not necessarily God."

"Oh! Now you've opened another whole can of worms."

What an appealing young man the doctor was! Might he be one of those possible beaus the rabbi had referred to? If I choose to stay, life as a doctor's wife certainly might be a viable option, just so long as I could also pursue the goal of becoming New York City's first female rabbi.

If nothing else, it's something to consider. I mean, what could possibly interfere with such a potential courtship? At this moment, I can think of nothing. Nothing at all . . .


SUNDANCE: MONDAY; FEBRUARY 18, 1901

"According to Berkeley's theory," said Emma. "Which I would describe as 'subjective realism,' there would be no sound."

"I don't get it."

"He proposes that sound exists only in the mind. If a tree should hit the ground, this would send out what he refers to as 'waves.' Now, if these should reach a human or animal ear, the natural mechanism inside such an organ must react to the intrusion. The ear does so by forwarding this raw information to the brain."

"Where the 'sound waves' are converted to sound."

"You got it!"

"Next thing you know," I marveled, "you'll be telling me that what I see with my eyes is not in truth actually there."

"If we had more time, that's precisely what I would say."

ETTA: MONDAY; FEBRUARY 18, 1901

"You're not sick. You're with child."

"Oh, my," I mumbled.

*Well, here's the answer to my sunpoken question of but a moment ago.*

*Always expect the worst you will seldom be disappointed.*

Momentarily, I froze up. Then I laughed hysterically! This took Dr. Weinstein back.

"I'll get you a mild sedative," he said, crossing to a glass and wood cabinet where a wide array of colorful bottles were arranged.

"I could use one," I chuckled.

He returned with a container of barbiturate. "Soon you'll feel a calm overcome you."

"In my case, doctor, I doubt even medicine can help."

"Please understand, I ask this question not out of casual curiosity but sincere concern. Are you married?"

"No."

"Do you know for certain the identify of the father?"

I considered, without speaking. It might be Butch or Sundance. Next, I thought of Enrico. A week had passed since we made love for the first time. I laughed out loud at the absurdity of my situation. At the very moment when I least needed further complications, they blew my way with the winds of life itself.

BUTCH: MONDAY; FEBRUARY 18, 1901

"You plan to do *what?*"

I did not expect a positive reaction from Kathryn when I told her I'd be spending the night with Etta and Sundance. But her sudden transition to a howling banshee did shock me.

"The three of us together, perhaps for the *final* time."

"Oh, Christ!" she shouted, slipping out of my arms, off the bed, and into her nightgown. Once dressed, she stomped about angrily. "You thought you'd do this under my very roof?"

"Well, now that you put it *that* way—"

"What other way *is* there?"

"I was hoping you might accept this as my way of saying 'farewell!' to one or the other. Likely, both."

"Then taking up again with me?"

"Something like that, I guess."

"Well, guess again! Listen now, mister. You have a choice to make here. Spend the night with them, and you're free to do whatever you want for the rest of your life. Find yourselves a love nest in New York, go to Bolivia or hell so far as I'm concerned. Or, stay with me tonight. Show them and prove to me that you've moved on. Then we'll proceed with our relationship. Your choice, cowboy."

ETTA: MONDAY; FEBRUARY 18, 1901

Joining Caleb in the hallway, my guardian sensed that I was deeply shaken. "I'm pregnant," I informed him. Caleb reacted with both relief and concern. On the one hand, I was not about to die of some disease. On the other, I was an unmarried though pregnant woman. Thus, essentially alone.

So what to do? Marry out of desperation? Tell the boys it might be either of them? Or Enrico? Take Rabbi Cohen up on his offer to mentor a lost soul, if he still wanted me after he learned of my current state?

Or, find a doctor to terminate this pregnancy. Here, though, was the latest irony. While I'd gladly crusade for a woman's right to choice I had no intention of seekingan abortion.

For *despite obvious difficulties, I wanted this child. Perhaps to be the kind of warm, loving mother I never had.*

SUNDANCE: MONDAY; FEBRUARY 18, 1901

"You look in rough shape," I told Butch as we met at the Washington Square Arch. He hadn't shaved; his suit might have been slept in. His eyes appeared hazey.

"Kathryn," he huffed, explaining their conversation of an hour and a half earlier. "She doesn't understand."

"How could she? The woman will bury her son today and is hoping against hope she'll begin a new future with you."

"Let's put that aside for now. As for today, I think it's best we ferry over to Jersey. Confront Lakeland. If he's the one who stole the evidence from DeFly's studio, do what's necessary to get our hands on the negatives."

"I'm with you."

"What should be our pretext for arriving?"

"Let's tell whomever we meet we'd like to play bit parts in Tuesday's shoot. Perhaps they'll need experienced riders."

"Well," I chuckled, "we sure do qualify for that."

## ETTA: MONDAY; FEBRUARY 18, 1901

"I don't want to go to the Garden yet, Caleb. Would you take me to the boarding house? I need to be alone for a bit."

On the way, we briefly paused at a bookseller's stall, as I longed for some fresh reading material. There, I spotted and purchased a copy of *Beyond Good and Evil*, the 1886 book by philosopher Friedrich Nietzsche.

We continued on. At the front desk, a temporary worker informed me that Mrs. Trumbell had left for the funeral. Once upstairs, I entered my room while Caleb again stationed himself outside the door. I lay down and slept for an hour. When I woke, I reached for the book. Bat had mentioned this controversial writer, saying here was a key work for anyone wishing to understand the current changeover in values. As I wouldn't be required at the Garden until two p.m., I flipped through the pages.

First: in the 20th century, 'reality' is no longer a concept that will unite people, rather drive us ever further apart. The most significant alteration in our perception of the cosmos is the conclusion that everything is subjective; objectivity merely an outworn myth. Here was an idea that had been formulating in my own mind for some time.

## BUTCH: MONDAY; FEBRUARY 18, 1901

"Regarding what Bat said last night," Sundance mentioned as seagulls circled overhead and mild waves sloshed against the ferry's sides, "had an opportunity to consider it yet?"

"Makes sense to me. The vast working classes in Europe, particularly in Russia? Existing on the edge of starvation, while the czar and a select few enjoy luxury in their crystal palaces? Henry, it ain't *right*."

"That's Russia. We live in America, land of dreams."

"What if they are impossible dreams?"

"I don't get you."

"Maybe democracy doesn't work anymore. Particularly when it's married to capitalism, as is the case in the U.S."

"I don't know. I like the idea that everybody has an equal shot at hitting the big time."

"Me? I keep thinking of all those who never will, yet cling to the illusion that success is right around the corner."

ETTA: MONDAY; FEBRUARY 18, 1901

"Everything matters," Nietzsche had written, "nothing's important." The irony inherent in that statement caught my interest. Seemingly a contradiction in terms, the couplet hinted at why that German intellectual committed suicide six months ago. How to resolve the two sides of this philosophic coin? Obsessing on such an absurdity could drive one to madness.

Other ideas present here might have been intended specifically for me. Notably, "No price is too high to pay for the privilege of owning yourself." Wasn't this what I'd struggled with over the past year? On another page the philosopher explained the subjectivity that I now embraced as my reality; particularly in a century which asked if God, as a concept or a being, might be dead, "You have your way. I have mine. As far as right and wrong, good and evil, or the truly correct and only 'way,' it does not exist."

Here, I grasped, in stark black and white, was the Modern view. "The Truth," once thought of as a hard fact, is elusive. If indeed it even exists.


SUNDANCE: MONDAY; FEBRUARY 18, 1901

"What's all the noise out there?" a gruff voice called from one of the lightweight buildings. Butch had been loudly whistling, while I was overtook by another coughing fit. From the half-open door, a short, stocky middle-aged man in a rumpled suit emerged. Even a pair of Wyoming hicks like us recognized him. For here was the man who revolutionized our world; Thomas Alva Edison.

"Sorry," I meekly whispered. "Won't happen again."

"Who are you, anyway?" he bellowed.

"Just a couple of would-be extras," Butch softly replied, "hoping to get hired."

"Recently arrived from the West. We're cowboys."

"Well, that'd qualify you more than any of the others we've interviewed. Most have never been in the saddle before."

"You'd have no problem with us regarding that."

"Certainly look rugged enough! You'd be portraying Butch Cassidy and the Sundance Kid. Ever hear of 'em?"

"Oh, sure," I snickered. "Hasn't everybody?"


ETTA: MONDAY; FEBRUARY 18, 1901

If, as Nietzsche claims, 'good' and 'evil' are outdated concepts, could there still be such a thing as a 'crime,' much less a 'sin'? I doubted that civilization could continue to function if such a vision won public acceptance. Humans might revert to the animalistic creatures they were before our ancestors first squatted together around fires, in time praying to something greater than themselves. Without which—or at least the belief in such a higher power—they could not continue with a sense that their lives meant anything beyond daily survival.

If Nietzsche were correct, then Lupo had as much of a right to exist as did as Joe Petrosino. Dare gaze into the heart of darkness and everything we'd been taught beginning in early childhood evaporated. How I wanted to reject this and somehow force such thoughts from my mind. But that would only replace modern nihilism with old-fashioned blind faith. And, for me at least, neither extreme would suffice.

BUTCH: Monday; February 18, 1901

"Well, as long as you're here, come on in and take a peek at what we're up to." With that, Mr. Edison ushered us into his ramshackle office. A projector sat on a worktable, facing a bedsheet tacked up on the far wall.

"So that's what the future of movies looks like!" I marveled.

"Pretty primitive. Our technicians are developing a more advanced variation, while others work at creating a higher quality camera to more vividly capture the world around us."

"And to think If we get hired, tomorrow we'll be in on American filmmaking from the ground floor."

"Here," he said, holding up a strip of celluloid. "This is our most recent picture, scheduled for release next week. Let me run this for you so you can grasp what we're up to."

Edison drew the shades, dimmed the electric lights, and started the picture show. We were astounded by the sight up there on the screen of fire engines roaring down a city street, then arriving at a burning building in which a frantic woman holding her baby screamed from the window for help. Firemen raised a ladder to rescue them. But if I expected the story to continue with a sequence in which mother and child were saved, I was in for a surprise.

Next, we witnessed this entire incident from beginning to end for a second time, only now from inside the smoke-filled room. It struck me that *Movies* could free the viewer from all previous notions of time and space as we conceive them. If the film's first half struck me as documentary, the second offered a carefully rehearsed drama. Considering the repetition—of events that occurred simultaneously presented to the viewer from different points of view—it took twice as long to watch the story unfold than would have passed in the real world. When the picture show ended several minutes later, Edison glanced to us for reactions.

"It was like *magic!*"

"Indeed. A new possibility for that ancient art. *Movie Magic!*

ETTA: MONDAY; FEBRUARY 18, 1901

I encountered yet another sentence that reached up from the page and grabbed hold of my mind, "People don't want to hear the truth because they fear that the illusions which sustain them will be destroyed." That was me, at this moment!

As to my shooting a man back in Wyoming and wounding another here? Nietzsche's warning, "Whoever fights monsters should be cautious he (or in my case *she*) does not become what he is trying to kill." After all the profound negativity, Nietzsche curiously concluded with a hint of hope, "Enjoy life. For this is not a dress rehearsal!" How fitting!

My life was indeed a play. Our days on the frontier had been the set-up for all to follow, Act One, more or less. Our subsequent time in the city, an ongoing combination of drama and comedy, the meaty Second Act. And now, as inescapable as the Third in a classic by Sophocles or a modern play by Ibsen, I anxiously faced the resolution of all that had gone before.

*The denouement was about to unfold itself, me a passive character or master of my fate. Which would it be? That I would soon discover . . .*

SUNDANCE: MONDAY; FEBRUARY 18, 1901

"Hello, again," the young man standing before the Black Maria's strangely-shaped construction said as we approached.

"Greetings. This is my pardner. Mr. Edison just informed us we're set to play Butch and the Kid tomorrow."

"Well, there's a great irony in that," Porter said with an agreeable chuckle. "Especially considering who's been cast in the roles of Siringo and Lefors."

This fits in with our plan, for we can keep an eye on Lefors and Siringo the entire time. They will mostly be interested in us as a means to an end, leading to Etta. She'll be hidden up at Madison Square, safe there from them.

"Where's Lakeland?"

"Mr. Lakeland is no longer employed by the Edison company."

ETTA: MONDAY; FEBRUARY 18, 1901

Stepping into the lobby, I found myself face to face with Mrs. Trumbell. She had returned from the funeral services and now stood halfway between the front door and the hospitality desk. Her demeanor implied a terrible sense of loss. And, if less obvious, a hopeful hint that she was free to begin her life anew.

"Hello, Mrs. Trumbell. This is opportune."

"That's one way of phrasing it."

"Well, we do need to talk things out. But if this is not the appropriate—"

"Step into my office." I signaled to Caleb with a wink that this should not present a problem. He nodded and again remained behind. I followed as Mrs. Trumbell led the way. Once inside her private little corner of the world, she pointed to a stuffed chair and sat on a couch across from me.

"Let's have it out," she announced. "Woman to woman."

BUTCH: MONDAY; FEBRUARY 18, 1901

After entering the Black Maria, E.S. marched to his desk, unlocked a drawer and opened it, withdrawing a large manilla envelope.

"What do you have there?" I softly inquired.

"Look for yourself," he wryly stated, handing me the package. Inside were the crucial negatives and prints.

"Henry and I broke into DeFly's office to steal and destroy them," I reacted, dumbfounded, "only to discover them gone."

"I arrived first, found 'em at once. Then brought them here this morning, showed 'em to Lakeland, and told him that his 'con' was finished. Gave him the choice of leaving, or me telling Mr. Edison about the blackmail scheme. He chose to go. Heaven only knows where to."

"Who will produce and direct the film?"

"Me! I'll get full credit. I'm a filmmaker now!"

"One thing bothers me, though. Did you have to . . . you know—"

"No. I don't."

"—kill DeFly?"

"What?" Porter's voice cracked. His face blanched.

"I mean, he didn't necessarily deserve to live, but—"

"Fellas, I have no idea what you're talking about. When I broke in, around eleven p.m. on Sunday, DeFly was not on the premises. What you're speaking of must've happened between my visit and your own."

"But, then, who . . ." I pondered.

ETTA: MONDAY; FEBRUARY 18, 1901

"You go first, Mrs. Trumbell."

"Address me as Kathryn. As for you, shall I call you Eloise or Etta?"

"Doesn't much matter at this point."

"Etta it is then. Everyone's still waiting for you to make the big decision. Stay or leave. Alone, or—"

"I won't know until tomorrow night, after my performance as Annie concludes."

"That's cutting the ribbon pretty close."

"I know. It's my 'way.' Always has been."

My mind returned to the night when, as a teenager, I ran away from home. Also, of when I abandoned teaching to ride off with a pair of handsome outlaws. Always, my life had progressed in fits and starts, each decision motivated by a current emotion rather than careful thinking. Apparently, it still did.

SUNDANCE: MONDAY; FEBRUARY 18,1901

After exiting the Black Maria and heading back to the compound's main gate, Butch and I noticed the door to Mr. Edison's office remained open. "Hi again," I said. "Just wanted to let you know that we checked in with Mr. Porter. We'll be here early tomorrow."

"Before you boys leave, come back in for a while."

"Sure," said Butch, as eager as me to spend more time with this avatar of the future.

"Let me ask a question. Did either of you realize that for five of the ten minutes it took us to watch *Life of an American Fireman*, the screen was blank?"

"No," I said, trying to grasp such a notion.

"We watched the whole thing. Non-stop action."

"Action, yes. But not non-stop."

"Mr. Edison, I don't get you."

He held up another strip of film. "Do you know how many individual frames must pass across the light source every second to create the illusion of continuous movement?" My pard and I both shrugged. "Twenty-four. Took us a while to figure how many were needed to create a proper sense of flow. Eighteen, too few; thirty, too many."

"But that hardly explains what you said about five of those ten minutes featuring only a blank screen."

"Let's try a little experiment. I'll run the film for you again, this time with slight variation as to speed."

ETTA: MONDAY; FEBRUARY 18, 1901

"Well, let's get down to it. Butch tells me he has agreed to spend tonight with you and Sundance."

"Correct."

"I assume this was your idea?"

"Right again."

"Care to explain why?"

"I should think that would be obvious. The three of us will move on together come Wednesday or part company once and for all. Seemed to me we ought to experience . . . well . . . *closure*, I guess you'd call it."

"You are aware that Butch might stay here with me?"

"I am."

"Do you expect me to accept him into my bed the following night, still smelling of *you*?"

"Maybe he could take a bath?"

"That's not funny."

"No, it isn't. In all honesty, I hadn't thought of the situation in quite that way."

"You were only considering what's best for yourself."

"True," I said, any sense of personal pride diminished.


BUTCH: MONDAY; FEBRUARY 18, 1901

Edison again screened *American Fireman*. Now, after a minute or so, he fumbled with the projector. "I'm going to diminish the running speed." As he did, I noticed the characters appeared to move in slow motion.

"I recall such a flickering effect from the Nickelodeon," I said, "when I failed to crank the machine consistently."

"Indeed! Now watch as I slow it down further still."

As Edison did so, each image was held considerably longer. And, between the appearance of each, a momentary blackness filled the screen.

"I told you that twenty-four frames pass across the light source every second. At that rate, how long do you imagine a single frame appears up on the screen?"

"One twenty-fourth of a second," I said without thinking.

"That's not possible," my pardner insisted.

"Why not?" Mr. Edison asked.

"Cause that doesn't allow for the time it'd take the machine to remove any one image, then replace it with the next."


ETTA: MONDAY; FEBRUARY 18, 1901

"Butch is free to do as he wishes. I have no hold over him. As for tonight? He must decide for himself."

"As a woman, I wish to maintain a sense of self-respect. In my case, it's all I have left."

"I don't mean to cut you off, Kathryn. But I'm already late for my rehearsal. Let me think all of this through—"

"My guess is that, deep down, he's still in love with you. If that's true, I don't want him. Call it pride—"

"No woman's more susceptible to *that* than me!"


SUNDANCE: MONDAY; FEBRUARY 18, 1920

"Right, 'Butch.' Say, you don't mind if I call you that, do ya?"

"Not at all, Mr. Edison," my pard chuckled. "Kind of fits, actually."

"So, ordinarily, each frame remains projected on the screen for one-*forty-eighth* of a second."

"Got ya."

"Now, how long would the changeover take?"

"Another forty-eighth of a second," I guessed.

"Precisely! During the forty-eighth of a second between each shot's time onscreen, what's up there?"

"Nothing," Butch deducted.

"I'm confused. While it's running at normal speed, why do we see the images but not the equal amounts of darkness?"

"Owes to a concept, realized over two thousand years ago by an Islamic mathematician, physicist, sorcerer, and philosopher named Ibn al-Haytham, better known as Alhazen. In time, the Greeks of the Classical Age would define this as 'Persistence of Vision.'"


ETTA: MONDAY; FEBRUARY 18, 1901

"I couldn't leave New York without saying goodbye," I told Susan and Elizabeth in their hotel suite. "I owe the two of you so very much."

"You owe us nothing," Susan replied. "We both of us adore you. And appreciate the remarkable person you are."

"And we still implore you to stay with us in New York."

"Despite our fundamental difference of opinion on the issue of abortion, Elizabeth?"

"If you remain here," she assured me, "we could agree to disagree on that."

"And focus on those issues that unite us," said Susan.

"Even concerning the vote, Susan, we have a problem. You're willing to align with Carrie Nation."

"One issue that might unite us is free access to birth control."

"Like you, I'm all in favor of that. But the Victorians still dictate public morality. And they resist sex education in public schools."

"Wouldn't this be a wonderful cause to unite us, then?"

"I can't argue with that, Elizabeth," I responded, stymied once again.


BUTCH: MONDAY; FEBRUARY 18, 1901

"I still don't get it," Henry continued. "If we clearly see the pictures, why don't we see the blank spots as well?"

"In a manner of speaking, you do. At least, your eyes do. But a person does not see with his eyes, rather his mind."

"I'm lost again," I sighed.

"You blink every five to seven seconds, correct?"

"Sure."

"And when you do, your eyes perceive the darkness of the lids as they go down and up. But the world doesn't go dark for you once every seven seconds. Your eyes are the equivalent of feelers on an insect. They pick up whatever information is out there. Raw material, 'unedited' to employ movie terminology."

"Sounds like what a wise lady told me about the way we hear. Not with the ears, but the mind."

"Wise, indeed. What the eyes perceive is conveyed by way of light waves. Then, once they've arrived, it's the mind's turn to process them. When a person sees something significant, this makes an imprint in the brain. And even if one should blink, we still hold on to that previous image. We ignore the blank spots as that's extraneous material. The brain overrides the eyes by picking out what maters and what doesn't, and focusing on that."

"As you mentioned earlier: persistence of vision."

"Describe that term for me, Butch."

"You don't have to be looking at something to see it!."

"True! Without which, *movies* would not be possible."


ETTA: MONDAY; FEBRUARY 18, 1901

"Look!" I said. "Up in the sky. Is it a bird—"

"No," Caleb informed me. "A hot air balloon."

Now, I understood why a considerable crowd had formed outside of Madison Square. The great showman James Anthony Bailey—who replaced his deceased partner P.T. Barnum as figurehead for "The Greatest Show on Earth"—was scheduled to bring his circus to the Garden even as Colonel Cody vacated. Bailey and his small companion Commodore McNutt would descend in a basket hung beneath the hydrogen-filled canvas contraption. This would precede the company arriving later that day by train. A glorious parade would sweep along Broadway, over to Third, allowing fans a free glimpse of the grand spectacle to soon appear.

"Barnum tried to sail it across the Atlantic," Buntline noted, stepping alongside us. "He found inspiration from a Jules Verne novel." We gazed upward in awe as a sudden gust of wind threatened to capsize the wobbly airborne device. "But even P.T. didn't possess enough hot air to pull *that* stunt off."

Meanwhile, a flurry of free passes for the show rained down, setting observers scurrying to and fro. That's when it struck me. This latest addition to those elements whirling about might provide a back-up plan for my escape tomorrow evening. In case Harry Houdini's escape tunnel did not function, In such a case, Bailey's balloon could whisk me from our performance down to the docks.

## SUNDANCE: MONDAY; FEBRUARY 18, 1901

"I've traveled all across, as well as up and down, this great land of ours," a large man in a cheap suit announced to several eager listeners while Butch and I were on the ferry back to Manhattan, "and I believe I've acquired wisdom which I'm happy to share with you."

The Walrus! Whom I'd met, ostensibly by accident, on that boat trip to Buffalo last month, though that seems years ago now. The fellow who'd explained to me why every barn in the country, and every building in the city, is dyed red. Now, with Butch off to find the restroom, I stood by myself, listening to the businessman share his wit and wisdom once again.

If I'd come to doubt 'fate,' suddenly I regained the sense that all things tie together. For this couldn't be a coincidence. Just now, the Walrus and I were reunited. And, incredibly, by boat. There must be some reason for that. And, if such a reason did indeed exist, doesn't that imply that every little detail of life is meaningfully tied to every other?

"Every year on Thanksgiving, Americans head to their local markets for turkeys to prepare for family and friends. Don't you do so yourselves?"

While his audience grunted and nodded in confirmation, I stepped up behind The Walrus.

"Then here's a question for you. Why turkey, of all possible choices?"

"Because that's what the pilgrims and Indians feasted on back in 1621."

"Good guess. But in fact, incorrect. There were no turkeys, wild or domesticated, in the Plymouth Colony at the time."

"Of course there were," another fellow shouted. "I've seen paintings of the event—"

"Those portraits were created during the past forty years. The turkeys are anachronistic."

"What does that even mean?"

"The artists included turkeys because it's a Thanksgiving staple today. They either weren't aware or didn't care that what our forefeathers partook of was fish and corn."

"Huh!" members of the growing crowd muttered in unision.

"Anyone else have an idea?"

"I do," I stated, coming up alongside the Walrus.

"Ah! My young companion of a fortnight ago. Reveal now what you learned from our previous conversation."

"Turkey is the cheapest meat available."

With that, the crowd laughed, recognition of the obvious truth now apparent in each man's eyes.

"Proving what?"

"That people are the same everywhere."

"Anything else?"

"Yes! That money makes the world go around."

Any chance that I may, like Butch, drift toward Marxism dissolved. However much I might admire the communist ideals, I am a realist. I don't believe Communism can work. Because it goes against the grain of what it means to be human, for better or worse. Marxism is based on the principle that human nature can change. I simply don't believe that. Not only are we the same all over. We always will be.


ETTA: Monday; February 18, 1901

Once the mighty balloon had been safely anchored on the street by several roustabouts, the lifelong victim of dwarfism known as Commodore McNutt hopped out and scurried down a rope ladder, smiling ecstatically and waving to the children. Then Bailey, appealing if not nearly as charismatic as his late partner Barnum, fumbled his way down as well. Topped with orange hair, his pink head rippled with sweat as he addressed the star-struck crowd.

"On Tuesday evening, Colonel Cody will conclude his stay at the Garden. I will follow that with a truly spectacular collection of international artists."

"Are you with the Wild West?" McNutt cautiously inquired, edging close while devouring me with his eyes.

"Well, yes and no," I smiled sweetly. "Commodore, how very much I would appreciate an introduction to your boss!"

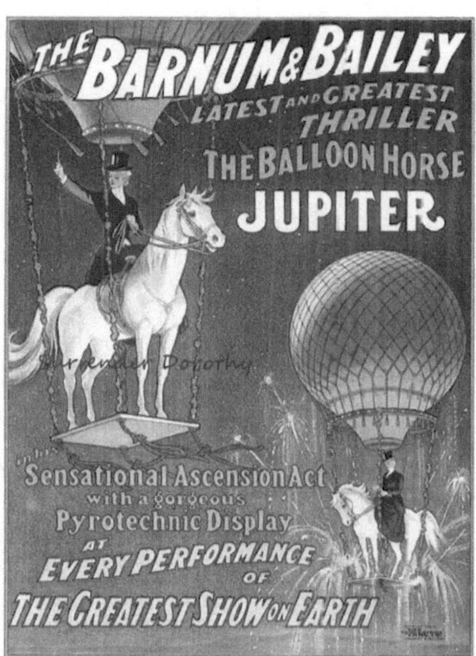


THE WONDER HORSE: To this day, it's unknown whether Butch Cassidy ever realized that Barnum & Bailey's star equine performer was in fact the same horse he had nurtured and raised in Wyoming years earlier.

"That can be arranged. Hoping to win a role in our show? With your looks, you could become one of the female trick riders. Though that would require tireless practice."

"In fact, riding is something I've had considerable experience with in the past."

## BUTCH: MONDAY; FEBRUARY 18, 1901

*My Dear Ship That Passed in the Night,* the letter began. I had returned to Trumbell's to wash up after the Jersey sojourn. A girl managing the front desk handed me a sealed missive. The letter had been sent c/o Colonel Cody at the Garden. Either he or Ned forwarded it on to the boarding house.

I'd known the moment I glanced at the return address—the Metropole in Cincinnati—who sent it. Also enclosed were two post-card reproductions of famous paintings.

*Likely, you were not expecting to hear from me again. Nor had I planned to contact you. Then I read about the last flight of the Wild Bunch. How fascinating to discover the man who shared my bed for one enchanted night was none other than that living legend, outlaw Butch Cassidy!*

*Of course, I had no idea as to where I might reach you. Then it occurred to me; you had mentioned Buffalo Bill's Wild West. It made sense that, were Cody and Cassidy in Manhattan at the same time, you two would come into contact.*

*I have not forgotten the confusion you expressed as to the future of our world, as well as your possible role in it. As an aficionado of fine art, I prefer to express ideas in the form of paintings rather than verbal discourse. So I include these oppositional visions of the shape of things to come in hopes they speak for themselves, and will aid you as to making the key choices you now face.*

*Au Revoir,*

*Your gone, but hopefully not forgotten, lover*

ETTA: MONDAY; FEBRUARY 18, 1901

"Can we talk?" Annie asked. After convincing Commodore McNutt to introduce me to Mr. Bailey, I'd hurried to the dressing room, only to find Annie patiently waiting.

"Sure. What's wrong?"

Annie handed me a copy of the New York *American*, Hearst's most popular East Coast newspaper. On the front page, and in block letters, the headline read: "ANNIE OAKLEY AND FRANK BUTLER READY TO SPLIT?"

"My lawyer explained that because they put a question mark at the end, I can't sue. Hearst's people know that by phrasing it as a question rather than fact, they are protected by freedom of the press."

I scanned the story, which implied that Frank had been hiding a pair of women in a West Side apartment during the Wild West's stay in Manhattan. Also that Annie, now aware of this, seriously considered a divorce.

"We can't let them get away with it! Maybe Bat—"

"Etta," Annie gasped, "this time, at least, it's true."

SUNDANCE: MONDAY; FEBRUARY 18, 1901

"Rabbi, may I disturb you for a moment?" I asked after a cantor greeted me and honored my request to meet the Jewish community's spiritual leader.

"All are welcome here. Don't I know you?"

"We met briefly that terrible night in little Italy."

"Of course. Henry? Welcome to my place of worship."

Anxiously, I seated myself across from his desk. "Etta insists you are a man of considerable wisdom."

"I fear your friend vastly overrates me."

"My guess is that she's point-on. I'm experiencing a crisis of conscience. Etta thought that you might be of help."

"In any way I possibly can."

So I confessed to the killings. Did this doom me to Hell? Raised as a Protestant, having listened to a sincere Catholic's advice, I wanted to learn if this other religion might help to guide me.

"Rabbi, I do know that Protestants, Catholics, and Jews all agree on our essential Covenant: The Ten Commandments."

"Yes, though many other issues deeply divide us."

"As I make ready for the next great journey of my life, I'm hoping you may help me to embark on that . . . well, odyssey . . . with a positive outlook despite what I've done."


ETTA: MONDAY; FEBRUARY 18, 1901

"I've suspected for a long time, but I wouldn't let myself believe it."

"Why now?"

"Because I saw the three together when I went shopping. They were laughing and flirting . . ."

Annie's anger, shame, and vulnerability hit home. If I were to accept Enrico's invitation, and by chance we passed Mrs. Caruso on some street in Italia, I'd inflict pain on another woman even as had happened to Mrs. Frank Butler.

I couldn't risk that. I've been many things in life that I'm not proud of. But I will not be a hypocrite, sympathizing with Annie, while offending another man's wife. I must tell Enrico 'no.'

"Your suggestion that we might trade places not only for tomorrow but beyond that. Is the offer still open?"


BUTCH: MONDAY; FEBRUARY 18, 1901

I reached for the first of the 4 by 6" post-cards, labeled "A Picnic in the Grass" or "The Bath." On its left side, the artist depicted a charming wooded area, a picnic lunch spread across a blue sheet; a young woman, nude; two suited men casually appreciating her beauty. On the right, and set farther back from her companions, another woman, partly masked by a translucent chemise, unashamedly stood in a pond, dressing. Thanks to my schooling by two knowledgeable females, I knew enough of art now to grasp the work's significance beyond compositional aesthetics.

However daring the sensuousness, Édouard Manet's style struck me as a conscious return to the formalism of the old masters Raphael and Rubens; a

THE PAINTER AS PHILOSOPHER, PART ONE: During the second half of the nineteenth century, France's Edouard Manet offered an early modernist vision of nature as a lyrical refuge from the pollution of ever encroaching big cities.

nod to the early realistic approach, now all but replaced by post-impressionism. The image wordlessly called out to me, 'Be among these gleefully indecent rebels,' at once contemporary, yet embodying a throwback to our pagan past.

Nature appears as welcoming here as the people who inhabit it. The nude's *Mona Lisa*-like gaze added to the sense of invitation as she considered each viewer of the work of art that contained her with vague disinterest. How I desired to pass from my real world into their perfect one.

ETTA: MONDAY; FEBRUARY 18, 1901

"Annie! You're serious?"

"I think so. Oh, I don't know. Etta, I'm so confused—"

"Join the club! I'm literally going around in circles."

"I *do* want to make it work with Frank. But I feel that I need . . ."

"A 'break'?"

"That's it! Maybe if I head off someplace for a while, he'll grasp what really matters."

"Of course, you're legally entangled with Frank. Marriage in the conventional sense of the term, compared to me."

"Still, that's why I came to you for advice."

"I can't offer any. You must choose for yourself."

"Okay. When the moment of decision arrives tomorrow, we'll determine which of us ought to sail away."

"At the last possible moment."

"Yes. As with the ending of a romantic novel."

"Indeed, And, sooner than later I'd guess, just like the Movies."

SUNDANCE: MONDAY; FEBRUARY 18, 1901

"Rabbi, the Sixth Commandment insists, 'Though shalt not kill.' Yet I did so. And not by accident."

"From what you've confided, the incident was predicated by dedication to family, as precious to we Jews as Christians."

"That certainly was the case."

"Now, let me share a detail few people living today are aware of. Most Jews and Christians who read the Bible believe the Fifth Commandment absolutely forbids killing."

"That's how I've always taken it."

"In truth, that's not the case."

The Rabbi reached backward and removed from a shelf what struck me as a rare and special item. From a rich purple sheath with yellow adornments, he delicately withdrew and then unrolled an ancient scroll. The paper, attached to hardwood handlers on either side, appeared so timeworn that it might crumple to dust at any moment. "This is the Hebrew Torah. It doesn't say what most people think."

ETTA: MONDAY; FEBRUARY 18, 1901

"You're pond scum," I all but spat at Frank once we'd completed two final hours of rehearsal.

"What?" he gasped, taken aback.

"However exaggerated and nasty the stories in Hearst's rags may be, they aren't fiction. You did cheat on Annie?"

"Yes," he admitted, embarrassed. "But—"

"No 'buts' about it! You betrayed her."

"You're a fine one to talk! Living with two outlaws."

"Never once did I betray a trust. Each man in my life has known of the other. I never lied to or deceived either."

"And that justifies your lifestyle?"

"To me it does. I feel no guilt."

"Well, then," he mumbled, "where does that leave things?"

"If Annie decides to remain here and work things out with you, that'll be her choice. But if she wishes to change places with me and sail off, I'll accept that."

"While you continue on with the Wild West?" he asked, dumbfounded.

"Perhaps. Should I decide to do so, there will never . . . under *any* circumstances . . . be anything between us other than 'professional.'"

"You'd reserve the right to involvements with other men?"

"With whomever I choose." As if to further confound him, I pointedly added, "Man or women."

"So! Anyone but me?"

"Bingo!"

## BUTCH: MONDAY; FEBRUARY 18, 1901

In 'The Picnic,' Manet projected that the human condition could still prove lyrical if we accept and practice his vision of nature as a peaceful garden. Contrarily "The Scream" by Edvard Munch portrayed the sky above as an ugly,

THE PAINTER AS PHILOSOPHER, PART TWO: As Modern Times approached, Norway's Edvard Munch presented an Existential Everyman, driven to madness by the daily routine of big city life.

angular series of horizontal stripes, blood-red, urine yellow; the mud below a fjord blackened by filth spilling forth from adjoining factories. If the French painting expressed an elite and unconventional community as a potential source of joy, the Norwegian's offered a nightmarish depiction of humankind abandoned and alone. Crossing a bridge from somewhere bad to an even worse place.

"The horror! The horror!" as author Joseph Conrad put it.

I grasped why my lover had chosen these two oppositional works. The choice was mine to make. I could scream in reaction to the Modern vision that insists we inhabit a cold universe, lost in the stars, no rhyme or reason to existence. Or I might force such a dark concept from my head and return to Manet's soothing woods with a male friend and female lover. Discover, as Wordsworth wrote, Splendor in the Grass, Glory in the Flower, God in Nature. Bliss!

The choice was mine. And, in truth, every man's.


ETTA: MONDAY; FEBRUARY 18, 1901

"However much I appreciate your offer, I can't accept."

"Let me speak?" Enrico pleaded. The desperation in his eyes expressed the Tenor's hunger to keep me in his life. "I sensed after leaving the last time that you would reject my previous invitation. I am not here to repeat it. Rather to say I'm in love with you. Completely—"

"*Unconditionally?*" I interrupted.

"Indeed! Therefore, I have come to the most difficult conclusion. I'll sacrifice everything, if you'll have me."

"You don't mean—"

"Yes! I'll divorce my wife. Abandon the Catholic church. Marry you in a civil ceremony. I will sign a legal declaration so this will be official and cannot be revoked."

"I don't know what to say."

"I beg of you, say *yes*."

"In all fairness, I'll *say* this: I'm with child."


SUNDANCE: MONDAY; FEBRUARY 18, 1901

"The Hebrew word for 'kill' is 'harag.' But that is not what Yahweh warns us against. For if it were, David's slaying of Goliath would have been a sin. Yet Yahweh rewarded the boy by paving the way for David to become King."

"I do know something of this story, Rabbi. And that later, as king, David purposefully arranged the death of his loyal subject, Uriah, so as to possess that man's wife."

"An evil which another commandment forbids: covetousness. How then does the Lord punish his once cherished David?"

"Yahweh turns David's son, Absalom, against him. The old king dies in guilt, misery, and shame."

"Our Good Book, in its original form, does not say 'harag' in the case of David destruction of Uriah, rather 'rasha.'"

"What does it mean?"

"'Murder.' The commandment says: Thou shalt not *murder*. Kill for personal gain. As David did to Uriah. Not the case with Goliath. For that was 'a righteous kill.'"

"Rabbi," I replied, feeling as if a great weight had been lifted from me, "I can't even begin to thank you."

"In that case, may I request something in return??" I nodded. "Please ask Etta to visit me one last time before departure."

ETTA: MONDAY; FEBRUARY 18, 1901

"I need to sit," Enrico responded in what struck me as a combination of a gasp and a sigh.

"Please do," I coolly, but not coldly, answered.

"Any idea who the father may be?"

"You, perhaps."

"But . . . not necessarily."

"I've been with each of my lovers, both of whom you've met. So it's a one in three possibility you're responsible."

Enrico hung his head low. "That's less than half."

"So! Does your invitation remain open?"

"But this changes everything. To give up my own flesh and blood son I adore—."

"This time around, Enrico, the choice is yours."

"If I'm able to accept your 'condition'?"

"I'll marry you. We might remain here in New York, or settle in Italy. Travel the wide world. Whatever you want. With me as your wife and my . . . possibly our . . . child as your son. Yes or no?"

BUTCH: MONDAY; FEBRUARY 18, 1901

"One last conference before push comes to shove," Bat announced. For the past several hours, Sundance and I sparred at the gym. When our practice match concluded, Bat insisted we three join Etta, as he had important news.

Once we gathered in her room at Madison Square, Bat drew a formal letter out of an inner-pocket.

"Oh, my!" Etta gasped.

Mailed from D.C., the missive had been sent by T.R. The vice-president elect planned to be with us Tuesday for the conclusion of our unfolding narrative.

"Says here," I noted, "Teddy believes he'll be able to coax the president into signing a full pardon for past crimes, seeing as we never killed nobody. Legally, we'd be free."

"How will T.R. convince McKinley to agree to this?"

"Butch, you and Henry will become 'display' prizefighters following your Tuesday night bout. Crowds across the country will arrive at auditoriums to watch a pair of legends box, then attend a free lecture by the former bandits on the need for law and order. That will justify your freedom."

"So far, so good," Etta cut in. "But what about *me?*"


ETTA: MONDAY; FEBRUARY 18, 1901

"That's trickier," Bat admitted, his brow now furrowed. "You would have to stand trial for the killing in Wyoming. But we might persuade the court authorities to relocate the trial here, avoiding prejudice from the deceased's friends."

"That'd be a plus," I acknowledged.

"Here's more good news. There's a brilliant young lawyer named Clarence Darrow who adores challenging situations. He might take on your case."

"What would I have to do?"

"To avoid a murder conviction, and possible execution, you'd plead guilty to a lesser charge. Second degree manslaughter, with extenuating circumstances. Darrow would call attention to the attempted rape. And as women now serve on juries, you could benefit from their potential sympathy."

"On the other hand, Victorian ladies might perceive me as a loose modern girl who had been asking for trouble, then shot down a respectable man, and throw the book at me."

"In court, Etta, there are no guarantees."

"What would my judgment likely be?"

"You'd receive a prison term of two to six years, with the possibility of parole after four."

"Four years in the prime of my life. For defending myself from a rapist? I appreciate your desire to help. So, thanks, but no thanks."

SUNDANCE: MONDAY; FEBRUARY 18, 1901

"Etta," I said, after Bat left, "remember the last night we three spent together, back at the Hole?"

"Menage-a-trois," she warmly recalled.

"Whatever one calls it," I said, "Butch and me simultaneously worshipped your body."

"I remember what happened, Sundance."

"My point is, we two made physical contact as well."

"Of course. That's inherent in such a situation."

"Ever since then, well . . ."

Unable to continue, I cast my eyes downward. That's when my pardner took over. We'd discussed how and when to tell Etta but hesitated. No longer. The time was now.

"We've been 'together,' without you."

"You don't think I grasped that?"

"We wondered," I stammered, "but couldn't be sure. We've been trying to work up the courage—"

"*That's* the big deal?" Etta roared with unrestrained laughter. "Don't you recall what I told you that day of your duel at the Hole?"

"*Anyone can see the two of you love each other.*"

"Whether it's me with either of you, you two together, or we three: we're *us!* Then, now, and always."

"I'm glad you feel that way," gushed Butch.

"Meanwhile, I've been looking for an opportunity to tell you: I've been with another woman. Two, actually."

Took me a little while to recover from this admission. When I finally did, I heard myself say, "I'm good with that."

"Me, too," Butch added.

"Congratulations. You've grown up. Belatedly!"


ETTA: MONDAY; FEBRUARY 18, 1901

"Do you believe that 'compromise' is a dirty word?" I asked Mrs. Trumbell after I'd returned to the boarding house.

"In all honesty, I've never given it much thought."

"Back when I still perceived life to be simple, I believed nothing could be worse than giving up on one's ideals."

"Now?"

"I'm a realist. And understand that the world is a complicated place. Compromise strikes me as the only way to adhere to one's own values while respecting those of others as well."

"I'm not certain where you're going with this."

"When we spoke earlier, Butch had a difficult choice to make. Spend the night with Henry and myself, or you. Then live with the consequences."

"Oh! I think I'm beginning to understand . . ."

"We do have another option. How about a foursome?"

## BUTCH: MONDAY; FEBRUARY 18, 1901

"Here we go again!" Etta laughed, if in a non-humorous manner as my pardner slipped into bed on her right side even as I crawled under the sheets on her left. Each of us knew that this might well be our last 'waltz.' But this time, with the trois expanded to a quartet.

"She'll be here soon," I said "Which allows us time to talk."

"As for tomorrow," Sundance added, "I do have trepidations."

"Let's worry about such things then. Tonight, we'll live for life itself. In the moment. Because that's the only thing we ever have for certain. Everything else is up in the air."

"So the surprises are all done with?" I asked.

"One left, boys. And it's a 'biggie.'"

"Shoot," Sundance replied.

"I'm pregnant."

## —INTERLUDE—

## BAT: OCTOBER 25, 1921

*Miss Etta Place's discovery that she was Jewish by birth adds a certain piquancy to her relationships with two of our key characters in this combination of fact and fancy. Harry Houdini's birth name was Erich Weisz; born in Budapest, 1874. At four years old, he immigrated with his parents to the U.S. to escape the anti-semitism prevelant in their homeland. First, the young man performed his illusions in lesser known stops on the wide Vaudeville circuit. Eventually, he moved on to Broadway thanks to Flo Ziegfeld's patronage. Houdini charmed, mystified, and delighted the masses with each successive show. A dreamer, at least early on, he hoped to challenge America's fear and loathing of Jews through his acts. If Catholics and Protestants adored him, Houdini reasoned, why could that not be extended to fellow members of his nation?*

*In comparison, Flo Ziegfeld's parents had long since arrived from Belgium, where they were minor figures of the local aristocracy. The family settled in our Second City, Chicago, their golden boy born in 1867 and baptized as a Catholic. Thirty some-odd-years later, Ziggy introduced Manhattan's mid-town theater scene to Jewish performers he had observed and adored while visiting Yiddish venues downtown. Flo and Harry clicked at once, despite different approaches to entertainment. Whereas Harry stepped out from the shadows of show business, Flo adored glitz, glamour, and beautiful girls. As to the latter, he had come to believe that the America evolving all around him was ready to cast off its Puritan heritage as well as recent Victorian values.*

CROWN PRINCE OF BROADWAY: Florence Ziegfeld all but created 20th century middle-to-upper-middle-brow entertainment with shows that balanced elegantly costumed beauties with comedy and music drawn from the city's diverse ethnic subcultures.

*Was the ever more diverse citizenry indeed ready for such an internationalization of our emergent culture? Ziegfeld introduced up-towners to the sentimental song stylings of Al Jolsen, born Asa Yoelson. In hopes of creating a delicate balance, Jolson performed in blackface, hoping to encourage a transition by which African American performers might in time also be allowed to appear in such respectable theatres. Flo featured mainstream stars as well, including Will Rogers, who brought the easygoing middle-American cowboy East with his cracker-baller homespun humor.*

*When the powers that be forbid female dancers of color to strut the Black Bottom, with its shake and grind movements, Ziegfeld found a daring young white woman, Ann Pennington, to perform it. Black and white, Christian and Jew, and if belatedly blacks all mixed together in what would emerge as our own Popular Culture. Drawing from many origins, coming together at that precise juncture in time as uniquely American entertainment.*

*Meanwhile, the development of the motion picture as an up-and-coming element in that now prevalent tradition, with the frontier a natural backdrop for this contemporary art form, allowed stories by Ned Buntline, the spectacle of Buffalo Bill's show, and paintngs of Frederic Remington to be showcased in our own unique contribution to the world: The Western Movie.*

*Which is precisely where our own story has been heading all along, and must necessarily reach its conclusion.*

# PART NINETEEN: AGAINST THE CURRENT

ETTA: Tuesday; February 19, 1901

"This may well be the final time we speak," I said, holding back tears when I met Emma at her place in the early morning, Bat already off to the newspaper. When I'd left the rooming house, my men were still asleep, with Mrs. Trumbell just beginning to stir. I guessed Butch would inform her of the latest news concerning the ever-unpredictable Etta Place's 'delicate' condition; Sundance had mentioned the previous evening that his first duty would be to bid farewell to his sister, Dag. What I most needed was the sympathetic ear of a big sister in spirit, if not bloodlines.

"Let's make the most of it," she encouraged.

I filled Emma in on all that had occurred since our previous meeting. To my surprise, I found myself talking about the religious and philosophic quandry now engulfing me. "One might claim Nietzsche has freed us from two thousand years of false 'truths.'"

"Are you certain that *free* is the correct term?"

"What else?"

"How about *chaos*?"

"Explain, Emma. That's why I'm here."

"Let's assume those rare citizens of the world who read books and magazines on a higher level than Ned's dime novels are exposed to Nietzsche. How might they react?"

"By becoming pessimistic or cynical, I'd imagine."

"Right! That 'everything matters but nothing is important' will in time trickle down to the common man. And woman. How will ordinary working people react to the notion that they need not follow The Ten Commandments? For if God is indeed dead, the how can there be the endless reward of heaven or the curse of hell?"

"I see. The question is: What, then, will motivate decent behavior among people?"

"There will be none," Emma solemnly pronounced.


SUNDANCE: Tuesday; February 19, 1901

"More likely than not," I told Dag as we stood together in a terminal at Grand Central, "this'll be our last parting."

"I know that, Harry," she responded, refusing to cry for fear of drowning our leavestaking with excess sentiment.

"Say 'hello' to the girls for me, if they even remember their uncle Harry."

"I will. And they do! Both speak often of the stranger from the far west who arrived on our doorstep."

"Be sure to take 'em to Cody's show. May not capture the way things were, but Bill surely keeps the legends alive."

"Guess this is it," Dag mumbled as porters swiftly loaded the final pieces of luggage and a conductor announced that any remaining ticket-holders ought to now board. "As to Etta?"

"Change of plans. Butch is willing to stay here with a woman he's met. So maybe I will box to win tonight."

"Don't let her get away, Harry. If you do—"

"—I'll never again know happiness," I finished for her.

"Nor will *she!*" With that, Dag kissed me on the left cheek, turned, and boarded without glancing back.


ETTA: TUESDAY; FEBRUARY 19, 1901

"Here's a story Bat once told me. T.R. related this to him after hearing it long ago from Cody."

"A folk tale in the making, so to speak?" I pondered.

"Back in the early days of our Republic, while residing in Boston, Ben Franklin received a letter from a Philadelphia intellectual. Like most others in our fresh bud of a nation, he considered Dr. Franklin the wisest man in America."

"No doubt that's true. I've read *Poor Richard.*"

"In this missive, the man—his name lost in the mists of time—shared a revelation. Following years of study in the sciences, he had concluded that God could not possibly exist. The fellow detailed the process of his 'discovery' and awaited a reply. Yet there was none, much to his disappointment."

"Got a feeling your story doesn't end there."

"A year or so later, this man arrived at a party in Boston only to encounter Ben Franklin. Excited, he hurried up, asking if the good doctor had indeed received his letter. Franklin admitted that he had. So the fellow asked, 'Well, what do *you* think?' Dr. Franklin stepped closer and confided, 'I have only one thing to say to you, having reached that same conclusion many years ago: Sssssssshhhhhhhh!'"


BUTCH: TUESDAY; FEBRUARY 19, 1901

"This changes everything," Kathryn gasped once I'd told her of Etta's pregnancy. The issue had not been raised when she joined us the previous evening for fear such an admission might spoil our brief, wondrous interlude.

"Not necessarily."

"Of course it does! LeRoy, this might be your child."

"We don't know that for a fact."

"If not, then it's Henry's. And if that's the case—"

"Etta's been with another man recently. Enrico—"

"I don't care. If there's even a chance it's yours, you *must* go with her. Or, if she chooses, stay here together."

"How 'bout you?"

"I'll survive. I always have."

"'Survival' isn't enough. You deserve to live fully—"

"What people deserve, compared to what they get, are more often than not two different things."

"But this time, I'm going to do something about that."

"You and Henry must support Etta. After the baby is born, and you have an opportunity to develop a deeper perspective, then decide whether you wish to remain with her . . ."

"Or?"

"Return to me. But considering your history together, you must be with Etta in nine months and help her through this."


ETTA: TUESDAY; FEBRUARY 19, 1901

"Tell people the truth," I mused, "and they'll revert to the hairy apes that preceeded us. Creating nothing; killing without qualms. Eating, defacating, and procreating. For if, as Nietzsche claims, God is dead, then civilization is nothing but a grand illusion."

"The Dark Ages will return, perhaps permanently."

"Do you believe that will occur, Emma?"

"I know it. Life is not a straight line but a circle. Everything that has happened before will again. And again—"

"So is this the choice I, like every citizen of the 20th Century, face? On the one hand, scientific realism that leads to despair. Or reactionary religion. A know nothing approach, seductive to simplistic people who recoil from the former."

"That's pretty much it."

"As to the first outlook. What do you call it?"

"Nihilism."


SUNDANCE: TUESDAY; FEBRUARY 19, 1901

"Now, you die," Lupo hissed, emerging from around the corner of a rectangular building not far from the ferry-station. The Wolf stepped directly into my shadow, his long stiletto held high.

"Didn't think I'd seen the last of you," I laughed with a weary fatalism I did not know I was capable of until now. Lupo arched his shoulders and edged forward with the brute force of a beast, incapable of conscience, motored by a rage to kill.

"No, no, no," Joseph Petrosino ordered, appearing as if out of nowhere to serve again as my protector. "Move and I'll shoot. And, make no mistake about it, to kill."

Lupo froze in his tracks as I cautiously backed away. Then the Mafioso threw down his long knife, shoulders slumping.

"Thank you, Joe," I mumbled.

"Thank *you*, Henry, for serving as the bait I needed to lure The Black Hand from his lair."

"No matter," the Wolf spat. "My lawyers will—"

"Not this time," Joe interrupted. "Yesterday, I received a judge's confirmation. Once apprehended, you'll be deported to Sicily. And that, as they say, is that."

ETTA: TUESDAY; FEBRUARY 19, 1901

"I'm so glad you came back," Rabbi Cohen exclaimed, rising from behind his desk in greeting.

"Henry mentioned you wished to see me. Though I would have returned anyway. We never completed our discussion—"

"First, let me apologize for storming out of that Red meeting the other night. I couldn't take any more."

"Do you have a problem with the cause of working men's rights and redistrubtion of wealth?"

"Not at all! I've always thought that the division of labor and capital is essentially unfair. Only, did Bat have to insist that for such a future, we must abandon God?"

"According to strict Marxism? Yes."

"As one who has firmly believed in Yahweh's presence all his life, and always will, I could never accept that."

"I agree."

"You do?" he asked, surprised.

"Most people need an incentive to do the right thing." "

"And religion provides the incentive: heaven."

"We must have faith in *something*. Otherwise? Chaos."

"Etta . . . Eloise . . . whoever you may be . . . please, remain here. Join our community. Together we'll attempt to 'reform' Judaism."

"Me becoming the first female rabbi?" I laughed.

"Why not? It has to begin with someone."

"All of this sounds wonderful. However, there's a new wild card in the deck that I must share with you before you go further."

As I explained my state of pregnancy, including the fact that any one of three men might possibly be responsible for my situation, Rabbi Cohen appeared to crumble like the proverbial cake left out in the rain. Apparently, this was too much for such a traditional person to deal with. When I finished my little speech, he tried to respond but could not. His eyes were not critical, or condemning. Rather, shocked and defeated. I did the only thing I deemed appropriate: rose, thanked him for his friendship and advice, then turned and swiftly exited.


BUTCH: TUESDAY; FEBRUARY 19, 1901

"We should've told Etta about . . . *us* . . . long before we did," I confessed.

"Agreed."

"Only stood to reason she would be comfortable with . . . 'us.'"

"How about you, Henry? I mean, you've never spoken about how you feel since we . . . you know . . ."

"Yeah," he cryptically mumbled. "I know."

"Still difficult to talk about, even though we now know that Etta's fine with it?"

"Shouldn't be," he admitted, "but it is."

"Maybe that has to do with our life in the West. Somehow, it don't seem like something that would happen to a 'cowboy.'"

"Then again, maybe it's time we stopped identifying ourselves by any one such notion of what it means to be a man."

"Now, you sound like Etta."

"Yeah. Took me long enough, but I'm gettin' there."

"Reckon you're right. Nobody gets to be a cowboy forever."


ETTA: TUESDAY; FEBRUARY 19, 1901

"Thank you for taking the time to speak with me," I said to Mr. Bailey after the Commodore had led me to his office. Following the meeting with the Rabbi, Caleb and I had boarded an uptown tram, arriving at Madison Square.

"Don't be silly," he insisted, grinning from ear to ear. "A true gentleman always makes time for a beautiful woman."

*If you had set out to say precisely the wrong thing to me at this point in my life, sir, you surely achieved your goal.*

"Commodore McNutt says you might be willing to transport me from Madison Square Garden to the Docks by way of your balloon."

"There is a problem. I have heard whispers in the halls. You are Miss Etta Place, the bandit queen! If there's one thing I don't want, it's to run afoul of the law."

"That shouldn't be a problem," said McNutt, joining us. "You see, Etta will impersonate Annie Oakley. So we'll be able to claim we were doing a favor for America's Sweetheart!"

*You sure don't look like Gawain from Arthurian legend, McNutt! Then again, maybe it's time I adhered to the advice I offer others. Don't judge a gift horse by its appearance. Saints and Saviours come in all shapes and sizes.*

## SUNDANCE: Tuesday; February 19, 1901

"Do you think this is a once in a lifetime thing?" I questioned Butch. Once again we were on the ferry, heading back to Jersey. "I mean, something special between you and me?"

"Meaning if we hadn't met, would either of us have ever experienced anything like what we've known? Now that you've asked, Henry, I have to admit: yes. Before we teamed up, I rode with a bronco-buster named Matt Warden."

"I recall he took a bullet during that disastrous bank robbery."

"What I've never told you is that he and me . . . well . . ."

"So you've experienced this before?"

"Twice. To reach back further, there was Mike Cassidy. On the trail, camped together. Late on a cold night—"

"Now that we're spilling the beans, I told you I ran away from home with my cousin?"

"I remember."

"Sleeping in thin blankets under a Conestoga wagon—"

"No need to finish, unless you choose to."

"Still feelin' awkward about it? Guilty, perhaps?"

"At last, I can comfortably say, Awkward? Maybe a little. Guilty? No!"

"Same for me."

## ETTA: Tuesday; February 19, 1901

"The Commodore informed me that you are an expert horse-woman. Would you ever consider joining my company?"

"One day ago, Mr. Bailey, such an offer would have been tempting. But I recently learned that I'm 'with child.'"

"Oh!"

"So for the next nine months, I would not be comfortable doing anything that might risk—"

"After you sail away," the Commodore suggested, "and have your baby, would you consider returning stateside? Perhaps under an assumed name."

"That's certainly a possibility."

"There'll always be a job waiting for you with the circus," Bailey assured me, "if you should so choose."

*That last phrase? Now, sir, you're talking my language.*


SUNDANCE: TUESDAY; FEBRUARY 19, 1901

"That's them," a child's voice shouted as Butch and I arrived at the Black Maria. "*They're* Butch and Sundance."

Turning, I recognized the kid I'd spoken with on that day back at Hole in the Wall when Butch and I had our face-off over Etta.

"Ponch?"

"Hi, Mr. Sundance. It's me."

"What are you doing here?"

"You told me to follow the 'straight and narrow' path. So, I offered my services to these lawmen."

"*No good deed goes unpunished,*" I spat.

"Alright, now," Siringo said, stepping forward. "You probably are aware that we have no authority to arrest either of you."

"I take it that's the good news," Butch guffawed.

"Yeah," Lefors said, coming closer. "But we still hold a warrant for murder against Miss Etta Place. And if she's here for this afternoon's shoot, we'll do precisely that."

"Don't try to interfere," Siringo added "We tossed away the blank cartridges we were provided for the play-acting. Our pistols are loaded with real bullets."

"Just to be safe," I whispered to my pard, "maybe we'd better do the same before the fireworks begin."


ETTA: TUESDAY; FEBRUARY 19, 1901

"I've re-checked the apparatus," Houdini told me after we'd practiced my upcoming escape within the completed tunnel. He stood beside Ziggy. "I can't imagine that anything could go wrong."

"If I've learned anything from life," I replied, "it's that something always can and likely will."

"That's where we'll come in," Mr. Bailey insisted, coming alongside us by the vast rectangular ring filled with sawdust.

"May I try one more time to convince you to remain here?" Ziggy asked. And so I had to again explain my predicament. "Well, if you ever wish, there'll always be a spot for you with my Ziegfeld Girls."

"And in your bed as well, I presume?" Blushing, he conveyed that my words were not all that far from his thoughts.

"Miss Etta," Houdini asked, "do you have any plans for the rest of the day?"

"I'm free until four p.m., when I must return here."

"Would you be willing to join me on the ferry, Caleb accompanying us, over to Jersey?"

"In truth, I was thinking about heading there."

"Great! I so want to see Menlo Park. Perhaps we'll even get to meet Mr. Edison."

## BUTCH: TUESDAY; FEBRUARY 19, 1901

"Alright, boys," Edwin S. Porter called out to the group of would-be movie actors standing beside the mounts they would ride in the robbery sequence, "let's see how this goes."

With that, the assembled city-slickers grabbed hold of their saddle horns, shoved their boots into leather stirrups, and struggled to raise themselves up onto uneasy horses. The effect resembled to Sundance and myself a clown show more worthy of Barnum and Bailey than anything resembling an accurate scenario from the West. The very thought that these dudes were expected to create a vivid depiction of the old days set us to chuckling. As did the possibility this incarnation of the event would convince the public this was the way things had been.

"Oh!" one tall fellow exclaimed as he lifted himself high only to fall down again on the steed's far side. Frightened, the confused horse bucked about. As the tenderfoot's left foot had become entangled in the stirrup, this might've led to the panicky mount dragging a greenhorn to his death. Henry and I clicked to our horses, dashed up on either side, and seized the reins of this dude's mount.

"Thanks, fellas," he gasped. "Thought I was a goner."

"Maybe you should excuse yourself from this sequence," I suggested as, after dismounting, we helped him regain footing.

"No, no. I won't give up until I master the process."

"Ain't worth dyin' for," Henry glumly responded.

"To me, Max Aranson, it is!"

ETTA: TUESDAY; FEBRUARY 19, 1901

"Mr. Edison?" I asked, recognizing the genius from his photos. Harry Houdini and I warily approached him as he exited his elegant home.

"Yes?" he snapped, clearly burdened with all sorts of concerns, likely involving the current film.

"I'm the actress who'll be portraying Etta Place."

"Oh, of course," he said, stopping in his tracks. "I saw your screen test. And was on my way over to the studio."

I guessed that Annie Oakley was inside that curiously shaped building, waiting for Porter to arrive back from the morning's outdoor shoot in the nearby countryside. Best, then, to talk with Mr. Edison here. If he were to enter the Black Maria and see me and Annie together, that might spoil everything.

"Here's a man who very much wants to meet you."

"No time for such stuff today. Maybe some other day—"

"Let me explain, sir. This is Harry Houdini."

SUNDANCE: TUESDAY; FEBRUARY 19, 1901

The Orange Express slowly emerged from behind a distant hill, chugging along as it did every day at this hour. Only now with a marked difference. In addition to the engineer and crew, along with the regular passengers, several of Porter's extras had been strategically placed inside the cars. When the actors playing outlaws rode up and halted the train, those planted inside would step down with hands raised high.

"Make ready to ride," Porter called out, signaling his cameraman to begin cranking. "And put some zest into it! I'd like to get this shot on the first try!" No question he was born for this! The once indescript man now appeared like a lord over his chosen domain: moviemaking.

Butch and I spurred our mounts forward and glided toward the oncoming locomotive. As for the others, the ride did not go smoothly. Their horses, with a horse's sixth sense that these were inexperienced riders kicked, bounced, and bolted. I reckoned it was up to us to save the day.

"Haaaaaaa!" I shouted, spurring my mount and galloping around the bucking broncos while Butch followed suit on the far side. Our horses understood that these were men who knew their business. Snapping to attention, they rushed toward the train as, on cue, the Iron Horse stopped at logs piled high on the tracks.

"Good, good," Porter shouted as we all moved forward. For a brief time, things remained calm. Then Max, the most awkward member of our company, fell off his mount. Fearful he might be trampled, we rode up on either side as the dude managed to rise. We seized Max by his arms from either side and carried him to safety.

"I think," Butch muttered, winded by the ride, "it might be better if you played one of the passengers!"

"I'll play anything," he responded, all but performing a happy-dance, "so long as I'm a part of this grand enterprise. Just think, boys. For all intents and purposes the American movie industry begins today. And we're part of it."

ETTA: TUESDAY; FEBRUARY 19, 1901

"What are *you* doing here?" Annie gasped after I left Caleb at the front door and slipped into the Black Maria. I'd found her waiting patiently, all crew members out on location.

"I wanted to check in person to make sure everything has moved ahead according to plan."

"I'm fine. And it's too dangerous for both of us to be here at the same time. Should Lefors and Siringo show up—"

"I'll be but a moment. I need to know. Have you yet decided about tonight?"

"No. But once I'm finished here, I *will* return to the Garden. With both of us there, it'll be more difficult for the lawmen to figure out who ought to be arrested."

"I appreciate that." I mentioned that there were now two routes of escape, the carriage and the balloon.

"Great! We'll throw them off, each taking an alternative route, then meet at the waterfront," she said. "There, we will decide who will stay and who will go."

BUTCH: TUESDAY; FEBRUARY 19, 1901

The train stopped and actors cast as passengers stepped down, forming a line stretching along one of the cars. Those women and men raised their hands, as several members of our group assigned to portray actors portraying outlaws dismounted and relieved one victim after another of their wallets and pocketbooks.

Then one of the fellows—I recognized him as Max Aranson, relocated by E.S. from the riders to play a passenger on the train—feigned panic and darted away, as if attempting to make a run for it. An outlaw fired his pistol, a considerable cloud of smoke adding to the excitement. At once, Aranson engaged in a bizarre pretend dance of death, spinning around in a circle.

"Don't you think he overdid it a bit?" Henry wondered.

"I told him to give it everything he had," Porter explained after the camera stopped clicking.

"Got to compensate for the lack of voices," Max said, hurrying up as he dusted himself off. "How'd I do?"

"Just fine," E.S. complimented him. "You may yet have a future in the movies. But stay away from the horses!"

"Not a chance!" Max chuckled. "Westerns are what I want to do."

"I have to tell you," I informed Porter. "Back in Wyoming, we never once shot a passenger. Or a lawman. Not that time, not ever. And certainly not in the back."

"No matter. Makes the film more thrilling. Got to give the public what they want!"


ETTA: TUESDAY; FEBRUARY 19, 1901

"I've been explaining to Mr. Houdini why I have doubts that his illusions will go over in the context of a motion picture." Edison spoke as I re-approached them, conversing in front of Edison's home.

"Really? I thought magic and movies would be a natural match."

"Mr. Edison wonders if what I offer will 'work' as a projected entertainment rather than on stage, in person."

"On Broadway, I watched the French film you screened."

"When Méliès performed that trick in his original stage act," Edison told us, "audiences were left breathless. But when Parisians saw the same 'gag' in a flicker, they were less ecstatic. The 'vanishing' might have been nothing more than a mechanical trick of the camera or assembled in the editing room."

"Well," I considered, "I must admit, such a thought did cross my mind. But when you repeated the act yourself after the screening I had no such doubts. So maybe Mr. Edison has a point. 'Movie magic' may be a realm unto itself."


SUNDANCE: TUESDAY; FEBRUARY 19, 1901

"Well," E.S. sighed, "we're all ready for the next shot." He referred to his vision for a spectacular conclusion in which two groups of mounted men, one led by Lefors and the other by Siringo, would come tearing over the hills to interrupt the robbery. "Where the hell are they?"

Though the camera-man and his team had shifted position so as to capture the approaching hordes, nothing happened. An odd stillness descended on the filming location.

"Something's gone wrong," I said. E.S. stood stock still, concerned that an unexpected event might ruin his exciting climax.

"Let's see what it is, pardner," Sundance replied. In unison, we swept ourselves up onto our mounts.

ETTA: TUESDAY; FEBRUARY 19, 1901

"I've got the solution to make everything work," Ned Buntline roared, greeting me at the entrance to the Garden.

"I'm all ears," I said as we stepped inside the stable where Rough Riders attended to their mounts.

"As soon as the Wild West concludes, while the rubes rearrange everything for the big fight, Cody's cast will congregate on the street outside, surrounding your carriage. You'll still be wearing the Annie Oakley costume. We'll do a night-time parade right down Fifth Avenue. Cowboys and Indians will escort our star: you."

"Where will the 'real' Annie be?"

"Up in the balloon with Bailey and the Commodore. Their team will steer that contraption down the avenue, above our entourage, as clowns and trapeze artists join in with us. If Lefors and Siringo are there, they won't be able to get close to you. Also, they'll be uncertain as to which of the two 'Annies' is the real one. How can it fail?"

—INTERLUDE—

BAT: OCTOBER 25, 1921

*As we wrap up this taller than tall tale, Moving Pictures become central. However modern they may seem, you can trace 'em back to the roots of civilization. Those advanced apes, standing upright more than 20,000 years ago, gathered in caves and left us a legacy. The Image. A wall-painting of a hunt often featured men with three legs and beasts with seven or more. No such creatures ever existed. And, likely, those primitive artists knew how to count. Had to, in order to survive from day to do. So! What did they wish to portray? Allow a viewer to believe he perceived the action in progress rather than one moment, frozen in time.*

*Then half a century ago came the still camera. One day in California, circa 1872, Governor Leland Stanford hired the British photographer, Eadweard James Muybridge, to help win a wager. As a horse cantered by on a race track, were all four feet ever off the ground simultaneously? Or did a single hoof necessarily remain earthbound for gravitas? At a heady cost of $20,000, Muybridge set up a line of still cameras along the track, each with a thread attached to its shutter, extended and tied to a pole on the far side. As the horse named 'Occident' tore through those strings, a succession of pictures were snapped. When developed, two images proved Sanford correct. Seeing is believing; now, everyone knew for certain that all four hooves are indeed airborne as a mount trots along.*

THE BIRTH OF MOVING PICTURES: Drawing on experiments by previous innovators, English-born photographer Eaedweard Muybridge all but created the concept of 'cinema' while settling a memorable race-track bet.

*End of story? Might've been, if not for a dream. While sleeping, Muybridge recalled an invention he'd earlier witnessed in Paris. Artist Christiaan Huygens had been inspired to paint on glass rather than canvas, creating images of a child skipping rope, each featuring a progression in movement from the previous picture. Huygens mounted these along the edge of a great wheel. Setting up a screen across from a light source, Huygens rolled the wheel. Gathered friends believed they saw a single flickering image of the boy jumping rope.*

*Muybridge rose the following morn and built his own magic lantern, this time featuring glass photographic plates. And so Occident hurried along, again and again. In fast or slow motion, depending on the speed with which Muybridge rolled the wheel. Competitors employed this device, dubbed the zoopraxiscope, to create similar Movies with lions, tigers, and bears. The form could not advance any further, though, until George Eastman created light, flexible celluloid film up in Rochester in 1889.*

*Meanwhile, down in East Orange, New Jersey, Thomas Edison invented a projector he called the Kinetoscope for a more advanced screening device. Then, in the mid-1890s, the Lumiere Brothers brought an end to the Nickeloden era when they unveiled their first motion picture theater in Paris. Shortly,* The Life of an American Fireman *proved the viability of such a device here in the United States.*

*Followed half a year later by* The Great Train Robbery. *Which drew our own cast of chracters together. And please do note, Lolly, if every word of this long-winded yarn isn't the absolute truth? Well, then, all I can say is:* it should have been!

# PART TWENTY:
# THE FIRST PICTURE SHOW

"Movies make you care, make you believe in possibilities
again. If someone manages to break through with a
film that speaks to you, suddenly the world makes
at least a little bit of sense once more."
—PAULINE KAEL

Side by side, we spurred our horses, rose up and over a slight ridge, and found ourselves gazing down at an entirely unexpected sight. Some thirty Ku Klux Klansman were spread out along the tracks, waving burning crosses and rifles. Several carried signs which announced, "Death to the devil's brood." To their right, Siringo, Lefors, and ten others playing The Posse had reigned in, their route toward the halted train blocked.

"God does not want this abomination to be filmed," one of the Klansman shouted.

"And we are God's good Christian soldiers on earth," another added. "Disperse, devils, and ride away."

Siringo appeared uncertain as to what he ought to do. His group of actors, mostly immigrants desperate for a job, were intimidated by the Old Order. For when the Klansman shouted "America for Americans!" they expressed their hatred of all newcomers to our nation.

"This is the land of free enterprise," Lefors howled back. "Edison has a right to create this new product."

"Take your foreigners and go back where you came from!"

"What's going on?" I asked, unable to hear the angry exchange over my sudden fit of coughing.

"Think back to the day we watched Lakeland and E.S. direct a flicker in Manhattan," Butch replied. "And recall that among the fascinated majority, there were those who felt threatened by anything that challenges the status quo."

"The ignorant forces always believe that anything new and different is dangerous. Will it ever stop, Butch?"

"No. The faces may change. But there'll always be those intolerants who hate what they don't understand."

"What should we do now?"

"As impossible as this might have sounded a year ago," he replied, holding his reins tight in his left hand, whipping out a pistol with his right and clicking to his mount, "I guess we'll have to give our old nemeses a helping hand."


ETTA: TUESDAY; FEBRUARY 19, 1901

"You have a special visitor," Bat said as he and Colonel Cody greeted Caleb and myself in front of my dressing room door.

"The vice-president is inside," Cody whispered.

"He came all the way back from Washington to see *me?*"

"During the past two and a half weeks," Bat explained while opening the door for me, "you have emerged as a figure of national significance."

"You're looking well, my dear," T.R. said as I entered.

"Even as you wear your success well," I replied.

"Thank you for that! I feel a bit worn following an all-night train ride to make it here on time."

"For what, T.R? I mean, Mr. Vice-President."

"I wanted to deliver this to you in person." With that, he handed me an envelope stamped with the presidential seal. Unable to form words, I fumbled to open it. Inside, I found a brief missive stating that I had received a full presidential pardon for all previous mis-deeds, even as had the boys.

"As to my shooting a man in Nugget—"

"In fact, several women of the town, respectable ladies all, have come forward with complaints as to the deceased's behavior. Apparently, he did not only menace working girls."

"I'm . . . *free.*"

"To start your life over again. I witnessed you falling in love with 'the city.' Now, it's your oyster to crack open."

"What a wonderful thought. Only . . ."

"Only what?"

"Now that the choice is truly mine, I'm no longer certain I wish to stay."

BUTCH: Tuesday; February 19, 1901

"Back off," I called out as I rode up to the Klansman, firing over their heads. "This is loaded with real bullets."

"Mine, too," Sundance added, following in my path. He shot at one fellow's high reaching hood, blowing a wide hole at the peak.

"We'll burn you on crosses before we're done," shouted their leader, easily identifiable by gaudy colored ribbons hanging from his sheet and an ancient crest, with a crucifix central, hanging about his neck.

"You'll do nothing of the sort," Siringo replied. The big man spurred his own horse forward, now committed to opposing these reactionaries. He and Joe drew their pistols and fired, nicking the tops of several pointed hoods. Now, the Klansman panicked.

"Don't be intimidated," the leader called out. With that, he aimed his rifle at Siringo. Before the Klansman could shoot, Sundance fired. His bullet slammed into the rifle barrel, sending it flying. As it did, a round went off, harmlessly flying past Siringo's head.

"Who else wants some?" I shouted. They turned and hurried away.

"We'd better get back with our group," said Sundance, turning his horse to rejoin our own team of pretend outlaws.

"Thanks, Kid," responded Charlie. "I owe you one."

## ETTA: TUESDAY; FEBRUARY 19, 1901

"Etta," T.R. asked, "do you have any idea as to the squalor and poverty that exists in rural Bolivia?"

"I have no romantic illusions about what might awaiting me. In truth, I have no romantic illusions left at all."

"Why, then—"

"There are other people to consider. Annie Oakley, for one. I promised to trade places with her if she wished. And Mrs. Trumbell! Butch offered to remain here with her. So that's a strong argument for me leaving with Henry."

"Anyone else?"

"Well, there's Butch and Sundance themselves—"

"Think of yourself first for once."

"There's that, too."

"Yet you still consider leaving with your lovers?"

"It's not so simple as that anymore. I'm still considering leaving with my *friends*."

## SUNDANCE: TUESDAY; FEBRUARY 19, 1901

"We heard shots," E.S. nervously remarked as Butch and I rode over the hill, rejoining the film crew.

"A minor nuisance," Butch said. "We can proceed now."

With that, Siringo, Lefors, and their posse appeared on the ridge, waiting for Porter to wave them on.

"Alright, fellas," E.S. shouted, hurrying behind the camera, signaling his cinematographer to crank away.

Everyone obeyed the director's commands. Those playing the Wild Bunch mounted then followed Butch and myself. I noticed Max once more riding with them. As lawman followed us toward a patch of woods, firing over our heads, I glanced back and watched as again the dude slipped out of his saddle, landing hard on the ground.

"Great! The audience will think that Max was shot off his horse!" E.S. announced. "That's a wrap."

## ETTA: TUESDAY; FEBRUARY 19, 1901

"Is it true?" Frank anxiously asked, coming up alongside me as I strolled along the rows of empty seats.

THE QUICK AND THE DEAD: The obscure 'extra' who played several roles, including a shooting victim of the gang and a fleeing gang member, would soon evolve into Hollywood's first cowboy star.

"What are you even talking about?"

"From what my wife told me this morning, she likely will take your passage on that ship bound for South America."

"You knew that was a possibility."

"Yeah. But now that it appears ready to happen, I can't stand the thought of losing her."

"Maybe you should've considered that earlier."

"Nobody's perfect, Etta. Not even you, I imagine."

"Believe me, Frank, I'm the least perfect of all."

"So why don't you get down off that high horse of yours and persuade Annie to remain here?"

"I might, if I believed you'd seen the light and were willing to 'reform.'"

"I've sowed my wild oats and admit the error of my ways. If only I could have a second chance!"

"That's what all of us most want from life, isn't it?"


BUTCH: TUESDAY; FEBRUARY 19, 1901

After bidding farewell to Max and the others, Sundance and I rode back to the Edison compound. E.S. and the crew had already departed for the Black Maria. And, as Siringo and Lefors were not around, I guessed they'd headed back as well.

"No idea what we'll encounter inside," Sundance mused as we trotted up to the studio. Dismounting, we spotted several worn horses. Inside, Charlie and Joe huddled in corner, watching as E.S. ran Annie, playing Etta, through her part. She tirelessly churned a tub of butter. Hat pulled low, even I had to look closely to be certain this wasn't the woman with whom we'd shared the past six years.

"Harder, stir harder," E.S. called out. With that, Annie performed even grander gestures of the work. "Good, good," E.S. said. "Now, head over to the fire. Throw another log on it."

"You understand," Siringo whispered as we sidled up next to them, "as soon as E.S. finishes, we'll have to arrest her."

"Thought you 'owed me a favor?'" Sundance replied.

"This is it! We ought to have put cuffs on Etta when she arrived. But we'll allow her to complete the scene."

"Well, take care, boys," I said, indicating for Henry to follow me back outside.

"How long will Annie be able to maintain the illusion?"

"Annie Oakley is one fine little actress. She'll hang her head when they come for her, refusing to make eye contact. Why, it might be another hour before they grasp the truth."

ETTA: TUESDAY; FEBRUARY 19, 1901

"Let's test my plan to make certain it works," Harry Houdini said after Frank and I practiced our shooting.

"Sounds good to me."

"You take your final bow, then step backward waving to the crowd while Bill and Bat move forward, blocking everyone's view. That'll give you a second to pull off the Vanishing Lady act, then hurry outside."

"If Lefors and Siringo are there to arrest you," Bat assured me as he entered, "they won't be able to get close thanks to all the cowboys and clowns surrounding you."

"Can't we just tell them about the presidential pardon? Once they're aware of it, wouldn't that end their pursuit?"

"Sure," said Bat. "But there will be a whirlwind of excitement. If I know them, they'll remain in hiding until ready to close in. By the time we're able to show them the papers, likely you'll have missed the departure."

"*If* you *do* decide to go," T.R. added.

SUNDANCE: TUESDAY; FEBRUARY 19, 1901

Once Butch and I returned to the Garden, we sought out Bat and Jack Johnson, who had agreed to run us through a final bout of sparring before the big event. Meanwhile, I mulled over whether it'd be best for me to sail, considering Dag's stern advice. And, as always, there was that other factor: the masculine raw instinct to win.

"Bat mentioned that T.R. was able to wrangle a full pardon for Etta," I said. "That changes everything."

"I know. With the law no longer an issue, might all three of us remain here?"

"Now that I've experienced more'n two weeks in the city, there's a part of me that misses the wide-open spaces."

" I hear you. My take on New York? It's a great city to visit, but I'm not so sure I'd want to live here."

"Let's talk a bit more on this with Etta."

With that, we headed for her dressing room. To our surprise, we discovered Etta outside, weeping at the sight of a note pinned to the door.


ETTA: TUESDAY; FEBRUARY 19, 1901

"You die tonight," Henry read the words on the page, bright-red, indicating it may have been written in blood.

"I don't get it," Sundance exclaimed. "Joe Petrosino insisted that the Wolf would not be released."

"Think it through," Butch explained. "With Lupo behind bars, he'll be angrier than ever. Wouldn't be difficult to get word to other Mafiosos and enjoy vengeance from stir."

"Now I have even more reason to leave," I said. "Then again, there's Annie—"

"The authorities won't hold her long," Butch pondered. "My guess? She'll join you at the docks, whatever her plans."

"So my future's in her hands now."

"Not if we tell her about this threat," said Sundance.

"But I'm not going to tell her. A deal is a deal."

"Everyone ready for the big night?" E.S. Porter asked, all but dancing with glee as he approached us. "My crew is setting up the camera right now. Just think, tonight you'll make history and I'll be there to record it for posterity."

Then E.S. noticed the dour mood of those assembled and softly asked what might be the latest problem to arise.


BUTCH TUESDAY; FEBRUARY 19, 1901

"So it's coming down to mano e mano between the two of us after all," I said to Sundance as we lingered in the shadows, attired in boxing shorts and gloves for our match. Meanwhile the Rough Riders took one last majestic sweep around the inner auditorium, to great applause from thousands of delighted New Yorkers. Momentarily, we would step into the limelight for the Wild West's grand conclusion: The Fight of the Century.

"Does that surprise you?" he replied. "In my mind, we—"

At that instant, the tone of the crowd altered from happy to horrified. Cheering ceased as a collective gasp possessed those gathered, from children with bags of popcorn or cotton candy sticks, to adults enjoying frankfurters and beer.

"Destroy their devil's drink," Carrie Nation bellowed, leading her reformers through the aisles.

"I'd almost forgotten about *her*," said Sundance.

"The bigger the event, the greater her notoriety."

Seated women and men found themselves accosted by the self-righteous forces rushing forward. Most of the Prohibitionists followed Carrie Nation's example, ripping drinks out of theater-goers' hands, then tossing the brew into their faces. Some people remained still, too shocked to move. Others attempted to fight back, or rose and fled. All the while, E.S. called directions to his team, instructing them to turn the camera from one point of interest to another, capturing those for posterity.

"Stay in your seats," Cody pleaded, though his strong voice could only barely be heard. "As our grand finale, Annie Oakley will now display her skill at marksmanship. So—"

ETTA: TUESDAY; FEBRUARY 19, 1901

Grasping what Cody required from me, I hurried into the spotlight, waving Annie's rifle high. Those in the audience seated far from the point of invasion and only vaguely aware of the nearby melee applauded. I must keep as many of those in attendance from falling into panic for as long as possible, even as security guards, recently arrived policemen augmenting their number, and denim-shirted circus rubes poured into the menaced areas. One by one they subdued and removed the screaming, kicking, and in some cases, biting Prohibitionists.

"We'll never let you have the vote after this," one male attendee yelped as the woman who had assailed him found herself dragged off by cops. He was cheered by other men who concurred.

*No, no, no! You don't understand. These are but a small number of radicals. They don't speak for all modern women.*

*Why can't I make everyone see? Violence is always counter-productive. I have learned that from harsh experience.*

"Make ready, *Annie*," Cody signalled. First he, then Bat, tossed empty pop bottles high in the air. I pointed my rifle and fired blanks. From his hidden vantage point, Frank shot, each bottle exploding. Those remaining viewers loudly cheered. The camera rolled on.

*This would be a night to remember. And relive over and over again, once E.S.'s film was developed and circulated.*

SUNDANCE: TUESDAY; FEBRUARY 19, 1901

"Ignore the voices of intolerance," Cody hollered through a megaphone. "These uninvited scoundrels will be removed."

While Etta as Annie continued to plug away at bottles, those in the bleachers appeared confused as to what they ought to do next. "This is counterproductive," Susan B. Anthony shouted at Carrie Nation. Impulsively, Susan abandoned her front row seat, hurrying up beside Etta.

"You'll make enemies, not win converts," Elizabeth added, joining the two of them.

"Keep out of this!" Carrie Nation shrieked.

Butch and I—with thick modern gloves rather than the outdated strips of leather on our hands—mounted the steps and entered the ring.

"Alcohol must be eliminated if we are to create Utopia," Carrie Nation insisted as a dozen policemen surrounded her.

"That will never happen," Etta as Annie responded. "We live in the real world. Where people, women as well as men, enjoy drinking."

As the situation calmed, Bat hurried into the ring. Jack Johnson had already joined us; now, both coaches were in place and the match could proceed. A side glance allowed me to catch Etta swiftly departing. But not before Susan and Elizabeth spoke with her for what might possibly be the final time.

ETTA: TUESDAY; FEBRUARY 19, 1901

"I'm so glad you both came tonight!"

"We're here to try one last time to convince you to stay," Susan said.

"Believe it or not," I laughed, "I haven't decided yet."

"That sounds very much like you!"

"Susan, I'm going to take that as a compliment." We all chuckled. "Have either of you seen Annie Oakley?"

"As you began your display," Susan acknowledged, "I spotted her entering the auditorium."

"Likely," I deduced, "she'll take the stairs to the roof and join Bailey at the balloon."

"Should you choose to go, we will pray for your return," Elizabeth insisted.

"And when you do, as we know you will, we'll proceed toward winning the vote."

"That's always possible when rational minds meet."

"And, as you like to put it, manage to create a happy compromise."

BUTCH: TUESDAY; FEBRUARY 19, 1901

At the sound of the bell, I lumbered toward the ring's center. From the far side, Henry hurried forward. A cheer of excitement echoed around the auditorium. Sundance and I halted as we met in the tight arena's middle. His slender frame hunkered downward in the manner of a cautious fighter. In response, I angled my shoulders back as I'd been coached to do. The two of us now played our assumed roles to the hilt; we would engage in what was advertised as a spontaneous duel.

"Murder him, Butch!" someone in a front seat hollered.

"Kill him, Sundance," yelped another eager sports fan.

Bloodsport! With fists rather than pistols. Bloodsport all the same, I realized as a hunger to emerge victorious overcame me. And, as I could see from Sundance's fiery eyes, he as well. Now, we were locked in a ritual old as time.

*Brother versus brother, like Romulus and Remus. Win or lose. Simple as that.*

ETTA: TUESDAY; FEBRUARY 19, 1901

"Here I am!" Caleb called, his carriage positioned on the street. As I hurried over and climbed up onto the seat beside him, I thanked God, Fate, or whatever may be out there that there were indeed those rare special people who still adhered to the Code of the Cowboy. The Way of the Westerner. In truth, the heart and soul of America itself.

*He had ridden with me. Now, he* stuck *with me!*

"Hello, Annie!" Cody greeted me from where he, mounted on his enormous horse, had stationed himself a few feet away. He deliberately addressed me by the 'wrong' name to confuse any foes skulking about. Meanwhile, the Rough Riders trotted up.

"Hello, Colonel," I shouted back, playing my role.

Even as Caleb slapped the reins and his horses pushed forward, various members of the Barnum and Bailey circus poured out of the Garden, joining the Wild West entourage. An army of clowns and vaqueros, Lakota warriors and lily-white trapeze ladies, unlike anything New York had ever experienced.

"To the docks!" Cody commanded.

SUNDANCE: TUESDAY; FEBRUARY 19, 1901

"Go for my jaw," Butch whispered, implying we might settle this without brutality, "I'll take the fall."

I knew what he was thinking: *Then you two will sail away together and at last become a true couple.*

"Speak for yourself, LeRoy," I muttered, moving in fast.

"Do what I say, or I'll end up flattening you."

"Think so? Bring it on."

That was the moment when each of us finally realized the 'show' had been called off. And that this, the big fight, however it might turn out, was for real.


ETTA: TUESDAY; FEBRUARY 19, 1901

Overhead, Bailey's legendary balloon set off from atop the Garden's roof. Onlookers heard the pump-like sounds of its departure and gazed up at sky, awed by the majestic flight that paralleled our movements below.

"Hi, Etta Place!" one well-attired woman shouted, waving at the magnetic female up in the basket beside Bailey and the Commodore. Annie dressed identically to me.

*It's working. No one can be certain who is who. At long last, and for once, things may turn out right.*


BUTCH: TUESDAY; FEBRUARY 19, 1901

Henry tightly crouched nearby, pummeling me with swift jabs to strategically wear the larger man down, bit by bit, so long as he isn't able to connect hard and fast. As I attempted to land one, he scurried away.

"Strike hard, Butch!" shouted someone in the crowd.

"Now, Sundance! Now!"

Caught up in the moment, the thrill of the sport, the enthusiasm of those surrounding us, the lights that drew everyone's attention toward us as if, at least for this indelible instant, we were the epicenter of the universe, I hungered for one thing: *victory.* Momentarily, absolutely nothing else mattered.


ETTA: TUESDAY; FEBRUARY 19, 1901

Suddenly, I noticed Lefors and Siringo in the crowd. Each pushing and shoving his way through the growing throng to reach me. Apparently, members of my team were not successful in intercepting them to explain there was no longer a reason to arrest me. So far as either lawman knew, I remained an outlaw. Their job was to bring me in, whatever the cost.

A greater shock hit my system when I spied a much more menacing figure skulking on the crowd's outer-edge. A tall man, dressed in black with a cape around his shoulders, a floppy hat's brow masking his face. As he slinked like a shadow from street to street, I sensed at once that this mysterious stranger had left the death threat.

SUNDANCE: TUESDAY; FEBRUARY 19, 1901

As Butch drew in for the proverbial kill, I stifled a sudden coughing fit, pulled myself back together again as best I could, and lunged forward, small fists pummeling his chest. The glare in Butch's eyes made clear he had read my strategy. Even as I hammered away at his torso hoping for a brief window when he lowered his paws I grasped that this mercy no longer remained viable.

The bell sounded. Each of us managed to restore some degree of restraint and retire to our respective corners.

*Tomorrow seemed like some inconceivable concept existing in a distant, unknowable future. All that mattered for either of us was to win at this isolated moment in our lives.*

ETTA: TUESDAY; FEBRUARY 19, 1901

"I didn't expect to see you here!" I gasped.

Our parade had just now reached the docks. We halted adjacent to the walkway that allowed access to the looming white boat. Simultaneously, the red balloon landed a short distance away. Bailey and the little Commodore frantically waved to New Yorkers who rushed to the point of contact. The Commodore slipped down, then reached up to help Annie. Hurrying to greet her, I found Enrico blocking my path. "I couldn't stay away," he admitted. "Just to see you one last time—"

"It's alright. I understand why you can't marry me."

"Nothing is more important to a man than his son. The legacy of a next generation is essential to we Neopolitans."

"To we Hebrews as well!"

"I want you to have this back," Enrico said, setting my Tiffany's clock-pin in place on my dress.

BUTCH: TUESDAY; FEBRUARY 19, 1901

Midway through the fifth round I found myself without the necessary energy to continue. Sundance's pummeling at my body may have felt like minor annoyances. Yet as the jabs accumulated, fatigue set in. Though I attempted to hold myself steady, I knew that unless I scored a square hit, I'd soon collapse. Through my clenched fists, I noted my opponent's eyes revealed much the same as to his stamina.

"Go for the knockout blow, Butch!" a voice roared.

"Keep it up, Kid," another fight fan shouted to encourage his favorite.

"ALL ABOARD!": Crowded by day and night, the New York City seaport offered a place of arrival and/or departure from Manhattan to the wide world.

Then, it happened! A powerful right-cross to Henry's head landed hard, even as his rat-a-tat strategy took its toll on my now severely bruised chest. I felt myself falling forward. Through clouding eyes, I perceived that Sundance was also heading for the mat. We fell into each other's arms, then down to the ground, side by side..

"A double knock-down," Bat announced. "I call it a draw!"

ETTA: TUESDAY; FEBRUARY 19, 1901

"Oh, Etta. A wonderful thing has happened. The lawyer who had planned to defend you in court, Clarence Darrow, offered to represent *me* in a case against William Randolph Hearst. And if we win, not only will I receive a handsome cash settlement but a full in-print apology."

"That's wonderful! So you no longer want to sail?"

"You are free to go, Etta. I'll be taking your advice! A woman *can* fight back, if she chooses to and believes in herself fully."

"As for Frank?"

"I'm not certain. I may stay with him or not. We—"

"Sorry to intrude," a familiar voice implored, "but I heard everything you said."

"Rabbi?" I asked as Annie hurried away and the rabbi stepped close, his eyes and manner apologetic.

"Since you left my office, I've done nothing but pursue Shanah, reviewing our Tanakh, the original text. Everywhere appear the terms Ga'al, Ratsah, and Selichan. In English, redemption, acceptance, and forgivenesss."

"Rabbi, there's no time now for—"

"I had no right to sit in silent judgment of you. You are a member of my nation and I implore you to remain here."

SUNDANCE: TUESDAY; FEBRUARY 19, 1901

"Where am I?"

"In the backseat of a carriage headed downtown," Bat said over his shoulder from up front. As I opened my eyes, I spotted Cody there as well, vigorously slapping the reins. A third person, seated between them, wore a bonnet. I attempted to focus on her as the cityscape rushed by on either side, also realizing Butch, now coming to consciousness beside me.

The street traffic was thin on Fifth Avenue at this time of night, allowing us to hurry along at a furious pace.

"Etta's already there," Cody added, "and Annie Oakley as well. We'll deliver you in time."

"I haven't agreed to go yet," Butch growled, sitting up.

"Oh, you'll go, believe me," said their female companion. She turned to glance back and I recognized her as Kathryn.

"But what about you—"

"I'll be fine. Go to Bolivia. Once Etta's had her child, decide if you want to remain there or come back to me."

"She's right," I assured him.

"Then we're free and clear?" I asked, still unable to think straight.

"Don't forget the threatening note on Etta's door," Butch reminded me. "Lupo—"

"I don't know who may have left it," said Bat, "but it sure wasn't the Wolf. Joe Petrosino's squad has been in the Mafioso's cell since his arrest, watching him closely. No way he could have slipped a message to his men."

"Then who . . . ?"

ETTA: TUESDAY; FEBRUARY 19, 1901

"Etta Place," a voice called out, "come to me!"

I had abandoned the safety provided by the crowd after spotting a stray dog, injured in the current chaos, lying on its side, whining. As in the past, here is my great commitment. "Bless the beasts and children," the wisest of rabbis once proclaimed. Whatever the risk to myself, I must care for the innocent.

As I crouched down, the cloaked figure I spotted during my coach ride stepped out from an alley.

"Etta Place!" a familiar voice announced from behind. Turning, I recognized Siringo and Lefors, methodically moving toward me. "Come to *us!*" Charlie commanded.

"Don't listen to them," the mysterious stranger warned. "Hurry to me at once. I'll protect you."

"Don't listen to him," Lefors insisted, waving for me to move in their direction. "*We'll* protect you."

Hesitating only to scoop the frightened pup up in my arms I closed my eyes. All logic indicated that I should flee the Pinkerton men and rush to the cloaked figure. Yet at this final moment of decision, I surrendered to emotion. My heart, as is so often the case for a woman, over-ruled my mind. So with my latest foundling held tight, I hurried toward Charlie and Joe.

"Thank God you made the right choice," said Charlie, wrapping his arms around me. Meanwhile, Joe ran forward, meeting the still yet unknown villain, who held a pistol. Even as he pointed the gun at me, Joe tackled the man, causing the shot to go wild. The two wrestled, falling onto the street, where the interloper's floppy hat fell off.

"Lakeland!" I shouted, recognizing him now.

"You ruined my life!" he screamed as Siringo darted forward. He and Joe cuffed Lakeland's arms behind his back.

"We just learned that you've been pardoned," Joe said. "When word reached us of this man's intent, we followed the parade to *protect* you."

"Etta!" Sundance called out, Butch beside him.

"Thank *God* you're alright," whispered Butch.

"So your faith is restored, James?" I chuckled.

"Perhaps the Bard you taught us to appreciate was correct," he laughed. "'There *is* a force that determines our destiny, however rough-hewn it may be.'"

Yet another carriage pulled up to the docks, allowing two more men to join us. "Stay," Flo Ziegfeld begged, "and I'll make you a headliner at the Follies."

"Remain here," E.S. countered, "and I'll make you a star of the silver screen!"

"Come with us," my boys simultaneously pleaded.

*Perhaps on occasion fairy tales do come true. For like the lady beloved by Gawain in that old tale, I'd been blessed with what every woman most desires: The right to choose for herself.*

# EPILOGUE

LOLLY: OCTOBER 25, 1921 AND BEYOND

"There are those who claim that everything breaks
even in this world of ours. As to ice? The rich
get it in the summer, the poor in the winter.
As for me, I just can't see it that way."

—WILLIAM BARTLEY ('BAT') MASTERON

Those words appeared on what had been the blank sheet of paper in Bat's typewriter. I noticed them after first excusing myself to use the restroom, then returning to hear the mighty story's conclusion. Once more seated, I initially believed my mentor had fallen asleep, as Bat's aged head tilted downward. But soon I recognized a stiffness to his body. My friend had passed over to the undiscovered country, from whose bourne no traveler returns. Our editorial board decided to print Bat's final statement verbatim in the following day's paper.

Four days later, at a funeral parade down Fifth Avenue attended by Bat's legion of fans, I walked beside Emma. Later, we held each other tight as the casket was lowered into Plot 185 of Primrose Section, Woodlawn Cemetery; the Bronx. When the services concluded, I headed home to the flat I shared with my young daughter Harriet, she the one bright spot of an otherwise disastrous early marriage and bitter divorce. Dutifully, I set to chronicling the intimate epic Bat had spun for me. Here was a writer's dream come true. A remarkable tale that had fallen into my lap, so to speak. The great irony, of course, had to do with something Bat had said: *You must choose, Lolly, whether to tell the story or remain silent.* In fact, though, a fly in the buttermilk (to borrow a phrase from those old-timers) limited my ability to bring this to the public, whether I should choose to or not. For with Bat gone, I could not provide a fitting conclusion to the piece. Whatever happened to Butch, Sundance, and, most intriguing to me, Miss Etta? Though tall tales of their adventures in South America had become the subject of lurid pulp fiction, there was no way of knowing what really happened. So I filed my notes and moved on with my life and career, revisiting the manuscript in solitude on occasion, wondering if this must forever remain the greatest story never told.

491

As to my profession, I sometimes wondered if perhaps Bat's passing had been an act of mercy. For above all, he warned me away from the Yellow Journalism favored by William Randolph Hearst, who kept 'actress' Marion Davies hidden away for clandestine meetings, despite his own marriage. A hypocrite who cynically employed his newspapers to preach old-fashioned morality to the masses during The Twenties, an era of radical change. I was of course aware that most non-Hearst reviewers dismissed Miss Davies' acting abilities, proclaiming that without this powerful man's influence, Marion would still be a member of that déclassé chorus line in which he'd discovered her. So, intent on succeeding in my chosen field, despite what Bat had so solemnly expressed, I requested an interview. In my *Morning Telegraph* column, I argued that 'Miss Davies might be something more than just another pretty face.' Marion—surprised that any indie journalist would say something positive—shared the piece with her lover, as I guessed she might. I was not surprised, then (if certainly pleased) when a letter arrived, inviting me to meet with them at Hearst's East Coast mansion.

At a late-night dinner party (Miss Davies serving as the hostess), this tall, stark, dominating mogul offered to hire me for his own New York paper. Aware that in doing so I betrayed Bat's sacred values, I accepted. Now I became part of a new breed—Bi-Coastals—regularly traveling back and forth between New York and Hollywood on the luxurious 20th Century Limited, always in pursuit of the next big scoop. When reigning superstars Doug Fairbanks and Mary Pickford dissolved their seemingly perfect marriage, my story on the break-up was the first to appear. Hearst syndicated the piece to his more than 70 papers nationwide. The next day, I was promoted to the position of national celebrity columnist.

I will admit, though, that to maintain my new status it became necessary to continue heaping high praise on Hearst's paramour. "Marion never looked lovelier," I noted on more than one occasion. As to the truly great stars, how intriguing it was to interview Harry Houdini. Mr. Edison's doubts aside, he had emerged as a popular screen attraction. I also met "Broncho Billy" Anderson, the first great star of Western films. Though I did not reveal my sources, I mentioned over lunch that I knew he'd been born to a Russian-Jewish father and a German-Jewish mother. Like Etta's parents, Max's had lived under an Anglicized name, in rural Arkansas, to avoid detection and persecution. Even as I promised to keep his secret, I shared with Broncho Billy my similar truth. In fact, I too was Jewish. My dark, some might claim exotic, good looks did not allow me to pass for Anglo. Instead, I'd opted for the lesser of two forms of prejudice, feigning to be Catholic, as the bigotry toward Mediteranneans, though potent, remained mild compared to what Hebrews had to bear. Listening to Bat back in 1921 relate Miss Etta's similar situation, I was struck by our parallel circumstances, as well as opposing strategies as to handling our identities. My plan had been to reveal my own birthright to Bat when I returned from the restroom only to find him deceased. Now, I wondered might I ever sum up the courage to, like Etta Place, come out of the ethnic closet, so to speak, and openly embrace my heritage?

I caught *The Great Train Robbery* at a revival house and was surprised to discover that all of her scenes set 'back at the Hole' had been eliminated. I asked Broncho Billy about it. Turns out, Thomas Edison decided that such cross-cutting slowed down the action so E.S. Porter trimmed the piece. Only G.W. Anderson and I were aware that 'Eloise Placer' had been the original face on the cutting room floor. Also, I attempted to track down the footage of that Fight of the Century, though no one could recall ever seeing this film. A meeting with Porter provided the answer; during the riot at Madison Square Garden two decades earlier, the cameras were overturned and the raw film exposed to the light, thus ruined.

"If something does not survive as a movie," E.S. sadly recalled, "it's as if it never happened." And so 'the fight of the century' gradually disappeared from memory.

* * *

Meanwhile, my career success continued. On November 19, 1924, filmmaker Thomas Ince died while partying on Hearst's yacht, yours truly also a guest. More concerned with my personal advancement than a journalist's unrelenting dedication to the truth, I 'buried' (in newspaper terms) what I'd witnessed: Mr. Hearst had discovered Marion Davies in the arms of her longtime lover, Charlie Chaplin. Drunk, Hearst pulled a pistol and, attempting to kill the comedic genius, shot Mr. Ince in the head. The incident was relegated to the back pages as a case of "heart failure." As Bat once claimed, the media doesn't report the news. The media *creates* the news. In some cases doing so by a dishonest silence.

A week later, my column went into national syndication, a reward for what Mr. Hearst called my 'discretion.' Bat would have condemned this as a failure of integrity. Shortly, I hosted my own national radio program, the *Hollywood Hotel*, and starred as myself in a motion picture version. Over the years, I became known as 'The Queen of All Media,' relishing perhaps more than I ought to such power and prestige. Ordinary people read me daily. And important folks feared me.

More than once, though, I woke in the middle of the night dreaming that Bat stood nearby, shaking his head sadly at the cynicism I had embraced in order to make my own American Dream come true.

* * *

One summer morning in the early 1930s something occurred that all but stopped me in my tracks. The upcoming race for president between the arch conservative Republican incumbent, Herbert Hoover, and liberal Democrat challenger, Franklin D. Roosevelt, dominated our political coverage. How significant to insert here that during the past thirty-plus years, the parties had reversed their identities. If Teddy Roosevelt had been the last great liberal Republican, F.D.R. helped initiate the Democrats' progressive wing. Though Hearst employees were expected to support Hoover, how intrigued I was that F.D.R., like his cousin before him, had once been governor of New York. Causing me to again recall Bat's tale.

At any rate, while sipping my coffee and flipping through the day's First Edition, I happened upon a story in which several of F.D.R.'s team members were quoted. Before I could turn the page, a detail caught my mind's eye. One of the people cited was named Eloise P. Long. There, in bold print, were her words, "I support the candidacy of F.D.R. because he has taken the once-marginalized views of socialist Eugene V. Debbs and, in the context of our current economic crisis, re-imagined them for today's masses."

*At that, my jaw dropped.*

* * *

"I'm surprised that you wanted to interview an unknown Roosevelt-worker like myself," the stately woman in her mid-forties said. We were seated together in the dining room of The Brown Derby on Hollywood Boulevard. This restaurant rated as my favorite West Coast haunt as it had been named after Bat's signature hat. If I'd had any doubts the person before me was indeed Etta Place, they were dispelled by enigmatic eyes that focused on the woman directly across from her. Also, an ancient Magen David dangled around her neck. The biggest giveaway, though, was a Tiffany's watch-pin, proudly displayed on her dress.

"In the future, I'll be expanding my column to include politics as well as entertainment," I fibbed. "Reading about the current Democratic campaign, I was fascinated by a statement you made and hoped to learn more on the subject."

For the better part of an hour, 'Eloise Placer Long' rambled on, apparently convinced here was a ripe opportunity to sing F.D.R.'s praises. His late cousin T.R. had succeeded Mckinley following that president's assassination. For eight years, Teddy supported those liberal causes this lady cherished: busting big trusts that represented capitalism at its rawest; championing our indigenous people; conserving vast areas of wildlands for future generations; crusading for the rights of women. And, particularly important to her, a high regard for the oft-maligned Jewish people. The former Rough Rider had opened America's doors to Eastern European Jews fleeing from violent pogroms in Russia, and picked a brilliant Jewish man as his Secretary of Labor, the first time such an honor had been awarded to a Hebrew.

Now F.D.R. spoke openly of his respect for the Jews. The Good Fight, apparently, continued on, if always with a new champion among the more enlightened of Anglos.

BUFFALO BILL, MOVE OVER!: "Broncho Billy Anderson" projected in early motion pictures the tall, dark, and handsome man of few words that Colonel Cody earlier incarnated in his Wild West show.

"What most caught my attention was your assertion that F.D.R. had incorporated the political theories of socialist Eugene V. Debbs, considered radical a decade ago, into the re-invented Democratic party's agenda."

Now enthused, my guest gushed on and on about socialism. "When I returned home after nearly twenty years abroad, even as The Great War came to its conclusion, Debbs—thought to be a dangerous Red by the moneyed class—was running his final campaign from behind bars. Jailed as a Bolshevik who threatened 'the American Way' with support of unions. For me, he offered a perfect middleground between abject communism on the Far Left and raw capitalism on the Extreme Right. Previously, as a young woman, I'd been unable to choose between the two, hungering for a happy compromise."

"Debbs' concept of socialism provided that?"

"Precisely! I realized there could be a balance between the virtue of individual initiative and a sense of respect for the *working* people."

* * *

"You appear intrigued by my stick-pin watch," she noted after observing my unintentional, if unrelenting, gaze. "I do understand that a member of Hearst's team . . . which nastily refers to my candiate as 'that Marxist cripple' . . . would be surprised a Roosevelt worker would display such an obvious status symbol while speaking about and for the lower classes."

"My guess is that it represents a special moment in your life that remains deeply important to you."

"Miss Parsons," my guest asked in a quivering voice after an awkward silence, "you know precisely who I am, don't you?"

"Yes," I softly admitted.

"Should I assume you're actually here to do an exposé in which you unmask a member of Roosevelt's team as a one-time wanted criminal in order to diminish F.D.R.'s viability?"

"I don't know how, or even if, I might convince you that's *not* case. You can't possibly imagine the deep sense of admiration I feel toward you."

"*Why?*" Miss Etta barely controlled her rising temper.

"First, we are both women."

"Don't imagine that would matter much to a Hearst reporter."

"Well, then, there's . . ." I pointed to the Magen David hanging from a chain and prominent on her chest. "Like you, I'm Jewish. Only secretly so."

"Everyone believes you're a Catholic." I explained my motivation for, in the past, concealing my origins. I had to succeed in my line of work, whatever compromises that entailed, though I was hardly proud at having done so. "But, Miss Parsons, may I ask: Why reveal this to me? And why now?"

"A dozen years ago, a great man took me under his wing even as he once did you."

"Bat?"

I nodded.

Her eyes all at once transformed from hard, cold objectivity to a genuine vulnerability. "I see. So . . . you know everything?"

"Not quite."

I explained that I'd been with Bat on the final night of his life, listening intently as he told me her tale. And that I knew what happened until the moment of truth when each must have decided about their departure for South America.

"You're here now to *learn* the final chapter?"

"If you will be so kind as to complete the tale."

"Why not?" she laughed, a touch of madness entering her tone. "As the ancient Greeks used to say, truth will out."

* * *

"I did indeed choose to travel south with my boys. My own daughter was born there. As she . . . I named her Bowdry . . . grew up, I decided to return so that she could attend college, as more schools opened their doors to female students."

"Like you, I had to raise a daughter on my own. So, again, we share a great deal."

"Now, Miss Parsons, you know the full story."

"More, at least, than I did an hour ago."

"You still have questions?" Etta laughed again. "Well, now that the cat's out of the bag, what the hell!"

Recomposing myself, I pursued the final details to finally unlock the puzzle. "Legend has it that Butch and Sundance attempted honest ranching in Bolivia but couldn't escape their reputations and reverted to outlawry."

"That's a bit of a simplification, but . . . true."

"In time, they went down in a blaze of glory, surrounded by federales, Cassidy and the Kid standing side by side until the very end."

"Well, that'd surely provide a proper grand finale."

"But that's not what happened?"

"No. They waited until things settled down back here in the states. Then, like myself, they drifted home once the pressure was off. Sundance . . . Henry, Harry . . . traveled out west and invested his money in an oil drilling company. When it struck black gold, he, under a new alias, became considerably wealthy."

"As to Butch?"

"He returned to New York. James, LeRoy . . . also with a new name. 'Robert,' now. And became a Bolshevik leader."

"Did he ever reunite with—"

"Kathryn? Indeed! They shared a happy existence together for nearly ten years until she passed away."

"Did you ever marry, Etta?"

"No. Though I still adore the finest sort of men—and women as well—I chose to remain single. Not that I haven't been asked, mind you!"

"And you have always worn your Star of David outside your dress for all to see? Knowing what sort of cruel prejudice you may face?"

"Yes! It is my birthright. I accept myself for who I am. Judaism is a part of that."

"I admire your courage."

BAT'S HAT: The legacy of Bat Masterson would be incarnated in the design of Los Angeles' famous Brown Derby restaurant.

"Do you?" Unhesitatingly, she slipped the Magen David from around her neck and handed it to me. "My gift to you."

"I'll wear it always!"

"Yes. But under, or over, your blouse?"

"Oh, my. That's a tough one."

"As it was for me in my time. In all truth, it's the most important decision you'll ever have to make."

A sense of quietude settled in at The Brown Derby at two in the afternoon. Is there any silence greater than a a restaurant during the lull between lunch and dinner? Most of the clientele had long since left this cozy recluse, returning to their daily lives. It was time for each of us to do the same.

"Anything else?"

"One last thing."

"Shoot."

"Ha! That word couldn't be more appropriate in terms of what I want to know. Who shot and killed DeFly?"

"What?" she gasped, truly surprised at my question.

"It might have been any of you. Bat, Butch, Sundance. I considered suspects as unlikely as Joe Petrosino and Kathryn Trumbell; Lupo. Harry Houdini or Edwin S. Porter." Halting momentarily, I cleared my throat before adding, "Or even you."

"So *that's* the missing piece which I might fit into the jigsaw puzzle?"

"I couldn't go to press without the final detail."

"Well," Miss Etta sighed, raising an eyebrow high, "maybe that's the one thing you never will know about all this. At least, not for certain."

I considered the situation carefully before responding. "So it will never reach the public. Perhaps that's for the best."

"May I ask why you say that?"

So I reiterated a story Bat told me, concerning a journalist who long ago learned the truth about a frontier legend. A hero of the people, known far and wide as The Man Who Shot Liberty Valance. In fact, Tom Doniphon, an acquaintance of the hapless 'hero,' had killed the bad man with his Winchester from an alley. But when decades later Senator Ransom Stoddard freely admitted this, ready to finally take his comeuppance, the reporter crumbled his notes and threw the paper away.

For the story, however mythic, meant something to people. An American fable with a hero and villain, the good standing boldly against the bad, and doing so for the very soul of a nation still in embryo. To dispel such a legend would undermine America itself.

And, for all our many faults as a country, there was indeed something good and true in our origination tale that ought to be preserved.

That editor believed so. As do I, at least now.

"*When the legend becomes a fact,*" I quoted Masterson citing the journalist, "*print the legend.*"

"Wow!" Etta replied. "What a wonderful idea for a possible short story."

"Yes. And perhaps, in time, a movie."

* * *

With a wry smile, Miss Etta Place rose and headed for the revolving glass doors. After I'd paid the check and walked onto the avenue again, twilight settling in, I spotted her one final time a block away. Etta Place stood near a corner, with a man on either side. Three people ogether as if they were meant to be, now and always. The men's wardrobes contrasted in style and, I guessed, substance. The larger fellow wore a wrinkled jacket of the type working men prefer. The other—a shorter, wiry man—was bedecked in the sort of tailored pin-strip suit favored by successful businessmen of the day. As neither wore a hat, I noticed that the taller man's hair was parted down the middle by what appeared to be an old scar, dark purple and prominent, while the shorter man's right earlobe was missing.

Something about the unspoken rapport among this trio caused me to linger a while, watching them stroll away, arm in arm. At the next cross-street, they stepped out of sight and my life forever. But before they did, one of the good old boys experienced a coughing fit. When he recovered, the other began whistling. I could hear the old tune "Oh, Susannah!" loud and clear.

*When you ride with a man, you stick with him. Clearly, though, that held true for a woman as well.*

The Magen David remained tight in my hand. I slipped it around my neck, knowing that I must decide whether I would tuck it under my blouse or proudly display rhe 'shield of David' for all to see. I chose the latter, wearing it in public for the remainder of my life. Mr. Hearst might not appreciate my gesture, but by now I had enough dirt on him in my files that he wouldn't dare fire me. More important still: if Bat were indeed peering down from some great ranch-house in the sky, he'd grin, wink, and nod in approval.

"WHEN THE LEGEND BECOMES A FACT . . . "; Louella Parsons, seen here in her office, had to decide whether to print what she had learned about the past or, as newspaper people put it, 'bury' the story to achieve a greater good.

# ABOUT THE AUTHOR

DOUGLAS BRODE grew up in Patchogue, Long Island, a suburb of New York City. From early childhood, he was fascinated by the bright lights of Manhattan, so near and yet so far, as well as the lure of the old west, readily available on TV, in movies and comic books and, in due time, 'serious' novels on that subject. *Meet Me in Manhattan* is his long planned work of historical fiction that combines those two adored subjects, as expressed through a retelling of the Butch Cassidy/Sundance Kid/Miss Etta Place legend. Brode's previous books for Sunbury Press include all three volumes of the PLANET JESUS trilogy, co-authored with his son Shaun, *PATSY: The Life and Times of Lee Harvey Oswald*, the graphic novel *SAND*, or *Once Upon a Time in the Jazz Age*, as well as the non-fiction *DISNEY-ANITY: Of 'Walt' and Religion.'* Brode is the author and/or editor of some fifty books on film studies including *Shakespeare in the Movies* for Oxford University Press. During his lifetime, Brode has divided his time between work as a professionl writer with such other endeavors of multi-award winning university professor, multi-award winning film, theatre, and television critic, regional theatre actor, produced playwright, motion picture screenwriter, magazine editor, radio announcer, TV talk show host, and multi-award winning journalist. In 2023, Brode received the Popular Culture Association's highest honor, the President's Award for lifetime achievement in the field. He and his wife, Sue Anne Brode, currently reside in San Antonio, Texas.